The Battle Immortal

KIRALYNN EPICS

The Silk & Steel Saga

Book One: *The Steel Queen*

Book Two: *The Flame Priest*

Book Three: *The Skeleton King*

Book Four: *The Poison Priestess*

Book Five: *The Knight Marshal*

Book Six: *The Prince Deceiver*

Book Seven: *The Battle Immortal*

Additional books by Karen L Azinger

The Assassin's Tear

Power Writing: Make Your Genre Fiction Soar

THE
BATTLE IMMORTAL

BOOK SEVEN OF
THE SILK & STEEL SAGA

Karen L. Azinger

KIRALYNN EPICS

Published by Kiralynn Epics L.P. 2015

Copyright © Karen L. Azinger 2015

First published in the United States of America by Kiralynn Epics 2015
Second Print edition 2016
Third Print edition Dec 2017

Front Cover Artwork Copyright Greg Bridges © 2015

The Author asserts the moral right to be identified as the author of this work.

All characters in this publication are fictitious and any resemblance to real persons living or dead, is purely coincidental.

ISBN Print book   978-0-9910297-4-7

ISBN e-book   978-0-9910297-5-4

Library of Congress Control Number: 2015915060

For Rick

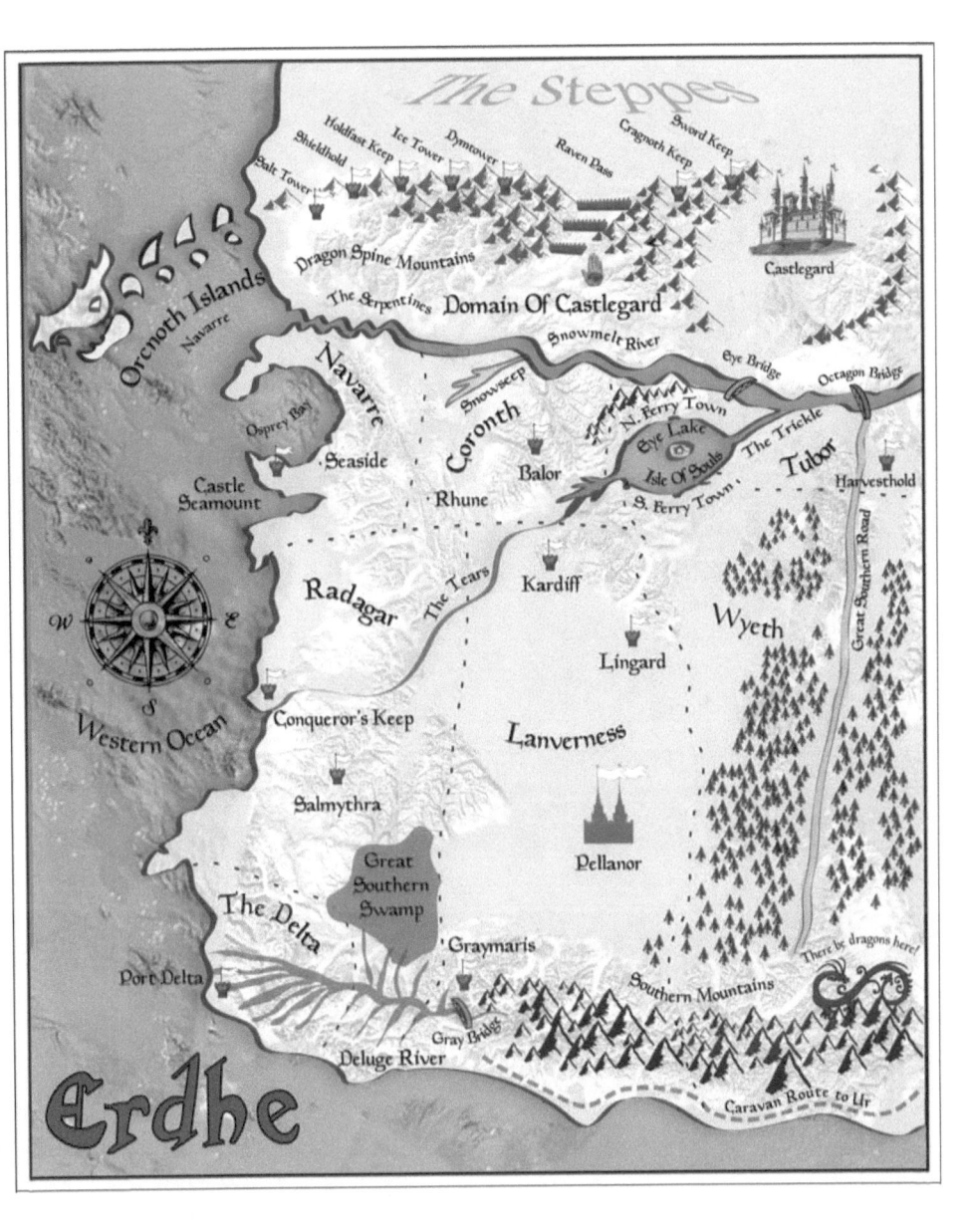

Prologue

Wings stretched wide, the great frost owl soared over the snow-clenched mountains. Sunlight warmed her wings and the rushing wind caressed her feathers, fitting tributes for a monarch of the sky. Gliding effortlessly on invisible currents, she surveyed the land below. Easy as breathing, the great frost owl glided above the lofty peaks, but to the monk-within, flying was ever wondrous, a glorious adventure, a breath-stealing boon of magic. Lenore gloried in every banking curve, in every updraft, riding the wind to dizzying heights. With a ten-foot wingspan, no other raptor could compete. She soared above the mountains with only clouds for companions.

The land spread wide below like a fine-stitched quilt.

Her keen avian eyes raked the countryside. The owl searched for a tasty meal while the monk looked for Darkness. From the lofty heights, the lands of Erdhe looked peaceful, but the monk knew otherwise. A red comet scarred the sky, foretelling the grim truth. The Battle Immortal had begun. Darkness wended its tentacles into the southern kingdoms, seeking to corrupt and conquer. The Kiralynn monastery stood as the last bastion of knowledge, a bulwark of the Light. In ancient times, the monastery had wielded many owl rings...now only three remained. As the lone guardian of the gateway, Lenore needed to be vigilant. Soaring across the Southern Mountains, she followed the trail to Drumheller Pass, searching for intruders. Rugged and forbidding, the mountain vastness provided a secret sanctuary, but the trail remained a weakness, a thin thread connecting the monastery to the kingdoms of Erdhe. Catching an updraft, she circled higher. Sunlight glinted on the ice below, reflecting an unearthly radiance. Glaciers and snowfields cloaked the tallest peaks, glistening in the midday light. Like a jagged line, the narrow trail zigzagged up the mountainside, climbing the heights to the pass. At the summit, a stony arch spanned a deep chasm, a knife-edged drop on either side. Hammer Glacier hung over the rocky span like a sapphire fist, a lethal trap for the unwary. Circling overhead, Lenore saw no sign of enemies, yet she felt uneasy. Heeding the warning, she followed the trail north.

Thousands of times she'd flown this route, yet she never tired of the gods-eye view. Gliding across the snowy peaks, she scanned the land below, matching details to her memory. Everything looked different from the air, patterns played out on a giant scale. Soaring on white wings, she saw the world from a perspective mere mortals could not fathom. Lenore marveled at the stunning display. Vivid colors swirled with intricate patterns as if the world held a grand design, a secret visible only from the air. She saw crystalline patterns stamped on frozen lakes, rocky cliffs embedded with colorful stripes, and glaciers carved with chasms that looked like blue glyphs. So often she glimpsed script in the patterns below, as if the gods had writ their very names upon the land. The elegant script teased her mind like a tantalizing riddle, written in a language she could admire but never decipher.

Banking left, she followed the trail north. Snowy ramparts of the lofty heights gave way to the deep green of cedar and pine forests. Rocky gorges cut the mountainsides, ripples of purple and brown carved like mighty sword strokes into the landscape. Waterfalls tumbled from the craggy heights, their spray billowing like false clouds. Rivers looked like ribbons, curling blue across the verdant land. Amidst nature's glory, men looked like ants, minor pieces toiling across the gods' chessboard.

Lenore pitied all those who were land-bound. Soaring higher, she delighted in the owl, yet duty never left her mind.

The trail snaked north, eventually joining the Great Southern Road, a paved wonder from another Age. The surrounding forest brightened to summer green, aspens and oaks appearing among the darker pines. Smoke rose in columns from cabins and holdfasts dotting the forest, proof the land was not empty of men. The dwellings were few and far between, most of them held by the Zward. Lenore soared above them without concern.

Farther north, the foothills smoothed to a dull flatness. Beyond the forest wilderness, summer colors embraced the lowlands, a patchwork of green and golden fields, ripening wheat rippling in the wind. Everything seemed at peace, yet a wary unease gripped her.

Catching a thermal, she spiraled higher.

The monk-within scanned the land, looking for the source of concern, but it was the owl who alerted her, instinctively spotting a rival raptor.

Mottled brown with distinctive tufts on its head, the great horned owl flew south at a determined pace.

An owl flying in broad daylight...it was unlikely...it was unnatural.

Lenore banked left, intent on following. Gliding more than a thousand feet above the suspect owl, she kept watch till the shadows began to lengthen. Below, the great horned owl flew on an unerring course. A fat rabbit darted across its path, yet the owl ignored it. Never deviating left or right, it flew above the Great Southern Road heading due south as if it carried a message...or sought a hidden refuge.

An unnatural owl seeking to spy, the conviction thundered through her.

Swift as thought, she folded her wings, falling into a steep dive. Silent as death, she plummeted from the heavens. Death from above, she aimed for the great horned head.

A heartbeat from the kill, the enemy owl swerved into an uncanny roll, curved talons raised in its own defense.

A man's face snarled from the feathers! The thing was a horror!

The abomination appalled her, yet she did not falter. The owl attacked, hitting with all the power of the stoop. Talons extended, Lenore struck the malformed creature, hitting with the punch of a sledgehammer. The fiend should have been knocked senseless, yet it locked its curved talons with hers, the sudden weight turning her tight dive into a plummeting tumble. Wings batting against the sky, she struggled to fly while straining to kill.

The fiend rasped, *"What are you?"*

She might have asked the same question were she not in owl form. Talons entwined, Lenore grappled for position, fighting a fiend straight from hell.

Fear riddled the fiend's voice. *"You'll kill us both!"*

So close, she smelled its rotting breath. It stank of corruption, it reeked of evil. Horrified, she struck at it with her razor-sharp beak, aiming for the man's pale blue eye. The creature tried to twist away, but her aim was sure. It screamed as the eye erupted in gore.

Twisting beneath her, it disengaged one claw and raked her underbelly. A searing pain ripped through her.

Lenore sought to drop the malformed fiend, but its talon remained tangled with hers. Locked in a death struggle, they plummeted towards the ground. The frost owl's instincts took over. Fighting with renewed frenzy, the owl-monk lunged for the fiend's throat, seeking to behead its rival. Her jaws snapped in a vice-grip, tasting feathers and sinew and bone. The fiend loosed an unearthly wail, struggling to break free. A clawing pain slashed Lenore's underbelly. The wound burned with a chilling cold as if infected with evil. Lenore shuddered with agony but the frost owl refused to release her prey. Clamping down hard, her curved beak worked to sever the malformed head. A cold wind buffeted against her, a warning that she fell in an uncontrolled tumble. Urgent with need, she renewed her effort. Her beak snapped shut with a satisfying crunch. A vicious twist ended the struggle. The gruesome head fell severed from the body. Lenore opened her talons, dropping the loathsome corpse.

Alarmed by the nearness of the ground, she spread her wings, seeking to soar, but a burning pain crippled her. Her left wing folded, flapping against her side. An upwelling of air gave her a moment's respite. Spying a pillar of smoke, she angled towards it, desperate for help, desperate to give warning. The fickle updraft abandoned her. Wounded, she fell into a tumbling plummet. The ground rushed towards her with frightening speed. She struck a tree, a searing agony spiking through her. Dazed with pain, she lost control of the magic. Light flashed bright, a nimbus surrounding her, and then she lost the owl. The forced change hastened her fall. Heavy with a woman's weight, she fell hard. Pine branches beat against her, snapping and crackling. Bruised and battered, she tumbled towards the forest floor. Clenching her fist, she refused to lose the owl ring. *I must warn the others, malformed fiends watching from the sky!* The ground punched her like a giant's fist. Her breath fled in a brutal rush, struck by a terrible agony. Battered and broken, she lay sprawled on the ground. Lenore struggled to move, to stay awake despite the pain, but everything dimmed to darkness.

Beyond Pellanor

1

Katherine

The *Sea Sprite* limped south under broken spars. Battered by wind and wave, her checkered sails hung tattered and torn, yet the valiant ship persisted, skimming across the turquoise sea. Sunlight glimmered on the waves, making the sea sparkle with foam-frothed diamonds, as if the south greeted the *Sprite* with a hero's welcome. *And well they should.* Kath hugged the ship's battle-scarred figurehead, watching dolphins ride the bow wave. Grown accustomed to the ocean's frolics, she leaned out over the bucking sea. A foam-crowned wave slapped the prow, throwing up a glitter of spray. Licking salt from her lips, Kath scanned the horizon, eager for her first glimpse of Navarre.

Navarre, the seaside kingdom held an almost mystical allure for Kath, the home of her sword sister, Jordan, the home of the ship's stalwart captain, Juliana, but most of all Kath longed to see the kingdom that had welcomed Duncan, giving him a haven to call home. Perhaps his room still held his scent. She longed to sleep in his bed and wrap herself in his memory. *Duncan,* she missed him so. Clasping his silver warrior's ring to her heart, she kept his memory close.

"Almost there." Danya joined her at the prow, the mountain wolf pressed close to her side. "Juliana says we're nearly there."

Halfway south, the wolf-girl had woken from her magic-induced slumber. Thinner by a stone, Danya seemed unharmed, but Kath saw shadows lurking in her gaze. She owed Danya much. They would never have won the Dark Citadel without her magic, but the long sleep had taken its toll. Kath wondered if the wolf-girl would ever dare her magic again.

"Port ho!"

The ship rounded the rocky headlands and entered Osprey Bay. Afternoon sunlight glittered jewel-bright across the turquoise waters. Kath gained her first glimpse of Castle Seamount. Hewn from basalt, the castle stood tall, rising from the shimmering sea like a dark sword. Surrounded by ocean, the crenellated battlements and tall towers looked impenetrable, the first war-worthy castle she'd seen south of the Spines. Impressed, Kath grinned, pleased that Jordan's ancestors had wrought so well.

"There's the city!" Danya breathed deep. "Fresh-baked bread and spit-roasted beef," she made a swoon-worthy face, "I can almost smell them from here!" Beside her, the wolf gave an excited yip.

Behind the stalwart castle, houses and shops built of white limestone climbed the bowl-shaped hills. The city sparkled in the afternoon sun, a glittering jewel overlooking the sea. Kath sighed with relief. On the long journey south, she'd feared the worst, imagining a war-torn land corrupted by the Mordant's influence, but Seaside looked peaceful, even prosperous. Sparkling white buildings embraced a harbor lapped by a bright blue sea. Kath had never seen a more beautiful city. Little wonder Duncan had chosen it as his second home.

A bell pealed a welcome, the merry tone ringing across the waves.

Sailors climbed the rigging, trimming the sails. The ship heeled to larboard, cutting a salty spray. Ragged sails flapped overhead, yet the ship cleaved a jaunty path to the harbor. Dolphins frolicked in the waves, riding escort at the bow.

Footsteps pounded the deck. Her painted warriors emerged from below, jostling the railing for a good view, all of them anxious to reach land. Bear forged a path through the gathering crowd to stand by her side. The big warrior towered over her, his great sword strapped to his back.

Kath watched his face, keen to see his reaction to the south, but Bear remained stubbornly impassive. "Impressive, isn't it?"

He flicked a glance toward her. "Beautiful...but soft. Such a place could never be defended."

His words rang true, yet Kath felt the need to defend her sword sister's home. "But not the castle, the castle looks strong and fierce, tall battlements protected by the sea."

He gave a grudging reply. "True," his gaze slipped towards her, a slight smile playing across his tattooed face, "perhaps the south is like the Svala, soft on the outside, but tough as steel inside."

Kath felt her face flame red, ambushed by the compliment.

"Bring her to port!" Juliana called orders from the rear deck.

Sails furrowed overhead and the *Sea Sprite* slowed. The harbor was crowded with ships. Most showed signs of a difficult voyage, their spars broken and their sails tattered, yet none looked worse than the *Sprite*. It seemed they'd borne the brunt of fierce storms and marauding MerChanters. Kath sent a prayer to the sea god, thanking him for the fleet's safe passage.

Lines were thrown and caught and the *Sea Sprite* was lashed to a mooring. Planks were run out to the dock, providing narrow walkways. Her painted warriors swarmed from the ship like starving men seeking succor. *Finally south,* yet Kath felt strangely hesitant. Her gaze sought the red comet. Time grew short, the red comet nearly quenched in the western sea. She dared not tarry. *"The Battle Immortal,"* Kath whispered the ominous words. Shadows and threats seemed to coalesce around her. She shivered, feeling the weight of a terrible fate.

"Come, Svala." Bear nudged her from her reverie.

"Not without Blaine and Zith." She saw them making their way across the foredeck, accompanied by Sidhorn and Neven.

Blaine grinned, his great blue sword rearing over his shoulder. "Land at last!" He'd grown a blond beard. It made him look older, bristling his sun-bronzed face. Kath supposed they were all older, worn by the journey as much as the war.

Blaine leaped the ship's railing. Landing on the dock, he flashed an exuberant smile. "Come on! Before the others pick the taverns clean as a bone!"

Blaine's excitement was infectious. Hoisting her small sack of belongings, Kath followed the others down the planking. Zith tottered like a drunk, still awkward with his missing left hand. Kath steadied him down the plank. "Take your time." The others waited on the dock, looking to her to lead, but Kath suddenly realized she no idea where to go.

"Ahoy the dock!" Marcus, the first mate, leaned from the ship's railing. "Go to the Eyrie, Juliana will meet you there once the *Sprite* is secure."

"The Eyrie?"

Marcus grinned. "A tavern where returning captains gather after a voyage. Best meat pies in town!"

Kath needed no further urging. "We'll see you there!" Giving Marcus a friendly wave, she led the others along the wood-planked dock. It felt strange to be on solid footing, Kath staggered for the first few steps, missing the ocean's rolling swells, but she soon grew accustomed to firm land.

Seagulls swooped and swerved overhead, the air laden with the sea's salty tang. Ships crowded the dock, swaying against their moorings. Most showed damage from MerChanter raiders, their hulls scraped and bashed by enemy rams. Navarre had paid a steep price to bring them south.

Kath reached the end of the dock and found a knot of painted warriors lurking in ambush. *"Svala!"* Fanggold engulfed her in a bear's embrace. First to board the lead ship, Kath hadn't seen him since the Dark Citadel. Ripe with the scents of sweat, leather and ale, he lifted her aloft. The big warrior did not know his own strength, crushing her tight against his chain mail.

"Hard to breathe!"

"Oh!" He set her down as if she was suddenly fragile. "Your ship lagged so far behind, we feared the sea had swallowed you!" Relief flooded his voice. "Svala, this south of yours is a strange place."

His odd comment made little sense. "How are the others?"

"Keen to fight."

"Did you lose many?"

"A few to waves, a few more to MerChanter raiders, but we showed them the bite of our swords." His voice dropped to a harsh whisper. "Svala, you must lead us to battle for we don't belong here."

She wondered at his impatience. "Soon enough, we need to find the Eyrie."

"I know this place, a great white sea eagle carved above the lintel, but it is meant for sailors not warriors of the north."

"We'll be welcome, show us the way." Fanggold led them along a cobbled street, the other painted warriors surrounding her like an honor guard. They chattered like children, talking about the journey south, marveling at the size of whales and waves, but as they walked through the bustling streets, Kath noticed the shopkeepers sent angry glares their way. A few made rude hand gestures while others muttered curses. The chilly reception shocked Kath. She studied her painted warriors with fresh eyes, seeking the reason for the cold welcome. Perhaps their faces looked too fierce. Predators tattooed in blue ink stared from their faces like nightmares sprung to life. Her painted warriors bristled with weapons, striding the street with the swagger of marauders, yet they'd come to save the south. In time, the merchants would be glad for their swords, Kath had no doubt of it.

The Eyrie was not far, a gable-roofed tavern overlooking the harbor, the limestone walls inset with bottle-glass windows. A wooden sign displayed the proud name in bold script. A menacing osprey with wings spread wide was carved above the lintel for those who could not read. Kath pushed open the doors and strode into a large airy tavern crowded with sailors. A brisk sea breeze followed her through the doorway, but it was the scent of sizzling meat that struck Kath like a war hammer. Her nostrils flared, suddenly ravenous for flame-cooked meat and oven-baked bread.

The conversation crashed to a halt.

Angry stares turned their way, hands reaching for weapons.

A burly tavern keeper with sea shells woven in his braided hair sent them a baleful glare. "We'll have none of your sort in here! Be gone, or you'll be leavin' bloody and battered."

Beside her, Fanggold growled.

Shocked, Kath stepped between them. "What kind of welcome is this?"

The tavern keeper snarled, "You flea-ridden parasites have worn out your welcome. No coin, no ale. Now be gone!"

No coin, and then she understood. Her painted warriors had never used coin. Accustomed to scavenging, hunting and bartering, they came south with empty pockets. Little wonder they found the south strange and unwelcoming.

Zith intervened, "Perhaps I can help." From the pocket of his midnight-blue robe, he drew a large purse. Holding it aloft, he set the coins to jangling. "We've gold enough to pay our way and to settle any debts."

"Gold?" The tavern keeper growled. "I'll be seein' this gold before I'll serve the likes of you."

A pathway opened to the bar. Awkward with one hand, Zith loosened the ties, spilling the contents across the countertop. Old coins, twice as large as those used in the southern kingdoms, clattered across the counter, bright with the rich gleam of gold.

Kath stifled a gasp, realizing they came from the Mordant's treasure hoard.

The gold coins had a mesmerizing effect.

Hardened sailors crowded the bar, gaping at the sight.

"Well, I'll be damned!" The tavern keeper broke the spell. Scooping a coin, he bit it. A smile spread across his swarthy face. "Gold, solid and true!" He stared at the coin, holding it aloft. "Ain't never seen a coin this size. What'd you do, raid the sea god's treasure trove?"

Zith muttered, "Something like that."

"Well, with gold like this, you're more than welcome. Take me best table." He gestured to a large round table in front of a roaring hearth.

"Keep that coin for payment." Zith scooped the rest into his purse. "We'll talk about settling debts later. Meanwhile, we'll have ales all around." Zith led them to the table by the fire.

Kath sat next to the monk, her back set to the warm blaze. Leaning towards Zith, she kept her voice a whisper. "Thank you. I didn't think about needing coins."

"Wealth is another kind of power. One you haven't learned to wield."

His words made her think of Queen Liandra. She wondered how the queen of coins fared against the Mordant. Shivering despite the heat, Kath made the hand sign against evil. "It's good you thought of it. Do we have enough coin for the army?"

The monk's voice dropped to a whisper. "We've two whole chests full."

Kath grinned. "Well done." She liked the idea of paying for her army with the Mordant's gold.

The tavern keeper limped towards them on a peg leg, carrying a tray brimming with tankards. "Me name's Scrimshaw Jones, former captain of the *White Eagle,* at yer service." He passed the frothing ales around the table. "Now what will ye fine folks be havin'?"

Kath answered, "I hear the meat pies are especially good."

"Best in town!"

After more than a moon-turn at sea, no one wanted fish, salted, dried, boiled or otherwise. "We'll have meat pies all around. And bring one for the dog." Calling Bryx a dog wasn't meant as an insult. People saw what they wanted to see, and a 'dog' was far more likely to be welcome than a wolf.

The tavern keeper flicked a glance towards the mountain wolf, but he raised no objection, proving gold was a powerful persuader.

Kath leaned back in her chair, savoring the fire's warmth, her muscles melting with pleasure at the hearth's fierce heat. Lulled by the heat, she was startled when a heaping plate plunked in front of her. She stared at an enormous meat pie, topped with a ladle of mashed potatoes, everything smothered in a rich dark gravy. The smell alone was enough to drive a starving man mad. Kath lunged at the pie. The first bite melted in her mouth. Flaky crust and tender beef swimming in a savory sauce, she fairly swooned at the taste. Licking a dollop of onion-flavored gravy from her fingers, she spared a glance for the others. No one spoke. Wielding table knives, they devoured their meat pies, licking gravy from their fingers. Beneath the table, Bryx gave a contented growl.

Tankards were refilled with a rich dark ale, and Blaine and Fanggold both ordered second servings of meat pie. Replete with warmth and good food,

Kath leaned across the table, intending to ply Fanggold with questions of the south.

Fists thumped against tabletops, rocking the tavern with a hearty rhythm.

Kath looked up to see Juliana and Marcus weaving their way through the tables.

Scrimshaw boomed, "The *Sea Sprite* and her bonny captain return!"

Someone yelled, "Raise a tankard for the *Sprite* and her sailors!"

Tankards were raised around the tavern, greetings and comments tossed back and forth like a windblown sail.

Juliana and Marcus joined them at their table. The two had barely taken a seat when Scrimshaw Jones limped towards them bearing a fancy tankard painted with an image of the *Sea Sprite*. Dripping with foam, he made a show of setting the tankard in front of Juliana. "Compliments to the captain!"

Smiling, Juliana raised the tankard. "Compliments to the Eyrie and all those who sail under the Osprey!"

"Drink! Drink! Drink!" Fists pounded tabletops, keeping time to the chant.

Juliana took a long, deep draught, drinking till she emptied the tankard. Flashing a satisfied grin, she clanked the tankard on the table and wiped the foam from her lips. "Always good to be in home port!"

As if on cue, tankards across the tavern were hoisted high. "To home port!"

The conversation returned like a tide rushing in.

Scrimshaw Jones said, "Shall I bring the usual?"

Juliana smiled. "You know what we want."

Scrimshaw carried the painted tankard away, hoisting it high as if it bore some special significance. It was only then that Kath noticed the long shelf behind the bar. More than fifty tankards stood in a row, each painted with the name and likeness of a different ship. Scrimshaw made a show of setting the *Sprite's* tankard back on the shelf with the name facing outward.

Juliana must have noticed Kath's gaze. "There's a tankard for each merchant ship of Navarre. While the ship's at sea, the tankard is turned so the name faces the wall. When the ship returns safely to port, the captain gets the first draught and then the tankard's turned outward, showing the name once more. With a single glance, patrons can tell which ships are safe in port."

Blaine said, "What if a ship never returns?"

Juliana sobered. "Then we have a keg night. Everyone drowns their sorrows in ale and then the ship's tankard is smashed, forever broken." Her stare settled on the shelf of mugs, sorrow creasing her face. "Since we're the last to return, the tankards tell me we lost three ships in the north, *The Smiling Jack*, *The Trident*, and *The Bonny Lass*. Good ships, good sailors...good friends too. All lost."

The words hit Kath like a punch to the gut. "I'm sorry."

Juliana gave her a grim nod. "They knew the risks, yet they chose to sail north." She studied Kath. "Your capture of the Dark Citadel proved Jordan's visions were true. We sailed north at the gods' bidding." She leaned towards Kath, her gaze intent. "Make their deaths count."

Make their deaths count...the words shivered in Kath's soul. She carried more deaths than the ships' crews. Her hand crept to Duncan's warrior ring. "I intend to."

Juliana met her gaze. "Good."

Scrimshaw returned bearing a meat pie for Juliana and a mound of spit roasted beef and mashed potatoes with leeks for Marcus. The two set to eating, but Kath burned with a thousand questions. "Do you think Jordan will be at the castle?"

Juliana shrugged. "Hard to say."

Kath persisted. "We need to know what's happening in the rest of Erdhe."

Juliana replied between bites. "The Eyrie is the best place to hear sea gossip, but for news of the kingdoms, you'd best go to the castle."

Blaine growled. "What are we waiting for?"

"The tides," Juliana grinned. "The castle is sea-locked till the tides run low, another reason to meet at the Eyrie." She took another bite smothered in gravy. "The castle knows we're here. They'll send horses once the tide turns."

Zith said, "What about our chests?"

"My men will see them safely to the castle."

Zith leaned towards Juliana, his voice dropping to a whisper. "The painted warriors have run up some debt."

The captain scowled. "Barely took two steps on land and I heard the rumors. The shopkeepers and tavern owners are mad enough to split skulls."

Zith plunked his purse on the table. "We've coin enough to settle all debts...but I'm not sure how to do it. Giving men who have never used coin a fistful of gold does not seem prudent."

Juliana considered the monk. "Hire Scrimshaw to serve as your agent. He's honest and well respected by the captains as well as the town folk. He can spread the word there's gold to pay. The others can bring their bills of laden to him and he can settle the deb. He'll know what's fair. Offer him a ten percent fee and you'll save time, coin and hassle. And you'll gain plenty of goodwill."

"Sound advice, thank you, captain." Zith pocketed his purse and went to speak with the burly tavern keeper.

A serving girl brought another round of ales. Sailors and other captains came calling to their table, seeking to speak with Juliana. Kath listened to the talk of the sea, drowsing by the fire's warmth. Sated with good food, she felt content. Turns of the hourglass passed. The setting sun speared the bottle-glass windows, sending circles of light dancing across the tavern, amber, olive-green, and brown.

A shadow blocked the colored light. Kath looked up, startled to see a tall blue-robed monk striding towards their table. He nodded towards Zith, but his gaze settled on Kath. "Are you Kath of Castlegard?"

She nodded, a shiver running down her spine.

"You've come late to the south. The Battle Immortal has already begun."

2

Ambrose

So strange to exchange his well-worn robes for a jerkin of dull brown leather and woolen trousers. For nigh on sixteen years, Ambrose had worn nothing save midnight-blue. It felt like a betrayal, as if he'd abandoned his vows, yet he had good reason. Darkness stalked the lands below, murdering monks despite their magic. Only a fool courting death wore midnight-blue in the southern kingdoms. Reluctantly, Ambrose gave up his scholar's robes for hunting leathers, committing to the long journey.

The sword lay on his narrow bed. *Invictus,* the name shimmered with legend, summoned to the monastery by Illumination. A boon and a riddle, the sword was an ancient weapon forged by the Order's last great wizard, a destiny awaiting the Battle Immortal. By ruling of the Grand Master, it was now his burden to bear. Only a scholar, never a warrior, Ambrose would carry it but not wield it. Knowing subterfuge was his best ally, he bound the five-foot blade in a length of carpet. It made for an awkward bundle, but he'd rather garner curious stares than covetous envy. Above all else, he dared not let the sword fall into the hands of Darkness.

An impatient knock sounded on the door to his sleeping cell.

Ambrose eased it open and met Master Rizel's piercing stare.

"Are you ready?"

Ambrose scoffed. "Hardly, yet I'm determined."

His friend and mentor slipped inside, a worried look scrawled on his weathered face. "This journey should be my burden, not yours."

Ambrose watched his friend pace.

"I argued for the sword to be sent to Castlegard. I should bear the risk."

"No." The steadiness of his answer surprised him. "The Grand Master has the truth of it. Your place is here."

"But..."

Ambrose forestalled him. "You dared the Mist. For the first time in nigh on three hundred years, you wielded a relic, waking the Staff of Summoning. You're needed here. You are the emissary to the King in the Mist."

"Emissary!" Rizel's lips curled in scorn. "The Guardian King summoned a storm, hurling me from the Mist like a scurrilous rogue. I escaped with the barest of answers." He shook his head, running his hand through his salt and pepper hair, his manner changing like quicksilver. Naked scorn waxed to deep concern. "Too many questions remain unanswered. We don't know enough, not nearly enough." His jewel-bright gaze locked on Ambrose. "You must solve the riddle and find a way to restore honor to the Octagon."

"Perhaps the sword is the answer."

"Perhaps." Master Rizel looked troubled. "Or perhaps it depends on the hand that wields it."

Ambrose felt his shoulders hunch at the daunting task.

"Either way, I've brought you this." From the depths of his pocket, he removed a coiled scroll of midnight-blue silk. "I found it in a musty corner of the armory, yet time has not dimmed it." Giving the coil a shake, he unfurled a twelve-foot battle banner. A shimmering field of midnight-blue, emblazoned with a radiant Seeing Eye embroidered in bright gold thread. The banner glimmered like captured starlight.

Ambrose gaped, entranced by the sight.

"A battle banner from another Age, yet it remains unfaded."

"Is it ensorcelled?"

"I think not, yet symbols have their own potent power." He coiled the banner and handed it to Ambrose. "Take it with you. The Seeing Eye may still bear weight beneath the mountains."

Ambrose took the banner. Tucking it deep in his satchel, he winced, cradling his right hand. The Seeing Eye stared from his palm, red and tender from the fresh tattoo. Turning, he showed it to his friend. "Even my third eye is red, too many late nights reading in the Great Library!"

But Master Rizel did not laugh. "Knowledge can be a sword *or* a shield. Never regret the gaining of it, for you know not how it will serve you, or how it might save you."

Ambrose sobered. "True enough."

"Take your robes as well. You may need to wield the full authority of the Order.

He added his midnight-blue robe to the satchel and then fastened the buckles, avoiding his friend's potent gaze.

"What is it?"

Shaking his head, Ambrose whispered, "I have my doubts."

"Don't we all. Yet, you show the courage of your convictions by taking the Seeing Eye."

"It seemed right." His worry escaped his lips. "But I have no magic."

Master Rizel gripped Ambrose's arm, conveying a firm confidence. "Yet, you serve the Light with fervor. Belief can be a potent magic. My sojourn in the Mist taught me that."

The words felt like a balm. "I'll remember."

"When the time comes, your belief will be your guide."

"The Light willing."

"The Light be with you." Master Rizel nodded. "Are you ready?"

"As I'll ever be." Ambrose took a last look around his small, spare cell. After sixteen years of study, he had few possessions to mark the chamber as his own, yet he'd always felt content, a scholar surrounded by limitless knowledge. With a sigh, he twirled a plain brown cloak around his shoulders, and then shrugged his satchel and the bundled sword onto his shoulders. Taking up a sturdy quarterstaff for a walking stick, he followed Master Rizel into the script-filled halls.

A contemplative silence shrouded the inner monastery, a hushed reverence that nurtured learning. They made their way through the mage-stone corridors illuminated with jewel-bright calligraphy. Ambrose's gaze clung to the walls, imbibing the beauty of knowledge entwined with great artistry. In many ways, the monastery was a temple to knowledge, history and prophecy inscribed on every wall. As a lifelong scholar, it pained him to leave, yet he would not shirk his duty. Fate had given him this one chance to foil the encroaching Darkness. Even scholars had their parts to play.

All too soon, they passed from the hallowed halls of midnight-blue to the open corridors of golden-yellow. Fresh-faced acolytes turned his way, stabbing him with suspicious stares. Their glares wounded him, till he realized it was because of his mundane clothing. Already he missed his midnight-blue robes. Feeling like a stranger in his own home, Ambrose hastened his steps, Master Rizel keeping pace beside him.

They passed through a rune-carved door stepping into the brisk morning light. Two blue-robed masters waited in the outer courtyard. One was tall and muscled like a blacksmith while the other was stooped and shrunken, a wizened figure smitten by age. Ambrose smiled to see them. "Master Vernius, Master Grimshaw, you honor me."

"The honor is ours." Master Vernius's voice cracked like aged parchment. "You've accepted a task bound for the annals of legends."

Ambrose felt his face flame red. "I'm not going to wield the sword, just carry it."

Master Vernius shook his head in admonishment. "You carry more than just a sword, you carry knowledge...knowledge that was long forgotten yet sorely needed, knowledge that may save us all. Use it well."

The words felt like a geas, adding an impossible burden to his shoulders.

As if sensing his uncertainty, Master Rizel whispered, "Trust yourself. Trust the Light."

Feeling as if he dare not tarry, Ambrose bid the others farewell and then turned towards the outer gates. A pair of guards pushed the massive gates open. They swung on silent hinges, opening a portal to the mountain vastness. Without looking back, he stepped into the wider world. A brisk wind snatched at his pale blond hair. Breathing deep the crisp mountain air, he strode down the timeworn path. Wispy horsetail clouds stretched overhead, ghostly banners marking the vaulted sky. A beautiful morning were it not for the red comet riding low on the horizon, a hideous reminder that Darkness sought to rule all of Erdhe. Leaning on his quarterstaff, he adjusted the burden on his back. Perhaps the sword would turn the tide, an unexpected boon of the Light.

Breathing deep the mountain chill, he followed the trail down the hill. A daunting wall of white lurked at the bottom, surrounding the monastery like a magical moat. *The Guardian Mist*...he wondered what visions waited to assail him.

A single blue-robed monk stood at the Mist's edge.

Stones rattled beneath his boots, skittering down the trail.

The monk turned, the blue hood falling back to reveal a shock of copper-bright hair.

His breath caught. *"Cynthia!"*

She gave him a brilliant smile. "I've come to see you off."

Her kindness ambushed him. They'd once been lovers but the pairing did not take. Reaching her, he pulled her close in a farewell embrace and found himself pressing a kiss that was more ardent than he intended. For half a heartbeat, she melted against him, raising his hopes, but then she stepped away. He studied her, noting the crimson flush in her cheeks, but he could not tell if it was embarrassment or passion.

She glanced away. "I've come to lead you through the Mist." Her guide's amulet glinted gold in the morning sunlight, a reminder that duty came first.

"Thank you." His heart bled into his words.

She raised her amber gaze, meeting his. "I heard you offered to bear the sword."

"To carry it."

"Ever the scholar, but now you've finally come out of the archives. I always told you there was more to life than musty tomes." Her gaze considered him. "You're braver than you know."

He dared to hope. "Perhaps when I return?"

"Perhaps."

She gave him a warm smile he intended to cherish.

"Come, your destiny awaits." Her words broke the magic. Duty called once more. She offered him the knotted end of the guide rope, her hand lingering on his. "Keep safe."

He gave her a solemn nod, suppressing the urge to kiss her once more.

She stepped into the Mist, disappearing in a wall of white.

The rope tugged at his fist.

Taking a deep breath of clear mountain air, he followed.

The world disappeared in a swirl of fog. White surrounded him, blinding him to all else. Even the ground beneath his boots disappeared, obscured by the sinister fog. Refusing to falter, he followed the tug of the rope, trusting his guide...but he did not trust the Mist. Since Rizel's return, he'd dreaded crossing the white gauntlet, fearing the wraith of the Guardian King. The dead were not always friends of the living. Pushing the dire thought aside, he kept walking. Peering into the mist, he longed for a glimpse of Cynthia's copper-bright hair. He searched for it like a banner of hope, but the guide rope vanished into a maw of white. Swiveling his gaze left and right, he stared in every direction, awaiting an assault of nightmares...but he saw nothing, heard nothing.

The white brooded, cold and silent. The endless nothing gnawed on his mind, an ambush waiting to pounce.

He felt as if he'd entered an ominous void, the whole world washed to white. *Like a page of blank parchment awaiting ink...but what nightmare will be writ upon it?* Not a single horror came calling. The blankness pounded against him, puzzling him...but then he had an insight. Perhaps the Guardian King kept watch, waiting to see if the monks kept their word. Emboldened by the thought, he dared to send a message to the King. "I bring hope to Castlegard, a sword to fight the Dark."

"Fight the Dark...fight the Dark...fight the Dark," his own words echoed back at him from every direction.

Ambrose raised his voice to a shout. "The Kiralynn Order keeps its vows!"

"Vows...vows...vows!" The single word echoed like a taunt...or a test.

A prickling sensation feathered down his spine. He felt watched. Sweat beaded his brow and his heartbeat thundered in his chest. He felt scrutinized; studied like a moth stuck in molten wax. And he did not like it. The feeling intensified, as if he and his fellow monks were on trial, awaiting judgment by the watchful dead. And then he understood. The grim silence made a strange kind of sense. The Mist would remain blank...until a decision was made...until a judgment was rendered. The insight weighed on him like a hanging threat. A bead of sweat trickled down his back. Under the gaze of the dead, he kept silent, knowing actions mattered more than words.

Tightening his grip on the rope, he followed its pull...and stepped into the light. Ambrose staggered to a stop, blinking at the brightness.

The Mist reared behind him, a seething wall of white where the dead kept watch.

Beside him, Cynthia coiled her rope, unaffected by the Mist.

He turned his back on the brooding fog. A great mage-stone hand towered in front of him, a statue from a bygone Age. In the stark landscape of rock and ice, the massive hand almost seemed like an illusion. Ambrose reached out, laying his palm on the statue, reassured by the presence of solid mage-stone.

Four strangers emerged from behind the hand, three men and a woman, all of them dressed in hunting leathers, all of them laden with weapons. They carried themselves with brazen confidence, as if they were accustomed to wielding steel. Without a word spoken, he knew them as members of the Zward.

The largest of the men, a bearded giant with a great sword rearing over his right shoulder, nodded towards Ambrose, his voice a deep rumble. "My name is Haythor, a captain of the Zward." He gestured to his companions. "This is Kren, Jada, and Tarlin. We're tasked with leading you to Castlegard." He gestured down the mountain. "We'd best get started. We've a long journey ahead."

Ambrose felt the Mist brooding watchful at his back. Nodding farewell to Cynthia, he followed the Zward down the steep mountainside. Leaving behind all he'd known and loved, he stepped into the Battle Immortal.

3

Katherine

Kath and her companions followed Aeroth out of the tavern and into the glow of the setting sun. Horses waited for them, along with a handful of guards in checkered tabards. Kath chose a sturdy bay stallion, swinging into the saddle with ease, but Bear, Sidhorn, Neven and Fanggold hung back. Fidgeting with their weapons, a look of trepidation scrawled across their tattooed faces. Her painted warriors milled around, staring at the horses as if they might grow fangs.

Kath turned her stallion. "You'll have to ride if you're coming with me. Might as well learn now."

Juliana gaped. "They don't ride and they don't use coin?"

Kath defended her warriors. "No, but they lived in the Mordant's shadow and their swords are fierce." From the corner of her eye, she saw the men straighten with pride.

Juliana sobered, "Just so."

Blaine and three of the castle guards heaved the painted warriors into saddles and then adjusted their stirrups. "Sit straight, keep your heels down, and use a light hand on the reins." Blaine positioned Sidhorn's boot. "Keep your weight balanced and your body loose." He shoved the reins into the big warrior's hands. "Squeeze both legs to start. Squeeze right to go left, and left to go right."

Sidhorn sat rigid atop the chestnut mare. "How do I stop?"

Blaine grinned. "Tug on the reins...or fall off." He vaulted into the saddle of a roan stallion, turning his mount in a fancy pivot. "Nothing to it."

Men, Kath struggled not to roll her eyes, but then she noticed her own thoughts mirrored on Juliana's face. Kath choked on a smothered laugh. "We'd best be going."

Juliana wheeled her horse and led them down the hill at a slow walk. They followed the cobbled street back down to the harbor, past the fishmongers' stalls, descending a ramp to the beach. Kath darted a glance behind. Her painted warriors sat stiff as boards on their mounts.

Juliana sent her a questioning look. "Shall we?"

Kath answered with an impish grin. "Sand is softer than stone." They thrummed their horses to a canter. It was not long before she heard a muffled fall and a loud curse. A riderless horse gamboled by. Kath turned her mount while Juliana caught the horse.

Bear lay sprawled on the wet sand. "Sorry, Svala. I'll try harder."

"Falling is part of the learning. We've all done it."

He climbed back into the saddle, his face intent.

One of the guards said, "We'll see them safe to the castle. You'd best not keep the king waiting."

"Take them for a gallop along the beach. Keep them in the saddle till they get the feel of it. They'll not find a softer place to learn."

The guard grinned. "As you wish."

Leaving her painted warriors in capable hands, Kath turned to Juliana. "Race you!" They urged their horses to a gallop, racing along the sea-kissed shore. It seemed forever since she'd ridden a horse. Kath loosed her long blond hair, glorying in the stallion's speed. She pulled away from Juliana, sprinting along the beach. The tide was out, exposing a colorful garden of corals and shells, like riding on the edge of a mystical land. At the far end of the beach, a pair of sentinel statues sat brooding at the sea's edge. Giant ospreys carved from black basalt, they crouched on the seashore, guarding the causeway to the castle. Kath slowed her mount to a halt. Turning her horse, she stared the length of the narrow spit, captivated by the view. As if by magic, a narrow finger of land rose from the shimmering sea, stretching from the shore to the castle gates. Built on a rocky outcrop, Castle Seamount jutted from the sea like a fresh-drawn sword. Beyond the castle ramparts, a golden sun sank into the sea, bronzing the ocean to a mirror-bright shine, as if the west beckoned with glory. Kath had never seen such a wondrous approach to a castle.

Beside her, Juliana grinned with pride. "It's something, isn't it?"

Kath nodded. "Something out of legend."

The causeway beckoned, the sinking sun blazing golden behind the castle like a path to glory. Kath thrummed her heels and her horse leaped to a gallop. *For Honor and the Octagon!* She raced along the causeway, pulled by the light of the setting sun. Kath's spirit soared. She reveled in the ride, as if touched by myth and magic. All too soon, she reached the castle's outer gates. Clattering up the steep ramp, she entered the courtyard.

A guard in a checkered tabard rushed to grab the reins.

Kath dismounted, flushed from the ride.

Juliana was close behind, hoof beats clattering on stone. The others cantered into the courtyard at a more leisurely pace. Blaine led, followed by Danya with the mountain wolf, Bryx, hard on her heels. Zith and Aeroth came last, riding close together, deep in conversation. Guards took their horses while Juliana led them into the castle.

Kath half expected the basalt-carved castle to be dark and foreboding, but it was not. Stone-cool ceilings vaulted overhead, everything swept with the salty tang of the sea. Kath found the castle to be a welcoming mix of comfort and martial practicality. Great tapestries embroidered with sailing ships added jewel-bright colors to the dark walls. A brisk sea breeze blew in through many arrow-slit windows, refreshing the air. They climbed the tower stairs to a pair of oak doors studded with seashells. Two flanking guards snapped to attention, spears held erect.

Juliana said, "Wait here, while I greet the king." She slipped through the seashell doors, closing them softly behind her.

Kath waited with the others. Her gaze strayed to Aeroth, impatient with questions, but the two monks had fallen silent.

A guard said, "Your weapons."

Kath unsheathed her short sword, shrugged off her throwing axes, and removed the steel daggers from her belt and her boot, but she stubbornly kept the crystal dagger. Blaine added his blue steel sword and two daggers, making an impressive pile.

The guard raised an eyebrow. "You expectin' to fight an army?"

Blaine answered. "Already did."

The doors opened wide. Juliana welcomed them in. "Come and meet the king."

They entered the king's royal solar, a circle of comfortable chairs drawn before a blazing hearth. King Ivor sat hunched in a carved chair, his face lined, his pale hair silvered to white, looking far older than Kath expected, as if he were Juliana's grandfather, not her father. Knowing she owed him much, Kath bowed low to the king. "We thank you for sending your fleet north. Without your ships, we would have been trapped in the Dark Citadel, our victory turned to a bitter stalemate."

The king studied her with sea-colored eyes. "You come clad in mismatched armor with an Octagon Knight by your side...you must be Kath of Castlegard."

"Yes."

"So Jordan's visions proved true."

"Just so." Kath leaped on her sword sister's name. "Is Jordan here?"

"She's marched north with the army to confront the Pentacle."

Apprehension squeezed Kath's heart. "What of the Octagon?"

"Aeroth can tell you better than I."

Kath looked to the monk but he said nothing. Her heartbeat quickened. "Then our swords are needed."

"Swords that eat much yet pay nothing." The sour words came from a dark-clad counselor standing in the shadows.

The king intervened. "Garth, not now."

"Yet, the shopkeepers are nigh ready to draw swords of their own."

Zith intervened. "We've brought gold. We'll pay all their debts and compensate the ship captains for any damage to their vessels."

"A generous offer." The king's gaze returned to Kath, "And yes, your swords are sorely needed despite their fierce appetites." He stood. "Come, I've called a war council." Opening a side door, he led them up a narrow staircase to a turret-shaped room. A large window overlooked the sea. Light from the setting sun flooded the chamber, burnishing the room to a soft gold. Kath's gaze flicked to the window, an excellent vantage point for spying any seaward approach to the castle.

A half dozen men stood near the window. One was dressed in midnight-blue robes of the Kiralynn Order. Kath smothered her surprise. *Another monk.* It seemed the monks flocked to Navarre like ravens. Standing beside the monk was a swarthy warrior in fighting leathers. The man nodded towards her, a welcoming smile on his bearded face. The remaining four wore blue and red checkered surcoats of Navarre. Their silver and gray hair declared their age if not their experience.

The king made the introductions. He gestured to the monk, a large bearish man who seemed more of a brawler than a scholar. "This is Master Yarl. The swordsman beside him is Thaddeus Tokheart. Both were Jordan's companions on her travels from the Southern Mountains."

"Well met." Kath's interest quickened. She nodded towards them and gained smiles layered with unspoken meaning.

"And these are my war advisors, Major Abernathy, Major Raul, Captain Ross and Captain Marvinth." The king gestured to the dark-robed man with the sour face. "And you've met my brother-in-law, Garth, who now serves on my small council."

Kath made the introductions for her companions and then the king led them to a large round table dominating the chamber's heart. The tabletop bore a map of Erdhe, painted bright with snow-capped mountains, deep green forests and turquoise seas.

Mapmaking was a military art prized by the Octagon. Drawn to the map, Kath studied the details. Her gaze swept the length of the Dragon Spine Mountains, noting the painted positions of castles, keeps and strongholds, marked with maroon octagons. One stronghold was missing and the locations of two others were wrongly positioned. Kath wondered what else the mapmakers had missed. North of the Spines, the map showed nothing but golden-grained steppes. The great sprawling grassland lacked the gargoyle gates and the Mordant's Citadel. Where the gargoyle gates should have been, the map simply bore the words, *"Beware Darkness."* Kath shook her head. The sentiment was chilling, but how could the Light defeat the Dark with such a vague notion of evil? The map's inaccuracies did not auger well for the battle ahead.

The king took a seat at the map table. The others gathered around. King Ivor gestured to one of his men. "Major Abernathy, your sword."

The major drew his sword, a rapier with a gleaming basket-weave hilt, and set it across the map.

"Aeroth," the king looked to the tall monk with silvered hair, "the map is yours."

The monk took up the rapier, using it as a pointer. From the way he held the blade, Kath knew he was not sword-trained.

Aeroth rested the tip on Raven Pass, a sword poised at the throat of Erdhe.

Kath braced herself, knowing the tale would be bitter.

"In the dead of winter, the Mordant sent his hordes sweeping south across the steppes to strike at Raven Pass. The walls held strong and the knights fought valiantly, but magic was their demise. Dark magic shattered the gates and the horde overwhelmed the Octagon."

Kath stiffened, for the monk's words confirmed the Mordant's cruel taunts in the dark cavern. "What of my father?"

Aeroth's face softened. "He accepted a challenge of single combat. The king thought he fought against the Mordant, but he was tricked. A turned-cloak knight wore the Mordant's armor. Wielding a cursed sword, he broke the king's blue steel blade."

"Impossible!" The protest burst from Blaine. "Blue steel never breaks!"

Aeroth gave him a grim look. "I tell you it is true. The king's blue steel blade shattered against the cursed sword. King Ursus died from the wound, buried in a cairn overlooking Raven Pass."

Kath felt a deadly cold creep through her. She knew of her father's death, but not the manner of it. The details deepened the hurt. "Death by deceit leavened with magic."

The monk nodded. "Just so."

Blaine's voice rang with bluster. "How do you know this?"

"I stood at the king's cairn and spoke to the Knight Marshal."

His words carried the weight of authority. Cold as a tomb chiseled in stone, the king's death was unchangeable. Kath shuddered at the grim tale. She'd heard the bitter truth from Duncan, but somehow this second telling made it worse, a dagger at her heart. Blaine slipped a comforting hand onto her shoulder. "The king will be avenged."

"Just so."

Silence held sway, a moment of mourning for the Octagon King.

Zith brought them back to the war. "What kind of magic sundered the gates?"

Aeroth looked grim. "The gates weren't just shattered, they vanished as if vaporized. I'm guessing a Wizard's Knock."

Zith gaped. "The ancient war magics?"

"Just so."

"Then we'll need more than swords to win this war."

Aeroth gave Zith a sharp look. "That was ever a certainty."

Bursting with impatience, Kath blurted her question. "What of the Octagon?"

Aeroth gave her a solemn nod. "They fought a winter war, hiding in the mountains, nipping at the horde's heels. They made a difference, whittling down the enemy's forces, but now the knights are in retreat, their numbers greatly diminished."

Blaine's voice was gruff. "But they fight on."

"Yes, but they've been forced to retreat."

Retreat, the word sounded like a death knell to her ears.

Aeroth swung the rapier across the length of the Spines. "Their main force has retreated to hold the Octagon Bridge while the Rose Army holds Eye Bridge."

Kath nodded, approving the strategy. "They're using the Snowmelt as a bulwark."

Aeroth answered. "Just so."

"And what of the enemy?"

"They've split their forces." Aeroth spoke for the better part of an hour, explaining what he knew of the enemy and the allied forces. The monk painted a grim picture, the allies outnumbered by more than ten to one. Kath wondered how he got his information but something in his eyes made her stay her question. Moving markers across the map, they discussed battle tactics as darkness encroached on the chamber. The talk of war continued till the night ruled the sky. Servants brought lanterns to brighten the chamber. Kath knew all the key decisions were made yet the men chewed on the details like dogs worrying a bone. Back and forth, they argued old ideas, seeking a way for a few to defeat many.

Weary of circular arguments, Kath said, "The numbers are against us. We need another advantage." She stared at the monks. "Do you have any magic that can help?"

Both monks gaped as if shocked by the question. Master Yarl sputtered, "It is not a question one asks."

"Against such odds, we're done with niceties." Kath speared them with her glare. "Well?"

Master Yarl paled, shaking his head no.

"And you?" She turned her stare to Aeroth.

"My knowledge is my gift to you."

So he wields magic...of some sort, but Kath did not press him. Some secrets had a value all their own. "Knowledge of the enemy is worth a great deal...assuming it's more accurate than this map." From the corner of her eye, she saw the Navarren officers bristle with offense. "If you have no magic, then we must find another advantage." She stared at the map, the wavy blue line denoting the tight twists and turns of the Serpentines. An idea gnawed at the back of her mind. "If the enemy seeks a crossing point, they'll most likely find it at a sand bar." Kath looked to Captain Ross. "True?"

The captain gave a terse nod. "True." In a defensive tone, he added, "Maps of the Serpentines are never accurate. In the west, the Snowmelt re-carves its banks every spring."

"And in spring the river runs jade-green instead of crystal clear, burdened with glacier melt?"

"True."

"Then I may have an idea for Jordan...but it will be tricky. I'll write her a scroll, explaining the trap."

The king's gaze speared Kath. "You're not going north with your army?"

She swallowed, feeling the trap of her own destiny closing around her. Kath longed to wield her sword yet fate had put a dagger in her hand. "I cannot."

"But Jordan named you a warrior."

Kath gave the smallest of nods.

"Then why?"

"They know." Kath pointed to the monks, but they said nothing. Her hand tightened on the crystal dagger sheathed at her belt. "Because the true battle lies in the south...in Pellanor."

The king gave her a puzzled look. "In Pellanor?"

Kath gave him a solemn nod, wondering if he could bear the truth. "In many ways, this war in the north is nothing more than a brutal feint."

"A *feint?* You call a horde of invaders a *feint?*"

With so many lives at stake, the truth felt obscene, yet such was the way of evil. "Yes, a feint we dare not ignore. A feint we dare not lose. A brutal and terrible feint that will cost more lives than I care to count, but while we confront this war in the north, the true peril lies in the south."

"Why?"

"Because the Mordant is there." His name fell like a doom across the chamber.

Kath held the king's stare. "Evil seeks to rot Erdhe from within."

The king's face crumpled. "I know. It's already visited my castle, striking a perilous blow at my family...at my heart." The king's voice firmed, showing the steel beneath his grief. "Where in the south?"

"To Lanverness. To Pellanor."

The king's voice was a hollow croak. "My daughter is in Pellanor. And her messages have suddenly fallen silent."

"Then I have another reason to make all haste to the south."

"Why? What can *you* do?"

Her fate came calling, wrapping around her like a shroud, yet Kath did not shirk from it. She unsheathed the crystal dagger, holding it up to the lantern light. "Slay the Mordant...or die trying."

4

Tybalt

Tybalt flowed through the classical forms, his quarterstaff whirling in calloused hands. A chill wind blew down from the snow-crowned mountains billowing his golden robes, yet the mage-stone courtyard held a comforting warmth. He stood in the back row, ranks of his fellow acolytes mimicking the master's forms. Sweat beaded his brow, yet his every movement was smooth and subtle. Mind and body attuned to a single purpose, Ty's gaze remained fixed on the blue-robed master atop the dais. He knew the routine so well that his mind was free to dance the heavens. Morning practice felt like a prayer. Around him, two hundred golden-robed acolytes twirled as one, the subtle whisper of their quarterstaffs the only sound, poetry in motion.

The harmony of the moment filled him with elation.

Only an acolyte, yet he felt euphoric. The quarterstaff was his true calling, as if he scribed words upon the very air, daring to write his own destiny. Perhaps he deluded himself with visions of glory, yet he longed to make a difference, to serve the only home he'd ever known.

Nimeria's triumph was on every acolytes' lips. The monastery fairly hummed with the telling of it, how a girl of sixteen had summoned a sword of ancient providence. *Invictus,* the name alone shimmered with power, igniting imaginations. Many of his friends swarmed to the scriptorium, yearning to repeat Nimeria's prodigious feat, but Ty found calligraphy tedious. He appreciated the beauty of illuminated script, but a feathered quill was not his best weapon. While others toiled with ink and parchment, Ty followed his own calling, wielding his quarterstaff beneath vaulting blue skies.

A blue-robed master descended the far steps, breaking the symmetry of the moment.

Ty was too far away to hear, yet it was clear the newcomer whispered something to the quarterstaff master. Despite the unexpected interruption, there was never a break in the master's elegant form, his every move imbued with power and balance. Ty burned with curiosity, yet he kept to the forms, his gaze locked on the master.

The quarterstaff master completed the form, twirling his ironwood staff with enduring grace. Strike of the Eagle flowed into Chasm's Drop, loosing a deadly blow to an imaginary foe. Coming to a serene stop, Master Christoff stood tall. His blue robes billowing like storm clouds, he bowed to his students, releasing them from morning practice. Ty and the others snapped to attention, returning the master's bow, but instead of dispersing, they lingered, brimming with curiosity.

"Come." Master Christoff's deep voice summoned them close. "You might as well hear it from me."

A puddle of golden-robed youths collected around the master's platform. Ty stood in the back, with the older, more experienced acolytes. Leaning on his quarterstaff, Ty's calloused hands took comfort in caressing the smooth ironwood shaft.

Master Christoff surveyed his charges. Tall and whipcord-lean, he stared at them with crystal blue eyes set in a stern face haloed by a wild shock of steel-gray hair. "You've all seen the red comet burning the sky like an angry eye. You've all heard the rumors, both fair and foul. A time of turmoil is upon us. A time of choosing." He paused, as if considering his words. "Debate rages within our cloistered halls, yet I for one believe war is coming. Not just to the southern kingdoms...but to the very gates of the Kiralynn Monastery."

Gasps erupted from the youngest acolytes, yet Ty found himself leaning forward, as if hearing a call to battle.

"The Kiralynn Order is the Light that opposes the Dark. Although many of you are still young, you have been caught by the turning of an Age. The time has come to make your choice." The master drew a solemn breath. "By order of the Grand Master, the Age of Requirement is relaxed to fifteen years."

Excited whispers leaped through the acolytes like chained lightning.

Ty's heartbeat raced. *Only seventeen, yet the choice is mine!*

The master raised a hand, stilling the chatter. "All acolytes fifteen and older are to make their choice. You can take your vows, becoming sworn monks of the Kiralynn Order... or you can leave, to return to your families, to your homes, or wherever fate calls you."

Leave! The word opened like a gaping chasm at Ty's feet.

"Those of you who wield the quarterstaff will be given a third choice."

Interest ignited around him.

"Adepts of the quarterstaff who do not wish to take midnight-blue robes, will be given the choice of joining the Zward."

The *Zward!* The name rippled through the acolytes like a legend. Admittance to the secret society was said to be hereditary...or by rare invitation.

Master Christoff's voice overrode the murmurs. "The Zward is an honorable calling, to serve the Grand Master with sword and staff instead of scrolls and magic. But swearing your life to the Zward is just as binding as taking vows with the monastery. Either way, your choice will be everlasting." The master's gaze softened. "You are young to have such a decision thrust upon you, yet your skills, your eagerness, your youthful hearts may make a crucial difference in the coming war. Think hard and choose well. You have a fortnight to make your decision. May the Light guide you."

The master turned, a swirl of midnight-blue robes.

All around Ty his fellow acolytes burst into excited chatter. *The Zward! The monastery! Home!* The choices were thrilling...frightening...and forever defining. Ty tightened his grip on his quarterstaff. He'd never considered the Zward. The prophecies predicted a turning of an Age was nearly upon them, and now it was *his* turn to make a decision, to decide how to fight...but some dreams died hard. Ty forced his way through the press of golden-robed acolytes. Friends called his name, others plucked at his robes asking his decision, but he ignored them.

Reaching the stairs, he took them two at a time, climbing till he gained the upper level. Across the courtyard, he spied Master Christoff talking with a pair of blue-robed monks. Slowing his hasty rush to a respectable walk, Ty hailed the quarterstaff master. "Master Christoff, can I have a word?"

"Yes, of course." The master moved away from the others, giving him a modicum of privacy.

Ty took a sobering breath, struggling to marshal his thoughts. "The Zward...or the monastery."

The master gave him a wry smile. "So you've narrowed it down to two."

"I want to fight."

"Careful what you wish for. War is a bloody business."

"I know."

"I doubt that you do, yet that does not diminish your courage, or your choice." The master sobered. "This war with Darkness will exact a terrible toll. Whether you choose the Zward or the monastery, your skills with the quarterstaff will be sorely needed."

"I never considered the Zward."

"It is an honorable choice. You will be taught many different skills of war and serve below the mountains. In times of peace, you might even take up a trade, living a seemingly normal life, hiding in plain sight, but peace is not ordained for these times."

The question burst out of him. "But what of magic?"

"Ah," the master released a knowing sigh. "Only sworn monks are given access to the Order's trove of focuses."

Ty held his breath, waiting.

"Magic has a way of ensnaring the imagination."

Ty flashed a hungry smile. "Especially if you grow up surrounded by walls brimming with legend and prophecy."

"So true." The master nodded, as if awarding a point in a sparring match. "But I must warn you, magic is often more of a dream than a reality. Few ever bond with a focus."

"But..."

The master raised a hand, forestalling his question. "All those who wield magic will form the tip of the spear in the coming conflict. I say this not as an enticement, but as a warning. Wielding magic against the Mordant's forces is perilous beyond telling. The Kiralynn Order has already lost two accomplished masters to this war. Both died hideous deaths."

Ty felt the need to defend such heroism. "But their deaths mattered." His voice rang with staunch conviction.

The master gave him a fleeting look. "In truth, it is too soon to tell."

The answer unsettled him, yet Ty refused to be deterred. "But if I take the blue, I'll be given a chance to earn a focus?"

"Youth is ever endowed with too much confidence and not enough caution."

Ty gave him a resolute stare.

"I know you younglings are all agog with Nimeria's great feat, and rightly so, but the girl pays a steep price for her magic."

He'd heard Nim remained in the healery, locked in magical sleep.

"There is always a price to be paid for magic. Great feats exact the greatest toll."

"But will I have a chance?"

Master Christoff nodded in concession. "Most assuredly. By decree of the Grand Master, all focuses, and even the ancient relics, are to be brought forth from the vaults and tested. Every sworn monk, young or old, will have a chance to bond with a focus."

Magic! The word shimmered in his mind like a long-held dream.

"But be forewarned, magic is not a good enough reason to take the blue."

"Yet, it magnifies one's ability to serve."

"Spoken like a master steeped in Kiralynn lore. Do you mimic others or speak for yourself?"

Chagrined, Ty blurted the truth. "The words may belong to others, but I agree with them."

"Good enough." The master gave him a measuring look. "Whether you choose the Zward or the monastery, your skill with the quarterstaff will be sorely needed." His voice dropped to a potent whisper. "And with continued study, you may one day become a master of the quarterstaff."

A master! Ty's head swam with the heady praise, but that was a dream for another day. He had his answer. Bowing to the master, he took his leave and went to find his friends. Ty had no doubt war was coming, yet he could not keep the smile from his face, for it seemed as if he stood on the edge of a great adventure.

5

Katherine

The war council ground to an uneasy stalemate. Candles melted to stubs, allowing a stealthy darkness to encroach on the tower chamber. They'd debated every strategy and tactic, but given the horde's size there were no easy answers. Kath thought the king looked weary, too many arguments chewed and gnawed like a pack of hungry badgers worrying a meatless bone. Kath would have ended the council hours ago but the men persisted. Juliana sent her father a worried glance. "Enough for one night."

No one argued. Rain pelted the tower windows, an ugly squall blown in from the sea. As the others took their leave of the king, Kath asked if she might have Duncan's room. King Ivor gave her a questioning stare but agreed.

Blaine and Kath reclaimed their weapons. Servants bearing lanterns led the others to their rooms. Darkness cloaked the castle, giving it a somber feel. A brisk sea wind whistled through the upper tower like a lost soul.

Juliana approached carrying a lantern, a halo of light surrounding her. "This way." She led Kath down through the tower to a small room facing the sea. "How do you know Duncan?"

How do I know Duncan? The question echoed in her soul. The aching emptiness felt like a raw chasm, yet Juliana deserved an answer. "Duncan came north with us."

Juliana raised an eyebrow. "And?"

Kath forced the words out. "He died a hero's death."

Perhaps her words conveyed her heart-struck sorrow, for Juliana's stare lingered, her face softening. "Oh. I'm sorry." She placed the lit candle on a desk table, such a small circle of light against the dark. "We all loved Duncan, especially the king."

Kath struggled to contain her emotions.

"This was Duncan's room."

"Thank you." Kath watched as Juliana turned for the door. She could not let the captain leave with the words unsaid. "And, thank you...for believing in Jordan's visions and bringing the fleet north." Her voice dropped to a whisper. "I'll find a way to make it all count."

Juliana held her gaze. "I know you will."

The door clicked shut and Kath was alone in Duncan's room.

His room. Such a small wedged-shaped room. A narrow bed pressed against one wall, a small desk sat beneath an arrow-slit window. A chamber pot and a sea chest were the only other items. The dark walls were blank stone, devoid of tapestries, nothing to distinguish this room from any other...yet Kath hoped. Closing her eyes, she breathed deep...yearning for a hint of his presence...but she felt nothing. Defeated, she sank to the bed. Pressing her head to the pillow she took deep breaths...but smelled nothing save lye soap. Her gaze roved the chamber, latching onto the sea chest. Hope drew her to the chest. She knelt, her hands hovering over the latch, sending a prayer to Valin. It wasn't locked. Opening the chest, she peered inside, and found a spare wool blanket. Kath hugged the blanket but it smelled musty. Beneath the blanket was a man's cambric shirt. Faded and worn, the soft pale-white fabric was crosshatched with clumsy stitching, clearly a man's attempt to repair a favorite shirt.

His! She knew it was his. Wide at the shoulders to fit his archer's broad build, the shirt had a vee-neck laced with a frayed cord and long dangling sleeves. Soft and well worn, she could imagine him wearing it. Kath hugged it close. *Duncan!*

A knock sounded on the door.

Kath laid the shirt in the sea chest and closed the lid. "Come."

The door eased open and Blaine peered inside. "I brought them."

"Good, we need to talk." She took the glowing candle from the desk and lit two more by the bed, creating islands of light.

Blaine ushered Aeroth and Yarl into the room, followed by Zith, a conclave of monks. Closing the door, Blaine leaned against it, an unmovable doorstop, his silver surcoat glimmering in the pale candlelight. The room suddenly seemed very small. Kath perched on the desk while Zith sat on the bed. The two monks stood on the edge of the candlelight, their midnight-blue robes dulled to black by the shadows.

Kath met Aeroth's pale stare. "You spoke of the enemy in the north...but you were deathly quiet about the south."

Aeroth's stare crossed hers. "How certain are you that the Mordant is in Pellanor?"

Answer a question with a question, such was the way of the monks, yet Kath granted him an answer. "From Bryce."

Aeroth gave her a puzzled look, but then understanding struck. He gaped at Zith, the older monk confirming Kath's words with the smallest of nods. Aeroth recovered his stony demeanor. "How?"

This was the hard part. Kath took a steadying breath. "One of our companions was captured by the Mordant...and tortured in his unholy crypt beneath the Dark Citadel." Kath's voice cracked on the telling. She swallowed, refusing to succumb to tears. "Somehow he was linked with Bryce."

Zith intervened. "We think the Mordant used the sacrifice to draw on the Dark God's power from a distance. Somehow Bryce used the link."

Aeroth's eyes widened, his voice infused with awe. "Then the host lives within the harlequin!"

Zith nodded, his voice betraying a mixture of pride laced with pain. "My son lives and serves the Light, spying on the Mordant...but I shudder to think of the cost."

Aeroth sobered. "The Grand Master must hear of this, both the news of Bryce and the Mordant's location. We thought the Mordant traveled with his army. If not for your victory in the north, the Order would be blind." Aeroth's voice turned thoughtful. "Although there have been signs. Your words explain a great deal. Pellanor has fallen silent." He turned to Kath, urgency in his gaze. "What else did you learn?"

"That he seeks to corrupt and destroy the Rose Queen, to rot Erdhe from within."

"Why?"

"Something about the greatest divide, but it made little sense."

Aeroth's gaze locked on Zith. "The Magdalene quatrain!"

Kath stared at the two monks. "What?"

Yarl explained. "Magdalene, an ancient seeress of the Order, foretold that the Dark Lord seeks to sunder mortals by provoking us to fight amongst ourselves, letting us do his dirty work for him. The Dark Lord urges his minions to divide mankind, driving us to commit acts of atrocity against one another for the slightest difference."

Kath nodded. "Divide and conquer, one of the first rules of war."

"The greatest Divide is by gender, pitting men against women, for it divides mankind nearly in half."

Kath nodded. "Hence his hatred of the queen."

Zith said, "It's more than that. The Kiralynn Order remembers while others forget. Over a thousand years ago, we bore witness to the Mordant's first atrocity, the destruction of the great city-state of Azreal. Imagine an entire city, and all its inhabitants, turned to ash." Zith visibly shuddered. "That cataclysm spawned the War of Wizards, plunging Erdhe into a feudal darkness, where warlords ruled by might instead of magic and justice. When swords rule, when might holds sway, women become chattel. Thus, the Mordant invoked the first Great Divide."

"The first? What are the others?"

"Divide by gender, divide by race, and divide by beliefs, these are the three Great Divides, the three greatest commandments of the Dark Lord."

Kath thought of Duncan's mismatched eyes and all the hatred they invoked. *Divide and conquer,* the first rule of war, yet she'd never dreamt such a tactic would be wielded by a god. Shivering, she gripped her sword hilt, thinking of the queen who ruled by guile and coins. "And Queen Liandra, a woman who rules the most prosperous kingdom in all of Erdhe, threatens to undo this Divide?"

Aeroth nodded. "Just so."

"The queen must be warned."

"It is worse than you know. Pellanor has fallen silent."

"What do you mean?"

"The Grand Master sent an open emissary to the Rose Court. Fintan was cruelly murdered, beheaded in the queen's very castle." Aeroth gave her a piercing look. "The killer was never found. A second emissary was sent, hiding as an apothecary in the queen's city. He too was slain, killed by his own magic." The monk shook his head. "Too much is happening. This war is spinning out of control."

Zith's voice was laden with worry. "Fintan wielded a powerful focus. What of his magic?"

"Lost."

"The Mordant has it?"

"We must fear the worst."

Kath interrupted. "Send another monk."

"We sent three, led by Master Numar...but all of them failed to make the last meeting."

Zith gasped. "Numar is dead?"

"Slain by fire."

Zith turned ghost-pale. "And the others?"

Aeroth shrugged, his face grim. "Dead, captured, or in hiding, either way we are blind in Pellanor."

Kath felt a terrible dread choking the chamber. "I must get to Pellanor."

Aeroth put a steadying hand on her shoulder. "First you must tell us all you know of the Mordant's plans."

"Little enough," Kath closed her eyes, recalling Duncan's dying words. "The Mordant went to Pellanor to unseat the queen, but I know not how. He strives to rot Erdhe from within." She bit her lip, remembering. "And there was something about an amulet the Mordant stole from your monastery. He counted it as one of his greatest achievements, something he'd been seeking for many lifetimes."

Yarl looked sick. "The stolen amulet, the key to the Guardian Mist. With that amulet, the Mordant can breach the monastery's greatest defense. There's more at risk here than you know."

The pieces fell into place. Kath stared at Yarl, her voice laden with certainty. "That's where the two thousand are headed."

The burly monk startled. "What?"

She turned to Aeroth. "You said that two thousand swift cavalry crossed Eye Bridge. The Mordant is sending a lightning force to raid and plunder the monastery."

Aeroth's face blanched pale. "The Grand Master must be warned."

"What of the queen?"

Aeroth stared at her. "We'll do what we can...but the fate of the queen may rest in your hands."

Her shoulders tightened. "The sooner we ride, the better." She glanced at Blaine and he gave the barest of nods.

Aeroth turned to leave, but Zith said, "Wait. There is one more thing you need to know."

Aeroth turned, his gaze intent.

"When Kath conquered the Dark Citadel, she gained access to the Mordant's treasure crypt."

Aeroth's mouth gaped. "His *treasure* crypt?"

Zith nodded. "A great hoard gathered through the ages. It was unlike anything I'd ever seen. Wealth spilled carelessly across the floor, coins from all ages. Great ironbound chests stacked to the ceiling, holding everything from swords and scrolls to goblets and crowns. Amongst the treasure, sat a throne, the throne of the Star Knights."

Yarl gasped. "We thought it destroyed!"

"All these long centuries, we deemed it lost, yet the throne was hidden away in the Mordant's hoard, cocooned in darkness."

Kath remembered the throne, and the flash of light.

Aeroth said, "What did you do?"

Zith shrugged. "The throne was too heavy and too valuable, so I left it there, hidden in the darkness. As to the rest, I had no way to separate the magical from the mundane, so I did the best I could. We brought three chests full of artifacts and two full of scrolls south with us."

Aeroth's eyes flashed bright. "You have them here?"

Zith nodded. "In my chamber. Perhaps we've stolen the Mordant's war magic."

"Well done!" Aeroth gestured to the burly monk. "Yarl will help sort through the scrolls, but we'll need to bring Andrew from the monastery to magic-sense the artifacts."

Kath's interest quickened. "He can sense magic?"

"Yes, but he cannot say what powers a focus holds."

Kath shuddered, remembering the magic-sniffing dwarf that had chased her through the forests of Wyeth. "Are there many with this talent?"

"Only Andrew and his focus." Aeroth looked distracted. "I must take word to the Grand Master." He stepped towards the door, but then turned and bowed to Kath. "You gained a great victory in the north, an unexpected victory. You may have caused more harm to the Mordant than you know. Far more harm than the Order ever foresaw."

Kath flushed. "That victory cost much." Sadness tinged her voice. "Too much."

"Great victories always have their price. Having gained the victory, we must wield what we've learned to best advantage." He nodded to Kath. "The Grand Master will be warned. We'll send what aid that we can to Lanverness." Aeroth took his leave, along with Yarl.

As they'd agreed, Blaine stepped outside the door to keep watch.

Zith began to follow, but Kath said, "Wait."

Zith softly closed the door on the others, and turned to face her.

"Thank you."

"Why?" Zith seemed genuinely puzzled.

"For not mentioning the Quickner...or the chests of gold."

"Ah," Zith shrugged, "the one is irretrievably lost, buried beneath the Dark Citadel. The other is yours to wield. The gold has already proven its worth. I suspect you may have more need of it. If not for the war, then to rebuild afterward."

"Will there be an afterward?"

"We must hope."

She gave him a slow nod. "And thank you for not mentioning the other."

His gaze sharpened. "You are the blade bearer, so it seems to me it is yours to do with as you will. Perhaps something from the Mordant's own hoard will be his undoing."

"Just so." Kath said the words like a promise...a promise to Duncan.

His voice softened. "Have you decided?"

"Not yet."

"When the time comes, you will know." He gave her a weary smile and began to turn toward the door.

"Wait, there is one more question." Kath hesitated to speak of it, a worry she'd borne on the long voyage south, but she needed answers. Resigned, she tugged her mage-stone gargoyle from beneath her jerkin. "When we battled the MerChanters on the *Sprite*, I felt a searing pain. I thought I'd been stabbed, but there was no blood. Later I found a red welt...in the shape of my gargoyle."

Zith's eyebrows arched. "Your gargoyle?" He stepped towards her, peering at the small mage-stone figurine held on her outstretched hand, yet he did not touch it. "I've never heard of mage-stone behaving in a such a way."

"It felt like a message," she hesitated to say it, "a message from the gods." She stared up at him. "It felt like an ill-omen."

Zith gave her a sharp look. "What do you think it means?"

"The gods speak in riddles." Kath shrugged in frustration. "I hoped you or your brother monks might know the meaning."

"The gods are not so easily deciphered." He sank to the bed, weariness lining his face. "Tell me again where you found it?"

"In the hidden passages beneath Castlegard. Some of the mage-stone towers are ringed in gargoyles, like sentinels keeping watch. This one is a smaller twin to a gargoyle atop Needle Tower." She fondled the small figurine. "I always thought of this as my good luck charm, a piece of Castlegard that belongs to me."

Zith stared at her. "From your own words comes the truth."

"Another riddle?"

Zith sighed. "There are too many riddles already." He gestured to her gargoyle. "Clearly your focus is somehow tied to the great castle."

Fear shivered down her spine. Kath gripped her gargoyle, her voice dropping to a harsh whisper. "But it felt like pain." A thought pierced her like an arrow shot to her heart. "As if the castle is imperiled."

Zith shook his head. "Mage-stone is eternal, impervious to war and weather."

Something nagged at the back of Kath's mind, something she should remember, but the thought evaded her. "Ask the others. This seems like a warning we dare not ignore."

"I'll speak to the others on the morrow. And now I must get some sleep." He cast her a weary smile. "I long for a bed that does not sway to the sea's rhythm." Turning, Zith left the chamber.

Blaine hovered outside the door. "Did you get the answers you wanted?"

"Some of them."

He gave her an odd look. "When do we leave?"

"As soon as the king gives us horses and supplies."

"Are you sure we should ride for Pellanor and not Castlegard?"

His question pierced her own nagging doubts. She belonged to the maroon as much as Blaine, yet the gods had given her a crystal dagger. "Someone has to slay the Mordant."

A troubled look flitted across his sun-bronzed face, as if he might say something more, but then he bid her good night and closed the door behind him.

Kath sank to the bed, alone at last. Weary beyond telling, she unbuckled her sword belt and tugged off her boots.

A soft knock came from the door.

Stifling a groan, she stood and opened the door a mere hand's width. "Yes?" A burly swordsman clad in leathers waited in the hallway, the one who'd traveled from the monastery with Jordan. Kath could not remember his name.

He gave a courtly bow, "Thaddeus Tokheart," and extended a sealed scroll towards her. "I know it's late, but Jordan charged me to give this to you."

"Jordan?" Kath accepted the scroll, fingering the seal.

"She counted me as a friend. A close enough friend that I gave her away at her wedding."

"Her *wedding!*"

"I'm sure she speaks of it in the scroll." He took a half step towards her. "May I come in? I find it awkward to speak in the hallway and I have a secret to share."

A night for secrets. "Yes, come in." Kath closed the door behind him and then sat cross-legged on the bed, the scroll in her hands.

He remained near the door, as if he did not wish to crowd her. "My men and I would like to ride with you to Pellanor."

"Your men?"

"I am a captain of the Zward. We serve the Grand Master with swords instead of scrolls." He extended his hand, revealing a small silver signet ring as if it was proof. "The Grand Master charged me to aid and protect Jordan for as long as she was vision-guided. And then he charged me to aid the bearer of the crystal blade. My men and I have been waiting for you."

"The Grand Master *knew* I'd come to Navarre?" Disbelief spiked her voice.

Thaddeus shrugged. "Hard to say what the Grand Master does or does not know, but I suspect he felt Jordan's visions were somehow tied to the crystal blade."

Secrets wrapped in riddles, the monks played a mysterious game.

"Perhaps we seem too secretive to you, yet we have survived the ages while so many others have disappeared into dust."

Kath gave him a level stare. "But now you've come to fight?"

"We've always fought. It's just that few have ever known."

"But this is different."

He gave her a solemn nod. "The red comet heralds the Battle Immortal, a time for swords and secrets to both make a difference."

She fingered the scroll.

"Will you let us serve you?"

"How many?"

"What?"

"How many men?"

"Three, besides myself." He stared at her. "You'll find we have many valuable skills."

"No doubt." Kath hefted the scroll. "Jordan has my trust, so your swords are welcome."

A hungry grin flashed across his face. "You'll not regret it." He slipped from the chamber, closing the door behind him.

Kath sagged against the wall. Her head ached, yet she opened the scroll, holding it toward the candlelight. Her gaze flew across the ink-scrawled words, reading a harrowing tale of god-given visions, daring rescues, and a hasty wedding in a ruined keep. Kath smiled when she read of the wedding. So Jordan had married her love...just as Kath had married Duncan. She wished her sword sister joy and a long marriage. Her own marriage had been cruelly short...yet the brief time she'd had with Duncan was precious beyond measure. Kath gripped his warrior ring, remembering their wedding night in the Shield Forest.

A strong wind buffeted the window. A shutter banged open.

Leaping from the bed, Kath closed and latched the shutter, muffling the storm.

Rain drummed against the keep, a storm howling outside. Safe and warm, Kath stilled, stretching her senses, seeking Duncan. Her spirit yearned for his. "I miss you," she whispered the words but there was no answer.

Sighing, she set Jordan's scroll aside to be re-read many more times. Kath shrugged off her clothes and pulled on Duncan's cambric shirt. Whisper-soft against her naked skin, the hem fell to mid-thigh. Snuffing the candles, she crawled beneath the quilt and nestled in his bed. *His bed.* She hugged the soft cambric shirt, imagining his arms around her. Kath closed her eyes and found Duncan waiting in her dreams.

6

Ambrose

After the monastery's brilliant vibrancy, the wider world seemed dull and unscripted. A cold wind whistled down out of the snowcapped heights, a reminder that death was only an avalanche away. Ambrose followed the Zward down the mountainside, nothing but shades of dull gray rock in every direction. At first there was no trail, at least none he could discern, yet the bearded giant, Haythor, led with unflinching certainty, barreling down the mountain with a ground-eating stride. Ambrose struggled to keep pace, the other three Zward following close behind. They scrambled down steep cliff faces and strode along gravel screes, the pebbles shifting treacherously beneath their boots. Ambrose watched a kicked pebble tumble to oblivion. A fall would be deadly. He sidled closer to the mountainside.

A growing ache pierced his side, yet he refused to lag behind. All those years of studying scrolls had taken an invisible toll. Perhaps he should have spent more turns of the hourglass wielding a quarterstaff instead of studying in the scriptorium. Wiping the sweat from his forehead, he adjusted the straps holding the bundled sword across his shoulders.

The Zward walked with a ground-eating pace. Colors began to appear, a splash of bright yellow lichen sprayed across a rocky outcrop, as if a painter had grown careless with his brush. And then they reached the trees, stunted pine at first, but the fringe of dark green was a welcome sign to the monk.

They descended through the pine scrub, entering a dusky forest. Birdsong flitted from the branches, serenading the whistling wind. Almost as if by magic, a trail appeared beneath his boots. They followed it down, always down, weaving through pine trees and scattered boulders. Steep and winding, the trail forked many times, designed to lead enemies astray, but Haythor never hesitated, walking with unflagging confidence.

The Zward never slowed, leaving Ambrose struggling to keep pace. Leaning heavily on his quarterstaff, he limped down the trail. His side ached, his feet hurt and his breathing was ragged but he refused to complain. At every turn, he yearned to spy the trail's end. For the life of him, he did not remember the path down the mountain being so long or so arduous, but then he hadn't walked it for a decade of years. Just when he thought he'd collapse, the trail leveled off. Emerging from the trees, Ambrose glimpsed the patchwork fields surrounding Haven.

Haythor clapped a meaty hand to his back, knocking the breath from his lungs. "You did well, laddie buck. Twice back there I thought I'd have to carry ya!"

The others chuckled, but Ambrose sensed it was good natured.

"Come, we'll spend the night at the inn."

Ambrose forced himself to shamble forward, perked by the thought of the inn's comforts.

Haven was a charming village nestled amongst tilled fields. Horses gamboled across spring-bright grass while domesticated reindeer moved in antlered herds across fenced pastures. Farmers worked the tilled fields sowing springtime crops in rich, loamy soil. From the forest's edge, it looked the perfect picture of peace and prosperity. Ambrose knew many of the Zward called Haven their home. A quiet place to raise families and hone skills, the villagers thrived beneath the enlightened guidance of the monastery. Ambrose quickened his steps, eager for a hearty meal.

The trail widened to a road as they neared the village, but instead of a serene sanctuary, the town hummed like a kicked anthill. The harsh rasp of saws and the staccato of hammers echoed down the lane. Men and women worked in the street building shutters to board up windows and doors. Others carried furniture and belongings from shops and homes, loading them into already-full wagons. Children watched from doorways, their faces stricken.

Ambrose's steps slowed to a crawl. "What's happening?"

Kren answered, his face grim. "They're preparing for war."

War here in Haven? Ambrose found the thought nearly unthinkable. Like the monastery, Haven was erased from the maps of Erdhe, yet the villagers feared war at their doorsteps! He shuddered, making the hand sign against evil. *If the town of Haven fears war, then what hope does the rest of Erdhe have?* It was for this very reason that he'd offered to carry the sword to Castlegard. His gaze swept across the village, noting the grim changes. The Light had to win, he swore it in his heart.

They climbed the steps to the inn. Passing through the doorway, Ambrose was waylaid by the savory smells of lamb stew swirling through the great room. Breathing deep, he could almost taste the tender chunks of spring lamb and carrots soaking in a hearty gravy.

Haythor appeared by his side, pressing a key into his hand. "Go up to the room. I'll be there shortly."

Tearing himself away from the mouth-watering smell, he found the steps and tramped up the stairs. The room was small but very clean with a mullioned window overlooking the main street. He dumped his satchel onto the floor and then shrugged the carpet-wrapped sword from his shoulders. Laying the bundled sword across the length of the bed, he knelt to tug off his boots. A pungent smell invaded the room. His socks were soaked in sweat, his feet aching from the long trek. Sitting on the floor, he wiggled his toes, relieved to be free of the torturous boots.

A knock sounded on the door. Before he could answer, a woman bustled into the room carrying a basin of steaming water. Haythor, the bearded Zward, followed behind, crowding the small room with his presence.

"Place it on the floor, next to him."

The young woman settled the basin next to Ambrose. Flashing a shy smile, she bobbed a curtsey and then left, closing the door behind her.

Haythor said. "Wash your feet."

"What?"

"One of the first things you learn in the Zward is how to take care of your feet. If you don't take care of them, they won't take care of you. We've a long trek ahead and I aim to get you to Castlegard. So wash your feet."

Ambrose peeled the sodden socks from his feet, dismayed to discover his heels were riddled with puffy blisters, sore and tender. He eased his feet into the steaming basin, sighing from the heat.

Haythor sat at the small table, flicking a flint to light a candle. Unsheathing a wicked looking knife, he held the tip in the candle flame.

Ambrose eyed the knife. "What's that for?"

"Your blisters will heal faster once they're lanced."

The monk braced, expecting it to hurt, but the big man had a deft touch, lancing the blisters with barely a pinprick of pain.

"So you're more of a scholar than a fighter."

"Yes." Ambrose felt his face flame red, embarrassed at his lack of fitness.

"Put clean socks on those feet. They'll be right as rain in the morning." Haythor cleaned his knife and then sheathed it. "So what do you study?"

Ambrose rummaged through his satchel, searching for clean socks. "History, philosophy, prophecy, lore. The monastery is a feast of learning. I could never settle on just one discipline."

"A jack of many trades, a master of none."

He felt as if the big man was lancing all his weaknesses. "Just so."

"And now you're posing as a carpet peddler." Haythor gestured a meaty hand to the bundle-wrapped sword. "Not many carpet peddlers treading the southern mountains."

Ambrose stammered, "It's...a secret."

"Obviously, and none too well kept either. Let's see the sword."

"How?"

"The shape alone screams what's inside."

Ambrose was reluctant, but if he could not trust the Zward, he was doomed. He cut the ties binding the carpet remnant. It fell away to reveal the sapphire-blue sword, a magic-forged legend gleaming in the candlelight.

Haythor whistled like a man spying a gorgeous woman. "She's a beauty."

Ambrose stood between the big man and the sword.

"Such a wondrous blade must bear a name?"

"*Invictus!*"

The name shimmered like a light-kissed jewel.

Haythor nodded. "The name alone invokes courage. What does the blade do?"

Ambrose did not answer, for in truth, he did not know.

"Keep your secrets." Haythor shrugged, his gaze locked on the sword. "You know the best place to hide something is in plain sight." He flicked a glance toward the monk. "But they don't teach deception at the monastery, do they?"

"No, they don't." Ambrose considered the question. "Do they teach deception in the Zward?"

Haythor beamed a hearty grin. "Of course! Most times we're outnumbered, and even if we're not, the Grand Master wants us to succeed without being seen, as if we're mere rumors, or ghosts. Makes our tasks damn bloody difficult at times. Deception is oft our best ploy."

"So how would you hide the sword?"

"Like I said, in plain sight." He pulled a tangled nest of leather strips from deep within his pocket. "Give it here."

Ambrose hesitated. "It's not meant to be wielded by the likes of us."

Exasperation rode the big man's voice. "Then we won't wield it, will we? We'll just hide it."

The monk passed the sword to the warrior.

Haythor weighed the blade in his hands, a wistful look on his bearded face, but then he began wrapping the hilt with faded leather strips. Starting with the pommel, he wrapped the two-handed grip and the coiled dragons riding the hilt, skillfully covering every telltale gleam of sapphire-blue. "Such a beauty. A pity to hide it." He handed the wrapped blade back to the monk. "I'll bring you a faded leather scabbard tomorrow. If you carry it like a sword, no one will give it a second glance." His face turned thoughtful. "But then you're not used to carrying a sword, are you?"

Ambrose clutched the sword. "No."

"Then tomorrow night, you'll start sword lessons."

"I'm just carrying it! I'm not meant to wield it."

"If you don't look like a man accustomed to wielding a sword, you'll draw notice. If you draw notice, then the sword becomes a prize instead of just a weapon."

Ambrose nodded. "I'll start lessons."

"Good." Haythor stood, his girth suddenly crowding the small chamber. "I'll have some stew sent up. Eat and then get some rest. We ride before sunrise."

Ambrose bundled the sword back into the carpet remnant and hid it under the bed. *Sword lessons*...he wondered if he'd still be a scholar by the time this quest was done.

A gentle knock sounded on the door.

He moved away from the bed. "Come."

The serving girl returned bearing a tray with a large bowl of stew, a frothy tankard of ale, and half a loaf of crusty white bread. Steam rose from the bread, proof it was fresh-baked from the oven. The monk fell on the meal, spooning mouthfuls of stew. The lamb was fork-tender, the gravy rich and flavorful. Tearing a chunk from the still-warm bread, he wiped the bowl, savoring every lip-smacking bite. Finishing the ale, he suddenly felt hammered with exhaustion. Falling into bed with his clothes still on, he succumbed to sleep.

"Wake up!" A large hand shook him.

It seemed to Ambrose that he'd only just closed his eyes.

"Get up!" Haythor gave him an insistent prod.

Night darkened the window, yet he rolled from bed, rubbing the sleep from his eyes.

Haythor thrust a worn leather scabbard into his hands. "For the sword. Where is it?"

And then Ambrose remembered his mission. Reaching beneath the bed, he reclaimed the carpet-wrapped sword and sheathed it in the scabbard, a perfect fit. With the leather straps hiding the hilt's true color, it almost looked like an ordinary sword. *Almost.*

Haythor helped him into the shoulder harness. Taking a step back, the big Zward gave him a critical look. "You still don't look like a swordsman, but we'll work on that. Come." Grabbing the monk's satchel from the floor, he turned for the door. "Time's a wasting."

The big man made his way down the steps with surprising stealth. Ambrose followed, trying not to disturb the inn's peace. They crossed the empty great room, embers glowing red in the hearth. Shrugging on his cloak, Ambrose stepped out into the brisk morning air, the dark just before the dawn. Stars rode the sky, the barest hint of light brightening the eastern mountains with a soft alpine glow. The others were already there, mounted on sturdy horses. Haythor gave him a leg up. Affixing the monk's satchel to his saddle, he turned and took the reins of a big chestnut stallion. Swinging into the saddle, he spurred his horse to a gallop. "We're away!"

Choking on the other's dust, Ambrose clucked to his horse. His mare lunged to a rollicking gallop. He struggled to keep his seat, adjusting to the horse's rhythm. Twice he almost fell, recovering at the last moment. Settling into the saddle, he followed the others. They rode through the village and surrounding fields and then up into the mountains. The road narrowed and turned steep, zigzagging up into the snowy heights. The pace slowed to a trot, but even then Ambrose feared it was too fast, worried the horses would be blown before they crossed the mountains.

Sunlight rose in glorious hues of gold, banded rays piercing the clouds like a benediction. The snow-crowned mountains blazed with color, reflecting the heavens. Ambrose found the beauty piercing. And to think he'd thought the world gray and unscripted. He'd spent too many years secluded amongst musty tomes, yet he missed the scholarly order of the monastery. Staring across the valley, he longed for a glimpse of home, but the monastery was hidden from view, lost in the mountain vastness. He prayed it remained so, invisible to friends and foes alike.

The sun crested the mountains, banishing the dawn colors. A brilliant blue vault stretched overhead. Even in broad daylight, the red comet was visible low in the sky, a scar blighting the day. Riding single file, Ambrose followed the others up the steep trail. Their quick start soon turned to an eternal plod. Ever upwards, they pressed on, winding their way up the mountain. Unaccustomed to riding, Ambrose discovered new aches. He fidgeted in the saddle, trying to lessen the hurt. His sturdy mare whinnied in rebuke. Midday approached, but the Zward never stopped, eating trail bread in the saddle. Ambrose longed for a break from the punishing ride, yet he grew deeply impressed with the Zward's determination and skills. Despite his newfound aches, his hopes began to soar.

They rode through the day, passing beyond the tree line. The trail narrowed, skirting up the mountainside. His mare stumbled, sending pebbles tumbling to oblivion. The mare was sweat-stained and blowing hard. He began to fear for his horse. "Perhaps we should take a rest?"

At first he thought his words were swallowed by the mountain vastness, but then Kren turned in the saddle. "Almost there."

Almost there! The words made no sense. He looked around, spying nothing but rock, gravel, and snow. The barren mountain wilderness drew close as a stranglehold, forbidding and cold. Confused and aching, Ambrose huddled under his cloak, giving silent encouragement to his horse.

Twilight fell like a hammer blow, the sun eclipsed by jagged peaks.

A muted roar pounded through the mountains. Somewhere, an avalanche fell, a killing wave of snow and ice. His heartbeat raced to a gallop. Ambrose scanned the lofty heights, but he saw no fell rush of snow.

His mare slipped on the scree. Regaining her footing, she struggled up the steep slope, blowing gusts of steam into the chill evening air.

And then his horse stopped. Startled, he looked up, surprised to find the others dismounting. Stiff and sore, he clambered down from the saddle, edging his way forward. "What's happening?"

Kren answered. "We're here, get your satchel."

Here? Befuddled, Ambrose turned in every direction, seeing nothing but snow and rock. "What do you mean, we're here?"

Kren shrugged a bulging pack onto his shoulders. "We've reached Drumheller Pass. By order of the Grand Master, no horses are to travel beyond this point."

"But why?"

"Boot prints are easy to hide, but puddles of horse piss and dung piles are not. Seclusion is the monastery's best protection. We'll walk till we reach the lowlands."

The meaning behind Kren's words hit hard. *War!* The threat overshadowed them all, dogging their every step. Ambrose returned to his horse. Giving the mare a grateful pat, he unbuckled his satchel and tugged it onto his shoulders.

A young lad appeared, stepping lightly down the trail. "I'll take your horse, sir."

"Where'd you come from?"

The lad flashed a gap-toothed smile. "Enid and I have been waiting. We'll take yer horses back to their pastures."

Even the children do their part. By the Light, we dare not fail. The sword suddenly felt heavy across his shoulders. Handing the reins to the lad, Ambrose pulled his cloak close against the brisk mountain cold. Shuffling forward, he made his way up the steep trail.

Haythor and the others waited for him, all of them carrying heavy packs and bristling with weapons. "Come, we've a long way to walk. Time's a wastin'."

Ambrose followed the Zward up the trail. They crossed the pass by starlight, descending into the darkness of the southern kingdoms.

7

Danya

Danya stared out the arrow-slit window at the wind-swept sea, wondering what the future held. Perhaps she'd spent too much time listening to the *Sprite's* sailors, becoming swayed by their superstitious lore. Since coming ashore, she'd been obsessed with the notion that she needed to have her fortune told, to seek the wisdom of the gods before venturing south with Kath and her maroon band.

"Come and eat." Neven flashed a warm smile. "You worry too much."

She returned to the table to sit next to him. Reaching for a scone, her sleeve pulled back, exposing the silver cuff incised with animal silhouettes. Danya yanked back her arm as if she'd been scalded, hastily tugging down her sleeve to hide the focus. A boon and a curse, she'd give it back if she could.

Beside her, Neven reached for the scones, passing them to her with a soft smile. "Have one." He put two on his own plate. "These southerners have strange ways, but their bakers make fare fit for the gods."

Her wolf-faced warrior, he'd risked so much for her, daring the perilous sea voyage south, daring the enemy, surely the gods would keep him safe. She took an oven-warmed scone and gave him an answering smile. "I'm glad you're with me."

"I know, *chera.*"

Chera, an endearment that meant *my heart.* Warmth flushed her face, always thrilled to hear the word pass his lips.

Beside her Gris said, "Better eat fast, we're wanted in the courtyard."

Danya scowled, feeling as if every moment with Neven was stolen. Tossing half the scone to Bryx, she slathered marmalade on the other half, stuffed it in her mouth, and rushed to follow Neven and his wolf-faced warriors through the castle hallways. Moving silent as wolves, they prowled through the great ironbound doors out into the shadowed courtyard. The sun was barely over the horizon, the morning air heavy with the salty scent of the sea, yet the courtyard teemed with saddled horses.

A tall man with long hair so pale it was nearly white strode toward her. "So you're the horse whisperer?" Clad in riding leathers, he smelled of horses and hay. "I was told you'd have the choosing of the mounts." He raked her with an ice-blue stare laden with disbelief.

Danya knew what he saw, a small petite girl with a pale face and a long straggle of brown hair, yet she refused to be discounted. "I know horses."

"Sure you do." He gestured towards the mounts. "Brought fifty of my best. I was told you'd be needin' thirty-five saddled for riding plus a few spares. Picked them myself, so they're all sound mounts. Can't go wrong with any of 'em."

"We'll see." Danya moved among the horses, keeping Bryx close by her side. Magic rose like a tide in her silver cuff, yearning to be released, yet she held the power to a trickle. Stamping hooves and tossing manes, the horses shied from the mountain wolf, till Danya eased their fears, introducing Bryx as a friend and protector. Running her hands along their silky coats, she murmured words of greeting while casting pictures in her mind. *Horses running, hooves pounding, manes rippling like battle banners,* she shared their love of a windswept gallop. A stallion nuzzled her, his muzzle soft, his large liquid eyes brimming with a warm intelligence, his heart full of courage. "This one for Kath." She found a gentle mare with a smooth gait. "This one for Zith." A showy roan nickered and pranced, tossing his mane as if he refused to be left behind. Smiling, she stroked his neck, surprised to find an even temperament beneath the glossy red coat. "This one for Neven." Danya worked her way through the horses, choosing mounts for each of her companions.

As she called their names, painted warriors came forward to claim their mounts. Uneasy around horses, they stared at their mounts as if they were fire-breathing dragons, yet they willingly sacrificed whole days galloping along the beach, determined to learn how to ride so they could follow their Svala south.

When she finished, a smaller herd was culled from the rest. "We won't be needing these."

The white-haired horse master sneered. "You say you know horses, but you didn't choose the Silver. He's the best of the lot!"

"The Silver is indeed a fine stallion, but he has a hairline crack in his left rear hoof. You'll need to get him to a good farrier before he pulls up lame."

The horse master gave her a squinty-eyed look. "His hoof is sound."

Danya shrugged. "See for yourself."

"I will." Ordering a groom to hold the silver, the master lifted the rear hoof, using a iron pick to clean it. His bluster turned to surprise, his gaze snapping to Danya. "How'd you know?"

In a quiet voice, she answered, "He told me."

His gaze narrowed, his voice laden with suspicion. "What else did they tell you?"

"The dun mare and the roan gelding both have bad manners and stubborn dispositions, not because they're bad horses, but because they had bad owners. They need patience before they'll be good mounts again."

"Anything else?"

A mischievous smile slipped across Danya's face. "Yes, the chestnut mare's with foal."

He gaped. "It's too soon to tell."

"Not for the mare."

He gave her a flinty-eyed stare.

Danya braced for scorn, or worse, the accusation of witchcraft, but the horse master surprised her. "Well, that darn beats all! Findin' that hairline crack without lifting a hoof and knowin' about the mare," his gaze turned to open admiration. "The castle said you was good, I should have believed them."

Relief ran through her. She gave him a shy smile.

Guards in checkered tabards poured into the courtyard. "Mount up! This is your last day and you've plenty to learn."

The last day. Her chance to have her fortune told was slipping away.

The painted warriors clambered into saddles. Most looked ill at ease, yet none of them shirked the chance to learn to ride. Neven winked at her from atop the showy roan, giving her a jaunty smile till the roan pranced sideways, tossing his dark mane. Neven stiffened, clutching the saddle horn. Danya sent the roan a stern look, *take care of him.*

Whinnying, the showy roan settled into a well-behaved mount.

Neven flashed a grateful smile her way.

The Navarren guards swung into the saddle, turning their horses towards the castle gates. "Let's ride!" Horses whinnied and nickered. Mounted men swirled through the courtyard, a clatter of hooves on stone. The guards led the warriors through the castle gateway and down the ramp to the long causeway. The last horse cantered through the gate, taking the noise and chaos with them, and then they were gone.

Danya watched till they reached the causeway's end, turning to gallop along the wide, curving beach.

In the courtyard, the horse master put his remaining mounts on a lead. "You're not with the others?"

"I'm with them, I just have something else I need to do." Danya crossed to the piebald mare she'd chosen for herself. Adjusting the stirrups, she swung into the saddle. Before her magic, she'd been a poor rider, uneasy in the saddle, but her skill no longer mattered. The silver cuff gave her a bond with all the animals around her. Having an understanding with the horse was the true trick to riding. Murmuring to the piebald mare, she rode through the gateway and down the ramp at an easy trot. Bryx followed close behind.

A brisk sea breeze whipped her long brown hair into a tangle. She chided herself for not braiding it, but Neven liked her hair long and loose. Her gaze followed the painted warriors as they galloped along the beach. Already four riders were down, sprawled on the wet sand. Neven would be sore tonight. They'd all be sore, yet they'd follow Kath south, iron pulled by an irresistible loadstone. Her gaze stole to the west, to the red comet riding low in the sky. Danya hated the thought of war, of more death and more battles, yet she'd promised to help. Perhaps the fortuneteller could ease her fears.

The piebald mare crossed the causeway without breaking stride. Danya marveled at the view. Coral gardens were exposed on both sides, orange and purple starfish glistening in the dawn light, treasures revealed by the retreating waves. Seagulls swirled overhead, the air laden with the birds' piercing cries and the sea's salty scent. Beyond the sandy shore, tiered houses climbed the crescent-shaped hills, a stunning backdrop to the turquoise sea. Clad in pale white stone, the city sparkled bright in the morning sun. Such a warm and welcoming city, as if the white-clad houses offered an embrace to the sea. Danya stared in wonder, for she'd never seen anything like it.

The sturdy mare knew the way, taking her across the causeway to the heart of the harbor. She found a hitching post near a clump of spring-bright grass and left the mare to graze. With Bryx by her side, she explored the harbor. People bustled to and fro with baskets on their hips, the soft murmur of conversation riding the salty air. Danya followed the bustle to the shops. The variety was amazing, selling everything from elaborately carved cedar chests, to beeswax candles, to seashell jewelry and clothing of all sorts.

Her belt purse hung heavy with golds, a gift from Zith, Danya decided to indulge in some gifts of her own. For Neven she bought a soft wool cloak dyed a deep forest green, a perfect complement to the dark woodsy brown of his eyes. For Gris, she bought a keen-bladed knife with an elk-horn handle. For the brothers, Balthus and Bardus, she bought leather belts tooled with images of running wolves. And for Severn, she found a flute carved of bone that had the sweetest sound. For herself, she could not resist a silver broach fashioned like a wolf's grinning face with green crystals inset for sparkling eyes. Aside from the silver focus, she'd never owned anything so fine. Pinning it to her cloak, she admired it in the merchant's mirror.

"What do you think, Bryx?"

The wolf chuffed in agreement.

While she bought gifts for Neven's den brothers, she plied the merchants for rumors of fortunetellers. One name was often repeated in hushed tones laden with a strange mix of fear and respect. "The crone's the one you want. Even Good Queen Megan, the gods rest her soul, sought the crone for her second-sight. Find the red door and you'll find your answers."

A shiver raced down Danya's spine like a trace of ghostly fingers. She gathered up her purchases and rushed from the shop.

Knowing she needed to return to the castle before the sea claimed the causeway, she left the bustling shops, seeking the crone's red door in the warren of back alleyways. Her footsteps slowed, growing hesitant. A part of her desperately longed for answers, yet another part wondered if the future was better left unknown. Her hand stole to the silver cuff hidden beneath her sleeve. She knew so little of magic and even less of the gods, yet she was caught by both, entangled in a fate that was not of her choosing. She longed to return to the far north, to take the full tattoos of the wolf den and marry Neven, yet she was committed to following Kath south. Her magic was sorely needed, yet she feared to be trapped by it. Magic took a heavy toll. The long life-stealing slumber frightened her. The attack on the Dark Citadel had stolen moon-turns from her life, time with Neven she could not retrieve. Even worse than the death-like slumber, Danya flatly refused to put any animal at risk.

Never again. A shudder passed through her, remembering the horses of the steppes.

Bryx yipped, darting in front of her, nearly tripping her.

Startled from her grim thoughts, she slowed her footsteps to a halt. "What is it?" Danya found herself standing in front of a rune-carved door painted bright red. "Oh."

A bell cord hung by the door.

Danya stared at it, considering if it was truly wise to seek the future.

Before she could decide, the red door burst open.

Startled, Danya, jumped back a pace.

An old woman with a halo of wispy gray hair peered from inside. "There you are! Knew you'd be coming. Come in, come in! I'm Matilda, the one you seek."

Such a warm welcome, Danya found herself following the old woman inside despite her puzzlement. "You knew I was coming?"

"The runes told me."

The crone's words held such quiet honesty they eased Danya's gnawing doubts.

Soothing scents of dried herbs and candle wax embraced her, pulling her deeper into the shop. Brightly colored bottles of all shapes and sizes cluttered the long shelves, proving the old woman was more than just a fortuneteller. Dried herbs dangled from the ceiling, tied with cheerful ribbons. Beeswax candles perched everywhere, on shelves, on windowsills, on wrought iron stands, as if the small shop sought every source of light. A star-shaped lantern hung in the heart of the cluttered room, dangling over a small round table. A fringed shawl draped the table, swirls of crimson and sapphire woven in an eye-catching pattern.

"I see you serve the Light."

Danya's stare jerked back to the old woman. "Why do you say that?"

"Because of the wolf."

Danya gave her a puzzled look.

"Oh, I know animals can serve those of Dark intent, but those poor beasts are usually twisted and warped by the foulness of those they serve. Find a vicious dog and you'll find a vicious master. Come to think of it, 'tis true of men as well as dogs." The crone gestured to Bryx. "The wolf looks hale and healthy and happy to be by your side."

Danya reached for Bryx, scratching the thick ruff at his neck. The wolf gave a satisfied rumble.

Flashing a knowing smile, the old woman fluttered about the room, lighting candles despite the morning sun pouring through the bottle-glass windows. "Have a seat. No need to stand on formality with me, my dear."

Danya sat at the small round table with Bryx curled by her boots. Uncertain what to do, she clasped her hands on the tabletop, the worn fringed shawl adding a splash of jewel-bright color to the room.

The crone sat across from her, her weathered face crisscrossed with wrinkles. "So you've come to cast the runes."

It was a statement not a question. "How do you know?"

"Such a healthy young lass, you don't look like you need a midwife or an herb witch, so I'm guessing you've come laden with questions."

"Oh," Danya felt vaguely disappointed.

The old woman flashed a kindly smile. "And the runes told me you'd be coming."

She began to wonder if this was all just a charlatan's ruse. "And did the runes tell you my future?"

"So you aren't a believer?"

The question caught Danya off guard. "I'm not sure. I know magic exists, yet can anyone truly see the future?"

"Yet you found your way to my door."

"Yes." *The crone had an uncanny way of seeing to the heart of things.*

"The gods see what can be. Sometimes they choose to share it with us poor mortals." The crone smiled. "If we ask nicely."

Danya wasn't sure if she believed in fortunetelling, but she decided to trust the old woman. "My life has changed so much, I hardly know myself. Some of the changes have been truly wonderful," she thought of Neven's warm arms wrapped around her at night, "but some of it truly terrifies me."

"So you seek to avoid the one and have more of the other?"

"Yes."

"Don't we all. If we live fully we can't help but get a dose of both." The crone opened a brightly painted cedar chest, removing a red velvet bag and a folded square of white linen. "Let's see if the gods choose to reply." She spread the linen square across the tabletop, revealing a twenty-pointed star painted in bright gold against the startling white linen. Her weathered hands smoothed the linen, running the length of each star point, as if invoking the gods from all directions. "Now, the petitioner asks for the blessing of her god."

Danya had never favored one god over another, so she prayed to the pantheon, to all the Lords of Light.

The crone held the velvet bag high above the center of the star. "The petitioner chooses seven runes."

Reaching up, Danya delved her hand into the drawstring bag. The smooth rune-tiles brushed cool against her fingertips. She swirled the runes, choosing seven.

"Now, the petitioner asks the question, casting the runes upon the many-pointed star."

Danya took a deep breath, asking the question pounding through her mind. *Show me how to wield my magic and survive.* She released the runes, casting them upon the star. Small tiles of colored glass scattered across the tabletop. Runes painted in bright gold shone from some of the tiles. Two landed face down, their dull side up. One of the seven teetered sideways, landing partially atop another, obscuring the lower rune. Danya reached to straighten it.

"Don't!"

Danya pulled her hand back as if bitten.

"The runes' positions say as much as the runes themselves. They cannot be disturbed lest the message be muddled." The old woman stared at the pattern, her eyes narrowed in thought.

Danya returned her gaze to the brightly colored runes, but they made little sense. Her gaze snagged on the rune sitting at the heart of the painted star. A rich amethyst in color, the tile was shiny-bright, which meant it was face-up...yet, there was no rune painted upon the tile. The rune was *blank*. A shiver raced down her back. "Why is that tile runeless?"

"That is the Wyrd rune, very powerful and very mysterious. So mysterious that its runic symbol cannot be drawn by the hand of mortals."

Another shiver claimed her, this one laden with dread. "Is it good...or bad?"

The crone's voice dropped to a hush. "Wyrd is the rune of fate. A very powerful rune, especially when it lies at the heart of the casting, at the very heart of the star." The crone pierced Danya with her stare. "You have come here on a matter of fate. And your fate matters to many."

A cold sweat erupted from Danya's skin, as if the gods peered over her shoulder. Shivering despite the room's warmth, she wasn't sure if she wanted to hear any more.

The crone pointed at the two runes lying nearest the star's heart. "Yours is a very rare and very ominous pattern, one I've heard rumors of but never seen. This rune teetering on the side of the Wyrd rune is Kauno, the Torch rune. Light on one side, Darkness on the other, Kauno foretells life or death, but in your casting it shows neither one nor the other. Lying balanced on your Wyrd, much will hinge on the outcome of your fate."

"What must I do?" The words whispered out of Danya.

"You must look to the other runes for answers. This red rune is Tir, the god of war."

"But Valin is the god of war!"

The crone's voice held a touch of rebuke. "Tir was the first god of war, far older than Valin, from before the dawn of time. The old gods and the new have a stake in this battle. Blood will flow ere it is done." Her boney finger roved across the table, reading the runes. "And this is Peorth, the rune of all things hidden. And this is Mann, the rune of many. And this upside down rune is Daeg, the daylight rune inverted to mean night and the need to be hidden." The crone shook her head. "Twice you are bidden to hide. The gods send you a powerful message, a powerful warning." The old woman gasped, her gaze suddenly becoming unfocused. She jerked upright, as if pulled by a giant hand. Grasping the table with both hands, the crone began to shudder and shake, as if caught in a fit. Runes tumbled across the painted star, destroying the pattern. The crone's voice dropped to a harsh rasp, *"Remain hidden! Use the many, use the small! Watch and seek and guide! Remain hidden lest the enemy gain your magic! Remain hidden or all will fail."*

Danya gaped.

"Heed the warning! Keep your magic hidden!" The crone shuddered and then slumped back in her chair. She looked somehow diminished, her face

ghost-pale. Shaking and shivering, as if throwing off a hand gripping her shoulder, the old woman seemed to come back to herself "The gods spoke." She blinked, her voice sounding mortal once more. "I hope you listen."

Danya stared down at the runes, but the pattern was ruined. The runes scattered across the painted star as if to wipe clean the message.

"The rune pattern is broken. I have no more for you."

With shaking hands, Danya reached for her purse. "What do I owe you?"

"Nothing." The old woman shook her head, her voice grave. "I'll take no coin to serve the gods."

Her heartfelt words only deepened Danya's fear. She started to rise, but the crone's hand snaked out, catching her wrist with surprising strength. "Heed the gods, or it will go ill for us all!"

The crone released her.

Danya ran for the door, Bryx on her heels. She fled the crone, she fled the god's voice. Racing through the cobbled streets, she ran blindly downhill towards the harbor...feeling as if fate nipped at her heels.

8

Tybalt

The hours of fasting and contemplation crawled by. Ty paced his sleeping chamber, his stomach grumbling in complaint. Seeking to soothe his festering nerves, he reached for his quarterstaff and began working through a set of forms designed for close quarter fighting. The steady whisper of his staff proved a comforting companion. Many of his friends had chosen the Zward, keen to wield their quarterstaffs in battle, yet despite their urging, Ty decided to remain with the Order. Never scrollish, yet somehow the ways of the monastery had seeped into his soul. He could not imagine leaving the script-filled sanctuary. His grip tightened on his ironwood staff, vowing to do all he could to hold Darkness at bay. Hours blurred as he worked the forms, defeating imaginary foes, yet when the knock finally came, it ambushed him, jarring his heart to a runaway gallop. Taking a deep breath, Ty set his quarterstaff aside and smoothed his golden-yellow robes, struggling to appear calm lest the masters change their lofty minds. Raking his hand through his unruly wheat-blond hair, he hastily cinched his rope belt with the simple knot of a novice. Taking a last glance at the small spare cell, Ty opened the door to his future.

Master Christoff waited in the hallway, his wild tousle of steel-gray hair tamed to a warrior's ponytail. "Are you ready to swear your life to the Seeing Eye?"

A shiver raced down his back, yet Ty held his voice steady. "I am."

The master gave him a knowing nod. "Then come, for it is time."

Ty followed the master down the cloistered hallway. Sunlight streamed through narrow windows, setting the illuminated walls aglow, more proof the hour was at hand. From time immemorial the monastic oath was always taken at the sun's zenith, when the full light of day dispelled shadows, a reminder that the Light would conquer the ever-threatening Dark if the Kiralynn monks held true to their purpose. And now those ancient prophecies would be put to the test. *The Battle Immortal*, Ty shivered at the powerful words. An orphan reared amongst legends and prophecies, Ty's gaze sought the comfort of calligraphy-filled walls. Elaborate script gleamed with golden highlights, the capital letters embellished with bright colors, every wall a stunning masterpiece. Entwined amongst the letters, heroes triumphed with raised swords while bards strummed their harps and castles stood stalwart with ramparts tall. Taken as a whole, the walls were a dazzling display, but the truth lay in the details. Ancient prophecies warned of a creeping Darkness, when an ancient evil would reach for all of Erdhe, and now that dire time, long foretold, was at hand. In truth, the prophecies scared him, yet they also made him bold. If ever there was a time for heroes, this was it.

Yellow-gold doors began to grow sparse, giving way to those painted a deep midnight-blue. *Midnight-blue,* Ty's gaze snagged on the forbidden color, a taunt and a tease. His imagination ran wild with possibilities, wondering what lay behind the forbidden doors. A smile split his face, knowing the mysteries would soon be his to explore.

Master Christoff sent a stern glance his way. "The monastery contains riddles wrapped in mystery. Taking your vows is only the first step. You have much to learn."

Ty wiped the smile from his face.

Cloaked in solemn silence, he followed the master through the hallowed halls, seeking the ancient heart of the Kiralynn Order. The walls narrowed, evoking a feeling of great age. Carolingian script changed to Gothic, the entwined embellishments becoming more sinister. Shadowy figures with red glowing eyes peered from the text. In the margins, stone gargoyles writhed upon pillars as legions in dark armor invaded the illuminated text. Ty shivered, feeling the potent threat embedded in the age-old message. His footsteps faltered, as if the shadows reached across time for him, but then the narrow hallways opened to vaulted ceilings. Dazzling sunshine beat against his face. Squinting against the brightness, Ty emerged from the shadowy corridor into the sunlit antechamber.

Soaring walls filled with calligraphy flanked the stairs leading to massive double doors. Clad in hammered gold, the doors shimmered like liquid fire. A pair of Seeing Eyes stared from the brightness like a great guardian keeping watch. Dark blue lapis was inset in the shimmering gold, the great eyes stared at Ty as if peering into his very soul.

"Come." Master Christoff gestured and a pair of blue-robed monks opened the doors.

Ty took a steadying breath before following him up the stairs. He'd been to the audience chamber once before, yet the wonders never failed to impress.

Stepping through the doorway, Ty struggled not to gape. The great mage-glass window spanned the left-hand wall, an impossible expanse of crystal-clear glass providing a perfect view of the valley nestled below. Opposite the window was the Star Screen. Over seven feet tall and twice as wide, the screen was a masterpiece of the monastery. Carved from a single slab of dark blue lapis, the polished stone was inset with faceted crystals. Delicate strands of gold wire connected the crystals into star constellations, forming a stunning map of the celestial night. Shimmering in the noon-day sun, the crystals glowed like diamonds set in a midnight sky.

But despite the dazzling wonders, it was the floor that truly held his attention. Beneath his boots the floor was painted a rich golden-yellow, but a few strides away a low knee-high railing split the audience chamber in half.

Beyond that railing, the floor was painted a deep midnight-blue. *Forbidden blue,* to Ty's knowledge this was the only chamber in the monastery with a divided floor, the sanctuary where the Order's inner wisdom met the inquiry of the outside world. He stepped towards the divide, drawn by the mystery.

Master Christoff gripped his arm, his words a whispered warning. "Take care."

Nodding, Ty sank to his knees before the railing. Struggling to still his racing heart, he stared at the Star Screen, tracing the constellations with his gaze. Knight, Dragon and Swan, he sought the familiar patterns of the midnight sky.

A chime sounded and a breath of incense wafted through the chamber.

A blue-robed master stepped from behind the screen. Wizen in stature yet his eyes were sharp and keen as a hunting hawk's.

Master Karidith, Ty nodded towards the venerable master, knowing names should not be spoken lightly within the ritual chamber.

The aged master sat cross-legged among embroidered pillows, taking a position to the right of the Star Screen. After striking a light to a brass brazier embedded in the floor, he turned and struck a small gong. The sweet note shimmered through the chamber like a blessing. "The Grand Master of the Kiralynn Order is present. Be aware that he sees you, he hears you. I am the Voice; in my tongue you will hear the words of the Grand Master." He raised his right hand to reveal the dark blue Seeing Eye tattooed upon his open palm. "Seek knowledge...Protect knowledge...Share knowledge." Lowering his hand, he peered at Ty. "A golden-robed acolyte has come before us seeking ascension to the blue. Who vouches for him?"

Master Christoff stepped forward. "I do."

"Is the acolyte worthy?"

"He is still young yet shows great promise with the quarterstaff."

Still young, the words pricked Ty's pride.

"And the choice of the Zward was given to him?"

"It was, yet he chooses to take his vows with the Kiralynn Order."

A pen nib scratched upon parchment. Ty watched as the Voice stretched a hand behind the Star Screen to accept a scroll. Snapping open the scroll, he began to read in a sonorous voice, "You are young to take our vows, but dire times require dire measures. We stand on the eve of the Battle Immortal. Darkness dares the final eclipse yet our Order ever serves the Light. Choices must be made. Every skill, every learning, every heart must be brought to bear if the Light is to prevail. On the cusp of such chaos, we ask if you, Tybalt Foundling, will take up a blue robe of the Kiralynn Order?"

The ominous shiver raced down Ty's spine, yet he would not turn away. "I will."

"Will you serve the Light through knowledge?"

"I will."

"Will you keep to our creed, ever striving to share our golden knowledge while protecting the secrets of the midnight-blue?"

The solemnity of the question washed across him. "I will."

"Will you keep our secrets even unto death?"

"I will."

"Will you serve the Order to the best of your abilities?"

"I will."

"Will you pledge your life to the Order from now till the Light claims you?"

Ty made his voice certain. "By the Lords of Light, I so swear."

A gong sounded, the silvery note shimmering through the air as if binding his vows.

The Voice gestured and a hidden gate in the low railing swung open, providing a path from the yellow-gold to the midnight-blue.

Ty's breath caught, knowing the true test was at hand.

Master Christoff draped a midnight-blue stole across Ty's shoulders, the fringed ends dangling down across his yellow-gold robes. Ty's heart thundered, awed to be wearing midnight-blue for the very first time.

The Voice intoned, "Cross the yellow-gold onto the midnight-blue to seal your vow, but know that you do so at your own peril, for the Light will strike you dead if your vows prove false."

Perhaps it was all the fasting, but Ty suddenly felt light-headed. Hesitating for half a heartbeat, he sent a quick entreaty to all the gods, asking for their support. Remaining on his knees, an age-old sign of humility, he took a deep breath and then shuffled forward. A humble supplicant, he moved from the ignorance of acolyte-yellow onto the dark-blue path of knowledge. Ty crossed the boundary, half expecting a jolt of magic...but instead he felt suffused with joy.

The sound of a gong shimmered through the chamber.

The Voice said, "It is done. The Light accepts your vows. Stand and take your place as a sworn monk of the Kiralynn Order."

Master Christoff helped Ty to stand.

Assaulted by a wave of dizziness, Ty swayed on his feet, his long day of fasting taking its toll.

The Voice stood, nodding towards Ty. "Welcome to the brotherhood of knowledge. How will you be known among us?"

Fresh-sworn monks chose new names to mark their rebirth in the Order. By tradition, most chose names from the Order's annals, honoring those who had gone before. Many of his friends had scoured the acolyte library, seeking names of by-gone heroes, but Ty chose differently. "As an orphan foundling, my birth name was never truly known. As a sworn monk of the Order, I choose to be known as Tybalt."

Master Christoff gasped at his impertinence.

Ty rushed to explain. "Since the name was given to me by a master of the order, I see no reason to change it."

The Voice gave him a withering glare but Ty refused to be cowed.

The sound of a pen nib scratching across parchment intruded.

The Voice retreated three steps, accepting a scroll from behind the Star Screen. Snapping the scroll open, he read. "It is fitting." The Voice scowled, but continued reading. "At the turning of an Age, old traditions will be set aside and new ones taken up. You shall be known as Tybalt, the first of your name. May you make this new name worthy of remembrance in the Kiralynn annals."

Struck by the challenge in the Grand Master's words, Ty's eyes widened with a mixture of relief and trepidation.

The Voice raised his right hand, revealing the tattoo of the Seeing Eye. "Seek knowledge, Protect knowledge, Share knowledge, for Knowledge is the Light in the Dark, the Slayer of Lies, the best Hope of mankind. Now go and don a blue robe and begin your journey into wisdom."

Numb from all that had transpired, Ty bowed towards the Star Screen and then towards the Voice.

Master Christoff put a hand on his shoulder, guiding Ty to a side door cunningly hidden in the midnight-blue wall. "You did well," his voice dropped to a low growl, "although your audacity is at times astounding."

Ty walked in a daze, scarcely aware that he trod dark-blue floors. The master led him to a new sleeping cell. Crystals inset in the midnight-blue door formed the shape of the Great Southern Swan, a symbol of seasonal change. Ty ran his fingers across the crystals and then entered the small spare cell. His scant belonging were already there, his quarterstaff leaning in the corner, his winter cloak hanging on a peg, his small chest stowed at the foot of his narrow bed...everything the same except for the color on the floor and the dark blue robe spread across the bed. *Everything the same, yet he'd gained a world of difference.* Crossing to the bed, he fingered the soft wool, smitten by the color and all that it meant.

Behind him, Master Christoff said, "Time to put off the yellow-gold of an acolyte and don the midnight-blue of a new destiny. Welcome to the sworn brotherhood of the Kiralynn Order. May your service be long and noteworthy."

9

Katherine

Kath fretted at every hour delayed. It took four long days to assemble the horses and supplies for their ride to Pellanor. Her maroon band spent the time doggedly cantering up and down the beach, determined to become capable riders. By the time the horses and supplies were assembled, her warriors were already bruised and saddle-sore, yet none complained.

While the supplies were assembled, each companion spent the boon of time in their own way. Kath remained closeted for long hours with Fanggold and the king's council, wrestling with strategies for the war. Zith dithered over the contents of their saddlebags, packing and repacking, trying to decide what treasures to bring from the Mordant's plundered hoard. Blaine sharpened his sword skills, sparring in the castle yard, fielding challenges from the king's guard. Of all the companions, only Danya seemed carefree, wandering the shops of Seaside as if she'd never seen a traders' city.

On the fourth day, they were finally ready. Kath bid farewell to Juliana, pressing a small cloth-wrapped bundle into her hands. "Keep this for me, till after?" Kath longed to take Duncan's shirt with her, but she could not risk losing it. "It's very precious to me."

Juliana accepted the package. "Till after." The two women hugged. "Come, I'll see you to the castle gates."

They found the king waiting in the castle courtyard with several of his advisors.

Kath bowed low. "Thank you for sending your ships north," she gestured to the courtyard filled with mounted men, "and for the horses and supplies."

"You brought an army south. Their swords are sorely needed." The king lowered his voice. "Find my daughter. See that no harm befalls her."

Kath found it hard to believe that Jemma was in danger. "If Queen Liandra still rules, then no harm will befall her. If the Mordant's gained the upper hand, then slaying the beast will cure many evils."

The king's voice turned fierce. "Then slay him and send my daughter home."

"The Light willing." Taking her leave, she accepted the reins of a chestnut stallion and vaulted into the saddle. Turning her mount, she looked for Blaine, Danya, Zith and the Zward captain. Ready to ride, they sat on their horses, beacons of calm amongst the anxious warriors milling on their mounts. Bear flashed her a determined grin, his hands white-knuckled on the reins. Kath prayed her painted warriors survived the long ride south. Nodding to her companions, she stood in the stirrups. "Let's ride!"

The castle gates swung open, admitting a salty breeze. Kath led her small troop down the ramp to the causeway. Sunlight dazzled the turquoise sea, incoming waves lapping on either side. A fresh breeze whipped her long blond hair into a battle banner, her maroon cloak fluttering behind. Keen to finish the god-given task, Kath spurred her mount to a gallop, flinging her war cry to the heavens. "*For Honor and the Octagon!*"

Seagulls churned overhead, their mournful cries the only reply. But then a great shout rose from the beach. "*For the Svala!*" Her army of painted warriors crowded the beach, more than two thousand brave swords who'd dared to come south, crammed into the holds of Navarren ships. They raised a din, their swords beating against shields and battle-scarred bucklers.

Kath's heart swelled to see them. Reaching the end of the causeway, she cantered between the two basalt-carved ospreys and then pulled her mount to a halt. Leaning from the saddle, she grasped Fanggold's arm in a warrior's grip. "Lead them north, Fanggold. Join the army of Navarre and show them the valor of your swords."

Fanggold flashed a predator's grin that matched the fierce wolf tattooed on his face. "It will be as you say, Svala." His grin widened. "Tell the Mordant we're keeping his Citadel."

"We're keeping more than that." Her grin answered his. "We're keeping all of Erdhe!"

"*Huzzah!*" A great shout rose from her painted warriors.

The fierceness of their reply flushed her heart with pride. Nodding to Fanggold, she spurred her stallion to a canter, leading her small band down the beach. Taking a last look at Castle Seamount, she turned her mount away from the sparkling sea, riding up into the cobbled streets.

10

Ambrose

Ambrose dodged left. Pivoting fast, he brought the great sword up for a two-handed parry. Steel struck steel with a mighty clang. Staggered by the savage blow, he struggled to hold on, the sword nearly twisting from his aching hands. Tightening his grip, he kept the blade raised against a second onslaught.

"Enough!" Haythor lowered his sword, flashing a toothy grin. "You've done well, monk. You're starting to find your rhythm."

Ambrose lowered the practice sword, his arms aching, his hands blistered with fresh calluses, his jerkin soaked with sweat. "I'm a scholar," his breath huffed, "not a swordsman."

"Yet, you learn to dance the steel! Think what you'll learn tomorrow."

"That's what worries me."

"Soon you'll be begging to join the Zward!"

Ambrose gave him a dubious look.

"Come," Haythor clapped him on the back. "That rabbit smells good enough to eat."

They made their way over to a campfire screened by a massive bramble bush. The others sat huddled in a crescent, absorbing the warmth of the flames. Kren handed him a plate piled with his share of supper. The crispy-skinned rabbit proved as tasty as it smelled. Hungry beyond telling, Ambrose folded the rabbit with the pan bread and scallions, shoveling the bundle into his mouth. *It must be the sword practice,* for he'd never felt such a fierce hunger. He ate in contented silence, licking the salty grease from his fingers.

Flickering firelight held the dimming twilight at bay. His gaze swept across his companions, all of them studded with weapons. Even at supper, they never relaxed their guard. The longer he traveled with the Zward, the more he appreciated their skills. Jada, the auburn-haired huntress, was an expert with her bow, keeping the cook pot filled with fresh game. Tarlin, the swarthy scout, built nearly smokeless campfires and showed uncanny tracking abilities. Haythor was an expert swordsman who seemed to know the land like the back of his hand. Only dark-haired Kren remained a murky riddle. Ambrose could not decide if Kren was a horse trader or a horse thief. Whenever their mounts started to lag from the punishing journey, Kren would disappear at twilight, returning before dawn with fresh mounts. Ambrose hoped the horses weren't stolen, but he did not have the heart to ask. Either way, they made good time traveling north across the low lands.

Tarlin doused the fire with dirt. "I'll take first watch."

In the seclusion of the Southern Mountains, they'd slept through the night without standing guard, but in the lowlands, they took turns keeping watch. Haythor worried about enemies, and Ambrose did not gainsay him.

They slept in their clothes, their weapons close at hand. Ambrose grew accustomed to sleeping with the blue sword harnessed to his back. If trouble came calling, he dared not lose *Invictus*. Staring up at the stars, his gaze sought the Knight, a bold shimmer of bright stars in the northern sky. *Castlegard*...he wondered how the Octagon Knights fared. He carried a gift from the monastery, a boon for their fight against Darkness. *Invictus*, the name shimmered in his mind. The great sword was meant for the hands of a hero, yet sometimes he wondered how much difference a single weapon could make. Forged by a wizard and summoned by an Illuminator, the sword had to be ensorcelled with powerful magics. Belief in the sword helped sustain him on the long journey, but sometimes his doubts grew, gnawing at him in the depths of the night. He'd carried the sword for more than a moon-turn, yet if the blade was magical, he'd felt no glimmer, no spark of latent power. *Perhaps the fault is mine, not the sword's.* Weary from the day's long ride, Ambrose curled into the warmth of his bedroll, seeking dreams, seeking answers.

"Time to ride." A meaty hand shook his shoulder.

Ambrose struggled to wake. Still dark, he crouched behind the bramble bush and then made his way to the horses. Strapping his bedroll and satchel to the saddle, he gave the gelding a pat and then stretched his aching muscles before mounting. *Dark before the dawn.* Riding before first light was a habit with the Zward. Stealthy and secretive, they avoided towns and villages, shadowing the Great Southern Road as they made their way north.

Haythor led, spurring his mare to a hard gallop. Cloaked in darkness, they made good time riding north along the empty roadway. They ate in the saddle, chewing on dried venison strips. Sunlight cracked the sky, slowly brightening the day. The ancient road ran straight and true, like a plumb line stretching from Castlegard to the Southern Mountains. A relic of another Age, Ambrose knew its history. Built when the Star Knights and the Seeing Eye served as one, long before the great cataclysm known as the War of Wizards. *History trod beneath ironshod hooves,* yet so few remembered the truth.

Leagues passed and still they rode, keeping their horses to a gallop. Fields of budding wheat stretched to the west, ripe farmland burgeoning with crops. On the eastern side, a dark forest encroached on the road, towering trees brooding with shadows. Light and dark, the ancient road seemed to forge a great divide.

Haythor raised his fist, slowing his mount to a halt. "Do you hear that?"

Ambrose tugged on the reins, slowing his gelding, puzzled by the question.

Tarlin leaped from the saddle, putting his ear to the road.

Their horses milled, ripe with tension.

Jada plucked an arrow from her quiver, priming her bow for a fight.

Tarlin sent an electric glance to Haythor. "They come from the north. Get off the road!" The swarthy man vaulted into the saddle.

Haythor led them into the forest. Ambrose followed, ducking beneath a low hanging branch. Trees swallowed the sunlight. Cedar and towering pine surrounded them, a fortress of bark and green. The soft forest loam hid the clop of hooves. Haythor wove a path into the depths and then called a halt. "Wait here." Dismounting, he threw his reins to Kren. "I need to see."

Ambrose clambered from his horse. "I need to see too."

Haythor gave him a piercing look.

A sixth sense compelled Ambrose to follow and see for himself. "You need a scholar's eyes." Meeting the big man's gaze, he refused to flinch.

Haythor groaned a burdened sigh. "As you wish, but stay close and stay quiet."

Ambrose nodded, his hands tightening the harness of the blue sword, making sure it was secure.

Haythor threaded a path back through the forest. Ambrose followed, seeking to emulate the big man, wincing every time a branch crunched beneath his boots. A raven cawed overhead, startling him. Pitch-black eyes stared from the pine branch like an ill-omen. Shrugging off his unease, Ambrose followed the Zward captain, trying his best to be stealthy. Haythor flashed the signal for caution. Dropping low, they crept towards the forest's edge. Crouched behind a cedar trunk wide enough to hide a horse, they kept watch on the road.

At first, Ambrose heard nothing, not even the chirping of birds, as if a fell stillness smothered the land. And then he heard it, the rolling thunder of many ironshod hooves. Ambrose froze, his hands clutching the cedar tree, his gaze fixed on the road. The ironshod thunder drew near like a breaking storm. And then he saw them, a mighty cavalcade galloped south. Golden pentacles gleaming on black armor, they rode in disciplined ranks, spears bristling in the sunshine. *Golden pentacles!* Shock pierced him like a sword thrust. Ambrose shook his head, denying his eyes, but the grim truth was there to see. *The Mordant's forces ride deep into the southern kingdoms!* Darkness invaded Erdhe! His mind whirled, fearing he was too late, fearing the Octagon Knights had already fallen. And then he spied the battle banner. Black silk, dark as sin, ending in a forked tail, bright red flecked with glimmering gold. *Darkness on fire!* His eyes widened, recognizing the battle banner from ancient tomes. "The Darkflamme!" The fearsome name whispered out of him like a nightmare.

Beside him, Haythor glared.

Ambrose pulled the big man close, whispering in his ear. "The battle banner of the Mordant!"

Haythor's glare turned to wide-eyed shock.

Slunk behind the cedar tree, they kept watch, counting as the dark legions rode past.

Their numbers were daunting, a raging river of steel.

Ambrose stiffened, spiked by fear. Amongst the lead riders, he glimpsed one clad in fearsome armor, a silver skull fashioned into a helmet, a lich king come calling. A wave of terror crashed against him. For half a heartbeat, he feared the skull rider had seen him. Ambrose wanted to run, he wanted to hide. Flee or hide, he could not decide, his heartbeat hammering as if to escape his chest...but then the lich king rode past, and the compulsion faded. Shaking and sodden with sweat, he slumped against the tree. Sketching the hand sign against evil, he wondered if the armored rider had been the Mordant himself. By the Light, this day could not get any worse.

Crouched in their hiding place, they watched the dark legion ride by, every man armed to the teeth. Shields, swords and spears, they clattered past, a legion of doom. The grim cavalcade seemed to stretch to forever. Ambrose estimated their numbers at two thousand or more. *An army come south*, and then an insight pierced him. He knew with unflinching conviction they were aimed at the monastery, at the Light's heart. He gripped Haythor's arm. "We must warn them!"

"Warn who?"

"The monastery!"

Haythor stiffened. "Are you sure?"

Ambrose gave him a solemn nod.

Haythor scowled, his gaze locked on the enemy.

The tail of the cavalcade came into sight, presenting a new horror. Ogres followed the horsemen, big lumbering brutes with yellow tusks protruding from their lantern jaws. Bulging with muscles, they carried spiked cudgels on their shoulders. Ugly and unnatural, they looked fresh-summoned from a ledger of demons. Lumbering at a pounding trot, the monstrous thud of their passing shook the very ground, quaking the trees.

Ambrose stared, gape-mouthed. *Ogres and ancient battle banners...*he made the hand sign against evil, feeling as if the worst of the ancient prophecies had sprung to life before his very eyes.

Haythor elbowed him. "Look there!"

Ambrose swiveled his gaze, noting a commotion among the ranks of horsemen. A dozen armed riders peeled away from the rest, galloping back north along the side of the road. They came to a halt not far from where the two men hid. A dwarfish man, seated behind one of the riders, clambered to the ground. Crouching on the roadway, the dwarf slew his head left and right, as if searching for something. Nearly crawling on all fours, he moved along the road till he came to a stop. Sniffing the roadway like a dog, he grinned, flashing teeth filed to wicked points. Clearly agitated, the dwarf spoke to the others...and then he pointed into the forest.

He nearly pointed straight at them!

Ambrose hissed. "I've heard of this! The dwarf can track magic!"

Haythor gave him a startled look. Pulling Ambrose to his feet, he shoved him towards the forest depths. "Run!"

Ambrose ran as if his life depended on it. Cedar, aspen and pine, the forest became a confusion of trees. A thousand shades of green dappled by shadows, he ran into the depths, seeking sanctuary. Ducking beneath a branch, he dodged a rabbit hole. An exposed root snagged his boot. Ambrose fell hard, cushioned by a bed of pine needles. Haythor yanked him to his feet, shoving him forward. The big warrior took the lead, weaving a path through the tree trunks. Behind, they heard the crack of branches, riders barreling through the forest. *Too close!* His heartbeat racing, the monk struggled to keep pace. And then they reached the others. Ambrose flung himself into the saddle.

Haythor hissed. "A dozen riders in black with a dwarf who can track magic! Tarlin, lead us away!"

To his credit, the swarthy man did not ask questions. Vaulting into the saddle, Tarlin led them deeper into the forest.

Riding single file, they followed the scout. Swerving around trees, Tarlin led them on a circuitous route, moving ever deeper into the forest. Ambrose strained to listen, but heard nothing save the thunder of his own heart. *A dwarf who tracks magic!* He knew what they sought. A chill slithered down his spine. *Darkness seeks Invictus!* Panic clawed his mind, yet he held it at bay, struggling to recall the whispers he'd heard in the monastery. Only a rumor, yet the answer terrified him. Ambrose knew what he must do. Spurring his mount forward, he rode abreast of Haythor. "The dwarf tracks the sword. *Only* the sword."

Haythor gave him a narrowed look.

Ambrose forced the words out. "You and the others need to get away, to warn the monastery."

Haythor growled. "Ride faster, monk."

Ambrose thrummed his horse, asking for more speed. The gelding leaped forward, flying through the dense green. He spurred ahead, riding just behind the scout. Branches beat against him, releasing the scent of pine. Ambrose clung to the reins, riding low in the saddle. The root-carved ground proved fraught with obstacles. Careening through the forest, they jumped fallen trees, ducked branches and swerved around a thick bramble patch. Ambrose prayed for his horse not to stumble. Death was only a mistake away. Riding low in the saddle, he clung to the reins, his gaze fixed on Tarlin. He followed the scout through the shadow-shrouded forest, hearing nothing but the drum of hooves and the frantic beat of his own heart. Flicking a glance behind, he spied the others strung out in a ragged line, weaving a path through the trees, but he caught no glimpse of the enemy. His gaze snapped forward, seeking the scout.

The scout was gone!

Before Ambrose could tug on the reins, he realized the ground fell away, a steep slope descending to a swift flowing stream. His horse stumbled, but then found its footing. They clattered down the slope, splashing into the stream. Crystal-clear and swift-flowing, the water was less than a foot deep. The gelding dipped his head to drink.

Tarlin hissed. "Stop him or he'll bloat."

The stalwart horse deserved a drink, yet Ambrose tugged on the reins. Whinnying in protest, the gelding shied sideways, fighting the bit.

Tarlin snapped. "Control your horse!"

Ambrose was not the horseman the Zward were, yet he struggled to calm his mount.

Haythor and the others thundered into the stream, throwing up a cold spray of water.

Kren was last. The dark-haired man flashed a warning look. "They're coming."

Haythor swore. "By Valin's stones!" His gaze speared Tarlin. "Keep to the stream. Lead the monk away. We'll do what we can."

Tarlin wheeled his horse, "This way!"

But Ambrose hesitated. He watched the others spur their mounts up the far embankment. Ironshod hooves digging into the soft soil, they galloped into the forest, leaving a clear trail for the enemy to follow.

"*Hurry!*"

Ambrose answered the urgent call. Turning his mount, he followed the scout, keeping his horse in the stream's heart. They rode at a fast trot, a dangerous pace in the stone-strewn stream, yet the horses did not balk, seeming to sense the urgency of their riders. Twice his horse stumbled, yet the gelding did not fall. *Dwarves that sniff magic!* Ambrose prayed the ruse would work, yet his mind told him otherwise. He stretched his senses, expecting to hear the clatter of hooves, expecting an arrow in the back. The blue sword weighed heavy against him. Whatever the odds, he could not let the sword fall to the hands of Darkness.

The stream began to twist and turn, taking a gentle curve to the right. Ambrose had no idea what direction they rode. A cathedral of green arched overhead, nothing but thick forest on either side. Even the birdsong had fallen silent, as if the forest kept watch.

Ahead, a fallen tree lay tumbled into the stream, the bark blackened as if from a fierce fire.

The forest crowded close, plenty of shadowy spots for ambushers. Pinpricks danced up and down his back. Amongst the spring green, he saw more than a few blackened trunks. Ambrose angled his horse around the fallen tree, making sure to stay within the swift-flowing stream.

Tarlin slipped from his mount. "Keep riding. Keep to the stream."

Ambrose hesitated. "What will you do?"

"Use the deadfall to set a tripwire for any who might follow."

The truth needed to be told. "They *will* follow."

Tarlin's gaze flicked to his. "You sure?"

Ambrose nodded. "The dwarf can sniff magic. They're following the blue sword."

"You told Haythor?"

"Yes."

"Then keep riding." The swarthy scout rummaged in his saddle pack, his jaw set in a stubborn scowl.

The Zward risked too much. "Can I help?"

The scout gave him a flat stare. "Will you give the sword to the enemy?"

"Never."

"Then ride."

Ambrose turned his horse. Thrumming his heels, he urged the gelding to a trot, keeping to the stream's heart. He did not like leaving the others, he did not like riding alone. He did not want to be a burden, yet the sword was his to carry. Icy pinpricks danced up and down his spine. His sixth sense played havoc with his imagination. He kept glancing over his shoulder, hoping for friends, expecting foes.

And then he heard a man's strangled scream.

It sounded like it came from back near the deadfall.

Tugging on the reins, he turned the gelding. Sitting statue-still, he listened hard.

A horse squealed in pain...and then he heard the clash of steel! Ambrose stiffened. If the others fought, he should join them, but the blue sword weighed heavy on his back. He dared not let Darkness claim *Invictus*. Caught between the need to protect the sword, and the need to fight, he dithered. *Delay serves Darkness,* Ambrose lashed himself for his indecision. And then he heard a horse galloping up the streambed towards him.

Friend or foe?

He reached back for the sword, his only weapon. His hand gripped the leather-wrapped hilt.

A rider approached.

Tarlin! Leaning low in the saddle, the swarthy scout lashed his mount to a desperate gallop. Blood streamed down his face from a nasty gash and he rode a strange horse bedecked with pentacles. *"Ride!"*

A thousand questions assaulted Ambrose, yet he wheeled his horse, urging the gelding to a gallop. Ironshod hooves raised a sparkling spray. His heartbeat ran riot. Riding pell-mell through the stone-riddled stream was sheer folly, yet luck favored the bold. Their horses kept their footing, following the stream's snaking twists and turns.

Tarlin pulled close. "Here! Stop here!"

Ambrose slowed the gelding, confused by the order. "Why?"

"Give me your reins and get down from your horse."

Tarlin made no sense, yet the Zward had earned his trust. Ambrose tossed the reins to the scout and scrambled from the saddle. "Why?"

"The dwarf is dead, but Haythor thinks the others will follow." The scout peered upstream, seeking enemies. "I'll lead them away while you hide in the forest. Stick to the rocks as much as possible. One of us will find you."

"One of you?"

Tarlin gave him a solemn stare. "Whoever survives."

Ambrose gaped.

"Run!" The scout lashed his horse to a gallop, the spare mount kicking up a sheet of spray.

Cool water drenched his already-soaked boots. Turning away, Ambrose scrambled up the embankment. He tried to keep to the water-smoothed stones but his boots kept slipping. Reaching the top, he ran for the forest.

Figuring distance was his best ally, he lengthened his stride, pushing for more speed. Secure in the worn scabbard, the blue sword thumped against his back like a goad. Racing through the towering green, Ambrose listened, stretching his senses. He feared for the others, he feared for himself, yet he heard nothing beyond the wild beating of his own heart. His stride began to slow, a jagged pain lancing his side. Gasping for breath, he stumbled to a halt. *Nothing but trees in every direction,* he leaned against a massive cedar, trying to catch his breath, wondering if he'd gained enough distance.

Shadows lengthened, choking the forest in shades of gray. He wondered if he should hide. *The dwarf is dead!* Ambrose clung to Tarlin's words, yet it paid to be cautious. Spying a gnarled pine, he decided to seek a better vantage. Knocking the mud from his boots, he began to climb. The ancient pine yielded plenty of handholds. He reached a thick branch and shimmied out. Lying flat, he surveyed the ground below. His gaze stumbled on a muddy boot print! Gasping in dismay, he searched for more. Finding another, his heartbeat lurched. Faint foot prints, soft scuffs, and slightly bent branches, told the tale. Most of the marks were subtle, yet the bird's eye view betrayed his passage through the forest. Cursing his carelessness, Ambrose sagged against the branch. Perhaps the enemy followed Tarlin, yet he could not wish such a grim fate on the scout.

Voices!

Ambrose peered through the branches, seeking the source.

Two men approached leading their mounts. Only silhouettes at first, but then he glimpsed their armor. *Golden pentacles emblazoned on black!* The enemy had found him.

11

Quintus

Spring was ever a time of renewal and hope...but not this year. Quintus feared the gods had forgotten the north. The winter snow was long gone, melted to mud, but the sky remained a dreary cast of gray, as if the world were locked in irons. Relentless rain pelted down, making everything sodden and miserable. Clutching his wool cloak against the wet chill, Quintus ran across the great yard, chickens scurrying to get out of his way. *Chickens in Castlegard's great yard,* more proof the war fared badly. Instead of the steady clang of sparring swords, the healer heard the forlorn bleat of a goat. Dodging puddles and barnyard animals, he made his way to the tower. At least the flood of battlefield wounded had slowed to a trickle, but the tide of displaced farmers and village folk brought challenges of another sort. Reaching the door, he rushed inside. Competing smells embraced him, the soothing scent of medicinal herbs warding against the underlying stench of excrement and blood. Healing was a fulfilling calling, but sometimes the task seemed never-ending. Sighing, Quintus stamped his boots to shake off the mud, and then hung his dripping cloak on a peg.

"Master Quintus!" Elise was there to greet him, a worried look scrawled on her face. Petite and pretty, her flaxen braid circling her head like a crown, the scullery maid turned healing assistant had proven a boon. "We've six more cases of fever," she leaned close, her voice dropping to a whisper, "and three of them are showing angry red spots."

Spots! The symptom could mean anything from flea bites to graveyard posies. He prayed it wasn't the latter. Plague killed more people than a horde of swords. "Show me." Washing his hands in a basin, he followed her up the stairs. Too many beds were full. Just when he thought he'd empty the tower of war wounded, the small folk came calling, a deluge bringing an endless assortment of ailments. Most complained of minor maladies, but this latest outbreak of fevered spots worried him. He made the rounds, keeping Elise close by his side, teaching her the art of healing. Two turns of an hourglass later, Quintus sagged with relief. "It's not graveyard posies but it's not flea bites either, something in between. Best dose them with yarrow tea, and get the lads to move those with spots into a separate chamber."

Elise nodded, an apologetic look on her face. "We're running low on yarrow."

Another problem. "Then give them fennel. I'll mix a potion of cloves and coriander for the ones with spots. We'd best keep a close eye on this." Rubbing his eyes, he suppressed a sigh, weary beyond telling. How he longed for this war to end. The knights fought with swords, while he fought with herbs, potions, poultices and hope.

Horns blared, beating against the tower. The strident call jarred him to motion. Berating himself for not learning the trumpet signals, Quintus went to the arrow slit window and looked out, but the slanting rain obscured the view. Three times the trumpets blared their summons. Quintus longed to ignore the call, but a dire secret gnawed at him. *The great mage-stone castle is not invincible!* He'd seen the impossible with his own eyes, how a wagon's axle had scarred the great castle's mage-stone walls. Distraught, he'd sent an owl-borne message south, seeking answers from the monastery. *Restore honor to the Octagon...*the reply made little sense. He'd shared the answer with one other, but the sharing did little to lessen his nightmares. For the sake of the knights' morale, he kept the dread truth locked in his heart, but every day he feared to find an enemy army encamped outside the castle gates. Burdened by the terrible secret, the blaring trumpets taunted him. Unable to suppress his unease, Quintus found himself needing to know. Leaving the sick and the injured in Elise's capable care, he made his way back down the tower stairs. Grabbing his sodden cloak, he stepped out into the slanting rain.

Chickens scattered as he crossed the great yard.

The inner portcullis was raised, the iron-toothed maw gaping open. A small crowd gathered by the gate, most of them aged veterans in maroon cloaks. Quintus stood at the rear, craning for a view. "What is it?"

A tall, gray-haired veteran turned. Spying the healer, Sir Darius gave him a respectful nod. "The trumpets announce knights returning from battle. We've come to welcome them home."

*Knights returning from battle...*to Quintus those words meant more wounded, yet he found himself relieved to learn the enemy was not harrying the castle gates. He stood with the others, silently keeping watch. Rain drummed down with a chilling beat, soaking cloaks and filling puddles, yet in time he heard the clop of hooves. Riders approached. A long line of maroon knights rode through the castle's killing corridor, but instead of proud heroes returning, they looked...bedraggled. Sodden battle banners hung limp from lances. Maroon cloaks draped tarnished armor. Shields that had once been burnished bright, were dented and battered. Instead of sitting sword-straight, most knights sat hunched in the saddle. Mud-spattered and travel-stained, their horses looked hard-ridden, and the riders hard-used.

The small crowd of gathered veterans opened a pathway for the vanguard. A grim mood descended on the watchers. They raised no hollow cheer, yet clenched fists snapped to their chests in stalwart salute.

Quintus stood mute with the others, bearing witness.

The mud-spattered vanguard trudged into the castle courtyard.

Near enough to touch, they rode past. Quintus got a good look at their faces. Gaunt, hollow-eyed, bearded, exhausted...they looked defeated.

Defeated! The raw impression shook his soul. And then recognition dawned. Amongst the vanguard, he spied Sir Lothar, Sir Gravis, Sir Rannock, Sir Blaze, Sir Adelmar...the knight-captains had returned to Castlegard, looking grim and hard-worn as if they'd ridden from the very gates of Hell. *The knight-captains have returned!* The realization hit like a death-knell. But then he noticed that one face was missing among the maroon-clad leaders. The knight marshal was not among them! Quintus clutched at the insight like a drowning man clutching at a log. Perhaps the marshal stayed behind to fight a rear action. Perhaps the maroon was not as desperate as it appeared. His imagination spun hope-laden scenarios.

"You have to tell them." The deep voice rumbled from behind.

Quintus spun to find Otto, the master swordsmith, glowering over him.

"The knight-captains have returned and they do not look victorious. War comes to the very gates of Castlegard." His deep voice sounded like a doom. "You must tell them."

"We need time to solve the riddle."

"Time is something you no longer have." Otto glared. "If you do not speak, then I will." Without waiting for an answer, the big smith turned and stomped back to his forge.

No time! The truth hit like a sledgehammer.

The castle courtyard erupted in swirling chaos. Knights dismounted, their maroon cloaks dripping puddles. Warhorses stamped and snorted. Orders were shouted. Stable hands, squires and pages came running to attend to their charges. A wagon trundled through the gateway. The cry of *"Wounded!"* went up, echoing against the castle walls.

The shout shattered his frozen thoughts. Spurred to action, Quintus rushed towards the wagon. He was needed. His healing skills could save lives, but he had no clue how to remedy the great castle. It seemed to him as if the end of the world had come calling. Mage-stone was broken. Castlegard was no longer invincible, yet the knights returned, seeking sanctuary. *Return honor to the maroon.* Valiant knights lay bleeding in the wagon bed, their stoic silence proof of their courage. His hands shook as he tended their wounds, praying for an answer to an impossible riddle.

12

Ambrose

Ambrose froze, his face pressed to the coarse tree branch. *Fight or flee!* The age-old question thundered through his mind. His heartbeat galloped as he watched the soldiers thread their way through the forest, clearly following his tracks. Their golden pentacles gleamed sinister in the waning light. Swords bared, they moved like veterans. *Too close!* His first instinct was to flee, but if he dropped from the tree they would hear him, find him, catch him...slay him. His only advantage was his position high in the pine...and the blue steel sword strapped to his back. *Invictus,* he wondered if the sword would save him. Ambrose had no illusions about his own sword fighting skills. Against a single veteran, he'd die flailing. *Two against one...*Ambrose knew he wouldn't last a handful of heartbeats, yet perhaps the sword's magic would waken in his defense. Scowling, he pushed the unworthy thought aside. He'd sworn to save the sword, not the other way around.

The lead soldier stooped, fingering a bent branch. *The dwarf is dead!* Tarlin's words pierced his mind. If the dwarf was truly dead then the enemy was blind to the sword's magic.

The grim clank of armor drew near. He was running out of time. Loosening the harness straps, he carefully shrugged the sword from his shoulders. The worn leather scabbard matched the color of the tree's bark. With luck, it would be found by someone worthy. With shaking hands, he strapped the sword to the pine tree, consigning the blade to the care of the gods.

Crawling further out on the stout limb, he crouched, waiting.

His heartbeat hammered so loud, he was surprised the enemy did not hear.

The soldiers followed his trail to the gnarled pine. "Looks like we treed him." Two grizzled faces stared aloft.

Taking a deep breath, Ambrose jumped, aiming his boots for the nearest face.

The soldier ducked but could not escape.

Ambrose fell like a lead weight, his boots hitting with a solid thud. He crumpled to the ground, landing on top of his target. With one soldier sprawled senseless beneath him, Ambrose rolled away, evading a sword stroke from the second soldier. Leaping to his feet, he lunged for the dangling reins of the dead man's mount, but the horse shied sideways. Ambrose followed, locking his fist on the reins. Using the horse as a shield, he pulled the mare to the left, blocking the swordsman. Forced to mount from the wrong side, Ambrose struggled to get his boot in the stirrup. Just as his boot got seated, he heard a loud smack. The horse bolted, throwing him to the ground.

Something hard struck his left shoulder. Winded, he gazed at a twilight sky.

Cold steel threatened his throat. "Surrender or die!"

Ambrose stared up into the sneering face of the second soldier.

"Where's your magic?"

So they don't know! Ambrose struggled for an answer.

The enemy's sword pressed against his throat, drawing a thin line of pain. "Where's your magic?"

Ambrose considered his meager possessions. "The stone...in my belt pouch."

The sword withdrew. A meaty fist punched his jaw, knocking the monk's head against the ground. Pain exploded in his jaw and the back of his head.

"Keep still."

Dazed by pain, he felt his belt pouch being rummaged.

Ambrose struggled to see straight.

"This it?" A meaty fist held a small oblong of dark gray stone in front of his eyes.

It was the whetstone Haythor had given him for the practice sword. "Yes."

The soldier growled. "It's not but a whetstone."

"Yet it holds great magic."

"What magic? What does it do?"

"It gives your blade a peerless edge."

The soldier fondled the stone, a gleam of avarice in his eyes, but then his stare snapped back to Ambrose. "If you be lying the snargons will know."

Snargons, so there were more dwarves who sniffed magic.

The soldier ripped the belt from the monk's waist. Rolling the monk on his side, he bound his hands behind his back, tugging the leather till it bit into his wrists. Ambrose struggled to no avail. "You've got my magic, let me go."

The soldier yanked the monk to his feet. "There be a bounty on magic and magic users, and I mean to claim both." He flashed a wicked grin. "And since ya killed Drog, the bounty'll be all mine." Reclaiming his horse, the soldier pulled a rope from his saddle bag. Quickly fashioning a noose, he slipped it over Ambrose's head. Tugging the noose tight, he leered. "Keep up if you want to live." The soldier swung into the saddle. Giving the rope a tug, he bound it to his saddle and then nudged his horse to a trot.

Ambrose began to run, the hangman's collar chafing his throat. Stumbling behind, he struggled to keep pace. *My lie will not survive the snargons,* somehow he had to get free. He fought his bonds, but his wrists were bound tight. The noose rubbed his neck raw, tugging him forward. His mind raced, seeking a solution, but he had nothing. And then he remembered the tattoo on his right palm. One look at the Seeing Eye and the enemy would know the truth. His boot snagged on a root. Ambrose tripped and nearly fell. Somehow he kept his balance. *One fall will be the death of me.* Perhaps it would be better to die, but he could not abandon the sword. Ambrose prayed to all the gods for succor, but he knew they seldom answered.

A bowstring thwanged.

The soldier gasped, an arrow sprouting between his eyes.

Jada! Ambrose looked for the Zward.

Dead, the soldier tumbled from the saddle.

The horse shied.

Realizing the danger, Ambrose rushed towards the horse, hoping to stop it, but his hands were tied behind his back. *"Whoa! Whoa!"* He sought to calm the skittish horse. The chestnut evaded him, his eyes wide with fright.

And then someone was there, grabbing the bridle, calming the horse.

Ambrose sagged in relief. "Thank you!" Saved by a stranger, but then a handful of leather-clad warriors stepped from the woods. Their bows were pulled taut, their arrows aimed at his heart. He gasped, struggling to understand, and then he saw their eyes. *Golden cat-eyes!* He'd read something in the archives. And then he remembered, using knowledge as a shield. "Children of the Deep Green! I come in peace."

Their bows remained taut, their arrows fixed on his heart.

"The pentacle is my enemy! The enemy of your enemy is your friend!"

Their faces remained stern.

He reached for a name, something he'd read in the archives, an odd title that had snagged his imagination. "The Treespeaker! I seek an audience with Treespeaker."

Several bowmen snarled.

Ambrose feared he'd misspoken.

"Why does a white-eye seek an audience with the Treespeaker?" The bowmen parted, making way for an older man with a chiseled face and flecks of gray in his auburn hair.

Ambrose swallowed, knowing much depended on his answer. "I'm a sworn monk of the Kiralynn Order and I seek an audience with the Treespeaker."

"Take care how you bandy her name, white-eye."

Ambrose refused to be cowed. "Darkness threatens this land. Will you ally with the Seeing Eye or fall under the yoke of the Pentacle?"

"This one is dead." The captain gave a contemptuous kick to the soldier impaled by an arrow. "And you look like a poult trussed for market."

An archer snickered.

Ambrose stiffened. His hands were bound, and the noose remained around his neck, yet he glared defiant. "Looks can be deceiving."

"And do you wish to deceive?" The captain leaned close, his gaze intent.

Unwilling to lie, Ambrose lost his bluster. "No."

"And you truly come from the Seeing Eye?"

Hope glimmered. "Yes. I bear the mark of the Seeing Eye on my right palm."

The captain leaned close, his nostrils distended as if sniffing the wind.

Ambrose refused to blink. Remaining statue-still, he met the captain's searing stare.

The captain scowled. "This one speaks the truth." He stepped away. "Remove the noose, bind his eyes, we'll let the Treespeaker decide."

Rough hands removed the noose from his neck.

"Wait!" Ambrose stepped towards the captain, but strong hands held him tight. "There's a treasure! It should not be left behind."

The captain turned, his gaze fixed on the monk. "A treasure?"

Words matter. Ambrose nodded. "A sword of peerless value."

The captain gave him an appraising stare. "Where is this *treasure*?"

"I refused to let the Pentacle have it, so I bound it to a tree."

Murmurs swirled through the bowmen, as if he'd said something of special import.

Ambrose held the captain's stare. "The sword should not be left behind."

The captain gave a slow nod. "Show me."

Twilight cloaked the forest, yet it proved easy for Ambrose to follow the horse's path back through the soft loam. The monk led the cat-eyed archers to the gnarled pine. A dead soldier of the pentacle lay sprawled beneath the ancient tree like an offering. "I killed this one, but could not evade the other."

The captain gave him a measuring look. "And the sword?"

"Strapped to the tree trunk."

"Sperry," the captain gestured to a slender youth, "fetch the sword."

Handing his bow to another, the youth shimmied up the tree, fast as a squirrel. "Found it." Moments later, he dropped lightly to the ground, a scabbarded great sword clutched in his hands. "Bound to the trunk, just like he said." The youth handed the sword to the captain and then reclaimed his bow.

Ambrose suddenly felt ill, uncomfortable with a stranger handling *Invictus*.

The captain considered the worn scabbard and the leather-wrapped hilt. He weighed the sword in his hands, a thoughtful look on his face. Grasping the hilt, he drew it forth. Sapphire-blue and etched with runes, *Invictus* shimmered in the waning light like a hero's blade.

Gasps escaped the archers. Even the bowmen knew this was a sword to be reckoned with.

The captain tore his gaze from the blade, seeking the monk. "For whose hand is this sword destined?"

The question rang like a query from the gods, yet Ambrose had no true answer. "I've sworn to bear it to Castlegard."

The captain considered the sword. "Yet, now it is in the Deep Green."

Horror gripped the monk. "You cannot!"

The captain sheathed the sword. "The Treespeaker will decide." He shrugged the harness onto his shoulders. "Blindfold him. Bring him."

"No, wait!"

The captain turned back. "You are full of delays...or do you have another treasure?"

"I have friends, four of them, a woman and three men."

"Those who enter the Deep Green unbidden, forfeit their lives."

Ambrose rushed to persuade. "But these four serve the Seeing Eye! They come as allies, not enemies."

The captain sneered. "And they need help?"

"Yes."

"You bring weak allies."

"I brought the sword."

The captain considered. "Describe them."

"One woman, three men." Ambrose described the Zward as best he could.

The captain nodded. "Word will be passed. Now come, the hour grows late."

Ambrose submitted to the blindfold. Archers gripped his arms, leading him forward. Shuffling between them, he expected to trip and fall, but his guides steered him true. *Perhaps they do not mean to harm me,* at least not yet. Walking blind, he considered all that had happened. He'd escaped the Pentacle, but now the sword was in the hands of a cat-eyed archer. Unsheathed, there was no denying the sword's great worth, yet he'd sworn to deliver it to Castlegard. Ambrose wondered if he'd made a grievous mistake. He replayed the encounter in his mind, clinging to a single name. *The Treespeaker!* The cat-eyed archers had responded to the strange name, proving it was more than just a myth. Ambrose racked his mind, seeking more information, but he recalled only scant scraps of old writings, some of it hard to believe. A chill shivered down his spine. *Knowledge is a two-edged sword.* He'd taken a chance, placing a wild bet on a half-remembered name, and now a riddle from an obscure tome would decide the fate of the sword...perhaps the fate of Erdhe.

13

The Knight Marshal

A bloody field littered with the slain stretched behind him, proving the prowess of his sword. An army of the living knelt prostrate before him, proving the power of his future. Roaring his triumph, the knight marshal raised the Dark Sword as if challenging the very heavens. *"I am the God of War!"* A savage strength surged from the sword, flowing through him, enough to slay ten thousand more, yet the commander had the truth of it. The God of War deserved an army.

Yes, the voice that he thought of as the sword's whispered in his mind, *let them serve!*

The marshal touched the commander's proffered sword hilt. "I accept your service. I expect your worship." He brandished the Dark Sword at the twilight sky. "For I am the God of War!"

His army stood, banging swords on shields, their voices raised in adulation. *"All hail the God of War!"* The cheering swept across the valley like rolling thunder, clamor enough to invoke the ire of jealous gods.

The marshal basked in their adulation and knew it was fitting.

"Come, my lord, let me show you the way."

The swarthy commander led him across the field. Soldiers fell prostrate to grovel in the mud as he passed. Their worship pleased him, but for efficiency's sake, he would give orders that bowing was enough...but not this day. On this day of his ascension, their worship was his due. Keeping the Dark Sword clenched in his right fist, the massive wall shield riding his left arm, he stalked across the blood-soaked field, accepting the adulation of his legions.

Twilight began to fade, flickering torchlight leading the way. On the far side of the valley, they reached an encampment of tents and pavilions. Canvas and silk glowed softly against the encroaching night. The marshal's military gaze swept across the long rows of tents, pleased by the vast number of swords they represented, as well as the orderliness.

"This way, my lord."

Commander Crull led him to the largest pavilion. The canvas was painted deepest black and embossed with golden pentacles, but it mattered not to the marshal. Symbols no longer held sway over him. Swords mattered far more than the color of shields.

Commander Crull rushed forward to hold the canvas flap aside. The marshal stepped inside and gawked for the first time, staggered by the luxury. Thick carpets woven in jeweled tones lay spread beneath his muddy boots. Braziers stood at the four corners releasing golden light and a welcoming warmth. A camp bed piled high with furs waited in the far corner. A table with chairs stood within the brazier light. These were luxuries he'd nearly forgotten, like a dream from some other lifetime. He reached forward, touching the chair, needing to be sure it was real. And then the smell hit him. He breathed deep the mouthwatering scent...spit-roasted beef sizzling over a fire. A wild hunger roared through him like a dragon unleashed. "Food, bring me food! Meat, and ale, and more meat!"

The commander snapped his fingers and an attendant went running. "Food will be brought, the best the camp has to offer. Meanwhile, let my attendants serve you. Your armor should be cleaned and polished. You'll find a velvet robe more comfortable than steel."

The marshal looked down. Blood and gore coated his mismatched armor, making death his new sigil. Amidst the sudden luxury, the gore felt profane. "Yes."

The commander snapped his fingers, and two attendants stepped from the shadows. "This is our new lord, treat him as you would the Mordant."

Blanching pale as ghosts, the two young men made deep bows.

The commander's voice was a lash. "Serve him well."

Keeping their stares downcast, the attendants approached. One reached for the Dark Sword.

"No!" The Dark Sword swung up, piercing the man's jugular.

Gasping, the attendant stood on tiptoes, the Dark Sword thrust through his throat. Blood burbled around the blade.

"Never touch the sword!" The marshal growled the words, yet he hadn't meant to kill. He jerked the blade free. The attendant collapsed, a corpse twitching on the carpet.

The other attendant fell prostrate to the floor.

"The sword is *mine!* Never touch it." The marshal spat the warning. With conscious effort, he lowered the great blade.

Blood dripped on the fine-woven carpet, staining the pattern.

Commander Crull watched from the shadows, his dark eyes glittering in the brazier light. "Get the corpse out of here."

The attendant scrambled to obey

The marshal grabbed a cloak thrown casually across the chair and used the fine wool to clean the sword. With long, tender strokes, he burnished the blade, wiping it clean. Beneath his hands, the Dark Sword glistened in the brazier light, keen and deadly. The marshal marveled at its lethal beauty. Forged dragons coiled on the hilt, as distinctive as legends. Runes ran the length, inscribed along the runneled blade. Most striking of all, the steel was the color of darkest midnight. A sword so dark it drank the light. A peerless sword, destined for a hero's hand...or even a god's. The marshal marveled at the blade, a weapon of lethal beauty. He'd heard once that the sword was the very soul of a knight...and this was *his!*

Smells intruded. Servants returned bearing a tray piled high with roasted meat smothered in gravy, braised leeks, and butter-browned biscuits.

Ravenously hungry, he leaned the Dark Sword against the camp bed. Shrugging the wall shield from his left arm, the marshal fell on the tray. Like a starving man, he shoveled slices of beef slathered with gravy into his mouth, nearly swooning from the savory taste. His mouth bulging, he struggled to chew, unable to eat fast enough to assuage his voracious hunger. He ate with his fingers, not bothering to cut the meat. Taking a long swig of rich red wine, he wiped the dribble from his beard, and returned to eating, using a slice of beef to wipe the gravy from the plate. A belch roared out of him, his hunger tamed but not appeased. "More, bring me more! And the bloodier the better!"

For the first time, he felt their stares. The attendants gawked at him as if a slavering wolf had slunk into the pavilion to gnaw on a fresh-killed lamb. Their stares stung.

"Have you never seen a god eat?"

Commander Crull was swift to answer. "No, they haven't." He snapped his fingers. "Serve our lord well, or lose your worthless lives."

The attendants scrambled to make amends. One took the empty tray. The marshal suppressed a snarl. With shaking hands, the others began unbuckling his blood-spattered armor. He stood, giving them access to the complex belts and buckles. Grieves, gorget, and the blood-encrusted breastplate came away, revealing sweat-soaked leathers. He smelled like a goat in heat. His armor littered the carpet, a metal man dismembered. It took two attendants to move the massive wall shield, more proof of its worth. The marshal growled. "I want that shield polished and then returned to me, a fitting shield for a god." The attendants bowed low as they struggled to carry it from the pavilion.

A servant returned with another heaping tray of beef.

Salivating, the marshal set to eating, but this time he wielded a table knife, chewing slow enough to savor the flavors. The wine was rich, tasting of sun-kissed vines. The beef was juicy and rare, just the way he liked it. The gravy was a rare treat, flavored with peppercorns and onions. He enjoyed the repast and then called for a third tray.

His hunger mollified, he stared across the table, studying the commander. A barrel-chested man with skin the color of burnished bronze, his dark hair was tied in a warrior's ponytail, his mustache long and curled. Stocky yet muscular, none of his features mattered save one. A deep scar divided his left cheek, an old sword wound that told the tale. The commander was a seasoned warrior who knew how to fight...and to survive. A fitting servant for the God of War. The marshal gestured to his almost finished plate. "You're not eating?"

Commander Crull gave a courteous nod. "I'll eat once your needs are met, my lord."

Servants entered, struggling to carry a copper tub sloshing with steaming water.

A bath! He'd nearly forgotten the luxury. Abandoning the nearly finished meal, he stood, letting the attendants remove his sweat-stained leathers. A terrible stink rose from the padded gambeson. Naked, his body revealed the pattern of his life, his skin crisscrossed with battle scars. All of the scars were old and faded, proof of valor gained before the Dark Sword. It seemed a lifetime ago. The marshal flexed his arms. Beneath his scar-crossed skin, he bulged with muscles, another boon of the sword. He enjoyed a rare vigor, robust with health despite his years. Stepping into the swirling steam, he sank into the water. Liquid heat soothed his aches, removing encrusted grime. The marshal began to relax, unclenching his guard. Attendants scrubbed him with soap and sponges, stripping away moon-turns of caked filth. They washed his hair, and trimmed his beard. He began to feel human again.

All the while, the Dark Sword remained within easy reach.

Pails of freshly heated water were poured over his head, the soothing warmth cascading down his chest. Finally clean, he stepped from the tub. Attendants swathed him in a warm robe of dark velvet. Across the pavilion, the camp bed piled high with soft furs called to him.

The marshal's one-eyed gaze sought Commander Crull. "Dismiss the servants, set guards on the pavilion, let none enter till I call for them."

"Yes, lord." The commander bowed, but the servants did not need to be told. They scurried from the pavilion like mice escaping a trap.

The commander strode to the canvas flap and paused. "What orders for your army?"

The marshal considered all that he'd achieved this day. "Have the dead placed in a massive pyre, but before they're burnt, I want every man in the army, regardless of rank, paraded past the mountain of the slain. Let my soldiers behold the power of the god they serve."

The commander's fist struck his breastplate in a brisk salute. "As you command." His gaze flickered to the Dark Sword, and then slid away.

The marshal bristled. "Know this," his voice turned hard as granite, "death comes swift to any who dare touch the Dark Sword."

"Yes, dread lord."

"Now go, and see to my army. I'll have need of them when I wake."

The commander bowed low, taking his leave.

Finally alone, the marshal crossed to the bed. Sinking into the seductive softness, he pulled the thick furs across his body. Exhaustion hovered close, yet his right hand snaked out, wrapping around the hilt of the Dark Sword. A jolt of energy whispered up his arm, connecting him to the blade. *Soon.* The word crooned through his mind like a seductive promise. He'd done well today, slaying thousands to claim an army, but his greatest task was yet to come. *Soon.* The Dark Sword sang to him, showing details of the deeds to come. Bathed in visions of glory, the marshal succumbed to sleep.

14

Ambrose

Time lost all meaning. Blindfolded and bound, Ambrose walked where his captors led him, ate what food they gave him, slept when they stopped. Wrestling with a thousand questions, he sought to engage his captors in conversation, but none obliged, leaving him to ponder his predicament in stony silence. So much had gone wrong. An army of the Pentacle rode unhindered through the southern kingdoms and there was no one to warn the monastery. Chased by a magic-sniffing dwarf, he'd lost his companions and then yielded *Invictus* to a band of cat-eyed archers. Despair dogged him. Locked in darkness, he feared for his friends, he feared for the fate of Erdhe.

And then something changed. The sounds around him grew muted, almost hushed, as if he'd entered a great cathedral. Rough hands pushed him to the ground. He sat cross-legged, his hands bound in front of him.

The blindfold came off.

Ambrose blinked at the blinding light.

Rays of golden sunlight streamed through the branches of a towering redwood. Staring aloft, Ambrose gaped at the size of it. Tall enough to pierce the sky, the immense redwood wore sunbeams like a regal raiment. Stately and majestic, the gigantic tree inspired reverence. Beholding the mighty giant, Ambrose understood the hushed silence. Like something out of legend, the great tree had a commanding presence, a sentient being cloaked in green, the undisputed monarch of the forest. Ambrose bowed his head in homage.

"Well should you bow, white-eye." His guards stood close behind him, but their longbows were unstrung, as if the great tree inspired peace. Ambrose hoped it was so.

His gaze took in his surroundings. Expecting dense forest, he was startled to see a crescent-shaped amphitheater rearing behind him. Tiered seats descended to an open stage surrounding the mighty redwood. But instead of carved stone, the amphitheater was living green, cloaked in a solid mat of vines, ivy, and moss. *An ancient ruin reclaimed by the forest!* Time lay heavy on the amphitheater, as if the tiered seats had witnessed more than one Age.

A shiver raced down Ambrose's spine. He felt as if he'd fallen into an ancient tome.

"So you come from the Seeing Eye." A woman emerged from behind the redwood's massive trunk. Tall and stately, she wore a magnificent cloak of white feathers and bore a wizard's staff carved of white aspen. Sunlight glimmered on the cloak's cascade of snow-white feathers, giving her an ethereal look. Her long silver hair was bound by a wooden diadem, an emerald stone winking at her brow. Her face was serene and unlined, making her age impossible to guess, but it was her eyes that truly startled. Her eyes were golden orbs, unmarred by any pupil. She should have been blind, yet she moved with the grace and confidence of the sighted. Suffuse with regal poise, she gave the impression of a powerful queen. Ambrose had no doubt he was in the fabled presence of the Treespeaker.

"You're real!" The awe-tinged words gushed out of him as he struggled to stand.

Her golden gaze fixed upon him. "Did you doubt it?"

Ambrose stammered an answer. "Some ancient histories read like myths."

Her voice was smooth as polished wood. "Yet, some myths prove true."

And if the myths are true, then the Treespeaker is a powerful sorceress! "Indeed." He felt like a stumble-mouthed acolyte. "I bring greetings from the Grand Master."

"Do you?" She tilted her head, as if considering him.

Chagrined, Ambrose bit back the lie. "No."

She gave him a knowing smile. "Do you mean me harm?"

"Never." He shook his head, his answer fervent.

"Untie him, for he is a guest beneath the great tree."

"But," one of his guards began to protest, but a single look from the Treespeaker silenced him. Pulling a knife from his belt, he cut the monk's bonds.

Ambrose rubbed his sore wrists. Emboldened by his new-found freedom, he dared to ask, "I came here with four companions, four friends. I need to find them."

The Treespeaker forestalled him with a raised hand. "There are other matters that must be discussed. Why are you here?" Her golden gaze bored into him, as if examining his very soul.

Fearing to be ensorcelled, yet refusing to flinch, Ambrose met her uncanny stare. "My companions and I were chased into the forest by soldiers of the Pentacle."

"Why were you chased?"

He hesitated, yet he had no answer save the truth. "For magic."

The great redwood rustled overhead, branches creaking.

Ambrose cringed, for he could detect no wind.

"And do you have this magic with you?"

His gaze was drawn back to the Treespeaker. Before he could answer, the captain of the archers stepped forward, the scabbarded great sword cradled in his arms. The captain gave a respectful nod to the Treespeaker. "To evade the Pentacle, the monk gave the sword into the keeping of a grandfather pine."

Into the keeping of a tree! The explanation sounded absurd, yet Ambrose did not gainsay the captain.

The Treespeaker stared at the monk. "Is this true?"

Ambrose hesitated. "More or less."

Her golden gaze turned to the sword. "I would see this sword that was entrusted to a grandfather pine."

The captain unsheathed the great sword. *Invictus* whispered from the scabbard, the sapphire-blue blade blazing glorious in the sunshine like a legend come calling.

The Treespeaker stared entranced. She approached the sword, gently laying her ringed hands on either side of the deadly-sharp blade. For the longest time, she said nothing, as if communing with wizard-wrought steel. Silence reigned beneath the great tree, as if the forest held its breath. Finally stepping away, the Treespeaker turned her golden gaze back to the monk. Her voice dropped to a husky whisper. "This sword and I are of an Age."

Impossible! Ambrose swayed, as if drunk on too much myth. "But that sword was forged during the War of Wizards!"

"So was I, my young friend. We were both forged in the same cruel crucible."

Ambrose could only gape, for he stood in the presence of an immortal.

"There is more at work in this world than most mortals realize. It is no accident that this sword comes here now, at the turning of an Age." She offered him a soft smile. "You may think you were chased into the forest by enemies, but this sword has come to my hand for a purpose." Her gaze returned to the sapphire blade. "Tell me what you think you know of its forging."

Ambrose felt like an acolyte being put to the test, yet he marshaled his thoughts in order. "Orin Surehammer was both the last great wizard of the Kiralynn Order and the first smith to unlock the secrets of blue steel. Plying his powers on the forge, he created indomitable weapons. Into the first blue steel sword he poured his powers, enchanting the blade with renewed stamina and peerless courage. With coiled dragons forged on the hilt, and runes engraved along the five-foot blade, the first blue steel sword was said to be invincible. Entrusted to the hands of a hero, Boric accomplished many great deeds, but he died in the far north and his sword disappeared, consigned to murky myths. Troubled by rumors of the missing sword, Orin became plagued by terrible visions. He believed the gods gave warning that Darkness coveted Boric's blade, subverting the sword to evil. Seeking to atone for his mistake, Orin forged a twin to the first blue steel blade, and into this blade, the last of his making, he poured all of his remaining magics. Named *Invictus*, the sword was hidden from the hand of man by arcane means, destined for the end of time, for the Battle Immortal." Ambrose gestured to the blue steel sword. "*Invictus* passed into the annals of myth and legend, remaining hidden for nearly a thousand years until it was invoked by Illumination, summoned a few moon-turns ago by a sixteen-year-old girl." Taking a steadying breath, Ambrose straightened his shoulders. "The Grand Master committed *Invictus* to the Battle Immortal. I've sworn to see the sword safe to Castlegard, to place it in the hands of a hero."

The Treespeaker's gaze remained fixed on the blade. "You speak the truth as you know it, monk, but this sword has been in the hands of the gods." She breathed deep, as if scenting a heady elixir. "I smell their divine touch upon the blade."

A shiver raced down his spine.

"Having been in the hands of the gods, its purpose has changed."

Changed! He stared, gob smacked. "Changed how?"

"That is the riddle." Her golden gaze pierced him. "Will you dare to learn the truth?"

He knew not the risk, yet he had but one answer. "Yes."

"Then together we shall seek the wisdom of the trees." The Treespeaker turned, the white feathers of her cloak shimmering in the slanting sunlight. Her staff in hand, she walked towards the ancient redwood with a stately grace. "Come, monk. Janthar, bring the sword."

Ambrose followed, wondering if he'd fallen into a god-given dream or a hellish nightmare.

15

Tybalt

Only a fresh-sworn monk, not yet accustomed to wearing robes of midnight-blue, yet Ty found himself awaiting a summons from the Grand Master. He paced his small spare cell, raking his hands through his wheat-blond hair, desperate to achieve a measure of calm. He should be meditating, but his mind kept skittering, plagued by ill-omened rumors. Some said Castlegard had fallen, others whispered the monastery would soon be under attack. Rumors ran rampant, and most of them grim. Infused with restless energy, he began to pace, wincing at every aching muscle. Before taking his vows, he'd thought himself an expert at the quarterstaff. A rueful laugh bubbled out of him, how little he'd known. After his first sparring round as full-sworn monk, he'd ached like a fresh-come novice. Mysteries wrapped in riddles, the dark-blue path was layered with endless depths of knowledge, yet he took pride in his vows. At seventeen, he was a full-sworn monk, a member of the Seeing Eye. Reaching for his quarterstaff, he ran his hands over the polished ironwood, determined to make a difference with his skills.

A knock sounded on the door.

Startled, Ty set his staff aside. Smoothing his midnight-blue robes, he checked the simple knot cinching his rope belt. Knots were important, for they told the level and expertise of the monk. His was only a single hitch, slightly more complicated than an acolyte's, yet someday he hoped to wear a master's braided knot.

A second knock sounded impatient.

Ty leaped to open it.

A short, stout, gray-haired monk waited outside. "I'm Master Digont. Please come with me." Without waiting for a reply, he turned and padded down the hallway.

Ty rushed to follow. Casting sideways glances at the master's roped belt, he read the knots. A *loremaster!* Ty's mouth went dry.

Rain pelted the casement windows, casting shadows across the illuminated walls. The master raised his hooded cowl, invoking the rule of silence. Stifling his questions, Ty followed the loremaster deep into the monastery. He soon grew lost, treading hallways he'd never seen. The master led him down narrow stone-cut stairs, as if seeking the very bowels of the monastery. Moisture beaded the inner walls as if they wept. Windows disappeared. Flickering lantern-light struggled to beat back the gloom. The stone-cloistered walls narrowed to a twisting labyrinth, the scripted text growing ominous with dark tidings. Battles raged across the ancient hallways. Ty felt secrets crowding the shadows. Turning a corner, he was shocked to find a pair of blue-robed monks standing guard with ironshod quarterstaffs. Ty shivered, feeling as if he trespassed on some inner sanctum.

The loremaster led him to the third door on the right. With a potent stare, he ushered Ty inside.

Light blazed from the room, dispelling the shadows. Squinting against the sudden brightness, Ty entered the chamber. When his eyes adjusted, he gaped, dazzled by the amazing artistry. Candles glowed in iron brackets along the base of the four walls, banishing every shadow. Painted a golden hue, the reflective walls were emblazoned with illuminated text finer than any he'd ever seen. Like pages from a long-cherished manuscript, the candlelight burnished the walls till they glowed golden with knowledge. Ty turned, staring, stunned by the artistry. The small square chamber was like an exquisite jewel box for calligraphy.

The master lowered his hooded cowl. "Please sit."

In the center of the chamber was a small square table and a single wooden stool.

Ty sat, clasping his hands beneath the table lest his nerves betray him.

The master gave him a leveled stare. "By order of the Grand Master, every sworn monk is to be tested for magic."

Magic! The word thundered through Ty's mind like a long-sought dream.

"Even the ancient relics are to be trialed."

Ty's heartbeat lurched with wonder.

"Bonding with a focus is rare. Have you ever felt the pull of magic?"

The question ambushed him. Ty struggled to control his galloping excitement. "No, I don't think so."

"Have you ever held a focus?"

"I don't think so."

The master raised a bushy white eyebrow. "Your subject of study is?"

Finally a question he could answer with pride. "The quarterstaff."

"Oh," disdain riddled the loremaster's voice, "so you're adept at bludgeoning." The master gave a long-suffering sigh. "Well, we'll expect nothing, and hope to be astonished."

Ty glared, teetering between anger and chagrin, too intimidated by the chamber to utter a tart response.

The pudgy loremaster turned and opened a door in the far wall, disappearing from view.

Ty gasped in surprise. The door was so cunningly hidden by the ornate illumination that he'd thought the wall solid. Glancing behind, he discovered that the door he'd entered had seemingly vanished, subsumed into the elaborate script. Even knowing it was there, he could not see it. *Illusion or magic?* Ty shivered, feeling like a mouse trapped in a magical box.

Master Digont returned bearing a wooden tray. "We'll start with these."

Ty realized it wasn't a tray, but a felt-lined drawer to a wooden chest. Within the drawer, spaced evenly across the green felt, was the oddest collection of treasures and junk. A gold coin sat next to a mangled spoon, a red-jeweled pendant next to a polished pebble. "Are these..."

"Focuses? Some are, some aren't, that is for you to decide."

"What must I do?"

"Touch them, feel them, fondle them, seek to find a connection. Take whatever time you need. If you feel the spark of magic, then I'll blindfold you and we'll see if the spark holds true." The master tugged a silken blindfold from his pocket. "If you can snatch the focus from the drawer while blindfolded, then it is yours to wield."

"And if I fail?"

"Then you're done."

Ty's mouth went dry.

The master gestured to the drawer like a shopkeeper presenting wares to a penniless customer. "Don't waste my time."

Swallowing his indignation, Ty silently swore to succeed. He stared at the trinkets, willing a connection. Starting with the red pendant, he methodically touched each one, praying to all the gods for a spark of magic...but he felt nothing unusual. Frustrated, the truth blurted out of him. "Nothing."

The master took the drawer and returned with another.

Ty leaned forward, eager to try again. He liked the detail of a miniature dagger carved from onyx, and a small shell with a delicate pink color kept snaring his gaze, but he did not know if 'liking' was enough. The question burst out of him. "Is liking enough?"

"Not nearly."

"Then what does magic feel like?"

"Different to different people, but above all you will feel a burning need to touch, to hold, to possess the focus. Such is the beginning of the magical bond."

Ty stared at the tray of clutter till a defeated sigh slithered out of him. "I don't feel anything."

With a knowing nod, the master removed the drawer. Disappearing into the far room, he returned with another. Twelve times the master presented drawers filled with clutter, and twelve times Ty felt nothing. His head began to pound and the small windowless room felt close, yet he refused to surrender his dream.

"The day grows late and you show no aptitude for magic. Are you sure you wish to persist?"

Ty stared at the master. "I'll keep trying till there are none left."

"Yes...but," the master hesitated, his lips clamping shut on unspoken words. He returned from the backroom bearing a deeper drawer lined with red silk.

Ty's heartbeat quickened feeling a sudden spark. He knew it as soon as he saw it. Amongst the clutter, sat a simple iron shodding. A common buttcap for a quarterstaff, yet Ty yearned to touch it. Full of need, he reached for it, afraid it was just his imagination, but once he held it, he knew it was meant to be his. Fondling the iron shodding, he studied it from every angle. Forged of ordinary iron, he could not find anything distinctive about it, but then he noticed the small maker's mark stamped on the inside. *The Seeing Eye!* This shodding was not some foundling object, it was forged by monks, a focus destined for war. Ty wrapped his fist around it. "This is mine!"

The master hovered beside him. "Are you sure?"

"*Yes!*" The word burst out of him with stunning conviction.

"We shall see." The master sounded dubious. "Return the piece to the drawer."

Ty tightened his fist, resenting the order.

"Return it." The master glowered. "You must pass the test or it shall never be yours to wield."

Reluctant, Ty unclenched his fist, returning the shodding to sit amongst the clutter.

The master bound his eyes with a silken blindfold. Without sight, his hearing seemed to sharpen. Ty heard the drawer being turned upon the table. He heard the items being rearranged. A throbbing silence returned, baited and full of questions.

Beside him, the master said. "Stretch out your hand, feel the focus, and snatch it from the drawer. If you cannot snatch it cleanly in one try, then it will never be yours."

Never, the word pounded against his mind like a battering ram. Ty stretched out his hand, wanting to believe, but a part of him felt it was impossible. He pictured the iron shodding in his mind...and then he felt it. Like a heated coal glowing beneath his palm, Ty sensed the shodding. He reached for it, cleanly snatching the iron cup from the drawer. Triumphant, he held it aloft, the thrill of magic rushing through him. "I got it!"

The blindfold fell away.

Ty blinked at the light.

Master Digont bowed towards him. "The relic is yours."

A relic! Ty felt lightheaded, his grip tightening on the shodding.

The master's voice turned courteous. "Do you know what it does?"

Ty grinned. "It's an iron shodding for a quarterstaff." He could not resist a poke. "Something we bludgeoners are familiar with."

The master had the grace to look chagrined. "No, I meant the magic inside."

Ty looked at the shodding nestled in his hand, overcome by a sense of rightness. "No, but it's meant to be wielded in war...and its name is Phade."

16

Ambrose

The Treespeaker led the monk to the edge of the great redwood's shadow. "At sunset, we shall seek the wisdom of the trees. Till then, you must not drink or eat lest you imperil your own life." Her golden gaze drilled into him. "Do you understand?"

Ambrose understood next to nothing about this strange encounter, yet he would not gainsay her. "As you wish."

"Till sunset."

"And the sword?"

She gave him an appraising look. "The great tree will guard it." Turning in dismissal, she gestured to the archer captain. "Janthar will show you to your friends."

My friends! Her words rang like a bell in Ambrose's mind. Bowing to the Treespeaker, he hastened to follow the archer, his footsteps quickened by hope. Birdsong twittered from the canopy, sunlight slanting through lofty branches. A leafy cathedral vaulted overhead, a thousand shades of green illumed by the waning sunlight, more beautiful than any stained glass window. They strode through a forest of towering giants that would have seemed impossibly tall save for the great redwood. Ambrose stared in awe. Tree trunks stood like living columns, some of them wider than the length of two horses. Their great girth implied a fathomless age. Humbled by the majestic conifers, he felt small yet strangely empowered, connected to an intricate web of life. *Forest* was too small a word for this lofty place. He'd entered a green realm, where monarch trees made dwarves of men's endeavors. Long-lived guardians of many Ages, the great trees stood like sentinels, endowed with ancient wisdom. Ambrose wondered what they remembered, what they knew.

Tantalizing scents of roasting venison intruded on his reverie. Breathing deep, his gaze tracked the scent to a cluster of domed tents sprung like mushrooms beneath the great trees. Murmuring voices and the clang of cook pots came from the clustered tents.

Janthar led him to the encampment's fringe, to a plain brown tent set before a campfire encircled by stones. A large bear-of-a-man sat hunched before the flickering fire, his left arm bound in a sling.

"Haythor!" Ambrose rushed to embrace his friend.

The big Zward stood, flashing a toothy grin, his face swollen by bruises. "They told me you lived!" Wincing at the monk's embrace, he shied away. "Careful, laddy buc, I've more aches and bruises than the archives have scrolls."

Ambrose released him. Bruised and battered, the big man looked like he'd been mauled. "Did the cat..."

"No, the cursed Pentacle."

Ambrose looked for the others, but the big warrior was alone.

"Jada's in the tent, badly wounded. She won't be walkin' any time soon."

"And the others?" He was half afraid to ask.

"Tarlin did not make it. The scout died fighting, skewered by a sword."

Ambrose mourned the taciturn scout. "He saved me. I should have stayed with him."

"If you'd stayed, you'd be dead, and all would be for naught." Haythor leaned close, his voice dropping to a whisper. "Kren got away. I sent him to warn the monastery."

A weight lifted from his shoulders, at least the monastery would be forewarned. "What happened?"

Haythor sank to the ground, using a stick to poke the fire. "Those soldiers were damned persistent. We set an ambush, killing the dwarf, and then we scattered, but they tracked us, dogging us through the forest. We regrouped, but they had us badly outnumbered. If not for the cat-eyed archers, we'd all be dead." He sent a pointed stare towards the trees.

Following his gaze, Ambrose saw three archers keeping watch from the shadows.

"They brought us here, tended our wounds, gave us food and shelter, but they're a damned skittish lot, always watching."

It was only then that Ambrose noticed the big man's sword was gone, and so were the knives at his belt.

Haythor gave him a slow nod. "They saved us, but we're not exactly welcome." Leaning forward, his voice dropped to a low growl. "The sword?"

"The Treespeaker has it. Or the redwood."

Puzzlement shown from the big man's face.

"I know. I feel as if I've fallen into a myth."

Haythor's stare narrowed. "They'll keep the sword?"

"I don't know." Ambrose's gaze drifted aloft, noting the angle of the slanting light. Time grew short, for the sun was nearly set. "I don't have much time." He leaned towards the Zward captain, keeping his voice to a low whisper, doing his best to untangle his encounter with the Treespeaker, the great redwood, and *Invictus*. "The Treespeaker says she's of an Age with the sword." Speaking the words aloud sent a chill racing down his back.

"That's daft!"

"I believe her." Ambrose chose his words carefully. "In the Great Archive, I stumbled across an ancient tome that spoke of a green power arising from the ashes of a once great city. Emerging during the War of Wizards, this reticent power was ruled by a woman, a Treespeaker. At the time, I thought it an odd title...not a person." He cast a sheepish glance at the warrior's face, but saw no ridicule. "If you meet her, you'll believe."

"And the sword?"

"She says the sword's purpose has been changed by the gods."

"*By the gods!*" The big man blanched pale. "You've dropped us into a divine tangle."

"Truly." Ambrose ran his hand through his hair. "But she says she can help discern its true purpose."

"And that's where you're going tonight?"

The monk nodded.

"Yet, you have doubts."

Ambrose sighed. "If something happens to me, you must take the sword to Castlegard." The Treespeaker's words nagged at his mind. "If she keeps the sword, then you must take word to the monastery."

The warrior growled. "I like it not."

Ambrose dropped his voice to a hush. "The Treespeaker says we are not here by accident but by fate."

"We're tangled in prophecy, that's for sure."

"All the more reason the Grand Master must know every detail of this encounter."

"I'm a warrior, not a scholar."

"Perhaps it's time to be both." Hunched before the fire's warmth, Ambrose recounted every scrap of conversation he'd had with the Treespeaker, seeking to understand the meaning laden in every word. All too soon, the sun set, plunging the forest into gloomy twilight.

A soft light bobbed in the forest depths. As Ambrose watched, it drew near their campsite. A cloaked man bearing a lantern stepped out of the gloom. "The Treespeaker awaits." Standing at the edge of the firelight, his golden cat-eyes glowed bright.

Eyes that glow like a demon's! Little wonder the cat-eyed people were spurned and feared across Erdhe. Ambrose stood. "I'm ready."

"Then come." The cloaked man turned and strode into the forest.

Casting a pointed glare at Haythor, Ambrose rushed to follow the bobbing lantern. Walking among the towering giants, his eyes adjusted to the gathering dark. Starlight crowned the great trees, glittering amongst the leafy canopy. The silvery light anointed the forest with a soft glow. Ambrose breathed deep the soothing scents of cedar and pine. Somewhere in the depths, an owl hooted. He embraced the wonder of the star-lit forest. Following the bobbing lantern, he expected to return to the great redwood, but the cloaked guide led him to a different giant, a massive cedar with a trunk the size of a small house. Light shone from an opening at the tree's base.

The hooded guide gestured towards the great cedar. "The Treespeaker awaits you within the Heart Tree."

Within the tree, unease prickled at the base of his neck. He imagined himself entombed in sap, like a fly stuck in amber. Taking a steadying breath, Ambrose stepped towards the great cedar. An angled gap at the trunk's base glowed with orange firelight. Following the light, he ducked low, entering the tree's heart.

Firelight illumed a small vaulted chamber of burled wood. Cozy and warm, the tree's hollow was like a small snug cabin. The Treespeaker sat on the far side of the stone-ringed fire. Her feathered cloak gleamed golden in the flickering light, matching the uncanny glow of her unblemished eyes. "Welcome to the Heart Tree. May leaf and bark enfold you in the peace and wisdom of the forest."

Ambrose took a seat across from her and then he noticed *Invictus* lying unsheathed on a bed of leaves. The naked sword seemed startling in the tree's hollow, as shocking as a woodcutter's axe.

"Yes, the sword. We are here to dream of it, and so it must be present." She handed him a wooden goblet filled with a golden brew. "Drink deep so that you may find your way into the dreams of the great trees."

Swirling the goblet, he sniffed the brew. It smelled of sap, of trees warmed by summer sunlight. Raising the goblet in salute, he quaffed the brew. Ambrose tasted trees! The golden potion tasted of oak-aged wine and a rich maple syrup and fine-ground pine nuts. A heady concoction of bottled sunshine and brewed bark, the elixir was as potent as the strongest brandy.

The Treespeaker began to hum, a low sound that vibrated through his bones.

Feeling drunk, his head swimming, his gaze skittered around the hollow. His stare settled on the blue steel sword, an anchor in the flickering light. Peerless sapphire steel, blue dragons coiled on the hilt, it was a sword sprung from ancient legends.

Tree roots emerged from the ground. Moving like fingers, they sought the sword. Delicate and fine, they wove a cocoon around the blade, a scabbard of living roots.

He should have been frightened, but somehow he found it fascinating.

"Time to sleep, time to enter the green dream."

Feeling lightheaded, he lay down next to the sword.

Something tickled his forearm. Roots sprouted from the ground, weaving a delicate web across his skin. Startled, he froze, but there was no pain.

"Accept the tree's embrace." Her voice was soothing as a mother's.

Root and song embraced him.

Lulled by the deep humming sound, Ambrose gradually relaxed.

Roots covered him like a protective blanket. A green song whispered through his mind. Succumbing to sleep, he dreamed.

17

The Knight Marshal

The knight marshal woke surrounded by seductive softness. Ambushed by the strangeness, he sprang alert. Fur blankets fell away as he leaped from the bed's warmth. The Dark Sword remained clutched in his fist. He snapped the sword upright, poised to strike. Crouched for battle, he searched for a foe, yet there were none to fight. The marshal stood alone in a richly appointed pavilion, thick carpets beneath his bare feet. And then he remembered. *So this is how the enemy lived while we built hovels in the mountains.* He growled at himself, annoyed by the intrusive memory. Shrugging off his mortal past, he focused on the present.

Starving, he prowled the pavilion. Daylight seeped through the dark canvas, providing dim illumination. Braziers in the four corners had long gone cold, holding nothing but spent coals. He found a chamber pot, sighing as he pissed a river, but his armor was not to be found, and there was no food, not a scrap anywhere. "Food! Bring me food!" He bellowed the order.

Like a djinn, Commander Crull stepped into the pavilion. "So the God of War finally rises."

"You dare mock me?"

"Never."

He heard sincerity in the commander's wary tone. "So I slept the night."

"Six nights."

"*Six?*" It explained his ravening hunger, yet the commander's answer made him feel strangely vulnerable. Scratching his beard, the marshal discovered it had grown.

"Magic has its price...even for a god."

"*Magic?*" His grip tightened on the Dark Sword.

"You slew thousands without taking a scratch. Such a prodigious feat must claim its due price."

"I won a battle, I needed sleep."

The commander gave him a flat-faced stare.

The invading scent of roast chicken goaded the marshal's hunger to a roar.

Servants appeared bearing flagons of wine and a tray piled high with a pair of roasted chickens and pan-fried bread. Before the tray settled, the marshal grabbed a drumstick, twisting it off. In three bites he gnawed it to the bone. Crispy skin, crackling with sea salt and garlic, he licked the grease from his fingers. The marshal consumed one chicken and then the other, bones piling on the tray. He ate with a relentless hunger, like a forge fire consuming charcoal. "More, bring me more." He reached for a goblet of rich red wine, his gaze turning to the commander. "Do you always eat so well?"

"Rank has its rewards."

"Is that why you fight, for rewards?"

"In the north, you first learn to survive, then you seek to thrive. Rewards are part of the thriving."

The answer sounded slimy to the marshal's ears, but he found he did not want to dwell on it.

Servants returned, setting a second platter of roast chickens before him. The savory smell renewed his hunger. Twisting off a drumstick, he pointed it at the commander. "Tell me about my army."

"At latest reckoning, your army stands at thirty-four thousand."

Thirty-four thousand, more than enough for his needs. "How many cavalry?"

"None, General Haith took all the cavalry south. Only the highest ranking officers retain their mounts."

"Archers?"

"Two hundred, minus the losses after your attack six days ago."

The marshal frowned. The total number of swords was stout, but the force was lopsided, missing cavalry and archers.

The commander said, "You still have one cadre of Taals."

"Taals?"

"Bulging muscles, slanting foreheads, tusks protruding from their lantern jaws, Taals are strong of arm and weak of mind. Birthed in the Pit, they're reared for war. The spiked cudgel is their preferred weapon."

"Ogres. I've killed those too."

"Nearly two cadre."

"How many in a cadre?"

"One hundred."

Not enough. "And what of siege engines?"

The commander's dark eyes glittered. "We brought none south with us. Wood is scarce in the far north."

So he seeks to test his god. "Yet the walls of Raven Pass bristled with trebuchets and catapults."

The commander gave him a knowing nod.

"How many survived?"

"General Haith ordered them brought down from the walls and positioned at the southern mouth of the pass."

"How many?"

"Five trebuchets, including one immense beast the troops named The Smasher, and eight catapults."

The marshal contemplated the number, weaving them into his plans. "Can the Taals move the siege engines?"

The commander shrugged. "They are beasts of great strength, they'll do as they're bid."

Servants bustled into the pavilion carrying his armor, everything shiny and polished. It took two men to bear the great wall shield. A golden pentacle shown from its curved front, the dark lacquer burnished to a shine. Drawn to his armor, the marshal inspected every buckle and clasp. The repair work proved superb, every nick and dent smoothed as if the metal were fresh-forged. Testing the bindings, he found them well oiled, the leather supple and smooth. Even his wool cloak was clean, the rents repaired and the stains removed. No longer encrusted with dirt and grime, the cloak showed its true color, a deep maroon. The marshal fingered the wool, caught in a distant memory, and then he stepped back to study the whole. Arrayed on the stand, his armor glittered formidable in the brazier light, awaiting the next battle.

Behind him, the commander said, "My lord, let me order you a fresh suit of armor, something befitting the God of War."

"No."

"At least a new cloak? Something embroidered with gold?"

"No."

"Do you have no sigil of your own?"

"I need none." He knew what the commander saw, a hodge-podge of symbols, maroon and silver mixed with black and gold, pentacles beside octagons, armor scavenged from many battlefields.

"But..."

He turned on the commander. "No, it is fitting, for all who wield a sword shall come to worship me...or die before their due time."

Retreating a step, the commander bowed low. "As you command."

"Now gird me for war." The marshal stood with his arms flung wide, watching as servants fitted him with a padded gambeson, leather, and finally a stout layer of armor. Lastly, they affixed his maroon cloak to his shoulder clasps. Encased in polished metal, the marshal tested every hinge and flange. Satisfied with the fit, he took up the Dark Sword. A savage strength roared through him. He raised the sword, as if to challenge the very heavens. "Time to test the mettle of my army. Sound the trumpets, rouse the legions, we march to war!"

Commander Crull said, "But what is the objective? Where do we march?"

In his mind, the Dark Sword whispered, *Time for the greatest glory!*

"There is but one conquest worthy of the God of War." Eager to claim his true destiny, the marshal strode from the pavilion into the glaring sunshine. The commander hurried in his wake as the marshal bellowed orders. "Sound the trumpets, call the men to the march. I ride to claim the greatest martial prize in all of Erdhe. I'll lead my legions east to war and glory." He felt the Dark Sword thrum with power, eager for blood and souls. His true destiny called. "Fabled Castlegard shall be mine."

18

Master Rizel

Blue-robed masters arrived in ones and twos. Master Rizel was one of the first to reach the audience chamber. Taking a seat beneath the great mage-glass window, he sat cross-legged on the golden-yellow floor, his midnight-blue robes puddling around him like a still pond. He watched as the others arrived, watched how they arranged themselves by factions. Those who argued for seclusion remained stubborn in their convictions despite the Grand Master's ruling, one of the many reasons he'd chosen the audience chamber as the site for the informal conclave.

A lingering scent of incense wafted through the chamber. He turned his gaze to the Star Screen. Dark-blue lapis inlaid with cut-crystal constellations, the great Star Screen dominated the chamber, a reminder that the Grand Master listened, keeping watch over all. Discussion and debate were encouraged, but ultimately the Grand Master decided.

The incoming stream of blue-robed masters slowed to a trickle. Masters Grimshaw and Vernius were last to arrive, taking seats near the outer doors. Rizel was relieved to see them. The conclave was open to all those who wore master's knots, yet only a fraction chose to attend.

The great gold-clad doors thudded shut.

A solemn silence cloaked the audience chamber. As was their custom, the masters sat statue-still in silent meditation, invoking the wisdom of the Light. After an appropriate time, Rizel nodded to Master Grimshaw. The scholar stood, a large, burly man with a bald pate and skin the color of ebony. "We meet in this chamber where the outer world seeks the Order's inner wisdom. Let those who have word from the kingdoms of Erdhe speak first. What tidings do you bring to the Seeing Eye?"

Two masters rose at once. One was expected, the other was not. Saklin, an aged quarterstaff master who kept contact with the Zward, was the first to speak, his words bubbling out of him. "Lenore lives!"

Relief rippled through the chamber. Like the others, Rizel was ambushed by the news. Lenore, the owl-guardian of the passes, had been missing for nigh on three moon-turns. She'd left the monastery on a routine patrol and never returned. Most feared her dead and her focus lost, both grievous blows to the Order. Word that she lived came as an unexpected boon. "How?"

The others stilled to hear the answer.

"One of the Zward found her broken near a crofter's cabin. Her injuries were so severe, he dared not leave her till now."

"Yet, she lives?"

Saklin nodded. "She lives but it remains to be seen if she'll ever fly again."

Murmurs of dismay whispered through the chamber.

Saklin raised an age-spotted hand. "There's more to the tale. Lenore was patrolling Drumheller Pass when she had a premonition, a warning of danger. As the owl, she soared north, down out of the foothills to the very start of the Great Southern Road. It was there that she spied a great horned owl flying in broad daylight." His gaze circled the assembly. In an ominous voice, he repeated the damning detail. "An owl in broad daylight, it flew on a straight path south, as if following the road. Soaring above the suspect owl, Lenore kept watch. Confirming the owl's unnatural behavior, she stooped to the attack...but it was *not* an owl. It was a fiend, an abomination with the feathered body of an owl and the face of a man!"

"*Soul magic!*" The words hissed through the chamber like a curse.

"The fiend spoke to her. They grappled and fought. Lenore beheaded the monstrosity, but it raked her side with corrupted talons. Gravely wounded, she lost owl form and plummeted from the sky."

Master Vernius said. "And the owl ring?"

"Locked in her hand."

Rizel breathed with relief.

Mistress Lurinda said, "Praise the Light that the Zward found her."

"Praise the Light." The words rippled like a prayer, yet a grim chill had entered the chamber.

Someone said what they were all thinking. "So the Mordant resumes his blasphemous ways."

"He must be stopped."

"It's worse than you know." Tamzin stood, the rumpled master of the owlery, his gray hair all askew.

Rizel settled back to listen to what he already knew.

"The far north brims with nightmares undreamt. To guard his domain, the Mordant created roving packs of gore hounds, twisted wolves with the cunning of men. He's breeding ogres, lumbering giants with horned tusks to serve in his armies. And he's found a way to infuse carved stone with the souls of men and beasts, creating gargoyles that serve." Tamzin cast a warning glare across the assembled masters. "As the Mordant's powers grow, so do his blasphemies. Zith believes there is nothing he will not dare."

More than a few masters went whey-faced, making the hand sign against evil, but Vernius latched onto the telltale name. "*Zith* said? How do you know what Zith said? Is he not with the blade bearer?"

Tamzin gave the barest of smiles. "And therein lies our hope. Zith was in Navarre with the blade bearer. It seems the girl found a way to conquer the Dark Citadel."

"The Dark Citadel!" Amazement leaped like wildfire through the assembly, but the initial burst of wonderment soon burnt out, leaving profound confusion in its wake.

Felix voiced the problem. "The fall of the Dark Citadel was never foretold in any of the prophecies."

Master Vernius said, "The prophecies are becoming unraveled. We've reached the turning of an Age."

Felix's voice dripped with horror, "The Mordant evades the Seeing Eye! The Order goes blind into the Battle Immortal!"

The chamber erupted in frenzied argument.

Master Rizel sat back, letting the argument rage, letting his brethren understand the true depth of the danger they faced. When the debate lulled, he stood. "There is still hope." His words sliced through their rhetoric. Silenced, they turned as one to stare at him. "Winged beasts with the faces of men, souls enslaved within stone gargoyles, gorehounds ensorcelled with men's cunning, these foul deeds fit what we have long known of the enemy. The Mordant wields soul magic in the service of the Dark. This, above all else, names him an abomination, a monster who must be destroyed. But the Order has always known this." He stared at his blue-robed brethren. "If not the details, then we knew his true nature. We of the Kiralynn Order have always known our true foe." He paused to let them consider. "But think of what was *not* foreseen. Look at what the prophecies did not foretell! *The fall of the Dark Citadel!* This is not an act of the Mordant, but of the blade bearer!"

His words sank in, knowing looks flashing between the blue-robed masters.

"Don't you see? The Mordant is trying to break the prophecies, but the blade bearer, she is beyond them! Think back to when we first saw the signs warning of the turning of an Age. We expected a blade bearer. Many in the Order thought it would be Princess Jordan of Navarre."

Felix interrupted. "The princess was god-kissed with visions. Visions that have made a great difference."

"None here will gainsay that," Master Rizel nodded the point to Felix, "but she was not the blade bearer. Kath of Castlegard was invited to the monastery because of her gargoyle focus, not for the crystal dagger. And now the Dark Citadel has fallen, proving the Mordant does not see her either. *He does not see her!"* Rizel gestured to his assembled brethren. *"We,* the Order of the Seeing Eye, did not truly see her."

"And this is cause for hope?"

"Yes." Conviction grew in his mind. "She is beyond prophecy. Kath of Castlegard writes her own destiny. She is the unexpected hero, a small petite girl whom others overlook at their peril."

"And being overlooked is an *advantage?"* Skepticism rode Felix's voice.

Master Rizel nodded. "Pray that it is. For we need every advantage for the coming battle. In the meantime, we dare not be slackers. The Kiralynn Order must do all that we can to defeat the encroaching Dark."

Debate rippled through the chamber, but this time it was more focused.

Tamzin stood, his voice rising above the others. "There is more news from the south."

A grim hush cloaked the chamber, everyone turning to stare at the rumpled owl master. "The Octagon, the Rose, and the Osprey are locked in a bitter battle with the Pentacle. They sought to contain the Mordant's forces in the north, but there was a breach. Aeroth reports that two thousand cavalry of the Pentacle crossed Eye Bridge, gaining entry to the southern kingdoms. War gallops south on ironshod hooves." His gaze swept the chamber. "The blade bearer believes this army is a spear tip aimed at the Kiralynn Order."

The chamber erupted in argument and accusations.

Felix's baleful stare speared Master Rizel. "And you sent *Invictus* away, just when the sword was most needed! If the monastery falls, it is on your head!"

Rizel parried the accusatory stare, putting iron in his voice. "If the monastery falls, it will be on *all* our heads. Destiny comes for us, whether we will it or not. Evil provoked this battle, but *we* must end it. Stand and be counted for our time has come." He met their stares, "For this is the Battle Immortal!" Suddenly weary, as if he'd carried a terrible burden for far too long, he sagged against the mage-stone wall, while his brethren erupted in argument. He'd finally roused the scholarly monks to war, making them confront the true dangers, but in the depths of his heart, he feared for the monastery. In truth, he feared for all of Erdhe. Invoking all the gods, he fervently prayed that a young petite girl could remain hidden long enough defeat an ancient evil, else all of Erdhe was lost.

19

Ambrose

Ambrose felt stiff, as if he'd stood in one place for an eon. Despite his stationary vigil, his roots had drunk deep, sampling the flavors of the world. His sap was rich with memories, a tasty tapestry of wisdom. Among the many memories, a blue steel tooth forged by wizarding-kind gleamed bright. The tooth was meant for rending, for bloody warfare against the Dark, yet the gods had added their transforming touch. Still a tooth, yet the blue blade held a divine-forged purpose. Wisdom wrought into steel, the blade would know. Only in the Light could a tree grow true. Ambrose shivered with understanding, quaking every leaf and bough. A great humming washed across him, a conclave of trees, the agreement of the forest. The sound swelled and then moved on, leaving him behind. The green dream receded, and he found himself gasping for breath, awash on a strange shore. Two arms, two legs, two eyes...he was small and contained and alone. Banished from the green song, he was mortal once more.

Ambrose woke with a start.

The encircling roots were gone, the fire dimmed to embers. Sitting alone in the tree's hollow, he felt bereft, abandoned, utterly alone. He missed the fellowship of the great trees, the deep wisdom of their roots, the sap-stored knowledge of Ages. Adrift in confusion, Ambrose felt his stubbled face, shocked to be human once more. He stared at his hands, strange yet so familiar. A Seeing Eye stared from his open palm. Memories trickled back into his mind, clear and rushing like a fresh mountain spring. He remembered his name, his purpose, a sworn monk of the Kiralynn Order. *Invictus!*

Turning his head, he spied the sword.

Horror gripped him. He stared speechless. Instead of a peerless blade, the sword was a rusted hulk. Red with rust and pitted with centuries of age, the sword was a ruined relic! He stared, aghast. Ambrose doubted the corroded blade would slice bread. This had to be a mistake, a cruel jest, yet the dragons coiled on the hilt were familiar. He reached for the blade, hoping to dispel the illusion, but his hands felt only corroded steel. So brittle, he feared it might break, his hands began to shake. The sword had the shape of *Invictus,* yet it was a rusted ruin.

The Treespeaker bowed into the hollow.

"What have you done?"

Unperturbed, the Treespeaker sank to the ground, regal in a cascade of white feathers. "Already you have forgotten the fellowship of the trees."

"*Where is Invictus?*"

"You hold the steel tooth in your hands."

"Blue steel *cannot* rust! *This is a ruined hulk! A mockery! A joke!*" Ambrose struggled not to shake the woman. "*Invictus* is the hope of Erdhe! My friends *died* bringing it here! Forged by a wizard, the blade was invoked by an illuminator! What have you done with it?"

"The gods have touched the sword. This change was not of my doing."

He shook the rusted sword at her. "This? The gods did *this*?" He gaped at her answer. "But why?"

"For the knowing."

Another riddle. He sagged with frustration. "I don't understand."

Her voice was gentle. "You belong to the Seeing Eye, not the Deep Green. You have entered the forest and dreamed deep, dreamed well, but now you must return to your singularity, living apart from the great forest. In time, you will remember, you will believe. For now it is enough to know that you must take the sword to Castlegard."

"This, a rusted hulk?"

"The blade is far more than what it appears. The sword is god-touched with purpose."

Her words lit a small spark of remembering in his mind, enough to soothe his outrage.

"Come." She rose, a study of grace and poise.

Shaking his head in vehement disbelief, he glared at the sword, yet it remained a rusted hulk. He felt betrayed, he felt a failure...yet some lingering memory whispered at the back of his mind. Soft as a leaf, a green memory brushed against his mind, offering succor. He'd fallen into a fairy tale, or perhaps a nightmare. Nothing in the archives had prepared him for this, yet the Grand Master had charged him with a task. Carefully cradling the rusted sword, he followed the Treespeaker from the Heart Tree.

Ambrose blinked, ambushed by the bright sunlight streaming through the branches.

"This is Martyn."

A green-cloaked man stepped forward.

"He will guide you to your friends. On the morrow, you will leave for Castlegard. Two hundred rangers of the Deep Green will see you safely to the great castle."

He stared at her, both puzzled and stunned.

"Know that I do this as much for the Forest as for you." The Treespeaker's face turned solemn, her voice ringing like an oracle. "An all-consuming Darkness reaches for Erdhe. The great trees feel it. Shuddering to their very roots, they spurn the poison, yet they are tied to the land. The end of an Age draws near. Much will change, much will be decided. My people are not plentiful, yet they will bend their bows to the Battle Immortal. Tell Kath of Castlegard to use them wisely."

Kath of Castlegard! Ambrose grasped the name. So the Treespeaker knew the blade bearer, yet the last he'd heard, the girl was on her way to Pellanor. He decided to keep the knowledge to himself, lest she rescind her offer of rangers. "As you wish."

She gave him a knowing smile. "Touched by the Green Dream, yet you are a monk once more, secretive of your knowledge."

Uncertain how to reply he kept silent.

"Take the sword to Castlegard and fulfill your destiny."

Ambrose felt fate-slapped, foolishly cradling a rusted sword.

"When you meet Kath of Castlegard, tell her the trees see her, they know her. The ceremony in the forest was well done. She is a true daughter of the Deep Green."

The words rang like prophecy, making his skin prickle.

Overhead, the great trees rustled and quaked though there was no wind.

Ambrose felt drenched in myth and legend.

"You feel it, the turning of an Age. A time when prophecies live and die, when magic runs wild, and legends collide with nightmares in epic struggles. To live in such times is both perilous and wondrous. May you evade the first and never lose the second."

"You see so much," he had to ask, "do you know if the Light will prevail?"

"Not even the great trees know this, but much will be risked ere this battle is decided." She made a sign of blessing. "May the wisdom of leaf and bark go with you." Nodding farewell, she turned and walked away, regal in her cloak of white feathers.

"Come." The voice of the green-clad attendant tugged at him.

Ambrose's gaze clung to the Treespeaker, wondering if he would ever see her again. *A rusted sword.* It seemed a cruel joke, yet he knew he would carry the blade to Castlegard. Despite the swords appearance, he would see the task done. Carefully sheathing the rusted sword in his shoulder harness, Ambrose followed the green-cloaked guide into the forest.

20

King Ivor

King Ivor summoned the monk to his council chambers. Master Yarl arrived in rumpled robes of midnight-blue. Prowling across the lapis floor like a fresh-woken bear, he squinted against the slanting sunlight. Burly and barrel-chested, the monk looked more like a brawler than a scholar, yet his red-rimmed eyes told a different tale. The king well knew the monk burned candles into the small hours of the morning, studying the trove of scrolls taken from the Dark Citadel. A prize laden with mystery and promise, the trove was the very reason he'd summoned the monk. King Ivor sought answers...and a distraction from his grief. "What have you learned?"

"Little enough." Bowing, Yarl took a seat at the table, wearily rubbing his eyes.

"Darkness threatens all of Erdhe. We need an advantage." The king pressed for an answer. "It's been nearly a fortnight. You must have learned something?"

"Many of the texts are old, the script difficult to decipher, but I can confirm that Zith had the truth of it. The Mordant is obsessed with mage-stone and soul magic."

"What is soul magic?"

"An affront to the gods. Some consider it the most powerful of magics, yet it has long been forbidden, a blasphemy for any wizard to wield."

The king of Navarre was no stranger to magic. "But what does it do? How is it used?"

The monk gestured to an ewer of wine. "May I?"

"Of course."

Yarl poured a generous goblet and took a long draught of merlot, wiping his mouth with the back of his shovel-sized hand. "Before he left, Zith told me something of his time in the north. He spoke of a Gargoyle Gate." The monk's gaze flashed to the king. "Have you heard of it?"

King Ivor shook his head. "The north is a dark riddle."

"More than you know." The monk took another swig. "Zith said the gates guard the entrance to the Mordant's domain. Great stone gargoyles, thrice the height of a tall man, affixed to stone pedestals. Each one different, each one grotesque, a mélange of beasts carved into stone." The monk lowered his voice. "When an enemy strides between the gargoyles, they waken."

"Waken?" The king stumbled on the word.

The monk gave him a solemn nod. "The stone gargoyles writhe upon their pedestals loosing an unearthly wail."

The king shook his head, rebelling at the conjured nightmare. "Not possible."

"Possible...with soul magic."

The king began to understand the monk's concern. "How?"

"By binding the souls of murdered beasts and men into carved stone, forever entombed in the gargoyles."

The king made the hand sign against evil. *"Abomination!"*

"Just so." Yarl rubbed his eyes, a weary gesture. "The prophecies say the Mordant will make all of Erdhe into a Dark Hell...unless he is stopped."

The king reached for his goblet.

The outer door eased opened. A guard in the checkered tabard of Navarre leaned inside. "A messenger from Pellanor, my lord."

The king's hope quickened. "Come."

The guard admitted a messenger clad in the emerald green of Lanverness. Travel-stained and smelling of leather and horse, the young man bowed low. "An urgent message from the Queen of Lanverness." Opening his courier's pouch, he removed a sealed scroll and offered it to the king.

"Only one?" The king had hoped for a message from his daughter. Jemma's reply was long overdue.

"Just one, my lord."

The king took the scroll and the messenger retreated a few courteous paces, waiting for a reply.

King Ivor ran this thumb across the raised seal. Imprinted with the royal sigil of Lanverness, the emerald sealing wax was unbroken.

Yarl said, "Shall I leave you, my lord?"

"No need." Breaking the seal, the king unrolled the scroll, his gaze imbibing the flowing script. *"What!"* Choking on the words, he read it again. Rage roared out of him. *"The queen's gone mad!"* He turned on the messenger. "What's the meaning of this?"

The lad cringed backwards, his face blanching pale. "I'm only the messenger."

"I want answers!"

Yarl interceded. "He's only a courier!"

"Yet, he must know something."

The courier cringed. "I swear I know nothing, lord!"

The king roared, *"Guards!"*

A pair of guards came running, their swords unsheathed.

"Take this lout to the deepest dungeon. I'll have the truth from him, one way or another."

The guards grabbed the messenger, dragging him towards the doors.

"Majesty, spare me!" Squirming, the lad kicked and punched, but he was overmatched by the guards. The doors thudded shut, silencing the lad's pleas.

Yarl glared, shock scrawled across his face.

The king thrust the noxious scroll towards the monk. "Read!" Raking his hand through his silver-gray hair, he paced in front of the windows. A brisk sea breeze blew in, but it could not quench his rage.

Yarl gaped. "The queen's *ransoming* your daughter for *magic?*"

The king rounded on him. "You see what I mean? The queen's gone mad! The woman is insane!"

"What magic?"

The king bit the words. "The magic to make a queen fecund. A legacy from the past, it is forever tied to our royal bloodline. It cannot be shared. It cannot be ransomed." He shook his head. "The queen's gone mad!"

Yarl's brow furrowed. He held the scroll towards the light. "Are you sure this is the queen's signature? Her handwriting?"

"I know it like my own." The king strode to a side cabinet, yanking open a drawer filled with scrolls. "See for yourself."

The monk moved to the cabinet. Removing scrolls, he methodically compared them, spreading them across the council table.

King Ivor paced at the window. A storm brewed on the northern horizon, but it would not hit till nightfall. His gaze cast across the cobalt sea, absently following sailing ships and their frothing wakes. Below, white-capped waves pounded against the breakers, sending a salty spray up the tower's basalt wall. The king's hands balled into fists, anger warring with grief. First his siblings fell to foul poison, then his beloved Megan...and now his dearest daughter! His house was cursed. His hand sought his pocket, fingering his wife's favorite bracelet, delicate seashells threaded on silver, but the charm could not hold his grief at bay.

"Everything seems correct."

"*Correct!*" The king rounded on the monk, spittle flying from his mouth. "Does the queen want a war with Navarre! For I'll not give up my daughter!"

The monk stood with his feet planted wide, as if braced for a blow. "My lord," he raised the scroll, "the handwriting is correct, but this message reeks of Darkness. This is *not* the queen."

"Her seal! Her signature! Who's to say what a queen will do when dogged by age!"

"This message is not from the Rose Queen."

The words roared out of him. "Then who?"

"The Mordant."

The Mordant! The name punched him in the gut. The king staggered backwards, gaping at the monk in disbelief.

"We know from the blade bearer that the Mordant has gone to Pellanor."

"*Pellanor.*" The king sank to the nearest chair. "Are you saying the *Mordant* has my daughter?"

The monk turned cautious. "Perhaps."

"Why would the Mordant want Navarre's birth magic?"

"I doubt he does."

The king narrowed his gaze. "Explain."

"Consider the intent behind the message. Who stands to gain most by this scroll?"

The king waited.

"Divide and conquer! If Navarre is provoked to war with Lanverness, then the south lies open to the Mordant's hordes."

The monk's words made a bitter sense. The king gestured to the foul message. "Yet, it bears *her* signature!"

"Perhaps the letter is forged...or the queen is coerced."

"Coerced?"

The monk gave him a hollow-eyed stare. "Pain, torture, blackmail, magic, all are tools of the Mordant." Yarl raised the scroll. "Or, this could all be a lie, an elaborate deceit designed to provoke you to war."

The king stood abruptly, his chair scraping across stone. He strode to the mullioned windows, putting his back to the sea. "And what if it's true?" He glared at the monk. "I'll not lose my daughter. I'll not lose my heir."

The monk gaped. "Princess Jemma is your heir?"

The king nodded.

"Who else knows?"

"None save the royal council and the princess."

"Pray that it remains so. As your heir, she's even more valuable to the Mordant."

Grief gnawed at the king, sharpening his fear for his daughter. "I'll raise an army to get her back."

"And you'll aid the Mordant if you do!"

"I can't risk my daughter." The king threw a daggered glare to the queen's scroll. "I can't ignore the threat."

The monk's eyes widened. "That's exactly what you should do!" Yarl began to pace, anxious as a baited bear. "Ignore the scroll. That's the best answer, majesty. Don't react to the Mordant's ploy. I'm certain he'll send another. Couriers take time, couriers get lost, even royal couriers. Meanwhile, you buy time for your daughter...and the blade bearer."

"But Kath does not know."

"I'll see that she does. The Kiralynn Order has its own network of couriers, far faster than yours, or the Mordant's."

The king chewed on the monk's words, wondering how far the Order's tentacles penetrated his kingdom. "I can't sit idly by."

"Then send men if you must, but send them in bands of five or six, without sigils or tabards of any sort, nothing to link them to Navarre."

"Of what use are a few handfuls of swords?"

"They can aid the blade bearer...or the Zward. Send them," the monk looked thoughtful, "to the Laughing Gargoyle, a travelers' inn to the west of Pellanor. The innkeeper, a man called Ort, serves the Zward. Once we hear more from Pellanor, we'll learn how your swords can best save the princess."

"Will we learn more from Pellanor?"

The monk gave him a solemn nod. "Most assuredly."

So the Order has tentacles through many kingdoms. King Ivor began to wonder if he could trust the monks.

"You can trust the Kiralynn Order, my lord." The monk's gaze was steadfast. "Darkness must be defeated. The Mordant is your true enemy, not the Kiralynn Order, not the queen."

"Yet, it is *my* daughter, *my* heir, who hangs in the balance."

"This scroll is a trap. To do anything else, aids the Mordant."

The king ground his teeth, grief cutting him like an open wound. "I'll heed your council, for now, but if this fails, your life is forfeit and Navarre shall forever curse your precious Order."

"Majesty, if we fail, there'll be none left to curse."

The Battle in Pellanor

21

The Mordant

Throne room to find the queen's castle in turmoil. Soldiers, servants and courtiers, rushed through the hallways chasing rumors, their furtive glances betraying their confusion. *Chaos is so easily seeded.* The Mordant suppressed a satisfied smile. Lifting his hooded cowl, he cloaked his face in velvety shadows. Clad in a long dark cape that slithered across the floor, the oldest harlequin glided through the marbled hallways, prowling silent as death.

The hallways provided a feast of rumors. Listening from the shadows, the Mordant sought lies worthy of embellishment and truths needing to be quashed. Chaos had so many flavors. Some feared the queen was dead, leaving the Rose throne vacant. Others whispered that a rebellious uprising had been narrowly thwarted, leaving the queen's tower drenched in blood. A few swore the queen had gone mad, ordering her own guards murdered. Everyone knew the knight protector was slain, an oft repeated fact that seemed to bolster all the other hearsay. Interesting how one grain of truth could spawn so many conspiracies. Fear and paranoia ran wild. Gathering threads of rumors, the Mordant strode the marble halls, supping on the confusion.

"*Lanverness is cursed! Darkness stalks the castle!*"

The Mordant came to a sudden halt. Startled to hear the naked truth, he scanned the vaulted chamber, tracing the voice to a gray-haired courtier standing atop the marble stairs.

"*A dark curse has befallen the Rose Court! The gods turn their faces from the queen's city!*"

The Mordant suppressed a snarl. Perhaps the man was truly god-touched, or merely drunk on delusion, but either way, the Mordant loathed truthsayers. "*Kill him...but make it appear an accident.*" The Mordant marked the courtier with a subtle gesture. An assassin peeled from the shadows to stalk the loathsome meddler.

The courtier persisted, his voice annoyingly righteous. "*We must repent! We must rally to the queen! Listen to me, for I have seen a vision...*" A shadow flickered behind the man, subtle and quick. A single well-timed shove sent the old man tumbling down the marble staircase. Screams battered the gilded walls till his head hit with a dull thud. Silence snuffed his screams, snuffed the truth. He came to rest with his head bent at an impossible angle, his eyes staring sightless.

The Mordant turned away. "What do you see now? The flames of Hell?"

Behind him, he heard the shocked murmur of courtiers, but there was no hew and cry. Clearly the bystanders deemed it an accident. The Mordant smothered a smile. *Mortals fool themselves when Darkness stalks their midst.* Even when the deed was done in front of their faces, they refused to see. They made it so easy, nothing more than sheep needing a herder.

Satisfied, the Mordant moved on. He roamed the gilded hallways, supping on chaos, but he knew such turmoil should never be wasted. The Great Dark Dance was a convoluted plan conspired over centuries. The Rose Queen's rule was an unexpected aberration, an abomination soiling one of his Darkest achievements. The woman deserved to be utterly destroyed, but in order to corrupt the past and twist the present, the Mordant needed to control the masses. Snapping his fingers, he summoned another assassin. "Bring me the traitor."

Nodding in deference, the dark-clad assassin scurried down the long hallway.

Rain drummed against the diamond-paned windows with a sharp staccato, as if the heavens wept. The Mordant lurked in a shadowy alcove. His hand reflexively sought the malachite coin nestled deep in his pocket. A focus stolen from a dead monk, he fondled the subtle engravings, certain its power would soon be his.

The assassin returned with the traitor in tow, a burly man clad in a dark robe.

The queen's spymaster was smart enough not to make any obvious signs of homage. Slipping into the alcove's shadows, the pug-faced traitor dropped his gaze, avoiding the Mordant's potent stare. "You summoned me, my lord?"

"This chaos must be harnessed. Spread the word that a ruthless assassination attempt on the queen's life was foiled." The Mordant embellished the tale, knowing the addition of small truths would garnish the greater lie. "The knight with the blue sword died valiantly defending the queen. All the assailants were slain, but the lord behind the plot remains elusive. Henceforth, the queen's security will be tripled." The Mordant grinned. "If anyone needs to see the queen, they should first approach you."

Raddock puffed like a predictable peacock. "It will be as you say."

The Mordant's voice dropped to hiss. "Take care lest you overstep. The court must believe the queen still rules, else her name cannot be sullied."

The traitor cringed. "Yes, lord."

"And once this chaos is turned to our purpose, you'll need to plan a state funeral for the slain knight. Lauding him as a hero will reinforce the need to protect the queen and keep her isolated from the court." The Mordant smiled. "Such a valiant death should not be wasted."

"Yes, lord."

"And find Hoit. I want a cadre of my personal swords to guard her at all times. Make sure all of them are clad in appropriate emerald."

The traitor perked. "Lord, the second squad can be trusted to guard the queen. They have been turned."

"Turned how?"

"A few were Red Horns who'd never truly reformed. I deftly herded them into the same squad. The rest were bribed with gold."

"*Gold,*" a sneer rode the Mordant's voice. "Those bought for gold seldom stay bought. I deal in souls, a much more potent currency. *My* swords will guard the queen. Under their watch, the bitch will remain caged."

The traitor backed away. "Yes, lord."

"It is time to turn this chaos to my purpose. A mountain of woes shall be heaped upon the queen's name. History shall curse her, forever spurning a woman's rule, but for my plan to succeed these sheep must believe the queen still holds power." He glared at the traitor. "Make them believe."

Raddock dipped his head, offering a subtle deference. A sheen of sweat beading his forehead betrayed his true fear. "Yes, lord."

The Mordant made a dismissive gesture. "Now be gone and do my bidding."

Bowing low, the traitor scuttled down the corridor like a cockroach fearing a boot.

The Mordant emerged from the shadows. A pair of dark-clad assassins glided in his wake. He strode through the gilded hallways, spinning convoluted plans. Even with a millennium of experience, he never tired of twisting mortals. Deceive, divide, corrupt and conquer, all of Erdhe would soon be his.

22

Liandra

Darkness stalked her court, an ancient enemy hidden in plain sight. Bloody images assailed the queen's mind. Liandra struggled to comprehend the terrible turn of events. From the brutal ambush in the hallway, to Sir Durnheart's shocking death...to the appearance of the Mordant. *The Mordant, the bane of Erdhe, here in our court!* His name sundered her mind like a thunderclap splitting the sky. A vivid nightmare resurrected from timeless myth, she made the hand sign against evil, but peasant superstitions would not avail her. *Till the castle sleeps*...the queen clutched at the Mordant's words, holding them close like a desperate hope.

Rain drummed against the casement window, darkening the pane yet it was still midday. Time was against her, she dared not waste a moment.

Assassins watched from the corners of her royal chamber, their stares tugging like lethal tethers.

Moving with measured care lest she startle the black-clad watchers to violence, the queen crossed her solar to join her women. Lady Sarah and the others flocked around like lost ducklings. Two of her women remained motionless, sprawled on the floor near the open window, felled by the assassins' ambush. *Ladies Martha and Cristal*...it hurt to see them sprawled insensate, crumpled like discarded dolls. Stiff in her ceremonial armor, Liandra gestured towards her fallen women. "See to them."

Lady Sarah obeyed. Kneeling, she gently turned Lady Martha.

"Does she live?" Liandra hovered over her stricken women.

Lady Martha moaned, answering the question, an egg-shaped bruise blooming on her forehead.

Relief coursed through the queen. "Give her water and help her to a chair."

Her ladies leaped to obey. Fluttering around the dazed woman, they gently helped her to sit near the hearth. Lady Sarah moved to the second puddle of unmoving silk. She tried to rouse Lady Cristal, calling her name and shaking her shoulder...till the brunette's head fell sideways, tilting at an unnatural angle. Lady Sarah gasped. "Majesty, she's *dead!*"

Murdered! Something in the queen snapped, unleashing a righteous rage. Liandra flew across the room, an accusing arrow aimed at the nearest assassin. "You *killed* her!"

The dark-clad watcher remained statue-still.

His indifference goaded her rage. "Is this what you do? Kill innocent women?"

The assassin's gaze locked on hers, his face impassive. "She got in the way." He shrugged. "She matters not."

"She *mattered* to *us!*" Fast as thought, the queen's bejeweled hand swept towards the assassin's insolent face...but the dark-clad man was faster. His hand pinioned her wrist, forestalling the slap. Shock speared the queen. "How dare you!"

His hand tightened, cruel as an iron shackle.

Pain erupted in her wrist, yet Liandra fought to ignore it. Reclaiming her regal demeanor, she glared at him. "Unhand us, for we are queen!"

"You're a puppet...you just don't feel the strings." He released her with a shove.

She staggered backward, shocked by his brute strength, yet she kept her footing. Her mind whirled, realizing the folly of her ways. Swallowing her rage, she gathered her wits, reaching for cold calculation. "You serve the Mordant." It was a statement, not a question, yet she sought to further loosen his tongue.

"As will you."

"Never." Her reply rang with cold certainty.

His insolent gaze bled past to stare at her women.

Her breath caught on the unspoken threat, yet she sought to understand her enemy. "Why do you serve him?"

The assassin gave her a dead-man stare.

The queen took a more slippery tack. "We have jewels. Enough to make you rich beyond imagining. All you need do is open that door and stand aside."

He remained unmoved, not even a twitch of avarice in his dark gaze.

"We ask this not for ourselves, but for our women."

For the first time, he truly looked at her, as if seeing something of interest...or perhaps something unexpected. His stare bored into her. She felt...*studied*. Suppressing a shiver, Liandra used her most compelling voice. "Let them go. As you said, they do not matter."

A stony silence was his only reply.

"Our jewels for their release?"

"None may leave." His voice brooked no argument.

She hadn't expected the bribe to work, yet she had to try. Her gaze dropped to her murdered handmaiden, the stink of death creeping through the chamber. "And what of the dead? Are you just going to leave her there?"

"After dark, when the castle sleeps."

When the castle sleeps...more proof that time grew thin. Liandra withdrew to ponder her position. She felt like a piece trapped upon a chessboard, beleaguered by the enemy's pawns. *A queen trapped by pawns, but in this game, all the pawns are lethal.* Balling her bejeweled hands into stubborn fists, Liandra drew her mind away from the immediate threat to consider the larger game. For the last fortnight, she'd suspected the traitor, weaving subtle countermeasures against him, but instead of ordering his arrest, she'd waited, seeking to catch the corruptor behind her shadowmaster's turned-cloak. Before she could act, the enemy sprung his own trap within her very castle. Regret tasted like bile in her mouth. At bitter cost, she'd learned the power behind the traitor. *The Mordant,* her mind shattered on his name like a storm-tossed ship breaking on lethal rocks. *So the legends are true.* She hadn't expected such an ancient evil to haunt her court. History ascribed many dark deeds to his name, the bane of Erdhe come calling. Laden with ill-omens, she told herself the legends were exaggerated, yet dire nightmares stalked her mind. Taking a deep breath, the queen resolved to force the nightmares away lest they cripple her thinking. *Remember, we won the second chess game...he can be defeated.* Drawing courage from that slender hope, the queen considered her secret advantage. The Mordant sought to cage her in her own castle, but her ancestors had wrought well. Castle Tandroth held secrets known only to the royal line. She'd shared the castle's secrets with a precious few, but never the traitor. The key to the castle's passageways lay nestled between her breasts. If she could just reach the hidden passages she could escape to mount a rebellion. So close but yet so far, she needed to bide her time and avert the assassins' prying stares.

"Are we to be a prisoner in our own castle?"

The assassin remained mute.

Realizing she'd get no further reply, Liandra drenched her voice in regal authority. "Then we shall repair to our bedchamber and change to more fitting attire." Turning from the assassin, she gestured to her women. "Attend us." She strode towards the far door.

"No." The assassin's voice cut like steel.

The queen ignored him, calling his bluff.

The shadows blurred with movement. The assassin appeared before her, barring the way. "No."

He moves like a phantom! Startled, her heart thundered. Forced to halt, the queen struggled to hide her alarm. "Stand aside."

The assassin crossed his arms, blocking the doorway.

"We *order* you to stand aside."

"You *order* nothing."

She drew herself up, jousting with her jailor. "Let us pass, for you dare not harm us."

A smile flicked across his surly face. "Hurting is allowed, but not to the face."

His words struck like icy darts. *Hurting is allowed...we have less leverage than we thought.* Liandra struggled to keep a stony facade. "Let us pass."

"You're ordered to remain here, in this room. And I am ordered to keep watch."

The queen clutched at propriety. "And how are we to change?"

He smirked. "Change here."

Her outrage flared, yet she sealed her lips in a prim line. Summoning a haughty voice, the queen said, "We have nothing to change into."

The assassin took a half step aside. "That's what your women are for."

So her women could go where she could not. The queen turned to her chief lady-in-waiting. "We'll have the green velvet gown with the dagged sleeves." Lady Sarah moved to obey, but the queen forestalled her. "And we'll wear our emerald necklace with diamond studs for our hair." Jewels were part of her regal image, a statement of wealth and power...but jewels were also easily converted into bribes. The queen intended to keep her jewels close.

Lady Sarah curtseyed, her face pale. "Yes, majesty." She soon returned, her arms bundled with a flounce of lacy undergarments, a beribboned corset, and an emerald-green velvet gown stitched with seed pearls and lined with shimmering cloth-of-gold.

The queen withdrew to the far corner of her solar, her back turned to the wall. "Attend us."

Her women swarmed around. Like an intricate dance, they removed shiny greaves and gorget and breastplate, replacing her ceremonial armor with soft layers of lace and silk and sumptuous velvet. The queen felt the assassins' stares, but her women interposed, deftly weaving a screen of fabric, armor, and their own bodies. Subtly gesturing Lady Sarah close, the queen whispered an order in her ear. Certain the assassins saw nothing, Liandra smiled, savoring the small victory.

Clad in comfortable velvet once more, the queen took the throne-carved chair by the hearth while her women coifed her hair into intricate swirls. Weaving diamond studs into her raven-dark locks, they set a constellation of glimmering stars alight in her hair. Much easier to wear than a heavy crown, yet the diamonds' sparkling nimbus created the same regal effect. Ropes of glittering emeralds carefully draped around her neck completed the regal ensemble.

Finished, her women stood arrayed behind the queen's chair, their bright silks offsetting the emerald green of her velvet gown like butterflies to her deep forest. Armored with her regal attire, the queen cast a commanding smile.

Image mattered. She was captured...but she was still queen...and she intended to wield every advantage.

Liandra felt the assassins' grinding stares. Standing rigid against the far wall, the black-clad assassins studied her, yet they showed no emotions, presenting a stalemate of sorts. The queen arranged her face in a calm facade, but her mind whirled, spinning plots within plots. Somehow she had to outwit the Mordant.

A steely silence settled over her solar, her rose oil perfume vying with the rising stench of death. Time slowed to a crawl, an abandoned chessboard awaiting the next move.

The door to her royal solar yanked open.

The queen's heartbeat skipped, yet by force of will she remained statue-still. *They did not knock.* Only an enemy would dare breach her royal chambers with such rudeness.

A tall man strode into her solar.

Not the Mordant, she remembered to breathe.

Emerald-green, he wore her colors, clad as a captain of her guard, yet his face was a stranger's, an enemy in disguise. Clearly a seasoned soldier, he walked with a predator's glide. A tall, barrel-chested man with salt-and-pepper hair, his gaze flicked to the assassins with silent acknowledgement and then settled on her. His eyes widened. For half a heartbeat he stilled, proving her image had the intended effect, but then he strode towards her without any sign of deference. She wondered if this one could be bribed.

His voice was gruff. "By orders of the Mordant, you're to be seen in the castle."

So we are needed. The queen considered the messenger. Such outright rudeness ruined his disguise. His parchment-thin act would fool no one, thus serving her own purpose, yet she needed to exert a measure of control.

"Did you hear me, woman? You're to be seen in the castle."

She gave him a frosty glare. "You wear *our* colors. Those who serve the Rose throne ask permission before entering. They bow in our royal presence. They make requests not demands."

Anger flared in his face. "You *bitch!* You're *nothing!*" He strode towards her, his hand raised for a backhanded slap.

Her women gasped, but the queen forced herself to remain statue-still.

His gauntleted hand sped towards her.

The queen glared, daring the blow.

The shadows moved...and then the black-clad assassin was there, catching the warrior's slap and turning it aside. "Not in the face!"

The warrior staggered back a step, outrage scrawled on his face. "You heard the bitch!"

The queen watched, amazed how the smaller assassin so easily manhandled the barrel-chested warrior.

"Not the face." The assassin stood between the warrior and the queen. The smaller man made no threatening gestures, yet it was clear he was poised to fight.

The warrior struggled to contain his rage. "You dare disobey the Mordant's orders?"

"*I* obey. Do you?"

"She's ordered to be seen in the castle."

"Then she shall be seen...without a mark on her face." The assassin stepped aside.

The warrior snarled, swiveling his gaze to the queen. "Come." He jerked his thumb towards the door.

It suited the queen's own purpose to be seen. Summoning her most regal bearing, she stood. "We are ready."

Her women crowded behind in a protective escort.

"Not them, just you." A sneer curled his lips. "I may not be able to mark you like you deserve, but if you fail to serve, your bright songbirds will pay." He spoke the threat with chilling certainty. "Understood?"

The queen gave a tight-lipped nod. Liandra understood very well. She walked a dangerous tightrope, needing to foil the Mordant's plans, needing to escape the trap, all without losing the lives of her women...or her own head.

23

The Mordant

Rumors from the castle wormed though the city on tentacles of gossip, whispers of bloody battles and assassination attempts. Some said the queen was dead, others said she'd caused the bloodshed. Mistrust and confusion spread like a plague. Few knew what to believe. The Mordant supped on the chaos as he walked through the cobbled streets, like drinking a fine wine. Smiles disappeared from faces and glances became suspicious. Commerce continued but at a more frantic pace. The steady stream of midday shoppers clumped into swirling knots and eddies. People moved in groups, uncertainty in their gazes. Awash in confusion, the queen's city was ripe for Darkness.

The Mordant waited till the depths of the night. Clad in a long black cloak, his face hidden in a deep cowl, he led a small cadre of snargons and assassins through Pellanor's back alleyways. One of the duegar carried a brimming bucket of blood brought fresh from a butcher's shop. The rich coppery smell cast a tang of death.

The moon was dark, nothing but a hole in the midnight sky, yet the queen's city glowed with unnatural brightness. Candlelight, torches, lanterns, braziers, the glow from homes and shops was obscene. Spilling into the cobbled streets, the light screamed of an excess of prosperity, an affront to the natural darkness, but this would soon change. He'd seen it many times before. Sow enough fear and the people cowered in their homes, their doors locked, their windows shuttered, their lamps perpetually dimmed. The Light would go out of the city, leaving everlasting Darkness to hold sway.

His time had come.

The Mordant swelled with the power of his first Dark Gift. Breathing deep, he roamed the streets, sniffing the air. In every direction, he scented delicious threads of Darkness. Even in the queen's city there were many who served the Dark God. Most served in lesser ways, but on this night, the Mordant did not seek minions or deluded rivals. Instead, he sought those who served the Light. He could not scent them. At best, he could only scent the absence of Darkness, but that absence was enough to mark their homes and their shops.

Snapping his fingers, he summoned the duegar carrying the bucket of lamb's blood. With broad brushstrokes, he marked the lintels and doorways of those who served the Light. Blood splashed crimson across the mitered stone. The design of the marks mattered not, yet it amused him to scrawl the symbols of impotent gods. Crude wings for the goddess of justice, a trident for the cursed sea god, a sword for the warrior god, a heart for the love goddess, a spiral for the misguided god of knowledge. In the light of day, the crude marks might be taken as blessings, or a child's amusement, but in truth, they marked the homes for death and torture.

The Mordant reveled in the task. He toiled through the night, but the queen's city was vast. In the allotted time, he roamed only a single sector. Even in the wealthy district, he was surprised by how many served the Light. The bucket of blood was soon empty, a good night's work.

At dawn's first glimmer, he returned to the manse. The audience chamber was crowded with soldiers and assassins awaiting his command. At the sound of his boots, they fell prostrate on the cold marble floor.

Crossing the chamber, he climbed the dais and took the throne in his true colors. "Time to begin."

Bishop Borgan bowed low, a smile on his portly face.

Soldiers and assassins snapped to rigid attention.

"The sun rises, yet Darkness dawns in the queen's city. Let the reign of terror begin!"

Fists punched the air in salute. "The Mordant!" A volley of two hundred male voices shouted their loyalty.

With a single gesture, the Mordant snuffed their voices to silence. "Clad in the queen's colors, you shall make your way to the homes and shops marked with blood. Waving parchments and wielding the queen's name, you shall break down their doors and take one member of each family. Take husbands for not paying tithes or taxes. Take sons for not serving in the army. Take wives and children for besmirching the queen's good name. It matters not whom you choose, or what charge you levy, but take one from each blood-marked dwelling. Kill those who fight back. Allow those who are passive to live, for they shall serve as witnesses." The Mordant's voice hardened, driving home the point. "We desire witnesses. Acts of terror must be witnessed to have their full effect. There must be plenty left alive to bleat their terror." His stern gaze roved his men, adding menace to his words. "And while you drag their loved ones away in chains, you must wave parchments and proclaim in a loud voice that you serve the queen's law. Every foul deed must be done in Queen Liandra's name. On this day, we smear blood on her legacy and make a mockery of her laws. Thus, shall the past be rewritten and the present forever twisted."

His men grinned like wolves keen for the hunt, but the Mordant was not yet ready to release them. "This task is of the utmost importance. For the deed to have its full effect there can be no mistakes. Just this once I shall take questions before loosing you to the hunt."

The men fretted, unaccustomed to questioning their lord.

"Ask now, or suffer the consequences."

A ripple of unease stirred through the ranks.

Finally a soldier in the back asked, "What if they want to read the parchments?"

"Ignore them."

"If they insist?"

"Kill them."

His men grinned. Another asked, "What shall we do with the prisoners?"

"Roll dice for them."

His men waited, their interest baited.

"The queen's justice shall be decided on a roll of the die. Roll a one and they hang by the neck from the castle walls. Roll a three and their severed heads are spiked above the castle's portcullis. Roll a six and their dismembered bodies shall hang from the city's sparkling white walls. Rape the women and release them to weep over their fate. Put the rest in prison, deep in the queen's dungeons."

"*Bak-hur!*" The men shouted their acclaim, keen for a feast of violence.

When the din quieted, an assassin asked. "Lord, are we only to take from the blood marked dwellings?"

"For now." The Mordant's voice remained stern. "There shall come a time when the true color of their souls shall not matter. When that time comes, true chaos shall claim the city. The queen's legacy will be indelibly besmirched, then all of Erdhe will be ripe for the taking."

Unsheathing their swords, his men clashed their blades against their breastplates, raising a terrible din. "*The Emperor of Erdhe!*"

Leaning back in the throne, he endured their acclaim, although they were grievously wrong. They hailed him as an emperor, when in truth he would be a god. *Mortals have such low expectations*...but he did not gainsay them. "Go and serve! Let the reaping begin!" The Mordant loosed his minions on the queen's city. The first wave of terror had begun.

24

Liandra

The queen emerged from her solar to find a dozen guards in emerald green crowding the hallway. Instead of bowing, they stared at her, their hands on their sword hilts. Their blatant rudeness told the tale, yet she found herself searching their faces. None were familiar. *Caged by enemies within our own castle!* She kept the bitterness from her face, desperate to escape the trap.

A tall, thin man with close-cropped hair the color of rusty swords strode towards her. Clad in emerald green, he had a captain's insignia on his shoulders. "I'm Commander Hoit." His face was pock-marked, his eyes sharp as daggers. "I'll be in charge of your security."

Her new jailor. She gave him a haughty glare.

"By orders of the Mordant, you're to be seen throughout the castle. Rumors of your demise serve no one." He leaned towards her. "You're to be seen but not heard."

And so the chains tighten.

"Remember, your women are held hostage against your good behavior. Falter and they die."

Liandra wearied of threats.

"This way." He made a gallant gesture but the glint in his eyes was laden with mocking. "Form up!"

Guards sprang to attention. Caging her in emerald and steel, they marched her down the hallway. The queen walked in their midst, surrounded by enemies. Liandra knew her presence served the Mordant's purpose, but she needed to survey her castle, desperate to gauge the corruption within.

Blood in the hallway. They'd removed the bodies, but blood from the ambush still splattered the marble floor. Her mind shied away from Sir Durnheart's death. Her gallant knight deserved better. Balling her hands into fists, she forced herself to focus on the practical. Her gaze fixed on the splattered blood. *Image matters*, yet these fools let blood mar our hallways, something she would never permit. Such mistakes were small, but they proved the Mordant was not infallible.

Her gaze slid to the rust-haired commander, wondering why he'd waited outside her chambers like a lackey...and then she understood. He'd sent a thug to summon her, to bully her, to make her pliant. *So he thinks he's clever.*

Liandra suppressed a smile, knowing he severely underestimated the steel of queens. She hoped his master did likewise.

They reached the end of the hallway. A pair of emerald clad guards snapped to attention.

These were hers! She recognized their faces, knew their names! Her footsteps faltered. She wanted to call to them but two against twelve stood no chance.

Beside her, the commander hissed. *"Majesty!"*

Hearing the threat, she kept walking. *Two against twelve,* her heart raced. They reached the steps and began to descend. Liandra walked without seeing, her mind awhirl with speculation. The presence of true guards in the Queen's Tower spoke volumes. *It means he does not have enough men!* More insights tumbled into place. Liandra realized her decision to engage the people of Pellanor had sparked the ambush. Forewarned by the traitor, the Mordant had sprung his trap and captured a queen...but perhaps she'd forced his hand before he was truly ready. Perhaps this wasn't a checkmate, merely a check. Heartened by the insight, she considered what she knew of her enemy. When the Octagon Knights fell, she'd scoured her library, reading every scroll and musty tome that mentioned the Mordant. A legion of horrors were heaped on his name, yet beneath it all he was ever the deceiver. Possibilities tumbled through her mind, looking at the chessboard from every angle. The queen was captured and her women held hostage, but perhaps this attack was parchment-thin. Perhaps her castle was ensorcelled by lies not substance. *Then her presence aided his deception, deepening his control,* the queen bridled at the thought, yet she needed to plumb the depths of his power. Her hand stole to her bodice, feeling the key hidden beneath velvet, her secret assurance. She need only reach the castle's hidden passageways to escape his hold, and then she'd turn the tables on the Mordant, pressing her own attack. Reassured by her ancestors' prudent secret, her attention snapped back into focus. Quickening her stride, the queen walked the halls of her castle, keen to take the measure of the Mordant's grasp.

Her jailors led her on a circuitous path. Liandra saw no other signs of bloodshed, save in her own hallway. Relief warred with bitter disappointment. *Was our capture so easily won?* She kept walking, absorbing every detail. Down marble stairways and along gilded hallways lined with vivid tapestries, her captors paraded her past her people. Soldiers snapped to attention, servants bowed low, and women dropped to deep curtseys. More than a few looked startled by her sudden appearance, hushed whispers following in her wake. Liandra longed to speak to them, but too much was at stake. Instead, she studied their faces, trying to judge their loyalty, trying to open their eyes to the truth. Too many tight-lipped lords refused to meet her stare, too many courtiers turned away, their faces flushed with shame. The queen kept a mental list. The loyal outnumbered the suspect by three to one...but those who were suspect held the most power. The Mordant had targeted his corruption well, a lethal acid corroding the most powerful. Anger warred with bitter resentment. Lanverness prospered under her rule, yet too many of her lords turned to Darkness. Their betrayal tasted more bitter than bile.

They reached a marble balustrade overlooking the castle's vaulted entranceway. Liandra paused at the railing, staring down. The bustle below slowly ceased, her people stopping to stare at their queen. Most looked confused. Some looked afraid. Their upturned faces beseeched her for answers, for guidance. Their need called to her despite the risks.

"My people," her voice echoed through the chamber with regal conviction.

Commander Hoit moved close behind her, a sudden menace, yet she dared to speak.

"You know us. You know how we rule. Remember both."

A dagger pricked her back. *"Enough!"*

Liandra doubted the dagger would plunge, yet she fell silent.

Commander Hoit hissed in her ear. *"You've just killed one of your women!"*

No! She whirled on him, but before she could protest, he whispered, "Speak and another dies!"

She glared at him in tight-lipped fury.

The commander gave her a lizard-cold smile.

At a gesture, the phalanx of soldiers tightened around her like an angry fist. Her jailors hustled her away. Liandra walked without seeing, shocked by the lethal threat. *To kill one of her women for a few innocuous words! Surely he did not mean it!* The sheer barbarity of the threat shocked her. Liandra struggled to grapple with the horror. She resolved to argue with the commander when they returned to her solar. Somehow she'd find a way to bargain for the lives of her women.

Her jailors led her deeper into the castle's heart. Their pace increased. Instead of a slow meander, they rushed her, herding down marble corridors. The commander seemed intent on a specific destination. Polished marble gave way to rough dressed stone. Laden with iron, the old stone walls glowed dull red in the fading light. Liandra stiffened. They'd reached First Keep, the oldest tower in Castle Tandroth. A fresh fear speared the queen. "Where are we going?"

She got no answer.

They reached a staircase and started up.

She felt the trap closing around her. "No." The queen came to a sudden stop. "Return us to our solar."

An arrogant smile flickered across the commander's face. "Keep climbing."

The queen stood her ground. "No, there's little point. Our people have seen us and we grow weary."

"Keep climbing."

"But this tower is rarely used."

"Exactly." His smile deepened to a malicious grin. "By orders of the Mordant you're to be housed in First Keep."

He knows! The thought struck like a thunderclap, sundering her mind.

Hoit gestured towards the stairs. "After you, *majesty.*"

Liandra climbed in a daze. A part of her wanted to kick and scream, to dash down the stairs, desperate to evade the trap...but she knew she'd fail. *Twelve against one*...she felt so alone. She felt so betrayed. Rough-cut stairs spiraled up into the old tower. They reached a door and her guards opened it, ushering her into a small, spare room with an arrow-slit window. Her mind rebelled at the betrayal. She turned to confront her jailors. "*How did he...*"

The door slammed in her face.

The key turned in the lock.

Trapped! Stunned, she stared at the cold stone walls. Her hand clutched at the key hidden beneath velvet, but it was useless, rendered impotent by the dull red walls. *How had he known?* First Keep was the oldest tower in the castle, built before her ancestors started honeycombing the walls with secret passageways. By choosing the tower for her imprisonment, the Mordant stole her secret hope. How did he know? For none now living knew the truth of the red tower save her. Not even the Master Archivist knew this secret. And then she understood. *None now living!* A deadly chill gripped her. The prince of Ur truly was the Mordant. *The Mordant!* Till now, she hadn't truly believed it was him. Tendrils of horror wormed through her mind. An ancient evil came crawling from musty tomes, Liandra sank to the bed, struck mute with terror. The oldest evil craved her kingdom. Within her mind she screamed.

25

Lady Sarah

Lady Sarah feared for the queen. She feared for herself and the other ladies-in-waiting. Truth be told, she was nearly petrified with terror, yet she clung to rigid decorum, her face a polite mask, knowing it was her duty to keep the others from crumbling to tears. Six ladies-in-waiting clad in bright silk sat close together on the far side of the chamber, sheep huddled against the wolves.

A lone man kept watch. Clad all in black, a baldric of nine knives across his chest, he stood near the door, his gaze sharp as daggers. A smallish man, short in stature with a broad chest, yet he looked like bundled violence.

Violence in the queen's chambers! Her mind skittered, shocked by all that had transpired. The queen captured by enemies in green tabards, an assassin climbing through an impossible tower-high window...and Lady Cristal killed with a single backhanded blow. Her friend's body lay crumpled near the window, covered with a blanket, yet death's foul stench permeated the royal chamber giving proof to the nightmare. Lady Sarah averted her gaze, lest her fear fester.

Calamity had struck like lethal lightning, turning the royal court upside down, yet the queen had managed to whisper a parting order before being taken away. Lady Sarah's gaze flitted to their jailor. *Was he truly a minion of the Mordant?* Her mind faltered on the name, the stuff of nightmares and ancient legends. She shuddered, making the hand sign against evil.

She felt his stabbing stare. The dark clad man kept a feral watch, yet the queen's last order thrummed through her mind.

Rain beat against the windows, the sodden drumming the only sound. Daylight began to fade, multiplying her worries for the queen. Darkness encroached, and still the queen did not return. The others began to fidget. A muffled sob escaped Lady Amy.

Lady Sarah stood, confronting their jailor. "Where is the queen?"

Their dour jailor did not answer.

She tried another tack. "May I light some candles?"

He gave the smallest of nods.

She found a flint and struck a light to the nearest taper, pleased that her hands did not shake too badly. Making a circuit, she lit every candle and taper, trying to hold the darkness at bay. A grim chill pervaded the queen's solar despite the light. Taking a chance, she knelt by the hearth. Adding pine logs and kindling, she built a roaring fire. A welcome warmth spread through the chamber, yet it could not dispel the lingering doom. She set a teapot to boil, the simple acts helping to soothe her mind and steady her nerves.

The outer door yanked open.

Lady Sarah startled.

A porcelain tea cup fell from her hands, shattering into a thousand shards.

A grim-faced man with reddish hair strode into the queen's chamber. Clad in an emerald green tabard, he carried an air of command, yet Lady Sarah did not know him. A pair of soldiers followed close behind, their hands on their sword hilts. They swept into the royal solar like a fresh menace...yet they came without the queen.

Without the queen! Lady Sarah retreated to stand with the other women, a flock of hens facing a sharp-toothed fox. "Where is her majesty?"

The commander's gaze flicked across her. "Your queen is unruly. She needs to be taught a lesson."

Lady Sarah stiffened, her outrage leavened with fear.

The commander's voice turned malevolent. "One of you will be that lesson."

Behind her, Lady Amy whimpered.

The scent of fear flooded the chamber.

Hands clenched, Lady Sarah forced herself forward. "Then let it be me."

The commander's gaze seared her. "You don't even know the price."

She forced her voice not to tremble. "Yet, I am her senior lady-in-waiting. I serve her majesty."

"Bravery in a woman, how odd." He strode towards her.

She struggled not to flinch.

Stopping a hand span away, he glared down at her, studying her as if she were a meal set before him on a platter.

Balling her fists, she met his gaze, refusing to be cowed.

"You're sassy." Turning away, he made a casual gesture behind her, pointing to Lady Cathor. "Take that one."

Lady Sarah's heart leaped with fear. "No, take me."

"I'll go." Lady Cathor stepped forward, her face as pale as porcelain.

"Yes, you'll do." The commander gestured and soldiers surrounded her, ushering the ill-fated woman towards the door.

"What will..."

The commander turned on her, impaling her with a dead-fish stare.

Behind her, Lady Amy erupted in sobs.

Gagged by horror, Lady Sarah watched her friend leave, noting the dignity in her posture despite the terror bleeding from her eyes.

The soldiers led her friend from the chamber.

Lady Sarah watched till she disappeared from sight.

The empty doorway gaped like a gateway to hell.

Terror pierced her. Her hands began to shake.

The commander flicked his surly gaze to the black-clad assassin. "Come. Your skills are needed." He strode through the door, the assassin following close behind. The door thudded closed. The lock clicked shut with grim finality.

Lady Sarah sagged against the queen's chair.

Behind her, the others dissolved into frantic weeping.

Somehow their sobs restored her resolve. Swallowing her own fear, she turned on them, her voice a stinging lash. *"Quiet! There's no time for weeping!"*

Shocked, they stared at her with liquid eyes.

"This is our chance."

Lady Martha asked, "To do what?"

"To obey her majesty. We must escape and remove the dagger from the queen's throat."

"How?"

Lady Sarah tugged the slender chain around her neck, revealing the skeleton key hidden in the depths of her bodice. "Her majesty gave me a key to the hidden passageways."

Their eyes went wide with hope. All had taken refuge in the castle's secret passageways during the Red Horns' ill-fated rebellion.

Lady Sarah snapped orders. "Time grows thin. Martha, you and Lindsey get the crown jewels."

"But we don't have the key!"

"Bring the whole chest! The two of you should be able to manage it. Amy, bring me a pillowcase. Beth, get a second pillowcase and gather the rest of the queen's jewels."

"But..."

"Just do it! Be quiet and be quick." The others leaped to obey. Lady Sarah's gaze flicked to the locked door, wondering how much time they had. Admonishing herself for the delay, she rushed to the queen's desk. Pressing a secret lever, she opened the hidden compartment where the queen kept Lord Robert's letters. Clutching the letters, she closed the hidden drawer. Lady Amy returned with an empty pillowcase. "Quickly!" Lady Sarah stuffed the letters deep into the silken sack and then added a striker and two unlit candles.

The others emerged from the queen's bedchamber. Martha and Lindsey struggled to carry a small metal chest between them. Lady Sarah's gaze flicked across the desk to the mountain of dispatches, but she dared not tarry. Snatching up a lit candle, she ran to the opposite side of the chamber. Ornate stonework decorated the wall. It took her a moment to find the right piece. Her hands shook badly, the candlelight jumping to the rabid beat of her heart. Turning a rose leaf carved in stone, she inserted the skeleton key.

A key rattled in the outer door.

Martha hissed, *"Hurry!"*

Her heartbeat hammering, she forced the key to turn.

The secret doorway hushed open. The others sped for the hidden chamber.

The outer door began to open.

Lady Sarah dashed inside, closing the secret door behind her. Lady Beth lowered the iron bar bracing the door. *"Did they see you?"*

Sarah did not know. Weak-kneed and sodden with sweat, she sank to the cold stone floor, her silk skirts puddling around her. The others did the same, their faces pinched with a mixture of relief and fright. A single wavering candle held the darkness at bay. They stared at each other, waiting for a pounding on the door. Heartbeats hammered, yet the silence held. Afraid the light might betray them, Lady Sarah blew out the candle. Darkness engulfed them, black and absolute and laden with nightmares. They sat huddled together, bound in silence, a handful of mice hiding in the castle walls.

26

Liandra

The queen paced the small, spare chamber, her mind harried with worry. Ensnared in a Dark trap, she feared for her kingdom, for her people, for her ladies-in-waiting...for her very life. *The Mordant,* his name thundered through her mind like an ominous storm. *He'd known the secret of First Tower!* She reeled at the thought. Impossible that he'd learned the Tandroth's royal secret. The queen shuddered, making the hand sign against evil. More myth than man, his very name spawned nightmares. How does one defeat such an ancient bane? And why did he stalk her kingdom? She needed more information. A spider queen cut off from her web of spies, she felt bereft. Somehow she needed to get free, yet she was trapped in the tower chamber, denied access to the castle's secret passageways. *Trapped in our own castle...and none know where we are!*

Liandra had never felt so alone.

She paced the small chamber, from the door, to the hearth, to the arrow-slit window.

Night darkened the rain spattered window and still no one came.

She began to wonder if her captors had forgotten her, leaving her to fester in the musty tower. Hunger gnawed at her, but her thirst was worse. Rain pattered against the glazed glass window as if answering her need. The narrow window was stubborn from disuse, yet she forced it open. Thrusting her cupped hands out, she caught raindrops, employing a child's trick. The meager drink wet her throat, yet it seemed like a cruel tease to her thirst. Shutting the window, she surveyed her prison. The bed was musty and stale, the hearth cold, without kindling or even a striker. Her captors had left her with no comforts, not even a candle against the gathering dark.

A key turned in the lock.

Her heartbeat jumped. Liandra turned to face the door. Drying her hands on her velvet gown, she struck an upright pose.

The door burst open, flooding the chamber with torchlight. Liandra blinked against the sudden brightness. Commander Hoit strode through the door. "Good evening, your *majesty.*" A mocking sneer rode his words.

The queen refused to answer, regal in her disdain.

The commander gestured and soldiers in green tabards entered. The queen searched their faces, but all were strangers. One brought an armload of kindling, another a lighted pillar candle and a chamber pot. A third carried a wine skin and a covered tray, setting both by the bed. The tray distracted her, the tempting smell of roasted chicken wafting like a tantalizing tease.

The queen's mouth watered, yet she remained statue-still. *So, the enemy brings comfort.* The woman in her sighed in relief, but the queen was dismayed, for it meant they intended to keep her imprisoned in the ancient tower. "We must return to our chambers."

Hoit gestured and the soldiers left.

She tried another tack. "Your ruse will not work unless we are seen. Return us to our chambers at once."

Hoit flashed a haughty smile. "How little you understand." He strode towards the door but then turned back at the last moment. "I nearly forgot." Snapping his fingers, another soldier entered the chamber. This one bore a metal wash basin, a towel draped across the top. "This is for you." With a flourish, he removed the towel, presenting the bowl towards her.

Liandra gagged, strangling a scream. A severed head lay in the basin...the head of Lady Cathor! Freshly murdered, her neck was crudely severed, her eyes bulging in terror. Struggling to swallow her bile, the queen's horror bled to outrage. "*Murderer!* How dare you! You murdered one of our woman for a few words!"

"*You* murdered her! You were warned yet you disobeyed! Learn to serve or pay the price. There are no idle threats with the Mordant!" Hoit gestured and the soldier withdrew, taking the gruesome head with him. Turning on his heel, the commander strode from the chamber.

The door slammed shut. The key turned in the lock.

Alone, the queen crumpled to the floor. *What have we done?* Her stomach was empty, yet she knelt, retching into the chamber pot.

27

Bryce

All his life, he'd wanted to be a healer. To ease pain from another's eyes seemed the highest calling. An acolyte of the Kiralynn Order, Bryce yearned to swear his life to the Seeing Eye, to gain access to the Great Archives, and become a learned monk. But those wants were like a dream from some forgotten life.

Sometimes he wondered if memories of that cloistered time were pure illusion.

For more than a year, he'd been held captive by the Mordant, a tortured soul subsumed by a thousand-year-old evil. Bryce railed against the cruelty of his fate. A prisoner within his own body, his mere existence was a living hell. Crouched in fear, he'd witnessed unspeakable things. Dark rites, foul torture, unbelievable atrocities, things no mortal should ever see, leastwise a healer. Steeped in nightmares, he'd watched as the Mordant spun a web of evil across Erdhe.

Did the gods not care!

Time was growing late.

Bryce felt it in the very marrow of his soul, yet no champion appeared to challenge the Mordant. Enraged, he beat against his cage, a butterfly battering steel.

Despair stalked him, yet he held it at bay. Clinging to hope, he prayed to the gods, for it was their favors that kept him sane.

Three times the gods had aided him.

The first boon came when the Mordant crossed the Guardian Mist to escape the monastery. Unbeknownst to the Mordant, the King of the Mist spoke directly to Bryce. Appearing as a star knight, with a winged helm and a face etched with wisdom, the king whispered words of ancient prophecy. And with the words came a gift, a pinprick of light, a spy hole into the world. The gift gave Bryce a narrow view of life, a way to eavesdrop on the Mordant. Crouched in his prison, Bryce spied on his unholy captor, seeking a way to foil a thousand-year-old evil.

The second boon came in the form of a cat-eyed man. Locked in his prison, Bryce kept vigil, memorizing the Mordant's every move. He brimmed with secrets untold, yet it seemed futile till he connected with the cat-eyed prisoner. Chained in the cursed crypt beneath the Dark Citadel, the Mordant used the man as a living sacrifice, his pain providing a conduit to Darkness. Perhaps the Lords of Light were affronted by the depravity, for they intervened when the Mordant slept, holding the conduit open. Sensing the man's suffering, Bryce connected soul to soul. Suddenly he had someone to talk with. Across the distance, he whispered the Mordant's most dire secrets. He took particular pleasure in revealing the Mordant's hidden treasure hoard, explaining how to find it, and then he divulged the Mordant's plans for the south. Bryce only had a short time before the connection shattered. Seared by the backlash of the Mordant's volcanic rage, he cringed in his prison, never knowing if the man had escaped or perished. Bryce fervently prayed the man still lived and that somehow the shared secrets would prove the Mordant's downfall.

Time passed and still no champion arose.

Despair engulfed him, but then, in Pellanor, the gods granted him a third boon. This boon came in the form of a malachite coin. *A coin from ancient Azreal,* he could sense the curse sizzling upon it, a heart-blood vow sworn by a sorceress betrayed. Vengeance reached out from across the centuries, yet the Mordant seemed oblivious to the curse. Knowing it was a powerful focus, the Mordant kept the malachite coin close, yearning to master the magic within. But Bryce knew such a bonding would never happen. Perhaps it was the curse, or the will of the gods, but either way, the focus pierced the gray void of his prison to bond with Bryce. And such a powerful focus it was. He marveled when he understood its purpose. But with that understanding came the warning that he could only wield it once, lest the Mordant wrest its power, wielding it for evil. Locked in his prison, Bryce bided his time, waiting for the perfect moment.

Three times the gods aided him with a boon...and now he prayed for a fourth. Bryce prayed for a chance to loose the curse and slay the Mordant.

28

The Priestess

The Priestess never knew tears could scald. Steffan's death proved a bitter lesson. Alone in her bedroom, she wept, pining for his dashing smile, his gambler's brash boldness, his endearing jealousy...and most of all for his searing touch. A tremor of remembered passion shuddered through her, leaving her gasping with want. Memories of their time together shimmered like summer heat in her soul, yet she could not afford such sorrow.

A single tear tracked down her cheek.

Anger shuddered through her. Tears were a damning weakness, a woman's weakness.

She resolved to put away her grief. Drying her eyes, the Priestess restored a stone-hearted facade. Beneath the carefully cultivated mask, her caged sorrow annealed to a seething rage. She owed a debt of pain to the Mordant.

Pulling her velvet robe close, she considered her position. She'd confronted the Mordant directly, plying her powers of seduction against his millennium of experience. The oldest harlequin wore a young man's body, fitting prey for her seductive ways, but beneath that youthful facade lurked a thousand-year-old evil. Jaded and cynical, he was heavily armored against her wiles, yet his soul reeked of fathomless power. The Mordant posed a perilous challenge, one she could not pass by. Answering his summons, she willingly went to his bed, intending to write her name upon his very soul.

She'd plied her powers through the night, ensnaring him with her seductive spell. Lacing passion with pain, she unleashed the succubus. Temptations blurred into a frenzy of delights as she rode the Mordant through the night. Taking him beyond ecstasy, she stoked his every lust, seeking to chain his soul with his own savage desires. Every caress seared his skin, every kiss enflamed his need...and then, just when she thought she had him chained, he proved impervious to her sorcery. Drawing on his own power, he rejected her wiles, subjecting her to a hellish pain. Stricken with agony, she writhed upon the floor...till he released her. Shocked and humiliated, the defeat bit deep. Never before had she been so thwarted, yet from their savage coupling, the succubus salvaged a secret advantage. In the depths of their passion, she'd drawn deep from the well of his soul. A river-load of stolen power combined with their tumultuous coupling invoked an unexpected magic. Their torrid passion fused the sundered pieces of Eye of the Oracle. No longer broken, the Eye emerged whole and fully restored. The great moonstone throbbed between her breasts, a secret power hidden from the Mordant. The Priestess fondled the Eye. Potent once more, the Eye renewed her power to scry. The Priestess reveled in her reclaimed magic, proof of the Dark Lord's favor. A serpent's smile played across her lips. *She* was the Priestess of the Oracle, the dark seductress, the midnight succubus, the mistress of the Dark Lord.

Their first encounter had gone to the Mordant, but the game was far from over.

Considering her tryst with the oldest harlequin, the Priestess realized her mistake. She'd confronted the Mordant directly...when she needed to be oblique. She'd been too obvious, too direct, ambushing him in his own bed, the very place where he most expected her wiles. Often ignored and overlooked, women triumphed by manipulating from behind. A hunter's smile graced her face. It was time to change the game. Deviousness became her armor and stealth her weapon. Wielding the Eye, she began to study his plots, seeking a way to unravel them. Scrying gave her a significant advantage, but scrying alone would not be enough.

Poison was another advantage, a woman's secret weapon. Never far from her hand, her serpent ring and coiled armbands glittered on the bedside table, poison-tipped needles cunningly wrought beneath enameled scales. She fingered the ring, caressing the hidden trigger. A needle snicked from the serpent's head, poison glistening on the tip. The lethal dose came from the Isle of the Oracle, from her garden of deathly delights. Each needle carried enough to kill a large man with a single prick. Death hidden beneath coiled beauty, the Priestess appreciated the duplicity, but once used the lethal dosage could not be renewed. The Mordant's henchmen had stolen her precious hoard of poisons. She snarled at the bitter loss, another debt that needed to be repaid.

Releasing the trigger, she returned the needle to its hiding place. Eleven sure deaths, her jewelry could give her that, but no more.

Eleven would not be enough, not nearly enough.

She needed a weapon of another sort.

Swathed in a velvet robe, a fire crackling in the hearth, the Priestess cast her mind back across her time in the Mordant's manse, seeking a weapon, seeking a weakness. And then it came to her. All those dark-cloaked assassins keeping watch. Jailors hidden in the shadows, their potent stares followed her every move. But beneath the Mordant's stern colors, they were still men, still susceptible to passion. The proof was in their stares. The way they lingered on her curves like cats licking forbidden cream.

Some were hungrier than others.

She recalled one in particular who stared like a starving wolf. Short in stature but corded with muscles...his dark stare could ignite a bonfire. The Priestess struggled to recall his name, and then she had it. "*Graylin.*" She tasted his name upon her lips, savoring it like a sweet treat.

Having made her choice, she set out to ensorcell him.

Keeping her stone-hearted mask in place, she spent her nights serving the Mordant with her bedroom skills. Seducing noblemen, she corrupted them to the Mordant's purposes while feeding the succubus. During the day, she found excuses to wander the manse, seeking one stare among many.

From across the room she felt his searing gaze like a burning brand. His need called to her, his manhood straining rampant against his dark leathers. For half a heartbeat, she met his gaze, giving him a smoldering look, and then she turned, a whirl of perfumed silks disappearing down the hallway. Trailing her scent like a dangling hook, she baited him, yet he never followed, always remaining rigid at his post.

For seven days she played the game of stare and smolder...and then she found him stationed alone outside her bedroom door. The heat of his stare seared her as she stepped into the hallway, yet she played coy, refusing to meet his gaze. Loosening her silk scarf, she offered a tease, revealing her plunging neckline. His stare sizzled across her cleavage. She slowed her steps to a seductive saunter. He leered from the shadows, his dark gaze consuming her curves. Tugging the scarf loose, she trailed it like a silken lash. Heat crackled around him like an oil-soaked torch. Keeping her gaze averted, she drew close enough to smell his musky scent. Pausing at the closed door, she waited.

Awakening to her need, he rushed to open the door.

So close, she felt the warmth of his breath.

He pressed against the open door as if her touch was lethal, yet his nostrils flared wide drinking in her scent.

She raised her gaze, capturing his. "I've felt your stare."

His breath caught.

"He's ordered you to watch." Her voice was low and throaty. "You *like* to watch."

A low growl escaped him.

"You watch *better* than all the others," she trailed her silk scarf across his broad chest, her voice deepening with earthy suggestion, "...so come and watch." She flicked her scarf, a silken lash caressing his neck. He shuddered beneath the soft enticement, yet he remained pressed to the door, maintaining a whisper of space between them. She let him keep his precious space, the better to tease him. Giving him a smoldering look, she sauntered by. Shedding a trail of silk, the Priestess crossed the chamber to the inner doorway. Refusing to look back, she focused every other sense on him, willing him to succumb.

She felt his stare.

She felt his hunger, a bonfire crackling at her back.

He hesitated, as if duty could somehow foil desire.

And then he made his choice. The door clicked closed. Determined boot steps rang behind her. He followed her into the bedchamber...yet he did not touch her, hovering at the inner doorway, as if denying his true intent.

Keeping her gaze averted, she slowly disrobed, making every movement a tease. "I know you, Graylin, for I've watched you too." Her inner sheath fell away. She stood naked in a puddle of silk, wearing nothing but the Eye. The great moonstone dangled between her passion-perked breasts.

He gasped.

She raised her gaze. With a single look, she beckoned.

Desire trumped duty. He crossed the distance, his face aflame, his gaze entranced.

The Priestess hid a triumphant smile. She hadn't even touched him, yet his soul was hers.

29

Jemma

A crown awaited her, yet she remained a prisoner, chained in a musty attic. *A queen*...she was meant to rule! Jemma stared at the slanting rafters, anger warring with bitter frustration. Her confinement started when Queen Liandra harried her for birth-magic that was not hers to give. In a fit of madness, the queen ordered Jemma confined to the dungeons. The *dungeons!* The word spiked her with nightmares, but her friends had saved her, spiriting her away to a forgotten tower. There she lingered in boredom, waiting for the queen to regain her senses, but release never came. Instead, an impossible nightmare came calling, crouched outside her tower window. *A man who looked like a spider!* Jemma shivered, making the hand sign against evil. She remembered a foul-smelling cloth pressed to her face. Darkness claimed her...and she woke here, wherever here was.

The space was large and round, the raftered roof rising to a conical peak. Wood beams radiated down from the peak, random nails sticking though the shingles in a patchwork of rusty points. The roof had a steep slant, making most of the space unusable. A tall man could stand straight near the center, but four paces away he'd be bent to a crouch. Dust shrouded everything, proving the place was never used. *An attic!* They'd chained her away in a tower attic, a trapdoor in the floor the only entrance.

A mattress, a musty quilt, and a chamber pot were her only comforts. She did not even have a candle and there were no windows. Light seeped in from the edges, where the wood roof joined the tower's stone walls. At times, the wind whistled through the rafters like a wailing ghost. Such a dismal and forgotten place, barren of comfort and hope.

Her anger spiked. She rattled her chains, a ghost in the attic.

Her left wrist ached, the skin rubbed raw. She'd tried forcing her hand through the manacle, gaining nothing but chafed skin nearly worn bloody. An eight-foot chain bound her to the central post. She'd scribed a circle in the dusty floor, testing the limits of the chain, seeking anything that might help her escape, all to no avail.

When she'd first woken in the attic, she'd screamed till her throat was hoarse, pounding the floor with her hands and heels, making a ruckus, but rescue never came. *Perhaps the tower is abandoned*...the thought plagued her.

Jemma did not even know whose prisoner she was. This was not the queen's doing, of that she was certain. Whoever ordered her abduction was sneaky, and evil, and malevolent. They hadn't even asked anything of her. Somehow that scared her worst of all. She had to get free.

Metal scraped against metal, the sound of a bolt being drawn back.

Jemma scuttled backward to the far edge of the mattress. Tucking her legs under her dress, she sat poised, gripping her chain like a weapon.

The hinged door swung upwards and back, laying flat with the floor.

During her first days in the attic, she'd attacked her jailor at the trap door, but that ended poorly. He'd merely jumped down from the opening, leaving her without food or water for four days.

Rungs of a ladder jutted from the opening. A head thrust up, swiveling till it found her. "Stay back if you want fed."

It was Coldeyes. He scared her even worse than Brute.

"Why am I here? Whom do you serve? My father will ransom me! He'll make you a wealthy man. Just let me write a letter!" She peppered him with questions leavened with bribes, but neither had any effect. Mute, he just stared at her with cold eyes, as if she was no more than a roach to be crushed beneath his boot.

He shoved a tray towards her. She watched as water slopped from the pitcher, regretting every spilled drop. He stooped to take the empty tray, the plate licked clean from hunger. Without a word, he turned and descended the ladder. She spied the keys dangling from his belt. One had to be the key to her manacle, the key to her freedom. He disappeared back down the opening. A cord tugged the trapdoor. It snapped shut like an angry mouth, leaving her in murky shadows.

Sighing, she pulled the tray towards her, careful not to spill a drop. Three biscuits, a mound of mashed potatoes and a roasted chicken, everything cold, grease congealing on the plate, yet she knew she'd lick it clean, hungry for every morsel. She'd learned to husband her food, never knowing when her jailors would bring more. It was almost as if they didn't care if she lived or died. The thought chilled her. A shiver ran down her spine, somehow she had to get free.

She ate a biscuit, forcing herself to chew slowly, making it last, and then she tore into the chicken. A bone pricked her finger, sharp as a needle. *A needle!* She worked the slender bone free. Licking it clean, she set it aside. All too soon, she finished her meager portion. Her stomach rumbled, wanting more, but her discipline held firm. Her gaze kept returning to the bone. Smaller than her little finger, yet the point was keen. *A chicken bone for a weapon!* The thought was absurd.

She sat in the waning light, confronting the bitter truth. No one knew where she was. No one was coming to her rescue. She'd have to free herself, but how? Darkness encroached, but she refused to be ensnared by the gloom. Pulling the quilt close, Jemma fixed her mind on solving the puzzle. She'd have to lure him away from the trapdoor, or she'd never get the key. And she'd have to wait for Brute to bring her food, for Coldeyes scared her too much. For the thousandth time, her gaze roved the attic. Squinting against the waning light, she sought a weapon, something more biting than a chicken bone, and then she saw it. Understanding struck. A feral smile slipped across her face. She'd use her prison against them, but she'd only get one chance to make it work. Jemma sat in the dark, scheming, waiting, praying for the gods to lend a hand.

30

The Master Archivist

The Master Archivist read the message by lantern light. Once more the queen bade him stay in Lingard, as if she no longer needed him. Grinding his teeth, he considered the scroll from every angle, inspecting her signature, her handwriting, and the royal seal embossed in emerald green wax. Everything looked flawless, save for the tone of the letter. He read it half a dozen times, mulling the words, considering the details, yet the fault remained more a vague feeling than a hard fact. He was not the sort of man to put more weight on a sixth sense than solid proof, yet the nagging doubt remained, gnawing at his mind.

What if the queen's messages are compromised?

Logic argued against his suspicion, for it would take a forger of uncanny skill to get every detail correct. *Every detail save for her tone.* Her love token gleamed in the lantern light, a simple gold ring emblazoned with his sigil. He wore it always. Fingering the ring, he sought reassurance against her message. Neither the queen nor her shadowmaster were inclined to commit blatant endearments to parchment. Such a thing would be unseemly and far too risky, yet subtle hints were often woven beneath their messages of state. It had become a game between them, to imply much while saying little. Of late, her dispatches had turned all business, with no hint of the warm heart behind the brilliant mind. His long stay in Lingard had begun to feel like a chilly exile. The more he thought about it, the more he worried.

He considered sending inquiries through his web of shadowmen, but decided against it. If the queen's messages truly were compromised, such an inquiry would only forewarn the forger. Far better to return to Pellanor and catch the foe red-handed...or learn the bitter truth from the queen's own lips. Anger warred with suspicion, he'd been gone from the Rose court for far too long. Sometimes duty was hard, but if the queen's messages truly were corrupted, then it was imperative he return. He considered the distance, begrudging every long league. By commandeering mounts he could cut the time by a third, riding quick as any royal courier. Crumpling the dispatch in his fist, he resolved to return to the Rose court, to see the queen and solve the riddle of her frosty messages.

Bidding an abrupt farewell to Lord Ronald, the heir to Lingard, he asked for the fastest horse in the lord's stable. Lord Ronald proved a generous host, gifting him with a spirited black stallion. Before the stallion could be saddled, another courier arrived. Galloping into the keep's courtyard on a lathered mount, he brought a message from the queen.

If the other messages worried him, this one alarmed him.

Just like the other dispatches, the queen's handwriting, her signature and the emerald seal embossed in wax proved beyond reproach. His alarm ignited from the queen's message. She spoke of a plot against her throne freshly uncovered by her shadowmen. Correspondence intercepted between the traitors spoke of their plan to assassinate the queen. Posing as traders from Navarre, the conspirators planned to meet at the Green Man Inn on the next dark of the moon. The queen's dispatch summoned her shadowmaster home, bidding him to kill the traitors and put an end to the plot.

Kill the traitors!

Kill not capture, the single word sent a shiver down his spine. The queen well knew the value of information. A hasty execution was both wasteful and lawless. Corpses never talked. The queen he knew would never issue such an order. And the sudden appearance of a plot against the throne deepened his unease for he'd heard no such tidings from his shadowmen. The dispatch smelled like a lie...it smelled like a well-oiled trap.

The implications chilled him.

Not only were the queen's messages compromised...but her very life could be imperiled.

Summoning the stallion, he vaulted into the saddle. Clattering through the cobbled streets, he galloped out of Lingard like a demon lit afire. The black stallion proved a princely mount built for speed. Racing against the dark of the moon, he rode long hours into the night, pressing the stallion for every league of speed. When his mount began to falter, he sought the nearest farmstead and used a royal writ to requisition another. Trading his lathered stallion for a chestnut hunter, he rode day and night, eating in the saddle, begrudging any delay. Rolled in a blanket, he snatched a few hours of sleep near the roadside, pausing only long enough to be sure he would not fall asleep in the saddle. A cloudburst caught him on the road. Rain beat against him, yet he did not slow. Leagues later, the storm clouds fled and the sun reemerged, the afternoon heat baking steam from his damp leathers. He followed the road south, galloping through a countryside verdant with green fields and rebuilt villages. Despite the ravages of the Flame War, Lanverness thrived once more yet his queen was imperiled. Riddled with worry, the shadowmaster burned through horses at a furious pace, gauging his progress by the celestial clock. The crescent moon continued to wane, a smiling sliver of light racing towards darkness, yet he made good time.

His unknown adversary had set him a daunting task, timing the delivery of the last dispatch to Lingard such that he'd be hard pressed to make the journey by the appointed night. The strategy was clearly designed to exhaust him, yet luck or determination favored the shadowmaster. Slowing his sweat-stained mare to a trot, he neared the inn, arriving a full day in advance of the dark moon.

The Green Man Inn stood at a busy crossroads, just a day's ride north of Pellanor. A prosperous way stop, the inn boasted a bathhouse and stables and had a solid reputation for clean rooms and hearty fare. Wealthy merchants and highborn travelers heading south to Pellanor used the inn to shed the dust of the road, donning silks and velvets before entering the queen's city. Those traveling north with coin in their purse often found they could not resist a last night of comfort before committing to the long road. Either way the Green Man prospered.

The shadowmaster rode to the stables, tossing a silver coin to the nearest lad. "Walk her, rub her down, and give her your best bucket of fresh oats."

The lad caught and bit the coin, a smile splitting his freckled face. "Yes, m'lord!"

The shadowmaster swung down from the saddle, stifling a groan as his boots hit solid ground, jarring his aching back. The long ride had inflicted more punishment than he cared to admit. Unbuckling his saddlebag, he crossed to the inn.

A weathered sign hanging above the door showed a man's face masked by green oak leaves. Painted bright green, the masked face held dark watchful eyes, reflecting the mystery of the forest. He'd passed beneath the sign countless times yet the leafed man's expression always seemed slightly different. Perhaps it reflected the mood of the beholder. This time the Green Man was laughing, but if it was out of mirth or derision, he could not say. *Tricks and traps,* the shadowmaster wondered if the joke was at his expense. For half a heartbeat, he considered donning one of the many disguises tucked in his saddlebags...but a good trap needed bait. Casually draping his hand on a throwing dagger sheathed at his belt, the shadowmaster strode into the great room, his dark leathers drawing stares like bees to a honeycomb.

The inn was crowded with noon-time travelers. His swift glance counted merchants, peddlers, a minstrel and a wealthy family but no obvious threats. Tantalizing aromas of spit-roasted lamb hit him below the belt, rousing a fierce hunger, but first he needed a room. He crossed to the counter, feeling the stares on his back. The young man working the counter was a stranger. "Where's Kirth?"

The young man gave him a wary look. "In the back room."

"Get him. Tell him Lord Highgate is asking for him."

"Yes, m'lord." His eyes widening, the young man scurried through the rear door.

It did not take long for the inn master to appear. A large bear-of-a-man with unruly dark hair and laughing green eyes, Kirth walked with a pronounced limp, his oversized boot hiding a club foot. "Welcome, my lord!" He flashed a jovial smile, an asset for any innkeeper. "What brings you to the Green Man?"

The shadowmaster slid a gold coin onto the counter. "I need a room for two nights."

"Our best room is already..."

The shadowmaster interrupted. "I want the rear room under the eaves."

"But..."

"Why don't you show it to me and I'll see if it suits."

Kirth gave him a knowing look, catching onto the game. Wiping his hands on his apron, he reached for an iron key. "Happy to oblige. This way, my lord." Limping, he led the shadowmaster to the rear steps. The staircase narrowed as they climbed to the third floor, to rooms tucked under the roof's slanting eaves. Formerly an attic, the top floor had been converted to a large dormitory where the poorest guests could spread their bedrolls for a few coppers. A quick glance showed the dormitory was empty, a sure sign the weather wasn't bad enough to coerce hard-earned coppers from the traveling poor. Ducking to avoid the slanting roof beams, the inn keeper led him to the attic's rear, to one small room that had been walled off to take advantage of the single window. Kirth opened the door, ushering him into the room. It smelled of dust and attic spaces.

The room was spare, a narrow cot pushed under the slanting eaves, a single rickety chair, and a chamber pot. The sole luxury was the large lead-paned window overlooking the rear of the inn.

"I can send a girl up to have it cleaned."

"No need." The shadowmaster strode to the window and threw it open, admitting a breath of fresh air. Leaning out, his gaze swept the back yard, satisfied with the lethal drop. "This will do." He tossed his saddlebags onto the narrow cot.

"Expecting trouble, my lord?"

Kirth had long served as a trusted member of the shadowmaster's web of informants, keeping a valuable eye on travelers flowing to and from the queen's city. Robert prowled the small room, taking its measure. "Heard anything from Master Raddock?"

"Can't say as I have, m'lord."

The innkeeper's answer deepened his concern, more proof the queen's dispatch was a forgery...and the meeting a trap. "Any word from Pellanor?"

Kirth shrugged. "More grumblings than usual about taxes and tithes. I guess the queen is keen to refill her coffers, but you look like you've come for more than rumors."

He gave the inn keeper the ugly truth. "I'm chasing a plot against the queen."

Kirth sobered. "How can I help?"

"I need food and sleep but I also need to be seen. I'll take my supper in the great hall. I want you to serve me, making loud use of my name to bait the trap. After the meal, I plan to sleep in the chair, but I need you to keep watch. If anyone approaches my table, I need you to wake me. I crave sleep, yet I dare not be caught by it."

Kirth's voice turned solemn. "I'll keep watch, m'lord. You can count on me."

"Good."

The innkeeper turned to go.

"And, Kirth?"

"M'lord?"

"Keep your eyes sharp and your cudgel close."

"Aye, m'lord."

Closing the door, the shadowmaster paced the small room, measuring the number of strides to the window while taking note of the angled roof, a hazard to his head. He checked the door's lock, not surprised to find that it was cheap and easy to pick, an invitation to his foes.

A knock sounded on the door.

He eased the door open, one hand on his knife. A serving girl waited outside. The master archivist accepted fresh towels and a steaming basin of hot water from the pretty chambermaid. He took the time to wash and shave, scraping away his grizzled beard, leaving nothing but a well trimmed mustache. His shirt stank, so he changed into a fresh one from his saddlebags, but over it he wore his leather jerkin. Travel worn, the dark leather smelled of horse and sweat but he valued its hidden protection. Supple chain mail hidden beneath padded leather, the jerkin had saved his life more than once. Checking the knife in his boot, and the one hidden at his back, he buckled on his sword belt. Three extra throwing knives were sheathed alongside his sword. Armed and armored, he made his way back down to the great room.

The crowd had thinned. Too late for the midday meal, too early for supper, yet the succulent scent of spit-roasted lamb lingered like a mouthwatering tease. The shadowmaster took a seat at a large round table set before the cold hearth. He sat in plain sight, his back to the river-stone fireplace, his view to the front door unobstructed.

Kirth limped towards him, bearing a large tankard frothing with ale. "Lord Highgate, you honor the Green Man with your presence. How may I serve you?"

He slapped a gold coin onto the table. "I'll have a double serving of the roast lamb and anything green you've got to go with it, and keep the ale flowing."

The innkeeper pocketed the coin. "Yes, m'lord." Kirth passed the order to a serving girl and then worked the great room, talking with travelers.

The shadowmaster sipped the ale, rich and dark and flavorful. A serving girl soon appeared bearing a platter of fresh-carved lamb smothered in gravy, a bowl of buttered leeks mixed with seed-pearl onions, and a small round loaf of fresh-baked rye bread still steaming from the oven. His hunger roared like an unchained beast. Tearing a chunk from the fresh-baked loaf, he sopped it with gravy and shoved it in his mouth, nearly swooning from the taste. Flavored with garlic, the lamb was tender and tasty. His gaze scanning the great room, he devoured the meal.

Kirth approached bearing a pewter pitcher. "More ale, Lord Highgate?"

The innkeeper was playing his part well. "Keep it full!" He settled back in the chair, sipping the ale. His gaze roved across the Green Man's patrons. If his foes hid amongst the other travelers, he could not tell. Content to let Kirth keep watch, he succumbed to exhaustion and the lulling lethargy of a tasty feast. His eyes fell shut.

The table lurched against him.

Startled awake, his hand slid to his dagger.

"More ale, Lord Highgate?"

The innkeeper's booming voice served as an anchor. Sitting up, the shadowmaster scanned the room. The Green Man had grown crowded with merchants, peddlers and a few families. A minstrel strummed a lute in the far corner, but he saw no obvious threat. Pushing his tankard toward Kirth, he said, "Top it off." As the innkeeper poured, he dropped his voice to a whisper. "Anything suspicious?"

"Not that I've noticed, but the hour grows late."

He flicked his glance to the darkened windowpanes. "Any traders from Navarre?"

"Not tonight."

The shadowmaster sipped the ale, watching as Kirth made the rounds, topping off tankards and having a word with his guests. Night had darkened the lead-paned windows, proving he'd slept for more than a handful of hours. His back ached from sleeping in the chair, but he felt refreshed from the hearty meal and the long slumber. He stretched, his gaze roving the inn. If his foes hid among the travelers, they were good, very good.

He dallied for the turn of an hourglass, sipping ale, listening to the minstrel, giving his foes a chance to find him. Tiring of the game, he slapped a gold coin on the table and made a show of flipping a second coin to the minstrel. Claiming a lighted taper, he lurched towards the stairs, pretending to be addled by ale. Feigning a drunken stupor, he climbed to his attic room, his senses on full alert. The taper gave only a small circle of light. Wary of an ambush, he searched the dormitory but it remained empty. Drawing a knife from his belt, he entered his small room...but it too was empty. He closed and latched the door, and then he arranged the deceit. Shoving the cot to the left side, under the slanting eaves, he rumpled the blankets, using his saddlebag and discarded clothes to make it look as if he slept in the bed. Satisfied, he closed and locked the window. Without the gentle night breeze, the room felt close and small and overly warm, but the closeness only served to magnifying his senses. Moving the chair behind the door's blindside, he snuffed the candle. His eyes adjusted to the dark. Sitting in the spindled chair, he tipped it back. Balancing the chair on two legs, he employed an old trick he'd learned long ago. If he fell asleep while on watch, the unbalanced chair would wake him. Prepared to wait, he played with his favorite throwing dagger, dancing the keen blade between his fingers, an exercise of skill and daring that kept his mind alert.

Beyond the lead-paned window, the night was velvety black, the waning crescent moon nearly snuffed to darkness. *The night before the dark of the moon,* he expected his foes to come early. In truth, he expected they were already here, waiting for the small hours of the morning when decent folk slept.

Straining his senses, he listened, his gaze patrolling the small room. Hours passed yet he remained alert. Nothing sharpened the senses like a lethal threat. Given the skill of the forger, he expected his enemy to be formidable. He wondered how many they'd send. His mind juggled the clues while his fingers balanced the throwing knife.

And then he heard it.

A faint scrabbling sound, no louder than a mouse or a rat...but it came from the window.

Perhaps it's a bird.

Puzzled, he slowly lowered the chair to rest on four legs. Statue-still, he gripped the throwing dagger by the blade. Braced to throw, he held his breath, every sense strained taut.

Another sound came from the door, a faint scratching at the latch.

He leaned forward, poised to fight.

The window eased upward, lifted by a slender blade.

The shadowmaster froze, *impossible!*

A tendril of cool night air flowed from the open window, shattering his disbelief.

Something crouched on the window ledge!

Clad in black, arms and legs bent like a spider, it perched on the sill like a demon come calling.

Beside him, the door eased open, betraying a second assailant.

Two against one, the shadowmaster hurled his knife at the fiend crouched on the sill. Without waiting to see it strike, he threw his weight against the door, bashing the lurker behind it. The door thudded against a solid body. Yanking the door open, the shadowmaster attacked.

A small man clad in black crouched on the far side, blood splattering his face.

Fast as thought, the shadowmaster hurled a second knife.

The small man blurred. Moving with a feral speed, he dodged the knife while raising a slender tube to his face.

The shadowmaster charged. Knocking the tube away, he tackled the small man, slamming him to the floor. Bringing his weight to bear, he pinned the assailant while reaching for a dagger, but the small man squirmed away. Writhing like a slippery weasel, the enemy reversed the hold, straddling the master. Fingers strong as steel tightened on the shadowmaster's throat, slowly crushing his windpipe. Desperate for breath, he lunged upwards, butting his forehead into the enemy's nose. Something crunched. Blood gushed hot across the shadowmaster's face. For a heartbeat, the enemy's grip slackened. Gulping air, the shadowmaster rolled, seeking to gain the top position. Sweat poured out of him. He'd never fought a foe with such uncanny quickness and skill. The two men grappled, rolling across the attic. The enemy unsheathed a dagger, plunging the blade into the shadowmaster's side, but the knife skittered harmless across his mail-lined jerkin. Grabbing his assailant's wrist, the master smashed his enemy's hand against the floor till the knife dropped from his battered fingers.

Footsteps pounded up the stairs.

The shadowmaster feared another assailant...but then he saw the torchlight. Kirth was there, a blazing torch in one hand, a massive cudgel in the other.

Flushed with advantage, the master hissed, "Surrender!"

The small man snarled, redoubling his efforts, reaching for something at his belt. The shadowmaster twisted, trying to pin him down. Kirth swung his cudgel, connecting with the small man's shin. Bones shattered beneath the cudgel. A stifled scream erupted from the assailant.

The shadowmaster straddled his foe, holding a dagger to his throat. *"Surrender!"*

The assailant's eyes blazed with defiance.

In the flickering torchlight, the master got his first good look at his foe. His face was blackened with soot. Blood streamed from his crushed nose. Clad all in black, a baldric of dark-bladed knives strung across his chest, he was small and wiry in stature, the perfect assassin.

"It's over." The shadowmaster pressed the knife blade to his enemy's jugular. "Whom do you serve?"

The assassin's face twisted into a cruel snarl. "I serve Death!" Lunging upwards, he sliced his own throat on the master's knife.

Blood spurted in a red font.

The shadowmaster jerked his knife away, but the deed was done. Hot blood drenched his leathers. Standing, he staggered backwards, shocked by the assassin's lethal resolve.

The body twitched in its final death throes, blood bubbling at the throat's gaping wound. And then the corpse stilled.

Kirth gaped. "Bloody Hells, who dies like that?"

The shadowmaster wiped the blood from his hands. "The better question is whom did he serve?" He thumped the corpse with his boot, making sure it was dead. And then he remembered the other one. "Come." He returned to his room, but it was empty, the window gaping open to the cool night air. Leaning out the window, he saw a body sprawled in the shadows.

Desperate for a clue to his foe, the shadowmaster raced down the stairs two at a time. Kirth lumbered behind, the torchlight jerking against the stairwell. Reaching the main floor, the master cautiously opened the inn's doors and peered out. Night held sway, the tree frogs serenading the waning crescent, but he saw no assailants.

Behind him, Kirth whispered, "Do you think there's more?"

"Could be." Pulling two knives from his belt, he slipped out into the velvety darkness.

The tree frogs fell silent.

Cursing their sudden stillness, he struggled to control his own breathing. Daggers bared, he crept to the back of the inn. His senses strained for any sign of movement, but the night seemed empty. He reached the rear. The body lay sprawled in the dirt, masked by the darkness. Using his boot, he rolled it face-up. *Another corpse,* his dagger impaled the assassin's throat, a killing throw.

Kirth lumbered around the side of the inn, his torchlight beating against the darkness. Pausing beside the master, he lowered the torch to illuminate the corpse. Clad in black, the small man wore a baldric of throwing knives across his chest. "Another one. Where did this one come from?"

"He climbed through the window."

Kirth raised his torch. Both men stared up at the attic window. Without ropes or obvious handholds, the climb looked impossible. "But how?"

"No idea." The master knelt, searching the corpse for clues. The assailant was well armed. In addition to the baldric of nine throwing knives, his belt held a wire garrote, a small grappling hook, a slender wooden tube, and pouches filled with darts. He sniffed a dart. "Poison!"

Kirth said, "Who kills with poison darts?"

The master had no answer. He finished the search, but found no other clues, till he noticed a mark peeking beneath the dead man's left sleeve. Slitting the leather, he rolled back the sleeve. Nine symbols were tattooed on the assassin's left forearm. They looked sinister...they looked like wizard's runes.

"What does that mean?"

The master archivist was a learned man, yet he'd never seen their like. "I wish I knew."

Kirth's breath caught. "Look!" He pointed at the master's jerkin.

A dart was imbedded near his neckline. Plucking it from the leather, he sniffed the needle, smelling the sharp tang. "Poison!" Death had come calling. He smashed the dart against the inn's stout wall, breaking the needle. "We need to bury the dead...and I need to copy those runes." *And I need to get to Pellanor!* He'd foiled the trap, but he'd failed to learn who was behind it. Of one thing he was certain, his queen was in deadly peril.

31

Jemma

Light speared through the rafters, illuminating her attic prison. Jemma stretched the chain shackled to her aching wrist. Moving in slow circles, she studied the slanting ceiling. Random nails poked through the shingles, creating constellations of rusty points. She found one patterned like the Big Ladle, another like the Southern Swan, and then she found a dense cluster. A feral smile slipped across her face. Comprised of short and long nails, she named it Mok, the Torturer.

Tugging on the musty mattress, she pulled it farther under the slanting roof, positioning it just beyond Mok. Retrieving the food tray, she sat on the mattress, nibbling a biscuit. Despite her gnawing hunger, Jemma forced herself to eat only her allotted portion. She'd learned to make her food last. All too soon, she finished and there was nothing to do but wait.

For three days, no one came. The water pitcher was nearly empty, the roasted chicken reduced to a pile of bones. Her stomach grumbled in protest. She began to wonder if they'd leave her to starve and then she heard it, the sound of a bolt being drawn back.

Her heartbeat leaped to a gallop. Hastily arranging herself on the mattress, she tousled her hair and pulled up her velvet gown to reveal a hint of pale white thigh. In such a dirty and disheveled state, she felt anything but beautiful, yet desperation drove her to the ploy.

The trapdoor swung open.

Jemma held her breath, waiting to see if it was Coldeyes or Brute.

A thatch of dark hair appeared. The gods were with her.

Her hand curled around the needle-sharp chicken bone. Casting a sloe-eyed glance his way, she said. "I thought you'd never come." Adding a hopeless quaver to her voice, a damsel in distress, Jemma steeled herself to do what must be done. "Please, I'm so hungry."

He stood near the trapdoor holding a food tray, a big hulking man with bad teeth and dark eyes.

She stretched her leg, a subtle tease.

Her movement snagged his gaze. His stare slid to her exposed thigh.

She twitched her dress to cover herself, a shy maiden.

His grin widened.

"Please," she lifted her hand in entreaty, her voice weak, "I'm so hungry."

He moved towards her, crouching beneath the slanting roof.

She gauged the distance, her heartbeat thundering so loud, she wondered he did not hear.

He crouched below Mok, setting the tray on the floor.

She lunged upwards, ramming the needle-sharp bone into his eye.

Gore gushed across her hand.

Screaming, he reared upwards, ramming his head into the roof of nails.

His scream twisted to an anguished squeal. His mouth sagged open, his eyes glazing.

For three long heartbeats, he hung there, and then he toppled forward like a felled tree.

Horrified, Jemma lunged to get out of his way.

Blood dripped from Mok.

Brute lay sprawled across her mattress, face down, the back of his head a ruined mess cratered with blood.

She'd killed him! Jemma froze, stunned by the horror of it, but then she gathered herself. Desperate to escape, she reached for the keys on his belt. *Three keys*, she tried the first, but it did not fit. With shaking hands, she tried the second.

The manacle clicked open, dropping from her wrist.

Elation rushed through her.

She crawled to the opening, but then went back for the keys, not knowing what waited below. Returning to the trapdoor, she scrambled down the ladder. Sunlight streamed through a pair of windows, making her squint. Bedrolls and trays of half-eaten food littered the floor. *Her food!* She glimpsed a door on the far side, the path to freedom.

Something glided from the shadows.

A black-clad devil!

She stifled a scream.

He stared at her, a surly smile on his face.

She ran for the door. Fear gave her speed. Two more strides and she was nearly there.

Something stung the back of her neck. She lunged for the door, but her legs buckled beneath her. *"No!"* Falling to the floor, she crawled towards the door. Jemma fought to stay awake, to win her freedom, but Darkness claimed her.

32

The Master Archivist

Roadside inns oft proved the best place for gaining new disguises. For a small purse of silvers, the shadowmaster bought a tinker's mule, complete with his stash of tools and fresh-patched kitchen wares. Trading his knackered mare for a gray-haired nag, he donned a moth-eaten cloak. Slouching his six-foot frame, the master archivist melted into the role.

Kirth, the innkeeper, saw him off. "You sure about this? That mare's worth far more than the nag."

"My life might depend on the nag. The mare's too rich for a humble tinker." Sighing, the shadowmaster settled onto the sway-backed horse, certain his back would pay a stiff price for the poor mount. "Take care and don't believe any correspondence save if it bears my sigil."

"Will do." Kirth pushed open the stable door.

Night cloaked the pre-dawn sky. While honest travelers slept, the queen's shadowmaster took to the road. Slumped in the saddle, he rode south to the annoying clang of pots and pans. The sway-backed nag stumbled to an amble, the reluctant mule tugging behind. The plodding pace frayed his already-worn nerves, yet he judged the disguise to be his best shield. *The queen is in danger!* The ambush at the inn proved the queen's dispatches were usurped by a master forger. He'd foiled the trap, yet the ambush was well planned, the assassins nearly lethal. Recalling the fight, his mind staggered at the assassin's self-murder, the way he thrust his throat at the naked blade. *Who dies like that?* He'd sought to capture the assassin, not kill him. This unseen enemy held his henchmen in a powerful thrall. Perhaps the wizard's runes inked on their forearms held a clue to their master's name, yet it was a riddle he could not decipher. The enemy's name remained a mystery, but his deeds painted a formidable picture. Canny, resourceful, convoluted, extremely dangerous, and most likely a wizard. *A wizard.* The conclusion chilled him. Fearing for the queen, he spurred the nag to a faster amble.

The sky brightened with the crack of dawn. Traffic along the road began to thicken. Farm wagons laden with produce lumbered past, oxen straining in their traces. This early in the morning, all the wagons and carts were full to burgeoning, headed south to Pellanor's peerless markets. Watching from beneath a floppy hat, the shadowmaster made note of every passing wagon. Merchants, farmers, peddlers, all were expected, but he saw no families, no gaggle of children perched in the wagon beds, as if Pellanor's draw was reduced to pure commerce. He liked it not. Kirth had warned him that the queen's city had changed, yet the raw proof compounded his worry.

By late afternoon, the road wound past a wooded knoll. Great oak trees spread their branches wide, crowning the hill with verdant green. A warning prickled down his back. The feeling intensified as he drew close to the woods. The shadowmaster felt watched. Scanning the trees, he saw nothing save leafy branches, yet he knew otherwise. After the Flame War, the queen had gifted the forest to the cat-eyed archers. Gazing at the green-crowned knoll, he wondered if Lord Cenric was back from the south. The shadowmaster was half tempted to veer off the road and seek out the archer lord, but urgency drove him forward. He needed to see Pellanor for himself. He needed to reach the queen.

Skirting the woods, the road curved south, affording travelers their first view of the great city. From a distance, the outer wall looked complete, though Kirth said otherwise. Sparkling white in the afternoon sunlight, the wall appeared more formidable than it truly was. Little more than cobbled buildings and hastily built walls, somehow the queen had found a way to turn an ugly necessity into an adornment, a white crown encircling her capital city. It was so like her, to find a way to marry function with beauty. She'd never wanted a walled city, yet the queen had found a way to make harsh choices palatable.

The sway-backed nag plodded forward, taking him home, taking him towards danger.

The city gates stood open, soldiers in green tabards patrolling the barbican, but something was amiss. To the left of the gate, red streaks stained the wall. The red stains puzzled him till he grew closer, and then they alarmed him. Disemboweled corpses hung from the merlons, their weeping innards staining the white walls blood-red. The shadowmaster struggled not to gape, his alarm spiking. His gaze roved the gates, seeking enemies, seeking friends. None of the faces looked familiar, but that proved little. Following a merchant's wagon, he slouched in the saddle, keeping his floppy hat pulled low lest someone recognize him. Pots dangling from the mule clanged loud, their discordant clamor adding to his disguise. He passed through the gates unnoticed.

Wagons laden with goods crowded the main thoroughfare. Posing as a poor tinker, he followed the tide of commerce towards the city's heart. His gaze roved left and right, taking the city's measure. The streets bustled but with grim intent. People went about their business, but they kept their heads lowered, their faces somber, their smiles gone. And then he noticed the children were absent, as if hidden from view. Bands of mummers and roving minstrels were vanished from the streets as well, as if all the brightness and cheer had fled the city. Pellanor felt cursed. The buildings and streets looked the same, but this was not the queen's city. His anxiety roared to a bonfire.

Farmers and merchants peeled off the main street seeking various markets, but the shadowmaster rode straight for the castle. A white confection of spires and flying buttresses, Castle Tandroth stood at the city's heart, a beacon of prosperity and elegance. As he drew near, he saw the queen's sigil flying from the castle's tallest spires, but colors could be misleading.

The crowd thinned and he got a clear look at the castle. The great gates stood open, guards in green tabards leaning on spears, but then he saw the red stains. Corpses hung from the walls, black crows pecking at the gruesome feast. A wave of stench wafted towards him, proving his eyes did not lie. Horror pierced him. Pellanor ran amok with death.

The queen! She had to be captured...or dead.

He yearned to gallop through the gates and rescue her, but he dared not be so brash. Clearly, this unnamed enemy had ensorcelled Pellanor. Given the dark state of things, he might be the queen's only hope. He dared not let her down.

Turning away from the castle, he rode back through the side streets, his mind churning. He needed information and he needed allies, yet he dared not misplace his trust. Knowing the queen's dispatches were compromised, he had to assume her senior officials were either corrupted or misled. Deciding to eschew the inner circle, he sought friends in low places.

Tugging his floppy hat low, he guided the sway-backed horse towards the murkier side of the city. Information was a shadowman's stock and trade. Always cultivating watchers and whisperers, they sifted dangers and opportunities from rumors and innuendo. As the queen's shadowmaster, he'd turned most of his sources and spies over to lesser shadowmen to run, but two he'd kept to himself. Both were trusted and true. He'd often used them as bellwethers to test the veracity of information trickling up from below, but in these dark times, they might prove his best hope. He considered his two sources. One was known to the queen, the other was not. Praying the queen remembered, he decided to seek out the first.

The Rusty Dragon was a tavern that straddled the border between respectable and ill-repute. A place where shady characters mingled with honest folk, providing a rich upwelling of gossip, rumors and hearsay. Over the years, the tavern had yielded a font of information, yet its true value lay in his deep bond with the Dragon's owner.

Stopping two blocks away, the shadowmaster abandoned the nag and the mule to a hitching post. Throwing his saddlebag over his shoulder, he was about to turn away when he noticed a man and three children crouched in the alleyway. They looked dirty and worn and they had no shoes. *No shoes in the queen's city!* There would always be poor, but the sight of their bare feet struck him as an ill omen. The Queen's Grace would have helped, not with handouts, but with a sure way to earn. *How had the city fallen so far?*

He unhitched the mule and nag from the post. The tinker's disguise had served him well, getting him safely into the city, but he needed it no longer. Pots clanging, he tugged the reluctant beasts towards the alleyway.

The man cringed backwards, his children huddled behind him.

"No, wait!" He offered the man the reins. "Take them, sell them, use them to help yourself and your family."

The man hesitated, his eyes darting like a kicked dog tempted by a scrap of meat.

The shadowmaster proffered the reins. "It's no trick. Take them."

Creeping forward, the man cautiously took the reins. When no blow came, he dared to smile, a look of wonder on his grimy face. "Thank you." He bobbed his head. "Thank you, sir."

"Thank the queen."

The man looked puzzled. "The queen, sir?"

"Prosperity flowed under the queen." He gestured to the man's bare feet. "This is not her reign. Tell the others." He gestured to the mule and nag. "That's how you'll earn them."

The man's eyes widened, his shoulders straightening with purpose. "Yes, sir."

He hoped the man understood, either way he'd done what he could. Turning away, the shadowmaster fixed his mind on saving the queen. Making his way through the tangled streets, he sought the Rusty Dragon. Slipping around a corner, he positioned himself in the shadows, keeping watch on the back door. From the rear, the tavern wasn't much to look at. A clapboard building weathered to a dull gray, the only distinctive feature was a cupola perched high on the roof. The tavern's namesake, a weather vane, stood atop the cupola. A great rusted dragon with wings spread wide, the weather vane soared above the tavern like a talisman.

He raised his gaze to the dragon.

The dragon flew south! Hope blazed within him.

Most folks thought the dragon was rusted solid, a weather vane in name only, but in truth, a cunning winch hidden in the cupola allowed the vane to be turned. It was not the wind that controlled the vane's direction, but a dire message. Normally the dragon flew north. When the dragon flew south, it meant an important message waited for him.

Circling to the front of the tavern, he kept watch for a turn of the hourglass. Seeing no signs of ambush or surveillance, he climbed the steps to the weathered dragon carved deep on the age-stained door.

Warmth and the smell of sizzling pork enveloped him. Colored light from bottle-glass windows illumed the great room with a soft glow. The soft light cast a cozy and welcoming feel, yet it permitted shadows to cloak the corners. The Rusty Dragon was the perfect meeting place for honest folk and denizens with shady skills.

A dozen patrons sat scattered across the tables, sipping tankards of ale and talking with murmured voices. He quickly scanned the room, yet saw no obvious threat. Keeping his shoulders hunched and his hat pulled low, he shuffled to a table in the corner. Putting his back to the wall, he took a seat, draping his dusty saddlebag over the nearest chair.

A barmaid with a saucy smile sauntered toward him. "What will you be having?"

"A plate of the roast pork and a tankard of ale." He let his gaze linger on her comely form as she walked away. She returned in short order with a plate heaping with roast pork and crackling, applesauce preserves and buttered carrots. His mouth watered, yet he kept to his disguise, paying with coppers, carefully counting each coin from his purse. Putting the last in her hand, he leaned forward, his voice dropping to a hushed whisper. "And tell Sam that Bardis has a ripe rumor."

Placing a foaming tankard in front of him, the barmaid never missed a beat. "You just wink when you want that refilled." Tucking the extra coins in her laced bodice, she sauntered back to the bar.

Ravenous with hunger, he dug into the meal, nearly swooning from the taste. The pork crackling burst with salty flavor, rich juices running down his stubbled beard. Wiping his face with the back of his hand, he took a long swig of ale, chasing away the dust of the road. The roast pork was excellent, the ale even better. The Dragon was known for its tasty fare, an added lure for honest folk. Wiping the plate with the last bite of pork, he finished the meal and gestured for a refill of the tankard.

The barmaid returned empty handed. "Sam will see you in the back room."

Pushing the plate away, he shrugged his saddlebag onto his shoulder and followed her to a side door, making sure to walk in a slouch. More than a few stares followed him, but such scrutiny was expected, all part of doing business in the Dragon.

The barmaid rapped three times and then opened the solid oak door.

He stepped into a small room without windows. Lanterns of all shapes and sizes hung from the ceiling, their bright glow dispelling the shadows. Paneled with dark wood, the room had no adornment save for a dragon head mounted on the far wall. Made of ceramic, the great dragon glared down at him, jaws gaping wide, glass eyes glowing in the bright light.

Taking a seat at the small table, the shadowmaster removed his hat. Setting aside his disguise, he straightened his shoulders, his penetrating gaze meeting the glassy-eyed stare of the dragon.

It did not take long for the hidden door to open. "Robert, you mangy old rascal, I feared you dead!" Samantha Caillas swaggered into the room like she owned it, which indeed she did. Clad in gray leather trousers, knee-high boots and a slender jerkin, she was tall and willowy without any noticeable curves. Obsidian-handled throwing daggers studded her belt, adding bite to her swagger. Her hair was close-cropped, blonde fading to silver. From a distance, she was often mistaken for a man, yet her face was heart-shaped, a single rippled scar marring her right cheek like a permanent tear. To most, Sam was a riddle, but her eyes told the true tale. Sharp as cut glass, they glittered with intelligence, humor, and a wary hint of coiled danger.

He rose from the table to clasp her arm. Her grip was firm and intense.

"Where have you been?" She stepped away. "The bloody dragon's flown south for nigh on a moon-turn."

A moon-turn, his anguish deepened. His queen had needed him and he hadn't been here. "From the queen?"

"No less." She removed a leather pouch from her jerkin, setting it on the table between them. "Glad to be rid of it."

His gaze fixed on the message pouch. Crossed white roses surmounted by a golden crown, the queen's seal embossed the supple leather. He yearned to reach for it, to read her words, but he needed context. "Who brought it?"

"A well-dressed woman. Gutsy to come here but clearly out of her depth. I'm guessing one of the queen's hand-maidens."

Lady Sarah! The choice of messenger told him much, screaming of danger laced with wary caution. Bridling his anxiety, he took a seat at the table. "Tell me of the city."

"You saw the corpses strung from the walls."

He replied with a dead-eyed stare. "By whose orders?"

"They're saying the queen. Criminals and miscreants rounded up in the dead of night, taken to the dungeons. Problem is, they weren't criminals, but honest folk roused from their beds. Two days later their mutilated corpses were strung from the walls, a lesson to us all."

Outrage rode his voice. "The queen never ordered it!"

"Yet, the corpses hang for all to see."

"And the people believe it?"

Sam shrugged. "The queen's standard flies from the castle spires."

"A ruse."

"Perhaps."

"Yet, the people don't see through it?"

Sam sighed, sinking to a chair. "Some do, some don't. Such a thing has never happened under the queen's reign. But it's happened in other kingdoms, other cities. The people are confused and frightened. Like sheep without a shepherd, they're not sure whom to believe, whom to trust. They mill the streets, going about their business, but you can see the terror riding just behind their eyes." She eased back in the chair. "I figure the only reason the city hasn't risen to a full bore panic is because most people cling to their faith in the queen. They see atrocities but they don't believe."

Willful disbelief...the fatal flaw of civilization. The shadowmaster grunted, his own observations matching her bitter assessment. "Whom do you name?"

"Rumor mills run wild with speculation." She gestured to the tavern's great hall. "I've heard every lord's name tangled with blame. Even yours."

"But?"

She arched a pale eyebrow in concession. "But this does not feel like petty ambition."

"What then?"

Leaning forward, she dropped her voice to a whisper. "It feels evil." She gave him a piercing stare. "Even the shady side of the city is quaking in its boots."

"Who then?"

"That's the riddle."

He waited.

She unsheathed a dagger, flicking it through her fingers with expert skill.

Unthreatened, he sat unmoving, knowing it was her way of thinking.

The dagger stopped, the obsidian handle flashing in the lantern light. "There's one gem in the dung heap. One name that garners mystery, admiration, and jealousy across the city."

"Who?"

"The Prince of Ur."

The name struck sparks in his mind.

"Spends gold like he's plundered a dragon's hoard. Hosts exotic parties to all hours. Spares no expense currying favor with lords and nobles alike...but there are dark whispers."

"What whispers?"

"Footpads and rogues speak of comrades gone missing."

The shadowmaster shook his head. "A weak argument."

"Yet, the whispers keep sticking."

He scratched the raspy stubble on his chin. "And when whispers stick, there's often more to the tale."

"True enough." Samantha sheathed her dagger, as if skewering the point.

Tugging a folded scrap of parchment from his boot, he shifted the conversation, passing the parchment to Sam. "Ever seen these?"

"No."

"Sure?"

She took a closer look. "Means nothing to me. Why?"

"These runes were tattooed on the left forearms of two very capable assassins."

She raised a pale eyebrow. "Sounds like a gang or a cult. I'll keep an eye out."

"You do that." Folding the parchment, he placed it back in his boot. "How's business?"

"Strangely enough, busier than ever. In troubled times the shady side seeks solace in gold, while honest folk seek the shield of shady steel." She shrugged. "The Rusty Dragon profits from both."

"More proof the city's in turmoil."

Samantha gave a slow nod.

The shadowmaster fingered the queen's message pouch, considering all that he'd learned.

"What do you need?"

"Ears, eyes, and a place to stay."

"Done."

He liked how she never hesitated.

Fishing through the pockets of her jerkin, she placed an iron skeleton key on the table. "Come back after dark. The room under the eaves is yours." Their hands brushed in passing, but the old spark was long dead.

"Thank you." He pocketed the key, his hands returning to caress the message pouch.

"I'll leave you to your queen."

For half a heartbeat, he wondered if she knew. Seeing her clear gaze, he dismissed the notion, for the secret was too deeply guarded.

"Stay for as long as you need. No one will bother you here." Rising she went to the far wall. Pressing an unseen latch, she disappeared through the hidden door.

Alone in the small room, the great dragon head stared down at him, like a trophy from a bard's tale. *It feels evil...*Samantha's words haunted his mind, echoing his own fears. He opened the message pouch, seeking word from his queen.

33

Liandra

Sunlight slanted through the arrow-slit window, proving it was late afternoon. Mired in worry, the queen paced her prison, moving from the door, to the hearth, to the narrow window. Hidden away in the musty tower, cut off from her shadowmen, her mind ran amok with nightmares. *The Mordant stalks Lanverness!* Without facts to weave a true tapestry, Liandra imagined a plague of grief visited upon her people. Somehow she had to get free.

A key turned in the lock.

Bristling, the queen turned to face the opening door, but instead of an enemy, she saw a friend.

Lady Claudia stepped into the room, her face deathly pale, a bundle of crimson silk clutched in her arms. "*Majesty!*"

The queen opened her arms in greeting. "How did..." but then she saw two black-clad assassins herding her friend from behind.

Closing the door, they took positions on either side, their hands resting on sheathed daggers. "You're to be seen."

Liandra was growing tired of threats. "You see us."

The taller assassin gave her a flat stare. "Change and make yourself presentable."

Alarm bells rang in the queen's mind. "Take us to our solar and we shall gladly change." She needed to see the rest of her women, to know they still lived.

"Change here, now."

Beside her, Lady Claudia crumpled to a curtsey, her voice quavering. "Majesty, they said I must help you change, or they will *kill* me."

Another dagger at her throat. The queen glared at the assassins. "Is this what the Mordant does? Threatens harmless women?" Her words beat against the stony-faced assassins. Silence was their only answer. Drawing herself up, the queen reached for her most majestic voice. "We need privacy to change. Leave us."

The taller assassin smirked, his gaze boring into her.

Neither man moved.

Lady Claudia tugged on the queen's ringed hand. "*Please,* majesty?"

Liandra would not risk her friend's life over such a small matter. "Come." Gesturing to the gray-haired woman, the queen retreated to the farthest corner. "We do what we can."

Lady Claudia did her best to be a screen, standing between the queen and the assassins' prying stares, yet Liandra felt exposed. Her anger fumed, yet she knew this latest demand served her own purposes. She needed to get out of this prison. She needed to learn what was happening in her kingdom.

Trading crushed velvet for bright silk, the queen mouthed silent questions, desperate to learn the state of her castle and her kingdom, but Lady Claudia only replied with wide, frightened eyes. The old woman either did not know or was too terrified to answer. Frustrated, the queen slipped into fresh silk. After days of captivity, a mere change of gown would not restore her regal appearance. Her raven-dark hair needed to be washed and carefully coifed, her paints and powders painstakingly reapplied to her face, her jewels artfully chosen to coordinate with her gown. Regal image was a high art form. The queen would never pair emeralds with crimson silk. Such a blatant fashion faux pas should have screamed a warning to her loyal lords, but she doubted they would notice. And then she wondered if she still *had* any loyal lords.

The door yanked open.

Lady Claudia stifled a shriek, melting to a curtsey, but the queen remained statue-still.

A tall man with iron-gray hair strode into her prison. *Another enemy clad in her colors,* the deceit galled her.

His cold, hard stare raked across her. "You'll do."

Another barbarian with no sense of fashion. The queen met his stare. "Your name?"

He cocked his head as if considering whether to reply.

"Surely your name is not a secret."

"Commander Trax." His voice was flat with disdain.

So she had a new jailor. "And where is Commander Hoit?"

Something flickered in the depths of his eyes, but the queen could not read it.

He shuttered his gaze. "You're to be seen and not heard." He gestured to Lady Claudia. "This woman will stand surety for your good behavior." His voice turned sinister. "Speak and she dies."

A muffled sob escaped Lady Claudia.

A cruel smile twisted the commander's thin lips. "In fact, for every word you dare to utter, someone in your service will die." He stepped towards her. "Do you understand?"

Liandra gave the smallest of nods.

Turning on his heel, the commander strode for the door without a backward glance.

Liandra gave Lady Claudia a reassuring look, and then followed the commander through the doorway. A pair of soldiers in green tabards waited outside. Neither bowed, confirming both were strangers. Hands on their sword hilts, they fell in behind her, jailors impersonating an honor guard.

Surrounded by enemies, the queen followed the commander to the stone staircase. Running her hand along the outer spiral, she considered the startled flicker in the commander's gaze when she'd mentioned Hoit. Perhaps her late jailor had suffered a stiff price for the queen's unruliness. No doubt the Mordant was a harsh master. A smile flitted across her face, until she remembered Lady Cathor's severed head. The queen suppressed a shudder. Her actions might have forced the Mordant to trade a knight for a pawn, yet it seemed an ill bargain to the queen. Somehow she had to foil the Mordant without endangering more of her people.

They reached the bottom of the stairs, the dull red stone giving way to polished marble. The commander strode through the corridors as if he knew her castle well. *So the Mordant's men have the run of our castle!* The realization hit her like a punch to the stomach. Hardening her resolve, the queen's gaze darted left and right, thirsting for details.

At first the corridors were empty, but then they came across liveried servants. Most gaped to see her. One dropped a tray, porcelain tea cups shattering across the marble floor. They stared at her as if seeing a ghost, too startled to even bow. She met their stares with an imploring gaze, desperate to impart a silent message. If any understood, she could not tell.

Her jailors whisked her along at an unseemly pace. The corridors became more opulent, vivid tapestries gracing the walls. Liandra spied a few minor lords in side corridors, but most would not meet her gaze. Bitterness stalked her. The queen began to wonder if there was any loyalty left in Lanverness.

Her jailors opened a thick door reinforced with iron banding. Ushering her through to the castle battlements, she strode into bright sunlight. For a handful of heartbeats, she walked in a daze, dazzled by the brightness. Sunlight warmed her upturned face like a forgotten caress. Her spirit soared to be outside, but then she heard the tumult of voices. It sounded like an angry crowd...it sounded like a mob! Hope quickened within her. Perhaps her people came to her aid, rebelling against the Mordant's tyranny.

Her jailors prodded her forward, but she did not need the urging. Rounding a corner, she reached the barbican overlooking the castle's main gate. Mounting the stairs, she strode to the crenellated battlement, keen to see her people.

She peered down at a sea of commoners besieging the castle gates.

Shouts answered her appearance, people pointing aloft.

One shout was louder than the rest. "*The Bloody Queen!*"

The hurled accusation stung her heart.

And then she heard other phrases. "Why?"

"Release them!"

"Let my son go!"

The queen gaped, sundered by understanding. She was being used, made a beard for the Mordant's foul deeds. But how could her people not know her? So many angry faces glared up at her, demanding answers. Liandra opened her mouth to shout a denial, but a dagger pricked her from behind. She reconsidered, doubting the crowd would even hear her voice, but she had to do something. Taking a risk, she made the hand sign against evil, gesturing to the commander standing behind her. Twice she made the sign, praying her people would see and understand.

"Enough." Commander Trax tugged at her elbow.

She gripped the balustrade, resisting, but the men soon pulled her away. Liandra prayed her people noticed.

Commander Trax glared. "Obey or suffer the consequences." Her jailors surrounded her, herding her back along the battlement.

The queen walked without seeing, her mind raging. Why were her people so angry? What had the Mordant done? Whatever foul deed he'd committed, it had been done in her name. A cold fist gripped her heart. For a dozen steps, she walked without thinking, her mind locked in a cold rage...and then one phrase beat against her. *The Bloody Queen!* Staring down, Liandra realized she wore a crimson gown. Understanding opened like a chasm yawning at her feet. Details mattered. While she'd worried about fashion faux pas, he'd used the very color of her gown against her! Images of the angry crowd assailed her mind. *The Bloody Queen...she'd* bet her life the shout had been planned, perpetrated by a servant of the Mordant. Her people were being manipulated. *She* was being manipulated. The queen's ringed hands tightened into fists. Liandra reminded herself that she played against the *Mordant,* a game where kingdoms and crowns hung in the balance. Every detail, every move mattered...and *he* was winning. Somehow, she had to turn the tables.

She found herself climbing stairs. They'd led her back to First Keep. Mired in angry thoughts, Liandra wondered if she'd missed an opportunity.

Her jailors returned her to her prison. Lady Claudia gasped to see her. At least her friend still lived.

Commander Trax gestured to the gray-haired woman. "Out."

The queen interposed. "Please, we wish to change. Velvet is much more comfortable than silk."

Commander Trax gave her a squinty look. "Fine." He turned to one of the assassins. "Keep watch. Bring the woman when she's done. You know what to do." The commander strode from the chamber, leaving two assassins to stand guard by the door.

The queen gestured to Lady Claudia. "Come, help us change back into the softer velvet."

Once more, the older woman served as a screen, her fingers shaking as she undid the many fastenings. The queen shed the silk gown, glad to be rid of the crimson color, a detail that served the Mordant. Raising her hands for the velvet, Liandra leaned close to the older woman, mouthing the words, *tell others!* She gave the woman a pointed stare, reinforcing the command. Lady Claudia gave the smallest of nods. The queen felt a measure of relief. Soft velvet cascaded across her skin. The velvet gown was no longer fresh, but at least the emerald color was hers.

Lady Claudia fluttered about, tightening fastenings and adjusting the queen's hair.

"Enough." An assassin interposed. Opening the door, he made a rude gestured towards it.

With a fleeting look, Lady Claudia bowed to the queen and then fled the chamber.

The two assassins followed.

The door closed and the lock clicked.

Alone, the queen sagged against the wall, exhausted by all that had transpired. *Her people*...she mourned for the deceit plaguing her city. The crimson gown lay puddled on the floor. The bright color suddenly looked loathsome. She kicked at the traitorous gown, vowing to feed the crimson silk to the fire. *Details matter.* Liandra reminded herself that she played against the Mordant, an ancient and terrible foe. But an old woman might be his undoing. If Lady Claudia whispered word of the queen's whereabouts in the right ears, she might yet get free. Liandra dared to hope.

A key turned in the lock.

The queen straightened, refusing to show weakness.

The door opened and an assassin entered.

He carried a basin, a bloody towel draped across it.

"*No!*" The queen shook her head in denial.

The assassin whisked the towel from the basin.

Lady Claudia's severed head stared up at her, her eyes bulging in terror.

"But I said nothing!" The queen protested, horror leaching into her voice.

"She knew too much." Draping the towel across the basin, the assassin turned away.

Something snapped in the queen. She flew at the assassin, clawing at his back.

The assassin whirled, his fist a blur.

An iron-hard punch struck her in the midriff. Like a paper doll, the single blow hurled her across the chamber. She hit the stone wall hard. Gasping for breath, she crumpled to the floor.

The assassin gave her a solemn nod. "Not in the face." Turning, he left the chamber, locking the door behind him.

Slumped against the wall, the queen struggled to breathe. Her midriff ached but her soul hurt worse. A sob threatened to escape, but she bit it back, refusing to succumb to weakness. She hadn't uttered a word, yet they'd killed Lady Claudia, severing her head out of cruel spite. Her anger warred with harsh reality. They lied. They broke their own rules. They thought they could break her. The queen's resolve annealed to hardened steel. This wasn't a game, this was war...and there were no rules. A cold certainty gripped her. She'd learn to play without rules...and somehow she'd find a way to win.

34

The Master Archivist

Sitting alone beneath the dragon, his hands caressed the royal message pouch. Taking a deep breath, the shadowmaster opened it. The pouch contained a single folded square of vellum embossed with emerald sealing wax. The wax bore the queen's seal. Leery of a forgery, he inspected the seal, but could find no fault with it. Breaking the wax, he opened the letter. Smoothing the vellum flat on the table, he exposed the words to lantern light. Her handwriting leaped up at him. Distinctive with elegant curls and swirling embellishments, he marveled that any forger could copy her hand, yet he knew it had been done. With a critical eye, he studied her signature, the slant of the writing, the confident penmanship, the familiar swirls. Everything seemed in order, yet the true proof lay in the message.

Leaning back in the chair, he began to read.

To Lord Robert Highgate, We have written you many times, bidding you return from Lingard, yet you do not come. We have sent royal couriers and even shadowmen to summon you home, and still you are not here. We worry some calamity has befallen you, yet we know how resourceful you are. Placing all our trust in your capable hands, we banish the thought that you are imperiled. Instead, we suspect that our messages have somehow gone awry. Since the bitter word of Prince Stewart's death, we have felt besieged and utterly alone. Except for our ladies-in-waiting, we begin to suspect all those around us, especially your deputy in black. We feel darkness surrounding us, choking us, reaching for our throne, yet the true threat does not yet bear a name. We have reached out to the monks, but they are dead or fled. We need you now, more than ever. Come to us in secret, but be wary lest your trust be misplaced. We pray this letter finds you safe and soon. Come to us, for our need is great. Liandra, Queen of Lanverness.

Shock hammered him.

He read the letter again, reading between the lines. Her words told more than she knew. Cocooned in a deadly web of deceit, she'd suspected the trap, but clearly her insights had come too late. His anguish bit deep. She'd needed him and he'd not been here. He cursed himself for tarrying in Lingard. He prayed to all the gods that he'd not come too late.

Standing, he paced the small room, considering all that he knew. The forgery of the queen's messages, the fanatic assassins at the inn, the state of

Pellanor, he had to assume it was all connected, a bitter web of darkness. The queen was imperiled, and he might be her last hope. A part of him wanted to rush to the castle, to kill any who stood in his way, but he dared not be rash, he dared not fail her.

He fingered her letter, reading it one last time. For a handful of heartbeats, his gaze lingered on her closing words. *Come to us, for our need is great.* Reaching up to the nearest hanging lantern, he opened the hinged glass and set the vellum inside. Her words burnt like an offering. He watched till every scrap of vellum was blackened to char, her words turned to smoke, Closing the lantern, he sent a rare prayer to the gods to lend him strength.

He strode across the room to the far wall, searching till he found the secret latch. Pressing it, he opened the hidden door.

Samantha sat in a light-filled room, sipping from a goblet. She looked up, meeting his gaze, but there was no surprise on her face. "You've decided."

It was a statement, not a question, yet he answered anyway. "Yes."

"What do you need?"

"A leather worker, the best craftsman in the city, and I need him to come here."

She did not balk at his odd request. "What else?"

"A few trusted swords."

She raised an eyebrow.

He shrugged. "I'll make do. But first the leather worker. The swords I'll need later, after I know more."

She stood. "I'll see to it."

"Thank you." His words were heartfelt. Giving her a grateful nod, he returned to the inner room to pace, and to scheme, and to wait.

35

Jemma

Her head ached and her mouth was parched. Jemma struggled to wake, assaulted by a horrible stench. A chain clanked as she moved, the sound of imprisonment. *Oh no!* Her gaze snapped wide, staring at the dim light. *Back in the attic,* her heart sank. Her left wrist was shackled, chained to the central post. Jemma yanked hard but the chain held firm. Bitterness rose like bile in the back of her throat, the snide smile of the black-clad devil haunting her. Two more strides and she would have reached the door.

The stench was appalling.

Her gaze circled the attic, and then she saw it. Jemma stifled a scream. A corpse was shoved deep under the eaves, his one-eyed face turned towards her, fixing her with an accusing stare. *The guard she'd killed!* A shiver ran down her back. They'd shoved the body under the eaves, leaving it to rot. But surely someone would smell the stench and come to investigate? Or, perhaps there was no one to come. The thought appalled her.

Jemma wasn't even sure she was still in Castle Tandroth...and no friend knew where she was. For the longest time, she sat hunched in the shadows, holding despair at bay.

Her thirst goaded her to move. She reached for the tray, pulling it towards her. The plate was empty, but she held hope for the pitcher. Liquid sloshed at the bottom. She drank from the pitcher, the water tepid and stale, but she did not care. Curbing her thirst, she forced herself to leave a few swallows for later.

The water helped clear her mind. Sitting cross-legged, she considered her prison. *No one is coming.* Somehow she had to get free.

Her gaze kept returning to the corpse.

Brute had worn a short sword and dagger sheathed at his belt. In the dim light, she could see that both sheaths were empty. Having taken the weapons, she was certain the keys would be gone as well, yet she wondered if something else might be of use. Time and again, her gaze returned to the corpse. The dead seemed her only hope.

Stretching the chain, she crawled towards the corpse. She kept her head low, lest she hit the rusty nails impaling the shingles. Holding her nose, she breathed through her mouth, appalled by the rotting stench.

The chain yanked her wrist.

Tethered, she tugged and stretched, but remained a few feet short.

Her feet! Removing her shoes, she stretched her legs towards the corpse. Her bare feet struck dead flesh. Repulsed, she flinched away. A sob threatened in the back of her throat, overcome by her plight. *No one will save me.* Taking a deep breath, she firmed her resolve. Reaching out with her feet, she levered her toes beneath his belt. Straining with her legs, she slowly pulled. At first he remained stuck, putrid slime oozing onto the floor. Twice, her toes slipped from the belt. On the third try, his head flopped forward, making a wet, sucking sound. Bile rose in the back of her throat, yet she persisted pulling the dead weight till he came within reach.

Panting, she stopped, listening for movement from below.

Hearing nothing, she turned to face the corpse. A shudder ran through her. Averting her gaze from his ruined face, she reached for his belt. Trying to still her trembling hands, she loosened the buckle and pulled it off. Both sheaths were empty and the keys were gone, but she already knew that. Her gaze roved across him. Finding nothing obvious, she resolved to check his pockets. Forcing her hands to delve each pocket, she found nothing save a few coins and a small ball of twine.

"You must have something." She stared at the corpse. Fighting her revulsion, she patted his jerkin and his pants, but her search proved futile.

Despair threatened to swamp her.

She'd expected the foul rogue to have something more, but then she had one last thought, one last hope. Jemma reached for his boots. Hidden in the right one, she found a slender dirk strapped to his lower leg. Elation thrummed through her. She drew the dirk, its slender length sharp and keen, perfect for her small hand. Jemma flashed a predator's smile, a princess with a sharp claw. And then she had another thought. Ignoring the stench, she removed the leather sheath from his leg. She strapped it to her own leg, high enough to be hidden by her gown. Sheathing the dirk, she used her feet to shove the corpse back under the eaves, and then she crawled to the mattress near the trapdoor.

Sitting cross-legged, she waited, her hand on the dirk.

She stank of death, the smell of it clinging to her hands and feet. Breathing the stench, Jemma hardened her resolve. She was still a prisoner, but now she was a prisoner with teeth.

36

Katherine

K ath spurred her horse to a thundering gallop. The countryside flew by, yet time grew late. Over her left shoulder, the red comet glowered low in the sky like a relentless goad. Setting a blistering pace, she led her small band south.

Riding from sunup to sundown, her painted warriors grew haggard, paying a harsh price for the punishing pace. Twenty-four of her maroon band, and another five wolf-faced warriors in Neven's den, set out from Navarre, all of them loyal and fierce, all of them strangers to the saddle. In the first few leagues, most took tumbles, gaining bruises and aches, yet they gamely climbed back on. Kath winced at every fall. She knew their swords would be sorely needed in Pellanor, yet she dared not slacken the pace. "Keep up or turn back. There's no other choice."

All of her warriors chose to climb back into the saddle.

Ignoring bruises and sprains, they clung to the pommels, grimly determined to follow their Svala south. But some injuries could not be ignored. Ash took a terrible fall, breaking his collarbone when his mare stumbled. Redlin broke his leg when his horse shied at a stream crossing, and Torlock died, his neck broken in a nasty fall. Kath settled the badly wounded at nearby farmsteads, offering a purse of golds to pay for their care. They buried Torlock under an oak tree, raising a rocky cairn over his grave, and then rode on. Kath mourned their loss, especially Torlock, but she dared not tarry.

Each day they rode their mounts to a lather, rubbing them down with fistfuls of grass at night. When the horses grew too weary for the grueling pace, fresh mounts appeared. Trotting from farmlands and village stables, the horses presented themselves to Danya, a boon of traveling with a Beastmaster. Danya greeted each new horse, pairing them with a rider. Giving thanks to the mounts that had served so well, Danya touched her forehead to theirs, murmuring words of praise, while the rest moved saddles and gear. Releasing their spent mounts with thanks, they rode on.

The Zward proved invaluable companions. Thaddeus and his men had a way of finding food and shelter while avoiding trouble. With the Zward serving as guides, Kath pushed the horses to a hard gallop, anxious to reach Pellanor.

Crossing a shallow stream, Thaddeus shouted, "We've reached Lanverness!"

Kath scanned the surrounding farmland, but she saw no difference between Radagar and the queen's kingdom. Leagues later she began to notice signs of the Flame War. Ivy climbed a burnt homestead, charred timbers poking skyward like fractured ribs. Summer lay warm and verdant on the land, but the green growth could not entirely hide the cost of war. Abandoned farmsteads, burnt villages, unexpected graveyards, it saddened Kath to see the scars of war upon the queen's countryside, yet she knew the Flame War was nothing compared to the Mordant's scourge.

"This way." Thaddeus steered them towards the southeast, skirting another burnt homestead.

For the most part, they shied away from roads, keeping to the back country. Her painted warriors looked too frightening with their fierce tattoos, and all of her companions bristled with weapons. To a stranger's eyes, they must look like a band of thugs summoned from nightmares. Kath doubted any would guess they served the Light. Perhaps the perception served them, for they met no trouble along the way.

The leagues flew by, but so did the days. Her painted warriors became competent riders. As they neared Pellanor, Thaddeus suggested they chance the roads at night, riding by moonlight. A half moon dipped behind the clouds, shuttering the land with darkness. Thaddeus steered the band towards a lesser-used road. "This way."

A large farmhouse sat back from the lane, flowering vines covering the front. Kath slowed her lathered mare to a walk. "Are you sure about this?"

He gave her a sharp stare. "We'll know soon enough." He slid from his horse, tying the reins to a post. Kath and Blaine joined him, both ready to draw their swords. Thad knocked on the door. "By the sword and the eye, open up!"

Lantern light bobbed in the side window.

They heard a bolt being drawn back. A small square cuff port opened in the door at eye level. The tip of a quarrel jutted out. "Who's asking?"

"Thaddeus Tokheart." Thad stepped forward, shielding Kath. "Is that you Ranoff?"

The quarrel disappeared and a brown eye gazed out.

For five heartbeats they stood in a stalemate till the moon slid from behind the clouds silvering the yard.

"Yep." The cuff port closed and another bolt was drawn back. The door opened wide. A gray-haired man with a pockmarked face lowered a heavy crossbow. "Come in. Can't be too careful these days."

Thaddeus offered his hand and the two men shook like old friends. "Where's Essie?"

"Watching the back door." His gaze raked across Kath and Blaine, lingering on their weapons, and then he glanced past them into the yard. "Tell the others there's a barn around back. They can put the horses in the pasture.

Most will have to sleep in the barn, not enough room in the house, but the hay is sweet."

Blaine went to tell the others.

The man's gaze fastened on Kath. "So you're the one."

A cold finger shivered down her back.

"Aeroth left a message for you." Easing the tension on the quarrel, he hung the crossbow on a hook by the door. "Come."

The narrow hallway opened up into a large kitchen, a cheerful fire blazing in the hearth. The smell of lamb stew pierced Kath, spiking her hunger. An older woman stood by the rear door, the loaded crossbow in her hands at odds with her checkered apron. Kath wondered when Lanverness had gotten so dangerous that honest folk greeted strangers with crossbows.

"It's them, Essie."

The woman lowered the crossbow, a smile creasing her careworn face.

"You best put more meat in the pot. We've got a horde to feed." Ranoff gestured to the large kitchen table. "Have a seat." While the woman diced carrots, he poured mugs of ale, placing one in front of Thaddeus and another in front of her. Next to Kath's ale, he placed a small bone tube. "This is for you. From Master Rizel."

Master Rizel! A second shiver traced down her back. Feeling the others' stares, she put the small tube deep in her pocket. "I'll read it later."

Blaine and Zith entered the kitchen, nodding a greeting to the woman. Blaine looked out of place with his silver surcoat and his great blue sword rearing over his right shoulder. Taking a seat at the table, he spoke to Kath. "Danya and Bear will join us once the horses and men are settled."

The woman ladled stew into wooden bowls, placing one in front of each of them. Swirling steam curled up, carrying the mouthwatering aroma of slow-cooked lamb and carrots. Kath breathed deep, savoring the smell. "Thank you for welcoming us to your hearth and home."

The woman smiled, a wisp of gray hair escaping from her bun. "You are most welcome. We all serve the Zward here."

Zith said. "All?"

"There's just the two of us now, and our son Keith."

Thaddeus tore a chunk of bread, dipping it into the stew. "Where's Keith?"

Ranoff answered. "In the city, scouting for you. He'll be back later tonight, the gods willing."

A plate shattered on the floor.

Essie jumped, stifling a scream.

Gripping her sword hilt, Kath leaped from her chair, following the woman's gaze.

Bear stood in the hallway, firelight playing across his tattooed face. "Sorry to startle." Standing half in the shadows, the big man looked like something sprung from myth.

Danya peeked from behind Bear, a hungry look on her face. "Is that stew?"

Essie flustered towards them, wiping her hands on her apron. "Yes, yes, come in, dears." She gestured them towards chairs, her gaze flicking towards Bear's face with a mixture of fascination and trepidation. "Sorry to be such a silly goose, but I've never seen your like."

Kath returned to her seat. "He's from the far north."

Ranoff groused. "That face will be a problem in the city."

Kath used a crust of bread to ladle a dollop of stew. "There's twenty-three more out back." The stew proved savory and flavorful, tasting even better than it smelled. "Bear and his men know our foe better than anyone."

Ranoff raised a bushy eyebrow.

Thaddeus said, "Tell us of the city."

Ranoff refilled their ales and then took a seat at the table. "Much has changed since you were last here." He told a grim tale, speaking of arrests in the dead of night, of executions without trials, of disemboweled corpses hung from the city gates. To Kath's ears, the litany of atrocities screamed of the Mordant. Her hand gripped the crystal dagger. "He's there." Her gaze swept her companions. "This is the Mordant's handiwork." A knot of fear tightened in her stomach. "We may have come too late."

Zith scowled, his voice vehement. "The red comet still rides the sky. We dare not lose hope." His gaze swiveled to Ranoff. "But what of the queen?"

Ranoff sighed. "Only the gods know, for the rumors make little sense. Some say she's dead. Others say she's gone mad, turned a vicious harridan since the death of her son. Either way the city is flush with fear."

Kath gaped. "Stewart's *dead?*"

"So they say, killed in a battle in the north."

"But, we heard none of this in Navarre!"

Ranoff shrugged.

Kath pushed her stew away, her stomach suddenly soured. She could not imagine Stewart dead. And Jordan, her heart ached for her swordsister. She gripped the crystal dagger, her words a deadly vow. "The Mordant has much to pay for."

The table talk stilled to ashes.

Blaine broke the silence. "More ale?"

Ranoff refilled their mugs while Essie took a pot of bubbling stew out to the men at the barn. Danya followed Essie, carrying an armful of bowls and two loaves of crusty bread. Ranoff stoked the hearth fire and then resumed his seat at the table.

Thaddeus said, "What else can you tell us of Pellanor?"

Kath sipped her ale, lost in thought, brooding over the ill-news, till she heard the word *wall*. "What? The queen has built a wall?"

Ranoff nodded. "After the Flame War, she raised a wall around the city, but it's not finished. There's a long gap in the west side." His gaze flicked to Bear. "Given the look of your men, I suggest you slip through it in the dead of night."

A wall. "Queen Liandra built a wall to protect her people...but the Mordant will use it to hold her people hostage." Her gaze slid to her companions. "That's the thing about walls, they're a two-edged sword. They can protect or they can enslave." Her voice turned hard as steel. "We'll enter Pellanor tomorrow night."

Ranoff stared. "And the Mordant? You know who he is?"

Kath answered. "We know his face, but not the colors he's wearing."

"So how will you find him?"

"We'll follow the evil."

The hearth fire snapped and crackled as if stirred, spitting sparks up the chimney.

"We'd best get some rest." Kath stood, reclaiming her saddlebag. "Can you show me to my room?"

Ranoff nodded towards her. Lifting a lantern, he led her to stairs at the back of the kitchen. "You and the brown-haired girl can share the large room at the back."

Kath shook her head. "Danya would rather sleep with Neven and the horses. Just give me your smallest room."

Astonishment marked his face. "It's little more than a cubby."

"If it has a mattress, it will be more luxury than we've had in many a night."

Shrugging, he showed her to a small room under the eaves. It really was a cubby, with a mattress on the floor and a chipped chamber pot in the corner, but the colorful patchwork quilt spread across the mattress looked warm and inviting. "This will be fine."

Ranoff lit a candle, placing it near the mattress. "You're sure?"

"I'm sure." She gave him a tired smile. "Thank you for your hospitality."

He lingered at the door. "Are you really the one?"

"Is it so hard to believe?"

He gave her a sheepish shrug. "Not what I expected."

"You thought Blaine would bear the dagger."

He did not answer, but the truth was written across his face. Chagrinned, he closed the door.

Kath sighed, her mind boggled by all the ill news. Sinking to the mattress, she dug in her pocket for the small message tube. *Master Rizel!* His name sparked hope. Kath needed counsel, but somehow she was reluctant to read the message. Removing the stopper, she teased the small roll of vellum from the tube. Spreading it flat on the floor within the candle light, she squinted to read the message. *He does not see you! Keep it that way!*

The words shivered through her soul, as if the gods heard her quandary.

Reaching for her saddlebag, she delved into the side pouch, removing the thick bundle wrapped in silk. Zith had found it hidden amongst the Mordant's treasure hoard. Telling no one else, he'd given it to her to use as she saw fit. Untying the gilded cord, she peeled back the silk layers, revealing a crystal dagger. The blade gleamed in the candlelight. Drawing her own crystal dagger from her belt sheath, she laid the two side-by-side. Hers had a slightly longer blade and the cross hilt was more rounded, but otherwise they looked nearly identical. Crystal wrought by magic, the blades were sharp and keen. At first glance, others might confuse the two, but Kath never would. She could feel the difference in her very soul. Her blade called to her with the siren's song of a bonded focus. She'd carried the second blade for nigh on several moon-turns, yet she'd never felt even a twinge of magic wakening within. Perhaps it was destined for other hands. Putting the Mordant's dagger aside, Kath fingered her own blade, feeling the call of potent magic. Kath knew the awesome power of the crystal blade, having wielded it to release the tortured souls imprisoned in the mage-stone gargoyles. She shuddered recalling their pain, souls trapped for centuries in cruel stone, enslaved to Darkness. The Mordant was a monster, but why would he keep the one blade that could damn him to Hell for all eternity? Kath stared at the second blade, unable to fathom the riddle.

She heard footsteps out in the hallway, certain they were Zith's. The monk was ever the first to seek his bedroll.

Swathing the second dagger in layers of silk, she tied the bundle with the gilded cord and hid it deep in her saddlebag. Taking the candle, she padded down the hallway, knocking softly on the nearest door.

Zith said, "Come."

She found him sitting on a bed, sorting through a tumble of golden jewelry.

Fingering a golden ring set with a huge ruby, he looked up, not surprised to see her.

Kath gestured to the jewelry, all of it from the Mordant's hoard. "Anything?"

A bitter look crossed his face. "Still nothing. I've kept these with me since we left the Citadel, even sleeping with them, but it seems I've no knack for magic." He lifted a golden torque cast in the shape of a dragon. "I like this one best. Such a showy piece, I wonder what it does." He settled the torque around his neck. The golden dragon gleamed from the hollow of his throat, wings spread wide, spiked tail lashing, inset emeralds glowing bright as eyes. "Fit for a king...or a sorcerer. What do you think?"

"Very impressive, if only we knew how to wield it."

"Even without magic, it will serve." Zith fingered the torque, his voice charged with a quiet vengeance. "I chose this one because it is so unique. The fiend is bound to recognize plunder stolen from his own hoard." His eyes flashed in the candlelight. "How angry do you think that will make him?"

She worried about him. "Careful what you wish for. You'll make yourself a target."

"Bait to catch a monster."

"Yes, but we need to catch him before he catches us."

"Just so." He fumbled adding rings to his one remaining hand, slipping his finger through them and then tugging them over his knuckle with his teeth.

Kath resisted the urge to help, knowing it would only raise his ire.

He glanced at her. "The message from Rizel?"

She handed him the small vellum strip.

He held it to the candlelight, reading it and then returned it to her. "Does this change your mind?"

"No, it adds to my conviction." She held the vellum to the flames, turning the words to smoke. "The Knight Marshal often said whatever the enemy least expects will be most effective."

"So you're planning to be unexpected."

"Yes and no. Against a thousand-year-old evil, I'm planning to be both." Sitting on the end of the bed, Kath whispered her plan.

37

Liandra

Darkness encroached, shrinking the size of her prison. Trapped by her own grim thoughts, Liandra knelt by the hearth, huddled in the small halo of light cast by the dwindling fire. She stared at the embers, at their red-hot glow. *Not the face*...the assassin's words twisted through her mind. Just this afternoon, she'd stood on the castle rampart listening to the crowd hurl accusations against her. What atrocities had the Mordant committed in her name? What nightmares plagued her city, her kingdom? She had to find a way to stop him, to foil his foul plan.

Not the face. The assassin's words were more than a warning, they were a clue.

The Mordant needed her as a pawn in his game of subterfuge.

Rage thundered through the queen, for she was no man's pawn, leastwise the Mordant's.

She stared at the embers, fascinated by the red-hot glow. One kiss of the embers to her cheek and her face would be ruined, blackened and burned, forever deformed. All who saw her would believe it was torture. They'd know she was captured. They'd know the deeds done in her name were lies. With a single burning coal, she could write the terrible truth upon her very face.

A raw hunger for justice pounded through her veins like a tempest.

Liandra leaned towards the heat, feeling the need to act. *To act*...the thought itself was seductive. As queen, she had a driving need to act, to steer the course of her own destiny, but could she ruin her own face?

The embers glowed red against the encroaching dark. She stared, both fascinated and repulsed by the possibilities. The pain she could endure, of that she was certain, but to be disfigured? To despoil her own beauty, that was the difficulty. *Image was her armor.* Could she give up her royal image, surrendering her beauty for the sake of justice?

Teetering on the edge of decision, one question plagued her above all. *Will our actions make a difference in this game of no rules?*

She pondered the question.

And then she wondered, would anyone ever know? The question pierced her. The Mordant was sly and slippery. Having no more use for her, perhaps he'd just order her killed, burying her body in an unmarked grave. Perhaps her death would help perpetuate his monstrous lies. She quaked at the thought.

Taking a deep breath, the queen considered everything she'd learned about her foe. *He lies. He plays by no rules. He is an ancient evil.* The truth was, if she sacrificed her beauty, he'd have her killed, nullifying her sacrifice. Her people would never know. Her sacrifice would make no difference. Cold logic did not lie. Such a dire gambit required an immediate advantage. Locked away in this god-forsaken tower, there was no advantage save to the Mordant.

At this point in the game, the embers were not a valid choice.

Robert, where are you?

Sighing, Liandra forced herself to stand, moving away from the heat. The queen began to pace, passing in and out of the light. Somehow, she had to find a way to foil the Mordant.

38

The Master Archivist

The Master Archivist slipped through the back alleyways, a black shadow hidden by a dark night. Alone, he made his way to the royal stables, a stone's throw away from the castle. Built during the reign of the third king, the stable was old yet solid, the stonework far too elaborate to house horses. Circling to the back, his fingers slid along the ornate wall, reading the carved embellishments. Counting seven rosebuds from the right, he depressed the eighth with his thumb while turning the nearest leaf. Beneath the stone-carved leaf was a keyhole. Keeping the chain around his neck, he inserted the skeleton key and turned.

A soft grinding sound issued from the wall. A hidden door eased open, releasing a breath of stale air. He slipped inside, quickly triggering the mechanism. The stone door ground shut, sealing the stairs in a tomb-like darkness.

Lowering his sack to the floor, he blindly searched till he found the hooded lantern and the striker. The lantern blazed bright, casting an island of light. Lifting the lantern, he inspected the steep stairway. Cobwebs blocked the path, telltale proof the queen had not used the hidden passageway to escape the castle. Donning his armor, he descended the stairs. The scent of mildew clung to the walls, a stone-cloistered chill reaching for him. Anxious to find the queen, he hurried down the stairs and along the narrow passageway.

From out of the darkness, the first face appeared. Carved on the inner wall, the jester had onyx eyes that glittered in the lantern light. Shuttering the lantern, the shadowmaster removed the onyx plugs, setting his face to the eye holes. The secret spy hole gave him a view of a castle corridor. Torchlight glinted along the marble hall. He recognized a tapestry, vivid reds and oranges showing an autumn hunting scene. Glancing down the hallway, he saw a pair of guards at the far door. *Guards in emerald tabards,* but were they friends or foes? The spy hole gave him nothing but more questions. Frustrated, he replaced the onyx plugs, unshuttered the lantern, and continued deeper into the castle.

Honeycombed with a labyrinth of secret passageways, Castle Tandroth was much more than a sumptuous palace. The queen's ancestors had wrought well, anticipating the need for hasty escapes, hidden refuges, and clever spy holes. A stone-carved secret preserved through the centuries, the castle served the Tandroths well, a hidden ally in times of turmoil. During the Red Horn rising, the castle had been key in crushing the rebellion. Now a threat of a different sort ensorcelled Pellanor. The shadowmaster prayed the queen had found safe refuge in the castle's hidden ways.

He yearned to sprint to the Queen's Tower, hoping to find her safe in the royal bolt hole, but he dared not get lost in the labyrinth. Raising the lantern, he checked the walls as he walked. The queen had taught him many of the castle's tricks, but not all.

Stone-carved faces stared as he passed. Their onyx eyes were tempting. At first, he tried them all, but he gleaned little for the time lost. The castle slumbered, any skullduggery put away for the night. The spy holes revealed nothing of the enemies plaguing Pellanor, and he caught no glimpse of the queen. Frustrated, he resolved to ignore the onyx eyes, racing to the Queen's Tower.

A stone crown marked the way. The passageway tightened to stairs spiraling up through the tower walls. The dust and cobwebs were smeared and broken, proving the passageway had been used. His hope quickened.

Reaching the top, he found a crowned king staring from the door. Inserting the key into the king's mouth, he unlocked the mechanism. The stone door shuddered open, revealing a finger of light. Unsheathing his short sword, he leaped through the doorway into the secret chamber.

A single candle on the far side revealed a splash of bright silk. Lady Sarah held a shaking sword, the other ladies huddled behind her. Terror filled their faces, their eyes wide with fright.

"Where is the queen?"

She pointed the shaking sword at him. "I'll not tell you, demon!"

Demon? The shadowmaster glanced down, seeing dust and cobwebs clinging to his leathers, and then he remembered his mask. Armor against the assassins' killing darts, he supposed the form-fitting leather mask must cast a frightening sight. He eased it up on his forehead. "Don't you know me?"

"*Lord Robert!*" The sword clattered to the floor. Lady Sarah raced across the distance, flinging herself into his arms. "You came! You came!"

Her desperate embrace ambushed him, proof of her dire fright. Awkward in her arms, he gave her a gentle pat. "I'm here now. Where is the queen?"

Stifling a sob, she released him. Taking a step back, she struggled to restore decorum. "Pardon, my lord, it's just that we've been so long alone."

"I'm here now," he made his voice soothing, "but I need you to tell me everything. Where is the queen?"

Fear spiked her voice. "That's just it, my lord, I don't know where they took her!"

"*They?*"

"The Mordant's men."

The Mordant! He shivered, feeling the threat of ancient Darkness. *Assassins with uncanny powers and arcane runes emblazoned on their arms.* He should have realized this foe was not of the southern kingdoms.

Lady Sarah's voice quavered, fraught with desperation. "I know it sounds impossible, but if you'd only seen him! He has the Evil Eye, the way he stares at you, as if he could damn your soul!"

"I believe you."

"You...do?" She gave him a hesitant look.

He guided her to a chair at the map-painted table. "I need you to tell me everything. The smallest detail might help me save the queen."

She took a steadying breath. "The Mordant is the Prince of Ur."

The revelation hit him like a punch to the gut. So the ancient bastard came cloaked in lies. He should have never left his queen. "Tell me everything."

She told a harrowing tale of a spider-like assassin crouched at the queen's window, of Sir Durnheart's valiant death, of ladies-in-waiting callously killed, of the Mordant confronting the queen in her own chambers, but nothing gave any clue to Liandra's whereabouts.

"And you've not seen or heard anything of the queen since then?"

"No, my lord," her voice turned tremulous, "but they've been tapping on the walls. With the way we disappeared, they must know about the secret passageways, searching for a way in."

"The Tandroth's built well. They'll not find this refuge without a proper key." He prayed he was right, for their enemy was the Mordant. *The Mordant!* His very name invoked terror.

The other women huddled close, as if they feared the shadows.

Lady Sarah said, "What now, my lord?"

"Now, I'll take you to a safe place in the city, and then I'll come back to search for the queen."

"And what of the Prince of Ur?"

His voice turned ice-cold. "The Mordant deserves death." *If such a fiend can be killed.* "But my first duty is to the queen. Her safety matters above all else." He spoke the words like a vow. "Come, time grows short." Taking up the lantern, he ushered the women towards the inner passageway. *Time grows short.* He felt the shadows nipping at his heels like a pack of slavering jackals. *The Mordant!* In the depths of his heart, he prayed the queen still lived.

39

The Priestess

T he Priestess glided down the staircase, trailing a scent of allure. Stares snapped towards her like iron to a lodestone. Guards and servants ogled outright while the black-clad assassins sent sly glances slinking her way. She gathered their stares, evaluating their intensity. Two assassins were already hers, but more would be better. A tall red-headed guard with broad shoulders looked particularly promising. The Priestess answered his stare with a smoldering look. Dropping her gaze to the bulge in his trousers, she wantonly licked her lips. He stiffened at his post, the bulge becoming more prominent. Raising her stare, she gave him a not-so-subtle smile, wondering if he'd dare make his way to her bedroom.

As if her smile was not enough of a lure, she glided close to him, her perfume trailing a tantalizing tease.

His stare hungered as she sauntered past, sizzling through her silken gown.

The Priestess smiled. Corrupting the Mordant's men had become her favorite pastime. Two could play at the game of souls. The Mordant was vastly older, and more powerful, but a Dark succubus was never to be trifled with, especially the Priestess of the Oracle. Seduction was her favorite weapon, but her threats were far more than just beauty-deep. Fingering her poison-tipped ring, an eager smile graced her lovely face. Vengeance would be hers, one way or another.

The Priestess dallied her way through the mansion, gathering stares while collecting snatches of conversations. Scrying showed her much, but she needed more, seeking the best way to spoil the Mordant's plans.

Suddenly fond of the rear rose garden, she'd taken to wandering the topiaries at all hours of the day and night, making a show of enjoying the fresh air and the summer blooms. Her culinary tastes grew sharply refined, prompting her to seek out the cooks in the kitchen, cajoling them into making her favorite dishes. Her most lucrative destination was the hallway between the kitchen and the throne room. Standing in the shadowy corridor, pretending to oversee the kitchen, she could eavesdrop on the Mordant as he gave orders to his minions.

Lingering over a fresh-blooming rose, she felt her guard stiffen as if he'd discovered a burr under his armor. Somehow they always knew when the Mordant sought attendance in the throne room.

Plucking a yellow rose, she meandered through the garden, returning to the manse. The tempting smell of fresh-baking cinnamon bread teased the hallway, drawing her to the kitchen. Sampling a taste of the fluffy white frosting, she flattered the cook, and then she slipped to her favorite post in the hallway. Standing deep in the shadows, she was obscured from the throne room, yet close enough to listen.

Her guard smirked, aware of her ruse, yet there were never any repercussions.

Perhaps he never told the Mordant...or perhaps the oldest harlequin cared not if she listened. Her pride bristled. The arrogant monster ignored her at his peril. Smothering her anger, she turned her head to listen.

The Mordant's voice pierced the shadows. "I will hear a report on the reaping."

A deep voice answered, most likely Major Tarq. "Two hundred and seventy-three citizens were arrested in the night's reaping. Of these, thirty-seven were women. As per your order, the women were raped and released. The rest are imprisoned in the dungeon, awaiting their fate."

The Mordant snapped. "Details, major, we need details. Speak of the arrests."

"All the arrests were made in the queen's name. Parchments were waved and crimes were cited. The accused were outraged, swearing their innocence. Some tried to flee, but most acted like sheep. Facing hardened soldiers in green tabards, they chose to submit while protesting their innocence. The night proved poor sport, for there was very little bloodshed."

"The pale milk-water of civilization flows in their veins. They rely on the rule of law instead of the rule of fear." The Mordant sounded smug. "What of the city?"

A different voice answered. "Rumors run amok in the markets. The people speak of the arrests, but their whispers seem hesitant, hushed, wary, as if they do not know what to make of the arrests."

The Mordant said, "They delude themselves, wanting to believe the arrests are lawful." She heard a predator's hunger in his arrogant voice. "Whom do they blame?"

"Most whisper the queen's name...but their anger is tempered with excuses. Many seem more shocked than outraged."

"So they do not yet believe. They cling to their delusion of justice. That will change once their loved ones hang from the city gates."

The Priestess grew bored, taking little interest in the city's suffering.

"What do the rumors say regarding the Princess of Navarre?"

A princess of Navarre! The Priestess stiffened.

A hesitant voice answered, "The rumors are scarce, as if the people do not believe the queen will harm her."

So one of her kin was in Pellanor!

"They'll believe when the scaffold rises in the marketplace." The Mordant's voice hardened to a command. "Spread rumors through the city that the queen holds a princess of Navarre hostage for birth-magic. Say she'll behead the princess, risking war for the sake of her empty womb."

Behead the princess! A towering rage roared through the Priestess. She began to back away lest her anger betray her. Her fists clenched, she climbed the stairs, seeking the seclusion of her chambers. Locked in a blind rage, she did not hear anything, she did not see anything. The Mordant trespassed on her family! A god-sworn threat whispered from her ruby lips like a blood-oath. *"No one kills my kin but me!"*

40

Katherine

Waiting till the small hours of the morning, they released their horses and crept on foot towards the queen's city. A barn owl glided overhead on silent wings. In a distant voice, Danya said, "The way is clear."

Kath gestured to the Zward captain. Crouched behind a bramble bush, she watched as Thaddeus led her small band of warriors towards the long gap in the wall, their dark cloaks blending into the shadows. A scowl rode her face. She hated waiting while others crept towards danger, but waiting was a necessary part of the plan.

The moon slipped from behind a cloud bank, silvering the landscape. Kath tensed, her hand on her sword hilt, but there was no cry from the walls. She watched as her hooded warriors slipped into the city. At least the moon had not betrayed them. Kath would have preferred a darker night, but time favored the Mordant.

Beside her, Blaine whispered, "How long?"

Kath settled down to wait. "As long as it takes."

The barn owl circled overhead and then glided to the ground beside Danya. The wolf-girl reached out with a gentle hand, stroking the owl's tawny feathers. "The city's a trap."

Kath kept her gaze on the long gap in the wall. "Of course it is, a trap set by the Mordant. But knowing it is a trap gives us an advantage."

Zith groused. "A slim advantage."

"Never forget we're playing against a thousand-year-old evil. We'll need all the advantages we can get." She'd learned much about her foe in the Dark Citadel. The throne basilica proclaimed his godlike arrogance, the hidden treasure hoard betrayed his lust for magic, while the cave-crypt beneath the Citadel screamed of his sadistic malevolence. Kath shuddered, remembering. But she'd also learned about the duegar, and how he used the snargon to sniff magic. Her lip curled with distaste, certain the queen's city was infested with twisted dwarves. *Snargons and black-clad assassins*...together they turned Pellanor into a potent trap. As soon as they entered with magic, the trap would be tripped, the hourglass turned. And time favored the Mordant. Kath gripped Duncan's warrior ring, sending a prayer to Valin.

Beside her, Blaine fell asleep, issuing hushed snores.

From her other side, Zith glared. "How can he sleep?"

"Sleep of the just." Kath smiled. "Let him sleep, there's no one near to hear."

The moon journeyed across the night sky, slipping in and out of clouds.

Just when sleep began to tempt her, a hooded lantern winked twice in the gap.

"They're ready for us." Kath woke Blaine.

The barn owl soared aloft, gliding along the gap in the wall.

Danya said, "All clear."

Kath rose to a crouch, pulling her sword from her scabbard. "Come on." Staying low, she led her companions towards the lantern light. The night remained hushed, a soft blanket upon the land. She reached the gap and found Thaddeus waiting. "The way is clear." With a deliberate stride, she entered the queen's city. A finger of unease trickled down her back. Kath shivered, knowing the trap was sprung, the hourglass turned. May all the gods grant her strength, for she'd reached the Battle Immortal.

41

The Mordant

Civilization created a heavy delusion, a sense of justice swathed in prosperity. The delusion ran deep in Pellanor. The people clung to the queen's laws, raising them like a shield against injustice. The Mordant intended to show the rabble the error of their ways. To change the past as well as the future, he'd shatter their close-held delusions.

Twice he'd roamed the queen's city at night, marking the lintels of the good with lamb's blood. His Dark Gift only enabled him to scent souls laden with Darkness, yet its absence was more than enough to condemn. Clad in emerald tabards, his men sought out the blood-marked homes. Spewing accusations of crimes, they arrested one member of each household, everything done in the queen's good name. Legal papers were traded for the lives of loved ones. Outraged, the accused swore their innocence. Some tried to flee, but most acted like sheep. Facing hardened soldiers in green tabards, they chose to submit, protesting their innocence with nothing but words. Such a feeble defense, the night proved poor sport, for there was very little bloodshed.

The bloodshed came three days later when one hundred and fifty nine citizens were dismembered and hung from the city walls. Blood and gore stained the queen's city, yet still the people did not believe. Seeing was not always believing.

The Mordant sent his duegars scurrying through the city, eavesdropping on markets and taverns. His listeners returned bearing bushel-loads of excuses. Some blamed the queen's advisors, a few said the queen had gone mad with grief, but many whispered the accused crimes had to be true. They argued that Good Queen Liandra would never execute the innocent, therefore the dead, by definition, were guilty.

The city turned sullen. The people went about their business, but they kept to themselves, burying their fears beneath hard-held delusions.

The Mordant kept watch, amazed by their naivety. He considered roaming the city a third time, marking more lintels with blood, but instead he decided to take a more insidious approach. Deceit was ever his best weapon. He decided to woo the city with lies.

From his ironbound jewel chest, he chose the medallion-shaped cameo carved from bone. Exquisitely wrought, the cameo portrayed a two-headed relief, a woman facing left and a man facing right. The two-faced focus was one of his favorites. Pinning it to his cloak, he invoked the magic within. In the mirror, his face appeared to melt. His hair turned iron-gray, his face elongated, a mustache sprouting over his lip. His skin withered with age, deep-cast lines of wisdom etched his face. His bright blue eyes darkened to brown, swirling with layered depths. The face of a young monk transformed into the face of powerful wizard, though none now alive would recognize it. Clad in gray robes, the Mordant added a stoop to his shoulders, completing the illusion.

A wave of dizziness swamped him, the price of magic. He leaned against the wall, gulping deep breaths until he recovered. The weakness passed, the magic steadying under his control.

The Mordant reached for the crystal of pain, placing it deep in his right pocket. In his left pocket, he placed the malachite coin. The coin still remained indifferent to his touch, but that would change with time. Taking a last glance in the mirror, he stepped from his solar.

Four assassins and a snargon braced upon seeing him.

Wielding the crystal, he speared them with pain, announcing his true presence. The snargon groaned, falling to his knees in agony, but the assassins only grimaced, their teeth clenched against the agony. Pleased with their response, he released them from pain. "Come, we have work to do this night."

He led them from the manse, out into the city streets. The night was still young, lantern light spilling from taverns and homes. The Mordant roamed the streets, listening to whispered gossip, but the pickings proved lean. The queen's people had grown tight-lipped, becoming wary of strangers, yet the taverns were full, overflowing with people seeking liquid solace.

Abandoning the streets, he sought out the more popular taverns. Roaming from the poor quarter to the rich, and back again, he stayed at each tavern for the turn of an hourglass, just long enough to plant well-wrought lies before moving on. His gold made him welcome, buying tankards of ale for those who would listen. Embraced by his new-bought friends, the Mordant joined the rowdiest tables, spinning tales against the queen. Whispering of innocents slaughtered and justice perverted, he claimed the crimes spouted by the queen's soldiers were trumped up lies. Reminding them of the dismembered bodies hanging from the city's walls, he painted the queen as a vicious and vindictive ruler, a ruthless woman controlled by vanity and her womb. Having tilled the soil, he planted the lies he most wanted believed. "I'll tell you something I heard in the marketplace."

They leaned forward, eager to hear.

"The queen is holding a princess of Navarre hostage for magic."

"Magic!" The word ensnared imaginations, echoing through the tavern. "What sort of magic?"

The Mordant lowered his voice to a whisper. "The sort that quickens wombs!"

Gasps echoed around him. Ensnared by a tale of magic spiced with sex, the listeners leaned in, demanding more.

"Age has nearly caught her. The queen is desperate for a fresh heir. So she holds the princess ransom, demanding that Navarre yield its birth magic."

Someone grumbled. "But Navarre is our ally!"

"The seaside kingdom is our friend!"

"What if they don't yield?"

It was the question he'd waited for. "Then the queen will behead the princess, sending a lesson to Navarre."

An older man, more sober than most, blurted. "But that will mean war!"

"True enough." The Mordant gave a solemn nod. "She'll drag your sons to war for the sake of her empty womb." He leaned towards his listeners, his voice low and earnest. "That's what comes from putting a woman on the throne."

"*Lies!*" The accusation hurled from the far side of the great room. "You lie!

The Mordant's listeners pulled away as if scalded, uncertainty washing across their ale-sodden faces.

On the far side of the tavern, a tall, lean man clad in brown hunting leathers stood. Pointing an accusing finger at the Mordant, his voice pierced the drunken murmurs. "You *reek* of lies! Do not listen to this one! Everything about him reeks of deceit!" In the lantern light, the man's eyes gleamed unnatural. They gleamed bright gold.

A truthsayer! The Mordant stood, keeping a tight rein on his magic lest he lose his disguise. He stared at his accuser. He'd seen such eyes before, in the cavern beneath the Dark Citadel. "You have the eyes of a cat, the eyes of a beast, yet you dare accuse me, a man of worth?"

"I am Zolten of the Deep Green and this one reeks of lies! Can't you smell his rot? He lies about the queen and he lies about himself. He is cloaked in lies! Believe him not!"

This was no mere drunken lout, but a god-touched truthsayer. The Mordant pointed a damning finger at his accuser. "This one is mine! Kill the rest! Kill them all!"

Patrons stared slack-mouthed, locked in drunken disbelief.

Assassins erupted from the shadows. Wielding blow guns and knives, they waded into the crowd, slaying everyone in their path. Screams erupted through the tavern. Some ran for the doors, while others cowered under tables, but there was no escape and there was nowhere to hide. Death came calling, spilling blood on the ale-soaked floor.

Amidst the chaos, the Mordant stood fast, his gaze locked on the cat-eyed man.

Across the room, the truthsayer drew a long knife from his belt. Accepting the Mordant's cold-eyed challenge, he pushed through the panicked crowd.

Seeing the knife, patrons lurched away, opening a path to the Mordant.

The Mordant smiled with ill intent. Magic rippled around him as he loosed his disguise.

"Even your face is a lie!" The cat-eyed man lunged, his long knife poised to strike.

Gripping the red crystal, the Mordant sent a bolt of pain at his accuser.

The truthsayer stumbled, his face a snarl of agony, yet he staggered forward, the knife clutched in his fist.

The Mordant doubled the pain. He imagined the man's spine being snapped in two.

A scream roared from the cat-eyed man, yet he crawled towards the Mordant. "What...are...you?"

"I...am...Darkness!" A final bolt of pain contorted the man till his bones snapped. The truthsayer slumped dead at the Mordant's feet, his golden eyes forever shuttered. The Mordant prodded the body with his boot, knocking the knife from the corpse's outstretched hand.

Around him, the screaming chaos subsided to silence.

Blood and bodies littered the floor.

Sheathing their knives, his assassins stood unscathed, awaiting orders.

"Torch it." The Mordant reached for the magic of the cameo. He changed his face, caring not what he looked like. Emerging from the tavern with two assassins as escorts, he made his way back through the night-shrouded streets. Behind him, the tavern burst into flames. *A truthsayer in the queen's city!* This was an enemy he could not abide. Rage thundered through him, for he sensed the interference of hostile gods. *A truthsayer!* The Light sought to meddle, yet their truthsayer was dead, and the Mordant was forewarned. This was *his* time, *his* destiny. Nothing would interfere, not even the gods.

42

Katherine

Kath stared from the shop window, watching the morning bustle in the streets. *Pellanor*...her hand drifted down to grip the crystal dagger. Watching but not seeing, she felt the sands of time running out. Pellanor was a trap within a trap. She'd followed the Mordant to the queen's city, come to outfox a thousand-year-old evil. Worry and doubt weighed her shoulders like a cast-iron cloak.

Something brushed against her leg. Startled, she stared down to find an orange tabby scribing runes around her boots.

"Meow!"

Kath gently shooed the cat away.

Blaine joined her at the window. "Anything?" Sheathed at his belt, he carried another crystal dagger.

"Not yet."

His great sword reared over his right shoulder, the hilt wrapped in worn leather to hide its true color. A hooded cloak of dark wool hid his surcoat, but to Kath's eyes it wasn't much of disguise. *When had his shoulders gotten so broad?* He looked like a champion, he looked like a hero.

"It's hard to wait."

"I know." The truth was, Kath didn't intend to wait. Keeping all their magic in one place made them a potent target. It made them bait. Far better to scatter across the city, to confuse the enemy, to weave many trails of magic. And while they scattered, they'd press their own hunt, seeking the Mordant. "We'll leave soon."

"You think the duegar will find us? Follow us?"

"That's what they do."

He fingered the crystal dagger at his belt. "And now I'm bait too?"

"I think so. But maybe not."

He gave her a puzzled look.

"The crystal daggers feel...different. Perhaps the duegar can't track them." Kath shrugged. "Or maybe they can. Either way, I'm most worried about Danya."

"Why?"

"Her magic is very old and very powerful. According to the monks, the Mordant has long lusted after the power of a beastmaster. I imagine her silver cuff leaves a potent scent for the cursed duegars. That's why I've asked the maroon band to protect her." Tension tightened across her shoulders like a taut bowstring. "The sooner we find the Mordant's lair the better." Kath rolled her shoulders, trying to ease the strain. "Perhaps Danya's learned something." Turning away from the window, she made her way to the rear of the cobbler's shop. Climbing the stairs two at a time, she nearly tripped over another cat. This one was dark as smoke from a chimney. Circling her legs, he followed her up the stairs.

Rapping three times, Kath entered the back room.

The dark cat bolted through the opening, making a beeline for Danya.

Neven tensed, his gaze on the doorway. Seeing Kath, he eased his hand from his sword hilt.

Kath nodded to him. They were all on edge. The wolf-faced warrior stood in a protective stance behind Danya, while Gris watched from the rear window.

The wolf-girl sat cross-legged on the floor, a dozen cats milling around her.

"*Cats?*" Kath stared at the swirling scrum. "Why cats?"

From the far side of the room, Bryx chuffed in disgust, as if he shared her question.

Danya gave her a distracted smile. "Some animals can see the true colors of our souls."

A shiver slid down Kath's back.

Danya gave her a knowing smile. "Not all animals, just the ones closest to mankind, the ones who are attuned to us, horses, dogs and cats. Dogs are the best at soul-seeing, but people notice them too much, so they don't make good spies."

"Cats are better?"

Danya snuggled an orange-striped tabby. "Most people ignore cats because they think cats ignore them."

This was one of the strangest conversations Kath had ever had. "So, you're saying cats don't ignore people?"

"No, they pay attention more than you think. They're great at pretending not to care. Some cats take indifference to an art form." She shrugged. "I guess it's how they keep their aloof sense of superiority."

"What about birds? Why not use birds as spies?"

"Because birds truly are indifferent to us. We're beings of the earth, bound to the ground, while they are beings of the air, soaring among the very clouds. When they fly, we're nothing but distant specks far beneath them. Birds see us the way we see ants."

"But you used the ravens to bring a warning to the Pit?"

"That was just a game to the ravens. Birds can't see our souls. To birds we all look alike."

"What about the giant frost owls the monks use?"

Danya looked away. "They're...different."

Kath did not want to ask. "So cats, then."

Danya nodded. "If you see a cat staring at you, pay attention."

"But I can't talk to cats."

"You'll figure it out. Animals have a way of communicating...when they have something to say."

Something soft butted against Kath's shin. She looked down to see two cats entwining her legs, one dusty gray and the other snow-white with black-tipped paws. Tails held high, they moved around her legs, weaving intricate knot patterns only cats could understand.

"They're remembering you."

This conversation was beyond strange. "If you say so, you're the beastmaster."

"I'm not."

Startled, Kath stared at her.

"The Painted People have the truth of it." Danya stroked an orange tabby, cradling it close. "I'm not a beastmaster, I'm a beastspeaker." She stared up at Kath, a hint of pleading in her warm brown eyes. "I'll talk with them, I'll explain about the Mordant, I'll ask for help...but I'll never ask them to kill again."

"I know."

Her voice dropped to a whisper. "You have to be Dark to be a beastmaster." She clutched the cat close. "I don't want Darkness in my soul."

Kath wanted to tell Danya that she'd lost the Quickner and that she needed more help...but she couldn't, especially when the wolf-girl had already done so much. "I know."

Danya smiled then, a mixture of warmth and relief. "I know you know, that's why I agreed to come south."

"Thank you."

Danya released the orange tabby. "They'll find the Mordant for you."

"And I'll do the killing."

"Just so."

She nodded towards Danya. "You take care."

"And you."

Kath turned away. Carefully stepping around the menagerie of meowing cats, she made her way to the door. Her hand sought the crystal dagger, needing to feel the solid assurance. Kath knew she'd never hesitate to strike a killing blow at the Mordant...but after talking with Danya, she wondered if it meant she had Darkness in her soul. Perhaps the gods and the beasts were the only ones who truly knew.

43

Tingold

Tingold flitted from roof to roof, watching the streets below. Dawn rose golden over the queen's city, waking the streets to a lively bustle. A maddening confusion of scents and sounds, the city was unbelievably vast, a sea of houses stretching to the horizon. Crowded and sprawling at the same time, it made him yearn for the wide openness of the steppes.

The south was such a strange place. Teeming with multitudes, they herded themselves into stone-walled cities, as if they feared the land. Soft and superstitious, southerners were an odd breed. Most flinched at first sight of his tattoos, not understanding the strength they gave him. Forced to hunt from the shadows, Tingold flashed a feral grin.

Reaching a cobbled crossroad, he climbed to the roof's pointy apex and perched like a gargoyle behind the stone chimney. The vantage gave him a good view of the crossroads and the market. People in colored cloaks swirled through the marketplace, trading stamped bits of metal for food. A sneer rode his face. Coins seemed so dishonest, for how could anyone ever know their true worth? Far better to trade goods for goods, where both parties saw the bargain's value. Coins were one of the many strange riddles he did not understand about the south.

Listening to the competing din of hawkers and hagglers, he scanned the crowd for dwarves. In the north, he'd hunted priests in the Dark Citadel with Blaine. In the south, he hunted snargons for the Svala. Tingold reveled in the hunt, but the two were very different. One was like hunting saber cats in their rocky dens, the other like stalking deer on the open steppes. In the north, the priests hid like vipers in the bowels of the citadel, afraid to show their faces. Here in the south, the Svala expected the swarthy duegar to blatantly roam the streets, mingling with the crowds, searching for magic. *Hounds of the Mordant!* A snarl rode his tattooed face. It shocked him that these soft southerners did not know what walked among them.

Crouched behind the chimney, Tingold scanned the crowd for prey. Sidhorn wanted to capture a dwarf and carve him till he talked, but Bear said the snargons were too deep in the Mordant's thrall to ever utter a word of betrayal. Tingold sided with Sidhorn, yet he'd sworn to obey. The Svala wanted the snargons followed, to find the Mordant's lair. Only if a snargon caught the scent of the Svala and her companions, was he permitted to kill.

It was a good plan, a wise plan. The Svala sought the battlefield, seeking to ambush the oldest enemy's lair. A hungry grin split his tattooed face. His knives were sharp and keen, but first he would watch. Crouched on the roof like a gargoyle, Tingold pulled his hood forward to shadow his face and settled down to wait.

44

Liandra

Boredom hounded the queen. Such an insidious torture, tedious days with nothing to do. Dull boredom slowly eroded her will and mothballed her mind. Liandra languished on the bed. All her life she'd been hardworking, and now her days dragged by, locked in a remote tower. There was nothing worse than a queen who did not matter. Never before had she felt so impotent, so alone, so forsaken.

A key turned in the lock.

Liandra straightened, keen for anything to dispel the boredom.

The door opened...and Commander Trax stood waiting. "Come."

Come, just come, no gowns, no serving women, no explanation, just a simple, naked command. Her mind quickened, tumbling the riddle. The answer struck like a dagger in the back. *He summons us to our death.* Taking a deep breath, she resolved to meet her fate as a queen. Smoothing her rumpled gown, her head held high, she followed him to the tower stairs. A pair of soldiers in green tabards strode close behind, another false honor guard.

The commander led her down and out of the ancient tower, into the castle's marbled hallways. Taking the less-used corridors, he wove a circuitous path, as if avoiding other people. *He does not want us to be seen!* The queen's heartbeat quickened, viewing the twists and turns as an omen of death. Her ringed hands tightened into fists. She expected to be led to the dungeons, but instead the corridors brightened with tapestries and gilded sconces. They'd reached the heart of the castle, entering the Queen's Tower. *Perhaps they need us after all!* Her hope soared as they climbed the stairs.

Soldiers in green tabards stood guard outside her solar doors. They snapped to attention. For half a heartbeat, she enjoyed the illusion.

Commander Trax gave her a piercing glare. "Do not disappoint."

The doors were opened and the queen swept alone into her solar.

Liandra hoped to find her women waiting, but that hope was soon dashed.

An enemy sat at her desk. A fat, toad-of-a-man, clad in sumptuous robes of imperial purple, the Great Wyrm embroidered above his heart like a bold-faced lie. He sat at *her* desk, fingering *her* quills. Outrage roared though her. She glared at him, feeling defiled.

"Ah, the queen." He waved her peacock quill, gesturing to a chair set before the desk.

The queen remained standing.

His fat, jowly face quivered to a smile. "Stubborn, yes," he flicked the quill in admonishment. "We all know you're stubborn, but that misguided choice will only bring you pain." Waving the peacock quill like a wand, he gestured to the chair, his voice dripping with mock courtesy. "Please, take a seat."

The queen remained standing, her stare boring into him, outraged that he touched her things.

His beady gaze flicked to the quill and then back to her. "This is your favorite, isn't it?" A hefty chuckle poured out of him. "I knew it! I recognized its firm line at once. You use it for your most important correspondence. A lovely quill, with a firm nib, a smooth ink flow, and the added flamboyance of a peacock feather. Yes, this quill is truly you."

Understanding struck. "The *forger*." She made the word a curse.

"Not a forger," he grinned in admonishment, "an artist!" His fat hands danced across her quills and ink bottles with covetous caresses. There was something obscene about the way he fingered her writing instruments, as if he defiled her very soul.

"Yes, you have a lovely assortment of the finest quills and inks." He flashed a satisfied smile. "As an artist, it's such a rare pleasure for me to sit at *your* desk, to use *your* quills, *your* vellum, *your* sealing wax. It elevates my art to another level. Almost as if I become you!" He laughed, his fat cheeks quaking. "And I must say, my dear, your script is one of the most elaborate I've ever attempted. All those swirls and elaborate curlicues, but I was equal to the challenge!" He beamed in triumph. "And now, with this," he gestured to her desk as if it held a feast, "my art will be perfected! No one will ever suspect!"

Rage engulfed her. She wanted to rush at him and claw his eyes out...but a dark-clad assassin stood guard, watching from the shadows. "What do you want?"

Her somber voice pricked his amusement. Leaning back in the chair, he sighed like a deflated bellows. "And here I thought we might have an amiable discussion of the finer points of calligraphy, but you are all dour, nothing but dull business. So be it." From the desk drawer, he removed a vellum document illuminated with elaborate script. Even from across the desk, she could tell it was a masterwork of calligraphy.

"Come, you are to sign this."

A cold chill feathered down her back. "Why, when you do it so well?"

A laugh burst out of his fat face. "I do! Don't I?" He sobered. "But flattery aside, the Mordant seeks your true signature."

She felt the trap closing around her. "He seeks my soul."

"Of course, it's what he does, collects, twists, shatters souls. Most succumb with a single glance." He gave her a piercing look. "So far you've avoided the anvil, but no longer."

The queen gestured to the vellum with her gaze. "And this is to be our anvil?"

He grinned. "No, this is your surrender." His gaze hardened. "The Pentacle will be your anvil."

His voice carried an ominous threat, yet the words made little sense.

"Deny the Mordant your soul, and your body will be fodder for the Pentacle." He flashed a sinister smile. "A sacrifice to the Dark God."

The queen stiffened.

"A most unpleasant way to die." His gaze drilled into her. "Heed the warning." He gestured to the vellum. "One signature and you escape such an ill fate."

One signature and we damn our soul. Fear stalked her, yet the queen remained statue-still. "What is the nature of this decree?"

"Come and read it for yourself."

Noting he was right-handed, she circled the desk, choosing to approach on his dominant side. He slanted the decree towards her, making it easy to read. Illuminated with gold and silver leaf, the calligraphy was both elaborate and exquisite. "Your work?"

"Of course."

Her gaze skimmed across the elaborate titles and hollow formalities, seeking the grim heart of the matter. She stumbled on a familiar name entangled with an old ploy. The queen read the hateful words aloud. "By choosing to withhold magic that would enable the Queen of Lanverness to bear a rightful heir, Navarre is declared an enemy of our kingdom. In recompense, the life of Princess Jemma is held forfeit. The Rose Crown hereby decrees...," Liandra raised her gaze from the vellum. "This is a death sentence."

He grinned up at her. "So it is."

Liandra felt ashamed that she hadn't thought of the princess in days. "The Mordant pushed this gambit before."

"That was subtle, this is not." He offered her the peacock quill. "Now you know the true depth of your woe. One signature spares you from a most dire fate."

The queen suppressed a shudder.

"If it's the princess you're worried about, you needn't concern yourself. Her fate is sealed whether you sign or not. She'll be executed on the morrow, her head sent in a basket to King Ivor, everything done with pomp and circumstance, all in your good name." He pressed the quill upon her. "Your stubbornness will not save the princess, yet with one signature, you spare yourself excruciating pain."

She felt detached, one part of her mind cold and calculating, the other dazed by the horror of it all.

"Take the quill and sign."

"Not the peacock quill." She reached for the raven-feathered quill. Inspecting the nib, she found it broad and sure, the sides sharp and keen as a knife. "Yes, this will do."

The forger grinned. "A bold choice." He unstoppered the gall-iron ink, moving the bottle towards her.

"No, not the black. For the signing of our soul, we'll use the vermillion."

"Ah, the red!" He stoppered the black ink and reached for the red. "I found this ink color to be particularly bothersome to copy."

The queen answered as if in a daze. "Yes, the color depends on the quality of the cinnabar. We purchased the mine, one of our many investments." She removed the stopper from the blood-red ink, carefully setting it aside lest it stain the vellum.

"But it's not just the cinnabar, it's something else, perhaps a binding agent?"

She loaded the quill with ink. "Tincture of arsenic."

Everything came into sharp focus, the fat forger leaning forward like a vulture, the assassin skulking in the shadows, the vellum scribed with a sentence of death. Her entire reign came down to a single stroke of the quill. For half a heartbeat, Liandra held the quill poised above the vellum. Changing her grip, she stuck like an asp, stabbing the quill deep into the fleshy vee of the forger's right hand. Breaking the feathered shaft from the nib, she left it embedded in his flesh.

"*Ahhhhhhhhhh!*" He squealed like a stuck pig. Blood spurted from the wound, staining the vellum. "*My hand!* The bitch stabbed my hand!"

"May you die of it!" She spat the curse.

The assassin was there, grabbing her from behind, pulling her away.

"Kill her! Kill her!" The forger raved, spittle foaming from his mouth, blood pouring from his hand. "Kill the bitch!"

The outer door flew open. Commander Trax rushed towards her. "What have you done!" His face twisted in rage, his hand cocked in a fist. "You've killed me, you bitch!"

Bound by the assassin, she glared at him, baiting him with her voice. "Not the face!"

He loosed the punch.

His fist connected with her jaw.

Her head snapped back, her face full of pain. The coppery taste of blood flooded her mouth. Darkness reached for her, yet she felt a spark of triumph. She'd poisoned the forger and ruined her own face, diminishing her worth to the Mordant. She was no man's pawn. Liandra knew she might soon die, yet she'd die a queen.

45

The Mordant

Behind him, the tavern burned bright, flames licking the darkness. Roused from sleep, people spilled from surrounding shops and homes, frantic to douse the flames. The Mordant sneered at their petty fears. They scrambled to protect meager belongings, while their very souls stood imperiled, for none would escape the Great Dark Dance.

Snapping his fingers, he summoned an assassin. "Have the traitor brought to the manse."

The assassin hesitated for half a heartbeat, and then rushed into the night.

The Mordant strode through the city streets, a gray cloak billowing in his wake. Releasing the power of the cameo, he let his features melt back to the monk's face. *A truthsayer in the city*, rage thundered through him. That cat-eyed bastard had seen through his deceits, ruining his web of lies. Fortunately, the man was fool enough to confront the Mordant directly. The thrice-damned truthsayer, along with every witness in the tavern, had paid with their lives, but it wasn't enough, not nearly enough. The Mordant released a snarl, his fingers caressing the crystal of pain, a litany of torments ringing in his mind.

His rage must have fueled his stride. In very little time, he reached the manse. Terrified servants rushed to open doors and bow their way from his gaze. Boots ringing on polished marble, the Mordant strode through the hallway to the throne room. Torchlight flickered from every wall, a dance of light and shadows. The Great Wyrm hung above the dais, glittering gold embroidered on imperial purple. Swathed in gray, the Mordant took a seat on the throne. Fondling the red crystal, he danced it between his fingers. Fortune combined with foolishness had revealed the truthsayer, but the Mordant trusted neither.

A rush of footsteps sounded in the hallway. A pair of assassins escorted the turned-cloak traitor into the audience chamber.

Clad in black, the queen's shadowmaster fell prostrate before the throne like a petitioning shadow. "You summoned me, my lord?"

The Mordant's voice was smooth as silk. "You never mentioned a truthsayer in the queen's city."

Raddock looked up, honest puzzlement scrawled across his face. "A truthsayer? I know of no such thing."

The Mordant fondled the red crystal. "You never made mention of cat-eyed men."

Raddock quickened, eager to please. "The cat-eyed archers come from the Deep Green. They saved the city during the Flame War. As recompense, the queen gifted them with a royal hunting preserve north of Pellanor."

The Mordant waited, letting silence serve as screws to the tongue.

Raddock stuttered. "They rarely come into the city. Now and then, one will visit a market or a tavern, but they seem to prefer the forest. They keep to themselves mostly."

The silence thickened to syrup.

Sweat beaded Raddock's broad brow. "Lord Cenric is their leader. He's on the queen's council, but he's often gone for moon-turns at a time." A whine entered the turned-cloak's voice. "They worship *trees,* my lord! And their cat-eyes are an affront to most god-fearing people." Raddock wiped the sweat from his brow. "They're good archers, but aside from that, they're of little account."

"How many?"

Raddock leaped on the question. "I've heard Lord Cenric say they are few in number."

The Mordant waited.

Desperation clung to the turned-cloak's voice. "In the forest, I'd say a dozen, maybe two dozen at the most."

"But you're not sure."

"No, lord, no one goes there! They're *tree* worshipers!"

The Mordant released the Darkness within, letting it flood his gaze. "Look at me." His voice roared with unleashed power.

Trembling, the turned-cloak obeyed.

The Mordant loosed the Darkness. Like a crossbow bolt it pierced the turned-cloak's stare, seeking his soul, flaying it for inspection. Such a small soul, flush with vengeance and riddled with spite. Long simmered in perceived wrongs, the shadowmaster brimmed with petty Darkness. The Mordant read the soul and then he raped the mind, laying bare the sins of the past. His victim thrashed upon the marble floor, drool running from his mouth. The Mordant ransacked the turned-cloak's mind, seeking knowledge of truthsayers, but he found none. Thwarted, his rage roared. He punished the shadowmaster with pain, sorely tempted to snuff his miserable life, but the Mordant drew back from that pleasure. *Serve or die!*

The Mordant withdrew. Darkness subsumed to the depths of his soul. Cloaking his power, he appeared mortal once more.

The turned-cloak twitched upon the floor as if plagued by nightmares.

The Mordant gestured to the stinking wretch. "Take him away and release him to the city."

A pair of guards leaped to obey, dragging the muddled man from the chamber.

The Mordant sat upon the throne. *Truthsayers in Erdhe!* It felt as if the cursed Lords of Light dared to meddle. He needed to know if the truthsayer was alone, a freak with unusual magic...or if he was many. His gaze snapped to the commander standing in the shadows. "You heard?"

Commander Tarq stepped forward, saluting fist to breastplate. "Yes, lord."

"Bring me one of these cat-eyed men, for I wish to flay his soul. Sedate him, gag him, and put him in one of the oubliette. Let him stew in entombed silence till I'm ready to break him."

"Yes, lord."

"And send scouts to probe this royal hunting preserve. I need to know the number of these cat-eyed atrocities." With a wave, he dismissed the commander to his task. Leaning back in the throne, he considered all that he'd learned. A lone truthsayer was easily dealt with, but if the cat-eyed people were endowed with a sense of truthsaying, then the entire race needed to be eliminated, every man, woman and child. A snarl rode his lips, for he could not abide truthsayers, the very antithesis of Darkness. Exterminating an entire race was nothing new to the Mordant, but it was how to do it. He'd only brought a small cadre of soldiers and assassins south to the queen's city. North of the Snowmelt, vast armies marched to his bidding, but in the city, his men were stretched thin. The cat-eyed people posed an unexpected obstacle. Perhaps he'd stoke the bonfires of hatred, setting the queen's people against the cat-eyed atrocities. The thought amused him. Eliminate a possible threat, while drenching the souls of the queen's people with Darkness. Deceive, divide, corrupt and conquer, the strategy had served him for a millennium of lifetimes. It would serve him now, at the hour of his triumph.

Dawn cracked the sky outside the window, brightening the chamber.

Bishop Borgan skulked in the entranceway, eavesdropping for crumbs of power. Pale and shivering, his right hand swathed in bandages, he leaned against the far wall, his silk robes sodden with sweat. The bishop was dying, *death by poisoned quill*. The Mordant would have found it amusing if not for the inconvenience.

He speared the prelate with his gaze. "Is all in order for the execution?"

The bishop stepped from the shadows. "The scaffold is nearly built, my lord."

"This is to be a royal execution. The scaffold's to be draped in banners of the queen's colors. Heralds will crisscross the city announcing the beheading. The queen's royal guard will escort the princess from the castle to the marketplace. Pomp and circumstance shall rule the day. Have Lord Cardig read the death writ, everything done in the queen's name. I want this execution forever etched in the people's memory, proof the queen put the needs of her womb above the welfare of her people."

"Yes, my lord."

"And speak to the executioner." A smile curled the Mordant's lips. "I want the first axe strike to miss, a showy spray of blood but nothing fatal. We'll give the people a good show. Three axe strokes to slay the princess, that should provide the gawkers with plenty of gore."

"As you wish, my lord."

"Remember, the head's to be saved. I want it sent to the king of Navarre with a note from the queen." He narrowed his gaze. "I trust the note's already written?"

"Yes, my lord, weeks ago." The bishop stepped forward, his posture submissive. "May I ask a boon?"

The Mordant's gaze turned cold.

"Given my lifetime of service, and my peerless value as a forger," he raised his bandage-swathed hand, his voice laden with pleading, "I humbly ask that you wield your great powers to heal me."

To heal! The Mordant swallowed a sneer. Healing was for lesser gods. Those who failed to serve deserved to die, yet it amused the Mordant to toy with the prelate. "I'll consider it."

The prelate's eyes widened, hope warring with desperation. He opened his mouth as if to speak and then thought better of it. Bowing low, he scuttled away.

The Mordant smiled, how easily mortals dangled on the barest thread of hope.

The bishop surprised him, turning back for one more word. "The queen, my lord," hatred rode his voice, "you'll make her pay?"

Finally a worthy request. "In ways she cannot imagine."

The bishop flashed a death's head grin. "Thank you, my lord." Bowing low, he turned and strode from the chamber.

A black-clad assassin appeared at the doorway.

It seemed the morning was full of supplicants. The Mordant waved him forward.

Bowing, the assassin approached the dais, a leather sack in his hand. "My lord, I've brought you something from the market." Reaching into the sack, he removed a severed head. Lifting it by the hair, he turned the face towards the Mordant. Set in a grimace, the sallow skin was etched with blue tattoos, a wolf emblazoned on the dead man's face.

The Mordant sucked air through his teeth. "Tattooed scum from the north!"

"I found him stalking a duegar in the marketplace."

"And you did not think to take him alive?"

The assassin paled. "The dart struck true, but he jumped to his death."

The Mordant ignored the excuse, his gaze fixed on the severed head. "This proves the monks' champion is here, hiding in the queen's city." A Dark rapture thrummed through him, all of his plans coming to fruition. "Find the knight." Through the eyes of the gorelabe, he'd seen the maroon knight, the despoiler of his Citadel. "Slay the others, but bring me the maroon knight whole and unharmed, for I alone shall craft his doom." The Mordant's gaze swept the chamber. "Summon my servants, for the time of my ascendance is near at hand."

46

The Priestess

Steffan was the man she missed, the man she mourned, but he was not the only man who'd sworn his soul to her service. Seeking solitude to ply her powers, the Priestess shuttered the windows and locked the door. Circling the chamber, she snuffed every candle save one. A velvety darkness embraced her. Chanting words of power, she poured water into the silver scrying bowl, a libation to the Dark God. Between her breasts, the great moonstone dangled. Potent with power, it throbbed like a second heartbeat. Kneeling naked before the scrying bowl, the Priestess removed the moonstone, gently lowering the Eye into the basin. Water spat and hissed, a clash of powers, but then subsided. Darkness triumphed, the crystal-clear water turning mirror-black, a perfect surface for reflecting Dark deeds. Summoning her powers, the Priestess cast her will upon the scrying bowl.

She dared not scry on the Mordant himself. She'd learned that bitter lesson the hard way, nearly losing the great moonstone, but his minions were fair game. For more than a fortnight, the Priestess plied the powers of the Eye, spying on his assassins and guards, seeking a prisoner princess of her own blood. Her quarry proved well hidden, but the Eye was not easily denied. Eventually, a guard led her to a petite beauty chained in a dusty attic tower. Glimpsing the girl for the first time, the Priestess nearly lost the image, for the girl's face mirrored her own, proof of the blood tie between them.

For three days, she scried on the guard, an invisible eye hovering over his shoulder. Memorizing his steps through the castle's twists and turns, she learned the way to the tower. Now, she need only summon her sworn lovers to put her plan in place.

Scrying only permitted her to watch and to follow, but for those whose souls were sworn to her, she could use the power of dreamspeaking. Suffuse with Darkness, the Priestess threaded her mind across the leagues, reaching all the way to Rhune. Garbed in gossamer thoughts, she entered the dreams of General Tarmin, issuing orders for the war in the north. As a parting gift, she gave her lusty general a dream he would forever treasure.

At the speed of thought, she raced back to Pellanor, seeking another sworn lover. She found him entwined in dreams of her. *Braxus!* Her voice pierced the fog of his lust. *Braxus, I have need of you!*

Her need snapped him into focus. *Mistress, my sword is yours!*

Gather the others. Erdhe teeters on the edge of Darkness. It is time to strike a blow at the Mordant. I shall have my revenge and then seek sanctuary at the Isle. She told him her plan.

So you will withdraw from Erdhe?

If the Mordant succeeds, he will not suffer another Dark Power in Erdhe, leastwise a woman. On the Isle we will be untouchable, and we will be close. If somehow he stumbles and falls, then Erdhe will be a ripe plum for the plucking. I will take my revenge and then I will wait and watch. Let the Dark God decide if he is a worthy heir...or a ripe sacrifice. Her voice held a malevolent purr. *Gather the others, the time grows short. Do not fail me.*

My life is yours! His pledge was potent with ardor.

A scream pierced her concentration. The Priestess pulled back, severing the link. Naked, she knelt before the scrying bowl. Beyond the locked door, she heard a second scream, one of her women in pain.

The door shivered in its frame.

The Priestess snatched the Eye from the scrying bowl and flung it under the bed.

The door blasted open.

The Mordant strode into her chamber, anger blazing from his face. "You dare to wield Dark magic unbidden!"

Pain racked her, as if hot pincers plied the bones from her body.

The Mordant's face contorted in hatred. "Did you think *I* would not notice?"

Somehow, the pain doubled. Locked in agony, she writhed upon the floor.

The Mordant's eyes blazed with fury. "*I* am the oldest harlequin! *I* am the Dark God incarnate! You are *nothing!* Grovel before me."

Screams roared out of her as the pain became a living hell. She thrashed upon the floor, seeking escape, but the agony consumed her. Battered, burned, flayed, he visited every agony upon her. She begged for death, she begged for release...and finally Darkness claimed her.

47

The Master Archivist

Castle Tandroth held many secrets, but only the queen knew them all. The Master Archivist slipped through the hidden passageways, peering through another spy hole. Like a grim ghost he haunted the castle, spending nights and days searching the musty passages, desperate to find the queen. He felt certain the Mordant held her captive somewhere in the great castle, bolstering the illusion that the queen still ruled, yet he found no trace of her. A nagging fear gnawed at his hope, yet he refused to believe she was dead. "Where are you?" His voice echoed in the narrow passageway, the only reply.

For the tenth time, he made his way to the royal hideaway adjacent to the queen's solar. His lantern light flickered against the smooth stone walls, holding the darkness at bay. Circling the round table painted with the map of Erdhe, he made his way to the spy hole near the hidden door. Shuttering the lantern lest the light betray him, he muttered a prayer to whatever gods listened to loyal assassins. Removing the onyx plugs, he set his face to the stone carving and peered into the queen's solar. A fire warmed the hearth, a pair of black-clad assassins standing guard near the outer doors. Candles glittered around the chamber, bestowing a welcoming brightness, but he saw no sign of the queen. Reluctant to admit defeat, he kept his face pressed against the spy holes, searching for any clue. Ink bottles and feathered quills lined the front of her desk, a stack of parchments waiting for her signature. A jeweled chess set sat arranged on a small table near the hearth, onyx and malachite armies standing in formation, awaiting an opening move. The royal solar looked much as he'd seen it a thousand times, yet the room felt starkly empty without the queen.

A shadow moved at the edge of his vision.

He pressed his face firm to the spy holes...and saw a *traitor!*

Clad in dark robes, Raddock strode across the chamber, seemingly indifferent to the assassins keeping watch by the door. "*Especially your deputy in black,*" the queen's warning pounded through his mind. The queen's letter named Raddock as a possible traitor. His presence with the Mordant's assassins proved it. The Master Archivist watched as the burly shadowman took a seat at the queen's desk and began reading through the stack of parchments.

A snarl rode his face, enraged to see *him* sitting at *her* desk. It hurt to watch a traitor defile her things. His gaze flicked to the assassins. *Three against one.* His anger was such that he might have risked the odds, but cold logic argued there was no need.

Easing back from the spy holes, he replaced the onyx plugs. Gathering up the lantern, he opened the shutter and made his way back through the warren of passageways. A turn of an hourglass later, he emerged in the alley behind the royal stables. Hiding his face within a cowled hood, he hunched his shoulders and affected a limp, making his way through the city streets.

A half moon silvered the queen's city, brightening the alley. He reached the Rusty Dragon without mishap. Entering through the back door, he limped to the great room. A minstrel strummed a lute in the far corner, the tempting scent of fresh-baked meat pies swirling though the tavern. His gaze roved the tables, settling on a thin man hunched over a pewter tankard. His stare was enough to draw the man's gaze. With three subtle hand movements he signaled his intent. The man gave a slow nod, turning his attention back to his tankard.

The shadowmaster's gaze caught the attention of a pretty barmaid. He pressed a silver coin in her hand. "Come wake me, Sally, in three turns of an hourglass."

She gave him a sultry smile. "For a silver, I'll do more than that."

"A tempting offer, but just wake me."

"As you wish."

He limped to the stairs, climbing to his small room beneath the eaves. He trusted the Dragon, especially its owner, yet he bolted the lock, wedging a small shim under the door for good measure. Tugging off his boots, he stretched fully clothed on the small bed, falling asleep nearly as soon as he closed his eyes.

A knock sounded on the door.

He sprang awake, his hand on a throwing dagger.

From beyond the door, he heard Sally's soft voice. "It's time."

"Thank you." He tugged on his boots, dashed cold water from the basin on his face, and made his way downstairs. The minstrel was gone, and so were most of the patrons, but the thin man remained, nursing an ale.

Since returning to Pellanor, he'd cautiously approached a few other shadowmen, the ones he trusted the most. Marstan was first among them. "Ready?"

The thin man nodded. "Aye, I'm past ready."

"And the others?"

"Out back." Marstan flung a fist full of copper coins onto the table and then swirled a dark cloak around his shoulders. The two men made their way to the back of the inn, their boots gliding whisper-soft across the plank floor. Stepping out into the moonlight, Marstan put his hands to his lips, calling the soft coo of a night dove. Four dark-clad men emerged from the alleyways, all of them bedecked with throwing knives. The shadowmaster greeted each man by name. "It's time to make a traitor sing."

Tolhard flashed a thin smile. "Which one? Filthy traitors are thick as starlings these days."

"Raddock, we're cutting the head from the snake."

Tolhard hissed. "Are you certain?"

The shadowmaster nodded. "No doubt. I saw him today with two of the Mordant's assassins."

Marstan said, "Kill or capture?"

"Capture, I need to find the queen." After explaining the plan, he led his small band towards a wealthier quarter of the city. Raddock had always been a creature of habits. The shadowmaster was betting the traitor's habits hadn't changed like the color of his cloak.

The mansion was large and pretentious, but the front garden was shoddy and overgrown. The owner, Lord Darway, had fallen afoul of gambling debts. He kept his mansion by moving his family to the ground floor, while renting the upper suites to affluent boarders. It was the type of arrangement that suited Raddock well, all the appearances of wealth without ever having truly earned it. Candlelight glowed from the top windows on the north side. The shadowmaster pointed. "Those will be Raddock's chambers. Remember, capture not kill."

Marstan and Blatt waited outside the front, the others following him around to the rear. The kitchen door was locked, but easily picked. Rubbing an oiled cloth on the hinges, he eased it open. A guard snored inside. *Camdor,* a shadowman turned traitor, more proof of Raddock's black heart. He'd expected to find a crop of traitors surrounding Raddock, but every one was a wound. Silent as death, he crept towards the sleeping guard. A single knife-slash and the traitor became a corpse. The Master Archivist lowered the body to the floor. Avoiding the pooling blood, he slipped down the hallway to the stairs.

He heard the creak of a floorboard. The sound betrayed the position of the second guard. Crouched low, the shadowmaster waited as the guard paced back towards the stairs. Rounding the corner, he hurled two knives. The guard gasped, *"You!"* and crumpled to the floor.

The shadowmaster reclaimed his knives, waiting to see if anyone heard.

The mansion remained quiet.

He gestured to Wilford and Tark. "Raddock is paranoid, more proof of his guilt. I expect you'll find more guards stationed outside his door. Dupe them and then slay them."

The two men padded up the stairs soft as shadows. Nearing the top, they made deliberate noise as if stealth did not matter.

The shadowmaster followed, but he did not turn the corner. Crouched with daggers poised, he listened. He heard his loyal men greet the traitors by name. A hushed conversation followed and then he heard a gasp. Rounding the corner, he saw two dead men being lowered to the floor.

He strode to the door and knocked.

At first, there was no answer.

He knocked harder, with more urgency.

The door yanked open. "What do you wa..." Shock riddled Raddock's face. "*You!*" He tried slamming the door, but the shadowmaster bulled it open.

"Surprised to see me?"

White-faced, Raddock fled backwards, scuttling across the sitting room, retreating to the inner door. His red velvet dressing gown flapped, revealing his skinny legs. It did him no favors. The inner door slammed shut, bolts thrown across the locks.

Instead of chasing, the shadowmaster just watched. He did not have long to wait.

The bolts were drawn back and the door eased open.

Raddock stepped back, his face as pale as curdled whey.

The master's gaze flicked around the sumptuous bedroom. Marstan crouched on the sill of the open window, a pair of throwing knives balanced in his hands.

Raddock retreated, setting his back to the far wall. "I didn't expect to see you..."

"...alive?"

Raddock swallowed hard.

"The ambush was clumsy."

Raddock whined. "I had no choice! He plucked the thoughts from my mind."

"He?"

"The...Prince of Ur."

"The *Prince of Ur,* is that how you delude yourself, accepting a false name?"

Raddock's gaze slithered sideways, seeking escape, but there was none. Pressing his back against the wall, he snarled. "You've no idea who you're up against." Cornered, the traitor began to babble. "The prince casts a long shadow. No one can escape his will. Not you, not your precious queen. When you meet him, you'll understand. His gaze bores into you, flaying your very soul. He knows everything, peeling secrets from your mind. I had no choice!"

"There is always a choice." The Master Archivist prowled towards the traitor. "Where is the queen?"

"The queen?" Raddock shook his head. "I don't know."

The shadowmaster lunged, pressing a blade to the traitor's thick throat. "Wrong answer."

Sweat erupted on the traitor's forehead. "I swear to you, I don't know."

"You must know something!"

"Somewhere in the castle!" The traitor gulped. "He holds her prisoner in the castle, but I don't know where. He trots her out now and then, garbed in silk and jewels, giving the illusion that she still rules, and then he bundles her away. No one knows where."

So the queen still lives! He embraced the thought, a balm to his heart, yet the traitor spoke of the queen as if she were a prized mare. Anger snarled his voice. "And you betrayed her."

"I had no choice."

He glared, sorely tempted to slit the traitor's throat, but instead he removed the blade. Grabbing a fistful of dressing gown, he shoved the big man towards the desk. "Sit and write. I want names, a list of every traitor turned. And lest you seek revenge by listing loyalists, I'll cut something off for every lie you write. The first thing I'll cut will be your manhood."

Sweat erupted on the traitor's forehead. Dipping the quill in ink, Raddock began to write. The scratch of quill on parchment never sounded so ominous. The list grew long, longer than he expected. The shadowmaster began to pace. Finally finished, the traitor offered up the names. The shadowmaster snatched it from his hands. Pacing, he began to read. Two-thirds of the way down, his gaze snagged on a name. *Marstan!*

Movement caught the corner of his eye.

The shadowmaster whirled, reaching for a blade.

"*Look out!*" A shoulder plowed into him, pushing him aside. Marstan grunted, a dagger protruding from his back.

The traitor ran for the door, but he was not fast enough. The shadowmaster loosed four blades, three of them embedding in the traitor's broad back. Grunting in pain, Raddock fell face forward, but his fat frame must have saved him, for he crawled towards the far door.

The Master Archivist followed. "You lied." Placing his knee between the traitor's shoulder blades, he bore down with his full weight. He grasped the traitors greasy hair, yanking his head back like a sacrifice to the slaughter. "Time to pay the price."

Raddock twisted, leering a wild-eyed glare. "You'll never be certain."

"I'm certain." He slit the traitor's throat.

Blood pooled across the floor, but he took no satisfaction in it.

He returned to Marstan, examining his wound. The traitor's blade had taken the shadowman in the fleshy part of the shoulder. "You'll live." He found a bottle of brandy and offered it to the wounded man.

Marstan took a long swallow and then handed it back. "He had a dagger hidden in the desk."

"I should have known. Raddock was ever slippery." Yanking the blade free, he doused Marstan's wound with brandy. "Why didn't you kill him?"

Marstan winced in pain. "You said capture, not kill."

"So I did." He bound the wound with bedding.

Marstan gave him a searching stare. "You don't believe him, do you?"

"If we don't believe in each other, then Darkness wins." He helped his friend stand. "Lean on me. We'll get back to the Dragon and I'll get Sam to summon a healer." They sidestepped the corpse, avoiding the spreading puddle of blood.

"And then what?"

"And then we find the queen." He made his voice certain, belying the questions haunting his mind.

48

The Priestess

The Priestess opened an eye and found herself alive. The revelation shocked her. The Mordant let her live! He'd made a grievous mistake...or else the Dark God had interceded. The Priestess sat up, taking stock of her body. Naked, she lay huddled in the far corner of her bedchamber, sodden with cold sweat. Her nose rankled, disgusted by her own stink. She'd soiled herself. Bruises mottled her entire body, probably caused by her own thrashing, yet nothing was broken. Her skin remained unflayed, her face unburned, her bones whole. She shuddered, remembering the excruciating agony. The Mordant had sought to break her spirit, not her body. He wanted her as a minion...as a plaything.

Anger sparked through her, proving he'd failed.

"Lydia!" Her voice was a harsh croak, her throat raw from too much screaming. *"Tara!"* She tried again, seeking help from her handmaidens.

No one came. No one answered.

And then she remembered the screams outside the door.

She tried to stand, but her legs buckled beneath her, every muscle bruised and sore. Like a worm, she crawled to the shattered doorway.

The coppery stench of death filled the outer room. And then she saw them, crumpled on the floor, their throats slit like sacrifices.

Her handmaidens!

Her resolve hardened.

She found a pitcher of water and cleaned herself. Her raven-dark hair was a tangle of knots, yet she refused to cut it. Her body was so sore that every movement hurt, yet she persisted. Finally cleaned and combed, she dressed herself in a low-cut gown of purple velvet. Searching among the wreckage of her bedchamber, she found her serpentine armbands and ring, poison hidden beneath the enameled scales. She slipped them on, the fangs of a serpent restored. Armored with death, she sought the Eye.

Reaching under the bed, she searched for the great moonstone. Flailing left and right, her hand found nothing. A shiver of fear pierced her. *What if the Mordant had the Eye!* Frantic, she shoved the bed aside. She found the great moonstone rolled against the back wall, swathed in cocoon of dust. Snatching it up, she cradled it close. The Eye knew her, throbbing like a second heartbeat at her touch. The Dark Lord had not abandoned her.

Whispering a prayer of thanks, she settled the chain around her neck, the great moonstone dangling in her ample cleavage.

Potent with magic and poison, the Priestess felt renewed.

Her mind turned to her plan, intent on vengeance. Much would depend on how many days had elapsed since the Mordant's assault.

Standing on wobbly legs, the Priestess went to the window and threw back the shutters. Twilight cloaked the rear garden in shades of rose and lavender. *Twilight, but how many days?* Standing at the window, she pondered the question.

Movement in the garden snagged her gaze. A dark-clad figure stepped from the shadows, deliberately standing in the waning light. The assassin stared up at her.

Graylin! She knew his face, she knew his soul. This one was sworn to her, her first conquest among the Mordant's men. The Priestess made a beckoning gesture and he nodded his assent.

The room was in disarray but it mattered not. Returning to the bed, she struck a tempting pose, watching as the colors bled from the sky. The shadows deepened from twilight to darkness. *Will he come? Is he a trap?* The Mordant had sensed her dreamspeaking, the most potent of her Dark powers, but could he also sense the succubus? Even if he could, did he care? He'd shown nothing but contempt for her feminine wiles, perhaps he thought she only plied the succubus on his behalf. A feral smile flashed across her face. Arrogance could be mortally blinding. *Will Graylin come? Will he serve...or is he a trap?* The Priestess pondered the question, life or death balanced on the answer.

A key turned in the outer lock.

She triggered the poison-tipped needle on her serpent ring, hiding the deadly sting beneath soft velvet.

Sensing stealthy movements in the outer room, she tensed, awaiting an answer.

Graylin appeared in the shattered doorway. His dark gaze drank her in. Dismay darkened his features. "What did he do to you?"

Relief coursed through her. With a subtle flick of her hand, she retracted the poison-tipped needle. "Nothing that lust can't remedy." Flashing a lascivious smile, she opened her arms to him. "Come, I want to rub my body all over your hands."

He came to her rampant with need.

Desperate to feed the succubus, she tugged on his dark leathers, wanting him naked. Skin to skin, she rubbed her body against him. Purring with hunger, she feasted on the delicious feel of him, her hands roving across his muscle-corded chest. Rolling on top, she pinned him to the bed. She straddled him, famished with need, taking him deep. The Priestess made it rough, riding him hard. Stroking up and down in relentless pleasure, she took his body while plumbing his soul. Her true name was there, scribed upon his very soul, proving he was hers, yet she used him shamelessly. Loosing the succubus, she worked her magic, endowing him with the stamina of ten bulls. Engorged, he arched his back, bellowing in ecstasy as she sucked decades from his lifespan.

Moonlight pierced the window.

Finally sated, she rolled off, scribing her true name in the sweat of his chest.

Power thrummed through her, the Priestess of the Oracle restored.

But with that power came a fresh fear. *The Mordant!* She dared not risk another confrontation. Time was of the essence.

Graylin snored on the bed, a satisfied smile on his face. She let him sleep as she dressed, hastily tucking the great moonstone into the gown's velvet-laced bodice. Clothed once more, she shook him awake. "Graylin, I need you."

Groggy from passion, he moaned in his sleep.

She shook him, desperate to know. "How long?"

He struggled to wake.

"How long?"

"A day."

Only a day!

"Everyone in the mansion felt the Mordant's wrath. I feared for you, yet you bid me obey him."

She heard the anguish in his voice.

"I kept vigil beneath your window, waiting to serve."

Another lust-struck swain, yet his vigilance may have saved her. "You did well. You did just what I asked. Now I need you to get me out of the mansion."

Concern darkened his gaze. "But Carlin and Veck stand guard at your door. Both are loyal to the Mordant." He stumbled from her bed, pulling on his dark leathers, a baldric of nine throwing knives settled across his chest.

"Surprise will be our advantage." She told him her plan. Releasing the hidden needle on her serpent ring, she followed him to the outer door.

Graylin gave her a nod and then yanked the door open. "Come, wench, by the Mordant's orders you're to attend him." He strode into the hallway.

Two black-clad assassins stood guard on either side of the door. Their gazes swiveled towards her, smirks twisting their faces.

She stepped hesitant from the room. "But I told you, I don't feel well." The Priestess feigned a swoon, slumping towards the guard on her left. He reached to catch her. She flicked her hand up, embedding the needle deep in his neck. He stiffened beneath her, his face contorted in pain. A fierce convulsion shook his body, foam flecking his mouth. The Priestess caught his dead weight, slowly lowering the corpse to the floor.

Graylin cleaned his knife, sheathing it in his baldric, the other assassin sprawled dead at his feet. He gestured to her corpse. "Poison?"

The Priestess smiled. "From my garden."

"Impressive." He glanced up and down the empty hallway. "Come."

Acting meek as a chastised prisoner, she followed him down the hallway to the marble stairs. Her footsteps faltered. Dark power beat against her. The brute force of it slammed into her, nearly staggering her. *The Mordant!* She felt him in the dark sanctum, working a powerful summoning, invoking the Dark God. How could he handle so much raw power? A tidal wave of Darkness washed across her, intoxicating and suffocating at the same time. The Priestess wavered on the stairs, nearly swooning from the strength of it.

Graylin took her arm. "Are you well?"

"Get me out of here." The Priestess struggled to clear her mind against the Dark onslaught. With such a powerful invoking, the Mordant could not have felt the succubus. The thought gave her hope, yet the force of his power deepened her fear. "Hurry!"

Supporting her weight, Graylin ushered her down the stairs and out into the jasmine-scented night.

Liveried guards stood at attention by the doors, but they did not interfere. In the Mordant's service, assassins outranked guards.

Graylin snapped. "Where is her carriage? Are all of you useless?"

Tarce, the red-headed guard she'd taken as her lover, saw her predicament and came running. "I'll see to the carriage." In short order, he drove through the gates, the dappled-gray team hitched to the open-topped landau. Graylin helped her into the carriage, taking a seat across from her. Tarce turned in the driver's seat. "Where to?"

Desperate to get away, she blurted the first destination that came to mind. "Lord Ferdic's mansion."

The whip cracked and the horses pulled away at a fast trot.

Distance gave her succor. The Priestess breathed deep, released from the smothering intoxication of Dark power. The strength of the Mordant's summoning boggled her. All the more reason she needed to get well away. But first, she'd strike a blow against him, exacting vengeance for Steffan as well as herself. The Mordant was the oldest among the harlequins, the oldest and by far the strongest, but she prayed his overweening arrogance kept him blind for one more night.

49

The Mordant

The Mordant descended the stone-carved stairs, entering the Dark sanctum. Braziers stood at the five points of the pentacle. Tortured figures cast in bronze, they held fire aloft. Shadows flickered across the sanctum, the gloom of Darkness pressing down. The vaulted chamber reeked of blood, sweat, and fear. Power prickled across his skin. The Mordant breathed deep the scent of magic, the indescribable aroma of power.

A lone figure was bound to the cold stone floor, chained spread-eagle to the pentacle. A tall muscular man, his skin was crisscrossed with flay marks, burns and deep cuts. Torture had transformed him into a work of art, yet he still lived. The Mordant had taken exceeding care with this one, a fitting sacrifice for the powers he sought.

His dark robes whispering across the mitered stone, the Mordant circled the sacrifice. "What do you smell now, *Truthsayer!*"

The man's eyes flashed open. They gleamed unnaturally bright, golden cat-eyes reflecting the brazier light. Spying the Mordant, the man stiffened.

The Mordant smiled, pleased by his reaction. "Yes, it is always so. The damned and their torturer share an intimate bond. Your pain has brought me much pleasure. Now, you will serve a higher purpose."

"No, please, no." The sacrifice began to babble.

"*Sarlant!*" The Mordant uttered a single command and the sacrifice clamped his mouth shut, bound by magic...but his bulging eyes betrayed his burgeoning fear. "Yes, that's much better. No need to speak, for you've already told me everything...yet your fear will serve a higher power." The Mordant circled the chained man. "Yours will be the perfect offering. Truthsayer magic in your blood shall make my offering all the more potent."

The Mordant began to dance. Muttering spells in an arcane language, he wove steps in an intricate circle around the sacrifice. Round and round, he danced the runes, invoking an ancient power. Flames erupted from the braziers, sending cascades of red sparks licking towards the ceiling. Darkness answered. An obscene power rippled through the chamber. The looming Darkness pressed down, drawn to the ritual like a beast slavering for a kill. The Mordant raised his arms, drawing power around him like a king's raiment. Swathed in Darkness, he circled the sacrifice one last time. His hands reached deep, drawing two silver knives from his robes. Raising the rune-scribed blades high, he twined them in wisps of velvety Darkness. Magic flared along the silvery blades, illuminating the ancient runes.

Smoke sizzled from the blades.

Silver was a conduit for Darkness. Throwing back his head, the Mordant convulsed with power. "*Sarlayon darkoth an! By my will, show me the future!*" He swooped down on the sacrifice, plunging the smoking daggers deep into the truthsayer's chest, seeking his heart's blood. The sacrifice convulsed, twisting in spasms of pain. Dark blood welled from the wounds, turned to smoke by the silvery blades. Power sizzled through the chamber. Writhing against his bonds, the sacrifice screamed, his mouth flung wide as if he could vomit all his pain...and then he lay still. His heart beat once, twice...and then stopped forever.

A corpse lay pinioned to the pentacle.

The Mordant stirred, his voice crackling with invoked power. "From beyond the grave, I summon answers. From the halls of Hell, I compel thee to speak. By rune and blade, I invoke the power of prescience. Let the future be foretold!"

Dead eyes flashed open, awakened by his call.

Instead of golden-yellow, the corpse's eyes were milky white, blank canvases tinged with flickering orange, reflecting the flames of Hell. "*Your enemies come!*" The voice was hoarse with a god's raw power. "*One shall be brought to you as a gift. The others shall come of their own will, cloaked in their true colors. They come bearing the very weapon you seek. An ancient weapon drenched in soul-magic. The one who wields it shall have the power to bind and unbind, to make and unmake, to sculpt souls into new forms. All shall be decided before the Pentacle. Cower and serve!*"

The eyes fell shut and the stink of death prevailed.

The sacrifice fell still, a corpse once more.

Drained of power and slick with sweat, the Mordant struggled to stand. He clutched his ringed hands to stop the shaking. Weakness would bedevil him for the next few days, but the soothsaying was well worth the price. A smile slithered across his face. An ancient magic long sought was nearly his. The weapon would grant him powers undreamed by mortal men. With it, he would fashion the world to his liking, carving enemies into nightmares that served. Gorelabes would be the least of his creations. A millennium of schemes was coming to fruition, the Great Dark Dance was nearly won. The Mordant laughed and the sound rang with Darkness.

50

Jemma

A sound woke her. Jolted from a nightmare, Jemma startled awake. Pitch-dark and not a shred of light to see by, she reached for the dirk strapped to her leg. The scrabbling sound came again. At first she thought it was rats. They'd grown bold, gnawing on the stinking corpse day and night, but then she realized it came from below.

Fear choked her like a cruel fist. *Come to kill me in the dead of night?*

Iron scraped against iron, the sound of the bolt being drawn back.

She tightened her fist on the dirk, a slender defense.

The trapdoor eased open, a slash of lantern light piercing the darkness.

Mastering her fear, Jemma hurriedly sheathed the dirk, knowing surprise was her only hope. Empty handed, she faced the trapdoor, her heartbeat thundering.

The ladder thudded into place. A dark-haired man appeared, holding a lantern high. He wore black leathers, a baldric of knives strung across his chest. A black-clad devil, her hopes sank.

Spying her huddled under the eaves, he gaped.

She must look a fright, a banshee locked in the attic.

"Just like her."

The comment made no sense. Befuddled, Jemma stared at her jailor.

"Come." He tossed a ring of three keys towards her.

Keys! She was so startled, the keys bounced off her, dropping to the mattress. The same keys she'd killed for. *Was this a trick?* She did not know, yet she'd take her chances. With shaking hands, she tried the keys on her manacle. The second one worked. Cruel iron clicked open, the manacle cuff falling from her sore wrist.

"Come." He disappeared down the ladder.

Anything was better than staying in the attic with the rotting dead. She crawled to the trapdoor and made her way down. Lantern light beat against her. Blinking, she turned, surrounded by men with swords, but they were a strange crew. One was a black-clad devil, one wore the purple and gold livery of Ur, while the others were clad in a hodge-podge of dark leathers. And then she noticed the corpses. Two of her jailors, their throats slit, lay sprawled in puddles of blood. Jemma retreated a step, uncertain if this was a rescue or murder. "What do you want with me?"

A woman strode from the shadows. Tall and statuesque, she wore form-fitting black leathers that clung to every voluptuous curve. Exuding a brazen sensuality, she moved with a predator's glide, but it was her face that truly startled. *Like looking in a mirror,* but this face was more mature, the beauty more potent, the green eyes hooded and cynical, the ruby-red mouth curled with a touch of cruelty. Jemma staggered back a step. *"Aunt Iris!"*

"Kin knows kin." Studying her, the woman rankled her nose. "You reek of death."

"They locked me with a corpse."

"Did you kill it?"

Jemma swallowed. "Yes."

"Good. I'd hate to waste my time on spineless kin."

Jemma was totally flummoxed, shocked to be rescued by her infamous aunt. "But you *killed* my mother!"

"Yes, and now I'm saving you."

"But why?"

"Life is complicated. You'll learn that in due time. Now come, if you want to live." Her aunt turned and strode from the tower chamber.

Thoroughly confused, Jemma followed, the armed men forming an escort.

Her aunt seemed to know the way, leading them through a labyrinth of twists and turns. At one point, she stopped, gesturing to the black-clad devil. Unsheathing a knife from his baldric, he glided around the corner, silent as death. Jemma strained to listen, but heard nothing save a slight scuffing sound. The black-clad devil returned, motioning them forward. Rounding the corner, Jemma spied two fresh corpses. *Both wore the emerald livery of Lanverness!* "But..."

A hand clamped over Jemma's mouth, smothering her words.

Her aunt glared. "Be silent till I give you leave, or I'll abandon you to your enemies." A cruel light glinted in her green eyes. "Blink if you understand."

Jemma understood nothing, yet she blinked.

The hand released her mouth, but the leather-clad guard remained close as a shadow, a potent threat at her back.

Jemma followed her aunt, her mind tangled in turmoil. Queen Liandra was her friend, yet she'd been imprisoned in Castle Tandroth. And now her dread aunt, the bane of her family, appeared from the shadows to rescue her? Jemma did not know if she should scream for help, try to run, or stay with her aunt. Nothing made a lick of sense, as if the world was turned upside down.

Her aunt gestured and one of the men opened an ironbound door. They stepped out into a night-darkened courtyard. Stars glinted overhead, bright as diamonds. Jemma stared aloft, overcome by the sight. So long imprisoned, she'd begun to doubt she'd ever see the night sky again. Breathing deep, she nearly swooned from the fresh air.

Swords whispered from scabbards as the escort encircled Jemma and her aunt. The guards stood poised, while the black-clad devil disappeared into the night. Jemma considered screaming, or making a run for it, but then the black-clad man returned, beckoning them forward.

They crossed the courtyard in a huddled rush.

More corpses lay slumped at the castle gates.

They passed beneath the raised portcullis and out into the city streets. Aunt Iris led them away from the castle. In a back alley, a man stood holding a dozen saddled horses. Her aunt chose an eighteen-hand stallion, swinging into the saddle with practiced ease. "Come, if you want to live."

One of the guards gave Jemma a leg up. She straddled the horse, her velvet gown bunched around her waist. Jemma barely had time to jam her feet in the stirrups and they were off, cantering through the dark maze of cobbled streets. Surrounded by armored men, Jemma had little choice but to follow. The ride was a blur of twists and turns. Few people roamed the late-night streets, yet light poured from many a window. Jemma peered into homes and shops, wondering who was friend and who was foe. Her horse lurched forward, stepping in a hole. With her gown bunched around her waist, Jemma struggled to keep her seat. And then they reached the city's edge, galloping through the unfinished wall into the surrounding fields.

Somewhere in the north, a wolf howled.

Jemma shivered at the primal sound.

Moonlight silvered the countryside. They rode for the turn of an hourglass, putting the city's lights behind them, and then her aunt reined to a halt. She circled her stallion back towards Jemma. "This is where we part ways. If you have any questions, ask them now."

Any questions? Her mind roared with confusion. Jemma stuttered a single word. "Why?"

"Why rescue you?"

Jemma nodded, her mouth dry.

"Because you're kin. Because I owe a debt of pain. Because my nemesis dares to style himself a god."

The answers made little sense. "But who?"

"The Mordant."

The name struck like a thunderclap. Staggered, Jemma clutched the saddle horn. "*Here?*"

Her aunt gave a solemn nod. "Make no mistake, the Mordant rules the city. If the queen still lives, I know it not."

So the slain soldiers in green tabards might have served the Mordant. "But why?"

"To rot Erdhe from within. To pit men against women. To despoil a queen's name so that a woman never rules again."

"But why me?"

"You were proof of the queen's madness." Her aunt settled her fretting stallion. "You were to be executed by the queen's royal writ on the morrow, your severed head sent in a basket to your father."

Jemma reflexively touched her throat, stunned by the shadow of an axe.

"You can best defeat the Mordant by evading the executioner." She gestured to two of her men. "Hugo and Tarce will see you to the border of Navarre." Iris turned her stallion. "The dawn comes. We must both be away ere the Mordant finds us gone."

Jemma recovered her voice. "Wait! Will I see you again?"

Her aunt turned back, a smile on her ruby lips, but this time it seemed genuine. "The family is better off without me." Her eyes shadowed, showing hints of sadness. "Tell your father, he might have been right about me." She gathered her stallion, but then she turned back for one last question. "Will you be queen?"

Jemma gasped to hear her secret spoken aloud. She hesitated, but her strange aunt had more than earned an answer. Jemma straightened in the saddle, her voice filled with quiet pride. "Yes."

"Good." Iris laughed. "There aren't enough queens in Erdhe." Her face changed like quicksilver, from gay laughter to a hard sharpness. "You owe me, niece. Someday I'll come to collect."

Jemma held her breath.

Iris gave her a shrewd smile. "Kin can be so complicated. Family can be a blessing, or a bane. Fare thee well." Putting spurs to her mount, she wheeled her stallion and galloped for the hills, her escort of men riding close behind.

Jemma watched till her aunt disappeared over the rise, uncertain if she was a boon or a curse.

The leather-clad man cleared his throat. "Shall we go?"

Jemma stared back toward the sprawling city, praying Queen Liandra prevailed. Perhaps she could help her friend and mentor by spreading the truth, but she'd not put her head back on the chopping block. She shivered, the shadow of the axe fresh in her mind. "Yes, to Navarre." Jemma turned her horse to the west, eager for home and the seaside crown.

51

Liandra

Her jaw ached and her head pounded. Liandra woke to find herself imprisoned in the same familiar chamber. Her spirits sank. She tried to console herself that it was not the dungeons, but First Keep was proving a formidable prison. Liandra fingered her jaw, wincing at the pain. Nothing seemed broken, but she suspected the bruising was spectacular. A pity she did not have a mirror to see the commander's brutal handiwork.

Remembering the fat forger, Liandra started to smile until she winced. At least she'd struck a blow at the enemy, driving the quill deep in his hand. *Vermillion ink bound with arsenic...*she hoped he died of it.

Rising from the bed, the queen began to pace, beset by all she'd learned. Her women murdered, the life of the princess imperiled, her people roused to anger, all of it the work of the Mordant. Her mind struck his name like a ship breaking on sharp rocks. How had it come to this? Searching for answers, she found none.

Isolated in the tower, Liandra felt like a spirit haunting her own castle. Twice a day, her captors brought food and wine and a fresh chamber pot, but the black-clad devils never spoke, refusing to answer her simplest questions. The combination of inactivity and not knowing rotted her hope. In the dark of night, her imagination spun vivid nightmares. Severed heads haunted her dreams, the bulging eyes of her women staring with reproach, yet the queen knew she could never obey the Mordant. Too many mornings, she woke in the chill grip of nightmares, but the grim light of day proved just as cruel. Languishing in the tower, she felt useless and unneeded. Queens should never be unneeded.

Liandra relied on her intellect to pass the dreary days. Setting an imaginary chessboard in her mind, the queen examined what little she'd learned of her enemy. Looking at the board from every angle, she grew certain the Mordant's game relied on deception and illusion and the breaking of rules. But if her conclusions were correct, surely the enemy would need her to prop up his charade. Surely, her courtiers and lords would clamor to see their queen. Lanverness was a complex kingdom, thriving on an intricate web of commerce and relationships. The kingdom did not run itself...yet no one came for her, neither friend nor foe.

Robert! She longed for her lover, for her shadowmaster, praying that her message somehow found him. Robert would look for her, Robert would find her. And if she could somehow escape this dread tower, she'd find a way to foil the Mordant.

A key rattled in the lock.

Her heartbeat quickened. Stopping in front of the cold hearth, she hastily smoothed her rumpled gown and then stood straight, assuming a regal pose. Friend or foe, she'd meet her fate as a queen.

The door slammed opened as if blown by a gale-force wind.

But there was no wind.

The Mordant strode in, anger in his gaze.

"*You!*" The queen flinched, struggling not to retreat half a step.

"You cost me my forger!" The full force of his stare hit like a battering ram. The queen staggered back a step, yet remained standing, refusing to yield.

The Mordant's gaze bored into her, as if he could tunnel into her mind. Unable to look away, yet she denied him with a force of will. Their gazes locked in a joust, time slowed to a torturous crawl. Light pulsed bright behind her eyes. Grimacing, the Mordant was the first to look away. Liandra sagged, remembering to breathe.

A fierce headache pounded behind her eyes, yet she forced herself to think, clinging to logic as a shield to her fear. *He comes clad as a prince of Ur, so deception still matters. He wants something. We are still needed!* The insight gave her strength. Determined to gain some advantage, she asked her most vexing question. "How did you know about the castle?"

His voice was winter-cold. "Your legends are my memories."

His answer opened a chasm beneath her mind.

"Woman, you know not whom you face." He made a simple summoning gesture...and the shadows answered. Darkness coalesced around the Mordant, weaving a cloak of nightmares. He seemed to grow in stature, like a demon come calling. "Darkness has come to claim Erdhe. There are none who can stand in my way."

Somehow the queen remained standing, her fingernails biting into her palms.

"Kneel!"

She refused.

Pain spiked her side. She ground her teeth against it.

The pain delved deeper, like a brutal dagger thrust beneath her ribs.

Stifling a scream, she dropped to her knees, clutching her side.

He loomed over her, a monstrous form cloaked in Darkness. "You are but a pawn set upon the board. Obey, or suffer the consequences."

The queen refused to bow her head. Grimacing against the biting pain, she stared up at him.

The air crackled around her like the prelude to a lightning strike.

Liandra thought she was going to die, felled by Darkness, but then he made a cutting gesture and the pain withdrew. Gasping, Liandra checked her side. She found no blood, yet she'd felt the plunge of a dagger. Dizzy with remembered pain, she swayed on her knees.

The Mordant's shadowy raiment dissolved, leaving her tormentor mortal once more.

Tap, tap, tap.

The sound came from behind, from the arrow-slit window. A cold foreboding slithered down the queen's back, yet she dared not turn away from the Mordant.

"That is for you." He gestured to the window. "A divine gift, a glimpse of your future." A smile crossed his face. "Behold and believe."

Tap, tap, tap.

"Serve and survive, or suffer the consequences as this one has." He flashed a sinister smile. "The next time we meet, you shall grovel in obeisance as you would to a god."

She stood, her fists clenched in slender defiance.

Tap, tap, tap.

He gestured to the window. "Look and learn my true nature." The Mordant turned, his purple cloak swirling behind him. In two quick strides he strode from the room. The door closed. The lock clicked shut. She was alone once more, confined to her prison, yet she dared not lower her guard. *Look and learn my true nature!* Liandra needed to understand her enemy, yet she feared the answer.

Tap, tap, tap, the incessant sound came from behind, from the arrow-slit window.

Five stories up, she could not imagine what it was.

Tap, tap, tap.

Liandra dreaded looking, yet she had to know. Standing, the queen turned to face the arrow-slit window. The narrow glass pane was so thick and so old, it let sunlight through but little else, offering a glazed and distorted view...yet she glimpsed something on the ledge.

Tap, tap, tap, the sound grew impatient.

Desperate for a weapon, she snatched a log from the cold hearth. Steeling her courage, Liandra went to the window. Opening the latch, she threw open the window and leaped aside, holding the log like a club.

Red feathers fluttered through.

A bird, it was just a bird, a red-tailed hawk! It fluttered to the floor, and with it came a horrid stench. She struggled not to gag. And then it looked up at her and spoke. *"Majesty!"*

The queen staggered backwards. Horror quaked her. The log dropped from her shaking hands. *It spoke! It had a face, a man's face!* A scream built in her throat. This thing was a horror, a nightmare come calling. But instead of attacking, it bowed to her.

"Majesty, don't you know me?"

She froze, trapped between terror and shock.

"Look at my face, look in my eyes, you know me!"

The fiend stank of putrid rot. Between its tattered feathers, the hawk body oozed puss and corruption, reeking like a long-dead corpse, yet the voice was vaguely familiar. The nightmare crouched at her feet, its wings spread wide in supplication. It stared up at her with pleading eyes. *That voice!* Liandra struggled to see past the monstrous abomination. Needing to understand, she focused on its eyes, a man's eyes, the window to the soul...and then she knew. A horrid gasp escaped her. *"Our Lord Sheriff!"*

"Yes." A single tear escaped his pale blue eye.

He is still human! The tear tore at her heart. Her strength fled, her legs suddenly weak. The queen melted to the floor, a sundered puddle of green velvet. "How?"

"He is the Mordant! He is Darkness incarnate!"

Look and see my true nature. Liandra shuddered. So this malformed creature was his herald, an abomination against man and beast. Bile rose in her mouth. The queen swallowed her revulsion, seeking to gain some insight into her enemy. "But how was this done?"

"Assassins captured me. I woke in a dungeon, chained to a pentacle. The Mordant tortured me, but I told him nothing!"

The queen believed him, smitten by his stalwart courage.

"He hurt me, but he never truly harmed me. And then his minions smuggled me out of the city. I woke in a farmer's field, bound beneath a night-dark sky." A shudder wracked him, raw terror erupting in his gaze. *"He summoned demons, he summoned Darkness...and then he did this to me!"* His gaze begged her for answers. *"How could he do this? How can the Lords of Light permit such an atrocity?"*

The queen had no answer. Emotions raged within her, an upwelling of horror, outrage, shock and sympathy...all twisted together with righteous anger. "The gods owe thee...and so do I."

A second tear coursed down his cheek.

Tentatively, she reached out with a single finger, wiping his tear away.

A sob escaped him.

The queen summoned her dignity, lest she cry as well. "What can we do for thee?"

"Kill me!"

The request rocked her.

"The Mordant forbade me to kill myself, but that only proves I can die!" He spread his wings, fanning a putrid stench. *"Look at me! The Mordant made me, but the magic did not take. From the very first night, this body began to rot."* A shiver passed through him. *"Perhaps an honest soul is not the proper clay for the devil's wheel."* He gazed up at her. *"I beg you, end this nightmare."*

She'd never killed anyone, not with her own hands, yet she owed him. He was her faithful vassal, and she was his liege lord. He deserved so much better than this. "How? We are a prisoner, without weapons of any sort."

For the first time, he looked around the small, spare chamber. *"Perhaps the log."*

She'd forgotten the log. *Bludgeoned to death!* The queen shuddered at the brutal cruelty. "You deserve better, far better."

"Yet, it seems the only way." He gazed at her with an unflinching stare.

She could not deny him. The queen reclaimed the log, holding it with two hands. It was heavy, yet she feared it might take several blows. Horrified by the thought, she smothered her mind, refusing to fail him. "Are you sure?"

"Please." He spread his russet wings wide, placing his head on the hearthstone.

The queen took a steadying breath. Tightening her grip, she raised the log above her head, fixing her gaze on his neck. *Wings spread wide*...the image thundered through her mind. Resolved to strike true, she whispered a prayer. "May the Light take you." Liandra hardened her will, lest she fail him. *There are no rules!* She brought the log down with all her strength...but a thought speared her. Tugging on the log, she missed, wood hitting stone with a dreadful thud.

Dazed, he blinked up at her.

"Perhaps your death need not be so cruel or so senseless." She took a steadying breath. "Will serve us one last time?"

Talons scraped on stone. He folded his wings to his side, crouched on the cold hearthstone. *"But I am a creature of the Mordant."*

"Your soul is still your own." Her thoughts quickened. "We seek a way to foil the Mordant."

"How?"

"We are imprisoned in our own castle, yet no one knows we are here. We need help to escape. We need our shadowmen." She told him where to look, and then she gave him a coded message. "Shout the message when you find them. You must make them believe you come from us." She gazed at him, her gallant lord trapped in a fiend's body. "Fly for us this one time. Be our herald instead of the Mordant's."

"Beware, my queen, for I could be a trap."

A bone-deep chill bit her. "How?"

"I can only speak my own mind because the Mordant gave me leave. He wants you to know who I am...who I was."

"He wants us to quake in fear."

"Just so."

She waited, certain there was more.

"Majesty, you don't understand the danger. Sometimes the Mordant invades my thoughts, tentacles of Darkness worming through my mind." The hawk shuddered, his russet feathers quaking. *"The Mordant speaks through me, he sees through me. I am his tool."*

A cold fear gripped her. "Is he here now?"

"No."

"Are you certain?"

"Yes. When he comes I taste Darkness, as if the whole world had turned to ash."

Liandra could not fathom how he endured such a cursed existence. *A trap*, she hadn't considered a trap. She stared at him, wondering if he was sent to betray her, but she saw no guile in his gaze. Such a dangerous gambit, to trust a creature ensorcelled by the Mordant, yet she made her choice. "You were sent to terrify us, to bludgeon us into obedience, yet we know you. We trust you. Your soul remains true." Her resolve hardened. "Will you do this for us? Will you be our herald?"

"*My queen, heed my warning! I am but a hawk to the Mordant's fist. If he summons me, I must answer. If he invades my mind, he will know. In this corrupted form, I cannot gainsay him.*"

She could well imagine the Mordant's volcanic wrath if he learned of this plot. "Yet you are our only hope. We will dare the risk if you will.

He stilled, as if considering her request, and then he bowed to her. "*The Mordant made a monster of me, yet you offer noble service. I thank you, my queen. It is an honor to serve you.*"

Liandra fought to suppress her tears.

His wings spreading wide, he leaped upwards. Two great flaps and he alighted on the window sill. Without a backwards glance, he launched into the air.

The queen ran to the window. She watched the hawk-fiend soar. He circled the tower once and then banked towards the northwest. "Fly fast and find him!" *Before the Mordant catches us both.* She sank to her knees, sundered by all that had transpired. *Your legends are my memories...the* Mordant's words pounded through her mind. *Look and learn my true nature!* A single red feather floated down from the windowsill, proof of the Mordant's fearsome powers. How could the Lords of Light permit such an abomination to exist? Yet, despite the Mordant's foul magic, his Darkness could not warp an honest soul. The Sheriff remained true despite his twisted form. And now he served his queen on one last mission. Perhaps the Mordant's own foul works would prove his undoing. *The Mordant is the true monster.* Liandra repeated the phrase like a litany, clutching the thought like a slender hope. He'd sent her a hideous fiend, but instead she'd found a friend. *There are no rules!* She needed a herald, she needed help. Liandra prayed the Sheriff was the key to unlocking her prison.

52

Katherine

Morning brightened the sky, another day to hunt the enemy. Kath reached beneath the neckline of her chainmail, touching her mage-stone gargoyle for luck. Tugging on a plain brown cloak, she reluctantly left the maroon in her saddlebag. Her magic was already a potent marker to the enemy, she'd not make it easier by wearing her true colors. Tightening the straps on the throwing axe harness, she glanced at Danya, but the wolf-girl remained in a trance, her gaze focused elsewhere.

Kath made her way down the stairs, a dusky-gray cat rubbing against her boots. Blaine waited at the back door, the hilt of his blue steel sword wrapped in worn leather, a dark gray cloak hiding his silver surcoat. He turned towards her, his blue eyes sharp and keen. "Time to hunt the enemy."

"Before he hunts us."

His gaze sobered, his hand slipping to the crystal dagger sheathed at his belt. "You honor me with this."

"Honor has always been yours." She met his gaze. "For Honor and the Octagon."

His fist clenched to his chest. "May it ever be so."

Her gaze dropped to the crystal dagger at his belt. "Be warned, by bearing a dagger, you may draw the duegar." So close to the Mordant, Kath had taken to hiding her crystal dagger in the secret sheath in her right boot.

"But you're not certain?"

Kath shrugged. "The magic feels different, not like my gargoyle, although who can say what a duegar can and cannot track. Just be careful." She leaned toward him, her voice charged with warning. "And, remember, maim the Mordant with your sword, but slay him with the dagger. Only the crystal dagger, or all this will be for naught."

"As you say." He swooped towards her, planting a soft kiss on her lips.

Startled, Kath staggered backwards.

Stepping away, he winked at her. "For luck."

Her face flamed red. She hadn't told him about Duncan. Perhaps she should, but now was not the time. "We've an ancient evil to hunt." Yanking the door open, she stepped into the morning sunshine. Annoyed, she did not wait for him, striding down the alley to the main street. Trusting him to follow, she joined the morning bustle. Her gaze roamed the street, seeking the foul duegar. *Hunt or be hunted,* they played a dangerous game, striving to find the Mordant before he found them. Much depended on the outcome. Perhaps, she should have put more faith in the stealth of cats, but Kath needed to get out, to take the measure of the queen's city, to track the ancient evil to its lair.

She turned right, threading a path towards the heart of the city. Seeing no sign of the magic-sniffing dwarves, Kath sought signs of evil. So much had changed since she'd last walked Pellanor's streets. The queen's city felt tainted. Smiles vanished from faces, replaced with furtive glances and suspicious scowls. Conversation dimmed to hushed whispers as if eavesdroppers lurked on every corner. Women huddled together, baskets clutched in their arms, scurrying to the markets like flocks of frightened hens. Merchants and peddlers wore swords, walking awkwardly with steel belted to their sides. Everywhere Kath looked, she saw signs of ill omens. Mistrust and worry claimed the city, the bitter fruits of fear.

Pellanor stank of the Mordant. She wondered that others did not sense it and run screaming from the city. Perhaps, their love of home blinded them to the evil slithering in their midst.

Reaching the first cross street, Kath turned left, trusting Blaine to turn right. By agreement, they planned to walk a braided path through the city, crisscrossing each other's path at every first, third and fifth crossroads. Kath hoped to weave a confusing trail of magic, while conducting her own hunt of the Mordant.

Meow, a black cat crossed her path. She wondered if it was one of Danya's.

Glancing aloft, she spied a cloaked figure hiding on the roof, proof her maroon band kept watch. She'd asked her painted warriors to protect Danya, while tracking the foul duegars. The wolf-girl remained safe, but the Mordant's lair remained a mystery. So far the hunt was an uneasy stalemate. Tension tightened across her shoulders like a drawn bowstring, knowing time grew late.

Kath reached the third crossroad, lingering till she saw Blaine on the far side. He gave her a secret smile as he sauntered past, his great sword rearing over his right shoulder like a potent threat. Tall and blond with broad shoulders, he looked a hero despite his dark cloak. Kath watched as the crowd ebbed away from him, opening a teardrop-shaped space around the knight. Blaine strode a straight path through the parting people, seemingly oblivious to the crowd's homage, as if it was his due.

"Look out!" A fat merchant barged into her.

Kath dodged left to avoid the merchant, narrowly saving her foot from being tromped. Dancing sideways, she evaded a bearded man carrying a barrel. Tossed like flotsam in a stream, Kath made slow progress. Axes were strapped to her back and a sword belted to her side, yet the crowd battered against her. It seemed short petite blondes were easily overlooked.

Blaine turned left as Kath fought her way through the crowd to turn right, both of them threading a path towards the castle.

*The queen's castle...*Kath expected the Mordant to lurk near Pellanor's seat of power. Perhaps he already infested the castle, a daunting thought. Kath feared for the queen, wondering if she still lived. She'd sent one of the Zward to seek an audience. Lucas had not yet returned, another worry. Kath's hand sought the mage-stone gargoyle hidden beneath her chainmail shirt. Darkness had already claimed too many good people. She prayed Lucas did not add to the tally. Resting her hand on her sword hilt, Kath prowled the cobbled streets, scanning for duegar, but she saw none.

Scents of cinnamon, cardamom, and saffron tickled her nose. She neared the spice market, the sound of dickering rising like birdsong from the great square. Even under the Mordant's grim cloud, Pellanor's markets never ceased to amaze. Commerce was the lifeblood of the great city, thrumming like a heartbeat through the spice market. Kath wove a path through the stalls, marveling at the enticing smells and vibrant colors. Pyramids of spices, yellow, red, orange, ochre and all hues of brown, crowned the stalls, dazzling the eye and bewitching the nose. A portly vendor sprinkled a concoction of spices on chicken skewers sizzling over red-hot coals. Mouthwatering smell pervaded the market. Two small boys dashed past, half-eaten skewers clutched in their fists. The skewers reminded Kath of the Isle of Souls, where she'd wandered wide-eyed through the markets, longing to have her fortune told. It seemed a lifetime ago. She'd been so young and naive.

"Hear ye! Hear ye!" Trumpets blared at the market's heart. *"Come hither and hear the words of your queen!"*

Kath dodged her way towards the trumpet's call. Spying a royal herald bedecked in the queen's colors, she moved towards him. The crowd thickened, pressing around her. Expectant faces turned towards the herald.

A trumpeter sounded a flare of notes. The emerald-clad herald snapped open a scroll. *"Hear ye! Hear ye! By order of her august majesty, Queen Liandra, the White Rose of Lanverness, the good people of Pellanor are summoned to the great market at noon of this very day to witness the queen's justice. By royal decree, an enemy of the realm shall be beheaded upon the scaffold block."* A murmur rippled through the crowd, yet the herald read on. *"For withholding birth-magic from the queen, Jemma, the Princess of Navarre is sentenced to death. The princess shall be beheaded..."*

Jemma! Kath staggered hearing her friend's name. *This was not the queen's doing!* She gaped at those around her, expecting a protest, but they seemed entranced by the herald, as if bewitched by Darkness. A chill gripped her...*the Mordant!*

"...submit to the headsman's axe. All loyal citizens are summoned to the scaffold to bear witness to the queen's justice. May Queen Liandra forever rule! All praise her majesty, the gods save the queen!" Snapping the scroll shut, the herald jumped from the stall, disappearing into the crowd.

"No, this isn't right." Kath protested but no one listened.

Roused by the herald's call, the crowd moved like a great leviathan. All around her, people surged forward, winding their way through the market stalls. Sluggish at first, but then the crowd thickened, gaining momentum, moving with a grim inevitability towards the city's heart.

Caught in the press, Kath was swept along like a storm-borne leaf.

Jemma! Kath struggled against the crowd, needing to get back to the others, to gather her maroon band and plan a rescue. Trapped in the crush, she made little headway. Bumped and jostled, she was carried along like driftwood. Kath glanced aloft, noting the position of the sun. *Nearly noon!* Even if she could break free, there was not enough time to set an ambush.

Frantic, she scanned the rooftops, hoping to signal her painted warriors, but she saw none.

An elbow bit into her side. Someone trampled her boot. Shoved and squeezed, Kath looked for Blaine, but she could not see him. Swallowed by the press, she tried angling to the side, but the swelling crowd's forward motion proved relentless. Realizing she could not break free, Kath decided to forge ahead. She'd scout the scaffold, searching for a way to save her friend.

Walking with the throng instead of against it, Kath was able to jostle her way forward, moving towards the head of the beast. The crowd followed the twists and turns of the street, spilling into the great market. A scaffold stood erected at the market's heart, a large wooden platform adorned with banners in the queen's colors. A chopping block waited atop the scaffold, a bucket positioned beneath the sinister curve in the dark-stained block. Kath grimaced to see it, bile flooding her mouth.

"This is not the queen's way!" She protested, but no one seemed to care.

Trumpets blared, echoing through the square, hastening the crowd to the deadly spectacle.

Time grows short! A cold shiver raced down Kath's back. Squeezed between two tall men, she saw little save the backs of taller people. The sour smell of sweat and ripe bodies compounded the strangling intensity. Drowning in a sea of people, Kath struggled forward. Murmurs whispered through the crowd, their tone equal parts curious and fear-laden. Above the hushed murmurs, Kath heard the clop of horses and the trundle of a wagon. Desperate for a better view, she ducked low, squirming forward. Something banged hard against her shin. She'd stumbled upon a mounting block. Climbing atop the stone block, she gained a view over the crowd. Someone shoved her, but Kath shoved back, refusing to relinquish her perch.

Horns blared as guards in emerald tabards trooped onto the scaffold, taking positions along the railings. *Too many swords...*yet Kath had to see.

An executioner appeared on the scaffold. His arms the size of most men's thighs, he wore a black leather hood over his face, nothing but cruel slits for eyes. Cradled in his arms, he held a massive double-bladed axe.

The crowd hushed to see him, a herald of death.

A gray-haired lord in crimson robes and golden chains of office strode to the front of the scaffold. Behind him, two emerald-clad soldiers half carried the prisoner. *Jemma!* Dwarfed by the guards, she looked frail and petite, a lace veil covering her face. Elegant as always, she wore a sapphire gown girdled in gold thread. A sumptuous velvet cloak was draped across her shoulders. Checkered red and blue, the cloak proclaimed the royal colors of Navarre.

"Jemma!" Kath shouted her friend's name, but Jemma made no sign of recognition.

The lord snapped open a scroll and began to read. *"Hear ye! Hear ye! By solemn decree of her most royal majesty, Queen Liandra, the White Rose of Lanverness, the prisoner, Princess Jemma of Navarre, is to be publically executed for withholding birth-magic from the Rose Crown, and thereby seeking to forever sever the Tandroth line. For this assault on the royal line, she is condemned to death. All ye citizens of Pellanor are summoned to witness the queen's justice. Bring forth the prisoner! Let the executioner strike swift and sure! May the Lords of Light grant mercy on her soul!"*

The guards moved the prisoner to stand before the block. One swept the velvet cloak from her shoulders, while the other removed the lace veil.

Kath gaped. *It wasn't her!* This girl had the same petite shape and raven-dark hair as the princess, but her face was a stranger's!

The guards forced the girl to kneel, pressing her head upon the block.

As if released from a trance, the girl suddenly snapped alert. Stark terror rode her face. Eyes wide in fright, she struggled against her guards to no avail. Mouth agape, she screamed a mangled wail.

She had no tongue! Kath was close enough to see that the girl's tongue had been cut out! Blood stained her teeth, proving the wound was fresh. Kath reeled in horror. The execution was a staged lie, a sick atrocity!

The girl began to squirm, but the guards held her down.

The lord gestured and the executioner raised the axe.

"No! This is wrong!" Kath raised a shout, but it was drowned by the crowd.

The axe swung down, the blade shimmering in the noontime sun.

Blood fountained bright. Red droplets splattered the front onlookers. A woman screamed. A child cried. The front row pushed back but there was nowhere to go.

Upon the scaffold, the wounded girl floundered and thrashed.

Twice more the axe struck.

It took three blows to sever the head, a gruesome death.

Kath stared, sickened by the travesty.

The executioner hoisted the severed head high, a look of terror forever frozen on the face of innocence.

The crowd began to seethe.

Someone screamed in horror, while others heaped obscenities on the queen's name. A few looked subdued while others looked terrified, trying to slink away. Fractured by raw emotions, the crowd began to disperse. The pressure around Kath eased, yet she had nowhere to go. The horror of what she'd witnessed rooted her to the ground. The Mordant had killed an innocent, staging her vile death like a mummer's farce. Clearly, he sought to besmirch Queen Liandra while invoking a war with Navarre. But did the stranger's death mean that Jemma still lived? Outrage and disgust thundered through Kath in equal measure. The Mordant had to die. But where was the beast's lair?

She stared up at the blood-spattered scaffold. Something told her to follow the severed head, guessing the Mordant would want to see the trophy from his vile play. Or perhaps he'd watched the beheading from the crowd? Kath quickly dispelled the notion, certain the Mordant would never sully himself with the stink of commoners.

The crimson-clad lord issued orders and one of the guards took the bucket with its gruesome burden. Kath angled sideways, slipping through the thinning crowd. Circling the scaffold, she kept the bucket in sight.

A rude, snuffling sound intruded, like a pig seeking a truffle. Kath looked down and found a dwarf pawing at her belt. *A duegar!* Repulsed, she pushed him away.

The little man stumbled, falling backwards. Glaring up at her, he flashed a wicked grin, his teeth filed to jagged points. "You smell like magic!"

Horrified by the execution, she'd nearly forgotten the foul duegar. Kath pounced on little man, grabbing his leather jerkin. He snarled, reaching for a dagger at his belt. Kath struck it from his hand. He squirmed, trying to get away, but she clung tight. He tried to bite her arm. Tripping him, she pressed his face to the cobbles, while grabbing him by the collar. "You're mine."

He squirmed, gnashing his pointed teeth.

Kath felt the prying stares of onlookers. Not wanting to be a spectacle, she deflected the curious with words. "*Thief!* Give it back, you filthy thief!" She dragged the little man away from the square, into the nearest alley. Throwing him against the wall, she drew her short sword, holding the blade to his throat. "Where is the Mordant?"

"Do you seek death?"

"Answer the question."

His squinty stare darted left and right, a weasel seeking escape.

Kath pressed the blade to his throat, drawing a bead of blood. "Answer or die!"

His stare snapped to hers. He snarled, flashing pointy teeth, but then he relented, his bluster fading to surly resignation. "I'll not say, but I'll show you."

Kath knew he was stalling. "See that crate at the far end of the alley?"

A grunt was his only reply.

"Imagine your head is the center of that crate." Keeping one hand on his collar, she sheathed her sword and reached for a throwing axe. A quick flick of her wrist and it struck true, hitting the crate dead center. She stared down at the duegar. "Run, and you won't have to imagine."

His eyes widened, a hint of respect on his swarthy face.

Unsheathing a second axe, Kath shoved him towards the crate. "Walk."

He skewered her with a shrewd glance, as if weighing his chances, and then waddled to the axe-killed crate.

Kath followed close behind. Tugging the first axe from the splintered wood, she returned it to her harness. "Now, the Mordant."

His nostrils flared wide, sniffing towards her. "What are you?"

"An angry woman with an axe."

"The scent of magic swirls around you, old and potent and nearly intoxicating."

"Walk." She shoved him forward.

He gave her a surly nod, and then turned the corner, waddling down another alley.

Kath kept careful track of the twists and turns. It seemed to her that they moved away from the castle, which doubled her suspicions. Perhaps the cursed dwarf was leading her astray.

Meow! A dirt-brown tabby darted from the shadows, rubbing against Kath's boots.

Startled, she stared down at the cat, praying it was one of Danya's. "Tell the others." The cat curled its striped tail around its paws, staring up at her with golden eyes. "The dwarf is leading me to the Mordant. Tell the others to bring their swords."

The duegar turned, his stare flicking around the alley. Seeing no one else, his stare settled on the cat. "You talk to cats?"

She heard no skepticism in his voice. Kath bit back a curse, knowing she'd have to kill him lest the Mordant suspected a beastmaster was in his midst. "Keep walking."

The duegar turned, waddling down the alley.

Kath cast a glance at the cat, but it made no acknowledgement...but then it was a cat. She chided herself for expecting something more. Hoping that Danya listened and understood, she nodded to the cat before following the duegar down the alley. Hefting her throwing axe, she urged him to hurry. "How far?"

"Not far now."

The noontime sun baked the alleyway. Avoiding a yellow puddle stinking of piss, Kath followed the duegar around a corner and heard a snarling hiss.

A massive black tomcat crouched in the alleyway. Hissing and spitting, he puffed his sides, his fangs bared. The duegar tried to skip past. The cat lashed out, claws raking the duegar's stubby legs. The dwarf yelped, but kept going. The cat turned and lashed at Kath, almost as if he was barring the way. Kath staggered backwards, flush with understanding. "This is a trap." Her gaze swept the alleyway, seeking a threat. Rain barrels, refuse, and closed doors, she saw nothing, yet the sense of danger thickened like a noose. She gestured to the duegar. "Come back."

Flashing a sinister smile, he turned and ran.

She needed him alive! Kath hesitated for half a heartbeat. *He knows Danya's secret!* Realizing she dared not let him escape, she drew back her throwing axe, taking aim at the dwarf.

Behind, she heard the crack of a broken roof tile.

Whirling, she saw a black-clad assassin crouched on the roof, a blow pipe set to his lips. Startled, she loosed the axe. Hastily thrown, she knew her aim was off the moment it left her hand. *Valin!* Turning, she ran, chasing the dwarf down the alleyway.

Something struck her arm. A dart impaled her leathers, saved from poison by her chainmail shirt.

Sensing the jaws of a trap, sweat bled out of her. Nearing the dwarf, she prepared to throw her remaining axe.

A second assassin dropped from the roof, barring her way.

Only one axe! Assassin or dwarf, her life or Danya's?

She hurled the axe with all her might, willing it to fly true. Unsheathing her short sword, she charged the assassin.

A dart struck her chest, but it did not penetrate her chainmail.

The dwarf screamed, falling face-forward, her axe embedded deep in his back.

Snarling, Kath charged the assassin. Howling like a banshee, she jinked left and right.

The black-clad devil never flinched. Raising his blowpipe, he blew.

Kath swept her sword blade in front of her face, a desperate defense, like trying to swat a fly from the air. Luck, or Valin, was with her, for something struck the blade, metal pinging on metal. Knowing she'd cheated death, a grin split her face. Kath raced two more strides, her sword raised for a killing blow.

The assassin dropped the blowpipe, reaching for daggers on his baldric.

Kath leaped, bringing her sword down in a two-handed strike.

The assassin crouched, his daggers raised.

Kath brought her sword down in a deadly chop. Blood spurted as Castlegard steel bit deep, cleaving through the assassin's neck. Surprise spiking his dying gaze. Shuddering, he sagged on her blade. Kath lowered the dead man to the ground. "Blaine said you were tougher to kill than that."

Placing her boot on his chest, she tugged her sword from the corpse. Wiping the blade clean, she strode to the dwarf.

Her axe had struck true, embedding deep in his back, but the duegar still struggled to breathe, not quite dead. Sheathing her sword, Kath yanked the axe loose, and then turned him with her boot. "Where is the Mordant?"

He stared at her, hatred glazing his face. "Come close," his voice rasped, "closer," a trickle of blood dribbled from his mouth, "and I'll tell you," his bloodstained lips curled in a sneer, "how to find...*death!*"

Something struck her throat, stinging like a bee. Kath whirled, tugging a dart from her neck.

A second assassin strode towards her. "We *are* hard to kill."

She raised her axe, but it wavered in her hand. Her vision swam. Her legs betrayed her. Kath crumpled to the ground, the axe falling useless from her hand.

53

Danya

An ancient power resided in the silver cuff, a brimming well of magic that yearned to be unleashed. Danya tapped into the silvery power, sending a silent call across the city. Choosing to beseech rather than summon, she asked for the help of feline kind. Cats from all quarters answered, swarming to the second floor of the cobbler's shop. Some came for curiosity, while others came seeking love and affection. With soft meows and tails held high, they wove runes around her, keening for her touch. Offering praise and soft caresses, she told them of a soul-reeking evil hiding in the city and asked them to search for death and darkness. Flattered and intrigued, many of the cats agreed. Underfoot yet unnoticed, the cats scattered through the city.

Having sent her small spies on their quest, she turned her thoughts to the local dogs. Seeking them in homes, shops, and back alleys, Danya asked them to be her guards, to keep watch for bands of armed men roaming the streets with ill intent. The dogs responded with eager tail wags and bright eyes, for guarding was play, duty, and fun, all rolled into one. Dogs of all shapes and sizes perked their ears, keeping eager watch on the streets surrounding the Zward's cobbler shop.

Feeling reassured by the circle of canine protection, Danya sat cross-legged on the floor, while Neven kept watch at her back. Drawing more power from the cuff, she entered a trance, her spirit roving from cat to cat, seeking an unfathomable evil.

From time to time, Neven woke her, pulling her from the trance to eat. Ravenous with hunger, she fell on plates piled high with meat and bread and gravy. She especially craved the meat, wanting it rare and red, greedily licking the grease from her fingers. After a short nap, she returned to the hunt, submersing herself in the silvery power of the cuff. Four-footed and small, she prowled the city on soft paws. Endowed with keen ears, keen eyes, and a discerning nose, she stretched her senses, always seeking.

So many cats roaming across the city, she asked some to watch over Zith hiding in his bolt hole, while others followed Kath and Blaine as they prowled the cobbled streets. Locked in a trance, Danya jumped from cat to cat, watching, listening, seeking, reveling in the four-footed form.

Awash in the cuff's intoxicating magic, time held no meaning. Sunlight slanted through the window, brightening and dimming and brightening again, yet Danya barely noticed, consumed by the hunt. She followed Kath for a while, but then lost her in the crush of a crowd. Reaching out to other nearby felines, Danya asked them to look for a blond girl who prowled like a warrior. Flitting to a gray mouser searching the queen's castle, she found nothing save marble hallways and courtiers' well-polished boots. And then she caught a sharp call from one of her spies. With the speed of thought, she was there, seeing through the eyes of an orange tabby. Fur raised in hackles, tail lashing, the cat hissed, flashing fangs. Melding with the cat, she smelled it, the scent of foulest evil. It rankled the nose, both enticing and repulsive, a sickening sweet scent of temptation overlaying the stench of death and decay. Terrified, the cat wanted to bolt, yet Danya held him firm, needing to see. Crouched in the shadows, she asked the cat to look up, seeking a human sigil, a signpost to identify the dwelling. Something hung on the wall over a throne-like chair, she strained to see the detail.

Another cat yowled for her attention. This one spied Kath in an alleyway, warning of a dark watcher on the rooftop. *An ambush!* Kath was in danger, yet the orange tabby had nearly discovered the Mordant's lair. Torn between the two, Danya swayed, stretched thin from following too many threads.

From a distance, the dogs began to bay.

Danya jumped back to the alleyway, to a fierce black tomcat. Melding with the cat, she did what she could to warn Kath, lashing out with fang and claw.

The howls of the dogs grew frantic, incessant for her attention.

The sound jarred her from her trance. "They've found us. They're coming."

Neven drew his sword, while Gris stiffened at the window. "We'll protect you."

Returning to the trance, Danya sought the braying hounds. Peering through their canine eyes, she found the enemy. A potent mixture of snargons, soldiers, and black-clad men stalked the streets with grim purpose. *Too many to fight!* "There's too many." Fear shivered through her. "A trap, the city is a trap!" The words of the rune-caster of Navarre spiked her mind with ominous warning. *Remain hidden! Use the many, use the small! Watch and seek and guide! Remain hidden lest the enemy gain your magic! Remain hidden or all will fail!* Danya burst to her feet, pierced by fear. "Entering the city was a mistake! We have to get out!" *Two legs instead of four...*she swayed with dizziness, unaccustomed to her own body.

Neven steadied her. "They'll catch us if we run, better to fight."

"No, there's too many to fight...and they're coming on foot." She made the decision, summoning four saddled horses from a nearby hitching post. "Take me outside. Trust the horses." Succumbing to beast magic, Danya fell into a swoon. Once more, she watched through the eyes of the hounds, yet she remained tethered to her body. Vaguely, she felt Neven's strong arms lift her, carrying her down the stairs and out into the sunshine. Cradling her close, he climbed into the saddle, settling her before him.

The hounds bayed, frantic with worry.

"They're coming." Directing the horses away, she threaded a path through Pellanor's busy streets. Bryx sprinted ahead, clearing startled bystanders. Unopposed, they cantered through the twists and turns of the cobbled streets. "Faster!" Neven's arms held her tight, swaying in the saddle.

The baying hounds fell far behind.

Reaching the gap in the western wall, they galloped out into the sunlit countryside, escaping the city, if not their pursuers. Danya knew the foul snargon would track her magic wherever they went, yet she had an idea where they might find sanctuary. Needing a view from the sky, she snared a red-tailed hawk with her magic. Spiraling upwards on wings spread wide, Danya gained a god's-eye view of the city and the surrounding countryside. Towards the north, she spied a forest crowned by mighty oaks. Releasing the hawk with thanks, Danya directed the horses to the wooded forest, a place where owls and wildcats both found refuge.

Dizzy from so many changes, yet she drew more power from the cuff. Strength flowed into her, filling her with potent magic.

Having set the horses on their path, Danya's spirit snapped back to Pellanor, desperately seeking the frightened cat. Crouched under the stairwell, hackles raised, she found him skulking in the shadows. Soothing his fears, she stared through his eyes, seeking a human sigil. A banner hung on the wall behind the throne. And upon that banner was embroidered an ancient symbol. Understanding struck. Releasing the cat, her spirit snapped back across the distance. Danya spoke the words aloud, before succumbing to exhaustion. "A dragon eating its own tail!" She struggled to get the words out. "Tell Kath, the Mordant hides beneath the Great Wyrm!"

54

Blaine

Blaine smelled the market before he saw it, the scent of cinnamon and other exotic spices tempting him forward. He turned the corner, expecting a busy noontime crowd, but the market was strangely deserted. An eerie silence smothered the great square. Devoid of people, the wooden stalls stood empty and forsaken, everything swept clean of spices. Only a few merchants remained, packing their wares, the spice-scent lingering like a ghostly remembrance.

The unexpected emptiness brought him to a wary halt, the silence punching him in the gut. *Noontime in Pellanor*...yet the market felt like a graveyard. His gaze swept the square, but he saw no signs of duegars, assassins or soldiers. *And no sign of Kath.* By agreement, they were supposed to wait at the spice market before pressing on. A feeling of unease slithered down his back.

Needing answers, he sauntered towards the nearest merchant. "Is the market closed?"

"No." A portly man with a ginger-red mustache, the merchant kept his head bent, scooping dried hyssop flowers into a burlap sack.

"Then where is everyone?"

The merchant flicked a wary glance to the hilt of Blaine's sword. "Gone to the execution."

An execution! The answer doubled his unease. "Whose execution?"

The merchant stopped scooping, giving Blaine a flat stare. "An enemy of the queen."

He heard fear riding the man's voice.

Plunging the metal scoop back into the hyssop, the spice seller hurriedly shoveled dried flowers into the sack. "Be there myself, but I have to look after my goods."

Blaine chewed the man's words, his gaze roving the empty market, wondering if Kath would have gone to the execution...but they'd agreed to wait. *Unless the execution was a clue to the Mordant.* His hand slid to the crystal dagger sheathed at his belt.

The merchant hissed a warning. "*Scat!*"

Blaine gave the man a stubborn look.

"Are you fresh-come to the queen's city?"

Blaine nodded.

"A word of advice, *best not to stand out.*"

Without the crowds, Blaine suddenly felt like a target. Nodding to the merchant, he sauntered back to a side street. Standing in a shadow, he slouched against a wall, keeping watch on the square. The merchants finished packing, loading sacks of spice onto carts and donkeys. The last one left and still there was no sign of Kath. A broken basket tumbled across the empty market, driven by a summer breeze. Blaine felt as if he was no longer in Pellanor, but some haunted rendering of the queen's city. Worry rode his shoulders. He turned away, retracing Kath's path.

At first, the streets were empty, but then he noticed faces peering from shop windows. He stared back, but the faces pulled away, watching but not wanting to be watched. Their stares did not feel sinister, just frightened, but the furtive watchers only made him more uneasy. Blaine lengthened his stride.

He walked for nearly a turn of an hourglass before a trickle of people returned to the streets. Women with empty baskets, men with swords belted to their sides, they walked with their heads bent and their faces averted, yet it felt as if the city breathed again. Blaine scanned the strolling crowd, looking for duegar, looking for Kath.

A cowled figure stared from an alleyway, disappearing back into the shadows.

Blaine veered towards the alley.

A wolf-faced warrior stepped from the shadows, his voice laden with worry. "Sidhorn sent me to look for you. The cobbler's shop is a trap!"

"A *trap?*"

Tingold scowled. "Danya and her guards fled. Not long after, a band of duegar and assassins appeared. They must have caught her scent. Some followed, giving chase, while others ransacked the shop. A handful never left."

A trap! Kath had warned him that the city would make for a strange battlefield, traps within traps. Pellanor was beginning to feel like the Dark Citadel, a hunting ground he knew very well.

"Where is the Svala?"

Lost...but he could not bring himself to say it. "We got separated. The others will need to keep watch on the shop, lest she return."

Tingold nodded. "Already done."

"And Danya?"

Tingold shrugged. "She summoned horses and rode west."

West...so the beastmaster had fled the city. Blaine knew they dared not let the Mordant get the wolf-girl's magic, yet he felt abandoned. Kath's plan was coming undone. He gripped the crystal dagger sheathed at his belt, a weapon to slay the demon. "Come, we need to find Zith." Blaine wove his way through the back streets, the wolf-faced warrior by his side.

55

Katherine

A heartbeat drummed through her head like thunder. Her mouth tasted like musty wool. Kath dared to open her eyes, squinting at the view. *The world is upside down!* Confused, she felt sluggish, like a moth trapped in molasses. It took her a moment to realize she was being carried over the shoulder of the black-clad assassin. *An assassin!* Her first reaction was to struggle, but she stifled the impulse, forcing herself to remain calm, a warrior assessing the odds.

Her hands were bound tight, dangling down in front of her. A slight twitch of her feet told Kath her legs remained untied, but her body felt leaden and slow. The effects of the dart still curled through her limbs like cold tentacles, slowing her reflexes and muddling her mind. Sleep beckoned but Kath struggled to stay alert. Her bound hands could reach the backside of the assassin's belt, but she saw no weapons, only tooled leather pouches. The pouches dangled like ripe temptations. Perhaps they held weapons, but Kath was no light-fingered thief. Tampering with the pouches would only serve to alert her captor. To defeat the assassin, she'd need the element of surprise as much as she needed a weapon. Better to feign sleep, playing the possum, waiting for the best chance to strike.

Relaxing her muscles, Kath hung like a sack of grain over his shoulder, her bound hands and long blond hair swaying to the rhythm of his stride. Despite his short stature, he carried her with apparent ease, a lesson to be cautious. The assassin stalked the back alleyways, keeping to the shadows. Kath cast sideways glances left and right, hoping someone might notice, hoping for a hue and cry, but she saw no one. Desperate, she looked for four-footed creatures, hoping to spy a cat, but none crossed their path. It seemed luck had forsaken her.

The assassin tightened his grip, adjusting her weight on his shoulder.

Kath struggled not to react.

A male voice said, "What have you got there?"

"A gift for our lord."

Panic spiked her, *the Mordant! She couldn't be delivered to the Mordant like a trussed pig.* For half a heartbeat she was tempted to fight, but it was too late to struggle, better to play possum. Kath bit her lip, her heart racing to a gallop. The assassin carried her through a doorway and into a marbled hall.

Savory smells of roasting pork and fresh baked bread swirled towards her, proving they neared a kitchen. The assassin turned away from the tempting smells, carrying her down a shadowed hall that opened into a large sunlit chamber. Peering through shuttered eyelashes, Kath caught glimpses of soldiers in purple tabards standing amongst black-clad assassins. *The Mordant's lair!* All around her, she heard the telltale jangle of arms and armor. Sweat erupted beneath her chainmail. Surrounded by enemies, Kath struggled to remain placid.

Jostling amongst the others, the assassin carried her towards the side, keeping to the rear. Shrugging his shoulders, he lowered her to the marble floor. His gentleness surprised her, or perhaps he merely sought to avoid a stir.

Lying on her side, her cheek pressed against the cool marble floor, Kath peered through a thicket of boots. Beyond the boots, she glimpsed a dais, and upon that dais sat *the Mordant!* A shiver of recognition speared her. His blond hair was longer than she remembered. He'd braided one blond lock and he'd grown a well-trimmed beard, yet she knew his face from the monastery. *Bryce,* she'd counted him a friend, an acolyte of the Kiralynn Order, yet the face of the young healer was utterly changed, overlain by a patina of fathomless cruelty. Possessed by a thousand-year-old evil, she wondered if the monk within still endured, a prisoner of his own body.

Boots shuffled sideways. A pair of soldiers in emerald tabards approached the dais.

Emerald tabards, proof he'd corrupted the queen's guards!

The soldiers bowed low to the Mordant. One carried a blood-spattered bucket.

The bucket!

The taller soldier said, "The deed is done, my lord. The girl panicked at the last moment, but it only added spice to the event. The executioner took three strikes to sever the head, just as you ordered. A royal execution, a pageant of blood and beauty, one the people will not soon forget."

The Mordant said, "Show me."

The soldier lifted a severed head from the bucket. Mercifully, all Kath saw was a tangle of raven-black hair.

The Mordant said, "Have it wrapped in the checkered cloak and sent by swift courier to the king of Navarre. By the time it arrives, decay will have obscured the features, doing the work of a dozen lies. Remember this day, when a single grisly gift sparked a war among allies, changing the past as well as the future." His lips curled in an arrogant smile. "So let it be done."

Anger spiked through Kath. She longed to attack, to forever rid Erdhe of the Mordant, but she could only watch, trussed like a goose bound for market.

Bowing low, the soldiers retreated. The Mordant leaned back on the throne. Kath glimpsed the sigil embroidered across his surcoat, a great golden dragon eating its own tail. Dredging a memory from her heraldry lessons, she put a name to the sigil. *The empire of Ur,* so he comes swathed in lies, hiding beneath the banner of distant Ur. A shiver passed through her. The Mordant truly was the prince of deceivers.

The Mordant stirred upon the throne. "Major Tarq, what word from the hunters?"

A deep voice answered. "The snargons tracked the scent to a cobbler's shop on the west side."

Danya! Kath feared for the wolf-girl.

"The quarry fled on horseback, but the snargons..."

Kath heard a sharp snuffling sound. Dirty boots blocked her view. Lying limp, she feigned sleep, peering through shuttered eyes. More boots appeared. Duegars surrounded her. Bending low, they crouched to sniff at her. One prodded her between her breasts. Kath lurched backwards, reflexively raising her bound hands in defense. A snide snicker acknowledged her movement. Having betrayed her ruse, Kath openly glared at them. Four duegars surrounded her, squat ugly dwarves staring down at her as if she was good enough to eat. One grinned a sinister smile full of pointy teeth. "What are you?"

A stern voice struck like a lash. "Jekal, you dare to interrupt me?"

The duegars stiffened, turning towards the dais.

The ugliest one, his face full of warts, answered. "Lord, this one reeks of high magic."

"High magic?" The Mordant's tone changed from annoyance to avarice. "What magic?"

Her assassin-captor grabbed Kath by the back of her cloak, dragging her towards the dais. "Lord, I caught this one stalking a duegar. I brought her to you as a gift."

The Mordant's stare turned her way.

Kath's heartbeat lurched to a thundering gallop.

His stare brushed across her, his voice full of disdain. "A girl? You brought me a girl who plays at swords?" He flicked his hand in dismissal.

Kath dared to breathe, spared by her sex, but then a gray-haired duegar sitting below the dais suddenly stood, his nostrils distended. His gaze fixed on Kath like a hound on the scent. "My lord, Jekal has the truth of it. This one reeks of ancient magic, powerful magic." The old duegar waddled close, sniffing at Kath. Repulsed, she tried to pull away, fearing he would find the crystal dagger, but the assassin held her firm. The duegar circled her, breathing deep, as if she were a prized pie at a village fare. Completing the circle, he stood in front of her, a crooked grin on his swarthy face. With a stunted hand, he reached out, tugging at the two leather cords around her neck. One held Duncan's warrior ring, the other her mage-stone gargoyle. Outrage flared through Kath as if he'd defiled her very soul. She flinched away, but the assassin tightened his grip. Oblivious, the duegar sniffed the silver ring once, and then dropped it, letting it dangle from the cord around her neck. Turning to her gargoyle, he fondled it with both hands. Breathing deep, he nearly swooned over the little figurine. "This is it!"

"No!" Kath lunged to her feet, her head butting the little man's face.

Yelping, he fell back, releasing her gargoyle.

Kath squirmed away from binding hands. Spying a doorway, she sprinted forward, desperate to escape. Footsteps followed. Somebody bulled into her from behind, slamming her to the floor. She fell hard, gasping for breath.

Too many hands grabbed her. Kath twisted and snarled, fighting like a rabid beast. A punch hit her square in the face. Her head snapped back and she bit her tongue. Blood swelled in her mouth. Dazed, she hung pinioned between two assassins.

"Show me."

Soldiers with drawn swords moved aside, opening a clear path to the Mordant.

He sat upon the throne, his gaze flicking across her. "Such a little wildcat, one wonders if you would be the same in bed." But there was no wonder in the Mordant's voice, just a cold certainty, like a torturer choosing an instrument.

Kath swallowed a shudder, remaining motionless, a mouse snared by a hawk's paralyzing gaze.

"Bring it."

The gray-haired duegar glared at her, his nose clearly broken, blood staining his ugly face. Waddling close, he yanked on the gargoyle, snapping the cord hard around her neck. With a flick of a dagger, he cut the leather.

Kath gasped, feeling the magic torn from her. She felt bereft. She felt a fool, watching as the duegar placed her gargoyle in the outstretched hand of the Mordant.

Feeling gut-punched, Kath hung between two assassins, a witness to her own failure.

The Mordant fondled the figurine, a smile alighting his face. "Mage-stone!" His gaze snapped to her. "In all my many centuries, never have I encountered a focus wrought of mage-stone." His voice turned hard. "How did you come by it? What does it do?"

Kath refused to answer.

The Mordant flashed a cruel smile. "In due time, you will beg to tell me. All your secrets shall be mine." His gaze turned to the gray-haired duegar. "Lasiter, tell me more."

The old duegar with the broken nose leaned forward, his gaze fixed on the little figurine as if he was bewitched by it. "My lord, it smells intoxicating, a focus of great age and power. Its strength akin to the oldest magics."

"A relic from the monastery?"

The duegar nodded. "Perhaps. It has the smell of a relic."

So he thinks it comes from the monastery! Somehow Kath knew the Mordant must never know it came from Castlegard.

The Mordant fixed his gaze on Kath. "How does a slip of a girl come to bear a relic?"

She did not answer.

"A riddle wrapped in the form of a girl." He gestured. "Bring her to me."

Still on her knees, the assassins holding her dragged her across the marble floor to the very foot of the dais. Someone grabbed her hair, forcing her head back. Kath felt like a sacrifice brought to the slaughtering block, her throat bared for a blade. She tried to remain calm, but her heartbeat galloped like a runaway horse. *Valin is my sword, Valin is my shield...*she fervently prayed to the god of war.

"Open your soul to me." The Mordant stared at her as if to flay her alive. The weight of a thousand years of evil beat against her.

Kath smelled the stink of her own fear. *Valin is my sword, Valin is my shield.* Afraid to even think of Castlegard or the Octagon, she clung to the simple prayer, repeating it like a chant.

Light flared at the back of her eyes, so bright it nearly blinded her.

"Ahhhh!" The Mordant howled in pain. "How dare you!"

Pain ripped through Kath. A scream burst from her lips. She writhed against her holders, feeling as if she were being torn asunder by wild horses. Her back arched, her bones grinding in protest. Her arms stretched wide, nearly torn from their sockets. Her screams turned to howls. She'd never felt such agony. Caught in a torturous rack, Kath roiled and screamed but there was no escaping the pain..and then it stopped.

Panting for breath, she hung limp between her captors.

"You...are...mine!"

Flinching at his voice, Kath looked at the Mordant, but his gaze was focused elsewhere, as if he was seeing something far beyond the walls of the audience chamber.

"Silence!" A fierce look filled his face. "I forbid you to speak!" Standing on the dais, the Mordant raised his hands like a wizard casting magic, but his gaze peered beyond the chamber walls.

A hushed dread smothered the audience hall.

All around her, soldiers and assassins shuffled backward, opening a moat of space around their lord.

Kath hung between her captors, trying to make sense of what she saw.

Anger flashed across the Mordant's face. His hands curled like talons, fingernails extended. *"Die!"* He slashed at the air, making raking gestures. Snarling, he turned, slashing left and right, as if he fought a ghost.

Kath stared, slack-jawed, wondering if the Mordant had gone mad.

No one in the hall moved.

Upon the dais, the Mordant fought an invisible foe, his face twisted in hatred. Suddenly the fighting came to a stop. Staggering back a step, the Mordant shuddered. "So be it." His gaze snapped back to the chamber, potent and cruel. "Dolf, with me. Time for you to kill a queen." He strode down the dais, his face dark as a thunderstorm. A path opened before him, assassins and soldiers cringing away. He'd nearly left the audience chamber when Kath's assassin-captor dared to speak. "My lord, what of the girl?"

The Mordant turned, casting a baleful glance her way. "Put her in an oubliette. I'll deal with her later." He strode from the chamber, an angry swirl of purple and gold.

56

Danya

Weary from holding so many different threads, Danya would have fallen from the saddle if not for Neven's strong arms. Suffused with magic, she was stretched too thin. Horses, hawks, cats, hounds, she darted between the different threads, keeping watch. A sixth sense warned her to let go, yet she dared not stop.

They reached the forest, mighty oaks upholding a leafy vault of summer green, but the enemy still followed. Once more she leaped to the sky, entering the red-tailed hawk. The wind caressed her feathers as she caught an updraft, spiraling higher. *To fly on pinioned wings...*the feeling was so intoxicating, soaring among the clouds, so easy to lose herself in the vast blue, but Danya forced herself to concentrate. Drawing more magic from the silver cuff, she tightened her bond with the hawk. Keen raptor-eyes raked the ground below and then she saw them. A band of men, coming on foot, led by a pair of dwarves. Like hounds on the scent, the dwarves slued their heads left and right, following a trail of magic. *Her magic!* The cursed duegars led the enemy north, towards the forest. By fleeing the city on horseback, Danya and Neven's wolf-faced band had gained a substantial lead, but the enemy persisted. They would come, of that she was certain. And when they came, there would be death.

"Who dares enter our forest?"

Neven's arms tightened around her, sending an urgent message, drawing her back to her own body. Danya swayed against him, struck by dizziness. So hard to be human after bonding with the feather-light soul of the hawk.

Neven spoke. "Like the animals of the woodlands, we come seeking sanctuary among the trees."

"Who are you?"

She saw them then, archers clad in greens and browns, their bows held taut, all of them staring with golden cat-eyes.

Neven's voice puffed with pride. "We are Painted Warriors of the far north, come to fight the Mordant in the Battle Immortal."

"Bold words for such a small band. Why should we welcome you to our forest, wolf-man?"

"Because we fight the same enemy...and we need your help."

Bryx stepped from the thick brush.

The nearest archers leaped away, turning their bows towards the big mountain wolf.

Bryx growled in warning, a low rumble, and then sauntered towards Neven and Danya. Taking a seat by their horse, he yawned wide, showing a fierce set of teeth.

The horses tried to shy, but Danya soothed them, holding them firm.

The dark-haired archer looked from Bryx to Neven. "So you walk with wolves?"

"*She* walks with wolves, and all creatures great and small. That is why we seek your aid."

The archers hesitated, conferring among themselves. Sensing they needed more proof, Danya reached for the red-tailed hawk. Answering her summons, the hawk fell into a stoop, plummeting towards the forest. Nearing the leafy green, he slowed with wings spread wide.

Danya shivered, returning to her own body.

A piercing call came from overhead. A red-tailed hawk swooped through the leaves, alighting on the ground next to the wolf. A proud raptor with bright plumage, he preened his feathers with a hooked beak.

Danya spoke. "Please, we need your help. *I* need your help. Enemies are chasing us, they follow my magic. Even if we leave now, they will still come to your forest."

An angry murmur hissed through the cat-eyed archers.

The tall dark-haired archer lowered his bow. "How many enemies and where are they?"

"They come on foot from the city, twenty swords led by two dwarves. They will be here within the turn of an hourglass, but they run blind, following the scent of my magic. If we work together, we can set an ambush."

The dark-haired archer stepped towards her. He breathed deep, as if he too was searching for her scent. He stared at her, studying her with his golden cat-eyes.

Danya held her breath, knowing much depended on the outcome.

"You speak the truth, although your tale leaves many questions. For now, we will work together. I am Carhain, captain of the Oak Grove. Come, and we will choose a place for this ambush."

Danya stiffened in the saddle. A wounded cry pierced her, sizzling through the magic of the cuff, but it was not any creature she'd ever bonded with. This one sought her, desperate for help. Something different, something else, a twisted, tortured creature seeking succor. She followed the thread, appalled by what she found. A soul of a man melded with a hawk, bound by foulest magic and unspeakable torment. She heard his cry, she felt his torment...and then the link snapped shut, as if sundered by Darkness.

Danya gasped, flung back to her own body. She felt tainted, soiled. "*Abomination!*" Danya shuddered, feeling the hand of a higher power. Her voice deepened, laden with the power of a god. "*Abomination! The Mordant breaks all laws of gods and men! He must be slain!*"

Bryx howled, a mournful wail.

Her mind was pulled towards a raven, as if the gods directed her vision. Through the raven's sharp eyes she saw the enemy approach the forest, a stunted dwarf leading the way. "They're coming! Beware!" Her vision burred, a great weariness assaulting her. Danya slumped forward, stricken by too much magic.

57

The Master Archivist

The Master Archivist trudged back from the execution, shame dogging his steps. Obsessed with the castle and his frantic search for the queen, he'd paid scant attention to the city, yet it was in the city that the Mordant wrote his worst deeds in a bold hand. The royal execution had ambushed him. He'd overheard rumors in the tavern, but he hadn't believed. Queen Liandra would never order such a foul murder and surely the Mordant would not dare.

The Mordant more than dared.

The shadowmaster felt like a fool who'd willfully poked himself blind. Recognizing the truth too late to recruit more men and mount a rescue, he'd forced himself to attend, standing witness to the grim spectacle. But the execution was much more than a mere spectacle, it was a statement of power. Instead of a princess, the Mordant brutally executed an innocent woman, all done in the queen's good name. The cruel pageant was an elaborate lie, yet the people of Pellanor seemed duped by the spectacle. Somehow the Mordant had gained control of the queen's city. Perhaps, the traitor had the truth of it, the Mordant cast a long shadow, and now the queen's city was eclipsed by foul darkness. The realization sickened him, but it also made him deeply fearful. If the Mordant dared to order such an atrocity in the public eye, then the queen's life was not worth a copper coin.

A shiver ran down his back. He was not normally a praying man, but he feared for his queen, he feared for his love. At least he knew the truth, the traitor unmasking the ancient evil. *The Mordant hides beneath the Prince of Ur.* Hatred curdled through the shadowmaster. Instead of searching the castle, he should have confronted the fiend who sought to steal her crown and corrupt her people. His hand stole to the throwing knife sheathed at his belt. *The Mordant!* His very name evoked nightmares, a legendary evil come to befoul Pellanor like a curse, yet surely he could be killed. Cut off the snake's head, and the snake must surely die. If he could not rescue his queen, then he would avenge her. The shadowmaster lengthened his stride, resolved to slay the Mordant.

He turned the corner, making his way back to the Rusty Dragon.

"Lord Highgate!"

The Master Archivist stopped, startled to hear his true name shouted in the street.

"Lord Highgate, I've come on behalf of the queen!"

He tracked the voice to the Dragon's tiled roof, but there was no one there, only a tattered hawk perched on the rusted weathervane.

The red hawk took wing, swooping down towards him.

The shadowmaster staggered back a step, for the thing was a horror, a man's face melded to a hawk's body.

"Crimson sword!" The hawk-fiend hovered overhead, each beat of its wings releasing a putrid stench. *"The queen is imprisoned in the oldest tower, in First Keep, beyond the reach of any passage. Crimson sword!"*

A woman screamed, pointing aloft.

The shadowmaster crouched, drawing a pair of daggers. "What are you?"

A man yelled, "A demon!"

Screams erupted from onlookers, people running away in blind panic.

"I was the Lord Sheriff."

The shadowmaster gasped.

"Save the queen!" Pain ripped across the fiend's face. *"The...Mordant...comes!"* Thrashing, the hawk fell to the ground, as if fighting some internal battle.

The shadowmaster stepped back, watching.

The thrashing stopped. The hawk righted itself, talons scraping on cobblestones. The bird crouched. Wings spread wide, it looked up at him, but the face was different, twisted with hatred, the eyes blazing with implacable cruelty. *"Die!"* The fiend launched itself at the shadowmaster.

Startled, the master loosed a dagger...and missed.

So close, the fiend was on him in a heartbeat. Talons flaring, it attacked his face.

Pain raked his cheek, the cuts biting like acid. He flinched away. Raising one arm as a shield, he slashed at the beast with his dagger. Putrid wings beat at his head. Cruel talons relentlessly slashed at his eyes. The shadowmaster dodged and turned, spinning away, but the thing followed. Blood poured from his forehead, the cuts stinging with pain. He stabbed at the unholy hawk, trying to keep it away. More than once, his dagger struck true, yet the fiend persisted, fighting as if it felt no pain.

"Down!"

Recognizing the voice, he threw himself to the cobbled street.

Thwak.

A feathered quarrel took the fiend in the head. It flapped to the ground, landing beside the shadowmaster.

He scrambled backward, but the fiend did not move.

Samantha stood in the doorway of the Dragon, a crossbow in her arms. "What was that thing?"

The shadowmaster got to his feet. "A fiend." He approached the sundered hawk. "Perhaps a friend." The hawk-fiend lay sprawled on the cobbles, its head shattered by the quarrel bolt. Putrid and stinking, it oozed green puss, rotting from within. The thing was an abomination, a horror, proof of the Mordant's foul powers. Proof that Darkness stalked Pellanor.

Smoke rose from the body.

The shadowmaster leaped back.

Tattered feathers ignited, the fiend bursting into flames...but the fire was pitch black, burning dark as midnight.

"Sorcery!" He spat the word like a curse.

Dark flames sizzled and burned, consuming the body till there was nothing left save a greasy mark marring the cobbles.

Samantha stood beside him. "Your proof's turned to smoke."

"Just so."

"Who has that kind of power?"

"The Mordant."

Samantha gaped. "Here in Pellanor?"

"Just so."

"Your face is a mess." Ever practical, she took his arm, steering him towards the Dragon. Shaken, he let her lead him to the tavern's great room. All the patrons were gone, fled or hiding. "It seems sorcery is bad for business." She pushed him into a chair, returning with a cloth and a bottle of brandy. "This will hurt."

It stung like hell, yet he remained stoic.

She talked as she worked. "What was that?"

"A message...from the queen."

She stared aghast. "That *fiend* brought a message and you *believe* it?"

"It knew the queen's code." He stared at her. "And I think I recognized it."

"You *recognized* it?" She made the hand sign against evil.

He gave her a solemn nod. "I think so."

Her face turned ghost pale. "So the Mordant *made* that thing?"

"I think so."

"The Gods help us." She sank to a chair. "What are you going to do?"

"The only thing I can do." He stood. "Save the queen and then kill the Mordant...or die trying."

58

Katherine

Kath had no strength left to fight. Drenched in cold sweat, her muscles twitching with remembered agony, she hung in the arms of her captors like a deadweight. It took all her will just to keep her head raised and her eyes open.

Her assassin-captors waited till the Mordant strode from the audience chamber and then they dragged her across the floor to a set of steps. Her boots thumped down the stairs, marking their number. The cool caress of stone-cloistered air stroked her sweat-drenched skin, making her shiver. The stairs led to a small wine cellar, barrels lining the wall. Kath stared at the wine casks, confused. One of the assassins fiddled with the latch on a mammoth man-high barrel.

The front of the barrel swung open, revealing a secret passage.

A potent stench wafted up from below, laden with the stink of sweat and piss, the raw reek of terror.

Kath flinched at the smell, struggling against her captors, but her efforts were feeble. They dragged her through the barrel's gaping mouth and down a short set of stairs.

Torchlight flickered below. The raw stink intensified, gagging her. Cages lined the walls. People stared from behind iron bars, men, women and children, their faces hollow and gaunt, their eyes empty of hope.

"What is this?"

They dragged her to the back of the chamber.

Two round stone plugs with embedded iron handles sat flush with the floor. An assassin took up an iron pry bar. Slipping the bar through the raised handle, he struggled to lift the stone plug.

Stone grated on stone.

He levered the plug aside, revealing a narrow round hole, dark and deep as a sightless eye.

"*No!*" Kath struggled against her captors. Summoning every last scrap of strength, she kicked and fought and gouged, but her captors prevailed. They forced her boots-first into the narrow oubliette. She fell hard, scraping against the side. Her boots struck bottom with a spine-jarring thud. Kath stretched her bound hands up towards the light, but it was too far to reach.

Stone grated on stone as they levered the plug back into place, like a moon eclipsing the sun.

"Nooooooo!" Kath screamed against her fate.

The plug fell into place with an ominous thud. Darkness prevailed. A bone-numbing cold embraced her. Kath beat against the walls to no avail. She screamed and hollered but no one came. Exhausted and heart-sore, Kath sagged against the walls, entombed in stone.

59

Liandra

Every time the key turned in the lock, Liandra flinched. She prayed for rescue while fearing the Mordant's retribution. His rage would be volcanic once he learned she'd turned his unholy herald to her own purpose. She shuddered remembering the corrupted hawk, her stalwart Sheriff ensorcelled in the putrid bird. Such a terrible fate, how could the gods permit such an abomination? Mired in worry and hounded by fear, the queen paced her tower chamber. Her gambit had to work, or she saw no way to escape the Mordant's lethal trap.

The key turned in the lock.

Suppressing a gasp, Liandra stood sword-straight, casting a haughty glare at the door. Whatever fate came for her, she would meet it as a queen.

The door swung open and a black-masked fiend leaped inside, bloody daggers bared.

She gasped, retreating a step.

"My queen!"

Recognizing his voice, she ran to him. *"Robert!"* Decorum be damned, she flung herself into his arms. He held her tight, lifting her off her feet. She tugged the leather mask from his face and then gasped. *"Your face!"* Ugly red scars crisscrossed his face, especially near his eyes.

"It matters not." He kissed her hard then set her down. "Come, we must go."

She needed no urging. Following him through the doorway, she found two black-clad assassins slumped in the hall, blood pooling on the floor. Stepping beyond the blood, she saw seven men, clad in a hodgepodge of armor, all of them wearing leather masks. "Why the masks?"

"The assassins' darts."

She remembered the darts, how they'd killed Sir Durnheart.

Robert tugged the tooled leather mask down over his face, nothing but slits to reveal his eyes. "Come." He hurried her to the stairs. The other men led the way, swords and daggers bared. Robert stayed by her side, keeping one hand on her arm as if she might disappear. They rushed down the carved spiral stairs of First Keep, meeting no opposition. Reaching the bottom, they entered a long hallway. The blood-red stone of First Keep gave way to polished gray granite. A wave of relief washed across the queen, finally free of the Mordant's insidious trap.

"*Halt!*" Soldiers in emerald tabards clogged the far hallway. Black-clad assassins stood among them.

Robert yelled, "*Run!*"

Badly outnumbered, they retreated back down the hallway.

"*Kill the queen!*" The enemy charged from behind.

Hearing the shout, Liandra knew her time had run out. Lifting her gown, she found herself in the lead. Refusing to be cornered in First Keep, she sped past the stairs, seeking another side corridor.

Steel clashed from the rear, the sounds of fighting coming from behind.

A man screamed in pain.

Robert hissed, "*Hurry!*"

Liandra raced down the corridor, searching the carved lintels above the doors. The fifth doorway bore the subtle mark carved in stone. "This way!" Thankfully the door was not locked. Flinging it open, she sped into a dusty storage room filled with crates, a narrow window giving just enough light to see by. Robert and three masked guards followed close behind. They slammed the door shut, piling crates in the way. While the men worked, frantic to block the door, Liandra raced around the room, her fingers following the narrow waist-high band of carved roses. Towards the back, she found what she sought.

A relentless pounding came from the door. The men worked to brace the barricade.

The queen turned the rose leaf, revealing a key hole. From the depths of her bodice, she tugged the chain holding the skeleton key. The key turned in the lock.

Stone ground against stone, and the secret door shuddered open.

"*Hurry!*" She hissed to the others, entering the dark passage.

The three masked men rushed past, one of them limping badly.

Robert came last.

A frantic pounding beat against the barricade, knocking crates to the floor.

Releasing the mechanism, the door ground shut.

Darkness swallowed them, muting all sound.

Liandra leaned against the wall, safe in the bowels of the castle. "That was close, too close."

"I knew I'd find you." Robert smothered her mouth with an ardent kiss. She clung to him, feasting on his strength, reveling in his touch, giddy to be alive. For a hundred heartbeats they indulged their passion, but then she remembered to be queen. "We need to get out. Our people need us."

"More than you know." Stepping away, Robert struck a flint, lighting a candle.

The other men shuffled forward, lighting candles from his till a small glow illumed the hidden passageway.

Robert handed her a candle. "Can you find the way out."

She smiled. "Of course." Her mood sobered. "But what of the city?"

"Corrupted by the Mordant's lies."

Anger burned through her.

He studied her face. "But some lies are more easily undone than others."

"What do you mean?"

Brushing a cobweb from her hair, he put a steadying hand on her arm. "Stewart lives."

"What?" Her heart froze, afraid to believe, but then her mind worked the puzzle. "The forger!"

Robert nodded. "The Mordant wove a web of lies around Pellanor, but in Lingard I read the true dispatches. Prince Stewart fought a fierce battle at Eye Bridge and lost, but the enemy did not stay to finish the fight. They crossed the bridge and galloped south. The prince took a minor wound in the battle, but he was not killed. The Rose Army regrouped and holds Eye Bridge against the north."

Her son lived! The knowledge unleashed a wellspring of strength within her...and a rage of vitriol at the Mordant. "Come," her voice sounded like silk over steel, "it is past time we slayed the Mordant's foul lies with truth." Holding the candle high, the queen led her loyal men out of the castle's secret passageways and into the city.

60

Katherine

Entombed in darkness, Kath sagged against the cool stone wall, every muscle aching. Battered and bruised, she took stock of her fate. Her weapons were gone, her throwing axes lost in the alleyway ambush. Both her sword and dagger sheath hung empty at her belt, her weapons taken by her captors...but they hadn't searched her boots. Pressing her right boot against the wall, she felt the crystal dagger tucked in the hidden sheath. A spark of hope surged through her, but it quickly dimmed. What use was the dagger if she could not escape? Trapped in stone, she needed her gargoyle. *Her gargoyle!* The gods had warned her never to lose it, yet she'd forfeited it to the very monster she'd sworn to slay. Despair beat against her. Shaking her head, Kath struggled to find a shred of hope. With bound hands, she searched her pockets and her belt pouches, anxious for anything that might help. Her captors had left her with a purse heavy with gold coins, a small ball of twine, a whetstone, a flint striker, and her signet ring. *Castlegard!* A pang of longing bit deep. Kath removed the heavy gold ring from her pouch and held it in her fist. If everything she'd heard was true, if her father and brothers were truly dead, then she was the last remaining heir to Castlegard. Duty and longing called to her in equal measure. If she died here, trapped in this stone hole, no one would ever know her fate. Kath set the signet ring on her finger. She clenched her hand into a stubborn fist, determined to find a way out.

Darkness pressed against her, heavy with a cold chill, as if to smother her resolve. The air smelled of dank stone but nothing fetid, implying she was the first victim fed to this godforsaken hole. *A fresh laid tomb...*Kath shivered. She bitterly regretted not carrying a candle stump in her pockets. Reaching for the striker, she raised it high above her head. One flick of the flint created a fleeting spark. A bright blink of white light revealed a glimpse of her prison. The walls were smooth, a cylinder carved into cold stone. She saw no cracks, no holes, nothing to give her hope. The plug that sealed the oubliette was out of reach. Even jumping, she could not touch it. Below her, the floor felt smooth and hard as stone, but she could not really see it. Somehow air seeped up from the bottom, but if there were holes, she could not tell. The oubliette was so narrow and close she could not sit, all part of the torture.

Finding no hope, she carefully returned the striker to her belt pouch lest she drop it.

Removing the whetstone, she stubbornly set to scraping the sharpening stone across her rope bonds. Sweat dripped from her forehead, despite the chill. Slow and sure, she sawed the whetstone across the rope. Unable to see, she tried to keep the whetstone sawing at the same place. Leaning her forehead against the cool stone, she strove for patience. It took forever, sawing back and forth, but finally the rope began to fray. She tugged and pulled to little avail. Frustrated, she returned to scraping.

A chill seeped into her flesh.

Time lost all meaning in the cold dark.

She must have dozed.

A loud clatter woke her.

Startled awake, she realized she'd dropped the whetstone!

"Nooo!" She searched with her boots and found it, but she had no way to pick it up! A cold rage roared through her. Kath bit at the frayed rope, gnawing at her bonds like a wild animal seeking escape. Tugging and yanking, she bit till the rope snapped asunder. Her hands won their freedom!

A thrill raced through her, a fleeting victory, but she remembered she was still trapped in stone.

Kath railed against her fate. This wasn't supposed to happen! How could the Light abandon her? No one even knew where she was! She prayed to Valin, to all the Lords of Light, beseeching their help, but the indifferent gods gave no answer.

The oubliette was silent and dank as a grave.

Kath sagged against the wall. The cold darkness gnawed at her mind, sapping her will. She prayed for rescue, she prayed for her captors to come. Her throat became parched, her stomach rumbled with hunger. She longed for a drop of water, for a glimpse of daylight, but nothing changed, as if her captors had forgotten her. She felt buried alive.

The muscles of her legs began to cramp. Kath squirmed, seeking relief. Unable to sit, she bent her knees, wedging her back against the wall. The position took some of the strain off her aching legs, but then her back and knees began to throb. Cramps racked her. Forced to stand, she leaned her forehead against the unyielding stone.

The oubliette proved an insidious torture. Trapped, she flailed against the walls, beating her hands till they throbbed. A sob escaped her, a prisoner trapped in stone.

61

Blaine

Darkness fell on the queen's city and still Kath did not come. Blaine paced the small chamber, fraught with worry. It was her plan to divide their magic into different bolt holes. Her plan to walk the city in braided paths, weaving confusing trails for the cursed duegar. He'd never known her plans to fail...yet they played against the Mordant. Doubt crept through his mind as turns of the hourglass passed. Waiting was always hard. Blaine yearned for action, for the feel of a sword in his hands.

Zith watched from a pallet on the far side of the room. "What will you do?"

Blaine combed his fingers through his blond hair. "Wait, for now."

"And then."

Blaine sighed, for it seemed as if everything was coming undone. "Kath said if something happened to her, I should do it my way." *But my way is the sword. Can swords defeat the Mordant?*

"We're running out of time. The comet is nearly gone from the sky."

Zith's words tightened the worry binding his shoulders. "I know. But first we need to find the bastard. Pellanor has countless hiding holes. The fiend could be anywhere."

Footsteps pounded on the stairs outside the door.

Blaine drew his blue steel blade. Bear and Sidhorn unsheathed their weapons, crouching beside the knight.

Three swift knocks followed by a delayed fourth implied a friend, but Blaine did not lower his guard.

Tingold opened the door, ushering another wolf-faced warrior inside. It was Gris, a member of Neven's den. Beneath his blue tattoos, he looked exhausted. Blood smeared his leathers and he stank of horse sweat. "I bear a message from Danya."

Hope ignited in Blaine. "So the Beastmaster lives?"

Gris nodded, struggling for breath.

Zith guided him to a chair. "Sit and tell us." Pouring a goblet of ale, he thrust it into the warrior's hand.

Gris drained the goblet. "We were ambushed," he paused for breath, "but the hounds warned Danya. She summoned horses and we rode from the city.

The enemy gave chase, but Danya led us north, to a forest crowning a hill. In the depths of the forest, we found allies, archers with strange golden cat-eyes."

Zith's voice held a touch of wonder. "The Children of the Deep Green."

Gris flashed a wolfish grin. "They're warriors. Together, we set an ambush for the enemy. They will trouble us no more." He stared at Blaine, his gaze sharp with urgency. "Danya sent me to find you. She said to tell you that the Mordant hides under the sign of the Great Wyrm, a golden dragon eating its own tail." Gris looked from Blaine to Zith. "Does that mean anything to you?"

Blaine recalled his heraldry. "A dragon eating its own tail...is the ancient symbol of Ur, but the empire does not meddle in Erdhe."

Zith said, "The Mordant hides beneath a lie." He turned to Tingold. "Run and get Thaddeus."

Nodding, the wolf-faced warrior hastened from the room.

"The Zward will know if an emissary of Ur lurks in Pellanor." The monk's stare turned hard. "We've found the Mordant."

Blaine nodded. "So Kath's plan *did* work."

Gris intervened. "Wait, there is more. Danya saw something else in the back alleys." His gaze turned bleak. "Kath was captured by a black-clad assassin."

"The Mordant!" Blaine made the name a curse. "Does she still live?"

"Danya said she held too many threads. She could not follow."

Bear and Sidhorn both issued a low growl. "We must save the Svala!"

Zith staggered to a chair. *"The blade bearer!"* His gaze sought Blaine. "If she is lost, then you are our last hope. You dare not fail."

Blaine straightened under the monk's searing glare. He gripped the crystal dagger sheathed at his belt. "The Battle Immortal."

Zith gave him a solemn nod.

"So be it." He turned to Bear. "Assemble the others. We attack before dawn."

The painted warrior leaped to do his bidding.

Zith gave him a puzzled look. "You'll just attack?"

"Someone has to, or the fiend will never die."

The monk stared, his face troubled.

"I doubt he'll expect it." Anger snarled Blaine's voice. "If you have another plan, I'll hear it, but time grows short. Kath's life may hang in the balance."

Zith had no answer.

Turning his back on the monk, Blaine strode to the window, gazing down at the night-cloaked city. *The Battle Immortal*...the name rang in his mind like a shimmering destiny. This was what he'd always wanted, what he'd dreamed of, yet now that the burden fell to his shoulders, it was heavier than he'd ever imagined.

62

The Mordant

Endowed with a virile young body and a restless mind laden with a millennium of experiences, the Mordant needed little sleep. Sated with sex, he roused the three young women from his bed, ordering them gone. Snatching up silk sheaths, they pouted, flouncing their perfumed hair, but they dared not disobey. Blonde, red-head, and raven-locked, they cast sloe-eyed glances his way before closing the door behind them. The Mordant rose from the bed, lighting candles around the room. Darkness mirrored the window, reflecting a youthful countenance with cynical blue eyes. He paused to consider his own reflection. Such a youthful body imbued with unfathomable wisdom, he reveled in the potent combination, a perfect state for his ascendancy.

Pulling on a dark velvet robe, he snatched up the two focuses that preoccupied his mind, a malachite coin from ancient Azreal and a small gargoyle cast in mage-stone. He could not resist touching them, fondling them, yearning to wake the magic within. The malachite coin remained stubborn. Despite keeping it close, he'd felt no flicker of magic from the obstinate coin, but the gargoyle was fresh come to his hand. *A mage-stone focus!* In his entire millennium of lifetimes, he'd never seen its like. His best snargon had named it a relic, endowed with the most potent of magics, a talisman from the ancient wizards. He yearned to fathom its secrets.

From the ironbound chest, he pulled a thick tome, one of the few he'd brought from the Dark Citadel. Adorned with ornate bindings worked in silver, he opened the latches, revealing vellum pages jeweled with color. An illuminated text, every page was exquisitely wrought, gold embellishments highlighting the elaborate script. The tome had once belonged to the cursed monks, but now it served him, as everything they'd ever treasured would soon be his. Turning the pages, he delved into the arcane details. An ancient grimoire of magic, the text spoke of forgotten powers. Fondling the small gargoyle, he turned the pages, searching for passages mentioning mage-stone.

A knock interrupted his reading.

Annoyed, he said, "Enter."

Dolf opened the door. "My lord, they come!"

A flash of excitement quickened in the Mordant. "The Octagon knight?"

"Yes, my lord." Dolf flashed a predator's smile. "He flaunts his colors, just as you said he would."

"My time is at hand." The Mordant savored the moment. "Rouse the men, but do it quietly. And then return to attend me."

"Yes, my lord." Dolf closed the door behind him.

A slow smile spread across the Mordant's face. He felt the long millennium of plots and schemes building to this moment, the culmination of the Great Dark Dance. Rising from the desk, he unlocked his ironbound jewel box, careful to avoid the poison-tipped trap. Nestled in velvet, his greatest focuses glittered in the candlelight. He chose carefully, adorning his arms with golden bracers and his fingers with jeweled rings. Armed and armored with magic, he set the crystal of pain into the prongs atop his iron staff. Raising the staff, the Mordant opened the link to each focus, reveling in the bounty of arcane power. He crackled with magic, adorned with the heady power of a god.

A second knock sounded on the door.

The Mordant reluctantly dimmed the magic. "Enter."

Dolf returned, bowing low. "How can I serve?"

"I'll have the wizard's robe of black velvet."

"Yes, my lord." The assassin served as his valet. The Mordant donned rich robes of black velvet adorned with arcane runes embroidered in gold. Into his pocket, he put the malachite coin and the mage-stone gargoyle. Satisfied with his preparations, he took up the staff of pain. "Come." He led the assassin from his chambers, down the stairs to the throne room.

The mansion hummed with men preparing for battle, yet they stopped and stared, bowing low as he passed. The Mordant swept into the throne room, the staff of pain clicking on polished marble. A cadre of assassins and snargons awaited him, falling prostrate to the floor.

The Mordant paused to stare up at the purple banner hanging behind the throne, the great golden Wyrm eating its own tail, the symbol of endings, the symbol of new beginnings. The dragon banner had served him well, but the time for deceit was over. "Time to come out of the shadows. Strike those false colors and raise my own."

A pair of assassins leaped to obey. Lowering the Great Wyrm, they discarded the purple silk. In its place, they raised a banner of darkest black, and upon that banner was a golden pentacle, the ancient symbol of power and pain.

The Mordant ascended the dais. Beneath the pentacle, he took a seat upon the throne. He felt a collision of powers building around him, a nexus of destinies. Strands of fate gathered so thickly around his throne, the Mordant felt as if he could reach out and pluck them, warping them to his will. "Let my enemies come to me. All of Erdhe shall be mine." Nothing could stop him, not the timid monks cowering in their mountain monastery, nor the Octagon knights in their crumbling castle, nor the impotent Lords of Light cringing beyond the gray veil. The Mordant breathed deep, crackling with Dark power, keen to attain his long-sought destiny.

63

Blaine

The time for subtlety was past. Instead of skulking in dull browns, Blaine would face the Mordant as a knight of the Octagon. Perhaps Kath would have done it differently, but this felt right. This was his way. His silver surcoat glittered over his chainmail, a maroon octagon emblazoned boldly across his chest. Swirling his maroon cloak across his shoulders, he shrugged on his sword harness. His blue steel sword reared over his right shoulder, the crystal dagger sheathed at his belt. No other weapons would be needed in this fight decreed by destiny.

Blaine followed Thaddeus down the stairs to the rear storeroom. The Zward had been busy since coming to Pellanor. Scouring the length and breadth of the city, they procured a small mountain of armor to defend against poisonous darts, the cowardly weapon favored by the Mordant's assassins. Bear, Sidhorn, and the other painted warriors sorted through the pile choosing bucklers, shields and chainmail. Blaine chose a gorget embossed with a rose to protect his throat and a simple barbute helm to guard his face.

Thaddeus brought him a kite shield cloaked in canvas. "I had this painted for you." Removing the canvas, he revealed a silvery shield painted with a maroon octagon.

Blaine tested the shield's fit, adjusting the straps. The weight felt good on his arm. Few knights could wield a great sword *and* a shield, but the incredible lightness of blue steel made it possible. "My thanks." Against the assassins, the added protection might save his life.

Thaddeus gave him a solemn nod. From the rear of the storeroom, he brought forth a second shield, but this one was smaller, a simple round shield emblazoned with a maroon octagon.

The painted warriors fell still, all of them turning to stare at the shield.

"I had this made for Kath." Thaddeus offered the shield to Bear. "I thought you might carry it in her honor."

The big man turned crimsoned-faced. Nodding to the Zward captain, he accepted the shield, settling it on his arm. "For the Svala."

"*The Svala!*" The words echoed through the storeroom.

Blaine noticed that all the painted warriors wore a tattered strip of maroon cloak tied around their right forearms, a symbol of Kath's maroon band. Making a sudden decision, he cut a thin strip from his own cloak, tying it to his right arm.

Nods of pride and approval rippled through the painted warriors.

Blaine waited till every man was armed and armored, nothing save their eyes showing. Uncorking a wine skin, he took a swig and then passed it around. "You've come from the north for a grim purpose. Tonight we finally wet our weapons with the blood of the oldest enemy." Blaine unsheathed his blue steel sword. "We slay the Mordant and rescue the Svala."

Swords hissed from sheaths. *"The Svala!"*

Blaine nodded to Thaddeus.

The Zward captain led them out into the night. In the rear alleyway, they found Zith mounted on a gray horse. The old man was transformed. His straggly beard was neatly trimmed and his silver-gray hair was combed straight to his shoulders. Clad in a robe of midnight blue, a jeweled dagger was sheathed at his belt. But it was the glittering jewels that truly transformed him. At his throat he wore a magnificent gold torque of a winged dragon and his right hand bore a fistful of rings. Steeped in dignity, he looked like a wizard summoned from a bygone age. Blaine prayed it was more than just an illusion.

One of the Zward took the reins, leading the horse.

Weapons bared, they loped through the city streets. Clouds dampened the moon and stars, deepening the darkness before the dawn. Still hours away from sunrise, the city slept, yet candles and lanterns glowed from a few windows, as if Pellanor clung to every glimmer of light.

Arms and armor jangled with each loping stride, proof of their deadly intent. The few rogues and sulkers who crossed their path ran at first sight. The maroon band comprised twenty-one painted warriors, every fighter a fierce veteran of the north. Five Zward who had traveled with them from Navarre, plus an additional seven men mustered from within the city. Blaine led a force of thirty-three against the assassins, guards, and duegars of the Mordant. He knew they'd be woefully outnumbered, but he was betting on surprise and ferocity to even the odds.

Thaddeus led them towards the wealthy part of the city. Shops and houses gave way to mansions surrounded by topiary gardens, the scent of jasmine perfuming the streets. Blaine flashed a chagrinned smile beneath his helm. Of course the Mordant hid beneath luxury, yet compared to the palace in the Dark Citadel, the mansions were hovels.

Thaddeus raised a fist, halting the troop. "It's best if we divide here."

Blaine clasped arms with the Zward captain. "We'll meet over the Mordant's dead body."

"May the Light make it so." Thaddeus gestured and a third of the force peeled away to attack from the rear. Sidhorn followed, leading Zith's horse.

Blaine turned to the others. "Check your armor." They took a moment to tighten buckles and straps, knowing any show of flesh could be lethal, and then they set off at a fast trot. Lucas led the way. Blaine ran behind the Zward guide, the kite shield on his left arm, his right wielding his blue steel sword. It seemed otherworldly to race through the city streets in full armor, yet they'd come to slay an ancient evil. A heady excitement gripped him, the elation of battle for a just cause. This was what he was meant to do.

Something pinged off his helm. Blaine spied a dark figure crouched on the roof. *"Assassins!"* He made the word a curse.

Darts pinged off shields and armor, a hail of death raining down, but none found flesh.

"For Honor and the Octagon!" Blaine roared his battle cry as he turned towards the Mordant's manse.

Guards in purple livery stood alert outside the door. Unsheathing their swords, they raised a warning cry as they crouched in defense.

At Blaine's signal, two painted warriors twirled slings, loosing stones. The guards dropped, felled at their posts, but more poured from the doorway. Like a kicked beehive, the mansion disgorged guards and assassins. Roaring his battle cry, Blaine waded into them. A single swing of his blue steel blade severed a guard's head. He stunned another with his shield while skewering a third with his sword. Blaine became a whirlwind. Stroke and parry, his blue sword cleaved shields and armor, seeking flesh. None could stand in his way. Leading the charge, he cut a path towards the doorway. An assassin ducked under his head-high swing, thrusting a dagger at his chest. The thrust felt like a punch, but the blade skittered off chainmail. Blaine brought his shield down, bashing the assassin's head with a sickening crunch. The assassin crumpled to the ground, another corpse piling by the doorway. Blaine leaped over the dead, slicing into the next defender.

He gained the doorway. *"To me! Rally to me!"*

Lantern light spilled across the entranceway, the marble halls proving wide enough to swing his blue steel blade. Enemies in purple tabards clogged the hallway, fodder for his sword. Blaine bulled into them, reaping blood and guts. Howling for their Svala, the painted warriors followed, fighting with a fierce savagery. The enemy fell back under the onslaught, blood slicking the floor.

Assassins leaned from the stairway, raining darts into the melee. Poisoned darts pinged off his armor like angry bees, yet none stung him. Blaine battled forward, ignoring the cowardly darts. Stroke and slash, he waded into the enemy, reaping a terrible toll.

Behind him, Tingold yelled, *"Above!"*

Blaine flicked his glance aloft, shocked to find a weighted net spiraling towards his upturned face. Shoving his foe aside, he raised his great sword like a spear. An ordinary sword would have been ensnared by the tangle, but blue steel sliced the heavy net as if it was gossamer. Shredded netting fell around him, the sticky strands clinging to his armor. He started to cut them free when a giant of a man rushed towards him, a battle axe raised in a two-handed strike. Unable to get his sword around in time, Blaine raised his shield. The battle axe struck with the force of a battering ram. The shield shattered into splinters. The axe sped through the shards, catching Blaine a glancing blow on the shoulder. Blunted by the shield's destruction, yet the blow drove him to his knees. Pain raged through his shoulder, numbing his left arm. Stunned, Blaine struggled to breathe.

Laughing like a berserker, the giant raised the axe for a killing blow.

Howling like a banshee, Bear barreled into the berserker, driving him back.

Blaine surged to his feet, joining the fight, wielding his sword with one good hand. Fighting beside Bear, the two of them pressed the attack. Steel clanged against steel with a ferocious beat. Bear's sword darted in, drawing the axe down to parry a low blow. Blaine stepped in with a head-high swing. Blue steel cut through armor, flesh and bone, severing the berserker's head. The head thumped against the wall with a sickening thud. Blood spurted from the neck, splattering the hallway. The corpse toppled to the floor, sprawled beside the severed head. Blaine kicked the head towards the enemy. Wide-eyed, they turned tail and fled.

Blaine gave chase, Bear two steps behind. *"For Honor and the Octagon!"* Bellowing his war cry, Blaine raced down the marble corridor, chasing purple-clad foes. The corridor opened into a large chamber with a vaulted ceiling.

The enemy turned, presenting a picket of swords.

Blaine skidded to a halt, Bear two steps behind.

"At last, the hero comes." A blond-haired lord clad in dark robes sat upon a raised throne, an iron staff held upright in his fist. Rings glittered on his hands, golden runes inscribed on his robes, he looked like a wizard stepped out of legend. Behind the throne, a black banner emblazoned with a pentacle declared the lord's true colors.

"The Mordant!" The name hissed out of Blaine like a curse. He leveled his blue steel sword at the fiend. "Fight me!"

The ring of swords tightened.

"That is no way to treat our guest."

Snarling, the guards retreated two steps, opening a space around Blaine and Bear, but they did not lower their swords.

From out in the corridor, the sounds of clashing steel echoed, yet no other warriors reached the audience chamber. Outnumbered, Blaine tensed, his gaze fixed on the Mordant.

The Mordant flashed a knowing smile, a spider lurking at the heart of a web. "Have you come to slay me with your blue steel sword?" He made a slashing gesture with his left hand while issuing a venomous hiss. *"Thanoth flamous!"*

Blaine's blue steel sword ignited with a cherry-red glow, as if stoked in a blacksmith's forge-fire. A volcanic heat beat against him, raging through his gauntlets, fierce enough to burn flesh from bone. Snarling, Blaine fought to ignore the pain, to ignore the blazing heat. He'd seen this foul trick before, in the bowels of the Dark Citadel, yet knowing it was a trick did not ease the agony. Pain roared through him, yet by force of will, he tightened his grip on the cherry-red sword, staggering towards the Mordant.

Behind him, he heard Bear gasp, caught in his own nightmare.

One step, two steps, Blaine struggled against the agony. Smoke rose from his gauntlets. The sword's glow intensified, glowing bright enough to blind. Blaine choked on the stink of charred flesh and scorched metal. Heat beat from the blade, so fierce he feared the sword would melt. Pain seared him. Clamping his teeth against the flesh-charring agony, he struggled forward. The sword wavered in his hands, glowing bright as Hell. He reached the foot of dais, but the pain was too great. Screaming, he flung the sword from his smoking hands.

Steel clattered against marble.

Blaine fell to his knees, cradling gauntlets blackened and charred. Frantic, he tugged off the smoking gauntlets, afraid of what he would find inside. The armored gloves clattered to the floor. He expected charred stumps, oozing blood, but his hands were whole and unburnt. Amazement and relief flooded through him, but then a snarl rose in the back of his throat. "*A trick! A lie!*"

Pulling the crystal dagger from its sheath, he surged to his feet and charged up the dais.

The Mordant gestured and pain spiked through him.

Blaine felt a sword thrust pierce his guts, skewering him alive. Groaning, he sank to his knees, impaled by steel. He looked down, but there was no sword. "*Another...lie!*" Grinding his teeth, he fought the agony.

The invisible sword twisted deep in his guts, ripping sideways.

Blaine hugged his middle, desperate to keep his insides from falling out, but there was no blood, no gore. He struggled to believe his eyes, yet the pain smote him.

"*Ahhh!*" A rasping scream escaped his clamped teeth. His spine snapped, bending him backwards, as if his body was bound to a wheel. Falling to the marble floor, he hit hard, driving the breath from his lungs. His arms and legs snapped wide, as if being pulled asunder. Every joint and sinew wrenched with pain, nearly torn from his body. Tortured by invisible hands, Blaine writhed in agony, yet somehow he kept a grip on the crystal dagger.

64

The Mordant

The Mordant descended the dais, the staff of pain blazing with a baleful red light. He circled the fallen knight, redoubling the pain. "So this is the hero they send against me." He gestured to a snargon. "Remove his helm. I want to see his face."

The snargon scuttled forward, tugging the helm from the knight.

Blond hair and pain-racked eyes, yet his mouth was a snarl of determination.

The Mordant hissed. "*You!*" He jabbed the staff towards the knight, sending a bolt of agony into his side. "I saw you in the sanctum beneath the Dark Citadel." He circled the knight, twisting his pain. "I saw you in my chambers in the Dark Palace. I prayed you would come, a champion sent to be sacrificed." The Mordant's voice hissed with hatred. "I owe you a lifetime of torment. Your payment is due." Anticipating the pleasure to come, he made his voice soothing with menace. "A knight of the Octagon shall be my vassal. Twisted into a faithful nightmare, you shall serve in forms you never dreamt possible."

The knight reared against his bonds, spitting hatred. "I'll never serve you!"

The Mordant laughed. "How little you understand the weapon you wield. Did the monks not tell you?"

The knight glared, fighting his bonds as well as the pain.

"No, they did not, did they? The monks are stingy with their knowledge." The Mordant circled the knight, holding him in a thrall of agony. "They never told you the potency of the dagger is tied to the life of the bearer. It's brilliant really. An amazing piece of magic linking the blade and the wielder, guarding against the champion's failure lest the dagger fall to my hands. The binding magic took many champions and many lifetimes to discern, but now the riddle is solved and you are mine!" The Mordant chuckled. "Long have I awaited your coming. Your pain and your life shall both serve me. For as long as you live the crystal dagger retains its soul potency, and you shall live a very long time. Wielding the power of the dagger, I shall remake the world!"

"I'll never serve you!"

"So strident and so naive. How little you understand what I can do with a soul-carver. By the time I am done, you will *beg* to serve."

"*Never!*" The knight bucked against his bonds, but invisible hands held him firm.

The Mordant bent to claim the crystal dagger.

The clash of steel intruded, warriors spilling into the chamber from the rear garden.

Annoyed, the Mordant gestured to the intrusion. "Stop them!"

Assassins and guards leaped to do his bidding. The enemy pushed to the very threshold of the audience chamber but no farther. The fighting was ferocious but brief. When the clatter of swords fell silent, Major Tarq approached. "My lord, you should see this." The major gestured and three captives were brought forward. The first two were warriors, battered and bloody. The Mordant gestured and their helms were removed, revealing tattooed faces. One bore the tattoo of an eagle, the other a wolf.

The Mordant snarled. "Tattooed scum from the far north, you should have stayed in your caves." But then he saw the third prisoner, a blue-robed monk of the Kiralynn Order. "I did not expect the Order to risk one of their own." The Mordant flashed a serpent's smile. "Bring him."

A pair of guards dragged the monk forward, forcing him to his knees.

Gold glittered around his neck, a torque fashioned into a winged dragon. The Mordant recognized the piece. Anger flashed through him. "How dare you!" Wielding the staff of pain towards the monk, he loosed a bolt of agony. "You plundered my hoard! You dare to wear *my* torque!" Twisting the staff, he quadrupled the pain. "My treasure hoard, how did you find it?"

The old man loosed a hideous scream.

Father!

The cry came from within, but the Mordant paid it no heed. Wielding the staff of pain, he flayed the monk, imagining his skin peeled from muscle, invoking a terrible torment.

The old man shrieked and wailed, thrashing in the hands of his captors.

The Mordant sneered. "You plundered my relics but you know not how to wield them!"

Green light blazed bright within the Mordant's mind. The light startled him, an ambush from within. The Mordant reached for his magic, but it was not there! A shield of green light shimmered around his mind, severing his will from all his magic. A thread of fear pierced the Mordant. He battered his will against the shield, seeking a weakness. The shield felt ancient, an unknown power buffering him. Something about it felt familiar, yet he could not put a name to it, a distant memory nearly forgotten. The Mordant battered the light but the green shield held, neutering his magic. Fear spurred his rage.

You shall not harm him!

The voice came from within, from the prisoner-monk. The Mordant turned his wrath upon the captured soul. *You betray yourself, for I need no magic to crush you!* Summoning the Darkness from within, the Mordant's soul grew in strength, gaining the power of an avenging god. Bloated with a thousand years of evil, he smote the captured soul. Darkness hammered down like an iron fist. With each blow against the monk, the green shield dimmed and cracked. Unleashing his full fury, he pummeled the monk till the captured soul howled in torment. Suddenly, the green light extinguished, snuffed like a candle. Magic roared back through the Mordant, as intoxicating as an heady elixir.

The Mordant opened his eyes.

"My lord, behind you!"

The Mordant whirled, his staff raised.

The knight was on his knees, the crystal dagger poised to strike.

Wielding magic, the Mordant turned his anger outward, striking the knight with the force of a lightning bolt. Magic smote the knight, hurling him across the room. The knight struck the dais hard, his body crumpling across the stone steps. The Mordant followed, invisible fists battering his foe. He flailed at the knight, till he realized his enemy's ploy. Bridling his rage, the Mordant withdrew his power. "You shall not die so soon...or so easily." He gestured to a pair of assassins. "Take him."

Assassins scrambled to subdue the knight.

He hung dazed between them, little more than battered meat.

"Take care, lest you snuff his life."

The Mordant looked for his prize.

The crystal dagger lay dropped on the floor.

"At long last." The Mordant swept down, claiming the dagger. Lifting it high, he smiled in triumph. A trickle of magic pulsed through him. Awakened by the dagger's touch, he felt his eyes glow with an unholy red light, revealing the harlequin within.

Assassins, snargons and soldiers dropped to their knees in homage. After a millennium of scheming, the time of his ascension was at hand.

"Take the monk and the knight to the sanctum." He fondled the crystal dagger, enthralled by the promise of the soul carver. "Put the tattooed scum in cages to await their turn." His men bundled the prisoners away, plenty of fodder for the soul carver. "At last, after a millennium of scheming, it is finally mine!" The Mordant followed, keen to wield the unchained power of a god.

65

Katherine

Kath woke with a start. *"Duncan!"* Dreaming of their wedding night in the shield forest, she longed to stay enfolded in his arms. Waking, she found herself entombed in stone, every part of her body aching and sore. *Trapped in an oubliette!* She leaned her face against the cold stone, bitter proof the nightmare was real. Her legs ached and her tongue was thick with thirst. So thirsty, she realized her captors had never returned with water, or food, or a scrap of light. Perhaps they'd forgotten. Perhaps they'd left her to die. Panic rose in the back of her throat, bitter as bile, yet she swallowed it down.

It could not end like this.

Time lost all meaning in the dark. She wondered if Blaine and the others even knew she was captured. *Cats in the alleyway...*she'd have to trust in Danya's cats. She laughed at the desperate absurdity, the sound echoing back with a tinge of madness. Kath shook her head, denying her ears. Perhaps Blaine would lead the charge and attack the mansion. She clutched at the thought, praying for rescue, but the stone plug remained stubbornly sealed, shut tight as a tomb. No one came, neither friend nor foe. Perhaps they'd attacked and lost. Despair filled the darkness. Kath could not bear to imagine their defeat.

Her own failure beat against her. Bound like a goose trussed for market, the assassin had brought her before the Mordant, dumping her at his feet like a gift. The humiliation rankled, her failure biting deep. And the Mordant, such a smug bastard, he hadn't even truly looked at her, dismissing her as a girl playing at swords. His arrogance stung, yet she'd gained by his smug ignorance. His men had confined her to this stone tomb without a thorough search. Sometimes it paid to be overlooked. Pressing her right boot against her stone prison, Kath proved the crystal dagger was still hidden in her boot sheath. She clung to the small victory, but what good was the dagger if she could not get out? She railed at the gods, pounding her fist against the cruel stone, but there was no answer.

Exhausted, she slumped against the wall.

Time stretched.

Darkness pressed down, weighing against her.

She grew feverish, dreaming of Duncan, but dreams of Duncan were a double-edged sword. She'd promised Duncan she'd put an end to the Mordant...and he'd promised to wait for her in the light. How would he ever find her if she died entombed in darkness? How could she ever face him if she failed to keep her vow? A tear slid down her cheek. She could not fail. She could not die in darkness.

"I have to save myself."

The words whispered out of her, like a message from her younger self. Startled by her own voice, she remembered her past, her time in Wyeth. Kidnapped by the Mordant's servants, she'd realized she could not wait for the shiny knights to rescue her. Life wasn't a fairytale. If she wanted rescue, she'd have to do it herself. But how?

Turning, she ran her hands across the mitered stone, but she found no blemish, no weakness. If only she had her gargoyle. The gods had warned her never to be parted from it. A memory teased her mind. Something Master Rizel had said. She struggled to remember, but it would not come to her, yet somehow she knew his words held the key she sought. Swallowing her frustration, Kath breathed deep, trying to still her mind. "Master Rizel," she whispered his name as if seeking to summon him. Building memories in her mind, she thought of the monastery, illuminated script shimmering from every wall. Kath stepped into memory, seeking the answers she needed. Following the jewel-bright script down a long hallway, she came to a door inset with a diamond-shaped window. Opening the door, she stepped into a garden, sunlight streaming through glass panes inset in the ceiling. *The garden of contemplation*...a marvel of the monastery. Kath willed herself to smell the verdant green, to be in the garden. She walked along the pathway, her hands brushing lush leaves. Towards the rear, she found the statue of the three monk-keys. *Hear no evil, see no evil, speak no evil*...Kath shivered, for she'd seen the cost of blindness to evil, but the statue's potent message was not why she'd come. Turning, she found him sitting on the stone bench, just as she remembered. A sun-kissed face lined with the wisdom of a life well lived, Master Rizel gave her a knowing smile.

I've been waiting for you. I knew you would come.

So real, Kath thought she might touch him, yet she withheld her hand, not wanting to break the spell. "Is this memory or imagination? Or something else?"

Does it matter? You've come seeking knowledge needed.

"Can you help me?"

Can you help yourself?

"I'm trapped in an oubliette...and I fear for my friends." Failure riddled her voice. "And I've lost my gargoyle."

Some things are never truly lost.

His words triggered a memory hovering just out of reach. Unable to grasp it, her voice turned frantic. "But I'm trapped in a stone tomb! It can't end here."

Have you given up?

Her answer came unbidden from the very depths of her soul. *"No."* Her voice was hard as steel.

Then this is not the end. He smiled. *There is more to you than meets the eye, Kath of Castlegard. Perhaps that is why the gods chose you.* His gaze turned solemn. *The answer lies within yourself. Remember what I told you about magic and the ancient wizards.*

A memory returned, sharp as swords. Pierced with understanding, Kath gasped, wondering if it could be so simple.

Master Rizel smiled. *There is nothing simple about it. Focuses were a tool for acolytes. An Age turns, and things that were lost will come again.* He stood, as if to leave. *Believe in yourself, and you will find a way.* The master began to fade, his image wavering like heat above a flame.

"Wait!" Kath struggled to hold onto him. "What if it does not work?"

It must work, and so it shall work, if you dare to believe. All of Erdhe depends on it. Like a candle blown out by the wind, the master disappeared.

The garden was gone. She was back, trapped in the oubliette, but Kath no longer feared it. Stone was something she knew very well, from the mighty walls of Castlegard, to the mage-stone halls of the monastery, to the Mordant's hideous gargoyles, to the tainted stone of the Dark Citadel. She'd walked through walls and ceilings, refusing to fail, refusing to be stopped. She balled her hands into fists, the gold signet ring a heavy reminder on her hand. She was the heir of Castlegard. She was the blade bearer. She would not be stopped now, especially when so much hung in the balance. Kath squared her shoulders. "I will not fail." Taking a deep breath, she thought back to the last time she'd held her gargoyle. She remembered the smooth seamless feel of it, mage-stone wings spread wide and claws carved small, details too intricate for an ordinary carving. *Her good luck charm.* Her talisman of Castlegard, she'd carried it since she was six. Kath imagined it nestled in the palm of her hand, every detail familiar. And then she imagined the magic within. She imagined it, she longed for it...she *felt* it! Magic sang to her, a song of stone, a song of power. Daring to believe, Kath embraced the power. "I will not fail." Opening her eyes, she stepped into the stone.

66

Blaine

S hackles clicked closed on his wrists. They'd stripped him of his surcoat and armor, leaving him bare-chested. Blaine tried to resist, but every muscle and joint ached, as if he'd been nearly torn asunder. He told himself the pain was just an illusion, but his body screamed otherwise. A groan escaped him as they hoisted him aloft. Pain lanced his arms and chest. Chains rattled overhead, pulling him upright till his toes just scraped the floor.

Fresh pain cut through the daze fogging his mind. Stone-cloistered cold puckered his bare skin. They'd brought him to some type of crypt, a silver pentacle etched across the floor. Bronze braziers stood at the five points. Twisted man-figures rising in tortured forms, they held flaming basins aloft, casting malformed shadows. *Not a crypt, an unholy chapel...*Blaine struggled to suppress a shudder.

"Strip the monk." The Mordant stood beyond the brazier light. Cloaked in shadow, he appeared as a sinister silhouette, dark without details save his eyes. His eyes glowed red like twin portals to Hell.

Assassins dragged Zith to the pentacle. They stripped him of his gold dragon torque and his rings. Cutting away his dark blue robe, they chained him spread-eagled to the silver pentacle.

Blaine kept his gaze on the Mordant. In the audience hall, he'd raged like an angry bull, hurling pain and magic, and then he suddenly changed, going cold as a slithering serpent. Somehow this cold Mordant scared him more.

"Leave."

Finishing their tasks, the assassins bowed low to the Mordant, and then scurried from the crypt. A door closed and it felt like a lid falling onto a sarcophagus, sealing away the living world. Blaine shivered, rattling his chains.

The Mordant glided into the flickering light. His staff was gone. In his hands he held the crystal dagger. "You sought to deceive me." His voice was smooth and soft and laden with menace. "Where is the true blade bearer?"

"I am the blade bearer."

The Mordant flew across the chamber, his dark robes fluttering like a great bat. He raised the dagger above his head for a lethal strike. Blaine flinched, expecting a fatal stab, but instead the Mordant slid the crystal blade across Blaine's chest, making the shallowest of cuts. Pain scored him, blood trickling down his torso like tears.

Standing lover-close, the Mordant hissed. "This blade is *dead*...and you know it."

Blaine struggled to concentrate, the shallow cuts leaving tracks of pain. "I know no such thing!"

"Then the monks lied to you." Hissing like an adder, the Mordant stepped away. Turning his glowing gaze to Zith, he began to circle the spread-eagled monk. "Both of you were in the Dark Citadel, yet it was you who plundered my hoard." The Mordant sneered down at the monk. "Amongst treasures collected through the ages, you found this dagger and you thought to deceive me. But the bearer of this blade is long dead, killed by my own hand." He raised the crystal blade, turning it in the flickering light. "The soul magic is long fled, leaving just enough residual in the crystal to betray my true nature." He lowered the blade, his red gaze slithering to Zith. "Did you really think you could deceive me? A mere mortal confounding a thousand years of evil?" Menace laced his voice. "I should drink your heart's blood and be done with you, but such a death would be too kind, too easy. I've always wanted a monk for a servant...for a gorelabe!" The Mordant swooped low, like a bat seeking blood. "You shall serve me!" Wielding the crystal dagger, he carved runes in the monk's chest. "*Scarmon tellerah clawth!* Tell me of the true blade bearer."

Zith shrieked in pain, the smell of burnt flesh reeking the air, but then he spat at the Mordant. "You...shall...not win!"

His red eyes glowering, the Mordant hovered over the monk, the crystal dagger poised for another cut. "So arrogant, yet you've barely begun to taste pain."

Blaine looked away, refusing to watch. Hanging helpless as a side of butchered beef, he fought his chains, desperate for a way to escape, but the iron shackles held firm, biting into his wrists. Sweat rolled down his naked chest despite the stone-cloistered chill. The monk's screams beat against him, a prelude to more pain. Trapped, Blaine's gaze skittered across the unholy chapel. *By all the Gods it cannot end like this!* Movement where none should have been snagged his attention. Something skulked at the edge of the flickering light, something low near the ground. As he watched, Kath rose out of the stone floor like an avenging angel. Blaine gasped to see her.

The Mordant's gaze speared the knight. "Will you speak and spare him the pain?"

Blaine snapped his gaze to the Mordant, afraid he might have betrayed Kath. "Yes, I'll tell you! Leave the monk alone, and I'll tell you."

The Mordant moved with a predator's fluid grace, rising to stand before the knight. "Tell me his name."

Blaine jerked away, deliberately rattling his chains. He swallowed, searching for words to distract. "I was only the diversion, the vanguard before the true attack."

"Give me his name."

"The true blade bearer..." Blaine twisted, clanging his chains, "is the heir to Castlegard."

"Another lie." The Mordant sneered. "Castlegard has no heir save the one *I* choose to make."

"You're wrong." Blaine spied Kath emerging from the floor behind the Mordant, the crystal dagger poised to strike. "There is one you overlooked. One you always overlook."

The Mordant snarled. "You lie to save yourself, but I will skin the lies from your tongue. Castlegard shall be *mine*."

"*Never!*" Kath rose up behind the Mordant, her face a mask of vengeance. "*I am Castlegard!*" She struck, driving the dagger deep into the Mordant's back.

The fiend stiffened, a look of shock and pain flashing across his face. He twisted, staring back at her, his voice enflamed with outrage. "A *girl!*"

Blaine gaped that the Mordant still stood! *She'd missed the killing blow!*

The Mordant flailed at Kath with the other crystal dagger, but the girl turned with him, keeping her blade buried deep in his back. "I'll flay you alive for this!"

Kath narrowly evaded the slashing dagger. "*By the Light, your soul is forfeit!*" And then she stepped into the Mordant.

Blaine gasped.

The Mordant crumpled to the floor, motionless as a puppet with cut strings...but the girl was gone, vanished from sight.

67

Katherine

Kath had learned much from the Mordant's foul gargoyles. Following the dark taint, she sought the fiend's soul-heart. Like a slug's trail, a foul wrongness oozed through the gray soulscape. She'd never felt such appalling Darkness, a soul drenched in a thousand years of evil. "*I walk in the Light. I walk in the Light.*" Shivering in revulsion, she whispered the words, holding the crystal dagger before her.

The dagger began to glow with a white light. Drawing comfort from the glow, she followed the foul trail. Kath found the Mordant waiting at the heart of Darkness. He stood in a vaulted crypt of stone, a silver pentacle etched across the floor.

"A mere slip of a girl." His face twisted in disdain. "They send a girl to slay a god." At first he wore Bryce's face, blond hair and blue eyes, but then his features began to melt and flow, changing into a blur of men. Wizards, warriors and kings, his face, form and garb changed, but his red gaze remained the same, implacable and seething with hatred. The changes began to slow. His flickering visage finally settled on a young man's face with long dark hair and dark eyes. Kath knew she beheld the true face of the Mordant, a man who'd lived a thousand years ago. A shiver passed through her. He might have been handsome, save for the stark cruelty radiating from his eyes.

"You've come to take my soul, but I'll reap yours instead!" The Mordant shimmered with power. An arcane glow melded to his body, forming a helm and armor. Burnished steel encased the Mordant, yet it was like no armor Kath had ever seen. The helm was fashioned into a fearsome skull, the breastplate engraved with skeleton ribs. Helm and breastplate, greaves and gorget, the armor was fashioned to resemble a lich king.

Terror radiated from the armor, beating against her.

Kath staggered back a step, fighting the need to cower.

A great sword grew from the Mordant's fist, the blade black as sin. The Mordant's voice deepened within the fearsome helm. "The knight said you are the heir to Castlegard. Come and taste the sword that slew your king."

"*Father!*"

The Mordant leaped to the attack. The dark sword came crashing down in a mighty two-handed strike.

Kath only had a dagger, *a dagger against a great sword*! Ducking low, she raised the dagger in a desperate parry. Light flared bright from the blade. The dagger shimmered and Kath found herself holding a crystal sword. Swallowing her surprise, she gripped the hilt, parrying the lethal blow.

Steel struck crystal and sparks flew.

Kath's arms shuddered at the savage blow, but the crystal blade held true. Twisting away, she sought an opening, casting sideways glances at her foe. The Mordant's armor was hard to behold, radiating a cringing fear.

The dark sword slashed towards her face.

She dodged away, evading the blade's lethal reach.

The Mordant rushed to the attack, raining blows. Kath gasped, twisting away, yet the Mordant pursued. Wielding the Dark blade with consummate skill, he fought with an intense ferocity. He fought like a sword master.

The realization spiked her soul, *a thousand years of evil!*

Dodging sideways, it took all her skill to evade the dark blade. Three times Kath parried the dark sword and three times she was driven to her knees by his fearsome strength. She rolled away, climbing to her feet. Her arms ached, her muscles trembled, yet she kept the crystal sword raised. Kath circled the enemy, seeking an opening. Somehow she had to find a way to get inside the black sword's fearsome reach.

"Surrender the crystal blade and I will let you live."

Kath ignored his lies, keeping the blade raised.

The Mordant circled. Within the fearsome helm, his eyes blazed Hell-bright. "You cannot defeat me. I was a master of war centuries before you were ever born. Your legends are my memories."

Kath leaped to the attack, but the Mordant moved with lightning speed, beating her blade away. A cut opened on her left arm, stinging like acid. Kath gasped, realizing the dark sword had sliced through leather and chainmail like a knife through churned butter.

The Mordant laughed. "Against this blade, you cannot win."

Kath slipped sideways, moving away from the dark blade, desperate for some advantage.

Behind the Mordant, a ghostly figure appeared. *Bryce!* Draped in chains, yet he gave her a determined look, tossing something towards her. It looked like a green coin, but when it hit the ground, it grew into a malachite shield. *For Azreal!*

The Mordant roared. "How dare you meddle!" He turned, sending a vicious stroke towards the shimmering figure.

Bryce disappeared in a howl of pain.

Kath lunged for the shield. Settling it on her left arm, she crouched to face the Mordant.

The dark sword crashed towards her with blinding speed.

Kath raised the shield, praying it held.

Dark steel struck the malachite shield. Green sparks flew and the dark sword quivered, issuing a terrible shriek. Twice more, the sword struck her upraised shield, and twice the malachite shield held. Trusting the shield, Kath blocked the dark blade and lunged towards the Mordant, penetrating his reach. *"For Castlegard!"* With all her might, she thrust the crystal sword towards his chest. The blade plunged deep, passing through armor, bone and flesh, seeking the Mordant's heart. Pulsing with white light, the crystal blade struck true.

The Mordant fell backwards, clattering to the floor.

His arms and armor disappeared in a swirl of shadow. A trickle of blood dribbled from his mouth. His eyes glowed red with a baleful light. "You shall not win!" He stared at her with a mixture of disdain and disbelief, spewing sibilant words like a curse. *"Taranth...darmon...rargarth!* I summon...the Dark God!"

Kath cringed. *He summons a God!*

The Darkness deepened. A Presence invaded the soulscape, something vast and dark and primordial. Oily and ancient, it oozed through the soulscape with implacable dread.

Strangled with terror, Kath crouched low. Afraid to breathe, she clung to the crystal dagger, the blade's light growing feeble against the gathering Dark.

At first there was only silence, the vast, dreadful silence of an open grave, the ominous stillness before a terrible storm...but then cruel laughter boomed from above. *Servants do not summon gods!* A thunderclap shook the soulscape...and the dread Presence was gone.

The Mordant gasped, shock stamped on his face. *"My lord! You cannot abandon me!"*

Released from the menacing terror, Kath stood. Exerting her will through the blade, she struck a deep blow. "By the Light, I cast out your soul!"

A wind appeared. Cold and dark, the wind began to howl, raging into a storm. A whirlwind of Darkness buffeted Kath, yet she kept the blade buried deep in the enemy's chest. The crystal sword began to vibrate and hum, burning with a fierce heat, yet she refused to release it, knowing the battle was not yet done. Clinging to the blade, she willed the foul Darkness into the Mordant. "Taste your deeds!" The Dark funnel swirled down, pouring into the Mordant's gaping mouth. He choked and gagged, yet the funnel was relentless. An ocean of sins poured into him, filling him till there was no Darkness left in the soulscape.

The rogue wind vanished, leaving nothing but a deathly stillness.

Bloated and dying, the Mordant turned his head. His face was withered and ancient, his dull red gaze seeking hers. "Mine...will be...the last victory. Castlegard crumbles under my will. All of Erdhe shall...fall."

Kath's heart quailed at his words.

He shuddered beneath her. His eyes went dark, the red light snuffing to eternal darkness like a candle forever blown out.

The Mordant's bloated body exploded in a shower of ash.

Battered and sore, Kath sagged to the ground, laying sprawled across the pentacle.

68

Blaine

Hanging from chains, Blaine gaped in shock. The Mordant lay crumpled on the stone floor, still as death, yet Kath was gone, vanished from the chamber. Blaine's heart thundered, his gaze skittering around the crypt, seeking enemies while praying for a glimpse of the girl. Shackled and chained, there was nothing he could do save watch.

"Zith, she's gone."

The monk gave no answer. Moaning, he lay shackled to the floor.

Blaine turned, dangling from chains, peering into the murky shadows.

The cold of the crypt seeped into him.

Red sparks erupted from the braziers, flames belching to the vaulted ceiling, as if opening a portal to Hell. Blaine twitched, his gaze darting around the crypt, yet he saw no reason for it. Bright sparks fell in cascades, hissing and spitting, sizzling across the cold stone floor. Shadows writhed around the braziers like tortured souls twisting in pain.

A screaming howl roared through the chamber, loud as a wounded dragon.

The flaming braziers suddenly dimmed as if snuffed.

Darkness encroached, ominous and suffocating.

An eerie stillness gripped the crypt.

Drenched in dread, Blaine shivered, his body erupting in a cold sweat. Hanging from chains like dangling meat, his toes scrabbled across the floor desperate for purchase. His gaze skittered left and right, seeking a friend, fearing a foe.

The flaming braziers leaped to life, returning light to the crypt.

The sense of suffocating dread eased.

Blaine dared to breathe. He blinked and Kath was there, lying next to the Mordant, the crystal dagger clutched in her hand. Yet she did not move. Still as death, her face was pale and haggard, as if she'd endured a great trial. Fear spiked him. "*Kath!*" He prodded her with his voice, her name echoing through the crypt.

Kath moved, answering his call. She rolled away from the Mordant, her groggy gaze seeking Blaine's face. She fixed on him like a ship seeking anchor in a storm-tossed sea. "His soul is gone, banished to Hell."

His breath caught, half afraid to believe. "*The Mordant is dead?*"

She gave him the barest of nods. "Yes."

Triumph blazed through him. "We've won! We're going to live! The ancient bastard is dead!" He flashed a rogue's grin. "I'd kiss you, woman, if I wasn't dangling from chains."

Kath stood, sheathing the dagger at her belt. Her gaze roved the crypt. "We need to get out of here."

Beside her, the Mordant stirred.

Horror pierced Blaine. "*He lives!*"

Kath did not seem disturbed.

Blaine yelled. "*Kill him!*"

Kath made a calming gesture. "He's the Mordant no longer. He's Bryce."

The Mordant sat up. Blue eyes fluttered open, but instead of hatred, they gazed with wonder. "I'm free!" He sobbed. "I'm alive!" He flexed his hands in front of his face. "My body is my own!"

Blaine hissed, "Are you certain?"

Kath drew the crystal dagger, but instead of striking the Mordant, she merely pressed the blade against his hand. "Look at his eyes."

The Mordant's eyes remained clear and blue and wide with wonder.

Kath smiled. "The red glow is gone. His eyes tell the truth. The Mordant is slain, his soul damned to Hell for all eternity. That threat is forever banished." She sheathed the dagger at her belt.

"Then it truly is done?"

"Truly." Her answer reassured, yet her face wore a worried look that said otherwise.

Bryce touched his face, as if to confirm the truth of his freedom. Turning to Kath, his voice was heartfelt with thanks. "I thought I'd die with the Mordant."

"I learned much from the Mordant's gargoyles. Some of the condemned souls were wizards who knew how to wield soul magic."

Bryce winced, struggling to sit.

Kath helped him. "I'm sorry for the wound to your back. I aimed to hurt but not to kill. You'll need a healer."

"I'll live." Bryce smiled and then grimaced with pain.

Zith roused, his voice feeble. Still chained to the pentacle, bloody runes carved in his pale chest, the old monk craned to see his son. "Bryce? Is that my son?"

"Yes, father. I'm here." Bryce crawled towards Zith, cradling his father's head in his lap.

Chains rattled as Blaine scraped his toes across the floor, struggling to take the weight off his aching arms.

"I have to find the keys." Kath stood, turning to leave, but Bryce said, "Wait!" Rummaging through the Mordant's robes, he removed three items, laying them on the stone cold floor: a malachite coin, a long shard of red crystal, and a mage-stone gargoyle.

"My gargoyle!" Kath snatched up the small figurine, holding it close.

"Take this as well." Bryce gestured to the red crystal but he did not touch it.

"No." Kath shook her head, shuddering in revulsion. "That focus is pure evil. It should be destroyed or thrown to the bottom of the sea." She looked at Bryce. "But what of the coin?"

"The coin belonged to a murdered monk. An assassin gave it to the Mordant but it bonded with me instead." Bryce reached out, fondling the malachite coin. "It came from ancient Azreal, carrying a curse of vengeance against the Mordant."

"Azreal?"

Bryce answered. "An ancient city destroyed in the War of Wizards."

Kath stared wide-eyed. "A potent curse."

Blaine rattled his chains, his arms lanced with pain. "The keys!"

Kath flashed a contrite look his way. Loping across the chamber, she climbed the stairs, disappearing into the shadows. Blaine felt the door open, as if the gloomy crypt drew a deep breath.

Bryce bent his head towards Zith. Father and son spoke with hushed voices. Blaine thought he saw tears on the old man's face.

Kath returned with Bear and Sidhorn and four rings of jangling keys. *Keys!* Blaine grinned, equally relieved to see the painted warriors alive. He'd feared he'd led them to their deaths. They both looked battered but whole. "How many survived?"

Sidhorn tried a key on Blaine's shackles while Kath knelt by the monk. "Too few."

Blaine needed to know. "How many?"

Sidhorn tried another key. "Tingold, Gris, Ruthgar, Tangor and Thaddeus are well enough to wield swords. Pren and Lucas live but both are sorely wounded."

Nine, so few! Blaine looked away, mourning the loss of so many.

Sidhorn said, "The Svala lives and the Mordant is dead, so they died with honor, they died with victory in their grasp. Their names will long be honored."

The lock clicked open. Released from the shackles, Blaine crumpled to the floor. His arms and shoulders ached and his chest wept blood, but he feared the fight was not yet done. "What of the Mordant's men?"

Sidhorn shrugged. "Thanks to the Svala, we hold the prison, but nothing more." The big man scooped up the mound of discarded clothes and armor and brought them to Blaine, helping the knight into a padded gambeson. Blaine tugged on his chainmail and his surcoat, feeling more like himself. "My sword?"

Sidhorn shook his head, handing him an empty shoulder harness. "We have but two swords between us."

Two sword! And the mansion was still overrun with the Mordant's men. Blaine shrugged on the harness. "We'll have to change that."

The last shackle fell open, releasing Zith. Wearing nothing but a loin cloth, he struggled to stand. Bloody runes carved deep in his pale chest wept blood. Bryce helped support his father, but Zith looked terribly frail, as if the rune-carved wounds had drawn years from his life. Zith tottered, nearly falling. Bear scooped the monk into his arms, carrying him like a child.

Kath said, "Come."

Bryce stopped her. "The crystal."

The red crystal lay on the edge of the pentacle. The shard glimmered evil in the brazier light.

No one wanted to touch it, as if the shard held a splinter of the Mordant's soul.

Kath glanced around. Gathering up a strip of blue cloth shredded from Zith's robes, she used the cloth to pick up the crystal without touching it. Wadding it in a small blue bundle, she stuffed it into one of her belt pouches and tied it tight.

She must have felt Blaine's stare, for she met his gaze. "We dare not leave it."

He gave her a solemn nod, yet he feared the way magic came to her hand.

Kath led the way from the crypt. They crossed the pentacle, climbing the steps to the door. Blaine followed close behind, yearning for his blue steel sword.

The door at the top of the steps gaped open. The raw stench of a prison poured out, hitting him hard, far worse than the stink of the crypt. People penned in cages like animals had a hellish reek. Blaine hoped to never smell its like again.

But the cages stood open, men, women and even children huddled on the floor. Filthy and gaunt, they looked frightened till they saw Kath, and then they looked awestruck, as if spying a hero from legend. Blaine turned away, chastened by the look on their faces.

He strode to Ruthgar. The boar-faced warrior stood guard by a closed door, a sword in his hand. "What happened here?"

Ruthgar scowled. "They captured a handful of us with their sticky webs, a cowardly weapon." His tattooed face flamed red. "I was ashamed to live, but then the Svala rose out of the stone. She slew the assassins and set us free." The burly man straightened, grinning like a berserker. "She put a sword in my hand again. I will not fail her."

"Weapons?" Blaine's gaze flicked around the dungeon, seeking a weapon.

"We have only the two swords, but plenty of daggers." Ruthgar drew a dark steel dagger from his belt and pressed it into Blaine's hand.

A dagger...when he needed a sword, but Blaine took it. Better to be armed than empty handed. "And beyond that door?" He'd been too dazed to remember.

"A cellar filled with barrels."

"A wine cellar." Blaine stretched, trying to relieve the terrible ache in his arms and shoulders. He glanced at the other painted warriors. Bruised, battered, and bleeding, none of them were fit to fight, but they did not have a choice.

Kath joined them, Bear and Sidhorn standing close behind. "We need to get out of here. But first we need to learn what's happening in the mansion."

She looked exhausted, her face pale and pasty, deep shadows bagging her eyes. Blaine doubted she'd survive another fight. "I'll go."

Kath gave him a grateful nod. "Remember, we don't have to fight our way out of here."

Blaine gave her a puzzled look.

She gestured to Bryce. "We have the Mordant. He can order our release." They turned to look at a young monk clad in dark robes. He sat on the floor, huddled next to his father. Somehow the menace was gone.

Kath said, "Fear of the Mordant runs deep. We'll play off that fear."

Blaine was doubtful. "Can he do it?"

"He survived the Mordant."

Blaine gave her a thoughtful nod. "But first we need to find out what's happening above."

"Just so."

"Sidhorn, Tingold, with me." Blaine gestured to Ruthgar. The big man eased open the ironbound door.

Kath laid a hand on his wrist. "Take care."

Blaine nodded, nothing but a dagger in his hand, feeling naked without his blue steel sword. His gaze slid to the others. "Get them ready to fight. This isn't over."

Kath gave him a burdened gaze. "I know."

69

Katherine

Kath sagged against the wall lest her legs buckle and her weakness betray her. She hadn't wanted Blaine to see how soul-weary she was. Morale mattered, so she sought to shackle her own fears, yet the Mordant's dying words plagued her like a Hell-spawned curse. She'd thought the Battle Immortal would be won with his death. A rueful sneer rode her face. How foolish, how naive. Only in fairy tales did evil die so neatly. The fiend was dead, but his treachery delved deep. *Castlegard!* She yearned to disbelieve his dying words, but somehow she knew he spoke the truth...a bitter truth aimed like a poisoned dart at her heart.

Kath scowled, knowing such distraction only served the Mordant. Smothering her fears, she turned her mind to the problem at hand. They needed to escape this prison, this trap. Their situation was perilous. Only a few battered warriors fit enough to fight, armed with little more than daggers, yet somehow they had to win free. Bryce was the key, yet he sat huddled on the floor wracked by tremors. The Mordant was dead, banished to Hell, yet the horror of his possession wrapped around the young monk like barbed chains. Kath shuddered, unable to imagine such a soul-crushing imprisonment. At least he had his father for comfort.

Zith looked terrible.

Kath worried about him. Sweeping off her cloak, she knelt, using it as a blanket to cover him. The monk shivered and shook, his face dead-fish white, foul runes carved deep in his chest, yet he clung to his son's hand. Kath gripped his arm, stifling a gasp. His skin was ice-cold yet slick with sweat. Kath tucked the wool cloak close. "He needs a healer."

Zith's fevered gaze found hers. "These cursed runes...leech my life."

Shock pierced Kath. She looked to Bryce. "Can you?"

His gaze was bleak.

She could not lose another companion, not now, not Zith. "Surely you can undo the Mordant's foul spell?"

"I don't know how." A hopeless pleading dogged his voice. "I spied on the Mordant. I heard his words, I witnessed his foul deeds, but I was a prisoner, never privy to his thoughts. When the Mordant carved these runes..." Bryce winced, taking a shuddering breath, "I felt his malice, his hatred for the Order, but I know not what the runes mean, or how they harm." Anguish rode his face. "I cannot undo this."

Zith's gaze sought his son. "Yet, you have done so...much. Always in the Light, enduring the worst evil. My son, I am...so proud."

Kath looked away, biting back tears, hearing words she never heard spoken by her own father.

"Take your vows." Zith gasped in pain. "Serve the Order."

"I will, father."

"Kath...my thanks."

Her tears broke.

"Father, *no!*" Bryce clung to his father's hand, tears streaking his face.

Kath prayed to all the gods, begging for help, begging for a favor.

Zith drew a rattling breath, and then was still.

Bryce tried to rouse him, to no avail. A sob escaped him. He whispered a prayer as he gently closed his father's eyes.

Kath crumpled to the floor, shocked by the loss. "No...not again." Once more the Mordant reached from beyond the grave to wreck vengeance. She'd come too late to the crypt. A friend, a mentor, an almost-father, she should have saved him. Loss and regret bit deep.

Bryce leaned huddled against the wall, his shoulders heaving, yet he made barely a sound.

Kath struggled to summon the last of her strength. Zith deserved to be mourned, but they had to escape the dungeon. Kath let Bryce cry for a handful of heartbeats and then she reached out to him. "His loss cuts deep, yet we must be strong or more will die."

Bryce recoiled from her touch, his face contorted by grief. "What do you know of loss?"

His words stung like a slap. Kath gasped. Swallowing her hurt, she wrapped her words in quiet dignity. "I lost my heart." She kept her words to a whisper, aimed for him alone. "The man in the Mordant's cavern, the one you reached out to, his name was Duncan. I tried to save him, but I was too late." Her voice broke. "Duncan was my husband."

Bryce gaped, sorrow spilling from his eyes. "I'm so sorry."

"I know." She reached out to him, and this time he accepted her touch. "We have to keep fighting, despite our loss, or evil wins."

Nodding, he wiped his face, struggling to master his grief.

Kath swallowed her own sorrow. Gripping the crystal dagger, she hardened her resolve. "The Mordant is dead, but his curse is not yet vanquished. We dare not stop or many more will die. The Battle Immortal is not yet done."

70

Blaine

Blaine stepped through the ironbound door, a dagger in his hand. A quick glance told him the wine cellar was empty of enemies. Barrels lined the walls, the prison reek banished by the pleasant scent of aged oak laden with wine. Breathing deep, he enjoyed the heady scent, cleansing his lungs. Silent as a cat, he crossed the cellar to climb the stairs, two painted warriors following in his wake.

The clash of steel echoed from above.

Hope quickened, perhaps more of the painted warriors survived to renew the fight. Blaine crept up the stairs, needing to know. Sunlight glimmered at the top. Blaine blinked, startled by the brightness. Down in the crypt, he'd forgotten about sunshine, as if all the brightness in the world had been snuffed out. He shook his head against the grim thought, tightening his grip on the dagger. Hugging the shadows, he reached the top, but he saw neither friend nor foe. Sounds of fighting came from the rear. He strained to listen, seeking a clue, but heard nothing save the clash of steel. With only a dagger, he dared not press his luck, yet it galled him to return without answers. Crouching on the stairs, he waited.

A shadow strode down the hallway.

Blaine ducked low, signaling the others.

A guard in purple livery rushed past without a glance towards the wine cellar stairs.

Blaine sprang from the shadows. Smothering the man's mouth, he pulled him backwards. Sidhorn punched him hard in the gut, knocking the breath from his lungs, while Tingold drew the guard's sword. They manhandled him down the stairwell, forcing him into the prison.

"I've got your answers." Blaine pinioned the guard's arms, while Tingold held a sword to his throat. "Now talk. What's happening above?"

The guard's wide-eyed stare raced around the prison, taking in the opened cages and the leering threat of the painted warriors, and then his gaze struck Bryce. *"My lord!"* His mouth flailed open, his eyes wide as coins.

For a handful of heartbeats, Bryce did nothing, his head bent over Zith.

Blaine feared the game was up, but then Bryce stood, the gold runes embroidered on his robes shimmering in the faint light. His voice turned hard, his gaze drilling into the captured guard. "Tell me what happens above."

Cries of alarm rang through the chamber. Released prisoners cringed in fear, adding to the effect.

Bryce glared at the captured guard, his voice a lash. "I said *speak!*"

The captured guard turned ghost-pale, words tumbling from his mouth. "We were attacked by rebels, my lord. Major Tarq ordered them to stand down, but they did not obey."

"Rebels? What rebels?"

"Most wear the emerald tabard of Lanverness, but they do not obey the coded commands. Major Tarq suspects an uprising."

Kath flashed a triumphant smile at Blaine. "The *queen!*"

The captured guard sent an indignant look towards Kath. "My lord, who are these rabble?"

Bryce grinned. "Champions of the Light." He dropped the charade, slumping against the wall, pain creasing his face.

Kath said, "Gag the guard." Sidhorn obeyed, roughly stuffing a soiled rag into the guard's gaping mouth. Kath stepped towards Bryce. "You did well, and I know you need a healer and time to grieve, but I need more. I need you to end this battle, to order the Mordant's forces to surrender."

Bryce grimaced. "It pains me to see their fear, to act like *him*, but if it will save lives, I will try."

"I need you to do more than try." She stared at him, her gaze as hard as steel. "I need you to succeed."

Bryce gave her a solemn nod.

"Good. And I will be right by your side."

Blaine gaped, for Kath looked weary enough for a stiff wind to blow her over. He gripped her shoulder, pulling her aside, his voice a harsh whisper. "You don't need this risk."

Kath stared at him, her gaze burdened with a heavy load. "I think I do."

"But why?"

"A sixth sense."

Her answer was vague, yet her voice was certain as stone. "But you slayed the Mordant? The deed is done."

"Just so." Her gaze turned beleaguered. "The Mordant is slain, his soul confined to Hell for all eternity...but we may have come too late." She gestured to a cloak-wrapped body. "Zith is dead."

The monk lay still, his face ghost-pale, the cloak covering him like a shroud. Blaine hissed, "How?"

"From the Mordant's foul runes. And there's more." Her face turned grim. "Castlegard is imperiled."

Castlegard! He gaped at her. "But how do you know this?"

"The Mordant said so."

"And you believe the prince of lies?"

She gave him a slow nod. "His words felt like truth." Kath stared at him, as if willing him to believe. "I know it sounds like madness, but somehow I'm certain that, if we tarry here, the Mordant will reach beyond the grave to gain a great victory. We dare not let that happen."

Blaine saw the conviction in her eyes. "Then the fight's not done."

"No, it's not. Slaying the beast was not enough. Somehow the Mordant's evil must be undone."

"And his evil reaches for Castlegard?"

She gave him a grim nod.

"Then what are we waiting for? I suppose you have a plan."

Her face was pale, yet she quirked a smile. "We haven't enough swords to attack. Bluff and bluster are our best bets."

"A risky bet."

"Yet, it's the best we have." She summoned the others close and told them her plan.

71

Katherine

Kath held out her wrists. Sidhorn settled shackles on them, but he did not click them closed. The big warrior hulked over her, a scowl on his tattooed face. "I don't like this, Svala."

"All part of the charade." She adjusted the shackles so they'd stay on her wrists. The crystal dagger was sheathed at her belt, and she had an assassin's dark dagger tucked in her boot sheath, but she felt naked without a sword. If it came to a fight, they were sorely outnumbered and badly under-armed. She prayed to Valin for their ruse to succeed.

Blaine squeezed into the captured guard's purple tabard, the Great Wyrm embroidered across his chest. It was a tight fit across his broad shoulders, so they cut a slit at the back, hiding the cut with the guard's cloak. Buckling on the guard's belt, Blaine drew the short sword. It looked small in his hands. "Are you sure about this?"

"It's our best bet." They both turned to stare at Bryce. Kath had bound his shoulder wound with strips torn from cloaks, staunching the bleeding, but he looked pale and shaken, sundered by his father's death and the terrible ordeal of his imprisonment. Only the Mordant's dark wizard robes embroidered with gold runes lent him any authority. Kath prayed it was enough. "Are you ready?"

Bryce nodded.

"Remember, you must make them believe you are the Mordant."

Revulsion flickered across his face, but then his mouth settled onto a determined scowl.

"Good enough." Kath looked to her painted warriors, needing their swords yet knowing their tattooed faces would betray the ruse. "Don't emerge till you hear the clash of steel."

Sidhorn gave her a troubled nod.

Kath gestured to the ironbound door.

Bryce led the way. Kath followed with Blaine holding a sword at her back. They passed through the wine cellar, crossing to the stairs. Sunlight blazed at the top, so bright against the prison's gloom. Kath cheered to see it, a ray of hope. They climbed the stairs as if leaving a tomb. The sound of clashing steel came from above.

Reaching the marbled hallway, Bryce stepped out without hesitation. Turning left, he strode down the hall, the runes embroidered on his robes gleaming bright in the sunlight. Kath and Blaine hurried to follow, keeping close as shadows. They entered the audience chamber. Bryce spoke, his voice bristling with command. "Major Tarq attend me!"

Soldiers and assassins snapped their gazes towards Bryce. Bowing low, they scuttled backwards, proving fear of the Mordant still held sway.

A tall, gray-haired commander gave a respectful nod. "My lord, you said you were not to be disturbed."

"The ritual is complete, but I emerge from the sanctum to hear the clash of steel. Have you failed me?"

The commander stiffened. "Rebels, my lord. A mixture of back alley rogues and guards in green tabards attacked while you were in the sanctum. The coded commands were given, yet they refuse to yield. They will be slain."

"This city should be mine." Bryce climbed the dais.

Kath did not like the way the commander stared at Bryce.

Taking a seat on the throne, Bryce said, "Fighting in the streets does not serve my purpose. Arrange a truce and bring their leaders before me to parley."

The commander hesitated.

"Go and serve."

The commander nodded. "Culver, Pesh, Granar, with me." His hand on his sword hilt, he strode from the audience chamber.

Bryce gestured to the black banner behind the throne. "Take this down. I will not show my true colors till the whole city bows before me."

A duegar hastened to obey. Releasing a rope, the pentacle banner fluttered to the floor like a wounded raven. The duegar gathered up the black silk and waddled away. The stone expanse behind the throne seemed naked without a banner, yet the absence of the pentacle was a relief.

Kath sidled towards the dais, standing in the shadows, Blaine by her side.

Major Tarq returned, his face grim. "My lord, the rebels refuse parley."

For half a heartbeat, Bryce looked startled. He gaped without a reply.

Kath stepped forward. "My lord, let me prove my worth by speaking to the rebels."

Major Tarq scowled. "What difference can a girl make?"

Bryce interceded, his voice firm. "Whatever difference *I* command." He made a perfunctory gesture to Kath. "Come and kneel before me."

Kath played along, kneeling on the lowest step of the dais.

"Look at me."

Kath raised her gaze.

Bryce leaned forward, staring at her as if he would pierce her very soul.

Sweat erupted on her skin. For half a heartbeat, she almost believed he was still the Mordant Reborn. Her hand twitched towards the crystal dagger, but then Bryce blinked and the spell was broken. Kath sagged in relief.

He leaned back in the throne. "Go and serve."

"Yes, my lord." Kath stood, holding her shackled wrists towards Blaine. He mimed unlocking them, removing them from her wrists. Keeping her gaze downcast, she walked towards the commander. "Take me to the rebels so I may serve our lord."

Anger roiled across the commander's weathered face, yet he turned on his heels. "Come." He led her to the rear of the manse, to a walled garden. Dead bodies lay sprawled amongst the topiaries, most clad in green tabards. The rebels had penetrated the garden only to be repulsed. Kath prayed their numbers were sufficient to win the fight.

At the garden gate, the commander barked an order. "Raise a parley pennant."

The soldiers looked dumbfounded.

Major Tarq glared. "Obey!"

A grizzled veteran said, "Sir, we have no parley pennant."

"Then get one!"

Soldiers snapped to action, scurrying into the mansion.

Kath waited beside the major. She kept her head bowed, meek and mild, but her gaze darted around the courtyard garden, noting soldiers and their positions. Sapphire steel gleamed in the sunlight. One of the guards held Blaine's blue steel sword. Kath suppressed a snarl.

A soldier returned bearing a torn white sheet tied to a spear. Leaning from the back gate, he waved the pennant.

For half a hundred heartbeats, they waited in tense silence.

From a nearby alleyway, a man yelled. "Surrender or die, we've got nothing to talk about." An arrow struck the lintel over the gate.

The commander sneered at her. "What will you do now, girl?"

"Obey the Mordant." Opening the gate, she stepped out with her hands raised. "I've come to talk. I'm known to the queen! Hear me out!" Her heartbeat thundered as she walked forward. Keeping her hands raised, Kath prayed she would not die in the alleyway, skewered by friendly arrows.

A man yelled. "Hold your arrows!"

She walked towards the voice.

A burly man in dark leathers stepped from a doorway. "In here."

Kath stepped into a overgrown garden and found herself surrounded by drawn swords.

"So you speak for the Mordant?" A tall gray-haired man with piercing eyes strode towards her.

Kath knew his face, struggling to remember his name. "Lord...Highgate, the master archivist to the queen."

He squinted at her. "How do you know me?"

"You know the truth. The Prince of Ur was the Mordant."

"*Was?*"

She gave him a slow nod.

"Who are you?"

"Kath of Castlegard," she quirked a smile, "for a brief time, I was fostered to the queen."

He studied her. "You've grown a thumb's width in height, and you've come into your curves, becoming a woman, but your eyes have a hard glint to them, as if you've known loss...or made difficult choices."

His insights both astonished and embarrassed her. Kath felt her face flame red. "You see much."

"Yet, I don't see why Kath of Castlegard serves the Mordant."

"I don't serve Darkness. I've come to save your men and mine." She told her tale simply and quickly. Doubt hovered in his steel-gray eyes, yet she could not blame him for it. "Even if you don't believe me, my plan has merit. I can get a half dozen of your best men into the audience chamber. Slay the commanders and I believe the rest will surrender." She stared at him. "But I need your word not to harm Bryce."

"You ask much."

"I ask this for myself as well as the queen."

"The queen? Explain."

"Bryce spied on the Mordant, watching through his eyes, listening to his words. He can help unwind the evil tangling the queen's city."

"How?"

"By naming the true traitors, culling the black hearts from those who were merely duped or misled. Would that not be worth a great deal to your queen?"

"It would."

"Then we must hurry, and you best keep him safe."

The master archivist barked commands, choosing five men. Others came forward offering daggers, dirks, wire garrotes and short swords. The six chose their weapons well, hiding a small armory of blades beneath their cloaks, down their boots, and stuffed in the rear of their belts. With so much hidden steel, Kath was surprised they did not clatter and clank with every move.

"Remember, the man in wizard's robes is not to be harmed, nor is his guard, a tall blond knight in a purple tabard." After the six nodded in solemn agreement, Kath led them out into the alleyway. They walked towards the Mordant's manse. Kath felt a hundred hostile stares trailing her every movement.

Major Tarq stood in the gateway. "Throw down your arms."

The six seemed to obey, removing all their visible weapons, creating an impressive pile.

"Culver, Pesh, search them."

Beside her, Lord Highgate bristled. Kath stepped forward. "No! There will be no search."

Major Tarq sneered. "What treachery is this?"

Kath gestured to the small mound of discarded weapons. "They have disarmed. They have shown trust. They expect trust to be shown in return."

Major Tarq gave her a hooded stare.

"It was part of the deal." Before he could argue, Kath added. "Ask your lord. He ordered this parley." Crossing his stare, she willed him to obey.

He hesitated for handful of heartbeats, but it seemed his fear of the Mordant still ruled. "Come," the major's voice was laden with warning. "I'll brook no harm to my lord."

His hand on his sword hilt, he led them through the garden and into the manse. In the hallway leading to the throne room, the major ordered them to stop. He went forward alone to speak to Bryce.

Kath waited with the others. The narrow hallway felt close as a trap.

Major Tarq returned to lead them forward. They strode to the very foot of the dais. Around the chamber, assassins and guards kept watch, their hands on their weapons.

Bryce remained seated on the throne, his face waxen and pale. Turning his stare to the six, he addressed the master archivist and his men. "There is no need for bloodshed among friends. We came to Pellanor in peace, seeking to strengthen ties between trading powers. Queen Liandra is our friend. There is no need for fighting, for bloodshed," Bryce raised his voice to a command, "therefore, as a show of goodwill, we order our own men to lay down their weapons, to prove peace is our true purpose."

Murmured confusion rippled through the chamber.

Kath tensed, feeling a warning shiver down her back.

Major Tarq roared, "The pentacle never surrenders!"

The master archivist struck, driving a dagger deep into the major's throat.

The queen's men sprang to attack, wielding hidden weapons, targeting assassins and commanders.

Kath lunged towards the nearest guard, slapping him hard across the face. While he gaped, startled, she plucked his sheathed sword and ran him through with it. Turning, she joined Blaine, raising her sword against an assassin. Two against one, they forced him back.

Steel clashed around her in a lethal battle. The throne room erupted in a whirlwind of fighting.

From the dais, Bryce bellowed, "Lower your arms. Surrender your weapons or die!"

The fighting was vicious but brief. A handful of commanders and assassins died, sprawled bloody before the dais. The others fell to the floor, bowing to their lord. A tense silence prevailed. Bryce slumped in the throne. "Sirken, go and command the others to surrender. There's been enough bloodshed this day."

A guard rose from the floor. Bowing to Bryce, he ran to obey.

Kath and the others stood in a rigid crescent in front of the throne, standing guard till the queen's soldiers poured in from the back garden.

Sundered by weariness, Kath sagged to the floor. "It is finished."

72

Katherine

The Mordant's men were led away in shackles, their fates to be decided by Queen Liandra with advice from Bryce. The dead were hauled to the garden, smears of blood staining the floor. Her painted warriors and the two surviving Zward came up from the prison like men resurrected. Blaine reclaimed his blue steel sword and his silver surcoat, returning with a confident swagger. Kath watched, seated on the lowest step of the dais, too weary to move.

The Master Archivist returned, striding towards Kath with a determined step. "That should be all of them, both the dead and the living." He gave her a pensive look. "That crypt below the prison reeks of evil."

"Just so. The queen should have it filled with stone and sealed forever."

His gaze slid to Bryce. A healer tended the stab wound in his back. Bryce had shucked the dark wizard robe in favor of a plain white shirt and brown pants scrounged from the mansion. The change made him look harmless and young. "Are you sure about him."

"Yes, I'm sure. The Mordant is dead, his soul banished to Hell, but Bryce is a treasure. What he's seen, what he's heard, will undo much evil. His knowledge will be a priceless boon to Erdhe."

"The queen is anxious to set her court aright."

"I need a day with Bryce and then I'm sure he will aid the queen." Kath's voice turned hard with warning. "Remember, he is a Kiralynn monk and should be honored for his fight against the Mordant."

"Sometimes that's hard to remember."

"I need your word. He's owed no less."

The master archivist gave her a solemn nod. "You have it."

Kath sighed. "My men fought hard. We have dead, too many dead. They need an honorable burial."

"All those who fought with you will be buried in the Ancestral Spire. It is our highest honor."

"You have my thanks."

"No, it is you and your men who are owed thanks. Twice we attacked the Mordant's mansion and twice we were repelled. It was your plan and Bryce's commands that toppled this foe. The queen will not forget."

Kath nodded, yet it hurt that she'd lost so many men, so many friends.

"Whatever you need, you have only to ask."

Kath gave him a grateful look.

"I've posted guards around the mansion, lest any of the Mordant's men seek to return, and there are two couriers stationed in the garden." He flashed a wry smile. "The queen is holding court in the Rusty Dragon. Send word if you need anything."

"In a tavern?" Kath could not imagine Queen Liandra holding court in an ale-soaked tavern. "Won't that tarnish her image?'

"It's safer till the traitors are rooted from the castle."

His words were a grim reminder the Mordant had long tentacles that burrowed deep. Kath shivered with foreboding.

"If there's nothing else, I'll return to my queen." Taking his leave, he strode from the chamber. His men went with him, till there were none left save her own warriors. Battle-weary, they sprawled around the chamber.

Kath sighed, leaning back on the dais, surrounded by friends. Her gaze roved her warriors, grateful for everyone who lived, while mourning those they'd lost.

Bear approached, carrying a sword cradled in his arms. "Svala, we found your sword. It bears the mark of Castlegard."

A smile lit her face. Kath unsheathed the sword she'd taken from the guard and replaced it with her own, a solid dependable sword of good Castlegard steel.

"We could not find your axes, but Gris brought your saddlebag." From it, he removed her maroon cloak.

Kath cheered to see it.

"Svala, you should wear your true colors."

"Just so." Kath stood and the big warrior affixed the maroon cloak to her shoulders.

Her men pounded swords against the marble floor, raising a great din. *"Hazzah! Hazzah!"* Triumphant shouts echoed through the Mordant's throne room.

Kath raised her hands and her men stilled to an expectant hush. "Tonight we feast! We celebrate those who died with honor, we celebrate a great victory. By coming south and defeating the Mordant, the Painted Warriors have truly won the north! May all the lands north of the Dragon Spines be forever yours!"

"Hazzah! Hazzah to the Svala!" Her men went wild with triumph. They looted the kitchen, bringing forth whole roasted hams, braised chickens, shoulders of roast pork with salty crackling, potatoes and leeks fried with churned butter, loaves of crusty bread and flaky pastries stuffed with ripe raspberries. Two of her men staggered back from the wine cellar bearing a huge cask of dark red merlot. Golden wine cups were passed and many toasts were raised. They drank to the living, they drank to the dead, but most of all they drank to victory.

Kath ate and drank her fill, enjoying the many delicacies of the Mordant's kitchen, but it was the joy of her men that truly filled her. Her gaze roved their faces, drinking in their smiles. Tattooed with bears, eagles and wolves, they were a fearsome lot, yet they were hers. Kath relished the comradeship of warriors, valiant swords in service of the Light. She missed Danya and Neven, thinking they should be here to join in the triumph, but then an orange tabby sauntered into the throne room like a feline prince, his tail held high. Spying the cat, Kath smiled, realizing Danya knew. Cutting a prime slice of ham, she threw it to the orange tabby. "You did well, beastspeaker. We all did." Kath raised a goblet in salute.

73

Katherine

Sunlight streamed through the great window, so bright Kath judged it to be noon. Wincing against the blazing brightness, she rubbed the last vestiges of sleep from her eyes. Snores rumbled through the throne room. None of her men had wanted to sleep alone, leastwise Kath, so they'd pulled bedding from the rooms above, spreading them across the throne room floor. Her painted warriors slept sprawled on feather mattresses, the remains of their victory feast surrounding them.

"No! Stop!"

Someone was tangled in nightmares. Kath traced the cries to Bryce. Grabbing a golden goblet, she filled it with wine from the cask. *Two casks*...she hadn't remembered them opening the second, little wonder her warriors slept late. Threading a path through the sleeping men, she made her way to his pallet. Crouching, she shook him awake.

Bryce lurched away from her, his eyes wide with fear.

"You're safe and well." Handing him the goblet, she made her voice soothing. "It's only a nightmare."

His wide-eyed gaze skittered around the chamber. "I'm alive," wonder flooded his voice, "and my body is mine."

"Your long imprisonment is over." She stood. "Come." Snagging another goblet, she filled it with wine and led Bryce out into the rear garden.

A courier and a guard in the queen's colors gave her a respectful nod and then slipped out the rear gate, giving her much sought privacy. Kath took a seat on a stone bench, Bryce settling beside her. Much of the garden was trampled, yet foxgloves bloomed around the bench, the scent of flowering jasmine perfuming the air. Sunlight glowed warm on her upturned face, birdsong chirping from the trees. So peaceful, it was hard to imagine a battle had raged here the day before, but Kath knew otherwise. She gripped Duncan's warrior ring, sorely missing him. "I need your help."

"You have it."

"You don't even know what I need."

Bryce shrugged. "You freed me from the beast. Whatever you need is yours."

Kath swirled the gem-encrusted goblet, the red merlot giving off a heady scent. Staring into the goblet, she dared to speak the words that haunted her.

"When I fought the Mordant in the soulscape, he said I'd come too late, that Erdhe would be his." She took a long swallow of wine, hating the admission. "I need to know his plans for the rest of Erdhe."

Bryce paled. He stared at his own goblet, as if all his nightmares could be drowned in merlot. "I fear for the monastery. On the night the Mordant chained my soul," a shudder quaked him, an echo of remembered horrors, "he murdered a guide and stole an amulet. The Mordant used the amulet to escape the Guardian Mist, but the amulet was the real prize, the missing piece he'd sought for many lifetimes. With the amulet and knowledge of the monastery's hidden location, his oldest enemy became vulnerable. The Mordant gave that amulet to General Haith, his most capable commander. He ordered the general to lead a strike force south, to slay the monks and ransack the monastery, to take their magic and utterly destroy the Kiralynn Order." Bryce gave her a beseeching look. "Erdhe needs the Kiralynn Order, the last bastion of true enlightenment. And I..." his voice broke, "I've lost my father, I've lost nearly everything. I can't lose my home."

Kath knew his pain all too well, yet she feared to speak the words. "And what of Castlegard?"

Bryce took a long drink of merlot, collecting himself. "The Mordant had a deep-seated hatred towards the great castle. I don't know why, but I know he meant to destroy it."

"Destroy Castlegard! But the walls are built of mage-stone!" Kath shook her head, her voice defiant. "Not possible."

Bryce stared at her. "We speak of the Mordant."

A shiver raced down Kath's spine. "How?"

He gave her a bleak look. "I know not. The plan was forged lifetimes ago, long before I was chained. It felt like something monstrous, something truly foul, yet he never spoke to his generals about it."

Castlegard imperiled! Somehow this threat had to be countered. "You must know more."

"If I knew more, I would surely tell you."

A grim silence settled between them.

Kath gripped the crystal dagger, plagued by nightmares.

Bryce swirled his goblet, his voice thoughtful. "Castlegard has stood unconquered for over a thousand years, the greatest castle in all of Erdhe. A stalwart bastion of the Light, the Mordant could never take it. The great castle must have felt like an infernal thorn in his side." Bryce turned his stare towards Kath. "Whatever the Mordant could not control, he sought to destroy. Yet to my knowledge, the Mordant never gave his generals orders to take Castlegard, so if the castle is imperiled, it must be by something magical, something powerful to break the ancient magic of mage-stone."

The magic of mage-stone! Bryce's words sparked a memory. Kath struggled to grasp it. "In the Dark Citadel, Zith collected every scroll and scrap of parchment he could find. When I asked him what he'd learned from the scrolls, he said the Mordant was obsessed with mage-stone, not in *making* it, but in *breaking* it." A second shiver passed through Kath despite the noontime sun. *Zith might have known the answer*...but he was dead, slain by the Mordant's foul magic. It felt as if the fiend was always a step ahead, reaching from beyond the grave to thwart her.

"And now my father is dead." Sorrow rode his voice.

"Just so."

They shared a silence filled with loss.

"Whooooooo!" A giant frost owl glided into the garden, alighting on the ground in front of Kath. A halo of soft white light shimmered around the owl. The glow intensified, the raptor stretching till a blue robed monk stood in its place.

"Aeroth!" Kath gaped, shocked to discover the monks were shape shifters. Or, at least this monk was.

"Kath of Castlegard." His gaze slid to Bryce, his right hand making the warding sign against evil. "Is it done?"

Drawing the crystal dagger, Kath pressed the blade to Bryce's arm. "See for yourself."

The young monk's eyes remained blue, unsullied by the red glow of Hell.

"So it's true!" Aeroth's eyes widened. "The host *can* survive the harlequin!"

Kath did her best to explain the battle in the soulscape.

Aeroth gave her a level stare. "So, the Mordant is banished to Hell for all eternity, but his evil remains, entangling all of Erdhe. The Battle Immortal is not yet done."

Kath's shoulders hunched as if against a storm. "You speak words I already know. What happens beyond Pellanor?"

"An army of mounted cavalry has entered the Southern Mountains. They seek the monastery."

Bryce gave warning. "Their general has the stolen amulet. The monastery is vulnerable."

"Then, it is as we feared." Aeroth's voice was heavy with foreboding. "War hurtles toward the very gates of the Seeing Eye. The turning of an Age is upon us."

"And Castlegard?" Kath needed to know. "What of Castlegard?"

Aeroth hesitated for a heartbeat. "An even larger army advances on Castlegard." From his robes, he removed a small bone-carved message tube. "Master Rizel sends word."

Master Rizel! Kath took the tube. Prying it open, she removed a small scroll of vellum. Taking a deep breath, she silently read the message. *The magic of Castlegard's mage-stone is crumbling. Restore honor to the maroon.* Alarm pierced her heart. *Mage-stone crumbling?* The message made no sense, a nightmare wrapped in a riddle, yet somehow she knew it was true. A cold chill crept down her spine. "Restore honor to the maroon? What does this mean? And how can mage-stone crumble?"

"There is more to the message." Aeroth's voice turned formal. "Kath of Castlegard, you are summoned to end the Battle Immortal, to undo the

Mordant's evil lest Erdhe succumb to Darkness. You are bid to come to the monastery...or to Castlegard. Come with all haste."

"Come!" She gaped at the monk as if he were mad. "If I rode a string of horses to death, I could not get to either in time to make a difference. The distances are too great!"

Aeroth gave her a penetrating stare. "I was told your magic is of stone. There may be a way, if you dare."

More secrets. The monks were full of secrets and hidden magic, yet there was nothing she would not dare for Castlegard. Kath squared her shoulders. "I dare."

Aeroth gave her a respectful nod. "Then come, for time is not our ally."

The Castle & The Monastery

74

The Knight Marshal

The war drums beat a relentless rhythm. The cadence echoed in his heart, a call to glory and conquest. The marshal hungered for war, for blood on his sword, for souls reaped and sundered. The Dark Sword whispered hungry murmurs, sheathed at his back, while the massive wall shield hung on his left arm. Gird for battle, he urged his warhorse up a steep trail, his entourage of dark-cloaked commanders following close behind. Pulling his horse to a halt, he gazed upon the valley below.

His army flowed like a dark river, vast and unstoppable, countless swords sworn to his service, yet the marshal knew Castlegard would not fall by swords alone. At the heart of his army, whips cracked and wood creaked. The massive siege weapons crept on. Taals grunted against the strain, their muscles bulging beneath leather harnesses. Yoked like oxen, they struggled to pull the catapults and trebuchet along the valley floor. It took twenty Taals to move the largest, the one they'd named the Smasher, but the monstrous siege weapon was well worth the effort.

The marshal grinned beneath his helm. The Octagon knights would never expect a siege. They thought their castle invincible. A millennia of history proved it so, but he'd come to smash history, to change the past and forge a new future. A new God of War had come to Erdhe and Castlegard would be his seat of power.

Hoof beats drummed on the soft loam behind. A small band of mounted soldiers reached the ridge top, all of them clad in dark armor emblazoned with gold pentacles. Snapping fists to breastplates, they saluted. "My lord, we found three spies lurking on an overlook." Three men bound and gagged, tugged on ropes behind the horses. Two wore the brown leathers of scouts, but the third wore the silver surcoat of a knight.

Feed me! The Dark Sword slavered for souls.

The marshal swung down from his warhorse. With a slow, sensuous movement, he unsheathed the Dark Sword, deep-carved runes flashing along the runnels. "Release the knight."

The guard hesitated. "But my lo..."

The marshal stepped towards the guard. With a single swing of the great sword, he took the man's head. The Dark Sword sighed in his hands, imbibing the soul. The headless trunk wavered, blood gushing across dark armor. Toppling sideways, the fresh corpse crumpled to the ground.

"Release the knight."

Guards leaped to obey. They cut the knight's bonds and removed his gag.

A young man in his prime, Sir Borax was tall with broad shoulders, fitting prey for the Dark Sword. "Name your weapon."

Sir Borax rubbed his chafed wrists. "Are you offering a fair fight?"

The marshal laughed. "Nothing is fair in this life, yet we *will* fight."

"A great sword."

The marshal gestured and a half dozen swords were presented hilt-first to the knight. He rejected the first two. Accepting the third, he swung it left and right, testing the balance. Satisfied, he raised the double-edged blade in salute.

Guards and officers scattered, opening a wide space around the two men.

The marshal waited, a helm hiding his face, the Dark Sword in his gauntleted fist.

Sir Borax leaped forward. Feinting left, then right, he brought his sword down in a two-handed strike. Steel rang against steel with a mighty clang. The marshal blocked the blow with the massive wall shield. The knight circled, raining blows, seeking an opening. The marshal turned, blocking every thrust with the shield. "Fight me, *damn you!*" The marshal toyed with the knight till the Dark Sword began to thrum with hunger. Discarding the massive wall shield, the marshal spread his arms wide, inviting a thrust to the heart. The knight lunged forward. Quick as summer lightning, the marshal parried the stroke. Ordinary steel screamed. The knight's sword shattered into shards. The Dark Sword swept forward slicing through chainmail, flesh and bone. Impaled, the knight groaned. "Who...are...you?"

"Don't you know me, Sir Borax?" The marshal tugged the helm from his head.

The knight gasped. "*You! A traitor?*"

"Not a traitor, a God." Twisting the Dark Sword, he took the knight's life, while the sword drank his soul.

75

Tybalt

Tybalt ran through the narrow defile seeking fertile ground for boots. Spying a muddy patch, he raced through it, leaving deep prints. Turning, he hopped from one stone to another, skirting his way back around the mud and he then ran through it again. Four times he retraced his steps, leaving a swath of tangled boot prints leading deeper into the gorge. Ty studied the trail, tempted to make a fifth pass, but that would be pressing his luck. The enemy was close, too close. Turning his back on his handiwork, he sped deeper into the narrow defile, his quarterstaff thumping against his back.

The steep-sided gorge angled to the left, towering rock walls on either side. A hawk screeched overhead, the wild cry befitting the rugged mountains. Racing around a stand of knotted pine, Ty skidded to a halt. The slotted gorge was a dead end, a sheer wall of granite mountainside blocking the way forward. Pursing his lips, he imitated the call of a mountain lark. Ty stared aloft, waiting, sweat beading his brow.

A dark-haired man peered from behind a boulder, tossing down a knotted rope.

Ty tested the rope, making sure it was secure, and then he began to climb. Hand over fist, his boots planted against the sheer rock wall, he climbed the gorge. His quarterstaff was bound to his back in a harness of his own making. Shod with a magical relic, he could not bear to be parted from it. The harness made the quarterstaff less cumbersome, bound diagonally across his back.

He neared the top, his arms aching.

A hand reached out, grabbing his jerkin, tugging him onto the trail.

"Thanks." Ty rolled to a crouch.

Barstin coiled the rope. Slinging it onto his back, he said, "Let's go." They raced along a mountain trail so narrow it was best fit for goats. At times, they took turns jumping ledges, daring a fall that would mean certain death. They reached the others in good time, ducking behind a large boulder overlooking the main trail. Ty found himself crouched next to Christoff, the master of the quarterstaff.

The gray-haired master gave him a wry smile. "Don't look so surprised. Those who teach can also do."

Like the others, the master wore a hodge-podge of brown leathers. They'd both put off their blue robes to lend their skills to the Zward. Only a fresh-sworn monk, yet Ty had served the last moon-turn roaming the Southern Mountains, setting deadfalls, ambushes, and false trails, seeking a way to thwart an army bent on destroying the Order.

"They come!"

Ty rose from a crouch, carefully peering over the boulder.

An army swarmed up the trail, a relentless line of mounted men in black and gold armor. The Zward used every trap and trick to erode their numbers and turn them away, but still they came, as if driven by the hounds of Hell.

Ty held his breath, watching as they approached the fork in the trail. The main trail was swept clean, giving the illusion it was seldom used. He willed the army to turn right, to follow the trail of tangled footprints into the slotted gorge, but they hesitated, scouts dismounting to study the signs.

A ripple of movement raced up the trail, parting the double line of mounted men. A battle banner flickered in the wind, black silk with a forked tail embroidered in red and gold.

"Darkness on fire." Beside him, Christoff hissed. "The battle banner of the Mordant."

A cold shiver raced down Ty's spine.

The enemy commander rode a strapping stallion, sunlight glinting on burnished armor. Something about his armor invoked a shimmer of fear. Ty had to look away.

"By the Nine Hells!" Targus, the Zward captain hissed a curse. "That one is smart. He's seen this ruse too often. He won't fall for it."

Ty risked a glance over the boulder. Sure enough, the enemy evaded the lure, keeping to the main trail. All his hard work was for naught.

Targus hissed, "Away with you. Get to the next choke point." He gestured to the boulder. "Pren, Cordon, see if you can move this boulder."

The two big men moved into position, levering iron pry bars under the boulder.

Ty did not wait to watch. He followed the others, scrambling up the steep goat track. Always they sought to stay ahead of the enemy, setting ambushes and diversions and then retreating to hide and strike again. The problem was, they were running out of mountain. Once they reached the treeline, there'd be nowhere left to hide. And a pitched battle would be nothing short of suicide.

Behind him, he heard the rumble of rocks and the screams of men.

He hoped Pren and Cordon got away, living to fight another day.

Ty loped up the steep trail, keeping pace with the others. He'd fight and die for the Order if need be, but he saw no way they could win.

76

Lothar

Lothar strode into the king's council chambers. A fresh breeze blew in from the arrow-slit windows, tattered battle banners stirring in the rafters. It felt strange to be clean-shaven, to smell of soap and leather, instead of sweat, and dirt, and grime. Stranger still to be in the council chambers without the king...or the knight marshal. He swallowed that thought, burying the bitter truth in his heart.

Standing with his back to the cold hearth, he watched as the knight-captains took their places at the round table. Most looked like scarecrows, their faces gaunt, their eyes sunken and shadowed, their hard-won muscles melted away by bitter living conditions and squirrel's rations. The winter war had taken a grievous toll. The cost was not tallied in corpses alone. Those who survived bore a stiff price. It was one of the many reasons he'd retreated to the great castle. Succored by Castlegard's stout walls and deep larder, they needed a chance to recover and regroup. Lothar refused to lead ragged scarecrows in a death march against the Mordant's army.

Sir Rannock was the last to arrive.

Too many empty chairs. Too many young ones promoted to take the place of dead veterans. He supposed they were all veterans now.

Lothar circled the table, feeling their stares, certain of their questions.

The tallest chair, the king's chair, remained vacant. King Ursus had died at Raven Pass, slain in single combat, valiant to his last breath. The king had lived a long and fruitful life, siring five sons, five knights of the Octagon, yet he'd died without a living heir, leaving the maroon rudderless in the storm. The throne of Castlegard sat empty. Lothar was not so proud or presumptuous. He passed by the king's chair, leaving the question of succession to be decided at another time.

By tradition, the knight marshal sat at the right hand of the king. That chair too sat empty. Lothar supposed he had more right than any other knight to claim the marshal's chair, yet he could not bring himself to surrender hope for his friend. He passed the marshal's chair, taking his usual seat at the marshal's right hand.

Murmurs rippled around the chamber.

Lothar scowled, knowing he'd poured lamp oil on flaming ambitions, but he refused to reach above himself. "I am the *acting* marshal." His voice was gruff, brooking no arguments. "Sir Rannock will be my second. The command will remain this way till we are certain of the marshal's fate." His stare darted across the table. "Honor to the Octagon."

"Honor to the Octagon!" The refrain echoed around the table, yet he saw more than one calculating look.

"Now," Lothar leaned back in the chair, "I will hear your reports."

Sir Rannock started, with each knight-captain giving a report till the circle was complete. Every aspect of the castle and the Octagon, from knights and squires, to arrows and swords, to horses and hay, to well water and ham hocks were discussed. Lothar listened, linking the details together like a suit of chainmail. "So it seems we have everything in abundance save for too few men, too few arrows and not enough healing supplies."

Grim nods circled the table.

Sir Tormund, a white-haired veteran spoke. "We've villagers and farmers in abundance too. Refugees keep pouring in from across the Domain."

Lothar's voice was firm. "Castlegard's gates will remain open to them for as long as the menace remains."

Sir Tormund groused. "But there are chickens in the great yard!"

"If the larders run low, you'll be grateful for their chickens." A few gray-beards chuckled, but veterans of the winter war remained stone-faced, for those men knew the true meaning of hunger. Lothar's gaze circled the table. "Castlegard is stocked with food aplenty till summer, if needs be. We will give our men time to regain their strength and vigor. Our scouts will shadow the enemy, keeping close watch. When the time is right, we shall ride out in force to strike a grievous blow against the pentacle." He looked for dissent but saw none. "Honor to the Octagon."

"Honor to the Octagon." The knight-captains rose, taking their leave.

A guard peered in from the doorway. "Sir Lothar, the master swordsmith and the master healer are seeking a word with the knight marshal."

Lothar sighed, expecting demands for more supplies. "Send them in."

The burly swordsmith and the pudgy healer sidled in. Standing huddled together like anxious supplicants, they watched as the knight-captains emptied the chamber.

"Stay, Sir Rannock." The knight nodded, returning to his seat. Lothar gestured to the healer and the swordsmith. "Come."

They hesitated, giving each other a sideways glance that bespoke trouble. Quintus said, "We've come to see the knight marshal."

So the rumors remain contained. Lothar kept his face impassive. "He's still afield. I'm serving as the acting marshal."

The two men looked at each other as if they were brewing a conspiracy. Quintus quietly closed the outer door and returned to stand next to the swordsmith.

His interest piqued, Lothar sat forward. "What can be so dire? We're running out of iron ore or healing supplies?"

"It's the castle." The healer blurted the words. "Mage-stone is failing. Castlegard is no longer invincible."

"What?" Lothar glared. "You're talking gibberish. Make sense, man."

Otto said, "No, it's true."

The smith's gravelly voice was heavy with certainty. Fear began to fester in Lothar's chest. "Explain."

The healer nodded, tripping over his words. "It started with a wagon." He told a tale about a scar on the castle's inner gate and about the smith's hammer wounding the forge wall. "So I sent a message to the Kiralynn monks asking for aid."

Lothar sent the pudgy healer a sharp look. "And?"

The healer turned thoughtful as if repeating a message he dared not get wrong. "They said that mage-stone is tied to intent. That Darkness has corrupted the Octagon. Restore honor to the maroon. Aid comes in the form of a sword."

Sir Rannock shot to his feet, outrage on his face. "The Octagon fights with *honor!* How dare you say we're corrupted by Darkness."

But Lothar heard something else. Putting a restraining hand on Sir Rannock, he said, "What do you mean, aid comes in the form of a sword?"

"I supposed it means the monks are sending a sword." Quintus shrugged. "I know no more than what the message said."

A sword to fight a sword. "Who else have you told?"

They both looked at him wide-eyed. "No one."

"Good." Lothar nodded. "Keep it that way."

Rannock glared at him. "Surely you don't believe them?"

"Their tale sounds impossible, but impossible things have been happening." Lothar shuddered, thinking of the Dark Sword. "And proof of their tale is at hand." He stood. "I think it is past time I inspected the castle for myself." He gave the healer and the swordsmith a stern look. "Go. If your tale holds true, we will speak more on this."

Nodding, the two men scurried from the chamber.

Rannock rounded on him. "You don't believe..."

Lothar forestalled him with a glance. "A sword to slay a sword."

Rannock gave him a furtive look. "To defeat the Dark Sword?"

"Just so." Lothar strode towards the door. "Come. Let's see if their tale holds true." He walked without haste, Rannock at his side. Exiting the tower, they strolled across the great yard, stopping to talk with the guards at the inner gate. Passing through the gate, they found the scar just where the healer said it would be.

Rannock gasped. "By all the gods!"

Lothar fingered the impossible scar, hoping touch would belie his eyes, but the scar proved real. Shaken, he made the hand sign against evil. "Come, I want to hear that message again." They returned back through the inner gate. Lothar strove to walk with a measured step, trying to appear calm, but in truth he felt as if the world was coming unraveled.

77

Tybalt

Trees were becoming scarce and scrawny, a sure sign they were running out of mountain. Ty pried a large rock from the steep-sided slope, careful to keep it from tumbling down the mountainside. Sweat dripped in his eyes despite the cool mountain breeze. His hands were rough and calloused. Filthy and tired, he was always hungry. He grunted, struggling to lift the rock. Ty staggered under the weight, carrying it back to the deadfall. Three stacked pine logs, supported by a boulder at one end and a stake at the other, formed a low dam holding back a small tide of rocks and boulders. He added his rock to the rubble, an avalanche poised to strike against a relentless enemy.

War was not what he thought it would be. Hit, run, hide and hit again, they stung the enemy like maddened wasps, but the long black snake never stopped, slithering its way deeper into the mountains. Soon they'd reach the crest and then the enemy would have the high ground. He shuddered, making the hand sign against evil.

Ty tipped his waterskin for a measured drink and then turned to hunt for another rock.

"That's enough." Prango, the Zward captain in charge of building the deadfall, waved them away.

Ty and the others took a seat in the shade of a twisted pine. Carl opened a satchel, removing two roast chickens wrapped in parchment and a loaf of brown bread. He fished at the bottom, removing a scrap of parchment. There was always a note. Carl read, "From Cherry, the innkeeper's daughter. May the Light guard you and keep you safe."

"To Cherry!" Ty's mouth watered. Cherry was one of the best cooks in Haven. The satchels had started arriving four days ago, more proof they neared Drumheller Pass. Carl took his share and passed the rest. Ty tore off a chicken leg, the skin crispy just the way he liked it, and a chunk of dark bread laden with raisins. They ate in silence, devouring every bite. Ty licked the grease from his fingers, wishing for more. Drythe passed a wine skin and they each took a few sips. Their hunger eased, they lulled under the sun-warmed pine.

A red-winged bird alighted on a branch, warbling a pretty song. For half a heartbeat, Ty imagined there was no war.

A soft whistle came from below, one of the signals used by the Zward. Ty and the others sat up, instantly alert. Ty scanned the craggy slope, spying movement amongst the twisted pines. "There." Rock-dusted leathers blended well with the mountainside, but movement was ever the betrayer. Master Christoff, Targus, and five younger men hustled up the steep slope. Their leathers were sweat-stained and one of the men had a bloody gash on his forehead. They reached the deadfall and crouched, breathing hard.

"They're coming." Targus surveyed the deadfall. "We've run out of mountain. This will be our last ambush before the pass." His dark gaze swept across them, a glint of approval in his eyes. "You've fought well, Zward and monk alike, but now it's time to run, to live to fight another day." His voice turned stern. "Take to the heights and don't look back. Cross the pass and serve the Order." His mouth turned firm. "The Zward's fight is done. Now it's in the hands of the Grand Master."

Ty wanted to protest, yet he knew an order when he heard one.

"Master Christoff will lead you across."

"No." The gray-haired master interrupted the Zward captain. "This ambush is mine. I claim the right as the oldest."

Ty held his breath, for the man who stayed behind always took the greatest risk. Less than half lived to fight again.

The quarterstaff master and the Zward captain crossed stares. The Zward captain relented, his words solemn. "An honor to serve with you."

"And you." They clasped arms like warriors.

Targus turned away, his craggy face set in a stern mask, his voice a rough bark. "Away with you! We've a mountain to climb. Daylight's a-wasting and the enemy draws near."

The others scrambled to get their bedrolls and satchels, but Ty approached the quarterstaff master, his mentor and his friend. His voice was rough. "Remember what the Zward say, live to fight another day."

Master Christoff gave him a wry smile. "But I'm a monk, an *old* monk." He tugged a midnight-blue robe from his satchel and pulled it over his head. "I'll live and die a sworn monk of the Kiralynn Order."

Ty wanted to protest, but his mouth was suddenly desert-dry.

"This is right. This is what I want." Master Christoff gripped Ty's shoulder, a reassuring warmth in his touch. "When the time comes to spend your life, pray the gods grant you a way to make a difference."

Ty turned away. He did not remember gathering up his bedroll or his satchel, yet they thumped against his side. Reaching the trail, he turned for a last look. Master Christoff stood proud beside the deadfall, his quarterstaff in his hands, his midnight-blue robes bright against the gray of the mountainside.

"Come." Targus gestured him up the switchback trail.

Ty followed the Zward, refusing to look back.

78

Quintus

Rumors swirled, whispering of an invincible army marching on Castlegard. Some said they were close, only a day's ride away. A few whispered the enemy brought siege engines. Plagued with worry and unable to focus on his work, Quintus took to haunting the castle's outer gates. The monastery's message said they would send aid, but so far he'd seen no sign of it, not a monk, not an owl, not a message of any sort. If aid did not come soon, it would be too late.

Mired in worry, Quintus trudged a path through the killing corridor, the walled gorge between the soaring mage-stone battlements and the castle's outer walls. Sunlight shone bright overhead, another fair summer day, but the bright weather could not dispel the corridor's grim gloom.

Ahead, the telltale creak of wagons and the murmur of voices echoed through the stone corridor. His heart sank, knowing what the sounds foretold. Rounding a corner, he saw a gaggle of farmers and peasants trudging towards him, their worldly goods piled high on carts. Pots and pans clattered, children following in the cart's wake. Bedraggled and filthy, they looked exhausted. They looked terrified.

Quintus wandered among them. "What have you seen? What do you know?"

"An army comes, too many to count."

"Devils in black armor, killing everyone in their path."

"They're coming! They're coming!" A pale-faced woman clutching a child ran past him as if ghosts nipped at her heels.

Hastening his steps, Quintus rushed to the outer gate. Nodding to the guards, he climbed the stairs to the barbican. What he saw added to his dismay. Villagers, farmers and peasants choked the drawbridge, jostling for entrance to the great castle.

Sir Cormin, one of the maroon-cloaked guards, joined him at the barbican. "It's been like this all morning. They come flocking like geese to spilled corn. Won't be a farmer tending the fields between here and the Salt Tower."

And that was another worry. Most fields were tilled, the crops planted, but who would tend them, and would there be anything or anyone left to harvest come the fall? Castlegard's storerooms and larders were stocked nearly to burgeoning, but would it be enough? Especially with so many extra mouths to feed. Quintus balled his hands into fists, shoving the added worry from his mind.

A cry rose from the press at the gates.

Sir Cormin pointed towards the west. "Look!"

Dark smoke belched from the village nestled in the valley.

War! The smoke screamed of war come to Castlegard like an inevitable doom. Quintus made the hand sign against evil.

"Their vanguard must have reached the village. Sound the first alert!"

Horns blared a volley of shrill notes.

People on the drawbridge panicked, screaming and shoving.

A guard shouted, "Clear the gates!"

Someone in the tower yelled, "Riders approaching!"

Quintus saw them, a handful of riders galloping pell-mell from the burning village, but they were too far to discern the color of their cloaks. He felt a burning tension gripping the men poised on the barbican.

Sir Cormin leaned over the battlement, glaring down at the peasant-cluttered drawbridge. "Get that bridge clear!'

Soldiers with spears herded the crowd through the gates.

"Get ready to raise the drawbridge!"

"*No!*" A premonition of dread choked Quintus. Once the drawbridge was raised, he knew with grim certainty it would not be lowered...and there would be no help from the monastery.

"Maroon cloaks!" A cry went up along the barbican.

"Sound the trumpets, knights returning!"

A blare of trumpets echoed against the castle ramparts.

Quintus could see it now, the riders wore maroon cloaks. Sunlight glinted on armor as they urged their horses to a frenzied gallop. Six knights and three scouts in leathers, they galloped across the greensward.

"Wounded! They've got a wounded man."

Hearing the shout, Quintus rushed to the stairs, making his way down to the press of shoving villagers. Babies cried, goats bleated, and pots clattered in a confusion of fear. Quintus pushed his way through the chaos, threading a path to the gatehouse. Hugging the shadowed entranceway, he stared across the greensward. The spiked portcullis remained raised, a farmer and his family rushing to cross the drawbridge.

Hoof beats approached at a wild gallop. The knights drew rein. Slowing their lathered mounts to a trot, they clattered across the drawbridge. Passing through the gatehouse, they dismounted, adding a swirl of sweat and armor to the chaos. "Wounded! We have a wounded man!"

Quintus shoved his way forward. "I'm here!"

The knights lowered a dark-haired man to the ground. Wrapped in a brown cloak soaked in blood, he raved, "*They're coming! They're coming!*"

Quintus knelt beside him, gently touching his forehead. The scout was feverish, his eyes glazed, his forehead burning. "Water, bring me water!" Peeling back the blood-soaked cloak, the healer stifled a gasp. The man had been tortured, his chest crisscrossed with flay marks and burns. And then he saw the scout's hands. Crippled and broken, his hands bore deep holes oozing blood. Quintus winced, for he'd never seen such cruelty carved into flesh. He ground this teeth, knowing there was little he could do save to make the scout's final moments less painful. "Water, I need water!"

A knight brought him a waterskin. "We found him nailed to a tree beyond the village, as if left as a warning. He's been raving since we took him down."

Quintus crushed a handful of herbs from his belt pouch into the waterskin.

"They're coming! More than you can count! A river of darkness! And the knight marshal leads them!"

"You need to drink."

Sir Taryl stayed the healer's hand. "What did he say?"

The scout's glazed eyes sought the knight, a sudden urgency supplanting his pain. "I saw him, the knight marshal! He slew Sir Borax and Sam and then ordered me nailed to a tree. He wants you to know."

Sir Taryl leaned in. "To know what?"

"To know he's coming."

"Are you certain it was him?"

"I'd know his face anywhere, that one-eyed stare." Blood bubbled at the scout's mouth. The light of reason fled. *"They're coming! More than you can count! A river of darkness! And the knight marshal leads them!"*

"Let me tend him." Quintus held the waterskin to the scout's lips, but he was too late. The scout shuddered and convulsed and then lay still. Quintus closed his eyes, another valiant soul lost to a brutal war. "May the Light keep you."

Sir Taryl stood, shouting orders. "Take the scout for burial. Clear the gatehouse! I want the drawbridge raised!"

"No!" Quintus shot to his feet, daring to lay a restraining hand on the red-haired knight. "Sir Lothar's ordered the gates to remain open till the last moment."

The knight speared him with a desperate glare. "I've seen what lies beyond the village. There's no stopping that dark tide."

Quintus clung to his courage. "Will you violate Sir Lothar's orders?"

Sir Taryl snarled like a hound on a leash.

"Ask Sir Cormin, or any of the knights on watch."

The knight stalked away, an angry swirl of maroon, but the drawbridge remained lowered. Quintus sagged against the shadow-cooled wall. He wasn't even sure what form the monastery's aid would take, yet he knew the drawbridge had to remain lowered.

Trumpets blared and more knights and soldiers surged to man the outer walls.

Shaken, Quintus climbed to the barbican. Seeking to stay out of the defenders' way, he claimed a perch beneath one of the gatehouse merlons. Leaning against the crenellated battlement, he stared out across the valley and stifled a gasp. The village was an inferno. Black smoke belched into the sky, forming an ugly cloud. He gaped at the sight. Such a senseless waste, such a needless tragedy...but then understanding struck. It wasn't senseless at all, but another a warning. Like the mauled scout, the village was a herald of fear. Darkness was coming, and there would be no mercy.

He clung to the stone barbican, staring out across the war-torn land, seeking some sign of hope.

Beside him, a young soldier said, "Do you hear the drums?"

And then he thought he did, like the rumble of distant thunder.

"They're coming."

So ominous those words. The healer crouched by the barbican, watching the billowing smoke.

The drums grew louder, the steady rumble enough to quake fear in ordinary men.

Somewhere below, a knight bellowed an order. "Raise the drawbridge! Seal the gates."

To Quintus, the order sounded like a death knell. "No, don't!" But his cry was lost in the chaos.

Chains clanked and rattled.

Wood groaned and the massive drawbridge began to rise.

Quintus sank against the wall, feeling lost.

Beside him, the young soldier stiffened, pointing south. "Look there!"

The healer stared south. At first he saw nothing, but then he spied a ripple of blue emerging from the Shield Forest. *Midnight blue!* It was a battle banner, midnight-blue emblazoned with a radiant Seeing Eye. Hope blazed within him. Two men rode under the banner. They cantered across the greensward, followed by several hundred loping runners clad in green and brown. "Hope comes! Lower the drawbridge!" But no one heard him. Frantic, he searched the barbican till he found Sir Cormin. "Friends from the south!"

The knight saw the band of men. "Sound the call for 'knights returning'."

The trumpeter raised his horn, blaring a trill of notes.

The cry of "knights returning" echoed up and down the wall.

The drawbridge halted, stalled in its rise, and then began to lower.

Quintus raced for the stairs, taking them two at a time. The chaos of the villagers was gone, replaced with knights and soldiers readying for battle. The portly healer dodged men in armor, determined to greet the newcomers. Reaching the shadow of the gatehouse, he waited, pressed to the stone wall, wondering if he'd recognize any of the men. He knew it was doubtful, given his time in the monastery was long ago, yet he hoped.

The drawbridge thudded level. The toothed portcullis remained raised. Quintus stared through the gateway, across the drawbridge, watching.

A pair of riders reached the drawbridge, the silken battle banner waving proudly in the wind, midnight-blue emblazoned with the radiant Seeing Eye. Quintus thrilled to see it, swelling with pride and hope.

The riders clattered across the drawbridge. The first was a giant of a man, with a bushy beard and a wild shock of dark hair. He wore brown fighting leathers, a sword hilt rearing over his shoulder, yet his left arm was in a sling, proving trouble dogged them. The second rider wore robes of midnight-blue... *a monk of the Order!* A slender man, yet he carried a sword wrapped in leather looming above his shoulder. Quintus stared at the riddle. Swords were never the weapons of monks. So befuddled was he, that the horses nearly passed before he stepped from the shadows. He raised his voice above the din. "Welcome to Castlegard, may knowledge be your guide!"

Turning in the saddle, the blond-haired monk sought his face.

"I'm Quintus, the master healer of Castlegard." He made a subtle hand signal identifying himself as a monk of the Order.

The blond-haired monk swung down from the saddle. "I'm Ambrose and this is Haythor of the Zward. We seek an urgent audience with the captains of Castlegard."

It was only then that he noticed their escort, archers clad in green and browns...and all of their eyes were golden yellow.

79

Katherine

Beyond Pellanor, summer lay soft on the land, as if peace was a season whose time had finally come, but Kath knew otherwise. The red comet was set, quenched in the west, yet the Mordant's influence hung over Erdhe like an executioner's axe. Armies of the Pentacle threatened Castlegard in the north and the Kiralynn Monastery in the south. If either fell, beacons of the Light would forever be extinguished, eclipsing Erdhe with Darkness. Kath shuddered against the grim thought. Putting spurs to her mount, she raced north with her small band, begrudging every turn of the hourglass lost.

They rode north at a blistering pace, thundering across the verdant countryside. Merchants and farmers scrambled to get off the road, making way for her small band of warriors. Galloping from dawn till dusk, they pressed their horses for every scrap of speed. Rising from their bedrolls at first light, they released their spent mounts with thanks, transferring their saddles to fresh horses. Kath gave Danya a grateful look as she vaulted into the saddle. The wolf-girl could have easily stayed behind, but she'd chosen to lend her magic to speed their journey north.

Thaddeus served as their guide. The Zward captain led them off the roads, cutting through ripening wheat fields and pockets of thick forest. Turning away from due north, he angled them towards the rising sun. Thaddeus led with unerring certainty, yet he carried no map. After a fortnight of hard riding, he drew rein, pointing towards a hilltop crowned with forest. "There, you can see it above the trees."

Kath settled her restless stallion, staring towards the northeast. Red ruins poked above the treetops, broken towers and crumbling walls, burnished bright in the waning light. The ruins called to her, echoing with martial splendor long lost. "What is this place?"

"You'll not find it on any map. Broken during the War of Wizards, the Crimson Keep is a place that time forgot. Once a mighty stronghold of the Star Knights, the local folk shun it as a haunted ruin."

The Star Knights! The very name echoed in Kath's soul. "So we seek the past to save the present."

Thaddeus gave her a knowing look. "Just so." He thrummed his heels against his mount. "Come."

They rode across ripening farm fields, entering a tangled forest of old growth trees. Massive oaks reared overhead, thick branches blocking the sun. Riding single file through the gathering gloom, they followed a deer track, spiraling upwards to the hilltop ruins. Tumbled blocks of blood-red stone appeared amongst the ferns. Some of the blocks dwarfed their horses, lichen mottling the red stone with veins of yellow and green. Kath marveled at their size, wondering what force could have torn them asunder. The track turned steep, and she gained a better view of the ruins, a broken tower spiking towards a sunset sky. The curtain wall was smashed, giant stones tossed down the hillside, yet the ruins held an age-old majesty, a memory of valor defeated but never quenched. Kath shivered, feeling as if ghostly warriors kept watch.

Thaddeus led them around the base of the curtain wall to a cave burrowed into the hillside. The gaping mouth was wide enough for five horses to ride abreast. "This cave once served as the stables to the keep."

A cloud of bats burst outward like an exhaled breath of dark smoke. Startled, their horses reared and stamped. Kath calmed her stallion as the bats swarmed into the forest. Swinging down from the saddle, she unsheathed her sword. "Any other surprises?"

Joining her on foot, Thaddeus struck a flint, lighting a torch. "Shouldn't be. The locals believe the tower is haunted." He led the way, holding the torch high.

The cavern proved huge, large enough to stable more than a hundred horses. The air smelled of bat droppings and old horse dung, musty but tolerable. A shaft of sunlight pierced a hole at the back, illuminating a ring of stones blackened by fire. "Someone's been here." Kath sheathed her sword.

Thaddeus nodded. "I brought Jordan here with a small band of Zward. She dreamed of this place."

Kath's breath caught.

"The gods guided us here. We rescued Prince Stewart and a young lord of Lingard." Thaddeus pressed his hand against the rough hewn stone, as if the walls held memories. "It was in the ruins above, that Jordan married her prince."

Kath's imagination caught fire. "I would like to see the ruins."

"Come, I'll show you."

They settled the horses, removing saddles and bedrolls. Ruthgar and Sidhorn took first watch, standing guard at the cave mouth. Gris and two of Neven's den went in search of firewood and small game. Bryx joined the hunters, chuffing at the musty smell of the cave. Bear discovered a cache of dry firewood, and started a small blaze in the stone ring. Danya, Neven, and the others settled their bedrolls around the ring, taking their ease before the fire.

Blaine joined Kath and Thaddeus, climbing a steep path up to the ruins.

The sun was nearly set, painting the sky vibrant reds streaked with gold.

Thaddeus carried a torch, his guiding light leading them through the shattered curtain wall into the heart of the ruins. The stonework was amazing, huge blocks of blood-red stone fitted seamlessly together. Kath ran her hand along the walls, imbibing a sense of the distant past, of silver-clad knights fighting for a valiant cause. She could almost hear the trumpet's clarion call summoning her to battle. "Can you feel it?" Her voice was reverent, hushed to a whisper. "The age-old struggle against the Dark. The stones remember even if men do not."

They reached the tower, the broken heart of the ancient keep. Fallen stones formed a giant staircase leading to a lofty view.

Thaddeus said, "This was where Jordan took her vows."

Kath could well imagine it, a wartime wedding held amidst the remnants of martial splendor. It seemed a fitting setting for her sword sister. Staring aloft, she spied the first star of the evening shining bright in the lavender vault. She wished Jordan well, praying the gods granted her a long and happy marriage. Gripping Duncan's warrior ring, Kath remembered their own wedding vows set amongst the Shield Forest. A sigh escaped her. She missed him so.

A figure stood silhouetted against the far wall.

Startled, Kath drew her sword.

"No need for that." Aeroth stepped from the shadows. "I've been waiting for you."

So owls fly faster than horses gallop. Kath kept the thought to herself, guarding his secret.

Blaine scowled at the blue-robed monk. "How did you beat us here?"

"The past holds potent secrets. Come." Aeroth turned, striding into the shadows.

They followed him to stone stairs so overgrown with bushes the entrance was nearly hidden. Climbing over fallen stones and pushing past scratchy thorns, they passed through the entrance, descending the stairs to a subterranean vault. The hallway was long and smooth-floored with a beveled ceiling. Thaddeus's torch flickered against the walls, the only source of light. The cellar felt ancient, yet well made, the mitered stone retaining an earthborn chill.

Thaddeus waved the torch in the open doorways, spider webs sizzling in the flames. "I remember this place. Brigands stored their ill-gotten gains here."

One room was piled high with casks and chests and the tempting smell of slow cured ham.

Blaine said, "What happened to the brigands?"

"Dead."

"Good," Blaine flashed a grin. "Then they won't miss their ham."

Beyond them, Aeroth hissed with impatience. "Come."

Following Aeroth's voice, they pressed deeper into the cellar. The last doorway opened into a small round chamber with a vaulted ceiling. Stars glimmered across the corbelled vault, facetted crystals reflecting the torchlight, the remnants of lapis-blue paint clinging to the stone. Beneath the starry vault, stood a mage-stone statue, a huge hand twice the height of a tall man. A Seeing Eye was chiseled deep on the open palm. Kath gasped to see it. "*Mage-stone!*"

"No, this is something far more rare and far more powerful. This looks like mage-stone, but in truth it is way-stone." Aeroth's eyes glowed golden in the torchlight. "This is why I summoned you here."

Kath's skin prickled, as if she stood in the presence of something very powerful. "I've seen these before, but they never felt like this."

Aeroth stared at her. "Then perhaps you've grown in your magic."

Kath swallowed, unwilling to explain how she'd escaped the oubliette. "What does it do?" Her right hand sought the mage-stone gargoyle hidden deep in her pocket, comforted by its touch.

"Way-stones were created before the War of Wizards. They allowed mages who had mastered at least one of the elements to travel."

"To travel?"

Aeroth gave her a solemn nod. "According to scrolls in the Great Archives, a wizard embraced his magic, envisioned the way-stone that he wished to travel to, and then stepped into the stone hand. A heartbeat later, he stepped out of the other way-stone, the one he held in his mind. Way-stones allowed mages to travel great distances in the blink of an eye."

Blaine barked a laugh. "Are you drunk or merely daft?"

Kath speared him with a warning glance. "I believe him."

Blaine glared at her.

"After all we've seen, all we've been through, how can you not believe it is possible?" Kath circled the massive hand, her voice dropping to a hush. "There is something ancient and powerful buried in this stone. It calls to me. I feel it."

"Then perhaps you can waken its magic. Master Rizel said your gifts were in the element of earth." Aeroth kept his golden gaze focused on Kath. "It is said that those who wielded earth power were best able to travel."

"You say 'perhaps'. So you don't know if the magic still works?"

Aeroth looked uncomfortable. "None have traveled the way-stones in centuries, yet the scrolls say the magic is sound."

"Scrolls?" Blaine spat the word. "You'd trust your life to musty scrolls?"

Kath ignored the knight's skepticism. "So this will take me anywhere?"

"No, only to another way-stone, and it must be one you've seen. Three are known to have survived the millennia of time. One stands just beyond the Guardian Mist, the threshold to the Kiralynn Monastery."

Kath remembered the great hand standing like a sentinel before the white wall of Mist.

"A second way-stone stands atop a balding mountain overlooking the southern entrance to Raven Pass."

Kath gasped. "I know that stone! I saw it when my father first took me to Raven Pass. Just a child, but I remember being dwarfed by the great hand, asking for the story behind the statue, but none knew the tale."

Aeroth gave her a solemn nod, yet he looked as if he did not approve. "The knowledge of the way-stones is a closely guarded secret. Few who wear midnight-blue ever learn of it, yet the Grand Master bid me to give this knowledge to you." He gestured to the great hand dominating the chamber. "This third way-stone remained forgotten until Jordan and the Zward rediscovered it whole and unharmed, though they knew not what they'd found." His stare drilled into her. "It is as if the gods give you the chance to choose. In the blink of an eye, you can travel halfway to Castlegard, or stand on the very threshold of the Kiralynn Monastery. The last bastion of knowledge and the castle of Light are both threatened by Darkness. Which will you choose?"

Kath felt a heavy weight fall across her shoulders. *Castlegard or the monastery!* Both deserved to be saved.

Aeroth said, "Think on it, for the way-stones should never be attempted by the weary."

Blaine's voice was blunt. "Why?"

Aeroth turned to him. "A weak mage will never be able to wield the magic of the way-stones. A weary mage may enter but never escape."

"Trapped in stone forever?"

Aeroth nodded, his gaze turning to Kath. "That is why I asked you if you dared. Only you can decide if it is worth the risk."

Blaine scowled. "Better to ride."

Aeroth's voice struck like a lash. "If you choose the mundane way, the safe way, then both Castlegard and the monastery will fall long before you ever reach either one of them. Only by daring the way-stones can your swords make a difference." His gaze fell on Kath. "Yours to decide."

80.

Katherine

Kath tossed and turned, restless with worry. Soft snores echoed through the cavern, proving the others slept. Light flickered across the sleeping forms, glinting off weapons kept close at hand. The bonfire had dimmed to only a handful of flames, the embers glowing cherry-red.

Tired of not sleeping, Kath tugged on her boots, grabbed her sword belt, and made her way toward the cavern mouth. Moonlight silvered the entrance, the stars spread in a glorious spray across the night sky. Nodding to the two sentries, she made her way to the path leading up to the ruins. The ancient keep shimmered in the moonlight, as if time was no barrier to valor. She breathed deep the stone-still peace, seeking answers to half a hundred questions. Beyond the curtain wall, she came across a fallen block twice the size of a horse. Climbing on top, she sat cross-legged, staring up at the glory of the stars.

A stone rattled on the path below. Kath heard the soft tread of footsteps, yet she sensed it was no foe. Waiting, she wondered which companion would come.

Moonlight glimmered on a silver surcoat. Blaine stared up at her perch. "May I join you?"

"Yes."

He climbed up beside her, sitting cross-legged, his blue steel sword jutting over his right shoulder.

Kath gazed at the stars, waiting for his question.

"Will you try the way-stone?"

"Yes."

His voice dropped to a hoarse whisper. "Can you do it?"

That was the question. "I won't know till I try." Kath fingered her mage-stone gargoyle. "But I think I can...if I believe."

"If you *believe?*"

"Much in this life depends on belief. Whether you believe in yourself, whether others believe in you." She gripped her gargoyle, thinking of her own life. Her golden signet ring weighed heavy on her hand, a reminder of her father. "Even if others don't believe, you can't let doubt riddle your life. Doubt is the precipice to failure."

"*Precipice!* Now you sound like a blue-robed monk!"

Kath laughed, and the laughter did her good. "I'm glad you came."

Blaine grinned at her, but then he sobered. "If the way-stones are such a deep dark secret, then why did the monk tell you with me there?"

Her gaze slid to his. "Can't you guess?"

He did not answer.

"Heroes are needed, both at Castlegard and the monastery. A grim battle awaits in either place." She turned towards him. "Aeroth wants you to come with me. He knows your blue steel sword is needed for the battle to come." She feared to ask. "Will you?"

Blaine hesitated.

"*I* will go with you." The deep voice came from below.

They both startled, ambushed by the painted warrior.

Bear stepped into the moonlight. "I will go with you, Svala."

His stalwart trust touched her deeply. "The risks are great."

"Risks do not matter, Svala."

"But you've never seen Castlegard or the monastery. To travel through the way-stones you must hold the image in your mind."

His blunt gaze never left hers. "Then I will think of *you*, Svala. That way I will travel wherever you go."

Tears threatened her eyes, touched by his staunch belief. "Belief matters." She whispered the words to herself as much as to him. "I am honored to have you by my side."

"Good." Bear crossed his arms, his legs planted wide, as if he intended to stand there till she came down.

Blaine said, "I will come too."

Her gaze slid to his. "I hoped you would. It will take both our swords to finish this journey we started so long ago." Kath stood, her own confidence bolstered by theirs. A weight seemed to have lifted from her shoulders. She hadn't realized how much she needed their companionship, their belief. "Come, we'd best get some sleep." Kath strode to the edge of the block and jumped. With two such warriors by her side, she dared not fail.

81

Lothar

Lothar stood atop the tower watching the enemy advance. War drums rumbled in the distance, heralds of a terrible storm. A dark tide crept up from the burning village, an implacable horde led by his friend. "Osbourne, what have you done?" Lothar's words whispered in the wind. He'd expected the enemy to attack one of the bridges, to cross the Snowmelt and plunder the rich southern kingdoms, yet here they were, a dark swarm advancing on an invincible castle. *Invincible!* His thoughts choked on the word. He hadn't believed the healer and the swordsmith, not till he'd seen for himself how the smith's hammer had cracked the forge wall. *Impossible!* He still found it hard to believe. Mage-stone had always been as sure as sunrise, forever solid, dependable, invincible, yet somehow mage-stone was failing, as if the castle had fallen under a terrible curse. He wondered if Osborne knew. Scouts reported the enemy had siege engines, catapults and a great trebuchet, as if their swarming numbers were not enough. Lothar sighed, feeling the weight of Erdhe falling on his shoulders.

Sir Rannock strode across the tower top, his maroon cloak billowing in the wind. "They're assembled and waiting for you."

Lothar figured he had half a day before the enemy settled into their positions, time enough to meet with the captains, the champions and the senior veterans. Time enough for his brethren to hear the words of the monk.

Sir Rannock gave him a grim look. "They know."

Lothar scowled. "Of course they know." In times of war, rumors moved faster than shit through a goose. He'd prayed for the knight marshal to remain true to the maroon, but the scout's dying words killed that hope. He would have kept the foul secret to himself, but the whispered words struck like sparks to dry tinder. Nothing could contain the rumor. One more problem he had to fight. He fingered the great battleaxe strapped to his belt. He'd never wanted to lead, not like this, and now the fate of the maroon rested in his calloused hands.

"Should I speak of mage-stone?"

Rannock looked away, considering. "No, they won't believe it."

"True enough. I'm not sure I believe it either." Lothar gripped his battleaxe. He'd met with the monk, Ambrose, in private. *Restore honor to the*

Octagon... the monk's remedy made no sense. And he'd not besmirch the maroon's honor by mentioning it. "We'll make the enemy prove it."

Rannock gave a grim nod. "The gods help us if it's true." He stared across the greensward at the gathering horde, his voice dropping to a hush. "What of the sword?"

"A rusted relic?" Lothar shook his shaggy head. "The monks have gone mad."

"Perhaps the whole world has gone insane, stricken by Darkness."

Lothar grunted. "Come." Turning from the battlement, he crossed the tower to the stairs. He took them two at a time, sunlight piercing the arrow-slit windows. Reaching the bottom, a pair of maroon-cloaked guards snapped to attention and then fell in behind. Lothar barely saw them, his thoughts mired in worry.

He wound his way through the castle to the massive audience chamber. Seldom used, the grand mage-stone chamber was built for an earlier Age when maroon-cloaked knights were revered across the land and Castlegard's king took counsel with other monarchs. A reminder of past glories, Lothar lingered in the shadowed wing of the dais, surveying the great room. Faded battle banners hung from vaulted rafters, distant memories of bygone triumphs. Stained glass windows, glittering with heraldry, added color to the dazzling spears of light illuminating the great hall. His maroon-cloaked brethren filled less than a quarter of the hall, bitter proof the knighthood had dwindled. And upon the dais sat an empty throne, the pale wood carved in the silhouette of the great castle. *An empty throne...*if only King Ursus had lived, but wishes were for children and fools.

Lothar strode across the dais.

An abrupt hush settled across the knights.

He felt their stares, he felt their questions. Perhaps they expected him to sit upon the throne, but he did not. Instead, he took a stance beside it.

Emboldened by his choice, his brethren hurled questions thick as spears.

"Is it true?"

"Has the marshal turned traitor?"

"Who will lead us?"

"Who will claim the crown of Castlegard?"

"Who is worthy?"

Lothar raised his hands, stilling the tumult. "The marshal made a choice. The winter war took a grievous toll, clawing away at our numbers, so the marshal grasped a desperate chance to save the maroon." They stood listening, their faces' solemn, not a sound in the great hall. "Many of you remember the high meadow where we found a hundred ogres slain by a single squire." Murmurs raced through the chamber. He raised his hands, demanding silence. "The Dark Sword that slew so many was gifted with great power...but it was also cursed. The marshal risked his very soul to wield that sword against the enemy." The bitter words choked in his throat, yet he forced them out. "The marshal dared to take the battle to the horde. That he now leads the horde against the Octagon is proof he lost that risk."

The chamber erupted in outrage.

Lothar let them rage, he let them argue, and when their words were spent, he resumed speaking. "We face the same Dark horde that we fought in the long winter war, but this time it is led by a friend." He stilled their anger with a stern glance. "Instead of setting ambushes in the mountains, this time we fight from Castlegard's walls." He choked on the thought of mage-stone, but he said nothing. "And this time we have unexpected allies." More than a few knights glowered his way, for many in Erdhe considered those with cat-eyes to be accursed, befouled, less than human. Lothar met their glowers with firm resolve. "Two hundred rangers of the Deep Green have brought their longbows to Castlegard to fight the Dark. Their longbows are sorely needed. *I* have made them welcome and you will as well." He raised his voice, overriding those who protested. "Any knight who insults our allies from the Deep Green, will be stripped of his maroon cloak and serve the duration of the war hauling rocks to feed the catapults." He glared at the assembly. "This is a promise, not a threat. Do I make myself clear?"

No one dared protest, but a few sent venomous looks his way.

From the rear, someone yelled, "What of the throne?"

"Yes, who will lead us?"

"We need a king!"

"*Silence!*" Lothar's roar echoed to the rafters. "For now, *I* lead the maroon. Once this battle is won, then the question of the throne will be decided."

"But how will it be decided?"

"Who will lead?"

"Who is worthy?"

They worried the question like a dog with a prized bone. Lothar had to give them something. "Perhaps a champion will emerge from the battle, a man worthy to be crowned king of the Octagon." That gave them something to consider. "When our allies rode through the castle gates, they came under the banner of the Seeing Eye. The Kiralynn monks have brought aid to Castlegard." He motioned to the wing of the dais, where the blue-robed monk, the healer, and the Zward captain stood obscured by shadows. "Master Ambrose of the Kiralynn Order claims to have brought aid from the monastery." Lothar gestured and the monk joined him beside the throne. The monk had a scrollish look about him, yet he carried a great sword wrapped in leathers. Lothar knew what the wrapped leather hid, yet desperation made him grasp at any straw. He gave the dais to the monk.

82

Ambrose

Ambrose surveyed the assembly of knights. *So few when history said there had once been so many.* Time and countless battles had dwindled the Octagon, yet perhaps a sword from the past could render a great difference. Sweat broke across his skin like a plague of worry. Ambrose knew he carried a rust-riddled sword. But he also knew what the sword could be...or at least he thought he did. The Treespeaker had said the blade was god-touched, he prayed it was so.

"I bring hope to Castlegard, though you may not believe me." Ambrose felt their stares and knew he'd started wrong-footed. He struggled to explain. "A sword was summoned in the monastery. The last blue steel blade crafted by Orrin Surehammer, it was forged a millennium ago, awaiting the Battle Immortal."

Murmurs of interest raced through the knights, for the name of the wizard-smith was laden with well-known legends.

Ambrose spoke above the murmurs. "Forged by the last great wizard, invoked by an illuminator in the monastery, and touched by the gods, *Invictus* is destined for the hands of a champion."

The great hall thrummed like a swarm of bees keen for honey. The knights fixed their stares on him.

Ambrose swallowed. He dreaded telling them the truth, yet that was his burden. "When I left the monastery, many moon-turns ago, this sword was sapphire-blue. Since then, it has been changed, transformed, touched by the gods, yet I believe its powers are undimmed." Words failed him. Resigned to their scorn, Ambrose began to unwrap the sword, like unwinding a shroud from a corpse. He started with the hilt and moved down to the coiled dragons, revealing the rust-pitted details.

Someone gasped.

Someone else sniggered.

Their interest sputtered to indignant anger.

A big red-haired knight snorted, "*That* is a sword of destiny? What tomb did you rob?"

The leather binding fell to the floor, revealing the rust-red hilt. Ambrose unsheathed the blade, revealing the rust-pitted great sword.

"What joke is this?"

"That blade will break on the first hit."

"Do you jest with us, monk?"

Insults were hurled his way. "We risk our lives and you bring us a rusty blade?"

Ambrose swayed under the assault. *They did not believe.* He'd dared much to bring the sword to Castlegard, yet he'd failed to convince them. *Invictus,* the name stirred in his soul, yet in truth it looked like nothing more than a musty relic from a forgotten tomb. He fingered the rusty dragons coiling the hilt...and then he remembered the Green Dream. Voices of the great trees shimmered through his mind with the clarity of a summer morning. *The sword will know. The sword will choose. The gods have decreed it!* Ambrose spoke with the force of destiny. His words rang through the great hall, cutting through their derision. "This sword is destined for the monarch of Castlegard! In the hands of the rightwise ruler, *Invictus* shall reveal its true form!" He raised the sword on high. "Who shall dare to wield this blade of destiny? Who will claim the throne of Castlegard?"

A hush descended on the great hall.

For half a heartbeat they believed...and then the knights snarled in derision. "Don't take us for fools, monk."

"Take that pig-sticker back to the tomb where you found it."

"We'll suffer no grave robbers here!"

Ambrose stood there, feeling foolish.

But then the huge red-haired knight pushed his way to the dais. "I'm the strongest! I'll dare the rusty sword to win the crown."

Sparked with a glimmer of hope, Ambrose offered him the hilt.

The knight grasped it with both hands, raising the blade aloft. "I claim the crown of Castlegard!" The hall stilled, watching, waiting, yet nothing happened. "Just a rusty blade!" Snarling, he hurled the blade across the dais. "Just a jape from the monks."

The sword clattered against mage-stone. Ambrose winced, half expecting the rusty relic to crumble to dust, yet it remained whole and unbroken. The monk retrieved the sword, wondering at its sturdiness, but the knights paid no heed, clattering from the great hall.

Quintus, the healer, approached. "You sounded so sure."

"I am sure." Ambrose lifted the sword. "Don't you see? If this blade were truly rusted, it would have shattered against mage-stone."

Quintus looked thoughtful. "Yet, that blade is so rusted it will not even cut cloth."

"Not in my hands, but this sword will be dauntless in the hands of the true king. I swear it is so." Ambrose crossed the dais. He reverently leaned *Invictus* against the throne. *An empty throne and a rusty sword...*he prayed the gods would keep their promise.

83

Tybalt

Forty-eight ragged men ran up out of the tree line into the barren heights. The switchbacks turned steep, stealing Ty's breath. He struggled to keep pace, his quarterstaff jouncing against his back. Every other switchback, he paused, stabbing a glance back down the rocky slope, hoping to spy Master Christoff, but the lower trail remained empty of friend and foe.

"Keep running!" The command came from behind. Targus, the Zward captain, herded them forward, his voice a lash. "Laggards die! I'll not lose more men to this mountain."

Ty fought his own weariness, struggling to increase his pace. In truth, he felt exposed without the trees, like a rabbit flushed from cover.

An eagle screamed overhead. Soaring on wide wings, the golden raptor spiraled out across the mountain vastness. The view was magnificent, jagged snowcapped-peaks stretching to forever. The mountains alone should have stopped the enemy, a labyrinth of rock and ice, yet somehow evil had ferreted out the secret path to the monastery. Once across Drumheller Pass, there would be little to stop them. The enemy moved like a long black snake slithering into the mountains, a relentless doom come calling. The Zward had dwindled their numbers, but it was never enough to turn them aside. He prayed the Grand Master had secrets potent enough to defeat an army.

Up, always up, the switchbacks climbed towards the heavens. His legs ached, yet he had no choice but to press on. The sun reached its zenith, blazing bright in a flawless sky, yet the air held a permanent chill, a cool breeze blowing down from the icy heights.

He reached the last switchback, climbing towards the pass. The trail grew level, and then he saw it, the last true chokepoint before the monastery. Drumheller Pass was a narrow knife-edge of stone spanning a dizzying abyss. A magnificent glacier overhung the pass, great crystalline swords of ice gleaming sapphire blue in the sunshine. Beautiful and deadly, the ice swords glittered bright, like weapons awaiting the hands of gods.

Ty was one of the last to cross the rocky span. Halfway across, he walked into the glacier's shadow. An ice-cold rain dripped down. Falling into the deep abyss, the gentle rain sounded like plucked harp strings. The sound was enchanting, belying the danger above. Sapphire-blue ice gleamed bright overhead, a frozen confection of the gods. Ty wondered that glaciers could be so ethereal yet so deadly. Tilting his head, he opened his mouth wide. Catching a few drops, he tasted the glacier. Clear, clean and cold, the melt water refreshed him.

Passing beyond the glacier's shadow, he reached the far side of the chasm. The trail snaked around a jumble of huge boulders. Emerging from the boulders, Ty was shocked to see a line of blue-robed monks toiling up the trail. Three of the monks carried a massive sixteen-foot horn between them. Runes scribed in silver spiraled the length of the wide-mouthed horn. Ty wondered if it was Ragdon, the mighty voice used for sky funerals.

Targus called a halt. "We'll rest here."

Grateful for the respite, Ty found a sunny spot just beyond the boulders. He collapsed to the rocky ground, sprawling with the others.

A gaggle of bright-eyed boys ran towards them, offering satchels of food brought up from Haven. The men delved into the satchels, discovering fresh-baked biscuits, sharp yellow cheese, and slices of smoked venison. Ty stuffed his mouth with a biscuit, nearly swooning from the buttery taste. The boys fluttered around like moths to a flame, pestering the weary men for tales of the war. No one had the stomach to tell them the truth.

Targus shooed the lads away. "Take your ease while you can." His voice turned solemn. "The pass is a rare place. A magnificent chokepoint where a single warrior can make a great difference." His gaze sought Ty. "Time to make your quarterstaff count."

Ty felt a prickle of destiny run down his back. He answered with a nod. It seemed the Zward was not yet done with the fight. Ty drew his quarterstaff from the harness on his back. A six-foot length of polished ironwood, the staff felt good in his calloused hands. He whirled the staff through the forms, and felt the magic thrum to life. The iron shodding was a relic from another Age. Ty knew its purpose, he knew its name. *Phade.*

84

General Haith

General Haith rode up out of the twisted pines into the clear mountain air. Above the tree line, there was no place for the enemy to hide. The barren heights reminded him of the open steppes, a type of killing field, a rocky anvil where only numbers mattered. He grinned, knowing he held vastly superior numbers, a hammer waiting to smash the killing blow. Like a hungry eagle, he scanned the barren heights. Nothing moved. Nothing save rocks and empty switchbacks stretched above, proving the pesky enemy had fled.

Putting spurs to his mount, he urged his warhorse to a trot. The *Darkflamme* whispered overhead, writhing in the cool breeze like a sharp-toothed serpent. His vanguard rode ahead, his army stretching behind, a creeping line of dark armor seeking to wet their swords. Harassed since the lowly foothills, the enemy sought to obscure the true trail, setting ambushes and snares. They'd bloodied his army, whittling his numbers, but in truth they served as a whetstone, honing his army to a battle fever. His men yearned for vengeance, for an enemy they could strike. When the battle finally came, there would be no holding them back.

Anticipating the bloodbath, the general grinned beneath the skeleton helm. He had the perfect instrument in the perfect place, an army poised to plunder the wonders of the Kiralynn Monastery. Power and glory would soon be his.

An infernal wail came from above.

Echoing against the rocky crags, it sounded like the caterwauling of a sick dragon.

Making a sharp gesture, he sent two scouts ahead. Whipping their lathered mounts to a gallop, they raced up the final switchbacks.

The scouts soon returned, grins splitting their swarthy faces. "It's a horn, my lord. A blue-robed monk sitting atop a boulder, blowing a massive horn." His grin broadened. "What are they going to do, serenade us to death?"

"And you saw nothing else?"

"No, my lord. The way is clear."

The way is clear...it sounded sweet, yet he knew the monks brimmed with tricks. "I will see for myself." The general spurred his stallion ahead. His vanguard made way before him, opening a path. His personal guards and his standard bearer kept pace behind.

Surmounting the last switchback, he reined his stallion to a halt. The view was breathtaking. The pass was nothing more than a narrow bridge of stone spanning a fathomless chasm, death on either side. A sapphire-blue glacier hung suspended overhead. Ice sculpted into crystalline forms, the glacier shimmered in the sunshine like a wizard's enchantment. Breathtaking and beautiful, it was the perfect place for a trap, yet he saw only two men. A blue-robed monk sat cross-legged on a far boulder, his lips pressed to a great horn.

Vooorooohoom.

The horn's voice was so powerful, he felt its pulse on the far side of the pass.

The other man stood midway across the narrow stone bridge. A young man, his pale blond hair tied at his nape, he stood with his legs spread wide, defiantly guarding the pass. Clad in rock-dusted leathers, he held a black quarterstaff in his hands.

Beside him, his second laughed. "A man with a stick!"

The young man raised his voice to a shout. "I am Tybalt of the Kiralynn Monks. By order of the Grand Master, this way is closed to you. Turn back if you value your lives."

His vanguard erupted in raucous laughter, but the general remained stone-faced, studying the pass with shrewd eyes.

Vooorooohoom, the horn blasted its bone-shivering wail.

General Haith gestured to his second. "Kill the arrogant bastard."

Commander Trollen unsheathed his sword. "With pleasure." Spurring his mount forward, he rode across the span. Turning his warhorse at the last moment, he slashed a vicious cut at the lone monk.

The young man moved like liquid lightning. Evading the sword slash, he landed a mighty blow on the horse's rump. Bellowing, the horse lurched forward, and found itself teetering on the edge. Commander Trollen struggled to get his boots from the stirrups, a look of horror on his face. The man with the quarterstaff struck again, slapping the horse across its rump. Squealing, the horse lost its footing. Horse and rider toppled into the chasm.

Vooorooohoom.

The horn's blare obliterated their screams.

The monk waited at the heart of the span, his young face calm as still water. His feet spread wide, he held the black quarterstaff balanced in his hands, awaiting battle.

Vooorooohoom.

General Haith sent a second swordsman. This one had the good sense to dismount. Unsheathing a five-foot great sword, he prowled across the span like an executioner. Feinting left, he unleashed a wicked attack. The black quarterstaff moved in a blur, blocking every sword stroke.

Vooorooohoom.

The monk ducked a head high swing. Striking like a viper, he unleashed a mighty blow against the guards ribs. A second blow pounded his helm. The guard staggered sideways, falling into the chasm.

Vooorooohoom.

The general scowled. "I'm done with this farce. Bring up two crossbowmen."

His command echoed down the line.

The monk waited patiently, blocking the rocky span.

Vooorooohoom. Vooorooohoom. Vooorooohoom, the horn marked time.

Two crossbowmen gained the top of the pass.

"Kill him."

Setting boots to their crossbow stirrups, the soldiers loaded their bows with iron-tipped quarrels.

Vooorooohoom.

The crossbowmen took aim, their fingers on the ticklers, waiting for the general's command.

The monk raised his quarterstaff to the heavens. Bowing his forehead to the dark wood, he began to chant. His image began to fray.

"Loose!" The general bellowed the order.

The crossbows bucked, loosing their bolts

In the blink of an eye, the monk faded to nothing. If the bolts found their victim, he could not tell.

"*He's gone!*"

"*Magic!*" The general snarled the word like a curse.

"He's there!" One of the crossbowmen pointed to a boulder beyond the narrow bridge. Somehow the monk had moved a hundred paces in the blink of an eye, a cowardly form of magic.

The leather-clad monk raised his quarterstaff in salute, a cocky grin on his face. Looking whole and unharmed, he stepped behind the boulder, disappearing from sight.

Vooorooohoom.

Commander Parn said, "The way is clear! There's nothing stopping us!"

The way *looked* clear, yet the general did not trust the monks. "Sound the advance." Trumpets blared, calling his army forward. He gestured to his third, "Take them across."

Saluting, Commander Parn led the vanguard across the rocky span, weapons and armor glittering in the sunlight.

Vooorooohoom.

Content to let his commander take the risk, General Haith watched as his vanguard reached the far side. Shouts and the clash of steel echoed back, proving the enemy was not so willing to surrender the pass.

Vooorooohoom, the horn continued to wail.

General Haith gestured to the crossbowmen. "Silence that infernal horn."

The crossbowmen set to loading their bows.

A great rumbling sound came from the glacier, like a giant chewing rocks. Cracks appeared, splitting the ice. The ominous rumbling grew to a roar.

"Sound the retreat!" General Haith turned his stallion, bellowing orders, but it was too late. The great glacier fractured, sending massive shards tumbling onto the pass. Sapphire-blue crystals, the size of small towers, thundered down, crushing men and horses beneath a frozen fist. The glacier flowed like a river, spilling an icy mountain onto the narrow pass.

The mountain trembled under the fearsome blow.

General Haith fought to control his stallion.

When the rumbling ceased, a fog of ice crystals hung in the air.

The general peered through the fog. An eerie silence betrayed the grim truth. His vanguard was gone, completely obliterated, crushed by the ice. The pass was blocked, a mountain of jagged ice crystals sealing the way forward. *So the monks sought to seal the pass!* General Haith seethed with anger. The monks thought themselves clever, yet they were not the only ones with magic.

85

Katherine

Kath woke to the smell of pan fried bacon. Enticed by a rush of hunger, she sat up and stretched. "Good morning."

Thaddeus sat by the fire, turning slices in a cast iron skillet. "Good afternoon."

Startled, she blinked at the shaft of blinding sunlight pouring straight down through the hole in the cavern ceiling. The pillar of white stood straight as a column. Sheepish, she realized it was high noon. "I guess I slept late."

"You needed it."

The others wandered in, carrying more booty from the brigands' ill-gotten hoard. Sidhorn opened a cask of red wine, filling four goblets and a battered tin cup. They passed the goblets and cup between them, sharing the rich red wine. Gris found a bag of walnuts, cracking them open and handing them around. Bryx gnawed on a ham bone, sitting contented next to Danya and Neven.

Kath looked at each of her companions, realizing this was farewell. Once she stepped into the way-stone, for better or ill, she would not be back. She stared at their faces, all of them dear. Kath could not find the words, yet she felt they knew.

Talking of small things, they feasted on bacon pan-fried with forest mushrooms and drank the brigands' dark red wine. As the wine flowed, her painted warriors competed to tell tall tales, exaggerating their first glimpse of the rolling ocean, of terrifying storms and towering waves, and battles fought on rolling decks. They ribbed each other, arguing over who fell the most when they'd first sat a horse, and who'd become the best rider. Kath listened, savoring every word, knowing it was their way of saying farewell.

When the last of the feast was consumed, Kath reached for a goblet topped with red wine. Standing, she turned, meeting each gaze. "This adventure we started could not have been won without you. Thank you for your swords, your courage, and your steadfast belief." She raised the goblet in salute. "Go home to the hard won peace of the north. And when you dangle your grandchildren on your knees, you'll have tales to tell the like of which they'll never forget...for you are all heroes." Her gaze settled on Danya. "The Light be with you."

"Svala!" Her painted warriors roared to their feet. Pounding swords against shields, they raised a fearful din. Bryx stood, adding a howl to the clamor.

Kath said goodbye to each of them, giving Danya the longest hug, and then she turned to Aeroth. "I'm ready."

Giving her a solemn nod, the blue-robed monk led her out of the cavern and up the steep trail to the broken keep. Blaine, Bear, Sidhorn and Thaddeus followed. Two of them would dare the way-stone with her, while the other two came as witnesses for the painted people and the Zward. Kath blinked against the noontime sunlight, so harsh after the shadowy coolness of the cavern. They reached the ruins, passing through the smashed curtain wall, into the heart of the keep. Tumbled blocks lay strewn everywhere, proof of a battle lost. The ruins seemed sad and forlorn without the glimmer of starlight. *The Star Knights fought valiantly...yet they lost.* The thought shivered like a warning in Kath's soul. She sketched the hand sign against evil. Perhaps the daylight made hard truths more harsh.

They reached the hidden stairwell, pausing only long enough for Thaddeus to light a torch. The Zward captain led the way down. Torchlight illumed the subterranean passage, flickering against the beveled ceiling. He led them straight to the rear, to the starry chamber. The great mage-stone hand reared in the torchlight, the Seeing Eye incised deep in the open palm. Kath stood before the hand, dwarfed by the way-stone.

Aeroth said. "Which will you choose? The monastery or the castle?"

"Both deserve to be saved, but for once, duty and my heart are aligned." She turned to face him. "I am Kath of Castlegard. There can be but one choice for me."

Dismay flickered across the monk's face, a fleeting emotion quickly suppressed. "I must warn you, a massive army marches on Castlegard. If they lay siege to the castle before you reach the gates, your choice may be for naught."

"Even a siege will not stop me."

Aeroth gave her a puzzled stare. "How can you be so sure?"

Kath smiled, oddly pleased that she knew something the monks did not. "Because there is a fourth way-stone."

Aeroth gasped, "Where?"

"In the hidden passageways beneath Castlegard. I found it as a child, though I knew not what it was." Kath laid a hand against the way-stone, feeling the shimmer of power within. "This way-stone will take me home."

Aeroth's voice was somber. "The gods favor you, blade bearer." Yet he tried one last time. "What of the monastery?"

"Your Order keeps many secrets and many hidden magics. It is time to wield them in your own defense."

He gave her a terse nod. "The Light keep you."

"And you." Kath stepped towards the way-stone, feeling the magic within. It called to her with a deep-throated thrum. *So much magic, but could she wield it?* There was no way to learn the answer save but to try.

Opening her eyes, she looked at the two men. "Are you ready?"

Blaine was whey-faced, yet he gave her a firm nod.

Bear's voice was a deep rumble laden with certainty. "I am with you, Svala. Always."

His steadfast words pierced her heart. "Then think of Castlegard, or think of me, but hold firm to the image, as if your very lives depend on it." She linked arms with the two men, the very same way they'd passed through stone walls in the Dark Citadel, yet this was different, so very different. Taking a deep breath, Kath thought of Castlegard, of ramparts tall and battlements stout, of soaring towers and invincible gates, of maroon pennants flying jaunty above mage-stone walls. In her mind's eye, she saw reflections of the battlements shimmering in the deep green moat, casting an image of enduring strength. *Castlegard...home.* Forcing all doubt from her mind, Kath clung to the image. *"Now!"* Reaching for the magic within, Kath leaped into the way-stone, her heart set on Castlegard.

86

Katherine

Kath leaped into the way-stone hand, expecting the cold, sedentary embrace of stone, but instead she was buffeted by a dark whirlwind. A howling storm raged within the way-stone, ripping and beating at her as if to tear her asunder. The maelstrom roared around her, fierce enough to scour flesh from bones. Kath feared the wind would eat her alive, scattering her soul to oblivion. Unable to sense her two companions, she battled the wind, clinging to thoughts of Castlegard like a ship tethered to a desperate anchor. Laughter riddled the maelstrom. Exultant and cruel, male laughter spiked the storm, mocking her efforts. The way-stone felt haunted. It felt *evil*. Battered by fierce winds and stalked by a malicious spirit, Kath reached for Castlegard. *Mage-stone spires impossibly tall, gargoyles ringing the tower tops, soaring walls and crenellated battlements, murder holes and portcullises, tricks and traps between the two walls, a placid green moat wide and deep reflecting lofty battlements, maroon banners rippling in the wind, catapults and trebuchets bristling the walls, an invincible castle, undefeated, unbowed...the place she dared to call...home.*

The wind spat her out.

She fell hard, sprawling onto a cold stone floor. Kath gasped for breath, every part of her battered and aching. The wind was gone, the air refreshingly still and cool, and smelling of cloistered stone. Kath sat up, straining to see, but the darkness was absolute.

"Svala, are we alive?"

Bear, his voice came from her right. "I think we're here." On her left, she heard a shuffling movement. Relief washed through her, knowing it must be Blaine. She gave thanks to Valin. "We made it."

A red light glowed in the chamber.

Kath stifled a scream.

Red eyes glared down at her, glowing with the light of Hell. *"At last...my long wait is ended."*

It was Blaine's voice, yet it wasn't.

Bathed in red light, the figure stood. He stretched, as if filling Blaine's body like a glove.

"No!" Kath's heart quailed, held spellbound by horror. *"Not Blaine!"*

The red-eyed figure loomed over her. "So many others broke their armies against the great castle's walls, but not *I*, for I, Ballial, shall succeed where they failed. Wielding stealth and cunning and a spider's patience, *I* shall take the great castle from within." The fiend laughed with a ravenous hunger.

Kath stared, frozen with horror. In the glowing red light of his eyes, she watched as the fiend drew Blaine's blue steel blade.

"My time has come!" Steel rasped against leather. "None shall stop me!"

"*Svala!*" Bear barreled into the fiend, knocking him backwards. The two men fought, grappling for the sword. Armor clattered as they fell heavy to the floor. Punching and kicking, they rolled against the far wall. In the red-tinged darkness, it was difficult to tell one from the other. Kath heard a loud thud and a sickening crunch.

One figure stood and the other lay still.

Red eyes glowed at her.

"No." Scrambling backwards, Kath drew the crystal dagger.

The fiend attacked. The blue sword swept towards her in a mighty two-handed strike. Kath rolled to the right. Blue steel struck mage-stone with a thundering clang, raising a spray of white sparks.

He means to kill me! Kath scrambled to her feet, dodging behind the way-stone hand. The thing that was Blaine followed, slashing and stabbing with the blue steel blade. The harlequin had Blaine's sword, but not his skill. He growled at her like a beast denied, the only light coming from his baleful red eyes. Kath knew she could not fight a blue steel blade, yet somehow she had to slay the demon within. Three times she circled the way-stone hand. The fiend gave chase, slashing the great sword towards her face. Kath narrowly evaded the blue steel blade, and then she took a chance. Backing towards the far wall, she cringed, nothing more than a frightened girl. "Don't hurt me."

The thing that was Blaine strode towards her, the blue sword raised over its head for a killing stroke. "Castlegard shall be forever *mine!*"

The blue sword descended swift and deadly.

Kath waited till the last moment. Stepping backwards, she disappeared into the mage-stone wall. Rushing two steps to the left, she emerged from the stone. "Castlegard is *mine!*" Ambushing the fiend, Kath leaped towards him. With all her might, she stabbed the crystal dagger into the fiend's side. Light flared bright. The crystal blade sliced through his surcoat and chainmail, biting deep into flesh.

The thing that was Blaine screamed and howled. He struggled to twist away, but Kath held the dagger firm. The fiend fell backwards, clattering to the floor, and she fell with him, keeping the dagger deep in his side.

"*Demon be gone!*" She roared the command. Willing her strength into the crystal dagger, she sought to smite the harlequin's soul.

Beneath her, the fiend convulsed.

Through the crystal dagger, Kath felt its great age. She shuddered, sickened by its madness, its lust for power, its infernal Darkness. Kath dreaded confronting another harlequin, especially one of such great age, yet she would not forsake Blaine. Gripping the crystal dagger, she sought the fiend within. Deep in the soulscape, she found it waiting. Pale faced and dark haired, it wore an enormously long dark cloak. Tattered and torn, the dark cloak fluttered as if in breeze, yet there was no breeze. Then Kath got a better look. Not a cloak, but writhing tentacles with great thorny hooks. The thing was a horror! As she watched, the tentacles grew, threading Darkness through the soulscape, imprisoning Blaine in a thicket of pain.

"Forever have I waited, lurking in the way-stone, waiting for the perfect host. And now my time has come!" It laughed at her, gibbering at the triumph of corrupting a knight, bragging of its scheme to lay claim Castlegard's throne.

Appalled, Kath slashed at the Darkness, seeking to sever the foul tentacles. *"Release the knight! You shall not have him!"* But for every one she cut, the tentacles multiplied, deepening their hold on Blaine. *"Demon be gone!"* Wielding the dagger's light, Kath sought to expel the Dark taint.

An oily foulness battered against her. *"What are you?"*

And then Kath realized she had a another weapon. She hammered him with the truth. *"The heir of Castlegard!"*

The fiend roared like a wounded dragon.

"You chose poorly!" Kath swallowed her own fear, daring to offer herself as bait. *"You know I speak the truth!"*

A shrewd look crossed the harlequin's pale face. Recognizing its mistake, the fiend loosened its hold on Blaine. Tentacles snapped back towards their master, writhing around the fiend like a living cloak. Spurting a plume of oily Darkness, it leaped towards Kath. *"Then I shall have you!"* Barbed tentacles spread wide, it sought to enfold Kath, to ensnare her and claim her soul. Instead of fleeing, Kath ran towards the trap. Leaping within the ring of tentacles, she sought the fiend's soul-heart. Wielding the blazing light of the crystal dagger, she struck true. Light pulsed from the dagger, shattering the demon. A booming sound shook the soulscape and Kath was thrown backwards. Severed tentacles writhed around her. Chunks of Darkness swirled like gore.

Battered and bruised, Kath crouched low, waiting.

Scattered soul-fragments sought to reform and return to Blaine, but Kath blocked the way. *"You shall not have him!"* Denied a host, the soul-pieces convulsed once, twice and then exploded in a shower of dust, fading to oblivion.

87

Lothar

Lothar climbed the steps to the gatehouse barbican, anger sparking his stride. The debacle of the throne room rankled. The rusty sword was a cruel joke, but the reaction of his brethren hurt even more. It shamed him that so many knights saw the Octagon crown as a prize, or worse, a right. A snarl rode his lips. According to the monk, the king's daughter still lived, so marriage could solve the quandary, but the girl was in distant Pellanor. Perhaps a betrothal would suffice, but to whom? An empty throne weakened the maroon, but he was no matchmaker. Meanwhile a dark tide lapped at the very gates of Castlegard. So many hopes turned to ashes, his head ached from thinking about it.

His captains clattered up the stairs behind, but he did not wait. Reaching the barbican, he strode to the crenellated battlement, steeling himself for the view. The truth hit him like a punch to the gut. A dark army surrounded the castle, swarming just beyond the greensward. So vast, their numbers counted beyond nightmares. Dark shields and black armor, the horde glittered like the carapace of insects, a dark pestilence come to overrun the gates of Castlegard. *"Not on my watch."* The words growled out of him like a vow.

Their numbers were nigh on invincible, but just as sinister were the siege engines encamped amongst the horde. Catapults and trebuchets stood poised to hurl massive stones aloft. The true strength of mage-stone would be tested ere this battle was done.

A loud crack, like the strike of lightning, came from the forest. A massive oak groaned as it fell. The enemy sought to use their own forest against them, building siege towers and spiked palisades. The battle was going to get bloody.

"Look." Rannock pointed to midfield.

Five riders cantered out into the greensward. One carried a spear topped with the white banner of parley. So they sought to talk, that surprised him.

He'd meet them halfway. "Lower the drawbridge." Lothar chose four knights as escort, all of them seasoned warriors. Turning to Rannock, he said, "The command is yours." Lowering his voice, he added. "Look sharp. At the first sign of treachery, raise the drawbridge." He glowered at his second. "At all costs, the gates must not be breached."

Rannock saluted, fist to his breastplate. "As you command."

Lothar strode to the stone stairs, his maroon cloak swirling behind him. Instead of his battleaxe, he carried the marshal's great sword, the blade that parried the Dark Sword. Perhaps that first encounter was mere luck, yet it seemed a prudent precaution. Lothar swung into the saddle, a mounted escort forming around him.

Chains rattled and groaned. The toothed portcullis winched aloft as the drawbridge lowered. A view of the greensward gaped before him.

Putting spurs to his mount, he rode through the tunneled pass-through and out across the drawbridge. His escort followed behind, hoof beats clattering across wooden planks. They cantered out into the greensward, meeting the enemy at the midpoint.

Five riders waited. One of them carried an immense wall shield on his left arm, an imposing feat of strength. That same warrior wore a strange mix of armor, some of it black, some of it silver. Affixed to his shoulders was a maroon cloak.

Lothar hissed to see it, proof the scout spoke true. Grim with dread, he drew rein two sword lengths away. "So it's you."

The warrior with the wall shield flicked his visor aloft, revealing a familiar scar-crossed face.

Lothar quailed to see the marshal, yet he kept his own face stone-still.

Around him, his escort's horses fretted and shied, proof their riders shared his alarm.

Lothar stared at his friend, shocked by the changes. He seemed younger, taller, stronger, more proof the Dark Sword was cursed. "Osbourne, this isn't you. Give up the sword and come back to the maroon."

The marshal smirked, his face full of disdain.

A long pause hung between the two men. Finally, Lothar said, "What do you want?"

"Isn't it obvious? Surrender the castle and swear fealty to me. All those who bend the knee will be spared."

Anger spiked Lothar's voice. "This isn't you! You never wanted to be king!"

"Not a king, a god!" He drew the Dark Sword, raising it to the heavens like a challenge. "With this sword I am the God of War! Grovel before me and serve!"

Lothar spat. "Go to Hell!" He wheeled his stallion, spurring for the castle, his escort galloping behind. His neck prickled in warning, fearing the horde would come charging, seeking to take the gates and breach the castle. Expecting treachery, Lothar stretched his senses, listening for an ominous roar, but all he heard was the marshal's cruel laughter. Somehow, the laughter scared him more than the horde.

88

Katherine

Kath collapsed across Blaine. *Blood on her hands,* his blood. Still as a corpse, the knight lay unmoving beneath her. At least the hellish red light was gone from his eyes, snuffed out, extinguished. She'd slain the harlequin, but she feared to find her friend dead. Fumbling in the pitch-dark, she sought his wrist. Willing him to live, she prayed to Valin for a heartbeat. Unable to feel anything, she pressed harder. *"Please!"* A faint pulse beat beneath her fingertips. Relieved, she sagged against him.

Darkness had ambushed them in the way-stones, a trap set in another Age.

Kath shuddered, feeling hounded by Darkness.

Desperate for light, she fumbled at her belt pouch. After her confinement in the oubliette, she'd taken to carrying candles, ransacking a handful from the Mordant's mansion. Dismayed at how badly her hands shook, she struggled to light the candle, flicking the flint striker. Sparks flared bright in the dark space. The wick held the flame, illuminating the subterranean space. A massive way-stone hand loomed over her, thrice the height of a tall man, but it was the walls of the small stone chamber that caught her gaze. The walls were mage-stone, proof she was home.

Setting the candle on the floor, she lit another.

Blaine was ghost-pale, his chest rising in jagged breaths. Kath tugged the crystal dagger from his side. Blood gushed across her hands. Somehow she needed to staunch the flow. She hacked a swath from his cloak, stuffing the wool into his wound, praying it would serve till she got him to a healer.

Having done what she could for Blaine, Kath crawled across the floor to Bear.

The big man lay unmoving, sprawled on his back. Blood coated his face, gushing from his smashed nose, but she could find no other wounds. "Bear, I need you." She shook him, desperate to wake him.

Groaning, his eyes fluttered opened.

For half a heartbeat, she flinched, but his gaze held true, unsullied by red light.

His eyes sought hers. "Svala, what was that?"

"A harlequin lurking in the way-stones, a trap from another Age." A shudder wracked her. "It's dead, its soul sent back to Hell, but Blaine is sorely wounded. I need your help."

Bear struggled to sit, but then groaned, clutching the back of his head. It seemed he was more injured than he appeared.

"I'll go for help."

"No." His hand gripped her wrist. "I do not wish to stay here. Give me a moment and I will come."

She sat beside him, huddled in the candlelight. Darkness gathered around them, cold as a tomb. Kath could not blame him for wanting her to stay. After the assault of the harlequin she did not want to be alone either.

Groaning, Bear struggled to stand. Swaying unsteadily on his feet, he leaned on her till he regained his balance. "Svala," the big man stared at her, his bear tattoo stark across his ghost-pale face, "as a favor, can we never 'travel' this way again."

Kath had no intention of ever again daring a way-stone. "You have my word."

Bear tottered, one hand reaching for the wall. "The knight?"

"Blaine lives, but he's sorely wounded. He needs a healer."

"Then I will carry him."

Kath wasn't sure it was a good idea, yet she did not want to leave Blaine alone in the subterranean crypt. Bear stooped, and she helped the big man heft Blaine over his shoulder. The painted warrior staggered under the weight, but then stood straight, his legs braced wide. "I will follow you, Svala."

Kath gripped his arm in thanks, humbled by his stalwart trust. She blew out one candle and then reached for the other.

"His sword."

Abandoned in a dusty corner, Blaine's blue sword glittered in the candlelight.

Since childhood, she'd yearned to wield a blue steel sword, but such a thing was always forbidden. Kath reached for the blade. Gripping the hilt with both hand, she swung the blade upright. Nearly as long as she was tall, the sword was unwieldy, swaying in her hands like a wind-blown sapling. *Blue steel*...a hero's blade. Such a wondrous sword was never meant to be wielded by someone like her, a short petite woman, yet the incredible lightness of blue steel made it possible for her to heft. For half a heartbeat, her imagination prevailed...yet when she opened her eyes, Blaine's great sword dwarfed her. Wavering in her hands, the sword's great size mocked her. Chagrined, Kath was thankful there was none save Bear to see, for the sword surely made her look ridiculous. A sigh escaped her. Leaning the great blade on her shoulder, she lifted the candle. "Come." Kath led Bear out of the secret passageways and up into the castle.

89

General Haith

The ram was finally ready. For three long days, his army encamped on the stony heights waiting for the Taals to bring up a felled log from the lower slopes. Stripped of branches, the ram was massive, one end chiseled to a crude point. Iron spikes driven into the sides served as handles. It took ten Taals to lift the brute.

Satisfied with the ram, General Haith removed the Wizard's Knock from an ironbound chest. A gift from the Mordant, he'd prudently saved the Knock for the monastery, knowing he'd need magic to defeat magic. Fashioned into a dull gray fist, the Knock looked innocuous, yet it packed the power of a god's punch. General Haith grinned, remembering how a single Knock had destroyed the gates of Raven Pass, smashing them to oblivion. He stared at the massive ice wall, betting on the power of Dark magic.

Summoning a priest, he ordered the Knock affixed to the tip of the ram. Securing the Knock, the priest bowed low and then scuttled away.

General Haith gave the signal.

The Taalmaster yelled, "*Lift!*"

Ten Taals squatted, hefting the massive ram. Powerfully built, yet massively stupid, the ugly beasts had their uses.

The Taalmaster roared, "*Charge!*"

Whips cracked and the Taals snarled. Lumbering to a run, they carried the ram towards the pass. Their footsteps thundered, quaking the very ground. Howling a guttural yell, they raced across the narrow span, hurtling towards the ice wall. Barreling with brute force, they plowed the ram into the ice. Light flashed blindingly bright. A vicious roar blasted the mountains. The general and his guards were knocked flat by an invisible fist. The ground shuddered and shook. Ice rained down in stinging pellets.

General Haith rolled to his feet. Shaking his head, his muffled hearing gradually returned. Ice pellets continued to fall, pebbling against the stony ground.

A white mist hung like a veil across the pass.

He peered into the fog but it was too dense for answers. Snapping his fingers, he summoned one of his guards. "See what lies beyond."

Saluting, the guard drew his sword. Cautious, he made his way out across the narrow span, disappearing into the frozen fog.

The rain of stinging pellets abated. General Haith strained to hear the clash of steel, but heard nothing save the vast silence of the mountain heights.

A lone figure appeared in the mist. The guard returned at a loping run, a grin on his swarthy face. "They way is clear! The ice wall is gone, smashed to splinters, and there are no guards on the far side."

So, the monks thought the ice wall would contain me. More fools they. "Mount up! The monastery is ours!" Cheers rose from his men.

His stallion was brought up. A soldier knelt to serve as a mounting block. Stepping on the soldier's back, the general swung into the saddle. He led his army across the pass, the *Darkflamme* streaming overhead. Nothing would stand in his way, not the monks, not their magic, not men fighting with sticks. He grinned beneath the skeleton helm. Power and glory would soon be his.

90

Master Rizel

Mired in worry, Master Rizel made his way to the audience chamber. He'd thought to arrive early, but Seraphina was already waiting. The silver-haired loremistress sat cross-legged on the floor, looking regal in her midnight-blue robes. Piercing green eyes set above high cheek-bones, the loremistress always carried herself with refined poise. He'd often wondered if she came from a royal house, but their pasts mattered not in the monastery. As a loremistress, she wielded a strange and powerful magic, a touch of beastmaster combined with the ancient art of scrying. Around her neck, she wore a silver torque fashioned into a great frost owl. Golden citrine gems were inset for eyes, great silver wings spread wide around her throat. In front of her sat a silver scrying bowl, a relic from another Age. Silver owls carved in flight flew around the bowl's rim, embedded jewels flashing like citrine eyes in the afternoon sunlight. The bowl and the torque were of an Age, crafted before the War of Wizards.

Nodding to the loremistress, he took a seat beside her, his robes forming a puddle of midnight-blue. Still as a pond, he sat in silence, waiting.

Others began to arrive, all of them blue-robed masters. They sat in circles rippling out from the silver scrying bowl. Master Rizel nodded to some of his friends, to Masters Vernius, Grimshaw and Tamzin, but no words were spoken. They sat in contemplative silence befitting the dire times.

For the last six days, ever since the enemy came within Seraphina's range, they'd gathered to keep watch over the battle for the Southern Mountains. The Zward fought with cunning and valor, winnowing the enemy's numbers, yet the dark tide crept ever deeper into the mountains, finally reaching Drumheller Pass. It was in the pass that ancient magic was brought to bear, bringing the dark horde to a sudden halt. Icefur's powerful voice woke the glacier, summoning the mountain's raiment to protect the monastery. Attuned to ice, the great horn's voice fractured the glacier, sending frozen shards cascading onto the pass. The massive ice flow crushed the enemy's vanguard and built an impenetrable wall. Judging from the sheer size, the jumbled ice flow would take several seasons to melt, sealing the monastery from the southern kingdoms, yet the enemy did not retreat. Encamped on the stony heights, they seemed to wait for something. Rizel and the other masters kept an uneasy vigil, praying for the dark tide to retreat.

The sweet sound of a gong shimmered through the chamber.

Master Rizel nodded towards the Star Screen, knowing the Grand Master kept watch.

Seraphina lifted a silver pitcher, pouring crystal clear melt water into the bowl. Her eyes looked weary, rimmed with dark shadows, proof of the toll she paid for her magic, yet she came to the chamber every afternoon. Reverently removing a white frost owl feather from a small cedar box, the loremistress waved it over the scrying bowl as if drawing a complex rune. Rizel knew the feather came from a particular owl's molt, a frost owl willing to link with the loremistress. Honed to a fine point, the feather's tine was sharp as a quill. Seraphina pricked her index finger, offering a drop of blood to create a bond. A single red drop fell into the scrying bowl, creating a ripple of power.

So close to the scrying bowl, Rizel felt a mountain breeze waft across his face.

Seraphina leaned over the bowl, murmuring words too soft to be heard. Gripping the sides of the bowl, she stiffened. A nimbus of light shimmered around her like a halo. Throwing her head back, she gazed unseeing at the ceiling. Her eyes changed color, the lovely forest-green eyes of the woman changing to the golden-yellow gaze of a giant frost owl.

Master Rizel bent forward peering into the scrying bowl. The crystal clear water shimmered silver, becoming a reflective mirror. Images began to appear. Feather, blood, and ancient magic linked Seraphina to a frost owl flying high above the snowcapped peaks. The scrying bowl reflected the owl's-eye view, silent scenes dancing across the mirror-bright water. At first the images were disconcerting. The land held strange patterns when viewed from the air. Fingers of snow reached down mountainsides, loosing melt-water rivers that carved runes deep in the rocky hillsides. Master Rizel fought a wave of dizziness. Taking a steadying breath, he read the patterns.

The owl spiraled lower. Rizel recognized Drumheller Pass, the narrow span of rock blocked by the massive ice flow. The enemy army remained encamped on the rocky heights, a dark stain on the mountainside. Movement caught the owl's attention. Ugly, brute-faced ogres lifted what looked like a massive ram. The image made little sense, for a single ram could never dent the massive ice flow sealing the pass, yet the ogres hefted the ram, racing across the narrow span. They hurtled the ram towards the ice wall. A blinding light blazed from the scrying bowl.

Stabbed by the harsh brightness, Master Rizel looked away. When he could see again, he returned his gaze to the bowl, but the scene made little sense. The view was obscured, nothing but white, as if a cloud shrouded the mountaintop yet he knew the sky was crystal clear, a faultless vault of blue.

The owl spiraled higher. The scrying bowl showed more of the pass, the overhanging glacier and the deep chasm delving on either side of the narrow span, but the white mist remained, a blot obscuring the ice wall.

A cold shiver traced down Master Rizel's back. As he watched, a soldier clad in dark armor crossed the span. Penetrating the white mist, he emerged on the other side.

"The pass is breached!"

Gasps of dismay rippled through his brethren.

The unthinkable had happened.

Master Rizel peered into the scrying bowl, confirming the grim tidings. Uncoiling like a sleeping snake poked awake, the vast dark army began to stir. Mounted soldiers crossed the pass. They rode straight through the white cloud, emerging safe on the far side. Rizel needed to see no more. Reaching out, he gently touched Seraphina lest she waste her magic.

Waking from the trance, the loremistress released the silver scrying bowl. Closing her eyes, she shivered. When she opened them again, they were changed. The raptor's golden gaze was gone, reverting to her natural forest-green. Sighing, she crumpled in a swoon.

Master Holbreth caught her. Lifting her in his arms, he carried her from the chamber.

It was always thus, the price of magic claiming its toll.

No one else moved. No one else stirred. His brethren sat in stunned silence. They'd all assumed the ice wall would hold, sealing the monastery from the southern kingdoms.

"Magic." Master Vernius said, "only Dark magic could obliterate so much ice."

Nods of agreement rippled around the chamber.

Master Rizel said what the others were thinking. "In less than a day, the enemy will take the town of Haven." His voice sounded like a doom. "The time has come. We must use our own magic to quell this threat."

Felix raised the only protest. "But once loosed, it can never be undone."

Murmurs swirled through the chamber, yet none raised a firm objection. The possibility had been discussed, argued, and debated till there was little left to be said. But argued possibilities did not hold the same cold dread as grim reality.

Taking a steadying breath, Master Rizel stood. "The turning of an Age is truly upon us. Darkness reaches for the Kiralynn Order. This decision can no longer be forestalled or debated. If the monastery is to survive, it is our last best hope." He turned towards the Star Screen. "If the Grand Master agrees, I will see it done."

The chamber stilled, as every blue-robed master held their breath.

The final decision seemed a long time in coming.

A chime sounded and Rizel knew he was released to the task. Bowing towards the Star Screen, he strode from the chamber.

91

Lothar

Galloping through the castle gates, Lothar bellowed orders. "Raise the drawbridge! Lower the portcullis! Seal the gates!"

Guards rushed to do his bidding, the great chains clanking.

Swinging down from his mount, Lothar took the stairs two at a time, climbing to the gatehouse barbican. He strode to the battlement, staring out across the greensward. The five riders were gone, retreated back behind enemy lines. The dark swarm roiled, yet they stayed beyond the greensward.

Rannock joined him at the battlement. "Was it him?"

Lothar dreaded speaking the words, yet the truth could not be denied. "The Dark Sword has consumed him. He styles himself the god of war!"

Rannock hissed, making the hand sign against evil. "So we fight?"

"Against that?" Lothar waved a futile gesture towards the horde. "No, we endure a siege." The word tasted foul in his mouth, for most knights preferred battle to a wasting stalemate, yet it was their only strategy. "Our stores are full to burgeoning. We've more than a year's worth of food and deep wells for water. We'll stay behind stout walls and let them hurl themselves against us."

Rannock's words dropped to a whisper. "But are they stout?"

That was the question. He looked at his second. "Believe that they are. We'll make the enemy prove otherwise."

Rannock nodded, but worry rode his gaze.

Lothar ground his teeth, fighting the plague of unsolvable worries by dealing with practicalities. "We need to husband our forces and mount a strong defense. Numbers are our greatest weakness. Knights fit for battle are the one thing we're short of. We need watchers on the walls and towers at all times. Graybeards and green youths can serve as lookouts. We'll form our best fighters into cadres. They'll need to be on alert, ready to repulse any assault. We'll need rosters, rotating the men, keeping the best swords sharp for battle."

A shout rose from the walls.

Lothar snapped his gaze towards the enemy.

A team of ogres struggled to drag a great trebuchet to the very edge of the greensward. Crouched like a chained dragon, the wooden beast was massive. He recognized it from Raven Pass.

Lothar cursed. "By the nine Hells, he turns our own weapons against us!" Gauntleted hands balled into fists as he watched the ogres struggle to load a massive stone into the trebuchet's sling.

A clenched silence descended on Castlegard's walls, all faces turned towards the mighty trebuchet.

Beyond the greensward, the great wooden beast convulsed, slinging a massive stone aloft. The stone tumbled upwards into the blue, and then fell, hitting the greensward with a ground-shuddering thud.

It landed well short of the castle.

Laughter rose in gales from the walls.

But Lothar did not laugh. He gripped the battlement, keeping watch.

The trebuchet convulsed again. Another stone tumbled into the blue. The size of a horse, this one fell short of the moat, yet the shock of its impact trembled though the outer walls.

No one laughed.

Another rock came tumbling. This one cleared the outer walls. Lothar watched it sail past, an ungainly weight of stone. Impossible that such a massive stone should sail aloft, death flying overhead. It lumbered over the outer walls, tumbling toward the inner mage-stone castle. It fell hard, crashing somewhere in the great yard.

"He knows." Lothar's voice was laden with dread.

Rannock gave him a questioning look.

"The marshal is targeting mage-stone instead of the outer walls. He seeks to break our spirit before he breaks our walls."

Beyond the greensward, the trebuchet convulsed. Another massive stone came tumbling towards the castle. Lothar watched the air-born rock, his gauntleted hands balled into fists. The stone stuck the king's tower with a thundering hit. Mage-stone trembled, but held.

A ragged cheer rose from the walls.

Rannock hissed. "It held!"

But Lothar had his doubts. "The swordmaster said the walls were still strong as stone, but not invincible." He shuddered, disliking his own fear. Raising his voice to a shout, he bellowed an order. "Loose the catapults and trebuchets! Rain stone on the enemy! We'll bury the horde beneath rubble!"

All along the wall, men scrambled to attend wooden monsters. The Octagon's catapults and trebuchets sprang to life, answering the enemy with a storm of stones. Rocks hurled across the greensward, thudding into the dark swarm, tearing bloody swaths in their ranks. The enemy answered, unleashing their own catapults. The sky grew thick with hurling stones. Castlegard's high walls gave the maroon's catapults greater reach, a sorely needed advantage. Stones tumbled across the greensward, dealing death to both sides. The battlements shuddered and shook from the pounding. Screams punctuated the falling stones, blood staining the ramparts.

It took courage to withstand the storm of stones, yet the knights and soldiers remained steadfast at their posts. Lothar stayed with them, pacing the outer battlement, watching the grim exchange.

The enemy was the first to flinch. Unprotected by walls, they bore the brunt of it. Horns blared along the enemy lines. The dark horde surged in hasty retreat. Yoking ogres to their siege weapons, they struggled to move their wooden monsters beyond reach of the maroon's catapults.

Lothar raised his voice to a shout. "Strike them hard! Aim for their siege weapons!" His orders echoed up and down the castle walls.

Catapults flung their arms aloft in answer. Stones ripped into the enemy's retreating lines. A massive stone struck an enemy catapult, smashing it to splinters. Men screamed, dying with the wooden beast.

A ragged cheer rose from Castlegard's battlements.

The dark horde retreated beyond reach of the falling stones. The added distance nullified all of the enemy's siege weapons save for the monstrous trebuchet. Made impotent by the added distance, Castlegard's catapults also fell silent, but the enemy's beast of a trebuchet kept hurling rocks. The great trebuchet owned the sky. Ignoring the outer battlements, it struck at the inner castle.

One at a time, the massive stones hurtled towards the king's tower.

Impossible not to watch as the great stones tumbled overhead.

Two more struck the tower, but caused no damage.

Lothar sagged in relief, but then the trebuchet hurled an even larger stone aloft. He watched spellbound as a boulder the size of a cottage soared over the outer walls. Such a thing should not be possible, yet the ungainly stone tumbled overhead like a god's vengeance. The shadow alone was enough to quake fear in men. Reaching its apex, it began to fall. It struck the king's tower like a mighty hammer blow, punching a ragged hole in the side. A cloud of debris rained down.

A hole!

Lothar gaped. He nearly wet his surcoat. *Mage-stone was sundered!*

And then he remembered his men. Staring the length of the battlement, he watched fear fall like a suffocating shroud across the maroon. The impossible had happened. Mage-stone had failed. Castlegard was no longer invincible.

92

Katherine

The secret door ground open and they stumbled into the light. Kath winced at the brightness. They stood in the castle's great yard, surrounded by soaring towers. *Home,* after all their travels and travails, it was hard to believe she was finally home.

Bear staggered and nearly fell.

Kath rushed to take some of Blaine's weight. His wound was bleeding again, blood staining his surcoat. Together they held the knight between them, staggering across the great yard towards the healery. A chicken squawked, fluttering across their path. *A chicken in Castlegard's great yard!* It seemed an ill omen. And then she heard the echo of horns, the strident call to battle. A great thump shook the castle, dust falling from above. Kath staggered, "What's happening?"

Something pulled her gaze aloft, and then she saw it. The king's tower was crumpled, a gaping hole in the side. Kath gasped. *"Impossible!"* The sight staggered her. She nearly fell. Mage-stone was said to be invincible. Kath shook her head, denying her eyes. Castlegard was her home. She could not imagine the great castle crumbling to rubble, as if the whole world were coming unraveled by a Dark curse.

Bear lurched forward.

Kath struggled to keep pace, her fretful gaze worrying the broken tower.

A handful of knights ran through the great yard, their arms and armor jangling, but none gave them a second glance.

"How is this possible?" Kath yearned to know what was happening but first she needed to get aid for Blaine and Bear. Both men had taken grievous wounds in the way-stone chamber. She steered Bear towards the healery. Without knocking, she kicked open the door. They stumbled inside.

Quintus stood, his mouth agape. "You! Here! How?"

They settled Blaine onto an open bed and then Bear sank to the floor, holding his head in his hands.

"They're wounded, can you help?"

Quintus shook off his surprise and knelt to help the knight. "What happened?"

Kath refused to speak of the harlequin, lest it taint Blaine. "We were attacked."

"In the castle?" Quintus gaped, his face turning pale. "Have they broken through?"

"*Broken through?*" She stared at the healer. "What's happening?"

The healer explained in broken sentences as he worked to clean and stitch Blaine's wound. "The castle is under siege. Surrounded by a dark horde led by the knight marshal."

"*The knight marshal!*"

Quintus nodded. "He's been corrupted by a cursed sword, a black blade that sunders blue steel. The monastery sent a monk with a sword, a blade that is supposed to foil the black, but it's rusted. *Invictus,* he called it. Claimed it's a hero's sword, but the knights don't believe it." Quintus gave her a dismal stare. "Can't say as I blame them, but somehow we're supposed to restore honor to the maroon or Castlegard's mage-stone will continue to fail." A great boom shook the walls, dust falling from the ceiling. Quintus flinched, but he kept working to staunch Blaine's wound. "The castle is crumbling under the assault, and there aren't enough knights to battle the horde."

Kath struggled to shut her gaping mouth. It sounded like a tale concocted by a bard, yet the grit from the ceiling proved at least part of the tale true. "How can this be?"

The healer's voice fell to a flat hush. "Ambrose says it's the Battle Immortal."

Evil echoed across all of Erdhe. Kath knew it lapped at the gates of Castlegard but she'd hoped to have more time. "What must I do?"

He gave her a beseeching stare. "Claim the crown. Restore honor to the maroon."

Claim the crown! His words beat against her with the force of a battering ram. Kath stood frozen, daunted by destiny. Through the open window, she heard the clarion call of battle horns. Her blood stirred to the stalwart sound. Kath fingered the heavy signet ring on her finger. *I am my father's only daughter...his only living heir!* She dared not let the great castle fall.

She looked to the healer. "Since the king's tower is sundered, where do the captains meet?"

"In the great throne room."

She gave him a slow nod. "See to Blaine and Bear, they are both heroes. They must live." Kath strode towards the door.

"What are you going to do?"

"What I must."

93

Katherine

Kath raced across the yard, dodging chunks of broken stone. Her heart quailed to see Castlegard's wounds. Wizard-wrought mage-stone was supposed to stand forever, invincible and enduring, yet the great castle was more damaged than she'd first thought. Shattered chunks of mage-stone lay broken in the yard, some of them stained with blood.

Reaching the doorway to Needle Tower, Kath raced up the stairs, seeking an eagle-eye view. She needed to understand the enemy, their numbers, their strengths, their weaknesses, their position. The spiral stairs seemed to stretch to forever, yet Kath never slowed her pace. She sent a silent prayer to Valin, thankful the tower remained whole. Reaching the top, she found the battlements empty save for the gargoyles. Stepping out into the sunshine, she joined the stone sentinels crouched at the railing. The view stole her breath.

A dark army surrounded the castle, their numbers vast.

She circled the tower, but spied no breaks in the horde. Darkness strangled the castle, a bristle of swords and spears enforcing an impenetrable siege. By numbers alone, they looked invincible. Kath shuddered, wondering if such an army had ever trod the lands of Erdhe. Never in her worst nightmares had she imagined such a vast horde, yet this was the foe she needed to defeat.

Impossible! Kath gripped Duncan's warrior ring, taking long, slow breaths.

She forced herself to really see the enemy, to look past the daunting numbers. Catapults and trebuchets were embedded in their front line, but only one flung stones aloft. A great wooden beast flung rocks the size of horses, hurling the massive stones as if they weighed nothing. She watched, mesmerized as a huge boulder climbed skyward, lazily falling into the castle's heart. The crash was deafening, tearing another hole in the king's tower. Kath reeled at the sight, feeling as if the rock had torn a hole in her soul. Mage-stone was shattered, broken, as if the world were coming unraveled. Shaking off the horror, Kath stiffened her resolve, turning her mind back to the problem.

Once more, she circled the tower, studying the enemy. "They have no horses." Given the battle was a siege, the advantage seemed of little consequence, yet she stowed it in her mind.

Having surveyed the enemy, she turned her mind to her beloved castle. Maroon-cloaked knights manned the outer walls, but they were too sparse, too few, no match for the enemy's daunting numbers. In a pitched battle, they'd be overrun. Shuddering against the dread thought, she turned her gaze to the castle. The mauling from the falling stones was hard to look at. King's Tower was broken like a jagged tooth and one hall was holed, the ceiling collapsed. The wounds hurt her heart, yet in truth the damage was inconsequential to the castle's defense. The enemy's intent was plainly scribed across the mage-stone castle. "They seek to shatter our will." In time, they'd aim their dread trebuchet at the outer gatehouse and walls, crumbling the castle's defenses. Time was against the defenders. A desperate need gripped her, yet the riddle seemed impossible.

"What would the king do?"

Kath leaned against the gargoyles, staring down at the great castle. A memory teased her mind. She'd once heard her father say that the great castle could almost defend itself. That the ancient builders had endowed Castlegard with eleven defenses. As a girl, she'd searched the castle high and low, seeking to solve the riddle, but she'd only ever discovered ten. Somehow she had to invoke the great castle's defenses, yet the elusive number eleven taunted her. Her mind worked the riddle...and then she knew.

94

Lothar

Lothar summoned the captains and the champions to the throne room. Around them, the mage-stone walls shuddered, dust falling from the rafters. An infernal pounding shook the great castle. The enemy had but a single trebuchet that could reach Castlegard's walls, yet the wooden monster was tireless, relentlessly flinging boulders the size of horses aloft. No one knew where the next stone would fall. No one knew when mage-stone would stand like a stout shield...or when it would crumble, crushing those who sheltered beneath. The great castle was no longer invincible.

Death fell from the sky and there was little Lothar could do to stop it.

His knight-captains clustered at a long table below the dais. The siege was barely begun, yet their eyes looked haggard with shock. Lothar's gaze circled the table. Veteran knights who'd endured the blood and gore of the winter war were daunted by the sight of crumbling mage-stone. The enemy had struck a devastating blow and he knew not what to do.

Sir Gravis, the oldest knight-captain, said, "How can mage-stone crumble? How is this possible?"

Sir Krismir hissed, "A curse, it must be a Dark curse."

"Mage-stone has ever been invincible!"

"Castlegard has stood for nigh on a thousand years and now it crumbles to a single siege engine? How can this be? How can the gods abandon us?"

Restore honor to the maroon. The monk's admonition pounded through Lothar's mind, yet the words made little sense. "Perhaps the monk can provide answers." He gestured Ambrose from the shadows.

The blue-robed monk looked hesitant, yet he came forward to stand by Lothar's side.

He turned to the monk. "Explain."

Ambrose gave a solemn nod. "Mage-stone is a powerful magic, making Castlegard nigh on invincible for over a thousand years. The wizards of old feared their most powerful workings might fall to the hands of Darkness, so they wove safeguards into their greatest magic. Creating complex bindings, they wove their power with intent. Break the intent and the magic fails."

"Speak plainly! Your words make no sense!"

Lothar spoke over the others. "But what intent?"

"For Honor and the Octagon." The monk's stare circled the knights. "Far more than just a motto, your words are proof of the very intent woven into Castlegard's mage-stone. Sully the honor of the maroon, and the magic fails."

Outrage ripped through the knights. "Our honor is unsullied!"

"We fight with bravery!"

Sir Lothar raised his fist, quelling them, yet his voice rasped with anger. "The maroon fights and dies valiantly, always a stalwart sword against the Dark. You dare not say otherwise."

"Valor and honor are two different things."

Sir Lothar growled. "You tread a fine line, monk. Explain."

Ambrose gestured to the empty throne. "The king is dead. The mantle of leadership fell to the knight marshal...but he has taken up the Dark Sword, committing atrocities against the Light. The honor of the Octagon is broken."

Sir Gravis said, "If we name a king, a true king, then honor will be restored?"

"I believe so."

Lothar rounded on the older captain. "But whom would you chose? Who is worthy of King Ursus's crown? Would you claim it, Gravis? Or you, Adelmar?"

Their faces screamed *yes,* but they did not have the courage or the audacity to say it outright. Anger burned in Lothar. A rebuke boiled within him, but before he could unleash his anger, the monk spoke, his quiet words spearing the chamber.

"That is why I brought the sword."

Covetous gazes turned to the rusty sword leaning against the throne. Lothar had forgotten the rusted relic, yet the breaking of mage-stone had shattered age-old beliefs, while opening the door to other possibilities. Impossible was a word that held less meaning.

Lothar dared confront the dragon crouched in the room. "Mage-stone crumbles over our heads and a Dark horde slavers outside our walls. As a remedy, the monks bring us a rusty sword...yet beneath the rust, the blade has the form of something greater." His gaze roved his captains. "Can any of you wake the sword and claim the crown?"

None came forward. Lothar wondered at their hesitation, but then he understood. Many of the knights shuffled with unease, proving they'd tried the sword and failed. A rare few had the grace to look shame-faced. "So you've all tried, yet the blade remains nothing more than a rusty relic." Lothar scowled, ambushed by the lost hope. "The sword is useless, so I suggest we stick to the practical. We have a siege to win."

Most looked chagrined, a few looked belligerent, yet they kept their arguments to themselves.

Lothar brought the debate back to practicalities. "We have to silence that trebuchet. Any ideas?"

Sir Rannock said, "It's beyond reach of arrows or our own catapults. If we sally forth to burn it, their numbers will swarm us before our men ever reach the beast." He scowled. "We dare not give them a chance to breach the gates."

The captains fell silent, haunted by the grim truth.

Sir Gravis's voice held a reluctant quaver. "Single combat?"

"Against the Dark Sword?" Lothar scoffed. "In the hands of a squire, that cursed blade shattered a blue steel sword and slew Sir Abrax, the maroon's champion. Sir Abrax was good, very good." Lothar scowled. "Better to risk the siege than to wager the outcome against the Dark Sword."

The outer doors flung open.

A girl marched in. Clad in mismatched leathers and chainmail, the girl had a tangle of long blond hair and striking green eyes. She moved with a warrior's confidence, a sword belted to her side, a maroon cloak affixed to her shoulders. Her face was teasingly familiar yet changed.

Lothar gaped. "The *princess?*"

The other knights stood.

Befuddled, Lothar said, "The monks said you were in Pellanor! What are you doing here? Where have you been?"

Sir Gravis scowled. "She's wearing a maroon cloak! Maroon is the mark of knighthood! Strip her of that cloak."

A pair of guards approached, but the girl slipped from their reach, defiance on her face. "I've earned this cloak!"

Sir Gravis spat. "Earned how? By pricking your finger with a darning needle! Rip that cloak from her shoulders! She dishonors us all!"

The girl evaded the guards. Leaping to the dais, she drew a short sword from her scabbard as if she knew how to use it. "I *have* earned this cloak! By taking the Dark Citadel and slaying the Mordant!"

Stunned silence reigned.

Sir Gravis barked a loud guffaw.

Laughter burst from the other knights.

Mocking laughter rolled through the great hall, beating against the girl.

95

Katherine

Kath gaped, their laughter flaying her very soul. *Laughter!* All the times she'd dreamt of coming home, she'd never in her worst nightmares expected laughter. Their mocking mirth beat against her, belittling her, turning her deeds to dust. Her mouth tasted like ashes. After all she'd done, all the dangers she'd endured, they *laughed* at her.

"I swear by Valin it's all true!" Against their ridicule, her words fell like wind-blown leaves.

Sir Lothar quieted the others.

A glimmer of hope beat within her.

The leather-faced knight-captain turned a kindly smile towards Kath. "Sheathe your sword, girl. None here will harm you."

In some ways his kindness cut nearly as deep as their laughter. Both belittled her, yet Kath sheathed her sword. Stubborn and sullen, she remained on the dais, standing near the throne, keeping a prudent distance from the others.

Sir Krismir flashed a grin he no doubt thought was charming, yet he looked at her with wolf-eyes. "Castlegard needs a true king. It's past time you were betrothed."

Betrothed!

Sir Adelmar said, "Choose a captain or even a champion, and settle the question of succession."

So they think of me as chattel to be married off, a stepping stone to the crown! She stared daggers at them, yet none seemed to notice. "I'm already married."

Sir Adelmar seemed undaunted. "To whom? No well-bred man would let a wife cavort in chainmail and leathers. Marriage to a lowborn knave is easily dissolved. You must wed a captain of the maroon."

Now they insulted Duncan. Kath hissed, "Come near me and I'll have your balls for garters!"

Sir Adelmar blanched, but then he quickly recovered, chuckling to cover his gaff.

More laughter. Kath fought to keep her hand from her sword. *Is ridicule their only weapon against a girl?*

Sir Lothar roared, *"Silence!"* He glared at the others. "She is our king's daughter. I'll brook no slight to her honor."

The others quieted, wolves biding their time.

Lothar gathered their attention. "Time is wasting. We need to break the siege. We need answers and we dare not be long from the walls." He flicked a weary glance toward Kath. "I'll speak with you later. We have a battle to win."

His curt dismissal hurt.

The maroon knights turned their backs to her. Standing in a circle around the table, they debated the enemy.

Ignored! Their indifference burned her. She'd come to help yet they made her feel invisible. Kath remembered why she'd left home. Her father had never truly seen her. The memories scalded. Yet Castlegard was imperiled, somehow she had to make them see her. She had to make them listen. "I know how to defeat the horde."

None turned her way.

She raised her voice. "I *know* how to defeat the horde."

A few turned towards her, but they gave her stone-eyed stares, as if she spoke in a strange language.

"The Dark Citadel fell!" She hurled the words against them. "Castlegard can be saved!"

Sir Gravis growled. "Stop your lies, girl."

Kath staggered as if struck.

Again, they turned their backs to her, resuming their futile discussion.

Kath gave their cloaked backs a baleful stare. She held the key to defeating the horde, yet they would not listen. Anger burned within her. Because she was a woman, they could not see the warrior within. Kath realized words alone would never sway them. Since they had not witnessed her deeds, they would never believe her, never acknowledge her, never truly see her. What must she do? Prove herself over and over again? But then she had a thought. "I brought witnesses! They can attest to my deeds!"

Sir Lothar stilled the others. "Witnesses? What witnesses?"

"Sir Blaine and a painted warrior named Bear. They're in the healery."

Questioning looks flashed between the knights.

Sir Lothar gestured to the guards. "Bring them."

The guards saluted, rushing from the chamber.

The knights resumed their debate, turning their backs to her once more. Only the blue-robed monk looked at her, raw speculation scrawled on his scholarly face.

Kath stood alone on the dais. Ignored, she felt like nothing more than a piece of furniture.

The sand grains of time seemed to take forever to fall, but then the outer doors burst open. Guards carried a litter between them. Behind them came Bear leaning on Quintus, and a tall lean man clad in green leathers. The stranger's eyes flashed golden in the spearing sunshine.

Golden cat-eyes! Warmth flushed through Kath as if she'd seen Duncan.

The guards carried the litter to the foot of the dais. Blaine struggled to sit up, giving her a wan smile.

A few of the knight-captains startled to see a painted warrior amongst them.

Sir Gravis said, "How did you enter the castle?"

Bear gestured to Kath. "With the Svala."

Sir Gravis's voice was cold as drawn steel. "I spoke to the knight."

Kath's hands balled into fists. *So Painted Warriors are invisible too!*

Sir Gravis repeated his question. "How did you enter the castle?"

Blaine answered. "The monks showed us a secret way, a magical way," his face grew grim, "but that way is perilous, too perilous to use."

Kath shuddered, making the hand sign against evil. After the harlequin's attack in the way-stone, she silently vowed to never dare them again.

Sir Gravis gestured to Kath, his voice laden with scorn. "The girl claims you've been to the far north. If the Dark Citadel is truly conquered, then I'll wager a maroon knight with a blue sword led the vanguard. This girl claims your victories for her own. Tell us the truth, Sir Blaine, for we will believe you."

Kath struggled not to gape. The old coot offered *her* victory on a silver platter to Blaine. The Dark Citadel would not have fallen without Blaine's courage, without his blue steel sword, but his heroism did not diminish her own. She stared at Blaine, imploring the truth.

But Blaine did not look at her. His stare roved the circle of captains, an odd look on his face.

The silence stretched.

For half a heartbeat, Kath feared some dark taint remained lodged in his soul. She knew he longed to be named a hero, to be accepted among the maroon captains, even feted. In truth, Blaine deserved a hero's accolades...but so did she.

Pride rode Blaine's voice. "The Dark Citadel fell and I fought in the vanguard."

Kath paled.

The knights murmured in amazement, triumph on their faces.

Blaine's voice hardened. "But it was Kath's plan."

The knights flared in outrage, but Blaine over spoke them. "Kath led an army of Painted Warriors against the Dark Citadel...and *won.*"

Shocked silence met his words. A silence as stubborn as strong walls.

Bolstered by Blaine's testimony, Kath stepped forward, her voice laden with quiet reason. "I know how to defeat the horde."

Their silence remained stiff as ramparts.

Kath stared at them, daring them to hear her. "I am my father's daughter. I bear a woman's form, but the heart of a warrior beats within. I know the path to victory!"

A surly silence was their only reply.

Blaine's voice dropped to an angry growl. "The Mordant only saw the girl, not the warrior within. He died for his ignorance. Don't let Castlegard fall for the same mistake."

The blue-robed monk stepped forward. "The gods don't forgive stupidity. They expect us to do our best. *She,*" he pointed to Kath, "is our best hope."

Sir Gravis said, "You want us to follow a girl?"

Sir Krismir growled. "Blaine woos her for himself!"

Sir Lothar banged a gauntleted fist on the table. "Enough." Stifling their protests, he turned to Blaine. "Will you swear to this, on your honor as an Octagon knight that the Dark Citadel fell...to the *girl's* plan?"

Blaine's voice was full of solemn dignity. "I so swear."

Sir Lothar turned to Bear. "And you, were you there?"

"I too fought in the vanguard for the Dark Citadel. It was as the knight said. The Svala won a great victory."

A loud boom thumped the great hall, shaking dust from the rafters. The ceiling shuddered from a ferocious impact as if struck by a mighty fist. Several knights cringed, staring at the ceiling as if they expected to be crushed. Magestone rumbled and shook...but the walls held firm.

More than one knight looked relieved.

The blue-robed monk spoke, his voice tinged with anger. "You bicker among yourselves, doubting the girl's worth, while Darkness wages war. Will you let the great castle be smashed to rubble around you?" He pointed to Kath. "There stands the true heir to Castlegard! It is for *her* that I brought the sword!"

Sir Gravis roared with anger, spittle flying from his mouth. "That *girl* cannot defeat the Dark Sword. That *girl* cannot vanquish the horde slavering beyond our walls! That *girl* makes no difference at all!"

"Perhaps I can." A few looked at her then, but their gazes were wary. She met their stares with cool conviction. "We fight with swords but we win by wits. I know how to defeat the horde."

Sir Gravis threw up his hands. "This is outrageous. A woman cannot lead the Octagon."

"Betrothal is the only answer."

"But who will claim her?"

"Only the strongest can lead!"

Arguments erupted in the hall, bitter words hurled between the knights.

Kath stared at them, appalled. Despite her words, despite her witnesses, their bone-deep prejudices prevailed. They thought of her as little more than chattel to be married, a prize to be bedded...a way to the crown. Finished with words, Kath let them argue. Turning away from the bickering knights, she sidled towards the throne, towards the rust-encrusted sword. *Invictus,* the name shimmered in her mind like a promise. Quintus had told her about the ensorcelled blade...but he'd neglected to say it was a five-foot great sword. Kath strangled a sigh. It seemed the fates conspired against her, yet the rusted relic drew her stare. Hard to believe the sword's tale given the state of the blade. So rusted it looked fragile, yet the details were alluring. Dragons coiled on the hilt, runes inscribed along the runnel. A five-foot great sword, it was forged for the hands of a hero. Her hope quailed, knowing the great sword would look ridiculous in her hands. The grim truth hit hard. If this was the true test to gain the throne, then it was a trap for a girl. Only a man full grown could wield such a sword. Perhaps the gods laughed as well.

Anger burned within her. *She* was the rightwise heir, her father's only living child, yet she needed the knights to follow her or all would be lost. Words alone would never sway them. She needed something else. Something to make them truly see her. Taking a deep breath, Kath dared to risk their ridicule. She stepped to the great sword. Grasping it with two hands, she lifted the rusty blade to the heavens.

Light flared bright.

The knights' arguments quenched to a stunned hush.

In Kath's hands, the five-foot sword shimmered and rippled, too bright to look at. She turned her face away from the sun-bright glare.

When the light dimmed, she dared to look.

Gasps echoed around the chamber.

The rust was gone, the true sword revealed. Kath stared in amazement. Crafted in sapphire-blue steel, the sword looked freshly forged, a thing of martial beauty. Dragons coiled on the hilt, runes inscribed along the blade, yet the sword was no longer a five-foot great sword, but a short sword, perfect for her hands. The gods had spoken.

96

Katherine

Kath held the blue steel sword aloft, giving thanks to Valin for his favor. Never had she thought to wield such a magnificent blade...or to earn the crown of Castlegard.

Sir Lothar dropped to his knee. "All hail the Queen of Castlegard!"

With a mixture of reluctance and distaste, the other knights knelt as well, but their cries of acclaim were tepid. "All hail the queen."

She heard how the word choked their throats.

Boom!

A thunderous impact struck the hall. Mage-stone walls shuddered and groaned, dust falling from the ceiling. A great lightning-shaped crack appeared, splitting the far wall from the vaulted ceiling to the stone floor.

Kath stared aghast.

The rumbles subsided. The great hall still stood, but the lightning-shaped crack screamed like a herald of doom.

Shock annealed to anger. The knights sprang to their feet, outrage on their faces.

Sir Gravis growled. "If she's the *true heir,* then mage-stone should be restored!"

"You *lied* to us!"

"More proof a woman cannot lead!"

Enraged, the knights turned on the monk.

Pale-faced, the monk had no answer.

Sir Krismir growled, "I'll not follow a girl."

And then Kath understood. The truth hit her like a punch to the gut. Her knowing stare raked the knights. "You bent the knee, but you never believed! Belief matters. Until you truly believe I am queen, mage-stone will not be healed." She lifted *Invictus,* pointing the blue steel blade at the great crack. "That crack proves the shallowness of your words. You wound the great castle with your stubborn disbelief."

They met her gaze, refusing to relent.

A stubborn stalemate settled across the chamber.

Even the sword is not enough! Kath sighed, yoked once more with the burden of proof.

Blaine said, "My sword is yours."

His words were like an unfurled battle banner, raising a glimmer of hope.

Bear said, "I serve the Svala!"

Silence hung like a balance.

Kath waited, tightening her grip on *Invictus*.

The golden-eyed ranger from the Deep Green stepped forward. "The Treespeaker sent our bows to aid Kath of Castlegard! We will follow this woman who is Queen."

Kath nodded to him in solemn thanks.

The monk raised his voice. "I brought the sword for her. *She* is the rightwise queen of Castlegard!"

Murmurs rippled through the knights.

Kath held her breath, hoping. Her questing gaze roved across the maroon knights in silent appeal, but most remained stubborn, doubt scrawled on their faces. She wondered why strangers from afar truly saw her, while those from her own home clung to their stubborn prejudice. Perhaps familiarity truly bred contempt, yet this was the hand the gods dealt her.

The silence stretched bowstring-taut, and she knew no others would come forward. Refusing to be cowled, Kath straightened her shoulders, putting steel in her voice. "You saw the sword change in my hands, transformed by the gods, yet still you do not believe. Then I shall give you proof of another kind. Deeds shall be my herald. Dare to follow me, and I will prove my worth." She gestured them close. "Come and I'll tell you how a legendary castle can defeat an invincible army."

97

Master Rizel

The reliquary was mesmerizing, a thing of great power and age. Master Rizel found it both eerie and compelling. Clad in burnished silver, the craftsmanship was peerless. A hundred faces peered from the four sides of the five-foot chest. Scholars, knights, wizards and monks, their faces pressed from the silver, so lifelike they looked as if they might speak. Master Rizel wondered if they would offer words of wisdom...or gibber in raving madness. Impossible to contemplate their terrible sacrifice made over a millennium ago. Shuddering to think of it, he ran his hands across the enchanted silver, intricate runes carved deep amongst the faces. Young and old, male and female, all of the faces were intriguing, but the most striking visage by far was the lone face carved on the lid. Stern and foreboding, the face held deep lines of wisdom melded with compassion. Silver eyes peered from the lid, watchful and knowing. Clad in armor, he wore the trappings of a Star Knight, and upon his head sat a magnificent winged crown...*the King in the Mist!*

Master Rizel shivered, recognizing the stern face.

A knock sounded on the door.

He opened the door to admit three blue-robed masters.

"So this is it." Master Grimshaw stared at the reliquary, naked awe scribed across his dusky face. "We're really going to do this?"

"There is no other way." His hand caressed the carved silver. "It seems fitting. The sacrifice from the last Age may save the monastery in this new Age."

Master Vernius said, "But will they?"

The question chilled him. "All we can do is ask."

Rizel saw his own fear reflected in their learned faces. "Waiting only serves the enemy. We dare not let Darkness prevail."

"May the Light ever guide us." Master Vernius's voice quavered with great age, yet a latent hint of steel flashed in his rheumy eyes. Despite his frailties, the old monk insisted on serving as a witness to the reliquary. "Live or die, I will see the prophecy fulfilled."

The others nodded in solemn agreement.

"Then let us begin."

Masters Grimshaw and Rordon slid stout staffs through the handles on either side of the reliquary. Both were strong men, yet they strained to lift the silver chest.

Master Rizel took up the staff of summoning. It looked ordinary, nothing more than a simple ironwood quarterstaff, but the master knew it was one of the greatest relics of the monastery. He ran his hands across the age-smoothed wood, remembering his last sojourn into the Mist. "May the Kiralynn Order ever serve the Light of Knowledge."

"Seek knowledge, Protect knowledge, Share knowledge." The others intoned the Order's creed.

Giving his companions a grave nod, Rizel opened the door and strode out into the knowledge-scribed hallways.

Solemn gazes snapped in his direction. Blue-robed monks and masters lined the cloistered halls, come to pay homage to the reliquary. All bowed low as the silver casket was carried past. Those with battle magic or adepts of the quarterstaff stepped from the long blue line to follow the reliquary. The Order would spend all of its strength against the enemy. Master Rizel prayed it would be enough.

With a measured tread, he led the growing procession past the watchful gazes of his brethren. Some nodded with silent approval. Many watched with grave concern, others with open anger, yet their silence showed their acceptance of the Grand Master's decision. He understood their fears. The silver casket was both a drastic hope and a dire risk. Either way, the monastery would be forever changed.

Sunlight pierced the windows, illuminating the jewel-bright script. Overcome with love for the monastery, tears stung his eyes. He could not imagine this temple of knowledge pillaged by Darkness, his brethren-in-learning put to the sword. For over a thousand years the Kiralynn Order had served as steadfast guardians of the Light. He found it unfathomable to contemplate the guardianship coming to an end. Master Rizel believed they'd served the gods well, but only the gods could say. Tightening his grip on the staff, he prayed to succeed.

Passing through halls of prophecy, they bore the reliquary from the learned seclusion of midnight-blue out into the common areas of golden-yellow. Rizel half expected to see young faces crowding the golden hallways, but then he remembered. All the acolytes had been given a choice, to take their vows to the Seeing Eye, to join the Zward, or to be sent home. The golden hallways were empty of youth, as if the future had fled. He shuddered, refusing to see the bleak emptiness as an ill-omen.

The rune-carved doors stood open, admitting the afternoon sunlight. He passed through the doors into the outer courtyard, a brisk breeze caressing his face. Blue sky vaulted overhead, crystal clear, unblemished by clouds or the Mordant's red comet. The comet was gone, banished from the sky, but the Mordant's Darkness lingered, a blight stretched across Erdhe. Master Rizel raised his face to the heavens, seeking the soothing warmth of the summer sun.

Monks with quarterstaffs rushed to open the outer gates.

Followed by a procession of masters and monks, they passed between the Seeing Eyes, carrying the reliquary down the time-worn path. Master Vernius leaned on his staff, breathing hard, yet his ancient face wore a determined look.

They reached the bottom, confronted by a wall of white. For over a millennium, the Guardian Mist had protected the monastery. Wrapped in legends and mystique, the magical moat was both a fearsome trial and a staunch defense. The monastery would be forever vulnerable without it. Standing on the brink of change, Master Rizel hesitated, wondering if the Mist would prove the Order's bane or salvation. "Come."

While the others stood watch, he led his three companions into the Mist.

Cool white fog rushed to surround him, embrace him, assail him. So dense, he could not see the stony ground beneath his boots. Cold and unfathomable, the ancient white pressed against his face like a smothering cowl. Master Rizel fought the temptation to recoil, to turn back and seek the sunshine. Gripping the staff, he hardened his will, striding boldly into the Mist. He trusted the others to follow, for he could not see them. This sally into the enchanted white required that they bring no amulet and no guide. The ancient rules required belief. Exposed to the risks, they dared the perilous Mist.

Master Rizel raised the staff. Striking the ironshod butt against the rock-hard ground, he dared to bellow, "*I summon the King of the Mist!*"

His voice rang hollow in the white.

The staff remained quiescent, nothing more than polished ironwood.

Malevolent words hissed through the Mist. *You enter the Mist unprotected! Your lives are forfeit!* Something feathered against the back of his neck. Whirling, he stared into the white. Figures darted through the Mist. Ethereal as ghosts, their ghostly raiment brushed against his face like cobwebs. He strained to see them. Fading in and out, their ghostly visages teased him. A monk in flowing robes, a learned scholar's elderly face, a beautiful woman, they seemed benign, but then their faces changed. A horrid wailing pierced the Mist. Ravaged by time and agony, they became hideous ghouls. They flew at him with hollowed eyes and fanged mouths, roiling around him like vengeful ghosts summoned from rotting graves. Anger and hatred beat against him, a fierce resentment against the living. *For a thousand years we've waited, protecting your precious monastery! A thousand years of servitude, bound to the White! Mortal, you've no idea what we've lost, what we've paid. Will you pay the same price?*

Will you pay...pay...pay? Snarling, they struck at him with clawed hands.

Pain pierced him, like a hundred daggers of frozen ice. Biting back a scream, he fought them with the staff. Never before had the white been so virulent. Perhaps the reliquary emboldened the spirits, giving them more substance. Summoning all his skill, he whirled the ironwood staff, holding the dead at bay. The ghouls flinched away, as if the staff's very touch stung. They cowered, scowling from the murky white. Unable to reach him, they drew back, skulking just beyond the staff's reach, slavering for the kill.

He'd gained a hard-won respite, holding them at bay with his whirling quarterstaff, yet he sensed the stalemate was his loss. Delay served the enemy. Taking a deep breath, he slowed the quarterstaff to a stop. Risking their attack, he stood spear-straight. Pounding the ironshod butt into the ground, he roared a command. "*I summon the King in the Mist!*"

Light flared bright, illuminating the staff with a blue glow.

The dead howled, disappearing in an angry swirl of white.

Instead of an ironwood staff, he held a golden scepter etched with silver runes and crowned by bright blue flames. Gratitude surged through him, proof the gods had not forsaken him. "By the Light of the Ethereal Flames, I summon the King of the Mist!"

The blue light of the scepter intensified, beating back the thick fog.

His companions staggered into the circle of blazing light. Masters Grimshaw and Rordon still carried the silver reliquary, and Master Vernius clung to his staff, yet all of them looked beleaguered. Slashes on their faces wept blood, proof they'd paid a price for daring the Mist.

Master Vernius sagged against his staff, looking weary to the point of collapse. "They're mad, vengeful. They've gone insane." He shook his grizzled head, his gaze bleak. "We dare not loose them from their vows. Our hope is lost."

In the depths of the Mist a horn sounded, a clarion call to battle. Spectral figures appeared, knights clad in armor, waging a long forgotten war. The details remained hazy, shrouded by fog, yet from out of the battle a lone figure strode towards them. With every step he became more substantial. Unlike the others, he looked real enough to touch. Clad in burnished armor, his breastplate bore the sigil for the Star Knights, and upon his brow sat a winged crown. Stern-faced, his eyes weary with wisdom, he stopped a sword-length away.

Master Vernius whispered with reverence. "*The King in the Mist!*"

The king surveyed the monks, his gaze lingering longest on the silver reliquary. "So the long-awaited time has come."

Master Rizel nodded, his hands gripping the scepter. "The turning of an Age is upon us. For nigh on a thousand years the Host of Guardians has served the Light, protecting the monastery from intruders, preserving the last bastion of knowledge from the Dark's covetous reach, but now the long foreseen threat has come. Ancient prophecies fall like hammer blows upon Erdhe. The Battle Immortal laps at the very gates of the Kiralynn Monastery. Your time has come. Your swords are needed. We humbly seek your aid."

"My aid." The king sneered. "Have you kept your word? Have you aided my bloodline?"

Master Rizel stiffened under the king's assault. "Aid has been given. *Invictus,* a sword out of legend, has been sent to Castlegard."

"And what of my heir, the last of my bloodline?"

"The blade bearer has been warned, given knowledge of the way-stones to reach Castlegard or the monastery as she so chooses."

The king's stare seemed to pierce his very soul, weighing his answer.

Master Rizel met his gaze, knowing much depended on the outcome. "We are brothers separated by an Age. We both serve the Light." He held his breath, waiting.

An eternity seemed to pass, the outcome balanced on a knife-edge.

"You speak the truth." The king nodded towards him. "Aid shall be given." He released a long-held sigh. "Finally, we who are sworn to the Mist will know the peace of the Light."

Master Rizel sagged in relief.

"So the prophecies come true at long last." The King flashed an eager smile. "The last battle awaits."

"The enemy is encamped outside the town of Haven. They number nearly two thousand."

"Their numbers matter not." The king sobered, giving him a piercing look. "Once released it can never be undone."

Master Rizel said, "A price we must bear."

Master Vernius stepped forward, his voice tremulous. "My lord, we were attacked in the Mist as if the sworn souls had gone mad, seeking vengeance. Can we trust them to harm only the enemy, or will they loose their wrath upon the monastery and our brethren in blue?"

The king sighed. "Long has been our vigil. Each soul freely accepted the burden, yet the price was far worse than any of us ever dreamt. Some have gone mad. Succumbing to the agony of time, they joined the wild hunt, yet they will answer to my summons." The king reached for his great sword. The blade rang as it came unsheathed, gleaming bright as a fallen star. "Our great sacrifice will have meaning." His voice stood firm as stone, carrying the weight of centuries. "I shall see to it."

Master Rizal bowed low to the king. "Then all those who bound themselves to the Mist shall be released."

Ghostly figures appeared. Scholars, monks, knights and wizards, they crowded around their lord, an ethereal host.

The king raised his sword. "Our time has come! The long-foretold battle awaits!"

A thunderclap shook the Mist.

Master Rizel tugged a chain from around his neck. Upon that chain was an ancient skeleton key. He used the key to unlock the silver reliquary.

A sigh whispered through the ethereal host.

Withdrawing the key, he threw back the lid.

Nothing but crumbled dust filled the reliquary. The bones had long since succumbed to time. He feared the backlash of the dead, yet he felt no anger. One at a time, the ghosts came forward, grasping a handful of bone dust. With each handful, the spirits glowed, as if anointed with stardust.

The king came last. "May the Kiralynn Order ever serve the Light." He reached for the dust with a gauntleted hand. Instead of glowing like the others, somehow the dust made him more real, more solid.

Horns rang triumphant through the Mist. Horses reared and battle banners appeared, held high on spears. A host of armed knights surrounded the king. He raised his star-bright sword. "For the Light! For the Battle Immortal!" His visage waivered, becoming as ethereal as the others. Mounting a white stallion, he rode to battle, surrounded by a ghostly host.

A wind sprang up. Swirling around the monks like a devil, it hurled grit in their faces. Shielding their eyes, they huddled against the storm, their robes billowing in the wind.

As quickly as it appeared, the wind died.

A calm stillness prevailed.

Master Rizel dared to open his eyes.

The Mist was gone.

He stood on a patch of bare rock, blue sky vaulting overhead. Turning, he saw the monastery set on the hilltop, mage-stone walls inset with gates adorned with the Seeing Eye. Below the monastery, a small assembly of blue robed masters waited, their faces grim. The Mist was vanished, the monastery made vulnerable, its golden gates revealed to the world. The time of hiding was done. Master Rizel sagged under the weight of the decision. Leaning on the staff, he startled, realizing it was ordinary wood once more.

Master Grimshaw said, "Look!"

The reliquary was wiped clean. Every face gone, nothing but smooth-beaten silver on every side.

Master Vernius crumpled to the ground, his strength spent. "It is done." He turned towards Master Rizel, his voice quavering with the burden of great age. "Do you think they will prevail?"

"They must." Master Rizel straightened. "One way or another, the monastery must be protected. I will join those who have chosen to fight. Who's with me?"

Master Grimshaw answered, his voice a deep rumble. "I will come. I will see this tale to its end."

Master Rordon gave a sheepish shrug. "I have no magic and my quarterstaff skills are sorely lacking. I'll help the old one back to the monastery."

For once, Master Vernius did not complain.

The others came forward. Battle mages and quarterstaff masters, they strode across the naked rock, their faces determined. Masters Rizel and Grimshaw took the lead. Gripping their quarterstaffs, they strode down the mountain, resolved to learn the fate of the Light.

98

Katherine

Kath sat straight-backed on the throne, *Invictus* unsheathed across her knees. In truth, it felt presumptuous to sit upon her father's throne, yet after enduring the ridicule of the knight-captains, she decided to take a lesson from the Rose Queen. Image mattered, especially for a petite woman. If sitting on her father's throne helped her rule, then she'd damn well sit on the straight-backed chair, even if it was uncomfortable.

She'd asked four of the knight-captains to join her on the dais, Sir Lothar, Sir Rannock, Sir Blaze and one other. The fourth was Sir Blaine, freshly raised to the rank of knight-captain. They carried him up to the dais, pale but proud on his litter.

The other knight-captains stood stern-faced below the dais, many of them openly glowering their displeasure. Doubters who would never support her, they thought her plan too risky, too wild, too dangerous, yet they had nothing better. Kath no longer cared what they thought, as long as they obeyed.

A host of knights and guards milled behind the captains, all those who could be spared from the walls. Janthar and his archers from the Deep Green stood to one side, leaning on their longbows, their golden eyes gleaming in the torchlight. The blue-robed monk, Ambrose, and the Zward captain, Haythor, stood with the archers. Behind those gird in armor, jostled the castle folk. Apprentices from the forge, lads from the stables, even cooks from the great kitchen crowded behind, craning for a view. Villagers and farm folk stood to the rear, nearly filling the long audience hall.

Whispers raced the length of the throne room. Her friends from the forge and the stable shouted to see her, beaming broad smiles.

"Kath!"

"The princess has returned!"

"Kath of Castlegard!"

Their smiles and warm greetings were a balm to her heart. If only the knights saw her worth like the castle folk. Kath buried the thought, keeping the regret from her face. Unbidden, her gaze slid to the mage-stone wall, to the lightning-forked crack running from ceiling to floor, ominous proof of the brutal power of Darkness. She had to save Castlegard...or they were all doomed. A bead of sweat ran down her back.

The latecomers slowed to a trickle and the outer doors finally closed with a resounding thud. Sir Lothar raised his gauntleted fist for silence. The crowd quickly stilled. Sir Lothar's gruff voice echoed the length of the great hall. "For too long, the throne of Castlegard has stood empty. An empty throne weakens us all, but now, in our time of great peril, King Ursus's last heir and only daughter, has come to take up the Octagon Crown." He gestured toward her. "All hail Queen Kath of Castlegard!"

"Kath of Castlegard!"

"All hail the queen!"

Loud cheering came from the castle folk and some of the guards and younger knights. The disgraced captains scowled in silence while the village folk were tepid and confused. Kath understood their reluctance. Warrior kings always sat upon the Octagon throne, and now they were presented with a petite blonde. Little wonder their cheers were weak, their faces riddled with questions. Kath grew weary of having to prove herself, yet she needed their support.

Standing, she raised *Invictus*, a symbol of her authority.

Hushed rumors raced through the hall at the sight of the sapphire blade.

Lowering the sword, she waited for the murmurs to subside.

Kath pitched her voice to carry. "Castlegard is imperiled. A Dark horde surrounds us, laying siege to the castle. They mean to break our walls, to take this great castle, to slay or enslave all within." She stared at them, seeing fear in their gazes. "But that will *not* happen. Not while I am your *Queen*." Kath gripped *Invictus*, willing them to share her conviction. "For nigh on a thousand years, Castlegard has stood as a shield against the Dark. The Octagon has long held Darkness at bay, but now a great trial is upon us. The Battle Immortal batters at our very gates. Against this new threat, the valiant swords of our knights will not be enough. Allies have come to our aid, archers from the Deep Green, monks with the tattooed Eye, and a Painted Warrior from the far north, but this victory needs more." Kath raised *Invictus,* the blue-steel sword glimmering in the torchlight. "I call upon every man, woman and child, every farmer and villager taking refuge in this great castle, to embrace the honor of the Octagon. I call upon you to lend your strength to the battle. Together we are strong. Together we cannot be defeated." She brandished *Invictus* aloft. "Trust in me and I will lead you to victory!"

Her friends from the forge were the first to cheer. *"Kath! Queen Kath!"*

Caught up in the moment, many villagers and farmers took up the chant. *"Queen Kath!"*

The walls echoed with their shouts, multiplying the tumult.

Kath's gaze raked across the armored host standing nearest the dais. Most of the knights remained surly and silent. It hurt her that they did not believe, yet she'd gained what she needed, a chance to save Castlegard.

99

Katherine

It took a full day to put all the elements of her plan into place. In truth, Kath craved more time, but time favored the enemy.

To defeat the horde, she'd need every able body in Castlegard, and even some that weren't so able. Villagers and castle folk, women and children, crippled veterans and stable hands, Kath summoned them to serve alongside the knights. Some manned the walls, sparing knights from lookout duty, while others served as message runners. Many toiled through the night, bringing up casks of oil, caltrops, and sheaves of spears from the castle stores. Others cleared the inner castle of rubble, fodder for the walls' catapults and trebuchets.

Castlegard hummed like a kicked beehive preparing for a desperate struggle.

Kath spent most of her time with the three hundred brave souls who'd answered her call to ride beyond the walls. Some were her friends, boys from the stable and apprentices from the forge, while others were maimed veterans with missing limbs. A few village women even stepped forward, swearing to their skill with horses. Young and old, male and female, Kath took every one, knowing numbers mattered. She'd need them all for her plan to work.

Her rag-tag army was outfitted with hastily cut maroon cloth. Unhemmed and crudely cut, yet drawn from the same swaths of cloth used to fashion knights' cloaks. Kath trusted the maroon cloth to complete the dire illusion. Farmers and apprentices, women and boys, she'd make them look like knights. A pile of armor was brought up from the stores, helms, vambraces, breastplates and gorgets. The apprentice boys took delight in trying on the armor but many of the villagers looked daunted, confronted by sudden fear. Kath walked among them, shoring their courage. She did not expect them to fight, but she needed them to look convincing.

With the armor sorted out, everyone was given a horse. Young boys needed boosts onto eighteen-hand warhorses. Some of the gray-bearded veterans had to be strapped into their saddles. Most of the old ones sat sword-straight with pride, their armor polished to a bright shine, a matching gleam in their eyes, keen to be called to the banners. Kath seeded the veterans through the column of her rag-tag army, expecting them to lend heart to the others.

Kath sought out Janthar and his small knot of cat-eyed archers. Most of the archers would remain stationed on the walls, but a few would dare to sally forth to slay the enemy's trebuchet. "Remember, wait for my signal. Loose your arrows and then turn and run like demons lit afire."

The cat-eyed archer gave her a solemn nod. "It will be as you say."

She gripped arms with Janthar, grateful for his presence, and then made her way forward to the vanguard. A cadre of the best knights in the castle were chosen to serve as her vanguard, the spear-tip of her plan. Already mounted, their silver surcoats gleamed in the afternoon light, their shields and helms burnished bright. Maroon battle banners waved from their lance tips. A few carried blue steel weapons. Their numbers were small, one hundred of the best, yet they represented the fearsome might of the Octagon. Pride swelled within her, honored to be among them.

Sir Lothar gave her a leg up, boosting her into the saddle. She'd chosen a nineteen-hand stallion, a showy mount with a snow-white coat and a silver mane. Kath wanted to make sure the enemy saw her. So much of her plan depended on deception and expectations. First she'd surprise the enemy with boldness, some would say foolishness, and then she'd give the enemy what they expected, what they thought they wanted. Timing would be crucial. Everything needed to fall into place like an elaborate puzzle. Kath prayed to all the gods for her plan to prevail.

A shadow of death fell across her. Kath glanced aloft, spying a tumbling boulder. Her stallion whinnied, sidling sideways, but the stone soared past, landing deep in the castle. A thunderous boom shook the walls. Kath shuddered, making the hand sign against evil. The enemy's trebuchet never stilled, an ominous threat falling from the sky, wrecking death, destruction, and terror. It was time to take the fight to the enemy. Sending a silent prayer to Valin, Kath raised her gauntleted fist. At her signal, the inner gates opened.

Kath led the vanguard into the castle's killing corridor. Held to a walk, the warhorses whinnied and neighed, shaking their bridles with impatience. The jangle of arms and armor echoed the length of the stone-sided corridor. The sun beat down with sizzling heat, setting arms and armor ablaze with light. Kath glanced back at the long maroon line, filled with pride that so few would dare to face so many.

Riding at a walk, it took nearly a turn of an hourglass to reach the outer gates.

Sir Lothar nudged his warhorse close to hers. "Do you think this plan of yours will work?"

"It has to." Kath raised her voice to a shout. "Open the gates! Raise the portcullis! Lower the drawbridge!"

Guards leaped to obey.

Chains clanked and the toothed portcullis began to rise.

Kath felt a flutter of fear in her stomach. With the gates open and the drawbridge lowered, the castle was vulnerable. She risked everything on this desperate gambit. Her plan dared not fail.

The drawbridge settled into place with a loud thud.

Kath stood in the stirrups. "For Honor and the Octagon!"

"For Honor and the Octagon!" The battle cry echoed through the killing corridors and along the castle ramparts, a brave shout daring the heavens.

Whispering a prayer to Valin, Kath spurred her stallion to a trot, leading the vanguard forward. Hoof beats thundered across the drawbridge. The vanguard emerged from the gates, maroon battle banners rippling in the summer breeze. The day proved warm and fair, a patchwork of wildflowers blooming in the greensward. The noon-time sun rode high overhead, bright in a cloudless vault of blue. Holding her stallion to a trot, Kath led her army out onto the field. She wore a silver breastplate embossed with a maroon octagon over her chainmail and leathers. A small shield sat upon her left arm and upon her head a crowned helm. The helm did not fit, too large for her head, but she did not intend to wear it for long.

Shouts rose from the enemy lines.

The frantic wail of horns gave warning.

Kath stared at the Dark horde, a roiling mass of spears and shields, too many to count. Their numbers alone were fearsome, enough to quell the courage of most armies. Confronted by the horde, Kath felt mortal. She did not want to die, she did not want to be hurt...but somehow the decision to do the right thing gave her a strange sense of strength. Not the invincible kind, but the inevitable kind, as if this is what she was meant to do all along.

Reaching the midpoint of the greensward, Kath signaled and her vanguard swung out on either side, opening like armored wings. Her champion knights presented a disciplined front, shields and lances held at the ready, their warhorses held to a trot. Behind them, her rag-tag army disgorged from the castle gates. Their spears held at all angles, they cantered across the greensward, giving the illusion of numbers.

Judging the distance to be right, Kath removed the cumbersome helm. Shaking out her long blond hair like a battle banner, she stood in the stirrups and waved the gaudy helm. Sunlight glinted off burnished silver, a signal to the archers running behind the vanguard.

Janthar and his handful of cat-eyed archers answered. Flaming arrows arched overhead, seeking to silence the trebuchet.

Discarding the awkward helm, Kath put spurs to her mount, asking for a gallop. Trumpets blared a charge. On either side of her, champion knights urged their warhorses forward, their lances couched. Ironshod hooves raised an ominous thunder, maroon battle banners streaming overhead. Unsheathing *Invictus,* Kath screamed her battle cry. *"For Honor and the Octagon!"* She led her small war host, flying across the greensward at a gallop. The battle for Castlegard had begun.

100

The Knight Marshal

Sieges were beyond tiresome, the most boring form of warfare. And while the siege held, there was little fodder for his sword. Restless, the knight marshal prowled his army, yearning for battle. Black-clad soldiers scrambled to get out of his way. He stared at them, seeking a challenge, seeking a fight, but none dared meet his gaze. The Dark Sword grew hungry, slavering for souls. He could almost taste its soul-lust.

No matter how many souls he reaped, the Dark Sword was never sated. The blade's ravening hunger bothered him not, but something had changed in the last moon-turn. Instead of just hungering, the blade *hated*. It seethed for vengeance. Against whom he did not know, yet when the reckoning came, the marshal was certain the blade would loose an incandescent rage. He shivered at the thought, like pumping glory into his veins. With the Dark Sword in his hands, none could stand against him. He truly was the God of War.

Shouts rose from the outer line.

Frantic horns blared in warning.

Sheathed in its harness, the Dark Sword keened to be fed.

The call to battle thrilled through him. Bellowing for his horse, the marshal pushed his way towards the front lines. What he saw staggered him with surprise. Maroon knights dared to sally forth from their castle. Riding across the greensward, sunlight gleaming on silver armor, a few dared to challenge many. The ploy was gallant and brave and hopelessly futile, a wasp provoking a hungry lion. His gaze swept across the greensward, counting their numbers, and then he saw the castle. The drawbridge remained down, the gates wide open. Worse than futile, this attack was stupid beyond telling, leaving Castlegard ripe for the taking.

"*My horse!*"

Commander Crull rode towards him, leading a saddled warhorse. Six mounted captains followed behind.

The marshal sprang to the saddle. Two soldiers lifted the massive wall shield. The marshal settled the great shield on his left arm, tightening the straps.

Flaming arrows streaked overhead. The marshal growled, knowing they sought the massive trebuchet. "Sound the drums!"

His orders echoed through the Dark host.

War drums woke, beating the summons to battle, a deep throbbing heartbeat.

Out on the greensward, trumpets blared the maroon's familiar call to charge.

Stunned, the marshal turned to watch, unable to believe so few would dare to attack so many. A vanguard of a hundred knights couched their lances, spurring their warhorses to a gallop. They thundered across the greensward, a line of silver death intent on battle, but behind them, the rest of their army panicked. Dropping their spears, they rode pell-mell for the castle gates. A low growl issued from the marshal's throat. The vanguard showed immense courage, while the rest showed good sense, yet their cowardice sparked his anger. *"I'll slay them all."*

Too far away to engage, the marshal watched the valiant charge.

Like a silvery eagle, the vanguard flew across the greensward. Unaware of the panic behind them, they smashed into the Dark lines. Mounted knights cut a swath through his foot soldiers. Lances broke and men screamed. Steel beat against steel. Warhorses bugled as they trampled the fallen. The Dark line bowed inward, taking heavy losses, but then someone in the vanguard must have realized they were exposed. A frantic horn blared the maroon's call to retreat.

The vanguard sought to disengage.

The marshal stood in the stirrups. "To me! To me! Sound the attack! The castle is ripe for the taking!" He drew the Dark Sword, brandishing it towards the heavens in challenge. Putting spurs to his mount, the marshal urged his warhorse to a gallop, racing towards the enemy.

Across the greensward, the knights' silvery vanguard retreated, but their order was broken. Pockets of knights rode together, racing back towards the castle gates. Some listed in the saddle, clearly wounded.

The knight marshal smelled blood. The Dark Sword thrummed in his hands, keen to feed. Putting spurs to his warhorse, he gave chase. Galloping across the greensward, he pulled a horde of screaming foot soldiers behind him. A mighty roar rose from his army, hungry hounds smelling the scent of bloody meat.

The vanguard's stragglers lagged behind.

The marshal spurred his horse, closing the distance, determined to claim the gates before the defenders raised the drawbridge.

One of the stragglers turned in the saddle, staring behind. For an instant their gazes met. Long blond hair and brilliant green eyes, *a woman, the knights let women fight for them!* A memory flickered in his mind, but he slayed it with a snarl. The octagon had grown weak. They were not worthy of the great castle.

The Dark Sword quickened in his hands, seething with hatred.

"To me! To war!" The marshal raced towards the drawbridge, keen for blood and glory.

101

Katherine

Kath turned her stallion, racing for the castle gates. Horns blared an urgent retreat. Most of her rag-tag army had fled the battlefield, but a few stragglers remained, galloping for the drawbridge. Kath urged them to hurry, lest they be ridden down by her own knights.

Retreating from the horde, her vanguard raced back across the open grass. Bloodied by the charge, some of the knights listed in the saddle. Maroon battle banners drooped, broken lances littering the field. A riderless horse sped past Kath's stallion. Another horse squealed, impaled by a spear. Kath mourned every knight lost, the bitter price of her plan.

Behind her, the Dark horde roared their vengeance.

The die was cast, her knights the bait in the trap. She dared a desperate gambit.

Riding at a gallop, Kath followed the others, her gaze fixed on the great castle. Sheathing *Invictus,* she put spurs to her mount, needing more speed lest the horde catch her.

A drum of hoof beats thundered behind.

Kath flicked a wary glance over her right shoulder, relieved to see a maroon knight riding close. His helm was closed, blood on his sword, but he seemed unharmed. Turning her gaze back to the castle, she leaned low in the saddle, racing for the drawbridge.

A warhorse rammed into hers, nearly unseating her.

Shocked, Kath struggled to stay in the saddle.

Her stallion shied away, but the maroon knight careened back into her, battering Kath with his shield. *"A girl...will never...rule!"*

Shocked, she knew his voice, a traitor-knight seeking to hide his foul deeds beneath the retreat's chaos. Kath reached for her sword, but his shield struck first, battering her hard across the chest. The brutal blow knocked her from the saddle. Kath landed hard, sprawled in the grass, the breath knocked out of her. Shocked and bruised, she stared as he galloped away, her stallion outpacing his warhorse. *Betrayed and left to die!* For a handful of heartbeats she lay there dazed.

A roar came from behind.

The Dark horde broke across the greensward like a raging storm. Berserkers led the charge, pounding towards her, their bearded faces wild with battle lust.

Too close! Fear spiked Kath. Anger followed. *"I'll not die by treachery!"* Kath scrambled to her feet. Her gaze skittered across the battlefield. Spying a riderless horse, she ran towards the roan. The mare squealed, shying sideways, its reins tangled in a dead knight's fist. Kath caught the reins, tugging them loose. Murmuring soothing words, she sprang into the saddle. The roan bucked, tossing her head, but Kath held sway. Putting spurs to her mount, she raced for the drawbridge.

102

General Haith

Beyond the pass, his army met no opposition. No ambushes, no traps, no diversions lurked beyond the sundered ice fall, as if the monks had vanished, disappearing into thin air. The cursed monks were slippery with magic. He trusted them not. Seeking a final battle, his army cantered down the trail, spears held at the ready. His scouts found a jumble of tracks but never the enemy. Unopposed, his army swarmed down out of the mountains into a verdant valley.

Birch forests gave way to lush farm fields surrounding a tidy village. Horses gamboled in paddocks and reindeer moved in herds across emerald green fields. Everything looked well cared for, the herds glossy and thriving, the fences mended, yet there were no people. So peaceful, the valley put the general's teeth on edge.

He led his army towards the village, the *Darkflamme* slithering overhead. Slowing his warhorse to a walk, he ambled down the main street. Stone houses and clapboard stores fronted the street, wooden signs depicting chandlers, bootmakers, a blacksmith, a bakery. Pink and purple flowers blossomed in boxes beneath well-polished windows, betraying a feminine touch. A large stable stood next to a prosperous looking inn, yet nothing moved. The street and stores stood empty and forlorn. The blacksmith's hammer sat silent. Not even a dog barked. The village stood quiet as a graveyard.

Beside him, his newly promoted second, Commander Jarthax, said, "Where are they?"

"That is the question." The general scowled. "I want the village searched. Anyone found alive is to be brought to me. Ransack the stores for food, but no looting or burning." His gaze swiveled to his commander. "Am I understood."

"Yes, lord." Jarthax snapped a quick salute, his fist striking his breastplate. "Will you take quarters in the inn?" Jarthax grinned. "A feather bed will be welcome after so many nights in the mountains."

The inn did look inviting...as inviting as a trap. "Stay hard, Jarthax, or I'll find another commander to promote."

"Yes, lord." The young commander sat rigid in the saddle.

The general pointed to a large grassy field beyond the village. "Have my pavilion erected in the center. Deploy the men in a defensive perimeter. Order them to keep their swords and spears sharp. The monks will not surrender without a fight."

"Yes, lord." Saluting, the commander turned, bellowing orders.

General Haith swung down from the saddle. His personal guards looked alert, their swords easing from their scabbards, their keen eyes raking the village. Surrounded by drawn swords, he entered the inn. The great room was large and spacious, a massive river rock fireplace at one end. The hearth was cold, nothing but ashes in the grate, but he could have sworn the kitchen held the lingering aroma of fresh-baked bread. It was as if the villagers had just walked out the door leaving everything intact. It spoke of stone cold fear...or confident calculation. When it came to the monks, it paid to be cautious. He'd not come so far and gained so much to lose now. Having seen enough, he strode from the inn.

One of his guards dropped to his knees, offering his back as a mounting block.

Stepping up, the general swung into the saddle.

His personal guards formed a phalanx around him, a bristle of sharp steel.

Keeping his stallion to an amble, he rode to the far field. His army swarmed the grassy expanse, guards evenly spaced around the perimeter. Shields and spears glimmered in the afternoon sunlight, a formidable force awaiting battle. Horses pawed the grass, picketed in a long line to the south. His pavilion stood at the field's heart, black canvas inscribed with golden pentacles. The general allowed himself a smile. Rank deserved its luxuries, even in the midst of war.

He swung down from the saddle. Servants rushed to offer him a goblet of chilled wine. A guard planted the Mordant's banner before the pavilion, the *Darkflamme* rippling in the summer breeze.

The general remained standing while his servants removed the fearsome skeleton plate. Beneath the plate he wore dark leathers embossed with a pentacle. Around his neck he wore a golden amulet that gleamed on his chest. A gift from the Mordant, the amulet bore the enemy's sigil, the radiant Seeing Eye. Servants cast furtive glances at the amulet, but they dared say nothing.

Sipping chilled wine, the general seemed to take his ease in a camp chair set beneath the pavilion's shaded awning, yet his gaze roved the camp taking the measure of his forces. Satisfied with their defenses, he fingered the amulet. He wore it always. Gold gleamed in the sunlight, a radiant Seeing Eye etched across the medallion's face. He fondled the amulet, the key to the monastery. If the Mordant's words proved true, the golden trinket would protect him from the monastery's defenses. It amazed him that something so minor could matter so much, but such was the manner of magic. Tonight he'd sleep under the stars. Tomorrow he'd claim the monastery, ransack the Order's magic and put every blue-robed monk to the sword. At long last the Order's trove of secrets and magic would be his, a fitting tribute to his martial prowess. Powerful beyond reckoning, he'd rule as the undisputed warlord of the Southern Mountains, owing fealty to none save the Mordant.

"My lord," a pair of soldiers interrupted his reverie, "we found him in a barn, tending newborn piglets." A young boy hung between them, a mop of dark hair obscuring his eyes. They shoved the boy to his knees.

The general surveyed the captive. He looked to be no more than eight. "Where are your people?"

The boy gave him a sullen look.

"Stubbornness will not avail you." He gestured to one of the guards. "You said he was tending piglets?"

The guard grinned. "Skewered them, my lord, tender roast suckling for your supper."

The boy whimpered.

The general grinned. "Take it as a lesson, boy. The strong always win. The weak always serve. Your villagers will never defeat my soldiers. Even the blue-robed monks will succumb to numbers and steel." He eased back in the chair. "Take him away. Stake him to the ground, but don't harm him. On the morrow, he'll lead us to his people or he'll die screaming."

The guards dragged the boy away.

The villagers must have a secret bolt hole nearby, else they'd fled to the monastery. He'd discover the truth on the morrow.

Clouds scudded across the sky, casting shadows on the field. His servants brought him dinner served on gold plate. The smell was enticing, roast piglet stuffed with wild grain and garlic. A few freshly promoted officers joined him at the table, eager to be noticed. Ignoring their earnest yammer, the general savored a rich red merlot while dining on succulent piglet. His gaze surveyed the lush fields and the tidy village. All of it his, the heart of his fresh-won kingdom.

Movement snagged his gaze. Something white crept down from the forest-shrouded foothills. A dense white mist roiled out of the trees. Like a ground-hugging cloud, the mist moved as if it had purpose, sweeping towards his encampment with uncanny speed. Large enough to hide a small army, the general saw through the monks' ill-disguised ambush. *"Sorcery!"* General Haith leaped to his feet, scattering plates and goblets across the table. "Sound the alarm!"

Officers and servants stared at him, startled, for none had noticed the uncanny cloud.

Screams rose from the edge of camp.

A trumpet blared, cut-off in mid-note.

"The enemy attacks!" The general bellowed. "My sword!" His servants came running with his sword and helm. He drew the sword from the scabbard and took the helm, but there was no time for more. "To me!" His personal guard formed a phalanx around him.

Screams and the clash of steel came from the uncanny cloud.

Confusion riddled the camp.

Seeking to thwart the ambush, the general led his veteran guards into the roiling mist. A dense, cold white surrounded him, shuttering his view. Chaos reigned, men screaming and fighting in the cloud.

"Demons! Slay the demons!"
"Kill the beasts!"

Figures darted through the mist. The general found it difficult to discern friend from foe. Sounds played strange tricks, adding to the confusion. The clash of swords and shrieks of the dying came from all directions. The general led his men forward, seeking the enemy...but then he realized no one followed. A cold chill prickled at the back of his neck.

"Kill the demons!"

All around him a battle raged. He heard screams, but saw no demons, only men in black armor. *They fight each other!* Gripped by madness, their faces twisted by fear, his men slaughtered each other. Slashing and hacking, they killed their own comrades as if battling monsters. Appalled, General Haith roared commands. *"Stop! Cease fighting! I command you to stop! This is madness! You're fighting yourselves!"* He bellowed and roared but none of his men listened, as if the mist held his army enthralled, poisoning their minds with battle lust. And then he understood. *"Magic!"* Somehow the monks had ensorcelled his army...yet he alone was unaffected. *The amulet!* He gripped the golden amulet, the only man immune to madness. Running through the mist, he sought to stop the senseless slaughter. Roaring commands, he stood in front of his soldiers, shouting orders, but they stared right through him, as if he was the lone ghost among the living.

Spying his second, he ran to the man. Evading a sword stroke, he gripped his arm. "Jarthax, stop this madness!"

Jarthax staggered to a stop. Lowering his bloody sword, he stared at the general, the light of sanity returning to his gaze. "Demons in the mist!"

The general clung to his commander. "There are no demons! Why do you attack your own men?"

"I didn't..." but then the commander's gaze widened in horror, ensnared by the carnage around him. "I *swear* I fought a three-headed monster..." he shook his head at the insanity of his words. "It seemed real, so very real."

"The cloud ensorcelled you, but this amulet protects me and any I touch." He tugged the commander forward, keeping a firm grip on his arm. "Help me save the others!"

All around him his army fought and died. Blood and guts churned the ground, but everyone they touched shook off the madness. The chain of sanity slowly grew. Gripping the amulet, the general led them forward, determined to save his army.

It seemed like the battle raged for an eternity...death shrouded in white, but then it ended in an instant.

The clash of swords fell sharply silent.

Corpses littered the ground...and all of them wore black.

The malevolent cloud began to disperse, revealing a twilight sky. The general staggered to a stop, finding it hard to believe that trees and pastures and cottages existed beyond the mist's killing madness.

The last of the white vanished with a long-held sigh.

General Haith shuddered, feeling as if a ghost had brushed against him.

The waning sunlight illumed the horrid truth. He stood on a field of carnage. His army was decimated, turned to corpses. Everywhere he looked, he saw death and carnage. His dark pavilion stood askew at the field's heart, leaning like a tottering drunk. The *Darkflamme* was gone, subsumed by violence. Tents were flattened, trampled into the bloody ground. Shattered shields and bloody swords gave testament to the bitter fighting. Corpses stared with sightless eyes, their guts strewn across the field. He stood in the midst of a battlefield lost, and all the dead wore dark armor.

Ravens circled overhead, dark wings spiraling down to the grim feast.

Released from the cloud's malignant spell, his men staggered about like drunkards.

Two hundred men out of two thousand! The general shuddered, appalled by the loss. He cursed the foul monks. *Tricked by magic,* yet he'd managed to salvage nearly two hundred battle-hardened veterans. He fingered the amulet, consumed by the need for vengeance. Perhaps his veterans would be enough to sack the monastery and put the treacherous monks to the sword.

"My lord!" Jarthax gave warning.

A host of blue-clad monks emerged from the foothills. General Haith estimated their numbers at seventy or less. Most carried quarterstaffs, but a few held swords and other weapons of ancient make. Many were graybeards. A few were women. A feeble lot, they looked no contest for his heavily armed veterans. If this was the strength of the monks, then victory was his.

Jarthax sidled towards him. "My lord, behind."

The general flicked a glance behind. A small band of leather-clad men loped out of the forest, the same rabble he'd fought through the mountain passes. Forty brigands, most of them armed with quarterstaffs, yet combining their forces, the enemy was still outnumbered. He'd show them the power of disciplined steel. "Form a square!"

His men hefted shields, spears and swords, forming a defensive square.

The monks approached, stopping a spear's throw away.

A tall blue-clad monk with salt-and-pepper hair and a sun-weathered face spoke, his voice firm with confidence. "The Mordant is dead! The Dark Citadel has fallen!"

Murmurs of dismay rippled through his men.

"Lies!" The general snarled, his voice a lash. "Stand your ground."

The monk pressed his advantage. "You have tasted the power of our magic! Put down your weapons and renounce Darkness. Choose life and follow the Light!"

"Lies! You spew foul lies seeking to trick us with words." The general bellowed his hatred. "We'll answer your lies with steel! Kill the monks!" His cadre of veterans advanced at a slow trot, a disciplined square bristling with weapons, yet his men muttered with unease, casting sideways glances.

Instead of running, the monks began to chant.

A woman in blue robes stepped from their midst.

A woman! The general rumbled with laughter, *women and songs, such a feeble defense,* but then the woman held a crystal orb aloft...and the orb began to glow with an unearthly radiance.

His armored veterans faltered and slowed, fear flickering across their faces. Many muttered oaths against magic.

"Advance! Sound the charge!" General Haith bellowed orders but his men balked, refusing to move.

The orb pulsed bright with light.

The monks' chant deepened.

An eerie cadence filled the meadow.

General Haith bellowed, "Sound the charge!"

A monk raised an iron wand and balled lightning crackled at the tip.

A moan rose from his men.

Jarthax fell quaking to his knees, surrendering his sword to the grass.

"How dare you!" Enraged, General Haith strode towards his second. "Stand and fight!"

Jarthax whined like a wild animal caught in a trap. "No more magic!"

"Coward!" The general's sword flashed bright. He smote at the commander's bent neck. It took three strokes to sever the craven's stubborn head. He kicked the grisly trophy for good measure. Blood-drenched, the general roared his fury. *"Attack!"* But his veterans had fallen into chaos. Bitten by fear, most abandoned their weapons. Cowards, they slunk away, seeking safety in the trees, while others knelt in surrender. A few shared their general's rage, hacking at their craven brethren. The general stared, appalled. He ranted and yelled, but even battle-hardened men could only be pushed so far. Magic broke his legion, the last of his Dark army frittering into chaos. A cold fury gripped him. He'd make the monks pay for their slimy-tricked treachery.

Roaring his hatred, he charged the monks. Alone, he raced towards their leader, the smug bastard with salt-and-pepper hair. He raised his sword like a scythe. Three more strides and he'd sow death among the blue-robed scholars.

Stepping from amongst the others, a gray-haired monk raised a crossbow.

Too close, Haith heard the soft click of the tickler.

Something punched him in the chest, a brutal blow that crumpled him to his knees. His sword fell from his slack hands. He looked down, shocked by the gaping hole. Blood, so much blood. A sudden fear gripped him, wondering what he'd find on the other side. Collapsing to the ground, the general fell into Darkness.

103

Katherine

L eaning low in the saddle, Kath asked her roan mare for more speed. Horse and rider tore across the greensward, tearing up clods of earth. She sped towards the drawbridge, a vanguard of death at her back.

A thunderous roar rose behind her. Swiveling in the saddle, Kath dared a glance over her shoulder. Berserkers in dark armor raced across the greensward, too many to count, as if the whole horde gave chase.

Hoof beats drummed behind, an enemy seeking to close the distance. Clad in mismatched armor, he bore an impossibly large wall shield...and his great sword was midnight-black. For half a heartbeat, their gazes locked. Recognition shuddered through Kath, *the knight marshal!*

Horror threatened to overwhelm her. She'd idolized the marshal since she was knee-high, and now her hero served Darkness. His betrayal shook her soul. Putting spurs to her mount, she raced for the drawbridge, as if fleeing the wraith of Hell.

Nearing the drawbridge, Kath raised her voice to a frantic yell. *"Raise the drawbridge! Seal the gates!"* Clattering across the bridge, she saw no movement at the barbican. Unguarded, the portcullis gaped open like a startled mouth. Keeping her horse to a gallop, she raced beneath the toothed portcullis, entering the twists and turns of the killing corridor. Mage-stone walls soared to her left, ordinary battlements on her right. Swiveling in the saddle, she glanced behind, looking for signs of pursuit, but she saw none.

Keeping her horse to a lathered gallop, she raced through the stone-walled labyrinth. Her roan mare caught up to the vanguard's stragglers. The traitor-knight was surely among them, but this was not the time. "Hurry!" Kath urged the stragglers forward, riding guard at the rear.

The killing corridor seemed endless, a labyrinth of twists and turns peppered with dead-ends, but Kath knew the way like the back of her hand. She herded the stragglers forward until the knights in front began to slow, their horses bunched together, their progress choked by the inner gate.

Fear shivered through her, they dared not get caught in the corridor.

She found Sir Lothar, his face grim. "Why are you slowing?"

"Your villagers and small folk are clogging the inner gates."

A chill gripped her. "Make them hurry. To be caught in the corridor is to court death!"

Sir Lothar saluted, spurring his horse forward.

Kath stood in the stirrups. "Sir Rannock, Sir Blaze, Sir Mellot, Sir Brindamir, Sir Galyad to me! Rally to me!" In the narrow confines of the corridor a valiant few could hold back many.

The knights and champions answered her call.

Kath drew *Invictus*. "Form a line. We have to buy time for the others to escape."

Weapons whispered from their sheaths as the knights moved into position beside her. They formed a thin line of maroon sealing the way to the inner gates.

Kath waited, sweat trickling beneath her armor.

Maroon battle banners hung limp, the wind stifled to a hush in the narrow stone gorge.

A roar thundered through the killing corridor. Kath heard the pounding of thousands of boots. Like a lethal tidal wave, the Dark horde crested through the stone gorge. "They're coming!"

Black-clad horsemen galloped around the far corner. One of them wielded a dark sword.

104

Blaine

Confined to a litter, his wound seeping blood, yet Blaine insisted on taking part in the battle. After succumbing to the fiend in the way-stone, he sought a way to atone for his failing. Kath relented, promoting him to knight-captain and entrusting him with the command of the castle defenses. Assembling a small squad of trumpeters and message runners, Blaine asked a pair of burly villagers to carry his litter to the top of Marshal Tower. A squat tower positioned near the outer walls, the battlement gave him a bird's-eye view of the greensward and the killing corridor below.

From the tower top, Blaine watched the silvery vanguard ride out, maroon battle banners rippling in the afternoon breeze. Knowing he should have been among them, it hurt to watch from the tower top, yet he lauded their stubborn bravery. Behind the veteran knights, Kath's rabble army of urchins in armor fanned out of the gates, giving the attack the illusion of numbers. Across the greensward, the Dark horde brooded behind their lines, a hammer poised above an anvil.

Kath led the vanguard, distinctive on her white stallion. Halfway across the greensward, the cat-eyed archers raised their bows, sending fire arrows streaking towards the monster trebuchet. At the archers' signal, the rabble army broke into a panicked retreat. Their disarray was planned but not feigned. Frightened, they raced back towards the castle gates while the maroon vanguard galloped to the charge.

Armor gleaming silver in the afternoon sun, the vanguard lowered their lances.

From the tower top, Blaine heard the mighty clash as lances splintered shields. The vanguard mowed into the Dark horde, cutting a deadly swath. Men screamed and horses squealed as death came calling. Their charge slowed to a standstill. The knights dropped their lances, unsheathing their swords. The silvery line dissolved into smaller battles. Mounted knights hewed into dark shields. The swarming horde surged around them, fighting on foot, bringing their numbers to bear.

Blaine tensed, muttering commands. *"Retreat, retreat!"* If the vanguard did not soon disengage, they'd be swallowed by the horde's relentless numbers.

A horn blared a strident call, and the vanguard began to retreat. Their maroon line was broken by battle, yet they pulled back, hacking at the dark-clad enemy. Swirling away from the horde, they galloped across the greensward.

Relieved, Blaine turned his gaze to the killing corridor.

The vanguard's charge had bought the rabble time. Most of the rag-tag army gained the outer gates. Strung out in a line, they raced through the killing corridor, seeking the sanctuary of the inner castle. *"Hurry! Hurry!"* He urged them forward, knowing time was of the essence.

War drums pounded a fearsome beat across the greensward.

A thundering roar rose from the enemy lines.

Like a dark storm, the horde broke. Countless thousands raced across the greensward, howling for blood.

The enemy had taken the bait.

The Dark horde chased the straggling knights towards the drawbridge, a race of life and death.

Blaine waited till the horde was committed to the charge. When the dark tide lapped at the castle's outer gates, he gave the order. "Loose the catapults! Pound them to Hell!" Horns blared the order. Young boys hoisted red pennants, frantically waving them from the tower top.

The catapults and trebuchets answered, hurling massive boulders into the horde.

Death fell from the skies, pounding gaping holes in the swarm, yet still they came, racing across the greensward, hurtling towards the castle gates like a plague of armored cockroaches.

The Dark horde swarmed across the drawbridge. Like an infestation, they raced through the stone corridors. So great was their number that they pressed into the dead-end corridors, crushing their own men against the buttressed walls.

Blaine watched the dark tide roll through the stone gorge.

Beside him, Sir Dorlin yelled, *"The inner gates are open!"*

Blaine heard the horror in the old veteran's voice. Spearing his gaze to the far end of the killing corridor, he saw Kath's rabble army was bunched at the inner gates, clogged with panic. The remainder of the vanguard stood as a thin defense, a hopeless stance of eighty knights. No matter how valiant, eighty could not withstand the horde.

Sir Dorlin yelled, *"Close the gates!"*

"No!" Blaine curtailed the command. Kath had given him strict orders to close the inner gates to protect the inner castle at all cost, but if he obeyed, the champions of Castlegard would die, ground to death by the horde. There had to be another way. "Close the inner gates but *open* the sally port."

Sir Dorlin gaped. "But..."

Blaine growled. "Pass the order! The valiant shall have their chance!" This one time, he'd disobey her, trusting the rest of her plan to prevail.

Messengers ran from the tower top bearing his orders.

Knowing the die was cast, Blaine watched the dark swarm roil through the corridor. It was time to summon all of Castlegard's defenses to the battle.

"Sound the attack!"

Horns blared a strident call.

Green pennants waved above the Marshal's Tower.

A mighty shout rose from Castlegard, as if the very walls had life.

Thousands of defenders rose from behind crenellated battlements. Knights, archers, smiths, castle folk, villagers, farmers, women, and children, they peered down from both sides of the killing corridor, seeking vengeance against the Dark. With a mighty shout, they attacked. Spears, caltrops, and stones rained down onto the enemy. Cat-eyed archers stood among the castle's defenders, loosing their longbows with uncanny accuracy. Feathered shafts whispered death into dark armor. Villagers struggled to lift pots of burning oil, spilling flames onto the horde. Screams erupted along the corridor, black smoke roiling into the summer sky. The stench of burnt flesh choked the castle. The narrow stone gorge became a lethal killing field.

Death claimed a fearsome toll, yet the horde continued to pour into the castle like lost souls seeking the gateway to Hell.

Castlegard obliged.

Corpses piled in the corridor, the dead amongst the dying.

Grappling hooks tangled the battlements but the knights were quick to cut them down. Defenders ran out of spears. More oil was brought up from the kitchens. Huge kettles of boiling water were lifted to the battlements. With each release, horrid shrieks rose from the swarming horde.

The Dark tide began to turn, retreating back towards the outer gate.

"*Drop the portcullis!*" Blaine yelled the order.

Horns bugled a strident cacophony of notes.

Defenders on the outer barbican rose from their hiding holes to release the portcullis.

The iron-toothed gate crashed down, pinning men beneath it, trapping the bulk of the horde within the castle.

Beyond the drawbridge, remnants of the horde fled for the forests. Broken and disorganized, they posed a lesser threat, brigands to be hunted down and slain after the battle.

Within the castle's corridor, the killing continued, a rampant chaos of death. Blaine gripped the merlon, searching for Kath. The Dark horde was broken, but not yet defeated. A thin line of maroon knights waged a bitter battle, fighting for their lives at the inner gates. Blaine stared at the roiling chaos, seeking Kath, hoping she lived.

105

Katherine

Kath parried the blow with *Invictus*. The blue sword rang like a bell, shattering the enemy's blade. Her follow through took him in the gut. Stepping over the fresh corpse, she raced to aid another knight. Two against one, they slew the foe, yet the Dark horde never slowed.

Weariness dogged her, yet Kath tightened her grip on *Invictus*.

A mace swung towards her head. Taking the blow on her shield, Kath stepped towards the enemy. *Invictus* sliced through chainmail and leathers, an unstoppable sword. The enemy died screaming.

She tugged the sapphire blade free.

A sixth sense warned her to duck.

A spear narrowly missed her head.

Chaos claimed the corridor, pockets of maroon knights battling berserkers in black. Corpses littered the ground, yet still the horde came, pressing for the gates. The enemy fought like fear-goaded madmen. Screaming battle cries, they raced through the stone corridor with bloodlust in their eyes. A few dared to stand against many, a silvery line against the Dark onslaught. Too many knights died, thinning their ranks. Kath saw Sir Adlemar, the traitor who'd attacked her in the greensward, fall to a berserker's axe. Justice claimed the craven, yet it was one less sword against the horde.

Darting to the left, Kath searched for the marshal, but she could not find him. Perhaps a spear or an arrow had slain him, but then she remembered he wore a maroon cloak. To those fighting on the battlements, he'd appear as a friend instead of a foe.

"Take the gates! Take the gates!"

Hearing the bellowed command, Kath recognized his voice. *He lived!* Luck or Darkness favored the marshal. She caught a glimpse of him through the melee. Wielding a massive wall shield like a battering ram, he knocked knights to the ground and then took their heads with a single stroke of the sin-dark sword. Helmless, his scar-crossed face was savage with battle lust. The marshal fought like a whirlwind. He fought like a monster instead of a man.

A spear skittered off her shield, a narrow miss.

Startled alert, Kath crouched in a defensive stance.

Twice her own defenders had nearly maimed her.

Kath glanced aloft and saw Gravis staring down from the battlement. *"Traitor!"* Anger threaded through her. Sheathing her sword, she grabbed the fallen spear and hurled it with all her might. It took him in the throat. Gagging on the spear, a startled look on his grizzled face, he tumbled over the battlement, a corpse falling into the killing field.

A sword whistled towards her.

Kath raised her shield, holding it aloft with both hands.

The great sword struck, shattering her shield into shards.

Rolling away, she sprang to her feet, unsheathing *Invictus*. The two swords met in a fearsome clang, but there was no parry, for the other sword shattered, broken by *Invictus*. Her follow through caught the enemy in the face. Blood spattered her armor. Yanking the blade free, Kath turned, desperate to reach the marshal.

Most of the knights had fallen back, fighting before the inner gates, but a knot of maroon was trapped, surrounded by churning black. The marshal waded into them, the Dark Sword reaping a terrible toll. The knights fought valiantly but only *Invictus* could withstand the marshal's cursed sword. Kath sought to reach him, pushing through the press, yet somehow he remained beyond reach. The battle ebbed and flowed, a swirl of death. Chaos conspired to keep them apart. Unable to forge an opening through the melee, she took another path. Dodging a battleaxe, she ran for the nearest wall. Invoking her magic, Kath leaped *into* the stone. Mage-stone surrounded her. The castle embraced her with a stone-cloistered chill, but Kath refused to be held. Staying within the corridor wall, she moved to the left. Stepping from the stone, she emerged deeper in the killing field. Gasping for breath, she pressed her back to the wall, seeking the enemy.

The marshal was behind her, a sword stroke away.

"For Honor and the Octagon!" Kath roared her battle cry, leaping towards him.

Fast as lightning, he turned to meet her charge. The Dark Sword snaked down with uncanny speed. She barely met it with the blue. The two swords clashed, steel clanging against steel. They hit like the ringing of a great bell...but neither sword broke.

Twice he struck at her and twice the blue sword withstood the black.

Glaring across locked swords, the marshal hissed, "What blade is this?"

"Your bane!"

He sneered. "Wielded by a *girl?*"

"A queen!" Disengaging, she whirled to her right, seeking an opening.

Three times she attacked and three times he parried her strikes. Unable to land a telling blow, she hurled words, seeking to sway the man within. "Remember your oath! You're the knight marshal! You serve the maroon!"

Hatred snarled across the marshal's face. Unleashing a mighty swing, he sought to take her head. She barely got her sword up in time. The Dark Sword struck the blue with a fearsome clang. The strength of his blow shivered down Kath's arms, nearly ripping *Invictus* from her hands. Kath gaped at the marshal's raw power. A master swordsman, he'd gained uncanny strength and speed. She could ill afford to trade blows with him. As if sensing her weakness, he attacked. A storm of blows beat against her.

"Your soul will be mine!"

Kath twisted away, evading his strike. Turning and dodging, she sought an opening, yet the Dark Sword was always there, half a heartbeat ahead of hers. The massive wall shield careened towards her, nearly bashing her head. She leaped away, barely evading the blow. The marshal wielded the shield like a battering ram, almost as deadly as the Dark Sword. Dodging and weaving, she sought to avoid both, desperate to find an opening.

Kath lunged forward, thrusting for the marshal's heart, but he parried the blow.

Fear stalked her. *This is the knight marshal!* She fought a hero of the maroon. The knowledge beat against her, betraying her resolve. *Invictus* withstood every stroke of the Dark Sword, yet she was losing. Slowed by weariness, every muscle aching, she twisted away, yet the marshal followed, never slacking his onslaught. Pain creased her left arm. He'd landed a glancing blow, the Dark Sword slicing through chainmail and leather, cleaving a crease along her forearm. The wound stung like acid. Only a shallow cut, yet her own blood stained her armor.

"Your blood!" The marshal licked his lips like a slavering fiend. "The sword *tastes* you! It tastes your *soul!"*

A chill slithered down Kath's back.

"You're the one!" Hatred snarled his face. "The Dark Sword *knows* you! It *seeks* your soul for slaying its maker!"

The Mordant reaches from beyond the grave! Her heart hammering, Kath retreated, keeping *Invictus* raised for a two-handed parry. She half expected the marshal's lone eye to glow bright red...but it did not. *"Only a man, only a man!"* She muttered the words like a desperate prayer.

Lightning-fast, the marshal leaped forward, unleashing a whirlwind of blows. He fought like a demon enraged, moving faster than a hell-spawned fiend.

Kath fought like she'd never fought before, yet she gave ground before the marshal's vicious onslaught. *Invictus* met the Dark Sword with a furious clang. Kath retreated, parrying every stroke, barely keeping the Dark Sword from her throat. The marshal never slowed, never showed any signs of tiring, while she withered under his relentless blows. Fighting for her very life, Kath summoned every scrap of skill. Sweat stung her eyes and the wound on her arm burned. Avoiding a vicious cut, she stumbled backwards, tripping over a corpse. The dead knight betrayed her. Kath fell hard, the blue sword clattering from her grasp. Empty-handed, she turned to face his blade.

The marshal snarled a twisted laugh. "The Dark Sword *lusts* for your soul. Forever shall you serve, enslaved to the blade." He raised the Dark Sword for the killing stroke. "Vengeance belongs to the Dark!"

Kath lunged for the blue sword, her gauntleted hand stretched out, but the Dark Sword was faster. The cursed blade whistled downwards. Kath lurched away, barely saving her arm. Where her hand had been, the Dark

Sword struck stone, raising a shower of sparks. Unable to reach *Invictus*, Kath rolled the opposite way. Springing to a wary crouch, she cast her gaze across the ground, desperate for a sword, any sword, but she saw none.

The marshal loomed over her. "Darkness will claim you!"

Anger sparked within her. "Never!" Kath reached for her only remaining weapon. Unsheathing the crystal dagger, she attacked. *"For Honor and the Octagon!"* Heedless of the danger, Kath hurled herself at him, aiming the dagger in a two-handed thrust.

The Dark Sword sped down in a defensive parry.

The two blades struck, steel against crystal.

Kath cringed, expecting the dagger to shatter...but the crystal held...and the Dark Sword *screamed!*

The marshal staggered backwards, a stunned look on his scarred face.

For half a heartbeat, Kath was thunderstruck with shock, but then she understood.

Light pulsed in the crystal blade...and the dagger grew into a sword!

A *sword!* She was meant to wield a sword. Kath attacked.

The marshal parried the blow.

Black steel struck gleaming crystal. A hideous wail rose from the cursed blade. The crystal sword answered, glowing with a fierce white light. Instead of attacking the man, Kath attacked the sword. She beat at the cursed sword, wielding soul-magic. *"I release you!"* Pouring all her will into the crystal blade, she sought to unlock the ensorcelled souls enslaved in bitter steel. The Dark Sword howled and screeched with every clash of crystal. The marshal stumbled backwards, seeking to escape, but Kath followed like justice unleashed. *"For Honor and the Octagon!"* Crystal beat against the tainted blade in a storm of blows. Smoke steamed from the Dark Sword. A legion of faces stared from the roiling smoke. A millennium of souls drunk by the sword bled away with every crystal stroke. Sighing with release, the ensorcelled souls fled, billows of smoke rising to the heavens.

The marshal groaned with agony.

His face became haggard, looking as if he'd aged decades.

Collapsing to his knees, he dropped the Dark Sword. *"Forgive me!"*

The cursed steel sizzled and smoked, releasing untold legions of souls.

The sword consumed itself, smoking and sizzling till there was nothing left save a dark sword-shape forever staining the stony ground.

The marshal sobbed, a broken old man released from a hellish curse.

Kath sagged to her knees, sundered by weariness.

The crystal sword pulsed with light, becoming a dagger once more.

Silence reigned

Kath realized the fighting had fallen still. Gazing the length of the corridor, she saw nothing save corpses and a small knot of maroon knights protecting the inner gates.

Sir Lothar limped towards her. "Your wits won."

Kath heard no irony in his voice and saw no ridicule on his face.

Retrieving *Invictus* from the ground, he offered the blue sword to her, hilt-first. "As did your sword. You truly are the Queen of Castlegard."

He finally saw her! The realization staggered her. All her life, she'd longed to be seen, especially by the maroon knights. If only her father had lived to see the day. Sheathing the crystal dagger, Kath stood, accepting the blue blade. *Invictus* felt right in her hands.

Sir Lothar held her gaze. "The blue sword was never the key to victory, *you* were." He knelt in homage. "All hail the Steel Queen!"

Tears threatened her eyes, for she heard nothing save honesty in his voice.

A great shout rose from the castle. All along the walls, defenders cheered, *"The Steel Queen!"*

Kath flashed a smile, raising *Invictus* in salute to those who'd fought from the castle ramparts. She stared up at their brimming faces, at the villagers, farmers and castle folk standing alongside maroon-cloaked knights. "We did it!" Elation thrummed through her. She brandished the blue sword to the heavens. "For Honor and the Octagon!"

Cheers thundered from the walls.

The great castle was saved, the battle won.

Maroon banners waved triumphant from lofty towers.

A chime sounded, a benediction from the gods. Castlegard's mage-stone walls began to glow with a radiant light. Stones clicked against stones. Mage-stone walls rumbled and shook, emitting a soft moon-glow shimmer. Cracks disappeared as if they'd never been. Walls knit together. Magic bolstered by belief healed the castle's mage-stone. Solid and unbreakable, Castlegard stood invincible once more. Honor was restored to the Octagon. Overcome with gratitude and relief, Kath stared in wonder at the great castle. She was home. And she finally belonged.

Epilogue

K ath woke with a start. *It's today.* She knew it in the depths of her heart. The conviction gripped her with undeniable certainty, a smile bursting across her face. Starlight still glinted on the arrow-slit window, yet she rose, too restless to wait for the lazy sun. Letting her squires sleep, she dressed in ordinary fighting leathers, something her father would approve of. Tugging on Duncan's lizard-skin boots, long-since cut to her size, she swirled her maroon cloak across her shoulders and belted her sword to her side. Peace cloaked the land, yet *Invictus* was never far from her hand.

Too excited for tedious scroll work, Kath roamed the great castle, stopping to speak to knights and guards and golden-eyed archers. The great yard stood empty, too early for sparing practice. Drawn to the peerless view of Needle Tower, she climbed the spiral stairs to the top. Stepping out onto the battlement, a summer breeze caught at her long silver hair. On this fair spring morning, she felt young despite her sixty-seven years. Standing alongside the gargoyles, Kath watched the sun rise. Golden rays speared above the Dragon Spine Mountains, casting an ethereal glow on the great castle. *Castlegard*, the name shivered in her soul like a blaze of glory. Her gaze swept across the soaring towers and proud battlements, taking in the splendor of every martial detail. *Mage-stone,* the key to Castlegard's invincibility had been restored after the Battle Immortal, all the cracks and fractures magically healed, but the gaping holes in the towers remained, as if magic had its limits. As queen, she'd summoned the finest stonemasons from across the southern kingdoms. Mage-stone could no longer be created, nor could it be mimicked, yet the stonemasons had done a fine job. Castlegard's daunting silhouette was restored, its proud towers rising unbroken, a symbol of enduring strength cast across the lands of Erdhe.

Soft footsteps scuffed the stairs behind her. A young girl clad in a squire's gray tunic burst out onto the battlement. Spying Kath, she gasped. "Sorry to disturb you, majesty."

Kath smiled, trying to soothe the girl's shyness. "Come, the view is the best in the castle."

"I know." The girl joined her at the railing. Giving her auburn ponytail a determined tug, she cast a sideways glance at Kath. "Majesty, can I ask you a question?"

Kath nodded, suppressing a smile.

"What is the castle's eleventh defense? I've searched everywhere," her young voice sounded vexed, "from the moat, to the drawbridge, to the highest towers, but I cannot find it."

A smile flitted across Kath's face, for all the newly accepted squires were tasked with discovering the great castle's eleven defenses. "The eleventh defense is not built in stone, but rather in the hearts and minds of men. Perceived as invincible, Castlegard's reputation is its greatest defense."

The girl's brown eyes went wide with astonishment.

"That is why you must never sully your own reputation, nor that of the maroon."

The girl gave her a solemn nod, yet a puzzled look filled her eyes. "But, majesty, how did you wield that defense in the great battle?"

Kath sighed, for she'd nearly forgotten how much it hurt to be discounted. "Because a truly invincible castle can only be defeated by treachery or incompetence. So I gave the enemy an illusion they were all too keen to believe."

The girl gave her a wide-eyed look. "I'll remember that."

"See that you do."

A trumpet rang out, a greeting to friends approaching the castle.

Kath's gaze swiveled to the north. She saw them then, a pair of riders cantering from the forest. And beside them loped a mountain wolf.

Bidding good day to the girl, Kath made her way down the tower. Eschewing the stuffy formality of the throne room, she decided to meet them in her solar, for this was a matter of the heart not the Octagon.

Maroon-cloaked knights snapped salutes as she climbed the stairs to the queen's tower. Her squires, Devlin and Sarah, squawked like mother hens, hovering about till Kath dismissed them with a wave of her hand. Finally alone, she stood with her back to the stone hearth, enjoying the soothing warmth of the crackling fire.

A knock sounded on the door.

"Come!"

The door opened and two painted warriors entered. Both were young and fair and in their late teens. Kath searched their faces, looking for echoes of Danya and Neven. A wolf tattoo graced the young woman's face, while the dark-haired young man bore a mountain lion. They both bowed deep with respect, and then the young woman stepped forward, presenting Kath with a bouquet of beautiful blue flowers. Intoning the same solemn words that were spoken every springtime, she said, "These are *Illania*, Maiden's Tears. They bloom only on the graves of heroes. As a token from the grateful north, accept these flowers from Duncan's heart to yours."

Tears crowded Kath's eyes, yet she refused to let them fall. *Duncan*, his name whispered through her heart. Every year the *Illania* bloomed on his grave, and every year the painted warriors brought a bouquet to her arms. Despite the great distance, they remained fresh, as if just plucked. Cradling the delicate flowers to her breast, Kath let precious memories wash across her. A warm silence cloaked the solar, unbroken save for the crackling of the fire. Taking a deep breath of the fragrant blossoms, Kath arranged them in a silver vase set before the arrow-slit window.

Summoning her squires, she ordered raspberry scones, honey cakes and tea, pressing them on her guests. Settling in a seat before the fire, Kath said, "Tell me of your grandmother."

The young woman smiled, her hair the same color as Danya's long locks. "Grandmother is well, she sends her regards," a shadow crossed her face, "but Grandfather Neven passed last winter."

Kath gasped, knowing the pain of losing a beloved husband. "My deepest sorrow for her loss and yours." So many of her friends were passing beyond the gray veil, yet they'd lived long and prosperous lives. "He will be sorely missed."

Thaya, Danya's wolf-faced granddaughter, gave her a solemn nod. "Tis true."

Kath kept the young people with her for the better part of the day, speaking of Danya, the painted people, the Citadel, the Ghost Hills, and wolf puppies. It seemed Bryx's line bred true, the new puppies always bonding with Danya's many children and grandchildren. "The north must ring with the cry of wolves!"

Thaya smiled, "May it ever be so."

The day passed in a pleasure of remembrances recalled and stories shared. Kath feasted the two young people in the great hall, serving slivers of meat from her own platter to the great mountain wolf lolling beneath the high table. Thaya and Chard stayed but a single night, anxious to return to the north. Burdening them with gifts and well wishes, Kath saw them to the castle gates, bidding them a fond farewell.

***

Kath woke to find the *Illania* wilted on her windowsill and knew it was time. The delicate blue blossoms always lasted a full moon-turn after reaching her hand. Some in the castle whispered of magic, naming them 'everylastings', yet nothing lasted forever.

Summoning her squires, she let them dress her in fighting leathers, affixing a maroon cloak to her shoulders. Kath buckled on her sword belt and then sent her squires scurrying for the horses and supplies. Unlocking her cedar chest, she removed a scroll written moon-turns ago. Signed and sealed, it held instructions for her knight marshal. Sir Barhold made an able marshal, especially in times of peace, but she sorely missed Blaine.

Lingering for only a moment, Kath made her way down the stairs to the great throne room. Her left knee ached worse than usual, but she strove to ignore it. As expected, the great throne room was empty, morning sunlight spearing the stained glass windows. It was here, so many years ago, that she'd claimed the right to her father's crown. She made her way to the dais, to the straight-backed throne carved in the silhouette of mighty Castlegard. She ran her hands across the carving. Kath was the last of the Anvrils. A knight not of her blood would rule the Octagon at her passing, but Kath had learned that it was not bloodlines that mattered, but spiritlines, the legacy of thoughts and deeds that one left behind. She'd renewed a sense of honor and courage in the maroon, instilling the will to win by wits not just by swords. Whoever led the maroon would walk in her spiritline, of that she was certain. Whispering a silent prayer to Valin, she hoped her illustrious ancestors were satisfied.

Kath unsheathed *Invictus*. The sword whispered from her scabbard, sapphire-blue steel shimmering in the light. Such a wondrous blade, amazingly light and forever sharp, the short sword was peerless, a perfect fit for her hand, a gift from the gods.

Speaking the words Ambrose had told her long ago, she raised the short sword to the gods.

Light flared blindingly bright.

Invictus shimmered and rippled with light.

When the light dimmed, the sword was changed. Once more a five foot great sword, yet now the blade was red with rust and pitted with age. It looked like a relic from a bygone age, yet she trusted the knights to remember.

Leaning *Invictus* against the throne, she left it for the hands of the next ruler.

She'd trust the sword to choose wisely, to choose someone of her spiritline.

Bowing to the great sword, she turned, a swirl of maroon, and strode out into the sunshine.

Her squires were waiting for her, the horses saddled, their saddlebags bulging with food and supplies. Shields emblazoned with maroon octagons were affixed to the saddles.

"Do you have the sword?"

Sarah bowed, "Yes, majesty." She handed Kath a short sword from the armory.

Straight and true, it was a simple sword of good Castlegard steel, much like the sword she'd carried so long ago. "This will do." Satisfied, Kath settled the blade in the empty sheath at her hip. "Come." She swung into the saddle, stifling a wince from the sharp pain in her chest. Taking up the reins, she led her two squires from the inner castle, through the killing corridor, beneath the toothed portcullis and out across the drawbridge. Knights and guards waved in greeting, unaware they were truly saying farewell.

Crossing the greensward, Kath paused to look back at the great castle. So many triumphs, so many dear friends, where had the years gone? She whispered farewell to all those who had gone before her. A summer breeze lifted the battle banners on the castle, stirring the maroon pennants to a jaunty wave, as if the spirits of Blaine, Lothar, Rannock and so many other gallant knights gave answer. Saluting them, she turned her horse to the south, taking the ancient road.

Kath set a leisurely pace, riding through a soft, summery land. Her squires proved good company, peppering her with questions she was glad to answer. The leagues passed with tales well told. They visited the Deep Green, paying their respects to the Treespeaker, and then they rode on, eventually coming to Wyeth for the turning of the full moon. *The Merrymaker* was just as Justin described in his scrolls, a prosperous inn with brightly colored banners bedecking the roof. Round stained glass windows depicted musical instruments, an invitation to bards and patrons alike.

While her squires settled the horses, Kath climbed the steps to the inn. Her friends were already there, seated at a round table before a roaring fire. Kath rushed to greet them, embracing her sword sister with a bear hug. "So good to see you, your majesty!"

Jordan flashed an impish grin. "And you, your majesty!"

They laughed like girls, marveling at the wonder of dreams come true.

"How is Stewart?"

"He's good, although he'd rather stay home with his hunting hounds than travel."

"And the girls?"

"Jenna's always got a sword strapped to her side. She'll make a fine general, but our youngest, Liandra, she has the old queen's gift for gold."

"Blood runs true."

Jordan sobered. "But it will make succession tricky."

Kath grinned. "The gods have given you a bounty of riches."

Jordan smiled, "Just so."

Arm in arm, they went to greet the others. Jordan had brought two of her daughters, Megan and Liandra, both in their early thirties. Justin sat next to his wife, Indigo. Jemma sat between two of the Royal Ks, her daughter, Kiris, and her son, Kyle. Kath embraced them all, lingering the longest with her dearest friends. They'd all gone silver or gray, except Justin who'd gone sparse, his bald head reflecting the ruddy firelight. Their faces held more lines, scribed with the rich experiences of lives well lived, but in many ways they looked the same to Kath. Their eyes were still bright, filled with warmth and mirth, and the memories of great deeds.

They talked and feasted till the sun set, and then the Harper King brought out his twenty-one string Cloyne. Setting the small harp on his lap, he went through the ritual of tuning the strings. Small talk vanished and the clatter of plates and tankards stilled. Bespelled by the promise of a bard, the whole inn hushed to listen. Setting his hands to the strings, Justin began to play. A lilting melody, soft at first, drew in the listeners, and then stirring chords took them on a soaring adventure. His hands flew across the strings, plucking notes of pure emotions. Loosing his silvery voice, Justin sang of Sir Tyrone, the black knight who held the tunneled pass-through at Cragnoth Keep. Courage hummed through the strings as the knight made his last stand, one against many. A cat-eyed archer joined the fight, threading arrows through the dark. Kath leaned forward, sitting on the edge of her chair. The song ended in a crescendo of notes. Sir Tyrone held the pass-through, dying a valiant and victorious death, a hero forever immortalized in song.

The inn shook with thunderous applause.

Wiping a tear, Kath whispered a heartfelt, "Thank you."

Justin nodded. "Valor must ever be remembered, especially the unexpected kind." Strumming a deep chord, he sang a ballad of a silver-haired grandmother who wielded knitting needles and knives. Defying her guards, the old woman leaped into the roaring pyre, wrestling the ruby amulet from the Flame Priest. The forge-hot fire consumed the priest, foiling a foul religion, but the price was steep. By the time the last chord stilled, even the bard was misty-eyed. Silence drenched the great room in solemn remembrance. Kath raised her tankard in salute. "To unexpected heroes." The others joined her. They drained their tankards, their hearts brimming with memories.

Pitchers of frothy ale circulated the table, but the bard was not done. His fingers rippled across the strings, launching into a jaunty tune. He gave them rollicking sea chanties and tender love melodies. Smiles lit the room as fingers and toes tapped to the lively rhythms. The Harper King played for a blissful turn of an hourglass, taking them on an adventure of songs laden with emotions. When the strings of the Cloyne fell silent, the entire inn was spellbound.

Enthralled, the inn's patrons sat in silence for three whole heartbeats and then the applause broke, coming in thunderous waves. *"Bravo!"* Patrons laughed and cried, begging for more, but the Harper King was done for the night. A grateful innkeeper brought brimming tankards and a platter heaped with fresh-baked gingerbread. Kath and her friends sat before the fire, talking till the wee hours of the morning.

For three short days and four blissful nights, they stayed at the inn, sharing delicious spit-roasted meals, entangled tales of daring feats, and wonderful music. All too soon, duty called her friends home. Crowns had a relentless pull on those who wore them. Kath was sad to see them leave, but grateful for their time together.

Kath bid them farewell and then stayed one more night at *The Merrymaker*. Rising early the next morning, she left a fat purse for the innkeeper and a sealed scroll for her squires. Saddling her horse, she rode alone into the forests of Wyeth. Trusting to memory, she left the road, forging a path through the old growth forest. Eventually, she came across the steep-sided gorge, the same gorge she'd jumped bareback as a girl. Older and wiser, the jump looked rash and foolhardy. Laughing at her younger self, Kath followed the gorge north till she found the crystal-clear stream. Her heart raced, knowing she was near. Riding against the current, she followed the stream to the ruins. A moss-covered stone shield lay half buried in the silt. Broken faces peered up through the crystal-clear water, marble ghosts from a bygone Age. Scanning the forest, her gaze sought the jumbled stones hidden by the smothering green. Beams of sunlight pierced the trees, illuminating the hillside. Overgrown with ivy, the broken keep was a tumbled ruin, yet it called to her.

Unsaddling her horse, she left the stallion to graze by the stream.

Kath climbed the hill to the ruins. Everything matched her long-held memories. Making her way past the jumbled curtain wall, she found the broken drum tower. Once a mighty tower, it gaped open to the sky. Hesitating at the doorway, Kath whispered a prayer to Valin. Her dreams of the tower had grown more frequent with age, as if the ancient tower called to her. Brimming with hope, she gripped Duncan's warrior ring and stepped across the threshold.

Kath entered the broken tower, but she heard no chimes, she saw no vision of another time. She held her breath, waiting, hoping...but there was nothing. Perhaps the magic was gone, faded with time.

Sorely disappointed, Kath sagged against the wall.

All these years, she'd felt so sure, so certain...but it was not to be.

Wild vines covered one wall, blossoming with blue trumpet flowers. Their vivid blue caught her gaze, reminding her of *Illania*. On impulse, she cut a single vine, braiding it into a wreath for her hair. Crowned in flowers, she explored the ruin. The forest sought to encroach, yet the old stones resisted. More overgrown than she remembered, yet in many ways it was still the same. The ancient oak tree stood proud in the drum tower's heart, a spread of green leaves providing ample shade. Spiraling around the outer wall, the great staircase climbed to nothing but open sky. Stone swords served as a railing, but less than half of those remained, a lingering hint of former glory. A wondrous mosaic adorned the tower's floor, blue and gold tiles depicting a map of Erdhe. The majestic oak grew from the map's mosaic heart. Paw prints tracked mud across the bright tile, yet the age-old wonders lingered, a touchstone for the imagination. So many details whispered of the Star Knights.

Kath circled the great oak, absorbing every detail matched to memory. Reaching the staircase, she began to climb. At the seventh step, she knelt. As she'd done so long ago, Kath tugged on the top step. Stone grated on stone. The step swung forward, pivoting to reveal a hollow beneath.

The hollow was empty.

For the longest time, Kath sat there, remembering, and then she tugged the crystal dagger from her belt. Wrapping it in a maroon battle pennant, she placed the dagger in the hollow. From around her neck, she removed the leather cord with her small mage-stone gargoyle. Perhaps the gargoyle belonged in Castlegard, yet Kath felt the need to bequeath it to the next blade bearer. A gift from the gods, the gargoyle had served her well, saving her life more than once. Fingering the small gargoyle one last time for luck, she set it next to the dagger, and then closed the step, hiding the treasures for another time, another hand.

"It is done."

Her voice disturbed a flock of starlings. Oak leaves shimmered as the starlings rose from the great tree, spiraling up into the heavens like a prayer.

Kath watched till they disappeared into the blue. Slumping to the stone steps, she rubbed her aching chest. Weary, she closed her eyes, resting her head against the tower wall, seeking dreams of Duncan.

A chime sounded.

Kath woke with a start, her heart thundering with hope. Golden sunbeams speared through the great oak tree. A tall figure snared her gaze. Standing on the edge of sunlight, *he* was there. *"Duncan!"* Mismatched eyes in a sun-kissed face, he was young and handsome, sculpted muscles beneath black leather. He gave her an all-consuming stare.

Kath's heartbeat raced. She rushed down the stairs, but then stopped short, fearful he was just an illusion. "Is it you?"

"Beloved."

His voice!

"I've hovered on the edge of the veil, waiting for you, my warrior of the Light."

Kath longed to throw herself in his arms, but she was fearful he'd disappear, vanishing at first touch. "All these years, I looked for you in the slanting of the light. Was it you that I first saw in this tower, so many years ago?"

"It is always me. Warriors of the Light are called back when they are most needed. You and I have loved in many lifetimes, battled side by side in many Ages, lived and died together, always fighting the Battle Immortal."

"But I thought the Battle Immortal was finished? The Mordant and all his evil slain."

"It is never done. Light against Dark is an immortal struggle. Darkness always strives to dominate, to divide, to subjugate and control. Those who serve the Light must be ever vigilant, lest Darkness prevail."

As a warrior, Kath well understood the need to be vigilant, to answer the call to battle, but being a warrior was not enough. Hungry for his touch, she stared at him, memorizing every curve of his dear face. "Will we remember?"

"We're always given a fresh start lest the memories of the past prove an overwhelming burden." He smiled that secret smile she loved so much. "But some things cannot truly be forgotten, for some bonds are stronger than memories, stronger than time." His voice was laden with longing. "One soul knows another and sparks fly."

"Like us?"

"Just so."

"Then I've known you before."

"Always."

"And in those many lives, do we ever have time for us?"

He gave her a radiant smile. "We have forever...and all the time between." Duncan held out his hand. "You can come with me now, Beloved, or you can have more years in this life." He gestured up towards the stairs. "Look."

An old silver-haired woman sat slumped on the stairs, crowned by a flower wreath, a smile on her weathered face.

Puzzled, Kath looked down at her hands, at her arms. Her skin was young and smooth, all the old pains gone. She was young again, as when she'd first met him. "I have a choice?"

"In the Light, there is always a choice." Duncan stood, waiting.

She turned to him and smiled. "Till the clarion calls." Kath took his hand and stepped into the Light.

The End

Dear Reader,

Thank you for taking this incredible journey with me! Thank you for following Kath, and Duncan and Blaine through the kingdoms of Erdhe. I'd love to know what you think of my books and what you'd like me to write next. So tell me what you liked, loved and even what you hated. You can contact me at k_azinge@hotmail.com or on Facebook at Karen Azinger.

I'd love to hear from you.

And now I have a favor to ask. Readers have the power to make a book or a saga successful. The fate of The Silk & Steel Saga rests in your hands. Please support my books by posting a review on Amazon or Goodreads or any other social network. Even a one sentence review matters. I'd love to see my books on the silver screen, but that will only happen if you show the world you care. Thanks for your time and your support, I write for you. For Honor and the Octagon!

ACKNOWLEDGEMENTS

W OW! My seven book *Silk & Steel Saga* is done, finally reaching its epic conclusion! I feel like I've climbed Mount Everest! I feel like I've fought and won a thousand battles! Thank you, dear readers, for taking this awesome adventure with me! I hope this journey was as amazing for you as it was for me. My dream of writing an epic fantasy saga could not have happened without the help of many, but there are two very special people I need to thank above all others. Without their help, enthusiasm, and endless encouragement, the dream of Erdhe would never have begun. Thanks first and foremost to my husband, Rick, who gives me the stars. We have forever, and all the time between. To my best friend and sword sister, Danae Powers, who listened from the very first chapter. To my alpha and beta readers who continue to cheer for my books, Mike, Nick, Bill, Peggy, Diane, Bob, Mary, Christine, Ruthie and Gina, your enthusiasm means so much to me. To my very first editor, Bill Johnson, a story really is a promise. To my good friend, Christine Miller, for insights on publishing. To her husband, Pat Miller, for invaluable help formatting the first book. To Greg Bridges for all the totally awesome front covers and the book spines. To Peggy Lowe, graphic artist extraordinaire, for all the back covers, the two maps and the logo, well done! I truly believe my covers are the best in the fantasy genre! To Robert Owen Williams for corrections. To Deborah Sanders for the eagle-eyed proof read. To Violet Lowe for my author photo. And to all of my readers and fans around the world who eagerly followed the saga through all seven books, I write for you. And to my mom, for everything, I so hope you know.

APPENDIX

LANVERNESS

Lanverness is an old kingdom, steeped in tradition, often relying on its wealth of natural resources and the shrewdness of its rulers to grow in prosperity and influence. Never fecund, the royal line of Lanverness has been forced to branch out several times over the centuries. The Rose Throne is currently held by the Tandroths. The Tandroths nearly lost the throne when the last king of Lanverness, King Leonid, failed to produce a male heir. The king survived a revolt and forced his noblemen to accept his only daughter, Liandra, as the heir to the Rose Throne on the condition that she marry a peer of the realm. Liandra is the only queen to rule a kingdom of Erdhe. Under Queen Liandra's stewardship, Lanverness has become the wealthiest kingdom in all of Erdhe.

The symbol of Lanverness is two white roses crossed on a field of emerald green. The seat of their power is Castle Tandroth, rising from the heart of Pellanor, the capital city.

QUEEN LIANDRA TANDROTH, ruler of the Rose Throne, also known as the White Rose of Lanverness, also known as the Spider Queen

> -her husband, **PRINCE-CONSORT DONALD TERREL**, chosen from among the noble families of Lanverness, Lord Terrel was raised up to be the Prince-Consort to the queen on condition that he forsake his name and his lineage. He died in a hunting accident shortly after the birth of his second son. The heraldry of house Terrel is a red unicorn rearing on a field of green.
> -their children:
> **PRINCE STEWART**, heir to the Rose Throne, promoted to general of the Rose Army, wields a blue steel sword
> **PRINCE DANLY**, spare heir to the Rose Throne, a condemned traitor
> **PRINCESS ASELYNN**, died at birth
> **UNNAMED PRINCESS,** died at premature birth, some consider it murder

-her councilors:

> **LORD ROBERT HIGHGATE**, the Master Archivist, the queen's shadowmaster, right hand to the queen
>
> **MASTER RADDOCK,** deputy shadowmaster serving the queen, was once a condemned thief, rescued from the dungeons by the Master Archivist
>
> **SIR DURNHEART,** the Knight Protector, raised to a knight after the Red Horn rebellion, wields a blue steel sword named *Loyalty*
>
> **LORD TURNER**, a former member of the queen's council, boiled alive for treason, a harlequin of the Dark Lord
>
> **LORD SHELDON**, the Lord Sheriff, leader of the constable force of Lanverness
>
> **LORD SADDLER,** a goldsmith raised to a lord after the rebellion, the Master of Coin on the queen's council
>
> **LORD CENRIC,** a cat-eyed archer, he sits on the queen's council when he is in Pellanor, leader of Clan Hemlock, his loyalty is to the Treespeaker and the Deep Green, he wears a cloak of peacock feathers
>
> **PRINCESS JEMMA,** princess of Navarre, a Royal J, wayfaring with the queen to learn the way of multiplying coins, sits on the queen's council as the representative from Navarre

-her ladies-in-waiting:

> **LADY SARAH JAMESON**, a distant cousin of the queen, principle lady-in-waiting to the queen
>
> **LADY MARTHA**, a lady-in-waiting to the queen
>
> **LADY AMY,** the youngest of the queen's ladies-in-waiting
>
> **LADY LINDSEY,** a lady-in-waiting to the queen
>
> **LADY CRISTAL,** a lady-in-waiting to the queen
>
> **LADY BETH,** a lady-in-waiting to the queen
>
> **LADY CATHOR,** a lady-in-waiting to the queen

-other members of the court:

> **SIR CARDEMIR,** fifth son of the Duke of Graymaris, the seahorse knight, sent by the queen as an emissary to the Kiralynn monks, murdered by the Mordant
>
> **FREDERINKO,** an emissary from the Empire of Ur

MASTER FINTAN, an emissary from the Kiralynn Monks to the Rose Court, mysteriously murdered in the queen's castle
LORD FERDIC, a minor peer of the realm
LORD CARDIG, a wealthy and influential peer of the realm
LORD DARWAY, a minor lord
LADY CLAUDIA, friend of the queen, wife of a lord

THE PEOPLE OF PELLANOR

MASTER NUMAR, a master of the Kiralynn Order and a skilled herbalist, he is posing as the master of an apothecary shop, The White Unicorn, in Pellanor, slain
MARSTAN, shadowman captain
TOLHARD, shadowman
BLATT, shadowman
CAMDOR, traitor shadowman
WILFORD, shadowman
TARK, shadowman
KIRTH, club-footed owner of The Green Man inn
SAMANTHA CAILLAS, also known as Sam, owner of The Rusty Dragon tavern
SALLY, a barmaid at the Rusty Dragon

LINGARD

Lingard is a fortress citadel, the second greatest fortress in Lanverness. The heraldic seat of the Rognalds. Their symbol is an iron fist on a field of yellow-gold.
LORD RONALD ROGNALD, son of Baron Rognald, ruler of Lingard, staunch supporter of Queen Liandra and Prince Stewart

THE MORDANT

With over a thousand years of life, the Mordant is the oldest of the harlequins. Imbued with Dark power, he is the god-king of the north, the ruler of the Dark Citadel. He wields the Staff of Pain, an iron scepter with a red crystal at the top.

The Mordant's time-worn seat of power is Dark Citadel, a forbidding fortress-city in the far north. Perched atop three hundred foot cliffs that overlook the Western Ocean, it is built upon a huge monolithic boulder. The tiered city has nine layers spiraling upward around the central stone monolith. Each layer holds a distinct class of people, with the poorest at the bottom and the palace of the Mordant at the summit. The stone monolith contains steps leading to a cave that underlies the Dark Citadel, an ancient sanctum to the Dark God, a source of Dark power.

The Mordant's domain also includes the steppes, a vast sea of grass that serves as a desolate greensward for the Dark Citadel, a barren killing field that becomes the anvil of winter. The northern steppes are divided from the south by a dark wall studded with ten Gargoyle Gates.

The domain also includes the Pit, a massive crater with near vertical glass-sheer walls. Slaves live within the Pit, toiling within the Mordant's iron mines. Female slaves are forced to serve as whores for the Mordant's army. Residual magic in the Pit results in the massive abnormalities of newborns. Two new sub-races have been born and bred in the Pit; the Taals, an ogre-like sub-race with massive strength and limited intellect, and the Duegar, also called the Hounds of the Mordant, dwarves with the ability to scent magic.

The symbol of the Dark Citadel is a gold pentacle emblazoned on a field of black. The Darkflamme is the Mordant's personal battle banner, twelve feet of black silk ending in two silken tails of bright red flecked with gold, creating the illusion of darkness on fire

SERVANTS OF THE MORDANT
> **BISHOP BORGAN,** a bishop of the Pentacle serving as the seneschal to the Mordant, a master forger

MAJOR TARQ, commander of the Eighth Fist, a cadre of elite guards from the Dark Citadel, sent south to serve the Mordant

DOLF, a master assassin of the Ninth Rank, posing as a manservant to the Mordant

FREDERINKO, formerly a chained servant of UR, the eunuch was kidnapped by MerChanters and then turned to Darkness by the Mordant, he serves as an emissary to the Rose Court

TOKAR, a snargon of the duegars

SORKON, a snargon of the duegars, Tokar's brother

GRAYLIN, an assassin

JEKEL, a duegar

CARLIN, an assassin

VECK, an assassin

TARCE, a senior guard from the Citadel

LASITER, a senior snargon

COMMANDER HOIT, commander of the Citadel guards

COMMANDER TRAX, commander of the Citadel guards

CULVER, soldier of the Citadel serving in the south

PESH, soldier of the Citadel serving in the south

GRANAR, soldier of the Citadel serving in the south

SIRKEN, soldier of the Citadel serving in the south

ARMY OF THE SOUTH

GENERAL HAITH- High General of the Army of the Pentacle, witness to the beheading of the Mordant in his prior life

COMMANDER TROLLEN, commander

COMMANDER PARN, commander

COMMANDER JARTHAX, young commander

DROG, soldier of the Pentacle

ARMY OF THE NORTH

COMMANDER CRULL, given command of the reserve forces in Raven Pass

THE ORACLE PRIESTESS

The Priestess is the ruler of the Isle of the Oracle, the guardian of the sacred well, the wielder of the Eye of the Oracle. She rarely uses her true name, but often goes by the name of Lady Cereus, a name given to her by Prince Razzur of Coronth. Beyond the Oracle Isle, she takes the phases of the moon as her symbol, gold on a field of purple. After the collapse of the Flame religion, she claims the southwest corner of Coronth for her queendom, establishing a capital in the ancient city of Rhune. She assumes the name of Queen Selene, the Lady of the Moon. Silverspire is her castle.

Hidden in depths of the Great Southern Swamps, the Isle of the Oracle is an ancient wellspring of Darkness, a place of power where the Dark Lord reaches through the Veil to touch his dedicates. At times of great prophecy, the Dark Lord releases his priest or priestess into the kingdoms of Erdhe to participate in the Great Dark Dance.

-her servants and soldiers:

> **LORD STEFFAN,** formerly the Lord Raven of Coronth, goes by the title of the Lord of Darkmoor, a dedicate to the Dark Lord, lover to the Priestess
> **GENERAL TARMIN,** a major of the Flame Army, sworn to the service of the Priestess and promoted to the general of her army, he commands her forces in Rhune, a lover to the Priestess
> **BRAXUS,** a lover to the Priestess, serves as her seneschal, also a skilled sword
> **HUGO,** captain of the guards, a lover to the Priestess
> **LYDIA,** dark-haired handmaiden to the Priestess
> **TARA,** blond-haired handmaiden to the Priestess

NAVARRE

The youngest kingdom of Erdhe, Navarre was founded less than four hundred years ago by a daring adventurer, Alaric Navarre, who rescued the youngest daughter of the king of Coronth from a band of sea pirates infesting the Orcnoth Islands. Gaining the king's confidence, and his daughter's hand in marriage, Alaric earned a freehold of land running along the Western Ocean where he later established his kingdom. His domain includes the Orcnoth Islands.

While defeating the nest of pirates, Alaric discovered a long-forgotten focus. The magic of the focus renders the royal house very fecund, enabling the queens to bear six to ten children in a single pregnancy. After using the magic, both the king and the queen become sterile. The focus is the secret strength of the royal house of Navarre, the bedrock for the succession to the throne. Alaric abandoned the convention of primogeniture, declaring that all of the tuplets have an equal chance to the throne. He instituted the practice of Wayfaring, a type of fostering where the heirs develop their greatest interests, striving to become excellent at a skill, a knowledge, or a trade, so that they can bring this knowledge back to Navarre and thus enrich the kingdom. After the Wayfaring, the King, together with the royal council, chooses the successor to the throne based on the talents, skills, and temperament that best fit the needs of the kingdom at the time. Navarre is well known for its uncommonly wise rulers…but with every great boon there is also a cost, the hidden focus brings with it the Curse of the Vowels.

The symbol of Navarre is a white osprey soaring on a checkered field of red and blue. The seat of their power is Castle Seamount, perched on a rocky outcrop on the edge of the Western Ocean. Navarre has always had close ties to the sea.

KING IVOR NAVARRE, the eighth ruler of the kingdom of Navarre
-his siblings:
PRINCE IRWIN, died of poison, believed to be a victim of the Curse of the Vowels

PRINCESS INGRID, fell from the rigging of a ship and died, believed to be a victim of the Curse of the Vowels

PRINCESS IRIS, accused of murdering her two siblings, exiled to the Orcnoth Islands, she murdered her guards and then disappeared

PRINCE ISADOR, Commander of the Army of Navarre, advisor to the king, nearly fell victim to the Curse of the Vowels, murdered at the poison feast

PRINCESS IGRAINE, Counselor to the king, court historian, tutor to the Royal Js, murdered at the poison feast

PRINCE IAN, Royal Bowyer, advisor to the king, murdered at the poison feast

PRINCESS IVY, Captain of a royal merchant vessel of Navarre

-his wife, **QUEEN MEGAN**, a princess of Tubor
-their children known as the Royal Js:

PRINCESS JEMMA, Wayfaring with the Queen of Lanverness to learn the way of multiplying coins

PRINCE JUSTIN, Sent wayfaring to become a bard, he receives permission from the King and Council to travel to Coronth to try and overthrow the Pontifax, also known as the Dark Harper

PRINCESS JORDAN, Sent wayfaring with the Kiralynn monks to learn the art of war, she is felled by the treachery of the Mordant. Healed by the monk's magic, she gains visions of prophecy and returns to Navarre. She is the sword sister to Kath of Castlegard

PRINCE JARED, Sent wayfaring with the Octagon Knights to learn the way of the sword, he is murdered by loyalists to the Flame

PRINCESS JULIANA, Wayfaring with Navarre's merchant fleet to learn the way of the sea, merchant captain of the *Sea Sprite*

PRINCE JAMES, Wayfaring in Tubor to learn to become a vintner

PRINCE JAYSON, Wayfaring in the Delta to learn the secrets of a new water wheels

his retainers:

MARY, Prince Ian's wife, murdered at the poison feast
GARTH, Princess Ivy's husband, elevated to the king's council
MATILDA, a wise woman, an herbalist, a midwife, and a fortuneteller, a friend to Queen Megan
MAJOR ABERNATHY, senior war advisor to the king
MAJOR RAUL, war advisor to the king
CAPTAIN ROSS, war advisor to the king
CAPTAIN MARUINTH, war advisor to the king
SCRIMSHAW JONES, owner of the Eyrie tavern, where returning sea captains meet

CREW OF THE *SEA SPRITE*

JULIANA, Princess of Navarre, a Royal J, captain of the *Sea Sprite*
MARCUS, First Mate

CASTLEGARD

Three hundred years after the War of Wizards decimated the kingdoms of Erdhe, a group of knights banded together to protect the southern kingdoms from the ravages of the north. They claimed Castlegard, the great mage-stone castle left empty after the War of Wizards, as the seat of their power. Adopting the shape of the great castle as their symbol, they became known as the Octagon Knights.

To bolster their cause, the knights were ceded land running along the length of the Dragon Spine Mountains. Stretching from Castlegard all the way to the Western Ocean, this land became known as the Domain. A series of castles, keeps, and walls were built along the Dragon Spines, allowing the knights to control the mountain passes and deny access to the southern kingdoms. The Domain also includes the only iron ore mine in all of Erdhe to yield blue ore, the rare ore required to forge the knights' fabled blue steel swords.

As a sworn brotherhood of elite knights, the candidates forsake their lineage and their past when they win their maroon cloaks. Their symbol is a maroon octagon emblazoned on a silver shield.

KING URSUS ANVRIL, King of Castlegard and the Knights of the Octagon, Lord of the Domain, bearer of a great blue sword named *Honor's Edge*.

> -his wife, **QUEEN PHYLA**, died giving birth to their only daughter
> -their children:
> **PRINCE ULRICH**, First-born son of the king, a sworn knight of the maroon, former commander of the wall at Raven Pass, bearer of a great blue sword named *Mordbane*, slain at Raven Pass
> **PRINCE GRIFFIN**, Second-born son of the king, a sworn knight of the maroon, former commander of Dymtower, murdered at Raven Pass
> **PRINCE GODFREY**, Third-born son of the king, a sworn knight of the maroon, former commander of Shieldhold, murdered at Raven Pass

PRINCE TRISTAN, Fourth-born son of the king, a sworn knight of the maroon, slain while leading a patrol into the steppes

PRINCE LIONEL, Fifth-born son of the king, a sworn knight of the maroon, former commander of Cragnoth Keep, murdered at Cragnoth Keep

PRINCESS KATHERINE, Sixth child of the king, also known as the Imp or Little Sister or Kath. As a female, the Octagon symbol of Castlegard is forbidden to her. Instead she uses the Anvril's ancient heraldic symbol of a red hawk attacking with talons outstretched on a field of white. Kath is hailed as the **Svala,** the war leader of the Painted People.

KATH'S COMPANIONS

DUNCAN TRELOCH - a master archer with ties to the Deep Green and Navarre

SIR BLAINE - a knight of the Octagon who wields a blue steel great sword named *Stonecutter* by the Painted People

SIR TYRONE- a veteran knight of the Octagon with skin the color of ebony, often referred to as the 'black knight', a hero slain at the battle of Cragnoth Keep

ZITH - a master monk of the Kiralynn Order, father of Bryce, loses his left forearm to the gorehounds

DANYA - a young woman who sought sanctuary in the Kiralynn Monastery with her mountain wolf, **BRYX**

ARMY OF THE OCTAGON KNIGHTS

SIR OSBOURNE, The Knight Marshal of the Octagon, right hand of the King, a one-eyed man with a scar-crossed face, he wields the Dark Sword

SIR LOTHAR, acting knight marshal, knight-captain of the Salt Tower, wields a battleaxe, close friend to the knight marshal

SIR ABRAX, champion of the maroon, wields a blue steel sword, guard to King Ursus, slain by the Dark Sword

SIR RANNOCK, champion of the maroon, serves as next in command to Lothar, wields a morning star

SIR BLAZE, champion of the maroon, wields a mace

SIR GRAVIS, knight-captain of Sword Keep

SIR ADLEMAR, champion of the maroon, wields a blue steel claymore

SIR BORAX, knight of the maroon

SIR TORMUND, old veteran knight

SIR CORMIN, knight of the maroon

SIR DORLIN, old veteran knight

SIR MELLOT, champion of the maroon

SIR BRUNDAMIR, champion of the maroon

SIR GALYAD, champion of the maroon

SAM, a scout serving the maroon

SIR TRASK, champion of the battleaxe, assigned to Cragnoth Keep as a punishment posting, slain at the battle of Cragnoth Keep

SIR TYRONE, knight of the maroon with skin the color of ebony, often referred to as the 'black knight', a companion to Princess Katherine, slain at the battle of Cragnoth Keep

ORRIN SUREHAMMER, legendary Master Swordsmith of the maroon, first forger of blue steel blades, some believe he forged magical abilities into his blue steel blades making them destined for the hands of heroes

OTTO, the current Master Swordsmith of Castlegard's forge, responsible for the forging of all blue steel weapons

QUINTUS, the master healer of Castlegard

ELISE, scullery maid turned assistant to healer Quintus

THE KIRALYNN MONKS

Founded over two thousand years ago by a group of scholars, knights, and wizards, the Kiralynn Order has always presented an enigmatic face to the world, a face that is open yet closed. One hundred years before the start of the War of Wizards the monks withdrew from the southern kingdoms, retreating to their monastery hidden deep in the Southern Mountains. As if erased from the minds of men, the monastery's location disappeared from the maps of Erdhe. The memory of the Kiralynn monks has slowly faded, becoming little more than legend and myth. Yet select rulers of the southern kingdoms still receive scrolls sealed with the symbol of the Order. History has proven that these scrolls contain an uncanny prescience. Kings ignore the advice of the Order at their own peril.

The symbol of the Kiralynn monks is a Seeing Eye in the palm of an Open Hand. Their seat of power is their mountain monastery. The motto of the Order is "Seek Knowledge, Protect Knowledge, Share Knowledge".

THE GRAND MASTER, the leader of the Kiralynn Order, his/her identity is a closely guarded secret
-monks and initiates of the Order:
>   **MASTER RIZEL**, a Master of the Order
>   **MASTER GARTH**, a Master Healer of the Order
>   **BRYCE**, an initiate of the Order, he studied to take his vows to become a monk and a healer but was subsumed by the Mordant's Awakening, becoming a prisoner in his own mind
>   **MASTER AEROTH**, an ambassador monk sent to the kingdoms of Erdhe
>   **MASTER ZITH**, a Master of the Order, accompanies Kath as one of her companions, he is the father of Bryce, he lost his left forearm in the battle with the gorehounds
>   **RAFE**, a sworn monk of the Order, he has worn the blue for five years, sent with Princess Jordan of Navarre
>   **MASTER YARL**, a master of the Order, an expert with a quarterstaff, sent with Princess Jordan of Navarre
>   **MISTRESS ELLIS**, loremistress, moon weaver

MISTRESS LENORE, loremistress

AMBROSE, sworn monk, friend of Master Rizel, offers to carry *Invictus*

CYNTHIA, sworn monk, Mist Guide

MASTER SAKLIN, old quarterstaff master, contact with the Zward

MASTER TAMZIN, master of the owlery

MASTER CHRISTOFF, master of the quarterstaff, trains acolytes

MASTER ADELBART, master of calligraphy, teaches acolytes in the scriptorium

MASTER TOLK, the Chronicler of the Order, a venerable elder

MASTER CARLISLE, half-blind master, a venerable elder

MASTER FELIX, a member of the seclusionists

MASTER GRIMSHAW, master scholar of ancient prophecies

MISTRESS SERAPHINA, loremistress

MISTRESS LURINDA, scholar of lore

MASTER VERNIUS, the loremaster for the Order, a venerable elder

MASTER KARIDITH, an ancient master who sometimes serves as the Voice

MASTER DIGONT, a loremaster, keeper of focuses

MASTER JULIAN, dead master to Vernius

MASTER RORDAN, master of the Order, scholar of history

MASTER HOLBRETH, master of the Order, friend of Seraphina

MASTER FINTAN, an emissary from the Kiralynn Monks sent to the Rose Court, mysteriously murdered in the queen's castle

MASTER NUMAR, a master of the Order serving as a hidden Wanderer in Pellanor, a skilled herbalist posing as an apothecary, he owns the White Unicorn apothecary shop, slain

NIMERIA HARPSINGER, sixteen years old, golden-robed acolyte studying under Master Adelbart in the scriptorium, longs to be an Illuminator

TYBOLT, an acolyte of the quarterstaff, raised to a sworn monk, also known as Ty, serves with the Zward

CARL, friend of Tybolt, a fresh-sworn monk serving with the Zward

THE ZWARD

The Zward are sons and daughters of Kiralynn monks who choose to serve by the sword instead of the scroll. An ancient and secret order, they serve the will of the Grand Master. Their symbol is a small silver ring emblazoned with a fist holding an upright sword. Their seat of power is the mountain village of Haven.

THADDEUS TOKHEART, also known as Thad, a captain of the Zward
DONAL, a sworn member of the Zward, serves with Thaddeus
BENJIN, a sworn member of the Zward, serves with Thaddeus
MARCUS, a sworn member of the Zward, serves with Thaddeus,
HAYTHOR, a captain of the Zward, charged with protecting *Invictus*
KREN, horse master of the Zward, serves with Haythor
JADA, master archer of the Zward, serves with Haythor
TARLIN, master scout of the Zward, serves with Haythor
TARGUS, commander of the Zward, leading the defense of the mountain pass
BARSTON, Zward serving under Targus
PREN, Zward serving under Targus
CORDON, Zward serving under Targus
PRANGO, captain of the Zward serving under Targus
RANOFF, hidden member of the Zward, owns a horse farm near Pellanor
ESSIE, hidden member of the Zward, wife of Ranoff
ORT, hidden member of the Zward, owns the Laughing Gargoyle tavern
LUCAS, hidden member of the Zward, a cobbler in Pellanor

THE DEEP GREEN

The Deep Green is an ancient power reborn from the ashes of the War of Wizards. Rising from the ruins of a great city, the forest grows with frightening speed. Trees at the heart of the forest are giants, growing to more than thrice the height of normal trees, while the dense tangle of underbrush forms a nearly impenetrable barrier. The forest protects its own, a race of people with golden cat-eyes. Calling themselves the Children of the Green, the cat-eyed people live within the boundaries of the forest in a confederation of clans under the leadership of the Treespeaker.

Outside of the forest, the cat-eyed people are shunned as evil abominations, said to be born from the perverse mating of man with animals. The cat-eyed people are persecuted across the kingdoms of Erdhe, and often put to death by the 'white-eyes'.

THE TREESPEAKER, as old as the forest, she is a seer, a witch, the embodiment
of the power of the Green. As the leader of the clans, she wears a cloak
of snow-white swan feathers.
-her clan leaders:

>**CENRIC**, leader of Clan Hemlock, he wears a cloak of peacock
feathers, volunteers to lead a war party to Pellanor
>
>**AGATHA**, leader of Clan Aspen, she wears a cloak of blue jay
feathers. She leads a faction that opposes dealings with the
white-eyes
>
>**BRAN**, leader of Clan Ash, he wears a cloak of raven feathers
>
>**CAMILA**, leader of Clan Maple, she wears a cloak of orange
kestrel feathers and is a member of the faction that opposes
dealings with the white-eyes
>
>**DEREK**, leader of Clan Redwood, he wears a cloak of red
woodpecker feathers and is a member of the faction that
opposes dealing with the white-eyes
>
>**CONRAD**, leader of Clan Spruce, he wears a cloak of brown
thrush feathers
>
>**LANA**, leader of Clan Oak, she wears a cloak of golden finch
feathers

-her people:

> **JANTHAR,** captain of rangers
> **MARTYN**, an attendant to the Treespeaker
> **JORAH SILVENWOOD**, a ranger of Clan Cedar, killed in
> the Mordant's fire

THE OAK GROVE

In thanks for their aid in the Flame War, Queen Liandra of Lanverness gifted her royal hunting preserve north of Pellanor to the Children of the Deep Green. This forest became known as The Oak Grove and contains a small settlement of archers and their families. .

> **CENRIC,** also known as Lord Cenric, is the leader of Clan
> Hemlock as well as the Oak Grove, an honorary member of
> Queen Liandra's royal council, he wears a cloak of peacock
> feathers
> **CARHAIN,** captain of the Oak Grove
> **ZOLTEN,** an archer from the Oak Grove

THE PAINTED PEOPLE

An ancient people, forgotten by most of Erdhe, the Painted Warriors are the descendents of escaped slaves and runaway soldiers. Living in the shadow of the Dark Citadel, the Painted People have forged a fiercely independent warrior culture that spans a thousand years. Outnumbered and poorly equipped, they strike back at the Pentacle in lightning raids across the steppes, reaping steel and armor from their enemies. They make their home in a secret labyrinth of caves hidden in the Ghost Hills. Deeply spiritual, they invoke the power of nature by tattooing their faces with the images of beasts and birds, a spiritual melding of man and animal. Divided into dens depending on their tattoos, they are guided by the Ancestor, a shaman of mystical memories, and lead by a Council of Leaders made up of representatives from all the dens. A secret and forgotten people, few in the southern kingdoms have ever heard of them.

THE ANCESTOR- Also known as the Keeper of Memories, the Old One. The Ancestor is always a woman, following a matriarchal line of mystical seers that stretches back for nearly a thousand years. As the spiritual leader of the painted people she is respected and revered but she does not rule as a queen. Instead she serves as a guide to the council of leaders.

VALDUR- a Taishan of the mountain lions, lost on a vision-hunter on a quest in the southern steppes. Attacked and left for dead by soldiers of the Pentacle, a patrol of Octagon knights found him and took him to Castlegard where he died in Kath's arms.

THE SVALA - After being tested in a trial by combat, **Kath of Castlegard** is hailed as the Svala, the foretold war leader of the Painted People.

THERA- leader of the ravens, master healer

FANGGOLD- warrior leader of the wolves

THE MAROON BAND

A brotherhood of painted warriors who claim the honor of protecting the Svala. Survivors of the original eighty warriors who witnessed Kath's trial at the Gargoyle Gates and then formed the vanguard for the attack on the Dark Citadel, they call themselves the Maroon Band. Their symbol is a tattered strip of maroon cloak tied to their right bicep. Their strips of maroon come from the extra length of Kath's maroon cloak, given to her by Blaine after the battle with the gorehounds. Led by Bear and Boar, they have become the personal guard to the Svala.

BEAR- a bear-faced warrior assigned to guard Kath, he refuses to reveal his true name, adopts the name of Bear and becomes Kath's personal guard and friend
BOAR- a boar-faced warrior assigned to Kath, refuses to reveal his true name, adopts the name of Boar and becomes Kath's personal guard and friend, wields a mace, slain
TORVEN- eagle-faced warrior patrol leader
SIDHORN -eagle-faced warrior, becomes second to Bear in leading the maroon band
TINGOLD- a wolf-faced scout, hunted with Blaine in the Citadel
RUTHGAR - boar-faced warrior, hunted with Blaine in the Citadel
TANGOR- a hawk-faced warrior
PREN -a bear-faced warrior
CLEMIT- a wolf-faced warrior
REDLIN -eagle-faced warrior
TORLOCK -wolf-faced warrior
ASH -owl-faced warrior

THE WOLF BAND

A band of wolf-faced warriors who have formed a den and are sworn to protect Danya.

NEVEN- the leader of the wolf band, a wolf-faced warrior hand-fasted to Danya.
BALTHUS- wolf-faced warrior, brother of Bardis
BARDIS -wolf-faced warrior, brother to Balthus
GRIS, wolf-faced scout
SEVERN, wolf-faced warrior

Other books by Karen L Azinger

Hungry to learn more about the kingdoms of Erdhe? Then consider reading my short story collection, *The Assassin's Tear*. The first story, *Prophecy's Twist*, explores the start of the War of Wizards, and the second signature story, *The Assassin's Tear*, explores the Dark Citadel from the perspective of a young thief.

The Assassin's Tear- Explore the medieval kingdoms of Erdhe, raid the tomb of the first emperor of China, survive an apocalyptic event Down Under, time travel to learn the secret of a famous scientist, and unravel the enigma of Dark Space in this collection of fantasy and science fiction tales from the author of *The Silk & Steel Saga*.

Power Writing: Make Your Genre Fiction Soar! - Fans of *The Silk & Steel Saga* will peek behind the curtain, gaining insights into the author's imaginings. Revisit the wonders of Erdhe with the author as your tour guide. Writers will learn how to color outside the lines and write bold genre fiction that will enthrall your readers and make your stories soar. *Power Writing* provides insights into many unique topics rarely discussed by other writing books. You'll find tips on writing magic, fortune telling, making maps and writing great battle scenes. Learn how to spice it up with romantic subplots and how to write with iconic images and tropes. Examples are drawn from genre masterworks like Tolkien's *Lord of the Rings*, Martin's *Game of Thrones*, Herbert's *Dune*, Rowling's *Harry Potter*, and the author's own *Silk & Steel Saga*, as well as examples from silver screen blockbusters like *Star Wars*, *Star Trek*, *Braveheart* and *Gladiator*.

The Front Cover artwork was done by the Australian artist, Greg Bridges. Greg's artwork has appeared on the book covers of many well-known fantasy authors. Thanks to Greg for the front cover, the spine, and the fabulous rendering of the Dark Sword used in the interior of the book. To see more of his art or to contact Greg, visit his website at http://www.gregbridges.com/

The Maps and the Back Cover were done by a graphic artist from Oregon, Peggy Lowe. Her illustration of the two maps helps to bring the kingdoms of Erdhe to life. Peggy can be contacted at her e-mail address, peggy@portfoliooregon.com

The dragon embellished T used on the back cover was hand drawn by Karen Azinger.

ABOUT THE AUTHOR

KAREN L. AZINGER has always loved fantasy fiction, and always hoped that someday she could give back to the genre a little of the joy that reading has always given her. Twelve years ago on a hike in the Columbia River Gorge she realized she had enough original ideas to finally write an epic fantasy. She started writing and never stopped. *The Steel Queen* was her first book, born from that hike in the gorge. Before writing, Karen spent over twenty years as an international business strategist, eventually becoming a vice-president for one of the world's largest natural resource companies. She's worked on developing the first gem-quality diamond mine in Canada's arctic, on coal seam gas power projects in Australia, and on petroleum projects around the world. Having lived in Australia for eight years she considers it to be her second home. She's also lived in Canada and spent a lot of time in the Canadian arctic. She now lives with her husband in Portland Oregon, in a house perched on the edge of the forest. You can learn more at her website, www.karenlazinger.com or at her Facebook page for The Steel Queen. She loves to hear from her readers!

www.ingramcontent.com/pod-product-compliance
Lightning Source LLC
Chambersburg PA
CBHW020926020726
47495CB00002B/360